Books in print by Blaine M. Yorgason

Gabriel's Well

Charlie's Monument

One Tattered Angel: A Touching True Story of the Power of Love

Ascending

Secrets

The Soderberg Saga

Hearts Afire:

Prequel - To Soar with the Eagle

Book One - At All Hazards

Book Two - Fort on the Firing Line

Book Three - Curly Bill's Gift

BLAINE M. YORGASON

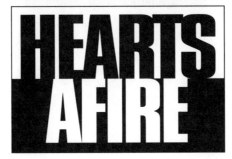

HEARTS AFIRE

BOOK THREE

Curly Bill's Gift

SHADOW MOUNTAIN®

Library of Congress Cataloging-in-Publication Data

Yorgason, Blaine M., 1942–
Curly Bill's Gift / Blaine M. Yorgason.
p. cm. — (Hearts afire ; bk. 3)
ISBN 1-57345-825-2 (hb)
1. San Juan County (Utah)—Fiction. 2. Mormons—Fiction. I. Title.
PS3575.O57C87 2000
813'.54—dc21 00-037541
CIP

Printed in the United States of America 72082-6720

10 9 8 7 6 5 4 3 2 1

For Karl R. and Edith Lyman,
dear friends and wise counselors,
who have taken the time to love us all

CONTENTS

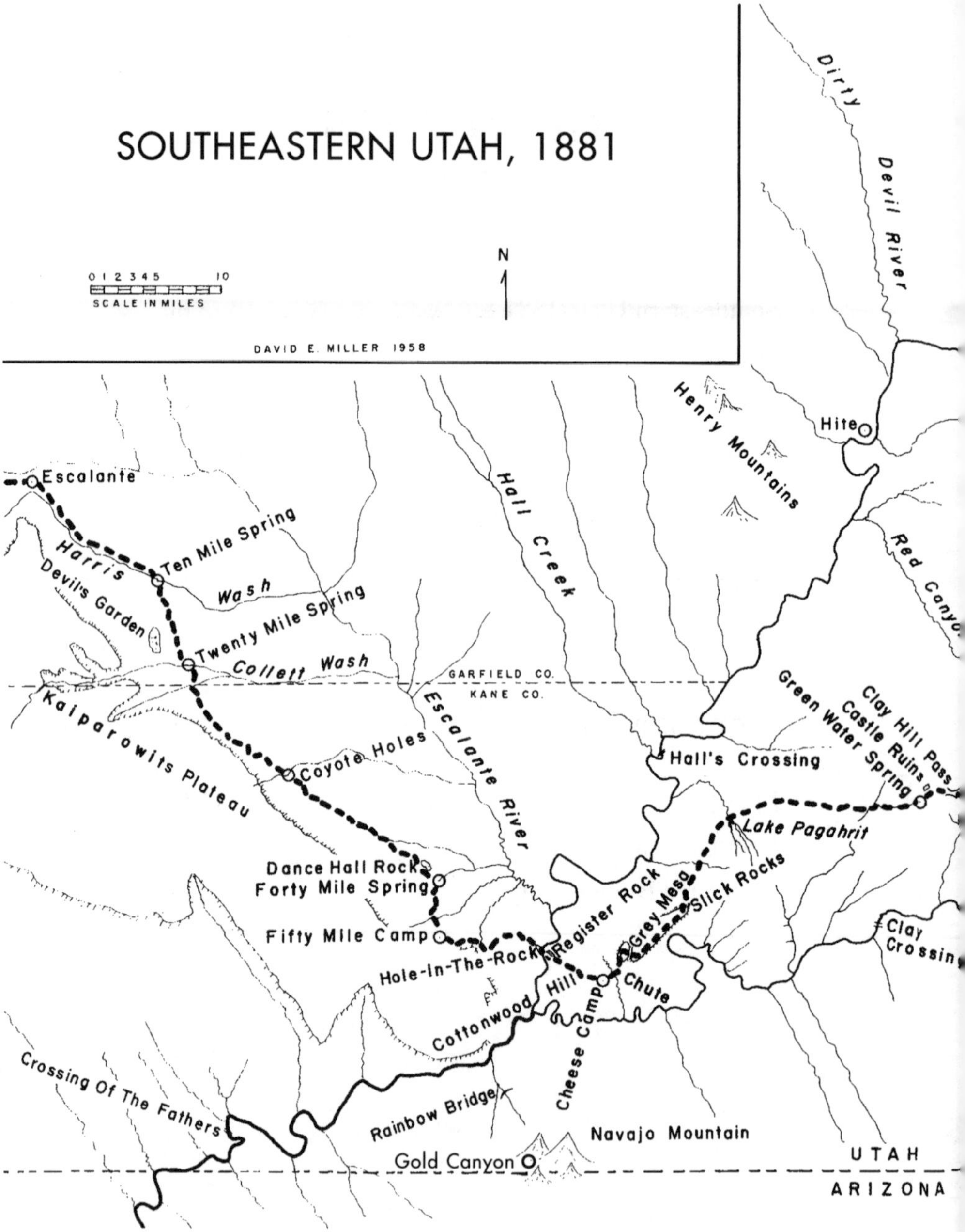
SOUTHEASTERN UTAH, 1881
0 1 2 3 4 5 10
SCALE IN MILES
N
DAVID E. MILLER 1958
Dirty Devil River
Hite
Henry Mountains
Red Canyo
Escalante
Ten Mile Spring
Harris Wash
Devil's Garden
Twenty Mile Spring
Collett Wash
GARFIELD CO.
KANE CO.
Hall Creek
Kaiparowits Plateau
Escalante River
Coyote Holes
Hall's Crossing
Clay Hill Pass
Castle Ruins
Green Water Spring
Lake Pagahrit
Dance Hall Rock
Forty Mile Spring
Fifty Mile Camp
Register Rock
Grey Mesa
Slick Rocks
Hole-In-The-Rock
Cottonwood Hill
Chute
Cheese Camp
Clay Crossin
Crossing Of The Fathers
Rainbow Bridge
Navajo Mountain
Gold Canyon
UTAH
ARIZONA

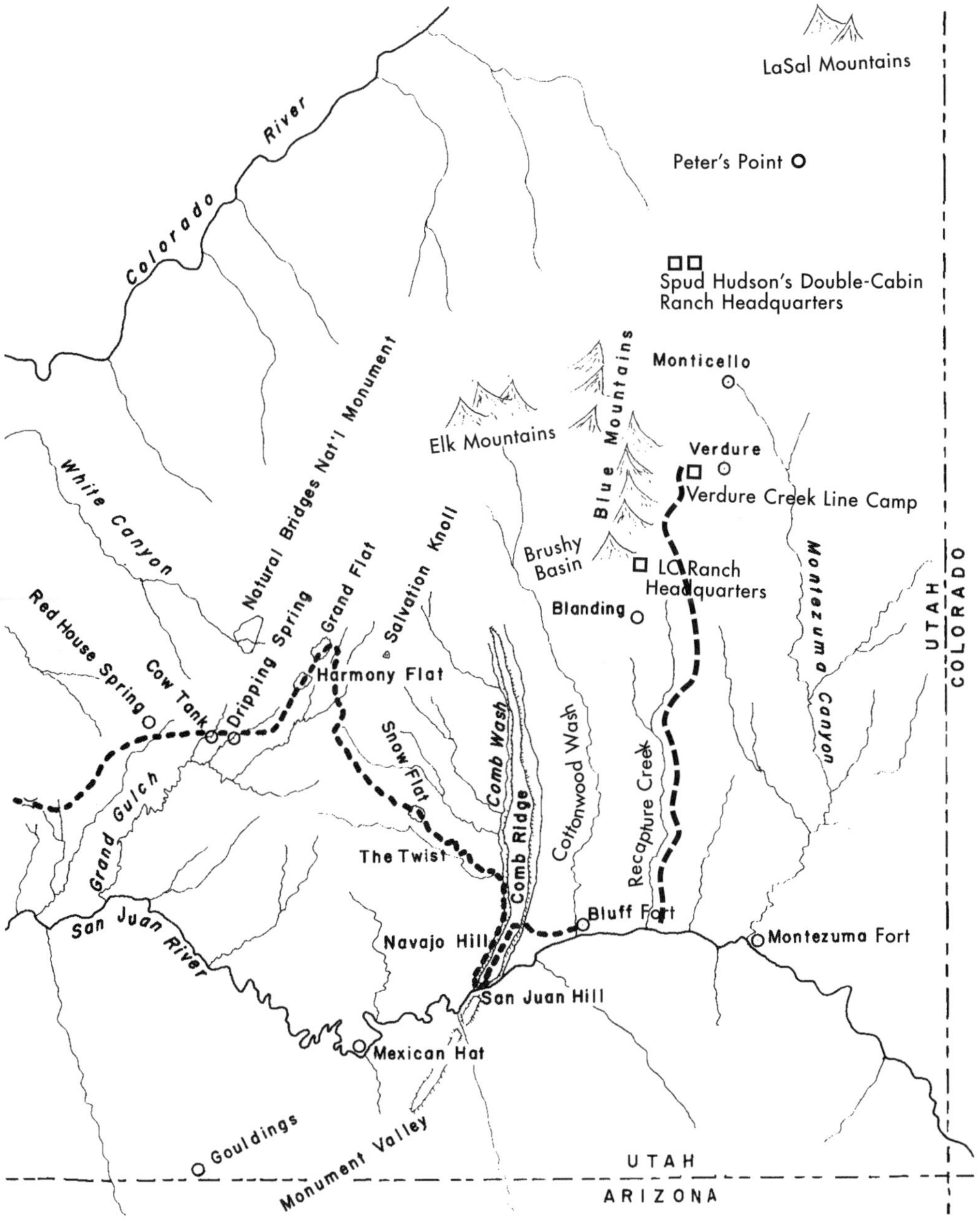

LaSal Mountains
Colorado River
Peter's Point
Spud Hudson's Double-Cabin Ranch Headquarters
Monticello
Blue Mountains
Elk Mountains
Natural Bridges Nat'l Monument
White Canyon
Verdure
Verdure Creek Line Camp
Brushy Basin
LC Ranch Headquarters
Blanding
Montezuma Canyon
UTAH
COLORADO
Red House Spring
Cow Tank
Dripping Spring
Grand Flat
Salvation Knoll
Harmony Flat
Snow Flat
Comb Wash
Comb Ridge
Cottonwood Wash
Recapture Creek
Grand Gulch
The Twist
Bluff Fort
Montezuma Fort
San Juan River
Navajo Hill
San Juan Hill
Mexican Hat
Gouldings
Monument Valley
UTAH
ARIZONA

Johnny Molander's Camp

PREFACE

Since the publication of *Hearts Afire: Book One—At All Hazards,* it has become obvious that the cast of characters involved in the settlement of the San Juan country is so diverse and so extensive as to be almost mind-numbing. Hoping to ease that malady (which I also suffered), I have prepared a list of the main characters for the second and third volumes, indicating whether or not they were historical, and telling a little about them. I hope this list will be helpful in your reading of the story.

CAST OF CHARACTERS

Billy, Eliza, and Willy Foreman: Fictional. However, their experiences are based on the journals and records of the actual San Juan settlers.

Mary and Kumen Jones, Bishop Jens Nielson, Annie Lyman, Lemuel Redd, etc. Actual historical characters, as are all the others who are mentioned as part of the citizenry of Bluff Fort.

Thales Haskel. Historical character, missionary to the Indians, and interpreter, who was assigned with his third wife, Margaret (Maggie), to assist the peace missionaries. Haskel was charged by Elder Erastus Snow to bring to a stop the thievery of the Navajos and Pahutes.

Posey. An historical character, who was a young teenager when the Saints came through Hole-in-the-Rock. For some unknown reason he very quickly developed an extremely antagonistic attitude toward the settlers, attempting to humiliate and/or physically hurt several individuals, especially women, during the first few years of the settlement. Despite periods when he became very friendly and helpful, Posey nevertheless made sporadic efforts throughout his life to kill the Mormons, though he was promised by Thales Haskel that he would never be able to slay any of them.

Too-rah. An historical figure, this young woman fell in love with Posey, who returned the favor with measure. Good-hearted and pleasant by nature, she was a delight to the citizens of Bluff.

Scotty, Old Chee, Poke, Mike, Tuvagutts, Wash, Bridger Jack, etc. The Utes/Pahutes portrayed in this story are all historical characters and were either involved in, or likely involved in, the incidents portrayed in this story.

Peeb and Jonah. Historical characters with fictional names, this young Pahute couple suffered the effects of Haskel's curse about as described.

Natanii nééz or Frank. An historical character, the tall Navajo was one of the craftiest thieves the Mormon settlers had to deal with. Finally, Thales Haskel pronounced a curse on him, as described, and when it took effect he came to Haskel pleading for relief just as Book Two portrays.

H'adapa. This is a fictional name for an historical Navajo woman, who came to raid but saw a starving Mormon child and took pity on it, thereafter making daily trips to bring fresh goat milk until the child was healthy again and becoming extremely close to the Mormon settlers in the process. Because we do not know her identity or that of the wife of Natanii nééz, who struggled with the consequences of her husband's activities just as the character in the story struggles, I have chosen to combine the two into one character, creating H'adapa. I was never able to find the actual identity of the starving child.

Dah nishuânt, Bitseel, Tsabekiss, Hoskanini, Hoskanini Begay, etc. All the Navajos are historical characters. Once again, care has been taken to present them with as much historical accuracy as possible.

Bill Ball. An historical character, who was the foreman of the LC Ranch, Bill befriended the Saints and did all he could to better their lives, including providing employment whenever he could do so.

Sugar Bob Hazelton. A fictitious character, he is actually a composite of four or five shadowy lawbreakers who left behind with their misdeeds neither their names nor the good feelings of the settlers toward them.

Curly Bill Jenkins. A fictitious character, he is also a composite—this time of several cowhands and adventurers who wandered into San Juan County, worked with and oftentimes befriended/assisted the Saints, and left behind them the respect and admiration of the settlers.

Erwin "Slim" McGrew, Bob Hott, and the other cowhands of the LC Ranch. Historical characters, these young men were involved in the cattle industry in Southeast Utah, no doubt interacting with Bill Ball and others. The Mormons of Bluff looked upon them as companions and friends, and in many cases learned the cattle business from them.

Walter Eugene "Latigo" Gordon. An historical character, he was an expert cattleman who was for several years the ramrod of the Carlisle Cattle Company. He was a typical Texas cowboy—tough-minded, fearless, and gun-toting. Though he was often at odds with the Mormons, in a later time Gordon married a Latter-day Saint woman and lived among her people.

Rob Paxman and Lug Santoni. Historical characters, who stole the Bluff herd of horses, with the consequences that are described. Rob Paxman's name is on record, but the name Lug Santoni is fictional because the man's actual name was not recorded.

The story that follows is a work of historical fiction. Whether the characters were fictional or real, whether the incidents portrayed were fictional or real, everything has been rendered fictitious through circumstances, interactions, and dialogue, which are solely of my creation.

That having been said, the major historical events portrayed in the following story did happen and occurred either on the dates given in the story or as close to those dates as I was able to determine.

The book is written chronologically, each chapter circumscribing one day in the lives of one or more of the four major groups of

San Juan inhabitants—the Mormon settlers, the Navajos, the Utes/Pahutes, and the ranchers/cowboys. Initially this format may seem a little confusing, but I could think of no other way to accurately represent the events occurring almost daily with each of these groups and which would have direct impact on the lives of one or more of the others.

From what follows, it should be obvious to the reader that all of these inhabitants were quite literally living their lives on the firing line of the San Juan frontier, where life-threatening danger was ever present and survival never guaranteed. This seems to have been especially so for the Latter-day Saint settlers, for whom the year 1881 was particularly difficult and in fact was pivotal for testing and trying their faith. I have done my best to portray that peril and their faith in the following story, *Hearts Afire: Book Three—Curly Bill's Gift,* which will finish the year 1881 and most probably conclude the series. Enjoy.

ACKNOWLEDGMENTS

In a work of this scope the list of contributors may be almost as long as the text, and in attempting to thank them all, some will be missed. For this I apologize and beg forgiveness. Nevertheless, certain individuals have given invaluable assistance that I must recognize: Albert R. Lyman, who came through the Hole-in-the-Rock as a baby and spent his long and productive life gathering and recording the details of the lives of the San Juan's inhabitants. Years ago, in a personal visit that lasted less than an hour, he imparted to me an enthusiasm that has never left me, for *all* the inhabitants of the San Juan, as well as the amazing land that helped shape them. Before his death, Karl Lyman, with his lovely wife, Edith, enthusiastically shared with me Karl's father's (Albert) research and writings, as well as their own perspectives on the country; since Karl's passing Edith has continued to do the same; and at their untimely deaths, Michael Terry Hurst and Pearl Baker kindly bequeathed me all their research on Posey and his relationship with the Mormons.

Karl and LaRue Barton, Karl's father, Clyde, and DeVar and Madge Shumway have housed me and then painstakingly—with horse, mule, and jeep—shown me the rocks and trees, the ruggedly beautiful mountains and valleys, the hidden arroyos and gulches that yet make up the San Juan country. With them and others, I have traversed nearly every inch of the old trail, save what is now beneath Lake Powell, examined the battle site in Pinhook Draw on the north slope of the LaSal Mountains, and wandered about the ever-changing San Juan River, majestic Monument Valley, the Blue Mountains,

Brushy Basin, and Elk Ridge, where the old Navajos, Pahutes, cowboys, outlaws, and Mormon settlers lived out their amazing lives.

Under the auspices of the Utah State Historical Society and California State University, Fullerton, Gary Shumway has spent years directing the gathering and publishing of wonderful oral histories of these inhabitants of San Juan County. These he has unhesitatingly shared with me. And his sister Francine Shumway Sumner has never stopped waxing eloquent, through all the years of our friendship, concerning "her" land and its people.

My publishers and friends Ronald Millett and Sheri Dew have encouraged me from long before the actual onset of this project, and I express deep appreciation to them, as well as to their talented editorial, artistic, and marketing staff, for making these volumes a reality.

Finally, I express heartfelt appreciation to my sons and daughters, who one after another accompanied me on my seemingly endless forays into the San Juan country; and to my eternal sweetheart, Kathy, who never once objected to the agonizingly long seven years it took to finally pull these three volumes, and their prequel, together.

PROLOGUE

Tuesday, August 30, 1881

St. George, Territory of Utah

Opening his eyes abruptly, Erastus Snow struggled to drag his mind out of a very disquieting dream. Fumbling with his spectacles he held his large pocket watch up to the moonlight. 11:33 P.M. So he hadn't been asleep very long at all, not more than an hour. Nevertheless he had dreamed a dream, or rather it seemed as if the Lord had given him a night-vision regarding the people in far-off Bluff.

A member of the Quorum of Twelve Apostles of The Church of Jesus Christ of Latter-day Saints, who bore direct stewardship responsibility for the Saints now living on the San Juan, Elder Snow believed implicitly in the power of the Lord to give him revelation in their behalf. The trouble was, already he could not remember the dream. All he could remember was a terrible feeling of uneasiness, of foreboding, as though some calamitous event or series of events had unfolded or was about to unfold around them.

Rubbing his eyes Elder Snow adjusted his pillow, wondering as he did so that the heat in St. George could be so oppressive. Even at night it was hot, and on this night even the slight bedding with which he had been covered seemed too much.

Tossing his bedding back he lay in the darkness with nothing covering him but his long nightshirt, doing his best to recall what he had dreamed. But when it wouldn't come, his mind began of its own accord to dwell upon the dear people he had called and sent into that desolate wilderness. For nearly six months they had endured the rigorous and terrible privations of a winter trek through unbelievably hostile country, overcoming obstacle after seemingly impossible obstacle as they had made their way toward the mission and destination he had given them. As one of them had recently put it in a letter, the Hole-in-the-Rockers, as they were now being called, had done the impossible simply because they hadn't known they couldn't.

Amazingly, their ordeal hadn't ended. They had now been on the San Juan nearly a year and a half, and their first season's crops had utterly failed and at last word the second season's crops didn't look much better. In order to provide some subsistence, the men had been forced to leave their wives and children to find work during the previous winter, and Elder Snow knew they were continuing their mission due more to sheer faith and pluck than because a way had been opened up for them.

Rising from his bed, he struck a match and touched it to the lantern on his nearby desk, turned up the wick, and began rummaging through a small stack of letters. "Ah," he breathed almost silently, "here it is. Platte Lyman's letter." It was dated simply July 1881, and as he held it to the light and began to read, Elder Snow wondered if this was the reason for his dream.

> I am grieved to report that for the second time this season the river has wiped out all our efforts to harness it. Twice now our five miles of ditch has been obliterated by mud and silt and the rampaging waters, we have lost our headgate once, and worse, our fields have been covered with a layer of hard blue clay that has killed most of our sprouting corn and other crops. We are now running three wagon loads of water-barrels all day every day to water what little we have been able to salvage, but it is nowhere enough and does little more than keep us too tired to think of much else.
>
> Plenty of folks are weak and discouraged, and some have pulled out and others are threatening to. We try not to be down in the mouth, but it is hard, and I promised the folks I would write and see if now is the time we might be released at last.
>
> May we hear from you at your earliest convenience.

Laying aside the letter, Elder Snow's fingers drummed a tattoo on the desktop as he pondered. Platte Lyman was a good man and an excellent leader. Like all leaders, he liked to put his best foot forward. In other words, he wanted the Brethren in Salt Lake to feel good about the Saints on the San Juan, and to not worry about them. Bishop Jens Nielson had done the same when he had visited Cedar City during the latter part of the previous winter. On the 6th of April an article in the *Deseret News* had quoted him as calling for more volunteers to go to the San Juan, telling them that water, soil, and climate were all good, and would abundantly reward perseverance, industry, and labor. Again Elder Snow drummed his fingers, staring at Platte Lyman's letter but not seeing it. For Platte to write such a letter as this, practically admitting failure and most certainly pleading once again for a general release for the people, had to mean that the situation in Bluff had become truly grave.

The question was: did his own troubling dream have to do with the events with the river that Platte Lyman had described so briefly, or was there something else—some terrible danger of even greater proportions, that the Lord was warning him about?

Of a truth, the elderly Apostle didn't know. But if nothing else, he thought as he pulled the cap from his ink bottle and took up his pen, it was high time he apprised the Brethren in Salt Lake City of the terrible difficulties the few remaining San Juan Saints were continuing to endure.

PART ONE

WOUNDS TO THE SOUL

1

Wednesday, August 31, 1881

Bluff Fort

"Say, Billy, you're sure making those old chips fly!"

Pausing, Billy Foreman lowered his ax and smiled at young Ben Lillywhite, who with his brother Joe and friends Will Mackelprang and Sam Rowley had been assigned the task of dragging firewood to the fort's chopping yard.

"Got to chop fast," Billy responded as he stepped over and loosed Ben's rope from the log the boy had snaked in, "especially if I'm going to keep up with you young bucks."

Sitting his dancing horse lightly, Ben Lillywhite expertly coiled his rope. "Then you'll be busier than ever, Billy! Bishop's called Charlie Walton to our crew, so now you'll have five draggers to keep up with!"

"Five? Glory be, son! You'll bury me alive!"

Ben laughed. "Not hardly. Pa says you're the handiest man with an ax he's ever seen. And you and Dick Butt are the only two in the whole fort who even try to use those old double-bladed wonders!"

"President Lyman uses a double blade."

"He does? Fancy that. I thought all he did was freight betwixt here and the Mancos. Well, Billy, I gotta ride. See you in a couple of hours with another log or two!"

At a trot Ben Lillywhite's horse exited the fort, its young master sitting firmly in the saddle with his two dogs trotting after. In admiration Billy watched, wondering that the boy made riding a horse look so easy. Had it been himself in the saddle, he knew, he'd be bouncing every which way, he'd be forever having to adjust his spectacles, and his mount, made nervous because of the poor showing of its rider, would about now be bucking him off into the dirt. No sir, Billy thought ruefully as he wiped his brow with his bandanna and turned back to the firewood he had been chopping, he and horses didn't mix. Didn't mix at all!

Next to the corral, he and the other Latter-day Saint colonizers of the San Juan country had built a wide overhang covered with brush, and under it was stacked, according to lengths, the dozens of cords of wood the community would need for the winter. Stockpiling that much wood was a huge project, and despite what had already been dragged in and chopped to length, Billy knew it was not yet half enough—especially now that he and the other men were going to be gone again, trying to earn a living elsewhere for their poverty-stricken families.

It had been an awful summer—long, hot and dreary, and fraught with frustration. Again and again the ditch had failed to hold water, and the river had been its typical monstrous self, either dropping away from the headgate to create drought, or flooding and sending so much silt into the ditch that it was quickly filled to the level. Worse, there were so few men and boys who could work on it anymore, that the settlers still had not dug it out properly since the last flood. The sad result was that the crops were sparse. Hauling water by the barrel to irrigate their plantings had helped a little but not enough, and the coming winter looked nearly as bleak as had the last one.

Not alone had the ditch and the river given the settlers fits, Billy thought, but with the exception of Hádapa's husband, Navajo Frank, who was now so crippled he could hardly move, the Navajos had kept up a continual round of thievery. The poor bishop and Thales Haskel, who had been off dealing with them practically every week of his life, were still trying to induce the headman Ganado Mucho to get his herd of five thousand sheep back across the river. Most likely, though, it was too late for there to be much winter range left for the settlers' livestock, for sheep grazed everything right to the earth, and according to Lem Redd, the hills of their winter range west of town and north of the river were now completely denuded.

Billy sighed wearily at the thought of the livestock starving, for it troubled him no end to see the poor animals go through any suffering at all. It was worse, though, seeing Eliza and now little Willy going hungry. No longer satisfied with just goat's milk, it seemed that the child had developed a hollow leg. He absolutely never stopped wanting to eat! Eliza was worried that he might be reduced to starvation before the coming winter was over—especially now that there would be such a poor harvest. And Billy could think of no good way to allay her worries.

To make things worse, the heat was continuing without letup! Even in the shade of the woodshed, as folks were calling the brushy overhang, there was no relief. Neither, on most days, was there the least hint of a breeze. Just unrelenting heat and the everlasting sun's glare off the bluffs above and the sand underfoot!

Again Billy wiped his face, and after taking a long pull at the jug of water he kept handy, and readjusting his spectacles and sweat-soaked hat, he lifted the ax and again began his rhythmical swinging, the chips flying off in all directions.

"So the boys think all I do is freight, do they?"

Startled by the unexpected voice, Billy pulled his swing and spun about. "President Lyman, where'd you come from?"

Platte Lyman chuckled. "Sorry to spook you, Billy. I was in the corral examining the cattle we just got in. I didn't mean to evesdrop, but I couldn't help hearing young Ben's comments. Or yours either, for that matter."

"I . . . I don't even remember what I said."

"You complimented my ax work," Platte responded. "Anymore, though, I don't think I could begin to keep up with you. Is that other double blade sharp enough to use?"

Billy nodded. "I sharpened them all last night."

"All of them?" Looking surprised, Platte took up the other double bladed ax and moved a log into position with his foot.

Nodding, Billy also toed his log into a better position. "That's right. Dick Butt once told me how inconvenient it is to start a day with a dull ax, and I've found he was right. So, whenever I get assigned to do any chopping, I always finish up my day at the grindstone."

Pursing his lips, Platte began swinging, Billy joining him, and soon the chips were truly flying.

"How's Eliza?" Platte asked as he worked.

"First-rate, except for a head cold she can't seem to shake. She figures the baby will be here in another two, maybe three weeks."

"Do tell? Does she expect it'll be a boy or a girl?"

"Boy. All along we've both been praying for a girl, but now she wants a boy in the worst way. Wants to name him after those young fellers killed by the Pahutes up at Pinhook."

"That'd be a nice gesture, all right. It was a real shame about those boys. A real shame. By the way, I got word a little bit ago that the Pahutes are back on Sand Island."

"They are?" Surprised at the news, Billy paused in his work. "That isn't going to make Eliza very happy."

"She's afraid of them, isn't she?"

Billy nodded. "With just cause. Besides what they did to Jimmy Heaton and the Wilson boys, that young fellow Posey and his brother have been like a nightmare to her personally. She believes in our mission and wants to do right by them and treat them kindly, but whenever they come near they're filled with such dire threats, that . . . Well, President, she isn't handling the situation very well, and that's a fact!"

Billy toed the log he had been chopping, his thoughts elsewhere. "I just wish the Pahutes hadn't come back, at least not this soon. Just a day or so ago Thales told me he thought they'd stay off in the mountains somewhere for another month, maybe two, most likely waiting for a posse to show up and plotting their next big ambush."

"Yeah, he told me that, too. Of course it's been more than three months since the battle in Pinhook, so they've probably wasted and used up all their ill-gotten gains, and are now looking for more."

"And we're the logical pigeons," Billy grunted. "Do you suppose any other posse ever chased them down?"

"Tell the truth," Platte responded, "I don't. Nobody's brought word of any such encounter to me out in Colorado."

"Nor to us." Once again Billy removed his spectacles and wiped his face with his bandanna. "I'd wager about anything that they spent the summer waiting in ambush, though. After all, this great wilderness of trees and rocks is their country, their home. They know every foot of it—every path, every trail, every seep and spring, every blind, every dead-end draw or gulch that might fool another man and leave him helpless and trapped forever. They know the way of the deer, the elk, the marmot, the badger, the eagle; every wide-pawed track of bear or puma or even of bobcat, every three-toed track of bird and lizard; and even the winding track of the sidewinder rattlesnake speaks volumes to them. According to Thales Haskel, in all this far-off and lonely country there is no place the Pahutes do not know, nothing they do not understand, nothing they do not know how to put to good use."

"Well put," Platte said as he leaned on his ax handle, his eyes never leaving Billy. "You've thought about them a lot, haven't you."

It was a statement, not a question, and Billy nodded. "Quite a bit. I wish there was a way to be friends instead of enemies, so we could exchange knowledge with each other. I'd love to know even a tad of what they do about how to survive in this country. It would make our lives here so much easier and more enjoyable. Besides, I'm assured our knowledge of the Lord and His ways would be of equal value to them."

"Yes," Platte replied as he bent back into the work of firewood cutting, "I'm of the same persuasion exactly."

For a time the two chopped in silence, and Billy could see that Platte Lyman was indeed an expert with the double blade. Each swing downward placed the blade exactly where he wanted it, each lift upward brought a rotation of the handle just exactly sufficient to bring the back blade forward and into line for the next cut. It was also how Billy chopped, he thought to himself as he watched, but not always was his blade lined up perfectly, and sometimes his cut was a little long or a little short, requiring an extra swing to bite out the chip and deepen the cut.

"Will you be going back to Colorado for the winter?"

"I reckon so," Billy responded without slowing his chopping. "It troubles me though, to think of leaving Eliza and little Willy again—especially with her caring for a new baby and all."

"Those who are left here will watch over her, Billy."

"I know that. Thing is, they were watching her last winter, too, and Willy nearly died."

"Yeah," Platte breathed soberly, "you have a point."

"I'm not blaming the Saints, mind you," Billy stated as he again paused in his work. "In that one area Eliza has a streak of pride a mile wide and a foot deep, and she plumb refuses to let folks know when she needs help. Of course she's first to offer help to someone else, but when it comes to herself, well—"

"She's about like the rest of us," Platte finished kindly. "It's a lot easier to give than it is to receive. I hear tell Dick Butt and George Ipson are planning to put in a sawpit up in the ponderosa pine country and will spend the winter cutting lumber. You thought of joining them?"

"I have," Billy grunted, once again putting his back into his work. "They've done a little exploring and found a couple of good sites, but I'm not convinced there's enough demand to pay three men. Them being single, it doesn't require as much to live, so they ought to do fairly well. But as for myself? Well, I've been praying about it ever since you made the announcement that we'd have to go away for the winter to find work, but so far nothing's come to mind. Nothing, that is, that will keep me close to home."

"If it's the Lord's will," Platte stated, toeing another log into place, "it'll come when it's time. By the by, have you looked at the new cattle Lem brought in as the latest assessment from the ranchers?"

"Only in passing," Billy responded without slackening his pace.

"There's quite a difference in the two bunches."

Billy grunted an agreement.

"What can you tell me about them?"

Sensing that Platte wanted verification of his own knowledge rather than knowledge, Billy kept his answer simple. "Bill Ball's are Texas Longhorns, while Spud Hudson's cattle are shorthorns, mostly Durham, I believe. At least they carry the coloring of Durhams—red to roan to white, or red-and-white spotted."

"Did you deal with both breeds when you ran the Co-op back in Cedar?"

"More shorthorn than longhorn, but there were some mixed breeds, too."

Platte's interest was keen. "Is one breed better suited to this country than the other, do you think?"

Billy grinned as Platte reached for the water jug and lifted it to drink, wondering how the president liked the foul, alkaline taste of his own well-water.

"Depends, I suppose," he finally responded. "Longhorns, which are wild cattle that came out of Texas and Mexico, are tall and leggy, and can travel miles and miles to water or good graze, and in a pinch can exist on cactus or most anything else. But their meat is tough and stringy, and on the hoof they don't carry a whole lot of meat per pound. They're also poor milk producers.

"On the other hand, shorthorns or Durhams originated in England and Scotland where graze is plentiful and water not hard to come by. They're shorter by a foot than most longhorns, and can't travel near as far or as well. But their meat is tender and well marbled with fat, and on the hoof they carry a whole lot more meat per pound. They're also good milk producers.

"Apparently most of our shorthorn herds came from animals President Young had trailed in from the Oregon country back in the 1850s. But there's another breed of real meat producers, Platte, one that the statesman Henry Clay imported from England back around 1817, as I recollect. The breed is called Hereford because it was developed around Herefordshire. I've only seen a couple of these animals, but as far as meat production goes, I do believe they'll be the cows of the future."

Platte nodded. "Interesting. Well, that explains why most folks in the settlements go for the shorthorns. Tell the truth, Billy, I'd never seen a longhorn before arriving in this country. But now that I've seen them, I'm thinking maybe we had ought to give them a little more attention. I mean, this is pretty much a desert country around here, too. Seems to me those longhorns would fit in mighty well."

Billy nodded. "Too well, in my opinion. Once those old mossy-backs get off in the rocks and trees of this country, they'll be just like the Pahutes. It'll take a legion of angels to root them out—and they'd be hard-pressed to do it even so. President, if we ever get past the

Pahutes and find a way to the top of Elk Mountain, we'll have plenty of graze and plenty of water, too. Besides which, our people have a natural need for good, rich milk. In my opinion we'd do well to get shut of what longhorns we have, stick to the Durham breed, and wait for the opportunity to pick up a few Herefords and maybe do some crossbreeding. That's what I'd do, anyway."

Platte nodded thoughtfully. "Put that way, what you say makes sense, and I appreciate it. By the by, I've got a horse I'd like you to take a look at—a nice stallion I picked up out in Colorado. Maybe you could ride him a little, if you don't mind, and tell me what you think."

Billy's look was instantly apprehensive. "I'll look at him, President. But to tell the truth, I don't know a whole lot about horses, and I can't ride them for sour apples."

"You're funning me."

"No sir, I am not." Billy was deadly serious, and he hoped it showed. "I even got bucked off one of the Butt brothers' mules this past spring, a gentle critter that's never bucked before nor since. But two crow hops, and I was in the dirt and feeling foolish. So, no, I am not funning you even a little."

Platte was astounded. "But . . . Dick told me you were a real horseman."

Billy sighed. "Dick has a highly inflated opinion of my abilities, I can tell you that. He watched me make a couple of good calls regarding buying some horses back in Cedar, which calls were more luck than otherwise. Then, too, now and then I was forced to talk a wild bronc into being a little more peaceful. I read somewhere that a calm human voice can be soothing to horses, and since I couldn't ride them any better then than I can now, talking soft and gentle was about the only way I knew to do. Occasionally it worked, Dick happened to see it a time or two, and that's why he goes around telling folks I'm what I'm not."

Platte nodded thoughtfully. "Now that I think on it, I haven't seen you do much riding."

"No sir, you haven't. But I'm a good teamster, President, and getting better right along. Give me a wagon and a fair team, and I'll take 'em wherever you want me to go."

"Well," Platte chuckled, "I'll keep that in mind. Howsomever, I'd still like you to take a look at my stallion when you get a minute. You know stock pretty well, and I do value your opinion." Platte paused, spinning the ax handle in his hands. "I'd also recommend that you do a little more riding, Billy. I don't know why, exactly, but the feeling is in me that you'll need that skill more than you can know."

Billy nodded thoughtfully as he tried to imagine what the stake president might be talking about. The two men then hefted their axes and returned to their task, and once again the air was filled with the sounds of chopping and the clean white chips that made such excellent kindling on a cold winter morning.

Bluff Fort

"Eliza, are you certain you're up to this? You do not look well at all!"

Glancing at Annie Lyman, Eliza Foreman did her best to smile. "Of course I'm up to it! Now stop all this blathering and let me finish."

The butter churn held steady between her legs, Eliza was working the paddle up and down through the cream that she, Mary, and Annie had pooled together, and already it was starting to set up. On the table beside her was a small bag of salt, and if she could keep up the pace, she would have finished butter, salted and paddled dry, within another thirty minutes.

Not bad, she thought grimly, unless she took into account her two friends, who for their part of the trade were out in the unrelenting sun, standing over a hot fire, laboring to make a huge kettle of soap. Of course she had helped leach the lye out of the ashes, and she had rendered and purified two entire kettles of grease over the past few weeks. But in her pregnancy, saponifying these ingredients by stirring them for hours over a hot fire, took almost more than she had in her to give, and just about everyone in the fort knew it. So the trade had been insisted upon, and Eliza knew she was being loved.

In fact, time and again through the latter half of the summer, someone had come to her with tasks she could do—mending, churning, and the like—to trade for tasks that she had simply not been up to. But that hadn't kept her from feeling guilty, burdened by a sense of shame that she was not carrying her own weight and that others were being forced to extra labor in her behalf.

Breathing deeply, Eliza paused to wipe her forehead with her sleeve, blinked her eyes against the sweat that dribbled down through her eyebrows, grimaced at the kicking feet of her unborn child, and readjusted herself in the chair. For the past hour or so the baby had been kicking against one particular rib, high up on her right side, and it was hurting so badly that Eliza wondered that she was able to churn at all. For a fact, she thought as she forced the paddle downward against the thickening cream, guilt or not, kicking baby or not, this task was plenty difficult for the likes of a swollen, old, crippled woman like her, especially now that she had come down with this miserable cold. She wouldn't have had the strength to do much more, no matter what she might have wanted!

For a moment Eliza burst into another fit of coughing. When it finally subsided, she said, "I . . . I'm sorry, Annie. It is not polite to cough so heartily when one has visitors—"

"Oh, stuff and nonsense! You aren't impolite, and you know it! But I will be, if I don't soon get back out to help Mary with that saponifying." Annie looked worried. "Do you need anything, dear? A hot mustard plaster? A drink? That cough is sounding positively awful! Honestly, I can't even imagine that we agreed to let you do that churning. You should be flat in bed, and you know it."

"I know no such thing," Eliza remonstrated weakly as she wiped her brow again, wondering that she was feeling so flushed. "But . . . if you wouldn't mind, some water would taste awfully good."

Smiling sympathetically, Annie ladled Eliza a drink, tenderly touched her cheek, and then went back out through the door, leaving Eliza alone. Even Willy was gone—off playing somewhere with little Albert Lyman and his older sister. Eliza breathed in relief at the welcome quiet.

Little Willy. How he was growing and changing. Every week seemed to make a difference, and these changes were becoming especially obvious to her now that the Lyman ladies had taken over his daily care. The child was talking more, his toddle had become a full-fledged—if still a bit clumsy—run, and there was nothing he was not curious about or poking into. In fact, Eliza worried constantly about rattlesnakes, for several had been killed within the fort during the hot summer, and she worried that it was only a matter of time before Willy would locate one in some dark, shady corner he was investigating.

Oh, how she missed her sweet Hádapa, the diminutive Navajo woman who had come to raid but had instead saved the life of little Willy and in doing so endeared herself to Eliza forever. She had been so wonderful with the child, and her sense of the land and its dangers had armed her with a natural instinct on how to protect Willy while at the same time helping him to grow. Of course Hádapa's terribly crippled husband needed her now, and Eliza understood that only too well. But, glory, how she was missed!

It was even worse when she thought of young Jimmy Heaton and his friend Isadore Wilson, the two young cowboys who had been so taken with little Willy. Their older brothers had been friendly enough, but those two had romped on the canvas floor with the child, carried him about on their shoulders, laughed and giggled with him. Well, they had *loved* Willy, and she and Billy had loved them! And now three of the four of them were dead, killed by the twisted, barbaric, and senseless cruelty of the Pahutes!

It had been a terrible thing, so unnecessary, so tragic! Even now Eliza wept as she thought of "her boys" being gone from mortality forever—never again to play with Willy or hold long and earnest gospel discussions with her and Billy.

With a sigh Eliza shook her head, pushed the churn away, and using her crutch, pulled herself to her feet. Somehow she had to stop thinking of these things, dwelling on them. It was time to stop weeping and grieving, and to feel a little joy in the eternal peace she knew Jimmy and Isadore had at last found. Then in another couple of weeks, when her newest child would make his arrival, she could at least partially immortalize the dear boys by naming him after them.

Besides, Eliza thought grimly as she dropped her crutch in order to pull the paddle and lid from the churn and lift it to pour off the buttermilk and expose the butter, that particular band of murderous savages, including the evil Posey, had disappeared into the mountains after the carnage at Pinhook. She hoped the government troops from Fort Lewis would have captured them by now, and they would not be coming back.

"Afternoon, Eliza," Adelia Lyman said as she breezed into the cabin with a smiling Willy in tow. "Willy said he wanted to come home a little early today, so here he is. I—Mercy sakes, woman, you look perfectly frazzled! Here! Give me that heavy churn, before you go into labor right here on the spot! Willy, be a good boy and fetch your ma her crutch so she can get to her rocker. That's a dear. Now I'll paddle the salt into this butter for you, Eliza, and you sit back and rest!

"Oh, by the by!" Adelia exclaimed, continuing her lively chatter. "Kumen brought in word to Platte a little bit ago that the Pahutes are back. He says there's a whole camp of them down on Sand Island. He said he saw Posey there, so I reckon we had all better start keeping our eyes peeled for that miserable boy again—"

Navajo Mountain, Navajo Reservation

The sun was less than an hour above the afternoon horizon when the Navajo youth Bitseel found the dead *belacani*—the dead white man. The first thing about it that surprised him, of course, was that there were no *jeeshóó,* no buzzards. In his land the buzzards announced the death of everything large enough to provide them life, and this white man certainly fit that description. He had also been dead more than long enough for the stench of his rotting flesh to ascend high and far, giving ample invitation to the carrion eaters of the skies. That they hadn't come, and were not now even circling, troubled the young Navajo warrior more than a little.

But not as much, he was thinking, as the second thing about the dead *belacani* that had surprised him. And that troubling thing, Bitseel knew without even a second glance, was that the dead one had been slain by another white man. He had been shot in the back while he had been seated at a small fire, and the force of the bullet had knocked him forward so that he had fallen face-first into the flames, where he had stayed until the fire had burned itself out.

Trembling a little, both from horror and from the natural fear of being near the dead, which fills the breasts of all the *Din'e,* Bitseel backed out of the shallow cave or sandstone overhang where the white man had been camping. It was in his heart to go—to throw himself on his horse and ride far and fast, and to forget that he had even seen this horrid sight. But the youth was on a desperate mission given him by his father, Tsabekiss, and the fading trail of that mission had led him to this place. Where else it might lead, Bitseel did not know. But in spite of the rotting corpse, he would not ride away to find his missing sister Naazbaa until he had the situation here sorted out.

In the dust below the mouth of the cave, Bitseel had already found the small prints made by Naazbaa's moccasins, and so he knew she had been to this place. For a fact, in the two days he had been unraveling her trail, the maiden had been to a great many places. But she was only twelve summers, and Bitseel knew it was natural for one of that age to show great curiosity without much judgment. Had she been a little older she would never have left her mother's sheep and goats alone, especially to go in pursuit of one lost kid. After all, the kid was old enough to fend for itself, and in due time would have returned to the flock.

Bitseel smiled then, a rather grim smile, for he knew his sister would not think such things. Instead her heart would go to the kid, and she would work out its trail and do her best to find it and return it to its mother and the rest of the flock. And that was just what she had been endeavoring to do, her older brother now understood. Her faint tracks showed that plainly, as did the less faint tracks of the missing kid. Unfortunately they also showed her boundless curiosity, as she had wandered here and there beyond the trail of the kid, looking at this and examining that before ever coming back to the tracks of the missing animal.

Such was the way of his sister, and no one knew it better than Bitseel, who had played many tracking games with her through the seasons. The trouble was, it had taken so long to work out Naazbaa's faint trail that the youth was feeling frustrated. And besides, deep down he was feeling that something had happened to her that was not good! In fact he was certain of it, though he had no real idea why. Except that she had not been seen for several days, not since she had walked away from the *hogan* of their parents to spend a few days with the sheep and goats. But those few days were now past—yes, and several more besides, and so old Tsabekiss had sent his son to track down the missing child and bring her back.

Squinting his eyes to more perfectly see shadows cast by even the most shallow depressions in the rocky soil, Bitseel moved across the hillside below the shallow cave. If she had gone up there, he was reasoning, she would most certainly have come back down again. An hour later, however, he was beginning to wonder if she might still be there somewhere, and he had missed her. He had found other tracks, of course—particularly tracks made by the notched sole of a white man's boot. But nowhere on that hillside had he seen any further sign of Naazbaa's footprints.

Though his whole soul revolted at the thought of returning to the place of that gruesome corpse, Bitseel steeled his nerves and angled back up the steep hill, looking everywhere for some small indication of his sister's passing. He was in the rear of the cave, however, standing near where the *belacani* had stood who had slain the other one, before he found another of his sister's tracks—in fact, several of them.

Now Bitseel looked on in wonder. Naazbaa had indeed been in this place, walking about and sitting, for there in the dust were the impressions made by her tiny feet and small body. But what alarmed the young warrior were the notched boot prints of the white killer, for in some places they were on top of Naazbaa's prints, and in other places her prints were over the top of his. Somehow Bitseel's younger sister had gotten involved with these—no, with *that* white man, and now Bitseel's heart began to feel true fear.

2

Thursday, September 1, 1881

Bluff Fort

"I swan, Eliza," Mary Jones declared as she stood before the fireplace in her cabin, stirring up a concoction of ground mustard, flour, and water, "you'd think at your age you'd know better than to stand out in that cool morning wind! Especially when you're in the grip of such a cold."

Trying to breathe through her congestion, Eliza Foreman did her best to smile at her busy young friend. "I was just saying good-bye to Billy and little Willy, Mary. That, and waiting for you. Besides which, the wind is only a breeze, and all I have is a silly cold."

Mary snorted as she stirred. "And you're closing in on fifty years of age and about to have your second baby, Eliza Foreman. Mercy sakes! Can't you see that you must start taking better care of yourself?"

Eliza started to respond but burst instead into a cough and ended up gasping for breath. For a fact her head cold had now dropped into her lungs, and it hurt like fury to breathe. It was strange, she thought, that she had come down with a cold in spite of the terrible August heat. To her it would have made more sense if she had taken cold during the previous winter, when instead she had been healthy as a horse.

Already the air in the cabin was hot, and Eliza wiped her forehead and then brushed a lock of graying hair behind her ear, not taking time to work it back into her bun. Outside the sun was glaring through the brassy sky, heating the sandstone bluffs and the sandy soil until it felt to everyone concerned as though they had settled in an oven. Worse almost than the heat was the intense brightness, which burned both the skin and the eyes and left the Saints longing for shade of any kind. It was a pity they had cut down so many of the cottonwoods along the river for fuel and lumber, though they were fast-growing trees and Eliza knew they would be back in a few short years. Still, with all her heart she missed the greenery of those trees, just as she still missed the cool, green forests of England and even the tree-lined streets of Salt Lake City. Lawsy, she would even have settled for the stunted junipers of Cedar City, for at least one could stand next to a juniper and get a little relief from the unrelenting glare of the sun. But in this horrid San Juan country there was no relief under sage or rabbitbrush or the ever-present sunflowers. The eyes of every one of the precious few of them who were still on the San Juan were red and blurred, and there were days when Eliza didn't think she could stand the heat and the glare a moment longer.

"Another thing," Mary said as if there had been no prolonged silence since her last comment, "are you drinking that raspberry leaf tea every day like Maggie Haskel told you to?"

Eliza made a face, then grinned guiltily.

In disgust Mary stomped her foot. "Eliza, you know very well that drinking that tea will make your childbirth easier. All the women say so—especially those who know anything about it. In fact, not drinking it during our trek is probably why you had such troubles giving birth to little Willy. And that reminds me of something else—have you put an ax or a knife under your bed yet?"

"No, I haven't." Eliza was trying not to laugh. "What on earth good will that do?"

"I don't have the faintest notion of an idea," Mary stormed as she put down the pot and spread a large cloth out on her table. "All I know is that women who've done it swear their labor pains were made less awful by keeping an ax or a knife under their bed for a few weeks before their delivery. Was it me, God willing, I'd do anything I could to make my labor less difficult."

"Mary, that's just an old superstition, and you know it."

"Of course I know it." Mary smiled knowingly. "Nevertheless,

Eliza, there's usually something to these old superstitions. Why, when I first started to liking Kumen, Ma told me to put salt on our fire seven mornings in a row and he would come sparking. I did, and he did. Happened every time I tried it."

"Coincidence, and you know it. By the way, why do folks call fellows and girls being together, sparking?"

"I've heard two reasons." Mary continued to stir vigorously. "First, because the sparks fly when they get around to their first argument. Second, and I think this is the real reason, a young couple up late with each other have to keep building up the fire in the fireplace, thus sending sparks up the chimney. Seeing this, folks quite naturally say they are sparking."

"Makes sense." Eliza blew her nose and then went to coughing again. "Joining the Church solved one superstition I learned back in London when I was a slip of a girl, though for the life of me I don't recall how I learned it. Probably from the Widow Burnham, who seems to have taught me all the other nonsense I ever picked up."

"What was that?"

"Just a little ditty about colors. It goes: 'Marry in white, you'll do all right. Marry in blue, your man will be true. Marry in brown, you'll live in town. Marry in green, ashamed to be seen. Marry in red, wish yourself dead. Marry in black, better turn back. Marry in yellow, got the wrong fellow. Marry in gray, you'll be sad someday.'"

Mary smiled. "You're right. It's hard to wear anything but white in the temple or the Endowment House, so the Church does solve that one. And 'Marry in white, you'll do all right' fits eternal marriages quite well, don't you think? By the way, have you ever heard that it's bad luck for a bride to cook her own dinner?"

"Yes, but that's because she's too nervous to do a decent job." Abruptly Eliza coughed again. "Oh, this is awful, Mary! Coughing is so uncouth!"

"Ma used to say, 'Cough on Monday, cough for fun. Cough on Tuesday, see a strange someone. Cough on Wednesday, get a good letter. Cough on Thursday, expect something better. Cough on Friday, cough for sorrow. Cough on Saturday, see your friend tomorrow. Cough on Sunday, the devil will be with you all week long.'"

"Well, this is Wednesday, so I suppose I should expect a good letter today."

"Maybe," Mary declared with a shake of her head, "but Ma said it meant when you started coughing. Did you start this morning, or yesterday?"

Eliza sighed. "Yesterday afternoon."

"Then get ready, because sometime soon you'll see a strange someone." Mary giggled. "Whatever that means."

Sitting in Mary's rocker with her kerchief to her mouth, Eliza watched as her friend finally got around to spreading the smelly, pasty concoction on the large cloth. Teach her to go out of her way to meet her friend, she was thinking. Now she was going to have to wear that awful hot mustard plaster.

"All right," Mary said forcefully as she took up her jar of tallow, "now we have to grease your throat and upper chest, my dear, after which you must wear this mustard plaster for ten minutes or until your skin turns pink, whichever is longer. Remember, though, wear it too long and you'll blister—not long enough and it won't root that cold out from your chest. With you being in a motherly way, well, you know how it feels every time you cough."

Eliza shook her head. "Mary, I can't just sit here in your home waiting for my skin to turn pink. We've all got work to do, and I need to fetch a fresh bucket of water besides."

"Then I'll fetch it for you," Mary declared brightly. "Because you won't be working today, I can tell you that. You've got to go to bed and sweat this thing out! Now undo those buttons at your neck, Eliza Foreman."

Moments later the two women were making their way across the rutted plaza of the fort toward the well, after which Mary had every intention of putting her friend to bed.

"Mary," Eliza suddenly whispered as she gripped her friend's arm, "have you noticed that man leaning against the meetinghouse wall?"

"How could I help it?" Mary's voice was as hushed as Eliza's. "He was there earlier, when I went to do chores. The way he stared at me, I was truly thankful I wasn't alone."

"I don't know why I didn't notice him. He looks positively evil!"

"Or strange." Mary giggled nervously. "Remember, Eliza: cough on Tuesday, meet someone strange. Well, there he is, stranger than anybody we've seen in a long time! Was it me, I think I'd start believing in superstitions!"

"Humph!"

"I mean it, Eliza. See how his nose has been cut off? Kumen says Apaches do that to their squaws when they've been unfaithful. I'll bet he was unfaithful to somebody, too."

"What an awful thing! Can you imagine a wife doing something like that to her husband?"

"No, but maybe it was his father-in-law. Was Kumen ever unfaithful to me, Pa might do that to him and even worse."

"The bishop?" Eliza asked in mock surprise. "Goodness me!" For a moment she was silent, watching the man out of the corners of her eyes. "Mary, I don't have a good feeling about him! What do you think we should do?"

"Walk faster!" Mary giggled nervously. "Actually, when Julie left me a little bit ago she was going to tell Pa about him."

"The bishop's at home?"

Mary nodded. "Uh-huh. He's about the only man who is. Everyone else is already out working on that awful ditch or up on the river helping to put all those cribs back together. But you're right, Eliza—that man is evil. I can feel it, too. I'll bet anything he's one of those awful outlaws we're always hearing about."

"Well, he smells evil enough," Eliza suddenly declared. "Phew! Why can't some men learn how to take baths once in awhile? Even with this head cold I can smell him!"

"That's because we're downwind right now," Mary giggled again as she held a handkerchief to her own nose. "Besides, Eliza, you mustn't speak so loudly! See? He's looking right at us! He's likely heard you, and now we'll be in trouble sure. Oh, look, here comes Pa! Let's walk slowly again, so we can see the show—"

Bluff Fort

Sugar Bob Hazelton was having trouble keeping his mind and body in one place. Or at least he thought he was. Sometimes he could still tell when his mind was switching about, jumping from one thing to another and playing tricks with the reality of it all. The rest of the time? Well, then everything in his mind seemed real whether it was or not, and nothing else mattered. For instance, at the moment he knew he was leering at two women, but anymore he didn't know if they were actually there, or not. Of a truth it had been so long since he had been with a real white woman, or even seen one, for that matter, that he could hardly remember it. But if his mind wasn't playing tricks again, here was a whole and entire fort full of Mormon women, white ones in real dresses, two of which were passing by and giving him the old once-over—

Just like that little Navajo squaw had done, he thought with a grimace that once might have passed for a smile. Yes sir, she'd given him the old come-on look, all right, and he'd done just that. She'd been good sport for him, too—up to the point when she had up and disappeared. Fact was, until then it had been almost like the old days with her—the days before Old Man Lacy had mutilated him so awfully—

To Sugar Bob it felt as though something had snapped in his head, for without warning he was no longer thinking of the vanished little squaw or even the two passing women. Instead his mind—in fact his very being, it felt like—was back on the slope of Navajo Mountain with old Fred "Dingle" Beston, his miserable, sorry, so-and-so of a partner.

Too bad, too. Dingle had sworn Sugar Bob off two or maybe three times in the past year or so, telling him he wouldn't ever partner with him again. He'd done it first in Texas, he'd done it again on the *Jornado del Muerto,* after both of them had been shot by that Mexican gunslick Espinosa, and he'd done it finally the day Old Man Lacy had cut him. Miserable, sorry fool! Three times! But when Sugar Bob had shown him the map and hunk of silver he'd taken from that nitwit wandering cowpoke—and Sugar Bob grinned as he thought of it—old Dingle had partnered up again in a hurry. Which had ought to learn him good, too! Trust your instincts, Sugar Bob's pa had always told him. Trust your instincts. Too bad old Dingle hadn't learned the same thing.

Of course the silver mine he and that little slip of a squaw had "discovered" turned out to be a lot of hard work, more than Sugar Bob had ever wanted to do in his life. And since that fool squaw had up and vanished on him, disappearing into solid rock the way she had done, and since Dingle was now dead and burned, Sugar Bob was forced to find a new partner so he could get rich off his wonderful discovery. And he'd get one, too—most likely from the LC, unless that fool Bill Ball was still ramrodding the outfit. Then he didn't exactly know for sure—

Sugar Bob Hazelton shook his head vigorously, trying to clear it, to think of something new, something like the two women who had been passing yonder when last he'd noticed them. But somehow his mind seemed stuck, and—

Bill Ball was the one man Sugar Bob feared completely, and he would never on purpose go anywhere near where the LC foreman might be found. Fact is, he didn't even like thinking about Bill Ball! Not unless he could think about finding some way of killing him. Still, he had to locate himself a new partner—

"Goot morning, my friend," a voice suddenly boomed from close beside him, totally unnerving the insane outlaw. "Iss der someting ve can do for you?" And frantically Sugar Bob spun toward the noise.

Cow Canyon

Almost all the way up the hazardous trail through Cow Canyon, Sugar Bob Hazelton was making good time. Still, he couldn't stop thinking of the old man back at the fort, and he was the only one Sugar Bob was thinking of. Nowhere in his heretofore fragmented mind was there even a single thought of the murdered and burned Dingle Beston, neither was there a thought of the new partner he needed so badly. Gone entirely from his thinking also was the fine little Navajo squaw who'd somehow escaped him in the canyon where he'd found that vein of silver ore. Even the two women he'd been lusting after back in the fort, the one tall and the other short, had ceased to exist. Nor did the fact exist that he had seen no other men in the fort to protect it—not one. All Sugar Bob could remember was that one solitary old man, and for some strange reason he was not going away from the insane outlaw's mind.

Spinning fearfully at the sound of the Danishman's voice, for it had so caught him by surprise, Sugar Bob had found himself staring upward into the calm blue eyes of maybe the tallest old man he had ever seen. He had worn a brush of white beard on his chin, his feet had been so gimped up he had to lean on a cane just to stand, and he had been smiling, kind and pleasant as could be.

But he had been so everlastingly tall—maybe a full foot taller than the unsettled outlaw—and Sugar Bob could hardly wrap his feeble and wandering mind around that fact. All his adult life he had thought of himself as pretty much the epitome of manhood—smart, dashing, handsome, tall, strong, quick, brave—just about everything anyone could want in a real man. Along his back trail there were piles of folks who would have agreed with him, too, women and men alike. And some of them, he thought with a smirk, were even still alive.

But of a sudden, standing next to that tall old man in the Mormon fort there on the San Juan River, Sugar Bob had realized he wasn't much of a specimen at all. Why, first the old fool had crept up on him, which Sugar Bob had allowed for years that nobody could do and still stay alive. Then, when Sugar Bob had whipped out his hogleg whilst he was still spinning in surprise, intending to shoot the old idjit sure, the old Dane had simply reached out, taken hold of his pistol by the barrel, and pulled it loose of his grip. Without so much as a by-your-leave he had tossed it into a water barrel that had been handy, after which he had used his one free hand to take Sugar Bob by the arm.

"You vill vant to be going now," he had said kindly, simply. And then he had turned Sugar Bob toward his horse and literally helped lift him into the saddle. And the grip the old man had placed on his arm as he had done so? In awe and disbelief Sugar Bob was still rubbing the spot where those old fingers had dug in, numbing his whole arm and making it virtually impossible for him to resist.

"Ya?" the Dane had said as he handed one trailing rein to the shocked outlaw and then the other. "Und you vill not come back und trouble dees people! No?"

Sugar Bob Hazelton, shocked that he was looking from his saddle practically straight into the eyes of the old man, had been able to do nothing more than nod his head in agreement.

And what else could he have done? he asked himself as he kicked his horse furiously up the narrow trail. His pistol had been gone, and his arm had been so numb that he couldn't get at his knife or his rifle, either one. Besides, there had been no fear in that tall old man's eyes, none at all. And Sugar Bob knew that despite the old fool was all crippled and worn tired with age, with his one free hand he could have reached out and lifted the outlaw from his saddle just as easily as he'd put him there in the first place.

That had once and forever unnerved the no-longer-handsome-and-dashing Hazelton. As much as the calm blue eyes and the amazing height of the man, what had startled Sugar Bob—in fact what had terrified him—was the old giant's amazing strength. That, and the fact—and Sugar Bob knew his mind was repeating this and would continue doing it for years to come—that the old man had evidenced not the smallest particle of fear. And there wasn't a man alive, at least a normal man, who did not fear Sugar Bob Hazelton!

And that, by all that was holy, was why he was riding now, spurring his horse up through Cow Canyon to get as far away from that fort as he could. For if the old man wasn't afraid of him, Sugar Bob's mind screamed at him from somewhere in its dark and murky recesses, then he was for sure and certain scared spitless of that powerful and mysterious old man!

Oola Bikooh, Navajo Reservation

If he hadn't seen the flutter of fabric in the small brush, Bitseel would have missed the opening to the narrow canyon altogether. He had been following the shod prints of two *belacani* horses, had lost the sign on a rocky slope, and had been casting about in widening circles trying to pick up the trail, when the cloth caught his eye.

Riding forward he was surprised to discover a deep crevasse cutting him off from the brush. And though it appeared that a solid mass of sandstone was all that awaited him across the crevasse and beyond the brush, when he examined the earth at the edge of the crevasse, there was unmistakable evidence that the *belacani* horses had paused here, and then vanished.

For a time Bitseel studied these things, thinking deeply. But it was only when he had climbed back on his horse in despair that he was able to see the logs on the far side of the crevasse—logs that had been cut and used as a primitive bridge and then pulled out of sight across the crevasse.

Picketing his horse, Bitseel easily jumped the crevasse and moved to the brush, where he discovered to his horror that what he had seen fluttering in the brush was his sister's woman-cloth—that which she had worn to cover her nakedness since becoming a woman a few months before—and which no woman of the *Diné* would ever willingly go without.

His heart now turning from fear to stone, the young Navajo warrior next found more prints made by the *belacani* horses, and he was not at all surprised to discover that the mass of sandstone was split in two, and that the hoofprints passed between the two abutments. Interestingly, the rock was formed in such a way that the split could not be seen from the far side of the crevasse, nor could be seen the narrow canyon that opened up beyond where the trail emerged.

Stealthily Bitseel moved forward, his rifle at the ready, and in a short time he came upon a small cluster of horses grazing quietly along the canyon floor—two of which were the *belacani* horses he had been following. Other than them, and a number of swallows that were darting through the air high above him, Bitseel could sense no other life.

He worked his way carefully down the widening canyon, and by the time he had reached the point where it narrowed again before plunging downward into the churning waters of the big river, he knew several things: First, this was the place where his father and old Hoskanini had come to gather their *beesh ligai,* their white iron or silver. He knew also that two of the horses belonged to Hoskanini, both he and his father had left other signs that Bitseel easily recognized. It was also obvious to the youth that white men, perhaps many of them, had spent a great deal of time in the canyon, over a great number of years, working the wide vein of silver ore he had found. Gazing upon the *beesh ligai,* Bitseel found himself rejoicing for old Hoskanini, for this would bring much prosperity to him and his family. Yes, this had to be the canyon called by his father *Oola Bikooh,* Gold Canyon, though where any gold might be, Bitseel had no idea.

But here and there he *had* found the notched boot prints of the *belacani* killer he had been seeking—those and the now barefooted tracks of his beloved little sister. More angry now were growing Bitseel's thoughts, more bitter his heart. Though the *belacani* killer and his sister seemed to be gone again, large in Bitseel's mind was growing the knowledge of what the man had most likely done to his sister. *Baadíishjááh,* he had taken her clothes from the very young woman, and that could only mean—

Bitseel was making his way almost blindly from the canyon, his hatred against the *belacani* raging within him, when he chanced to see the ancient and faded cross that had been carved low down in the sandstone wall—that, and beneath it, the tiniest corner of blue fabric protruding from the sand. Almost he passed by it, almost. But then with a cry of anguish he moved forward and pulled it free, to discover not the body of his sister as he had expected, but only her long flowing skirt, sewn by the loving hands of his mother.

Frantically Bitseel began to dig with his hands, throwing sand behind him as he sought his sister's body. Instead, however, he found an opening under the sandstone overhang, a sort of cave that led inward. Worming his way forward he was astounded to find himself in a larger room where he could stand without difficulty. Using *belacani* matches to light a candle set on a stone shelf near his head, Bitseel inched slowly forward into the tunnel, growing ever more fearful. And it was at the very end of the tunnel, where wire gold glittered all about him, that Bitseel found the battered, mutilated body of his little sister, cowering even in death from the *belacani* horror she had only through death been able to escape!

With haunted eyes Bitseel removed his shirt and covered his

sister's nakedness, and then with a heart of stone he turned and made his way back into the sunlight. He would ride to the *hogan* of his parents with the news, he vowed. But after that, the evil *belacani* killer with the notched boot print, would never again know rest. More, no others of the despised white race would find mercy at his hands—

3

Friday, September 2, 1881

Bluff Fort

"My goodness, Eliza! Do you realize that you and Mary actually saw the infamous Sugar Bob Hazelton? And lived to tell about it?" Annie Lyman chuckled more from nervousness than humor. "Rumor has it that not many have, you know."

Eliza nodded soberly. "I know. I've heard the rumors, too."

"Were you frightened of him?"

"Eliza frightened of Sugar Bob?" Billy chuckled as he finished lacing his boots. "If that poor soul had known the sheer grit of the two women he was leering at, he'd have cut and run long before the bishop arrived."

Looking up at her husband, Eliza smiled weakly. "That's not so, Billy, and you know it."

"I know nothing of the sort. None of you women know how brave you are—how full of pluck. Look at you, Eliza, pioneering in this howling wilderness day after day with almost no resources, carrying your second child at the same time, and facing untold dangers from every direction with nothing but faith and an iron skillet for your weapons! Glory be, hon-bun! If that isn't true bravery, I don't know what is."

Helplessly Eliza looked up at her smiling friend. "Pay no attention to him, Annie. In his spare time Billy's fixing to be a dime novelist, and you know the aversion of those fiction writers to the truth."

"I don't know, Eliza." Annie's grin was wider than ever. "It sounded like the gospel truth to me."

"Humph! Goes to show what either one of you know. For a fact I was scared to death, not of the man so much as of the perfectly awful feeling I had when I was looking at him."

"Did you have any idea who he was?"

Soberly Eliza shook her head. "I didn't. Had I known, or if I'd been alone, then I'm certain I would have been terrorized." Pausing, Eliza took a deep breath and pushed at her unborn baby's feet, trying to move them away from her sore ribs. "But I didn't and I wasn't, Annie, so I wasn't really frightened. To tell the truth, the worst thing about the man was his stench. Even with this silly cold I could smell his horrid odor, and I'm grateful I didn't have to get any closer than I did."

"So am I," Billy stated as he rose to his feet, clapped on his hat, and hefted the burlap-shrouded water jug he had carried daily throughout the summer. "Annie, it's mighty kind of you to come over so early, but you know Eliza. She sees something to do she'll do it, consequences be darned. But maybe if you'll stick with her and force her to stay off her feet—"

"Don't worry, Billy. She'll be fine. I've brought Brother Lyman's mending, and she has yours and Willy's, so we both have more than enough to keep us busy."

"Good." Billy smiled, leaned down, and kissed his wife, and then stepped to the cabin door. "Remember, I'll be at the woodshed if you need me, or if the baby decides to come early. That's why the bishop's keeping me here in the fort, you know."

"Oh, for heaven's sake!" Eliza groaned with exaggerated frustration as she lifted up her shoe to throw it. "Go chop some wood, Billy, so we poor women won't freeze to death this winter!"

With a playful yelp and a grin Billy ducked the poorly aimed shoe and slipped out the door. Thank goodness, he thought as he strode toward the woodshed, that Bishop Nielson had agreed to keep him close by—

San Juan River

Posey's heart was not good. For most of the day he had sat on a rock overlooking the big river, listening to the whispered song of *pah,* the water, and rehearsing in his mind what had occurred early that morning. Once again, as had happened during almost every turmoil of his mind since that flight up the steep canyon of the LaSals the previous spring with the hand of the comely Too-rah held tightly in his own, the difficulty had managed to come down to her.

Pu-neeh! That's what the old grizzly Poke had called him when they had happened to cross paths a little after sunrise. It had been a surprise meeting, too, and without thinking he had smiled at Poke's favorite and only younger sister, Too-rah, who had been following a little behind. *Pu-neeh!* Skunk! the surly Poke had snarled. And he had sneered the name particularly loudly in the direction of Too-rah, whom he had then grabbed and dragged away by the arm. The whole thing—the name, Too-rah's enforced slavery, Posey's terrible fear of Poke—all of it put together was infuriating to Posey, not to mention humiliating, and he had absolutely no idea of what to do about it!

In his mind Posey went back to the big raid on the horse ranch in Colorado, and to all the power and glory of the next few weeks as Mike's band, Poke's band, Wash's band, and all the other bands that had been involved, had battled and slain the cursed *mericats,* taken their wealth from them, and then thrown it in every direction.

Yes, during the weeks-long foray some things had gone badly, but Posey was certain he knew why that was so. He was just as certain that, after he had become chief of his own band, and he knew that day was coming, no such mistakes would be repeated.

Despite those things he looked longingly backward in his memory, thinking of the glorious summer on the back of Elk Mountain where he and the others from all the nearby bands had slept and played *ducki,* games of chance with the white man's face cards, and rent the air with their piercing shrieks and exulting chants while they danced around their fires at night. It did not matter that they either lost, used up, or abused every scrap of their ill-gotten wealth, which by late summer had left the Pahutes as ragged and poverty-stricken as before. All of them knew that successful raids could be conducted again, great raids! And in the meantime there were always the mormonee, the foolish people in the unfinished fort along the big river. Anything could be stolen from them, anything at all, and at almost any time. So for the people who were calling themselves Pahute, life through the past summer had been good, very good.

For Posey things had been even better. One morning while Mike, old Chee, Poke and his brothers, Mancos Jim, and the others were still in the back reaches of Elk Mountain, continuing the celebration of their great victory, Posey had caught sight of himself in a still pool of water. That had become a transforming moment, for he had suddenly seen himself as he looked to others—as he looked to Too-rah.

Cutting the sharp leaves of a yucca bush and binding them with a buckskin thong to form a sort of comb, Posey had begun to work the years of tangled snarls and knots out of his faded green hair. It had not been easy, and several hands full of hair had lain strewn about the earth when he had finished. Yet, with it parted in the middle and braided into two whips down behind each ear, over each shoulder, and onto his chest, and with a strip of gaudy red cloth woven into and around each braid, he was more than pleased with his appearance.

From an ugly old Uncompahgre woman he had cajoled a pair of beaded moccasins and some fringed buckskin leggings. And from Tobuck-ne-ab, who was now called Mancos Jim, he had traded one of his best stolen ponies for a fiery red shirt that had come from the body of one of the dead *mericats* in the LaSals—a red shirt complete with a darkened bullet hole in the left breast. All this, plus the fine hat he had taken from one of the two young white brothers slain on the top of Harpole Mesa, as well as dabs of blue and red paint on his face, made Posey look every bit the chief he had always thought himself to be.

Having discovered his own striking image, no longer was he afraid of being seen by Too-rah. No longer did he drop his eyes in shame and duck out of sight whenever she came near. Instead he had strutted proudly, this way and that through the encampment, and there was no doubt in Posey's mind that the *nan-zitch,* the girl, had noticed and was paying particular attention.

It was quickly proven to be so, for within a day of his acquiring his new appearance and becoming a true man of the People, Posey had managed to sneak Too-rah away into the trees and once again spend a little time holding her soft and willing hand. Every day or so through the summer, that great and wondrous thing had been repeated, until Posey had come to expect that it would always be so.

To make matters more interesting, Too-rah, who was the last child of Norgwinup's old age, was being reared by her grizzly brother Poke, who did not hesitate to enlist the aid of his fearsome brothers, Hatch, Sanop, Bishop, and Tehgre, in seeing that their baby sister was never allowed in the presence of the warrior Posey. Such restrictions made courtship a risky proposition, for had he been caught, Posey felt certain he would have been shot to death on the spot. But by stealth he got in to see her, and he got out again by the same dangerous trail. Through the summer he had never been caught, and in his mind the love-struck youth was now living through each of those brief but sweet encounters once more, glorying in the knowledge that Too-rah felt just as strongly about him as he felt about her.

Now, though, the insults and the threats and the keeping of Too-rah from him, were becoming to Posey less and less like a game. Somehow it seemed that the young girl should be his, though of a truth he had no real idea of what that might mean. Still, it was comforting to have her nearby, to see the sidelong glances of dark eyes or the flutter of long lashes, and to hear her voice as she spoke quietly but with conviction of his own magnificence and greatness. These things Posey craved, and with all his soul he wanted them to continue.

The trouble was, with the approach of yellow leaves, shortened days, and colder nights, the Pahute bands had left the mountain and come to the big river. It was customary for them to meet with the Navajo there, to trade or gamble venison and tanned buckskins for that which would make life more bearable and even beautiful—the silver ornaments and woven wool blankets manufactured by the *Diné*.

It was normally a good time, too; even a fine time, filled with more nights of dancing around the fires and more *ducki* during the day. But despite those things that all were looking forward to, here on the big river the brothers of Too-rah had grown more vicious, more insulting, more determined to keep the youth at bay, and Posey had not been able to spend even one moment alone with the lovely *nan-zitch*. This troubled him greatly, though he could think of nothing he might do that would make things better.

There was also a third thing that was distressing Posey, something that even his great mind could not exactly define. With the big raid of the previous spring, he had tasted what to him seemed true adventure—true living. He had seen white men put under the grass, and he had seen how easy it was to do. And as each of the days of their fleeing from the *mericat* posse had passed, the Pahutes all the while leading them to where the ambush had at last unfolded in the LaSals, murder and high adventure had begun to feel normal.

But then, with a suddenness that was surprising, the greatest adventure of Posey's life had ended! All summer he and the other warriors had watched from the rocky brow of their mountain retreat, hoping fervently that more posses of rich *mericats* would be coming after them. All summer they had shot their rifles and ridden their ponies in preparation for another great battle, for surely the white *mericats* would not allow so many deaths to go unpunished. And when those *mericats* did come, they chanted and shrieked to each other around their fires at night, the warriors of the People knew the perfect trails to lead them along, the perfect box canyon traps into which the foolish whites could be led.

But despite that wonderful knowledge, no one of the whites had come to the San Juan to challenge them, to satisfy their lust for more blood! Not once in all the long summer had there been even a hint of dust on the distant eastern horizon! Even the blue-coats on the other side of the Blue Mountain had returned to Colorado. And so now Posey and some of the others had grown restive. They, and he, wanted action! He wanted more horses, more saddles, more guns, more of everything the whites seemed so easily able to obtain. But mostly he wanted to see more white men being put under the grass! Only from such a battle would he feel again the excitement that had daily filled his breast during the spring. Only from such a battle, he was also certain, would he ever get the fine rifle he was still dreaming of, the rifle which would finally give him the power to take on the peculiar whites he had come to despise the most—the mormonee in the unfinished fort only a mile or so upstream from where he now sat.

Only, there had been no battle, not even a skirmish. So how, Posey wondered for the hundredth time during that day alone, could he find for himself the fine rifle of his dreams? Without such a rifle, how could he ever fulfill his destiny and become chief? And how—and of a sudden this was by far the most important question—how, without a fine rifle, could he get such things for the lovely Too-rah as would impress her enough to leave the fearsome grizzly Poke and her other brothers, to be with him?

Abruptly Posey's mind went to the fort of the cowardly mormonee. It would be from them that he would get his fine rifle, he now realized. Yes, and it would be from them that he would obtain the fine things that would turn the mind of Too-rah away from her brothers and toward him. But where—?

And suddenly Posey knew! The husband of the tall mormonee woman, who walked with a stick, the frail mormonee who wore glass before his eyes, had held he and Scotty under the muzzle of a fine new rifle. *Oo-ah,* yes! Surely that had been a sign that the rifle was to be his, and that he would use it with as great a power as had the small mormonee.

For an instant that thought gave Posey pause, for he had no desire to face the man again. Truly that one had shown no fear. But if he were not present in his foolish log *wickiup*; if his tall, ugly squaw was there alone, then Posey had no doubt he could quite easily take the rifle from her. *Oo-ah,* yes! Without doubt he and Scotty could conduct a successful raid upon that one log *wickiup*!

But not now, he thought, as he scrambled to his feet, his mind filled with resolution. It was too close to darkness, and not a warrior of the People would be so foolish as to make a raid on the mormonee *wickiups* at night. Night was when they came together. Night was when all the men returned from where they had spent the hours of daylight in their foolish labors. No, Posey grinned as he turned back toward the encampment of Poke's band, darkness was the time for making raids on the mormonee horses and mormonee cattle. Daylight, he thought as his grin grew wider, would be the right time for making his raid on the log *wickiup* of the tall and ugly mormonee woman—

Dalton Springs

Curly Bill Jenkins had just finished his supper—a can each of beans and peaches—when he heard the movement out in the early evening darkness. Without moving, the tall, cadaverous-looking, thin man with the sad eyes listened, and when it came again a moment or so later, faint and almost not a sound at all, he knew he was being watched. Casually, he rose to his feet, stretched, spread out his bedroll, and emptied the pot of coffee onto the fire, dousing the flames even as he silently cursed the waste of his perfectly good brew. Back at his bedroll he bunched it up some, stuffing under it his saddle blanket and saddlebags. Then in the darkness he took his rifle and backed silently into the brush that surrounded his lonely camp, to settle down and wait.

Curly Bill—given that moniker down in Texas on account of his completely bald dome—had been hanging onto the business end of a rifle and shooting squirrels for his ma's dinner pot since who flung the chunk, and maybe even before that. Born in Cajun country along the border of Arkansas and Louisiana and raised on fiddle music and blackstrap molasses, Curly had somehow grown into a peaceable sort of young man. Righting a wrong one night, he had found himself drifting west into Texas ahead of some mean-spirited citizens who had not appreciated his interference in their midnight necktie party, and who had decided to hang him instead. But being at least as innocent as the man he had liberated, Curly at length had voiced his objection through the business end of his rifle, leaving at least one Louisiana vigilante who would never knot another rope. And of course after that, Curly Bill could never go back.

In Texas he had adapted well to the cattle business and had become a top hand with both a horse and a rope, and about all anyone could ever say against him was that he was too easygoing, and would walk an extra mile just to avoid a fight. Some criticized that, but Curly Bill had seen enough trouble in that one night to last him a lifetime, and so he did his best to avoid it. But when trouble came to him, like it was right now as the figure of a man moved across the darkened clearing and up to his bedroll—well, under those conditions Curly Bill had no trouble taking a stand, no trouble at all.

"Here, there!" the man in the darkness growled as he poked Curly Bill's bedroll with the end of his rifle. "Get up afore I blow a hole clean through you!"

There was a moment's silence while the bedroll did not move, the man cursed violently, and without the least hesitation he began firing, levering round after round into Curly Bill's bedroll, totally destroying it.

"Well, I done warned you!" he grunted after his rifle had clicked on an empty chamber. "Too bad, too! Now I got to find me a partner somewhere's else."

"You might have tried asking," Curly Bill breathed from where he had risen to his feet. "Now toss down that rifle, mister, and get your hands up where I can see 'em!"

Spinning, the man dropped his rifle and slapped his hand toward the weapon at his side. But his pistol was not even out of the holster when Curly Bill's bullet tore through the fleshy part of his hand, bringing forth a howl of pain and almost endless profanity.

"Mister," Curly Bill drawled as he stepped forward to the edge of the clearing, "you do learn slow. Now stop all that caterwauling and toss a little wood on them coals. I've a hankering to see who the devil can be so all-fired stupid."

Still swearing ferociously the man obeyed, and a few moments later, when the flickering light had revealed the man's face, Curly Bill began to chuckle.

"Sugar Bob Hazelton, as I live and breathe. Looks like old I. W. Lacy really did take his knife to you. Improved your appearance, too, if I do say so myself."

"Yeah," Sugar Bob snarled as he gripped his wounded hand, "and paid for it a'plenty! You'd be that useless coward Curly Bill Jenkins. Old Dingle always liked you, but he never had no more sense than a little beggar with a big navel, and now he lies rotting in a stupid cave to prove it. Too bad you wasn't under them blankets that I just shot to doll rags. Now you've gone and ruint my hand for the second time this week, the first being when a miserable old fool of a no-good Mormon like to have twisted it clean off my arm."

Vehemently the insane man then began cursing the Mormons, almost shocking Curly Bill with the pure venom of his speech. "Them and their fearsome ugly women," he snarled as he wound down before lapsing into a troubled silence, "are the spawn of the devil hisself, and that's a natural fact!"

"Ordinarily," Curly Bill replied conversationally, "I'd argue to the death with the likes of you over most anything at all. But when it comes to Mormons, Sugar Bob, I'm forced to agree. I ain't never heard a good thing about 'em in my life, and I don't expect I ever will. But then, you gut-shrunk, sorry excuse for a woman-killing worm, you can't be much different from the worst of them, and that's another natural fact for you to chew on!"

But Sugar Bob, far from listening to the mostly accurate and well-chosen insults of his newest captor, had felt the snap in his mind and was gone again. As far as he was concerned, Curly Bill Jenkins and his rifle no longer existed, nor did the small fire in the well-hidden camp. Instead he was back in the Mormon fort on the San Juan, leaning against the wall and leering at the two passing women.

That tall one, he was thinking, the one with the crutch, looked to have more wrinkles than a hard-boiled shirt, and she'd been pinched so thin she must have been weaned on a pickle. Like a snake on stilts, his warped mind snickered as his leer grew wider, with a bulging belly like she had swallowed a melon. Horrors!

But that other one prancing along beside her, now, the short one—mercy, mercy! She was purty as a little red heifer in a flower patch. Sure as a belch after a big meal, that little filly would make him a fine blanket companion—

Abruptly Sugar Bob remembered the way Old Man Lacy had cut him, and his leer changed to a frowning snarl of venomous hatred. Because of Lacy, his mind screamed in frustration, women weren't good for nothing anymore; nothing, except to maybe paw around a little and then carve up the way I. W. had done him, just exactly like he'd done with that little squaw down on the reservation. Of course she hadn't actually been old enough to be a real squaw, but she'd been old enough, by Tophet, for him. Only somehow she'd snuck off on him, her trail had vanished against a huge sandstone cliff, he'd buried her dress there just to show her, and—

But, Sugar Bob furiously reminded himself, that'd been down near Navajo Mountain, down where he'd found that famous silver mine everybody was calling Peshleki. This was here, up under the Blues, and he was trying to get a new pardner to mine that silver. Only now this fool Curly Bill Jenkins had shot up his hand—

The Navajo girl, and even the two women at the fort, abruptly forgotten, Sugar Bob Hazelton growled and snarled in helpless anger and frustration. Curly Bill grinned at the man's antics, and was just getting set to fetch his rope and tie the wanted man up for the night, when with a wild howl Sugar Bob spun completely about, pulled a terrible face at Curly Bill, and then ran shrieking into the darkness. And Curly Bill was left with his rifle at the ready but the trigger unpulled, absolutely dumbfounded by the strangeness of what he had just seen.

4

Sunday, September 4, 1881

Bluff Fort

"All right, brothers and sisters. Any questions?" Platte Lyman smiled as he waited. The Bluff members of The Church of Jesus Christ of Latter-day Saints had concluded their worship services earlier, and he had just finished outlining the tasks that all of them must accomplish within the next few weeks if the community were to be ready for winter. Or at least, he thought ruefully, as ready as they could be. "Yes, Annie?"

"You'll be leaving for Colorado in the morning?"

"That's right. Before daylight, if all goes well. I'll be taking little Albert R. with me, so you know it won't be a long trip. As some of you know, before we came out here, Billy Foreman was called by the Brethren in Salt Lake to put in order the cooperative store back in Cedar. The past two days he and I have been cording firewood at the woodshed and at the same time organizing all we'll need to establish a cooperative store here in Bluff. While the weather's good, I'll be going after supplies for the store, and after my return we'll officially capitalize it and make certain every one of us has as much stock ownership in it as he or she desires."

"How do you propose to pay for these supplies?" someone called out.

Again Platte smiled. "Somehow, George, the Lord has managed to soften the hearts of several of the Gentile merchants in Durango and thereabouts. They've seen the sort of work we've done for

Mr. Mears on the D&RG Railroad, they've become acquainted with Elder Silas Smith and others of our people who came through the Hole and have now settled on the Mancos River and in the San Louis Valley, and they are aware of the integrity of Latter-day Saints from Moab and elsewhere who have taken up work in the mines or in the freighting business along the western slope of the Rockies. In short, they have decided that we are a people who can be trusted. I'll have no difficulty in obtaining credit."

"The trick," someone murmured to a round of grim laughter, "will be to pay them all back again."

Platte nodded. "That's exactly right. But brothers and sisters, if we have faith and do our duty here where we have been called to serve, even that will be given to us—"

Bluff Fort

"Mercy sakes, Eliza, you sound awful!" Ann Rowley, who because of an ill child had skipped the business meeting following worship services, was doing her best to sound upset. "You should be home in bed, taking care of yourself."

Trying desperately to breathe despite the aching heaviness in her chest, Eliza shook her head to show her disagreement. Truly she did feel terrible, and even Billy had tried earlier to convince her to stay in bed. In fact through the early morning she had done just as Billy had directed, staying in bed and trying to get some rest. Thing was, her chest hurt just as badly when she was laying down as it did when she was standing up, so why not, she reasoned, be up and attending worship services with her husband and son?

"I . . . I just can't bear to be abed when everyone else is . . . in meeting," she replied, her voice sounding terrible even to herself.

Ann Rowley looked perplexed. "In your condition? Merciful heavens, woman! Not alone are you hardly a week away from delivery, but you look and sound positively awful. What did you think you could do? Stand up and lead the singing?"

"I don't know. I . . . I—" Abruptly Eliza began to cough, a long, wracking series that doubled her over and left her gasping for breath and dripping with sweat.

"I . . . I'm sorry, Ann," she breathed as she used her crutch to pull herself upright once more. "I don't hardly know what's gotten into me—"

"Eliza, you are not well, and I'm not funning you even a little. Has Maggie Haskel seen you lately?"

"Not . . . not since—" was all Eliza could get out. Then she was coughing again, a dizzying bout that not only doubled her over but left her totally starved for air. Her eyes wide with fear, Eliza hit her chest with her free hand, and as she began the wrenching process of inhaling a little air between coughs, she was startled to hear a distinct whooping sound with each short intake of breath.

"Oh, lawsy," Ann whispered as she reached out to steady her friend, "that sounds terribly like the whooping cough—Eliza, honey, I don't know whether to take care of you or go get Billy and Maggie. But you've got to get back in bed!"

Feeling not alone lightheaded, but now in pain low down where her baby was, Eliza nodded. "I . . . I can get back. Bring . . . bring Billy. And hurry, Ann. P . . . please—"

Bluff Fort

"As usual," Platte Lyman was continuing, "Bishop Nielson will be in charge of the fort. He's put his counselor, Kumen Jones, in charge of the harvest, such as it is. Kumen, would you please stand and tell the folks what's been planned?"

"Certainly." Kumen was on his feet in an instant, his ever-present walking stick held before him with both hands. "Brethren, we'll be getting the corn in, the cane, and the wild hay up on Recapture. We'll also be storing in the cabin we've prepared as an icehouse any squashes, pumpkins, gourds, melons, and potatoes that have made it to maturity. Sisters, you'll—"

"What's to keep the Pahutes out of the icehouse when they come snooping around?" someone interrupted.

"A stuffed rattlesnake has been donated to the cause, all coiled up and ready to strike." Kumen grinned, for everyone knew how diligently the Pahutes worked to avoid contact with rattlesnakes. "We're going to have it laying in the dirt just outside the door. We just don't want any of you folks shooting it or beating it to death again with a broom. One death had ought to be enough for any of the Lord's creatures, rattlesnakes included.

"As far as the corn goes, we'll be storing it in that empty cabin next to where the store will be. We also have a little wheat and barley that lived long enough to head out, and we'll have bins for those, too.

"You sisters will be in charge of rendering molasses out of the cane, and the bishop and some of the boys will make certain you have plenty of firewood for the purpose. We're also going to need more soap, so I've asked my wife to be in charge of gathering all the fat drippings from everyone so it can be saponified."

"Won't we need our drippings for our rag lanterns?"

Kumen smiled. "Not this winter. President Lyman will be bringing back sufficient lard or tallow and other materials to pour hundreds of candles, which give better light and do not put off such a foul odor. I've asked Sister Eliza Foreman to take charge of that project. We also have a limited amount of coal oil for the lanterns, but of course that will be used sparingly. So, no more grease lights, at least this winter.

"Brethren, we have a few hogs that we'll need to butcher, and Sam Rowley and Josh Stevens have promised they'll have a smokehouse finished by the time the sisters can have the hams, tongues, and side meat salted and cured. Molasses will take the place of brown sugar in the curing. We don't have any hickory wood, either, but Sam assures me dried corncobs and juniper will do fine. We'll also be smoking all the fish we can catch, so remember to set your lines each night. When that net we've ordered comes in, we'll use it instead, and hopefully we'll have more fish. Oh, that's right. We'll also need to move the outhouses again, so we'll need two new pits dug. The bishop will be making those assignments in the morning."

"We're also going to be butchering and jerking the meat from some of our long-legged Texas cattle," Platte added. "My brother Walter and whoever else accompanies me to Colorado will be herding the others along behind, so we can sell them and rid our range of them in favor of the more productive shorthorn breeds."

"That's a fine idea," Kumen stated in agreement. "I hate like fury trying to milk a longhorn cow!"

"Or any other kind of cow!" someone quipped.

"What about the water?" Mary Ann Perkins called out to end the quiet laughter. "That out of the well is every bit as terrible as what's in the river!"

Kumen nodded his agreement. "I know that, Mary Ann. But short of digging another well and most likely finding the exact same water, I don't know what to recommend."

"We could make charcoal filters out of several barrels," Billy suggested.

"Do you know how to do that?" Kumen asked.

"I've seen it done, and it isn't difficult. A dozen would probably keep all of us in fresh water—that is, if we used it only for drinking and cooking."

Kumen turned to Platte Lyman. "President, what do you think?"

"Sounds wonderful. I'm as tired of drinking alkali water as the next person. Brothers and sisters, all who would be willing to use filtered water sparingly, raise their hands. Let's see. That's unanimous. Thank you. Billy, will you accept the assignment of putting these barrel filters together?"

Billy nodded. "I'll get on it as soon as you return from Colorado. We have plenty of barrels, but I'll need at least a dozen spigots. And someone to burn up some charcoal."

"I'll pick up what I can in the way of spigots in Durango, and Kumen will have somebody on the charcoal project by morning. Won't you, Brother Jones."

Kumen gave his best easygoing smile. "Whatever you say, President."

"Thank you." Platte grinned in response. "Anything else, Kumen?"

"Likely, but right now my mind's drawing a blank."

"Sorry to hear that," Platte teased. "Brother Lem Redd? Or Bishop Nielson? Anything more from the bishopric?"

Both men shook their heads.

"Very well. Brothers and sisters, are there any other questions before we adjourn?"

"Yeah! What do we do about all those Indians down on Sand Island?"

"That's right, Pla . . . I mean, President Lyman," someone else called out. "There are quite a bunch gathered there. Are you sure this is the best time for you to be leaving?"

"It is if we're to have those supplies. As for the Pahutes who are camped on Sand Island, Brother Haskel has the apparently eternal assignment of keeping his eye on things. Thales, can you tell us what is happening?"

Slowly the Indian missionary and interpreter rose to his feet. "It's a powwow," he replied simply.

"How do you know that?"

Thales' piercing blue eyes impaled the questioner. "Henry told me."

"You'd trust the word of an Indian?" another asked.

"More than most white men." Thales was deadly serious, and it showed. "Besides that, Henry's a fine boy, one I'd be proud to call my son. The Lord's given him some interesting dreams about himself and his people, so he knows quite a bit about what they've lost over the centuries. He also understands our role in this country at least as well as most of us, and far better than the rest of us.

"Finally, he knows that those who insist on stealing from us are going to be destroyed, and the thought frightens him. He is very concerned that his people learn to make wise decisions—that they find their way back to Christ."

"As if he knows the Lord," someone snorted.

"Sister Delia," Thales said by way of reply, "why don't you tell 'em a little more about Henry."

"He is a wonderful young man," Adelia Robison Lyman stated when she had reached her feet. "I know, because I've been probing his thinking. As a child I learned the Paiute tongue, which is about the same as the Ute language these folks speak. So Henry and I have had several long discussions. I have also been reading to him from the Book of Mormon, and he accepts everything in it—and everything else I tell him. More, his prayers to *Shin-op*, their name for

Jesus Christ, are among the most sincere and humble petitions I have ever heard. Henry is as dedicated to righteousness as anyone I have ever known, and is being greatly blessed with various gifts of the Spirit. For that matter, old Peeagament and his wife, Peeats, are about the same. Peeats is a wonderfully conscientious worker, and I feel terrible that some of her children—in fact all but Paddy Grasshopper—are making her old age so miserable."

"Thank you, Sister Lyman." Thales glared about at the small group of Latter-day Saints. "For a fact, despite the false traditions of their fathers, a good many of our Lamanite neighbors are the same as Henry—honorable men and women. But like us white folks, they do have a few bad apples in their barrel. They're the ones that Henry knows are going to start dying. Too bad somebody hasn't placed the same curse on us."

Again the old Indian missionary paused, looking around. "As far as this powwow is concerned, there're only Pahutes there now. But shortly I reckon the Navajos will show up, and then they'll spend a week or maybe two, gambling and trading with each other. They do this every fall, and it seems to me like a mighty civilized way for them to carry on their endless wars against each other."

"Maybe they'll combine against us," someone suggested, ignoring the elderly missionary's sarcasm.

"I doubt they could muster that much intertribal unity. Happen they do, though, it won't be much different from what's been going on steadylike since last spring."

There were chuckles and sighs of agreement all around, for everyone present knew that if it hadn't been one sort of attack or setback, it had been another, and the situation showed precious little promise of changing.

"I don't suppose—"

"Billy Foreman," Ann Rowley interrupted as she stuck her head in the door of the meetinghouse, "Eliza needs you. Quick! Maggie, she'll be needing you, too."

Looking rattled, Billy rose to his feet.

"Billy, before you leave, you'll need to find someone to watch your son," Maggie Haskel declared as she also arose. "Then you get home, and I'll be along directly—"

Bluff Fort

"Heap hungry!" Posey growled in his deepest voice as he glared at the tall woman who walked with a stick, but who was now laying on the bed in her square *wickiup*, her ugly face dripping with sweat. He and his brother had entered the fort running, and to their surprise had encountered no one. Thus no one knew they were in the cabin with this woman, and Posey was exultant with the anticipation of success.

Besides, he knew this woman was afraid of him, for he could see the fear in her eyes. It was good to see such fear, too, for it gave Posey the courage he thought might have fled from his heart. *Oo-ah,* yes, when the man with the glass before his eyes—the one who was this woman's husband, had held him under his rifle at the place called Boiling Springs, Poesy's heart had trembled. His fear had not been a big thing, of course, but it had been a troubling thing, one that would not let him alone during times of darkness when he lay without sleeping, trying his best to think instead of the comely Too-rah—

"Heap hungry!" he repeated angrily as he rubbed his stomach, at the same time looking all around for the rifle he knew must be there. "All-the-same *tick-i,* all-the-same eat!"

Slowly the trembling and desperately ill woman twisted off the bed and pulled herself to her feet, adjusted the stick she walked with, and staggered to the box on the wall that served as her cupboard.

"*To-edg-e-tish,*" Posey sneered at his brother while the woman did her best to slice the bread and spread butter liberally across it, "a long time ago I thought perhaps I would fear this *shan-gee,* this lame woman."

"She seems ill," Scotty replied as he watched warily from near the door. "And I am wondering where her fearless man might be."

Posey made the sign of having heard, never for one second ceasing his silent scrutiny of the cabin. "You speak truly, my brother. She is ill, but it is because of her fear of the great Posey! *Wagh!* For *to-edg-pe-nun-ko,* a long time to come, this squaw and her man will be my enemies!"

"Do you see the *aukage,* the rifle?"

Posey made the sign that he did not.

"Perhaps the one with glass before his eyes has taken it with him," Scotty suggested. "After all, what warrior of the People leaves his weapons in the *wickiup* of his squaw?"

Stunned, Posey realized that Scotty had spoken truthfully. If the frail man were not in this place, then neither would his fine rifle be here. It would be with him, wherever he was, and it would be ready to be used! But what else was there in this *wickiup* that he could raid? What fine thing could he present to the comely Too-rah?

Taking the slices of bread the woman was suddenly handing them with trembling hands, Posey and Scotty quickly devoured them and just as quickly demanded more. And it was while the woman was preparing two more slices that the Regulator clock on the wall chimed, and Posey was instantly smitten.

"*Tabby-nump,*" he said, pointing with excitement to the wall clock. "My brother, this *tabby-nump* will be what I present to the *nan-zitch* called Too-rah." And as he spoke, Posey could still remember the wondrous feeling of Too-rah's hand in his own as they had fled the guns of the *mericats* over in the LaSal Mountains the previous spring.

But Scotty was shaking his head firmly. "No, my brother, that thing is too big to steal. The white woman will see that we are taking it, and she will send her husband to kill us."

For a moment Posey thought, and big in his mind was his memory of the woman's husband, his fine rifle held steady in his hand.

"Once again," he breathed, "you speak truly." Reaching into the pocket of his stolen red shirt, which besides the bullet hole was already soiled almost beyond recognition, he pulled forth two blood-stained greenbacks he had managed to keep for himself since the previous spring. There were also five silver dollars and some change in the pouch that hung from his neck, but these silver coins he would keep for more important things.

"Heap good greenbacks," he said as he tossed the two bills onto the table in front of Eliza. Pointing to the clock, he declared, "Much greenbacks! Posey buy him *tabby-nump,* Posey buy him clock!"

The woman's eyes widened with comprehension and surprise,

and then without warning she burst into a terrible fit of coughing, struggled for breath that she could not find, dropped her crutch, and then she slowly crumbled onto the canvas floor.

Dumbfounded, Posey lost precious seconds simply staring at the gasping woman. But then remembering his business, he was just turning to remove the clock from the wall when the voice of the woman's husband carried in from somewhere close by.

"*Pikey! Pikey! Tooish apane!*" Scotty yelped as he ducked for the door. "Come on! Come on! Hurry up!" And without another word he was out the door and running for the nearest gate.

For only an instant Posey hesitated, torn between his desires and his fears. But then, when the fearless mormonee with glass before his eyes called again, sounding closer, the suddenly anxious young warrior forgot the clock, grabbed his two crumpled greenbacks from the table, and leaped out the door after his fleeing brother.

Bluff Fort

"Billy . . . Oh, my darling husband, what have I done?"

It was late now, nearly midnight, and Eliza had been struggling for hours. Billy, sitting on the edge of the bed beside her, hardly knew how to respond. Her voice was filled with anguish, that was sure; maybe more than he had ever heard in anyone's voice. And though she hadn't done a single thing that was wrong, he had no idea how to convince her otherwise. The Lord knew he had tried, for most of the past several hours, as a matter of fact. He had even brought Bishop Nielson in to help give her a blessing and had listened as the bishop had spoken wonderful words of comfort to her. Eliza had been promised that all would be well with her unborn child, and to let her mind be at peace. But poor Bishop Nielson might as well have been whistling into the wind—

"You haven't done anything wrong, hon-bun," Billy responded with as much tender love as his voice could hold. "I've told you that again and again, and it's time you believed me. All you did was faint from loss of breath."

"And . . . from fear! Why does that boy terrify me so badly? I . . . I don't understand it! He wasn't even armed!"

"Hon-bun, he was still threatening—"

Her eyes closed, Eliza was not listening to her husband. Rather she was thinking once again of Posey, and of the fact that he had carried no rifle. Surely he had been one of those who had slain Jimmy Heaton and Isadore and Alfred Wilson in Pinhook Draw—and then left his old rifle on the ashes of their dead fire! And she was thinking, also, of the two one-dollar greenbacks he had offered in trade for Billy's clock, the two greenbacks that were stained dark with what she absolutely knew was a white man's blood. Was that Jimmy's blood, she wondered? Or Isadore's? And in Posey's eyes, she could see as clearly as if he were yet standing before her, still burned the terrible spirit of hatred and murder that had driven him to commit such bloody deeds!

"Besides," she gasped, trying to force her horrid thoughts from her mind, "Ann Rowley says I've caught the whooping cough—" Abruptly Eliza dissolved into another fit of coughing.

"She's right, Eliza. You have. But that isn't your fault, either, and Ann didn't say it was." Tenderly Billy wiped his wife's feverish brow with a damp rag, holding her until the spasm of coughing had subsided. "She loves you most as much as me, hon-bun, and would never on purpose criticize you or try to hurt you."

"But Billy—"

Gently Billy placed his fingers on Eliza's lips. "Don't talk anymore, Eliza. You've got to save your strength."

"But—"

"I mean it, hon-bun. Don't talk. Everything's going to be just fine."

"Billy, I . . . I must tell you something!"

"Not now, hon-bun. Just try and rest—"

"But there isn't any . . . any movement."

"What?" Billy focused his mind, trying to understand what Eliza was saying.

"The baby has st . . . stopped moving, Billy. I haven't felt it since I passed out in front of Posey and Scotty."

Billy stared at Eliza's protruding tummy, and then he reached out and put his hand where he had always before felt movement. "The baby's probably asleep, Eliza," he said when he felt nothing. "They have to rest, too, you know."

"It is not asleep." Eliza's eyes were suddenly dry, her voice almost wooden. "Our baby has died, Billy. I . . . I have killed it."

"Eliza! Don't say such things."

"With my own foolish fear I killed it, Billy. I was—"

Eliza suddenly burst into another fit of coughing, a fit that seemed to go on, the spasms contorting her tired body. And it was during the last of her coughing spasms that Billy realized his beloved wife's water had just ruptured.

"Maggie!" he yelped as he bolted from the bed, his heart in his throat. "I . . . I think the baby's getting ready to come—"

5

Monday, September 5, 1881

Bluff Fort

"Billy." Maggie Haskel's voice was soft as she tenderly held the newborn child. "You and Eliza have a beautiful little daughter."

Still holding his wife's hand following the pain and difficulty of delivery, Billy hardly dared look. But Ann Rowley, Mary Jones, and Annie Lyman did, and all were almost instantly weeping.

"Is it . . . I mean, is she—"

"Yes, Billy, she is dead. From the blueness of her lips, I would guess she passed away a few hours ago."

"I . . . I knew it!" Eliza cried, her face twisted in agony. "I did it! I killed my precious baby!"

"Eliza," Maggie stated rather sternly, "that isn't so, and if you'll wait another minute I'll show you why."

Carefully but quickly Maggie Haskel cut the cord, nodded for Ann to take over waiting for the afterbirth, and then she rose to her feet and carried the tiny child around to where both Billy and Eliza could see her.

"I want you to look at this sweet little daughter of yours, both of you."

Her face now without expression, Eliza turned with Billy toward their dead child.

"First," Maggie declared, "so far as I can tell, your little daughter is absolutely perfect. Toes, fingers—every tiny part of her looks just right. She's a little small, about five pounds, I would guess.

Nevertheless, she is one of the most beautiful babies I have ever seen. Look at this, Eliza. Her face is the spitting image of her mother's face—of you. I'm pretty sure I can guess how pleased Billy is about that."

Pausing, Maggie turned the baby a little more toward Billy. "In case you've never seen one of these, Billy, this is called the umbilical cord. The baby's food and air come through it while the child is in the womb. Sometimes babies, in the early months of their growth, are very active, twisting and turning about in the womb."

"She was!" Billy breathed. "We used to wonder at it."

"I'd imagine you would. When a baby is active like that, it isn't unusual for the cord to become wrapped around its neck. Look closely, now, and count with me, for I have never seen anything like this. Your little daughter has the cord looped around her neck two, three, four—five times! Amazing."

"Five?"

"That's right. Five. And look here. Do you see where the cord—right here—has been pressed or pinched tight? When she was born this spot was right against her little shoulder. I can't say this for certain, but it looks to me like those loops around her neck shortened the cord so much that when she dropped into the birth canal getting ready to be born, the cord had no slack left and was pinched tight between her shoulder and Eliza's pelvis. Most likely this happened yesterday, Eliza, or maybe during the night before."

"When I fell after Posey frightened me so badly—"

"No, my dear, that fall yesterday afternoon couldn't have caused this. It happened perhaps a day before that, and it happened during the natural process of the baby dropping into the birth canal and preparing for birth. In my opinion that is both when and why this little child died, or at least that's likely the mortal side of it."

Maggie Haskel paused, her eyes looking fierce. "Eliza, listen to me now, and Billy, don't you let her forget this. Your daughter's death had nothing to do with your fainting or falling down yesterday, or with anything else either of you may or may not have done during the past eight months or so. This death was set in motion way back, maybe even before you knew you were expecting—"

Another spell of coughing brought on more contractions in

Eliza's abdomen, and moments later Ann Rowley nodded with satisfaction. For the next few minutes, while Billy tenderly loved his wife, Maggie, Annie, and Mary gently and carefully cleaned and then dressed the tiny baby.

"All right, you two," Maggie said softly as she laid the tiny body in Billy's suddenly trembling arms, "here is your daughter. Hold her, cherish her, and get to know her. Her spirit may have fled this tiny body, but I've a feeling she's still here and very much involved in this blessed event. She is pleased with this body the two of you have produced for her, and she knows that this is the body in which she will be raised up during the resurrection. On that great day you and she will be reunited, and if you remain worthy, both of you will be given the supernal privilege of helping this exalted being grow with her glorious body and learn how to use it."

Again Maggie Haskel smiled tenderly. "Remember, she loves you dearly, as only one of our Heavenly Father's angels could, and I can just imagine how desperately she wanted to stay and bask in your love. So give it to her now. Let her know what her name is. And after all of us are gone, talk to her. Tell her of your hopes and dreams for her. Weep over her all you wish. And because you are both grieving so deeply, tell her of that, too. I am absolutely certain she will understand."

For a moment or so Billy held the little body close, gazing at her while tears of both joy and sorrow streamed down his face. Then, very tenderly, he reached down and placed the child in Eliza's arms.

At first unresponsive, Eliza did her best to hold her face expressionless. But then, somehow, the beautiful spirit of her tiny daughter reached down into her heart and tugged, and with a wail of sorrow that could only come from a perfectly loving mother, Eliza lifted the tiny child to her face and began to sob.

—o—o—o—

Bluff Fort

"She . . . she's so beautiful, don't you think?" Eliza was holding her daughter's little body in her arms, doing her best to appreciate and love and memorize every perfect feature. It was approaching morning, and the people of the fort were already beginning to stir, but for Eliza there was no sleep, no peace. Not only did the whooping cough continue to wrack her exhausted body, but there was a lot of pain in her abdomen as her uterus and surrounding muscles were continuing to contract.

"Billy, darling, I . . . I've . . . never seen a more lovely child."

Billy smiled tenderly. "She's mighty near perfect, all right. I keep thinking she's going to open her eyes, either that or twist that little mouth and start in to telling us she's hungry."

Eliza wiped her eyes. "It's so hard to imagine that she . . . she's dead! Oh, Billy, why couldn't she have breathed, even for a few minutes? All I'd have needed was an hour or so—"

"No, hon-bun, you'd have wanted more, and then even more after that. We both would. I . . . reckon the good Lord knew that, and took her when it was best for all of us."

"I don't believe that!" Eliza's burst of anger brought on a new fit of coughing, and only when it had subsided, could she continue. "How can . . . everything be all right?" she whispered hoarsely. "The bishop promised me that in his blessing, you know! He and you! Look at her, Billy! She isn't all right. Why, the dear little thing suffocated! How can that possibly be best for her? Oh, lawsy! How she must have suffered! Look how the skin of her neck is raw from fighting against that awful cord. She suffered horribly, Billy! I know she did!

"Why would God do that? Why would He allow someone so tiny and so perfect and so . . . so innocent—" And while her suffering husband remained mute, having absolutely no idea of how to respond, Eliza burst once again into a combination of coughing and tears.

Sand Island

The Pahute warrior who had taken upon himself the white man name of Jonah, did not know what to do. All the day before he had worried, during the time of darkness he had lain next to his woman with his hand upon her belly, feeling the movements of her unborn child and worrying still, and now the sun was showing again and he was still of two minds concerning both of his immediate problems.

The first, and no doubt the most serious, had to do with disquieting rumors about a terrible curse that had befallen the tall Navajo raider known as Frank—the same curse, some were saying, that had been spoken by the mormonee called Haskel against all the People of *pah,* the water, who continued to raid the white people in the new fort. Jonah knew he himself had taken advantage of every opportunity to make such raids, and so might be susceptible to the same cursing. What he didn't know, was whether the tall Navajo who had been as a friend to him, to Poke, and to the others, had actually been cursed.

The second problem he was grappling with, had to do with his woman. Because she was growing large with child she was no longer able to travel easily, and yet the band was soon to leave for a lengthy journey into the land of the *Dinê*. Jonah knew they would be expected to travel along, and this troubled him.

A member of the fearsome Poke's band, Jonah had long looked upon the one known as the grizzly as almost more than a man. From before he could remember he had been following Poke, first as a child seeking joy and getting into all sorts of mischief because of the older youth, and now as a man who followed Poke as his chief. He had followed him during the Big Raid of the previous spring, had fought beside him in the LaSals and the draw called Pinhook, had spent the summer with him on the back side of Elk Mountain in glorious idleness, gambling, feasting, and waiting for an attack from more white posse members, an attack that had never come. And of course he had taken every opportunity to participate with Poke in the raids on mormonee horses and the slaying of mormonee cattle.

But it was there in the grass and timber of the high mountain where they had spent the summer encamped, that Jonah's problem had begun. Just as he had followed the older Poke through all the seasons of his memory while Poke's father Norgwinup had been chief, so, too, had he grown close to Poke's youngest sister, the *nanzitch* known as Too-rah. In fact, when Jonah had taken to himself a woman he had chosen, the one called Peeb, who had also grown up in the band of old Norgwinup, Peeb and Too-rah had been as sisters, almost inseparable from each other, and each a favorite of old Norgwinup. And though Peeb was now his woman, she remained close to Too-rah and seemed to know of Too-rah's heart. And it was this heart thing, Jonah had concluded, that lay at the beginning of the problem.

All through the summer he had heard the chattering of his woman as she had described Too-rah's warm longing for the young warrior known as Posey. At first it had been happy chatter, but as the season progressed, the chatter had become sorrowful, until now there was nothing but sorrow on the countenance of either woman when Posey was discussed. For some reason the great Poke had taken a dislike to Posey, though as far as Jonah could tell Posey was a fine warrior, a willing gambler, and a hard fighter. Yet Poke would not countenance his sister Too-rah's interest in Posey; neither would he permit Posey to so much as come near her. When that happened he breathed out terrible threatenings against Posey, and three times now Poke had beaten Too-rah until she had lost consciousness.

Of course a man had a right to do those things to a woman who was not the property of another, and Jonah knew that. His right was especially strong when the woman was of his own family, for then he also had a responsibility for her behavior and for seeing that she was given to the best possible man. If that took a beating or two to correct her thinking, so be it. And Poke had indeed made his decision: Too-rah was not to be given to Posey, but was to be sold for a great and unimaginable sum to a youth of the *Diné,* who lived far across the big river to the south—the very destination for which they would soon be departing. This troubled Jonah for many reasons, and now as he sat idly stirring the coals of the fire he was doing his best to sort through them.

Across the fire the woman Peeb, whose name meant *feather,* was laboring over a new shirt of buckskin, which Jonah would soon be wearing. This pleased Jonah greatly, not so much because he would soon have a fine new shirt, but because his woman gained such happiness from doing it for him. Jonah knew this, for every movement she made, every look on her comely face, proclaimed it. This thing that she felt for him filled him with wonder. He also wondered at the feelings he was experiencing within his own heart—feelings of pride in the more than lovely Peeb, and feelings of anxiety to do all he could to please her and bring even greater happiness to her countenance.

Jonah did not even have a name for these feelings, neither did he believe they were common to the others of his people—the warriors particularly. And so he kept still about them, speaking of them to no one. But nevertheless he shuddered whenever a warrior did to a woman what Poke had done to his youngest sister, and he vowed again and again that he would never hurt his woman in such a manner.

This thing especially Jonah did not understand. Heretofore there had been nothing he would not have done for Poke, no place he would not have gone, no enemy he would not have destroyed. Somehow that had now changed. Each time Jonah looked at Poke, he saw only the beating of Too-rah, that and the continual urging to make more raids upon the mormonee. These things were troubling the lowly warrior more and more, until now he was wondering at the wisdom of his and the woman Peeb's even remaining with the grizzly's band.

Concerning what Poke intended to do with the *nan-zitch* Too-rah, Jonah could do nothing and he knew it. But concerning whatever else the fearsome chief might have planned, especially as those plans involved more raids upon the mormonee in the big fort, Jonah knew he had only to take his woman and depart.

The problem, of course, was that forever afterward he would have to either avoid or else face the dangerous grizzly's anger. But was that worse, he was wondering as he poked idly at the fire, than incurring the anger of *Shin-op*—the anger that Henry said had been spoken of by the mormonee Haskel? Jonah did not know, but this morning he was feeling not only the urge to take his woman and leave Poke behind, but also to go to the *hogan* of the tall Navajo and see for himself whether the rumors of the power of Haskel's terrible curse were true.

———o—o—o———

Bluff Fort

"I've been studying on it, hon-bun," Billy said as he placed the little basket next to his wife on the bed, "and I believe I know how we have to look at things."

Bleary-eyed from coughing as well as despair and lack of sleep, Eliza looked from her daughter to the anguish-filled countenance of her husband and then back again. She knew that the fabric-lined little basket was to be the child's final abode, and she knew as well that the Saints would soon be coming to bear her daughter away to the rocky hill where she would be buried, never again to be viewed by mortal eyes. But the finality of it all was too terrible for Eliza to accept. She couldn't! There had been too little time for memories to form, too little time—

Hours had passed since her baby's birth. It was now full day again, and in her exhaustion and pain Eliza was already starting to forget certain things. Convinced that it would be the same with memories of her daughter, she was fighting against sleep, determined to have every possible second with her baby that mortal time would permit, and to lock every precious view in her mind forever.

"First," Billy said as he sat beside the basket that Eliza herself had woven only a month before, "her spirit's here, I'm certain of it. And I'm just as certain she'd like to have us name her, just as Maggie suggested."

"I'm calling her Mary," Eliza declared with finality, her voice hoarse and raspy. "I . . . I promised Mary Jones if she was a girl—"

"I love that name," Billy responded tenderly. "And her middle name should be Eliza, after the sweetest and most wonderful woman in the whole world!"

"Billy—"

"Well, it should! Mary Eliza Foreman. That's a fine sounding name, hon-bun, and I'm certain our daughter's pleased with it." Billy reached out and caressed the baby's tiny fingers. "I . . . I think she'd also be pleased if her mother and father would do their best to rejoice in her happiness."

"Billy, don't you dare ask me—"

Patiently Billy waited for his wife's fit of coughing to stop, then he continued. "I don't mean we shouldn't grieve or miss her, Eliza, either one. But I think we should remember that she's now where pain and hunger don't exist, and where the devil can't ever tempt her to sin. That must be what the Lord meant when He promised you in your blessing from the bishop that everything would be all right."

Billy smiled brightly through his tears, trying to force a happiness onto his countenance that he did not for an instant feel. "Glory be, Eliza, think of it! We have a daughter who is already exalted in celestial realms, and who now dwells in the presence of the Lord God. What comfort that knowledge should give us!"

Taking a deep breath, he continued. "Here's another thing. Just think of the assistance Mary Eliza will be giving us now that she's an angel. All along we've believed in the ministry of angels, and now just like that we have our own, a sweet eternal being who no doubt loves us even more than we can love her. Why, I doubt our mortal minds can even comprehend all the ways she'll be blessing and helping us. You've been saying right along that Willy's becoming a real handful, and now you'll have all the help with him you need—the sort of help that only an angel can give."

Pausing, Billy swiped at his eyes, fighting desperately not to be overcome with his own sorrow—fighting to provide the strength for his wife that he knew she needed. "Surely the . . . the Lord must love us, too, hon-bun, to honor our little family with . . . with such a wondrous daughter."

Tenderly Eliza looked up at her husband, realizing for the first time that he was also grieving. "I . . . I know you're right, Billy. But . . . but after she's buried, how will I ever manage to remember her? And how, oh, how will I ever fill this aching that my arms, my heart, already feels?"

Knowing that her neighbors would soon be coming to bear the tiny body of her daughter away, Eliza once again dissolved into coughing and tears. And Billy, feeling the same concerns and too filled with sorrow to resist it any longer, finally succumbed to his own loneliness and grief.

Sand Island

It was late in the day when the elderly Pahute warrior called Tuvagutts rode down off the bluff, through the shallow water, and into the encampment on Sand Island. He was followed by the warrior called Sanop, one of Poke's brothers. Both of them were grinning widely, and each was leading a horse that, not two hours before, had been in harness and pulling a mormonee wagon.

"Ungh!" old Tuvagutts grunted as he lifted his leg and slid from the back of his own pony. "You see how it is, brothers?" His voice was loud, and quickly a crowd of fifteen warriors and perhaps half that many squaws gathered around. The warriors had been listlessly playing cards, waiting for the Navajo to show and having no actual idea of when they might arrive. The women, on the other hand, had been diligently working at their never-ending chores, serving in one way or another their lords and masters, who sat at cards. Now, though, the women paused to rest, and felt gratitude even though it might only be for a minute or two.

"Ho! With two men only we conducted a raid. *Oo-ah,* yes! With this knife I cut this fine horse from the straps that bound him to the *o-yem-pongo,* the wagon. And I did it, brothers, while the foolish mormonee sat in the wagon, watching."

Sanop nodded his agreement. "Brothers, it is so, even as Tuvagutts has said. Both fine horses were cut free, and that mormonee who was dressed as a man but who must have been a squaw, did nothing more than make pleadings with his mouth. Ho! That, and stay seated in his wagon. It is truly as Poke and the others have said! The mormonee are all weak, too fearful to fight."

The two continued their exulting boasting, while among the warriors who had crowded around, three were listening but experiencing vastly different reactions. The young man called Henry, who had been feeling so hopeful that the warriors of the People would no longer steal from the mormonee, was now suddenly feeling afraid for the safety and well-being of his people. Big in his mind were the remembered words of the mormonee Thales Haskel, and he knew, as he listened to the wild boasts of Tuvagutts and Sanop, that those warning words would now begin coming to pass.

Haskel's terrible words were also big in the mind of the warrior now known as Jonah, who had begun trembling as if with a fever the instant the warrior Henry had first repeated those words to the People. Jonah didn't know what had caused his trembling, but he did know that he had to get across the big river—to go to the *hogan* of the tall Navajo and find out for himself what had actually happened to the man!

And near Jonah, but thinking nothing of those strong words of Thales Haskel, the agitated Posey could not take his longing eyes off the big guns carried by the two Pahute thieves. In spite of his failure in the mormonee *wickiup*, somewhere, somehow, he had to get for himself one of those big guns—

6

Tuesday, September 6, 1881

Sand Island

Revelry on the island had reached a fevered pitch, with the beating of drums, the chanting, and the shrill war cries of the dancing Pahute warriors rending the evening air. For some time the elderly Indian missionary and interpreter had been seated on his horse in the darkness, watching. No one had seen him come, and no one had noticed him since his arrival. Thales Haskel wasn't certain how that worked, at least not exactly, but over the years since his calling nearly three decades before, there had been numerous times when he had been in the midst of Indians, sometimes throngs of them, and had not even been noticed. He took it as part of the promise of complete protection he had been given when President Brigham Young had set him apart. Of course that promise had been conditional, too. He could neither fear the Indian peoples nor thirst after their blood. Interestingly, he had never felt fear, and instead of hating them he had found himself filled almost constantly with a mixture of admiration and sorrow.

Just as he was feeling tonight, he thought as he watched the exulting throng grow larger and the celebration more frenzied. There was such vitality in these people, such simple joy, and most of them were filled with great integrity—at least as it applied to their own peoples. Who could not admire such characteristics, which quite often seemed to be utterly lacking in the white race?

Though the Pahutes did not have much of a culture, the same

was not true of the *Dinê*. The Navajo culture was very organized, very formal, one that had been established over literally centuries of experience. There was a rule for everything, and from infancy Navajo children were taught these traditional rules at every opportunity. As long as a Navajo youth, male or female, followed these rules, there was no doubt that they would turn out just as had their parents—strong, success oriented, and filled with a desire for *hózhó,* or balance, in their lives.

The Pahutes, on the other hand, seemed to have abandoned nearly every aspect of Ute culture when they had revolted against the tribes in Colorado and fled into this San Juan wilderness. The squaw dance had disappeared, the bear dance had disappeared, even the sun dance, which they had borrowed long before from the Sioux and Cheyenne, had disappeared. In fact, the only thing Thales could discern that the Pahute men had maintained, besides their singing and rhythmic dancing to drums around their fires at night, was their propensity for raiding. And even in this, they had carried it to an extreme, substituting it and gambling for every other form of obtaining a livelihood. Among these San Juan renegades, even hunting had deteriorated into a happy accident, accomplished only when an animal literally stumbled in front of the sights of their guns.

Of course life remained much the same for the Pahute women as for the women of the Colorado Utes, and so they had abandoned nothing. Which was too bad, Thales thought with sadness. For the women, life was an unending round of labor and brutality. Many of the men beat their wives and even other women at will, and for those rare souls whose men were kind to them, life wasn't much better. From daylight to dark they were farming small crops of corn and beans and squash here and there, harvesting it and cooking it either for storage or for immediate consumption, gathering berries and nuts and anything else they could find for the same purpose, cleaning animal carcasses and working skins into leather, and any of probably hundreds of other tasks that no man would ever think of doing.

And during all this heavy, difficult labor, while the men were gambling or sleeping or playing their games of warfare or hunting, the women remained totally responsible for the needs of their lords and masters, the men, and of course all the children. They served in virtual slavery almost all their lives, and when they finally reached the point where their aged and exhausted bodies had nothing left to give, they were simply left beside some trail to die. Of course weakened old men and sick children were abandoned in the same way, but still—

Anyway, Thales Haskel thought with sorrow, this was why he had come to think of the Pahutes as pagans—people without rule or order, whose only ambition was to satisfy their own immediate desires. In sharp contrast were the Navajo, who with their rules and regulations and rigid social structure—but who had no belief in an individual, personal afterlife—reminded him of the New Testament group called the Sadducees.

How strange it was, he thought, that both the Pahutes and Navajo had gathered to this same wilderness area at this same point in time, and that the Lord had called him and a few others of the Latter-day Saints, to try and somehow establish peace between everyone by returning both Navajos and Pahutes to a knowledge of the resurrected Christ—a knowledge their ancestors had so clearly been given. Yes, and to somehow teach his fellow Church members to make themselves worthy of the glorious burden of responsibility they carried.

Sighing at the seeming impossibility of the mission to which he had been called, Thales Haskel noted that the group around the huge fire was no longer growing larger. It was, therefore, time for him to ride into their midst and deliver, for the final time, his warning.

Sand Island

"My brothers," Thales Haskel said in the tongue of the Utes, speaking only when the revelry had vanished into utter silence, "my heart is heavy, for you have not listened to my words." Slowly he looked around the assembled crowd of warriors, his gaze lingering upon each face.

"Tuvagutts, you are old and should have wisdom, and yet you foolishly continue to steal from the mormonee. Wash, you do the same, and Jonah, so do you. Mike, you also steal from the mormonee. Chee, you and your sons do the same. Poke, you lead Hatch and Bishop and Tehgre and Sanop, yet you lead them to destruction because you delight in stealing and murder. Baldy, your son Henry has been doing his best to stop you from stealing, but you will not listen!

"Wash, Mancos Jim, Bridger Jack—all of you steal from the mormonee and everyone else so you will have more to gamble away. The great *Shin-op* is not pleased with this way of living.

"The *Diné* across the big river are no different, and all of you know this. Natanii nééz has been the worst, for he has gone about telling his relatives and others how easy it is to steal from the mormonee. But I ask you all to look around and tell me where that tall thief is. Do you see him among you? Do you see the great wealth of horses he has accumulated? These are things for you to consider.

"My brothers, I speak for the mormonee, but I speak because *Shin-op* has given me these words to say. *Shin-op* loves the mormonee. *Shin-op* loves all others who love the mormonee, and who are friends with them. *Shin-op* has told the mormonee to stay in this place and be friends with all of you. He has told the mormonee not to fight you, not to hurt you. *Shin-op* has promised to protect the mormonee so that you cannot kill them. He has said that if you fight the mormonee, or hurt them in any way, then it is *Shin-op* himself who will turn and do battle against you. If you go on stealing the horses of the mormonee, or killing the cattle of the mormonee, or taking anything from the *wickiups* of the mormonee, you will die. These are the words of *Shin-op*."

The old Indian missionary paused, his piercing eyes going from one countenance to another. "Maybe you will get sick and die," he continued slowly, speaking or grunting the words with all the guttural inflection of a native Ute. "Maybe you will kill each other. Maybe *Shin-op* will send the lightning to strike you. Maybe you will rot away in a white man's jail. Maybe he will reach out with his unseen hand and touch you, and like the Navajos Peokon and Natanii nééz, you will wither up like grass under the burning sun."

Again Thales Haskel paused, looking around, letting the absolute silence around the huge fire give emphasis to his words. "If you steal mormonee horses or kill mormonee cattle," he thundered once more, shocking them because none had ever heard him raise his voice, "you will die! These are the final words of *Shin-op* to you, and he will speak them no more, forever!"

Bluff Fort

"President Lyman!" Billy was truly surprised as he opened his door, and it showed. "I thought you had departed for Colorado."

Platte Lyman smiled tenderly as he entered the Foreman cabin. "Well, I stayed for your baby's service yesterday," he explained after he had once entered the cabin. "Then today other things continued to pop up, delaying me. I'm finally on my way."

Billy nodded, wondering that anyone would want to start such a journey so late in the evening. But then there were a lot of things he was wondering about lately—wondering about and struggling with. Life seemed to be getting harder right along, much more difficult than he had ever supposed it might, and he could not understand that. Neither could he understand why the Lord—

"It was a beautiful service yesterday, Sister Eliza." Platte Lyman was holding his hat in his hand, not knowing whether to stand or to sit. He didn't think of himself as being much good at socializing, preferring instead to be off in the rocks and the trees discovering new trails and new country. In his calling as president of the San Juan Stake, however, he was also expected to mingle with the Saints, and to sustain and comfort them as he could. And goodness knew the Foremans needed a little comfort right now. If only he were more adept at providing it—

"The sisters' voices were beautiful as they sang Sister Eliza R. Snow's hymn," Platte continued, wishing Eliza would at least try to smile. Of course she had lost her child, he thought, and so her grief was understandable. Still and all, though, the baby had not lived but had been stillborn, so in Platte's studied opinion the whole experience shouldn't have been so devastating for either Billy or Eliza. After all, the child hadn't even taken a first breath—

To Platte's mind then, came thoughts of his own three children, their bodies now moldering in lonely graves hundreds of miles away in Oak City. Alton, his firstborn, who was the light and hope of his life; Eliza, a dear little child who had been named after his own mother; and happy, bubbling baby Lydia. Alton had been born after five childless years—years when he and Adelia had about given up hope of ever becoming parents. And then to have him and three daughters seemed like the greatest of all possible blessings.

But then had come the dreaded grim reaper, sparing Evelyn but taking Alton, Eliza, and Lydia in such a short time, when none of them had hardly even had time to grow or develop at all. The loss of his children had devastated Platte and Adelia, and there were times when he found himself still struggling with the loneliness and grief of their loss.

But at least, his mind suddenly realized, his children had lived long enough to make memories, and to leave those memories behind when they had been taken. Poor Eliza, on the other hand, had no memories to which she could cling. Neither did Billy, for their little child had been taken before any memories could be formed—

"Kumen was eloquent in his praise of you and his witness of the life of tiny Mary Eliza," Platte went on, his heart suddenly feeling drawn out to this dear couple, "and Bishop Nielson bore a powerful testimony of Christ and His saving grace. I am so sorry you were not there to be part of it."

"They . . . sang one of Sister S . . . Snow's hymns?" Eliza questioned weakly.

"Why, yes, they did. *Your Sweet Little Rosebud,* it was called. And they sang it beautifully, too."

"Eliza and Sister Snow were once dear friends," Billy explained softly. "Are you familiar with that hymn, hon-bun?"

"I am . . . not."

Reaching onto the shelf where their precious few actual books were kept, Billy took down a tiny hymnal, the 1877 edition of one published by Brigham Young, Parley P. Pratt, and John Taylor in Manchester, England, in 1840. The name on the front of the hymnal was Fanny Emma Lee, and it was she who had given the hymnal to Billy.

"This is the hymn, Eliza, but changed to the way they sang it yesterday. The words were:

Your sweet little rosebud has left you,
To bloom in a holier sphere;
He that gave it, in wisdom bereft you;
Then why should you cherish a tear?

Your babe in the grave is not sleeping,
She has joined her dear loved ones above;
Bright beings now have her in keeping,
In a mansion of beauty and love.

She's a treasure you've laid up in heaven,
For a season removed from your sight;
To your bosom again she'll be given,
With fulness of joy and delight.

She's gone where life's ills cannot find her,
She's secure from each danger and snare;
O how cruel the love that would bind her,
To years of affliction and care.

Look up and you'll find consolation,
Which God by his Spirit will give;
And through faith, the rich manifestation,
That this gem, your sweet daughter, yet
lives.

Putting the hymnal back on the shelf, Billy wiped his eyes and blew his nose, embarrassed that he was not as able as Brother Lyman and others to control his emotions. It had been the same the day before at little Mary Eliza's funeral service. He had wept as he closed the lid of the basket Eliza had woven from rushes and sealed with pitch, the basket that would for the rest of mortal time serve as his only daughter's little coffin. He had wept when the women had sung; he had wept during Kumen's remarks as well as during the testimony of the bishop; and he had hardly been able to control himself when Lem Redd and Dick Butt had lowered the basket into the grave and begun filling it in. For a fact he seemed to be weeping more than Eliza, though she was still desperately ill with the whooping cough and likely wasn't completely aware of what had happened. It was—

"Platte . . . I mean President Lyman, may I . . . ask you a question?"

"Of course, Eliza." Platte was still twisting his hat nervously, wishing with all his heart he was on the trail again.

"A brother and his wife st . . . stopped in here today, while Billy was . . . back at the cemetery. He . . . told me that since little . . . Mary Eliza had never had a chance to use her . . . her body, God would send her spirit back into another one—give her another chance at mortality. Does . . . that mean I'm going to have another baby, and . . . that it will be Mary Eliza again?"

Stunned, Platte stared down at the ill woman. "Some fellow from here told you *that?*"

Eliza nodded. "From Montezuma Fort. He . . . said he had been a bishop before he came here to the San Juan, and one of the Brethren had taught him that doctrine."

Shaking his head, Platte sat down on the edge of the bed. "Not one of the Brethren of The Church of Jesus Christ of Latter-day Saints, Eliza. That's nothing more than the doctrine of reincarnation or transmigration of souls, which puts at defiance Christ's atonement and the resurrection of the dead. Joseph Smith said such doctrine was of the devil, and as I recollect, St. Paul agreed when he told the Hebrews it was appointed unto man *once* to die, and after that the judgment."

"President Lyman's right," Billy declared. "Alma says we can only die once and then no more as our spirits and bodies are reunited in the resurrection. And in the forty-ninth verse of section sixty-three of the Doctrine and Covenants the Lord says that all people shall rise from the dead and shall not die after."

"What . . . he said . . . frightened me," Eliza whispered. "I . . . I don't think I will have any more . . . children, President Lyman. I . . . I'm just too old to go through this . . . again. And I can't bear the thought of little Mary Eliza going to . . . to another mother because she . . . she can't come to me!"

"That won't happen, hon-bun." Billy was adamant. "Mary Eliza is our daughter! We were sealed to each other through the holy priesthood of God, and even though she was stillborn, she was born within that covenant we've made and entered into. And whether she took mortal breath or not, God had already joined her spirit and her body together. We both know that, for we have felt her kicking and moving around in your tummy, independent of you, for months. Besides, in the Doctrine and Covenants the Lord says that not one hair of any body he has created, neither mote, will be lost, for it is the workmanship of his hand."[1]

Abruptly Billy stopped, and then he opened his leather trunk and began fumbling through his stack of daybooks. "Somewhere in here," he mumbled as he searched, "I wrote down what President Young said about when the spirit entered the body. If I can just find—Ah, here it is! Now, I—Well, what do you know. This goes to show how bad my memory is getting." Billy looked up, grinning sheepishly. "This is actually a note I copied from one of President Young's talks, though I'm sure I also remember him speaking of it in the office one day. I . . . uh . . . I don't recollect why it so impressed me then, but now I believe it bears directly on our little daughter.

"According to what I have written, President Young said: 'When the mother feels life come to her infant it is the spirit entering the body preparatory to the immortal existence. But suppose an accident occurs and the spirit has to leave this body prematurely, what then? All that the physician says is—"It is a still birth," and that is all they know about it: but whether the spirit remains in the body a minute, an hour, a day, a year, or lives there until the body has reached a good old age, it is certain that the time will come when they will be separated [to] . . . take a sleep in the dust [and then] . . . come forth immortal in the day of the first resurrection.'[2]

"Do you see, hon-bun? Mary Eliza's spirit and her body had been united for several months that we know of before death separated them, so obviously she will be privileged to take that same

1. D&C 29:25
2. *Journal of Discourses,* 17:143.

body up again in the resurrection. Don't you agree, President Lyman?"

Slowly Platte rose to his feet. "I do agree," he solemnly declared. "Stillborn babies, miscarriages, babies dying after an hour of life—well, it appears that it doesn't much matter. Every child of God has value and is alive after God has created it, and as Billy said a few moments ago, none of what God has created, can be wasted. Why in the world any of us would suppose the Lord would be willing to discard or throw away such a perfectly formed little body as belongs to Mary Eliza—well, that makes no sense! This doctrine feels right to me, Eliza, not alone because it came from President Brigham Young, but because I can see that it is consistent with the scriptures.

"Now, you need to forget what that brother told you this afternoon, because he is wrong. I feel to promise you that the day will come when your precious little child, Mary Eliza Foreman, will be resurrected—her glorious spirit reunited with that beautiful little body that now rests peacefully in her grave on the hill. Then if you are worthy she will be yours eternally, and you and Billy will be given the privilege of raising up a celestial child."

Platte smiled, turned as if to go, stopped, and turned back again. Seemingly deep in thought, he said nothing for several moments. Then he spoke: "Uh . . . There is one other thing, Eliza. I also feel impressed to tell you and Billy that in this life you *will* raise up a daughter."

PART TWO

FATEFUL DECISIONS

7

Wednesday, September 28, 1881

Sand Island

"Pikey! Tooish apane! Come on, hurry up!"

Frantically, Posey was shaking his sleeping brother, so upset that he could hardly contain himself. "In the darkness the grizzly has taken the *nan-zitch* and ridden across the big river! Hurry, for we must follow!"

"Mmmph," Scotty mumbled as he forced open his eyes. Suddenly they opened wide. "My brother," he questioned, his voice filled with surprise that it was Posey who knelt beside him, "where is it that you have been?"

"Hunting *te-ah,*" Posey growled impatiently. "Hunting the deer." He had no intention of telling Scotty or anyone else that he had spent the past many days cowering in the thick willows a mile upriver, fearful that the mormonee with glass before his eyes would come hunting him. Things had gone from bad to worse when he had attempted to kill an old mormonee cow so that he might eat, and had been gored by the animal's horn. His hiding had then grown even more fearful, and he had spent his days keeping mud on his wound and his nights fearing that the old cow might have belonged to that same fearsome mormonee—who surely wished to put him under the grass.

Oo-ah, yes! Truly that one with the tall, ugly woman was a devil, a man to be avoided at all costs. But how could he have known—

"Hunting the deer?" Scotty was questioning in disbelief. "When there is *ducki* to be played? Or the *nan-zitch* Too-rah to be seen? And with what weapon did you hunt, my brother? Did you not leave your big gun on the dead ashes of that fire?"

"My knife!" Posey snarled, wishing for the hundredth time that he had not been so rash about leaving his rifle behind in the LaSals. Why, the prestige of carrying even a useless rifle was better than the ignominy of showing himself with no gun whatsoever. "And here," he continued angrily, "you see the wound the deer inflicted while I bravely waited for it to die."

"*Wagh,*" Scotty breathed in awe as he sat up on his blanket. "I would hear more of this great thing."

"*Katz-shu-mi,*" Posey growled, growing more frustrated by the moment. "I have forgotten these things already. Now *pikey! Tooish apane!* They have *katz-kar-ra,* they have gone away! In the darkness that fool has crossed the river into the land of the *Diné*. We must follow!"

"Who? . . . Who has crossed the river?" Scotty was trying desperately to understand.

"Poke!" Posey growled with terrible animosity. "The grizzly. He and his band have taken Too-rah across the big river, and we must follow them!"

"But . . . it is not yet even light," Scotty protested.

"Their going awakened me where I slept, my brother, and so I ran and found their ponies gone. Yes, and I also found the tracks of their ponies going down into the water. Now *pikey! Pikey!* We must hurry, for if the rains come, we will have no idea of where they have gone!"

With a heavy sigh, Scotty rolled from the *wickiup* and into the cold, predawn darkness. He was tempted to say *nene kotch,* not me, but he knew his older brother too well, and so he wisely held his peace. Instead he took his weapons, wrapped his warm sleeping robe about himself, did his best to ignore the occasional icy stings of rain that were already coming ahead of the fall storm, and stumbled off toward where their horses were kept. Somehow he knew that Posey would already be mounted and moving toward the river, and that he was going to have to move quickly if he had any hope of catching his agitated and no longer missing brother.

Cane Beds, San Juan River

"I had no idea, back when we left Cedar two years ago, that I was going to be spending so much of my future chopping." Talking to himself, or maybe grumbling a little, Billy Foreman dropped the short, curved-blade sickle, straightened his aching back, lifted his dripping old slouch hat, and wiped the rain from his face and thinning hair. It had turned off cold, too cold for September, and the lowering sky gave no hint that any clearing might be in the works. Worse, the sandstone walls that loomed over the wandering and untamed river seemed to intensify the gloom and reflect it downward, until a man felt almost as if he were heading into mortal danger.

Sighing with discouragement, Billy rubbed his back, stretched it as well as he could, and tried to wipe the water from his spectacles. Slowly then he bent back over, lifted the sickle, and again began swinging it into the bases of the sweet sorghum stalks, which the Bluff citizens called sugar cane. Found growing wild by Isaac Haight shortly after their arrival the year before, the cane was of sufficient quantity, on this bottom and the few others where it grew, to produce molasses enough to satisfy the Saints and even to sell in Colorado. In fact, somehow the Bluff Saints had scraped enough money together to purchase an old sugar press, a heavy piece of machinery that Platte and others had freighted to Bluff from Colorado. This machinery rendered a fair grade of molasses out of the chopped cane, which molasses—and Billy smiled ruefully at the irony of it—had so far been their only cash crop.

A flock of black crows passed overhead, their raucous cries echoing between the bluffs, and as they disappeared over the cliffs to the south, Billy found himself wondering again at the silence and desolation of the country. He didn't usually mind it, not at all. Yet there were times, especially when he had been working alone like he was now, when the quiet of the land got to him. Then it became almost threatening, a vast and unending stillness broken only occasionally by moaning winds, creaking cottonwoods, murmuring water; yes, and even the distant splashes as sandbanks toppled into the river. These and other little sounds, always startling because they could never be anticipated, began to unnerve him, and then he found himself imagining all sorts of things that thus far had turned out to be nothing.

Of course, Billy thought with a grim smile, *it doesn't help that the country is filled with so many potential enemies.* It was true. Navajos, Pahutes, Sugar Bob Hazelton and other white desperadoes of his ilk—all part of a vicious two-legged wolf pack that seemed constantly endeavoring to destroy the Saints. Being completely alone caused a man to think on such dangers, at least a little, and to wonder what he might do if such an enemy were to present himself for battle.

Naturally a man would do whatever it took to protect his family, he thought as he ignored the rain and began swinging again the dulling blade of his sickle against the stalks of cane, toppling two or three with each new swing. Maybe he didn't carry a gun—most of the brethren didn't. But that didn't mean he was defenseless. No sir, not by a long shot! Why, besides his faith, he held the holy priesthood, the very power of God, and he knew it would stop such enemies in their tracks—provided of course that he was worthy to use it and that it was the Lord's will that it be used in such a manner. Then there were the angels they had all been promised as protection—the same heavenly but unseen beings who had most assuredly protected them all at Boiling Spring a few months before, when the Pahutes had been so bent on their destruction.

Billy had no doubt of the reality of these guardian angels, especially now that his own Mary Eliza was one of them. Sometimes, though, he found himself wondering why the angels didn't take a little firmer action, or perhaps act a little sooner. In his mind, a lot of trouble could have been prevented the past year or so, and a lot of useless work avoided, if those same angels had been a little more quick to their tasks. That they hadn't been, occasionally troubled him.

He also found himself wondering, from time to time, at his own responsibility in that regard. Would he ever be called upon to actually fight? To actually lift and fire a weapon in defense of his wife and son? After all, the righteous people he read about in the Book of

Mormon had certainly been required to take up arms in defense of their families and their liberties; yes, and to die and even to kill in such battles. Could he and the other Saints on the San Juan reasonably expect to avoid such trials and tribulations?

Unfortunately, Billy didn't know the answers to such questions. He couldn't even get any feelings about them in prayer. All the Lord seemed willing to tell him, whenever he thought to ask, was to keep exercising faith and that all would be well—whatever that meant. So to the best of his abilities that is what he had been doing, leaving the fighting to the Lord. After all, he'd reminded himself again and again, he'd not been called to *fight* the inhabitants of this country but to help *bring peace* to them, and the only time he had trouble accepting that mission, the *only* time, was when he thought of that miserable Pahute boy Posey—the one who had so thoroughly terrorized his precious Eliza.

Grunting with the stiffness in his back Billy straightened again, his thoughts not so much on his own discomfort but rather on the fort a few miles downriver. How his heart was aching for his beloved Eliza. From daylight to dark all he really did was worry about her, wanting to be close and yet knowing that no matter how he tried to help, nothing seemed to change her condition. Though the whooping cough appeared to be over, and though she was recovering nicely from the strains of birth, their baby's death had ripped out Eliza's very heart, leaving her without ambition or even hope. Worse, no matter how hard he tried or how fervently he prayed, Billy seemed powerless to help. It was as though Eliza's soul had become a hollow shell, and nothing could fill her back up.

In some ways their tiny child's passing had done the same to him, though with all the work that needed to be done to get ready for winter, Billy's grieving came only in moments of quiet—moments when his brain was not needed for the task at hand. And Billy was grieving, that was sure. The least thought about little Mary Eliza's tiny dead body brought instant tears to his eyes, and there was always within him an empty feeling, a hollowness, such as Eliza seemed to feel, and a loneliness. In less than a heartbeat his little daughter had come and then gone, leaving not so much as the smallest smile to warm his heart, or tiny fingers curling around his own to give him memory and ease his pain.

Billy knew that if he could remain worthy, he and Eliza would be with their infant daughter again. And whatever such a concept might mean, they would also be given the privilege of rearing her in the hereafter. But the hereafter seemed so confounded far off and unreal, he thought grimly, while in this life the dreary days seemed to drag on and on!

Taking a deep breath Billy closed his mind against the despair it seemed so easy for him to feel—the same despair that was obviously stealing the life from poor Eliza. For her it didn't take mortal enemies such as Posey and Sugar Bob Hazelton, not at all. Instead, she was being destroyed by her own loneliness and grief, unseen enemies that were just as real as the angels who had been assigned to protect them.

And that, Billy thought grimly as he once again attacked the cane, was why he hadn't been able to help her. No matter how hard he worked, no matter how hard he prayed, he was filled with the same sorts of tragic, overwhelming emotions. And the despairing grief they each felt, seemed somehow to feed the seemingly hopeless sorrow of the other.

So where, he thought for the thousandth time, was the Comforter both he and Eliza had been promised? Or the angels, for that matter, who could just as easily guard against an inner enemy as a mortal one? Where, oh where, was his beloved little angel daughter?

"Oh, dear Father in Heaven," he breathed fervently as his heart seemed to once again tear itself apart, "for whatever reasons, you took our little Mary Eliza before we even had a chance to know her. We're doing our best to accept that, but won't you please help poor Eliza and me, to feel a little comfort . . ."

Bluff Fort

"Morning, Eliza!" Jane Walton, who was serving as Relief Society President of the Bluff Ward, stepped into Eliza's cabin and closed the door against the drizzling rain. "Thank goodness for fires," she said as she stepped to Eliza's fireplace and extended her hands to the warming flames. "I don't know what's wrong that I chill so easily, but Charlie says it's on account of me having too many children—with each birth, I lost another internal furnace, and now I'm down to none, which he says he can tell when I put my cold feet up against his back of a night." Jane chuckled. "Of course, he complains over the silliest things . . .

"Eliza, dear, you are looking much stronger! How are you feeling?"

Looking up from her rocking chair, Eliza attempted a smile. "I believe I'm doing better, Jane. I hardly ever cough anymore, and . . . and . . . Well, glory!" she declared as her eyes filled with sudden tears. "I don't know what's the matter with me! It's been practically a month now, and the least little thought of Mary Eliza, and I . . . I . . . Oh, mercy, look at me! Bawling like a baby—"

"You aren't a baby," Jane soothed as she pulled a chair forward and sat down. "You're a grieving mother, Eliza. You've lost a precious child, and you have every right to cry."

"But . . . I ought to be able to control myself—"

"Jesus didn't. When he saw the grief of Mary and Martha over the death of their brother Lazarus, the scripture says he wept. And that was in spite of the fact that he knew he was about to raise Lazarus from the dead. If he wept, Eliza, then I suppose we also have a right to weep in our grief."

"How long will . . . will it last?"

Jane Walton shook her head. "I don't know, dear. As long as it takes, I suppose. That is, for the weeping to stop. As far as grieving the loss of your daughter, that will never end—at least not in this life. She's your flesh and blood, Eliza, and so it's natural for you to pine after her—until you and she are finally reunited in each others' arms."

"But, Billy seems to be mostly over it. I haven't seen him cry in two, nearly three weeks."

"And mostly you won't," Jane responded, speaking tenderly. "Men are like that, dear. They sorrow and grieve, all right, but usually they do it down inside where other folks can't see. They do other things, too, that take their minds away from it. When my Charlie gets to grieving, he gets out his violin and starts in to fiddling, and that's especially so if it's night and a storm is howling. Could be you've heard him?"

Silently Eliza nodded.

"His fiddling bothers some folks, but I don't say a word because I know that's my Charlie's way of crying—of letting the Lord, and I suppose the whole world besides, know how sorrowful lonely he is for the little ones we've been forced to lay away."

Eliza didn't respond, and for a moment or so both women were silent, watching the fire and listening to the water drip through the dirt roof and onto the factory muslin that Eliza had draped above them as the ceiling. There, at the moment, at least, the rain was being absorbed.

"Are you feeling any better about our mission here on the San Juan?" Jane abruptly asked.

"I . . . I don't know." Eliza's expression was bleak. "I was doing much better, thinking more positively about it. But then Posey came back to threaten me, and then Mary Eliza died—in practically the same day, and since then the least little thing . . . well, life in this awful place feels too large for me to handle. I try and exercise faith, Jane, and I swan if Billy doesn't give me a blessing almost once a day. But that old feeling of terror keeps on flooding back to join my grief, and I just don't know if I'll ever make it—"

"Of course you will!" Jane reached over and took Eliza's hand. "Why, already you are doing wonderfully better, and I know the Lord will bless you with continued improvement. But there are some tricks the Lord has given us, Eliza—things we can do to help ourselves. Yesterday I was reading the account of General Moroni in the Book of Mormon, where he was readying his people to defend themselves against the Lamanites, and three verses seemed to jump out at me—two verses in the forty-eighth chapter of Alma, and one in the forty-ninth. As I read them, I thought how amazingly appropriate they are for us. Would you like to hear them?"

Without enthusiasm, Eliza nodded slowly.

"Good! That's the spirit!" Jane smiled warmly. "In the first of the three verses—verse seven—we learn that Moroni had been preparing the minds of the people to be faithful unto the Lord their God. We must do the same, Eliza. By diligently praying, and by nourishing our souls through both studying and pondering the good word of God, our minds are prepared to be faithful.

"In the second of the three verses—verse nine—we read that Moroni strengthened their weakest fortifications with the greatest number of men. In our current war, which is really a conflict with Satan and his spirit army, our weakest fortifications seem to be ourselves. So we strengthen ourselves by accepting the combined strength of each other—diligently attending our meetings, inviting in and listening to the block teachers, accepting and filling our own callings, and simply loving and serving each other. And you do that so well, Eliza, especially in your calling to love and instruct our young women. You have no idea how much strength you have imparted to them over the past couple of years."

"They are all wonderful girls."

"Yes, and they have been strengthened by a wonderful woman. In the last of our three verses—verse five of the next chapter—Moroni teaches the Nephites to prepare places of security. In our day, obviously, our greatest place of security is the temple."

"But . . . that is so far away!"

Jane nodded. "Yes, it is. One day, perhaps, that will change, and we will have a temple of our own. Until then, we must take the correct principles we are taught in the temples and put them to use in our own homes. We must recollect the laws we covenanted to live, and assist ourselves and our children to live them. In that way, Eliza, our homes will become places of security, just as are the temples."

"I don't see how that can stop individuals such as that evil Posey!"

Jane clucked her tongue sympathetically. "Perhaps he or others can burst through your door, Eliza. But has he hurt you yet? Or has he hurt Willy or Billy? No, for you have all been protected, just as have the rest of us. Do you see, my dear? Your home is already a place of refuge."

"It certainly doesn't feel that way!"

"I understand why you feel as you do. And perhaps in that sense none of us will ever feel completely secure. For the moment, at least, that seems to be the nature of this mission of ours to the San Juan. But even so, my dear, the Lord promises us that we will yet enjoy a better world." Reaching out, Jane took up Eliza's copy of the Book of Mormon. "Here," she said as she quickly turned the pages, "this is what the other Moroni wrote, here in Ether, chapter twelve, verse four: 'Wherefore, whoso believeth in God might with surety hope for a better world, yea, even a place at the right hand of God, which hope cometh of faith, maketh an anchor to the souls of men, which would make them sure and steadfast, always abounding in good works, being led to glorify God.'

"Do you see, my dear? This harsh and frightful existence is only temporary, and with your wonderful faith and good works you may be sure of obtaining that better world Moroni speaks of, and of there being reunited with your precious Mary Eliza."

And Eliza, once again overcome with grief, could not begin to respond.

Cane Beds, San Juan River

"Yo, Billy Foreman!"

Looking up, Billy was delighted to see his friend Dick Butt riding toward him along the bank. Taking his hat off he waved it, and then with another grimace of pain he stretched his aching back muscles as he waited for Dick to arrive. The rain, which had fallen fairly steadily since the night before, had first eased off a little and had now stopped altogether, though the clouds remained low and threatening.

"Sure seems like the Lord pulled the cork," the young horseman grinned as he drew rein and shook the water off his slicker. "Yes, sir, Billy, she's wet enough to bog a snipe."

"And cold enough to freeze the beard off a mountain goat," Billy groused in reply as a breeze chilled his thoroughly wet body. "You and George Ipson back from seeking out a site for your sawpit already?"

William George Willard Butt, who wished to be known only as

"Dick," slapped his wet hat against the fender of his saddle and then calmed his startled mount. "Back, and George is already dryin' hisself in front of a warm fire at the fort. When I heard you was out here cuttin' cane, though, I thought I'd amble on out and see if you had grown web feet, or was you instead, ready to load 'er up and call 'er quits."

Billy grinned. "I reckon I've cut about two wagon loads, and so far there isn't a sign of webbed feet anywhere. That's a mighty pretty horse you have there."

Looking down at his mount, Dick grinned. "Ain't he, though? I saw a cowboy riding him north of here a ways, feller name of Curly Bill Jenkins, and you know me and hosses. I had to have him. My nag and an old Walker Colt was all it took for the swap, and I've been pleased as punch ever since. He has a gait like velvet, Billy, smooth and easy. Here, take him for a little jaunt, why don't you?"

Billy shook his head and chuckled. "You know me and horses, Dick. I'll admire him from a distance, and that's good enough."

Dick gave an exaggerated sigh. "I can see you made a poor bargain with me back in Cedar," he scowled. "You cleaned up my grammar by a lot more than somewhat, Billy, and even taught me to cipher. But I never even made a dent in teaching you to ride. Thing is, with your way with animals, you had ought to be a fine rider. And would be, if you gave yourself a chance. Besides which, a man in this country that can't ride—well, in some ways he ain't hardly more'n half a man. I don't mean that disrespectful, but I reckon you know what I mean."

"I do. Platte's told me the same thing. Only, I'd hate like fury getting bucked off and breaking my spectacles, and for some reason that bucking routine is the first thing a horse likes to pull with me. I tell you, the very thought of not having my specs scares me half to death. Even old Wonder bucked me off last spring—like to have broken my neck and my specs, too—and you know he hasn't bucked more than twice in his whole sorry life."

Dick shook his head. "It's your fear them animals are responding to, Billy. Animals can sense fear, and hosses can sense it better'n most on account of they're smarter'n most. You stop fearin', and for the most part they'll stop buckin'."

"Even in the mornings?" Billy was grinning.

"Aw, Billy, you know as well as me that of a cold morning, hosses have got to get their kinks out. But that ain't hardly buckin', nohow. A feller just has to wrap his legs around 'em and hang on, and after a couple of hops, they're fine."

"Not for me," Billy responded tiredly. "I suppose I'll stick to being a teamster and leave the riding for others. Speaking of which, now that I look at it, I reckon I have a good two loads cut here."

Dick grinned widely. "Then let's load those wagons yonder and get you out of this old river bottom afore the rains come again! You want to fetch the teams whilst I cut a little more cane?"

Without waiting for a reply Dick dismounted and ground hitched his horse, took the sickle from Billy's hand, and commenced cutting and neatly falling the sorghum stalks. Nodding his thanks and still rubbing his back, Billy strode off toward the cottonwood stand where he had left his teams and tandem wagons earlier in the day.

Cane Beds, San Juan River

"I saw Eliza whilst I was at the fort," Dick said without preamble as Billy pulled the two wagons to a halt a few moments later. "She's still looking mighty peaked."

"You're right, she doesn't have much strength," Billy admitted as he set the brake with his foot, leaped down, and bent painfully to begin gathering armloads of cane to lift aboard the wagons. "But at least she's up and about, Dick, and Maggie Haskel says she's thrown off the whooping cough for good."

"I figured so, else you wouldn't be this far out from the fort. She over grieving for the baby yet?"

Instead of replying, Billy was suddenly overwhelmed with his own raw emotions, and for a moment could do nothing but attempt to regain control of himself.

"Aw, dad-gum it, Billy," Dick remonstrated as he saw his friend's expression, "I didn't mean to upset you thisaway. I . . . I'm plumb sorry I said anything—"

"It's all right." Billy gulped and tried to smile. "If it hadn't been you it would've been someone else. I keep thinking I'm going to get over it myself, and then something happens or somebody says something and bang, in my mind I see that sweet little child again, her tiny neck chafed and her lips all blue and cold in death, and . . . and . . . well, I sure am an emotional old fool!"

"You ain't nothin' of the sort! Why, I ain't even married and started on a family, but just thinkin' on maybe one of my future children passing on the way little Mary Eliza did, without even having the chance to take a breath or anything, and my whole insides come near to chokin' off entire. I'd hate it something fierce.

"More, the way you keep carrying on with the work no matter—well, I take back what I said about ridin'. You got real hair on yer brisket, Billy Foreman, and I mean that sincere!"

Billy nodded his thanks and buried his face in another armload of cane to hide fresh tears. *This is crazy,* he was thinking. At least for Eliza's sake, somehow he had to get over their child's death.

"You and Julie fixing to tie the knot this fall?" Billy asked, trying desperately to get his mind on other things. Dick Butt and Julie Nielson, the daughter of the bishop and his first wife, were in love and everyone knew it. But nobody knew what they intended doing about it.

"I wish!" Dick replied emphatically. "But no, I reckon not until next spring, after the winter's work is behind us." Soberly the young man shook his head. "Thing is, Billy, I should have gone to the settlements with her and her pa last fall instead of going with you and George to cut them railroad ties. That would've put us at the temple in St. George, and we'd a been a happily married couple right this minute. Me, though, I was thinking dollar signs, thinking a woman wouldn't want no man who was broke and poorly fixed as me."

"Those things don't seem to bother a woman the way they bother a man," Billy quietly declared.

"Don't I know it now! Trouble was, I sure didn't know it then. And now I got to work another winter, not on account of me and Julie so much as on account of there ain't hardly enough of us men left in Bluff to find jobs and earn sufficient to hold each others' bodies and souls together, let alone get comfortable and drop a few extry dollars in our pockets."

"Well, I hope it works out for you soon, Dick. You and Julie'll be happy together, that's sure. By the way, did you find any good timber for a sawpit?"

Dick grinned. "Good timber? Billy, that high-up country is crawling with good timber—that and the finest graze for cattle a body ever did see! It ain't no wonder them Colorado and Texican cattle barons have taken up the country and filled it so full of beef."

"You're talking about the Blue Mountains?"

"As ever! Some folks call them the Abejo Mountains, I found out, but I just call 'em rich. And just two fellers own practically all of it! Spud Hudson controls the northeast slopes and on back around to the northwest, and Bill Ball and his LC spread are closer, here to the southeast on Recapture. Someday I aim to see what's over behind the Blues, to the west, but this trip George and me just didn't have time."

"West? You mean up on the Elk Mountain?"

"Sure enough. What I meant was, I'd like to see what the Elk's like up on top. But that's Pahute country, and after last spring's sorry little war here and up in the Pinhook Draw country of the LaSals, George and me just didn't feel up to exploring 'er on our own."

Billy nodded. "You know that Platte, Joe Barton, and Orrin Kelsey actually got up there and walked for miles across it—all the way to the Bears Ears."

"I heard that—heard it was a wondrous tableland of a country with freshwater springs and grass that never seems to quit. Heard too that Platte's been worryin' somethin' fierce about our graze since all those Navajo sheep ate down our winter range. He figures the Elk Mountain country had ought to make a good summer range, and that all he needs is to find the way up."

"Yeah, and fight off the Indians while he's looking," Billy offered.

Dick grinned. "Well, he never ran into a single one that first trip. Of course neither did he find a trail beyond what they called First Valley—at least not one fit for hosses or cows. Orrin says once they left their hosses they had to scramble up some mighty steep cliff rocks to get on top, and that twice he figured he wasn't going to make it at all. Thing was, on top they found Injun pony tracks all over the place, so they know there has to be a trail. If I'm around when Platte goes back lookin' for it, I'd love to ride with him. What I heard of that country sure did whet my appetite."

"It does sound wondrous. And you say you found lumber?"

"All sorts, and not where it is so hard to get at as up on the Elk. George and me figure on diggin' a pit in the ponderosa country, which is down east off the Blue Mountains, along Recapture or one of the other drainages. We figure we can work the trail to the LC into a passable wagon road, and do a good business hauling out sawed lumber for the folks here and over in Colorado. You . . . uh . . . you figure on working with us again?"

Soberly Billy shook his head. "No, Dick, I don't think it'd be right. I've been going over the figures, what two men can do as opposed to three, and how much can maybe be earned in a winter if even an average paying market can be found. Tell the truth, two men might make a profit, but not three."

Dick was silent for a moment, studying Billy's face. "You sure of that?" he finally asked.

"Dead sure."

"But Billy, you can't go back to Colorado—not with Eliza sufferin' the way she is! Tell you what! You and George work the lumber pit instead of me. That'll be some closer than Colorado for you, and—"

Billy's headshake was adamant. "No, Dick, you and George Ipson are partners, and can both outwork me three ways from Sunday. The sawpit was your idea, and you need to be the fellers who do it."

"But we need your head for figuring, and—"

"No buts, Dick Butt," Billy said with a wide smile, "and no pun intended, either. Eliza and little Willy and me will be just fine, I'll help you whenever I can, and next spring we'll all rejoice to have a little straight lumber to turn into floors and maybe even roofs. One, such floors would certainly slow down the rattlesnakes from inviting themselves for dinner, and Eliza will be mighty thankful for that!"

Dick chuckled as he threw the last of the cut cane aboard the second wagon. "I heard she was some upset by snakes, all right. Very well, Billy, no sawpit for you, at least not this winter. But that doesn't mean you should go to Colorado, either. I've got my eyes peeled and my ear to the ground, and you can bet I'll rustle up some sort of job for you afore I leave for the hills—a job that's closer to home by a lot more than somewhat. You can count on it!"

Billy grinned. "Whatever you say, Dick. Whatever you say." And clambering aboard the lead wagon, he kicked off the brake, took up the lines, and snapped the teams into movement. And realized, with another wry grin and a tug on his old hat, that the rain had started again.

8

Thursday, September 29, 1881

Jackrabbit Canyon, Navajo Reservation

"My son, I am troubled much by that which I see in your countenance."

Old Tsabekiss sat in his *hogan* in the traditional place of honor, his face to the eastern opening. Next to him sat his son Bitseel, his eyes straight ahead, while across the cooking fire and near the doorway Tsabekiss's woman sat in her traditional place, her hands busy even as her mind wandered backward along the old but joyful trails of her daughter. It had been a hard thing for old Tsabekiss to learn from Bitseel of the little one's troubling death, for truly she had owned a place close to his heart. But his sorrow had been nothing compared to that of his woman, who had said nothing but could not possibly hide from him her suffering.

Neither had the old man supposed that the thing would have hardened the heart of the young man Bitseel the way it had done. But then, who could know the strange ways of the heart? Who could know—?

"On the morrow I will take up the trail of the *belacani* with the notch in his boot," Bitseel snarled by way of reply. "I will do to him even as he did to the little one who is gone, only more so, and I will do the same to every other *belacani* that I find! They are an evil people, my father, and I will do what I can to destroy all of them!"

Tsabekiss grunted. He did not argue with the youth, for that was not the way of the *Diné*. Besides, Bitseel was now a man, and in all things could choose for himself. Yet the old man felt troubled, for his son had become as one possessed, and seemed to have lost his *hózhó,* the balance in his life that all of the People considered to be of greatest importance.

"It is said that the *nóódái* will reach this place by the morrow," the father finally replied.

Bitseel made the sign that he had also heard this thing concerning the despised Pahutes, but that it was of little consequence to him.

"They are coming to tell us it is time for the gathering at the big river," Tsabekiss continued. "They are coming to tell us they are ready to be stripped of their wealth and to be left the beggars and fools they have always been."

Tsabekiss knew how skilled Bitseel had become in the playing and manipulation of the white man gambling cards. The Tall One, his wife's cousin Natanii nééz, had seen to that. Until his terrible sickness, no one among the People had been a better gambler than Natanii nééz, and he had taught the youth Bitseel all he knew. More, Bitseel loved card games, and would ride many days in order to play. Now old Tsabekiss was hoping the thought of playing the despised Pahutes would take the anger from the heart of his son and restore a little of that all-important balance he had somehow lost.

Making the sign of utter disgust, Bitseel kept his gaze from his father. "Those that come are the band of the sniveling dog Chee, he who created so much misery before we drove them from the mountain. It is them for whom we held the Enemy Way sing."

"Yes, my son, though I have heard that the young one who hates you has not yet died."

Thinking angrily of the cowardly whelp Posey and his evil, darting tongue, Bitseel nevertheless made the sign that he was no longer concerned with such things.

"It is said that one of the *nóódái* has expressed a desire to sell his sister so that you may take her to wife."

Bitseel chuckled without humor. "It is he who is called Poke, my father. He had the same foolish desire when he came to this place one year ago; yes, and also the year before that. The girl is called Too-rah, but not only is she of the cursed *nóódái,* she is also very young and not very pretty. Perhaps this time I would have taken her as a slave, but I will not be here."

Tsabekiss made the sign that he understood his son's determination, though he had not yet given up hope that he could persuade him otherwise.

The old man continued, "When we rode with Natanii néêz and Zon Kelli after the mormonee horses across the buckskin mountain of the Kiabab," he then ventured, "my own heart was set hard against the *belacani,* all of them, and I, too, wished for their destruction. I wished not only to raid, my son, but to destroy, for I hated the whites for all the suffering they had inflicted upon the *Diné*. I especially hated the *belacani* called mormonee, for they seemed to be of such cowardly ways."

Bitseel remained silent, listening and remembering.

"Returning to *Diné tah,* we crossed the horses at the place the Spanish call the Crossing of the Fathers, and it was there in the water, my son, that this *chinde,* this devil, took control of my leg and turned me into an old man."

Without looking at his father's twisted and shriveled leg, Bitseel made the sign that he remembered.

"The *chinde* will not go away," Tsabekiss concluded softly. "It has much power, my son, and is slowly eating away my life. Even that Blessing Way chanted by Dagai Iletso, old Yellow Whiskers, has not taken away the *chinde's* power."

Thoughtfully Tsabekiss fingered his *jish,* the small medicine bundle that hung about his neck. "Now," he continued quietly, "it is in my mind that perhaps I am suffering even as Natanii néêz. He says he set his heart against the *belacani* mormonee. I have done the same. He says also that it was the mormonee god the *nóódái* call *Shin-op* who did that great evil to him."

"I do not know this *Shin-op*!"

Tsabekiss nodded. "I do not know him either. But this much I do know, my son. No *chinde* ever touched me until I set my heart to destroy those *belacani* mormonee. No devil ever took hold of me until I gave up my *hózhó,* my balance, in that great quest."

"What is it that you say to me, my father?"

Tsabekiss took a deep breath. "I say, and my words are true, my son, that except perhaps in the heat of battle, no man is meant to hate or destroy another. To do so, especially to slay because of anger and hatred, is to give up all balance with the universe. And that, my son, is a terrible and dangerous thing. I knew this, for it is the old way of the *Diné,* the traditional way. Yet somehow I forgot it, and now I wish I had not."

"But . . . that *belacani* with the notched boot is evil, and deserves to die!"

Tsabekiss acknowledged that Bitseel's words were true. "Yes," he declared softly, "and because of that, he has also given up whatever *hôzhô* he himself might have had. Now he will forfeit his life just as surely as did the great Peokon or our cousin Natanii nééz, who may be dead even as we speak."

"Then it is I who will be the one who brings death to the *belacani* of the notched boot!" Bitseel declared.

"Perhaps you will, my son. But do not seek it, I beg you. Leave it to the *Yei,* and to those other sky people who watch over the affairs of the *Diné*. Keep intact your balance with all living things, and no *chinde* will ever have power to destroy you. More importantly, in time all things that are needful will come to you, including, perhaps, the slaying of the evil *belacani* with the notched boot. Let your mind walk away from it, my son, and you will see that I am right."

Old Tsabekiss grew still, and in the silence of the forked stick *hogan* in Jackrabbit Canyon the youth Bitseel thoughtfully fingered his own *jish,* his father's words growing ever larger in his mind.

Bluff Fort

"Hot water coming up!" Lula Redd called as she and Leona Walton staggered from one of the cabins with a large kettle of steaming water held between them. "Which one of you sisters needs it most?"

Waving her hand, Eliza smiled at her young friend. "Over here, Lula!"

"We're on our way!"

"Eliza," Anna Maria Decker exclaimed from where she knelt

next to her, "I still say it is too soon for you to be doing such hard work. I can do that for you—"

"Thank you, Anna." Eliza smiled again. "I'm feeling well enough to do something, even if it is only Willy's diapers."

"Well, let that be all you do. I mean it, Eliza. I'll be happy to do the rest of your washing!"

"And I'll help!"

"So will we all!"

In gratitude and wonder Eliza looked around at the women—her dear friends—and recalled for a moment the words of Jane Walton from the day before. Surely they were all strengthening each other.

"If we had more stoves in this fort, we could get more hot water." Lula Redd was grousing good-naturedly, but everyone knew the benefits of having cookstoves instead of fireplaces. It was just that they were so expensive.

"Lawsy," young Leona Walton exclaimed as she looked into Eliza's tub, "are those Willy's diapers?"

"They are, Leona. Stinky, huh?"

"Stinky, and almighty colorful!" And with that observation she and Lula turned and ran giggling toward the well, where they would refill the kettle and get it back over a fire.

Now that the rain had stopped, and before the work of processing the sorghum cane into molasses was begun, a goodly number of the women in the fort were attacking their neglected washing. In the cabins water was being constantly heated as the children fed wood to the fires and three stoves that now graced the fort, and outdoors the several washtubs were kept at least half full of warm, clean water. Leaning over their washboards, propped against the inside of the tubs, the women soaped and scrubbed their clothes by rubbing them up and down the rippled boards, up and down, into the water and back out again, in and out, in and out, constantly turning and wringing each piece of fabric until most of the dirt was left in the water of the tubs.

The washboard was next placed in a rinse tub where the process was repeated until no more soap was evident. Then each piece of clothing was wrung by hand as tightly as possible, shaken out, and hung on one of several dozen lines that had been strung here and there throughout the fort for that purpose. It was grueling, back-breaking work, and yet it needed desperately to be done, both for cleanliness and to preserve the clothing for as long as it would last.

"Look at these poor diapers of Willy's," Eliza abruptly exclaimed. "Practically every one of them is threadbare, and the only passably good ones have 'Pride Of Durango' printed across them. No wonder Leona and Lula giggled."

Nellie Lyman laughed. "Their underwear probably says the same thing. So does half the children's underwear in this fort! One thing's for sure—with that many young people wearing unmentionables made of flour sacks, nobody needs to wonder where we Saints purchase our flour."

"I don't mind seeing the flour sacks and knowing they're covering the children's backsides," Mary stated quietly. "What's difficult for me, is seeing how thin and patched everybody's outer garments are getting—Kumen's, most especially. And that's despite the fact that every one of us is spinning and stitching up homespun at every available opportunity. I swan, but our whole and entire community seems destitute, and after two summers we still haven't managed a harvest sufficient to sell for more than our own barest subsistence. Worse, I don't see a whole lot of hope for the future."

"Billy's and my clothes are the same as Kumen's," Eliza admitted. "Thin enough, almost, to see through. And everything little Willy wears, was something else before it wore out and got restitched."

"Well, it's too bad one of us doesn't have enough money to help the others out."

Eliza was jolted by a sudden pang of guilt. Though Billy knew of her shares in the Cedar City Co-op, she had kept secret from him her large and untapped savings account in the bank in Salt Lake City. Only occasionally did she allow herself to think about it, and then it was only to feel guilty because she was saving it for when the San Juan Mission would fail—for when she and Billy would need funds to start over somewhere else. Now as she remembered this, she thought again of Jane Walton's scripture-based admonition that each of them needed to strengthen and bless the others.

Oh, glory—

Sand Dunes, Navajo Reservation

"Beautiful sunset, ain't it?" Johnny Molander stretched as he stood with his back to the growing fire, looking about. The sun was just setting over the mesas to the west, and in the clear air it seemed to Johnny that he could see forever. "Folks back at the LC warned me this desert country was a harsh land, and it may be. But I'll be dogged if it ain't just as beautiful as it is harsh. Don't you think that's so, Bob?"

The other man, of darker visage, did not reply. Rather, his mind was occupied with thoughts of the new rifle protruding from Johnny Molander's saddle scabbard. It looked to be a fine weapon, and he wondered how the easygoing cowboy had ever been able to afford it.

"Well," Johnny continued, "as my old *segundo* Bill Ball likes to say, daylight's a burning. Reckon it's time I relieve this ol' hoss of his saddle. Mighty good of you to invite me to camp with you for the night, Bob. A feller never knows when some Navajo warrior will sneak up in the dark and dust him one."

"They'll do that in the daylight, too." The man who called himself Bob was nonchalant. "I've seen me the remains of half a dozen fellers scattered here and yonder, every one of them shot in the back. And every one of 'em thought he was safe from the Navajo when it happened, more'n likely because he didn't have enough eyes to see everywhere all to once."

"A man traveling alone is at a disadvantage, all right." Johnny Molander, who had tied his horse's reins to a creosote bush, was fiddling with his latigo strap, smoothing a rough edge with his pocket knife.

"I had me a pardner," Bob continued, "but he passed away out west of here. Mighty sad doings. I bin alone ever since. Two, three times the Navajos have nearly got me. It's pure, dumb luck that they haven't."

For a moment all was silent. Then, finally, Johnny asked, "Which way did you say you was going?"

"I didn't."

Quickly and easily Johnny pulled his new rifle out of its

scabbard and checked the action. Turning around, he stepped back to the fire. "No, Bob, you didn't say, and neither did I. But I'll tell you what. You look like you've had some hard doings in your life and are in need of a break, and in spite of that my nag's saddled and ready to ride, I don't want to go no further acrost this reservation alone. So if you want to pardner up with me for a spell, why, you're welcome."

"You still didn't say where you was going."

Resting his rifle in the crook of his arm, Johnny Molander grinned. "You ever heard of a lost mine called Peshleki? Fabulous silver mine, or at least that's what they say. Well, Bob, I'm going after it."

Bob, his interest in the new rifle suddenly forgotten, watched the other carefully. "It's a big country," he said at last.

"It is." Johnny grinned as he tapped his breast pocket. "But I got me a map. Won it in a poker game over to Fort Lewis. I also won me this." Reaching into the pocket of his jeans, he withdrew a small lump of ore, which he tossed to the man on the ground. "That's silver, Bob, practically pure. It come from this lost Peshleki mine. You pardner up with me, and half of what we find will be yours."

Bob studied the silver but did not reach to pick it up. "How do you know the map's any good?"

"It is."

Slowly Bob rose to his feet, wondering if this was a man he could partner up with. Goodness knew he needed one. But that hunk of ore—well, it was troubling his mind, it surely was. It looked too much like . . .

"If you're that sure," Bob growled abruptly, his mind made up, "then I reckon you can camp with me tonight, and we can pardner up tomorrow. These Navajos throw the fear into me, they surely do."

Feeling satisfied, Johnny Molander turned back to unsaddle his horse. Behind him he could hear his new partner stirring about the fire, and so he did not hurry. Rather, and he did this for no other reason than that the evening was so clear and calm, he passed by his mount and climbed afoot to the top of a sandy hummock.

This is *a beautiful country,* he thought as he looked about from this more lofty vantage point. Almighty dry and forbidding, and filled with danger because of the Navajos. But beautiful! Off to the northwest rose the looming bulk of Navajo Mountain, where his map said he was headed, and abruptly Johnny Molander was filled with excitement. In another day, maybe two, he would be in the hidden canyon where the fabulously rich Lost Peshleki was located. And now that he had himself a good partner who would cover his back—

"You never did say what your last name was," he called to the man behind him.

"Nope. I didn't."

A smile on his face, Johnny Molander turned to ask why, and in hardly more than a heartbeat, two bullets smashed into his forehead, striking with such force that they spun him over and around to fall face downward on the far side of the hummock, his new rifle flying out before him and burying itself in the sand. Johnny felt no pain at this abrupt ending of his plans, nothing but surprise, and for a fraction of an instant he wondered what had happened. But then his eyes dimmed and it didn't matter anymore.

Toiling over the sandy hummock, Bob slid down to Johnny Molander's side, toed him over onto his back, and saw that his most recent new partner was dead. In the next instant he reached down and removed the map from the man's shirt pocket. Quickly it was unfolded, and Bob was amazed to see that it pointed the way to the hidden canyon on the southwest slope of Navajo Mountain.

"Knew there was a reason you had to die," he grumbled as he thrust the map into his own shirt pocket. "Too bad, too. I could'a used you working that mine, but I'll be a twice-blinded polecat's dung afore I'll work that mine for *you*!"

Abruptly Bob burst into raucous laughter. "So long, pardner," he cackled as he made his way back up the hummock of sand and down the other side, where he kicked out the fire. "Oh, yeah. Since you asked, my last name is Hazelton—Bob Hazelton. Or Sugar Bob Hazelton, if you'd like. Least that's what my friends used to call me." And with another cackle he mounted his horse and rode away into the gathering darkness, his insane mind already dismissing the valuable horse and rifle he was leaving behind.

Bluff Fort

With a satisfied smile Eliza dusted the ink on her two short letters, folded them carefully, and inserted each into one of her few remaining envelopes. The first of them she carefully addressed to the president of the bank—her bank—that was shepherding the funds she had earned through her millinery business and its subsequent sale, accomplished just prior to her marriage to Billy. The second letter was made out to the co-op in Cedar City. If she were giving all her money away, she had decided, then it would certainly be appropriate to trade some of her stock for a new cookstove.

Wouldn't Bill be pleased that she had finally rid herself of her selfishness? And wouldn't it feel good to also be rid of her guilt? Of course, she thought with a continued smile, once her funds were officially transferred to the bank in Durango, they would prove a great blessing to the community. And that's what she would do with her money, she had already decided. She would give every penny to Bishop Nielson, and then he could disburse it as needed or as he felt inspired. The stove would remain hers and Billy's, but even so it would be a blessing to every family in the fort.

Yes, Eliza thought as she sealed the envelopes, that would be the Lord's way, and he would no doubt be pleased by her decision. Billy would also be pleased, but he didn't need to know about it—not yet, at least.

Almost laughing out loud at the thought of such great surprises, Eliza wondered if everything could be completed by Christmas. Yes, if she could find someone who would freight the stove out from Cedar. Wouldn't her modest wealth make wonderful gifts for everyone, she thought? Yes, indeed, and a blessing such as every one of them had been desperately praying for, practically since the day of their arrival in Bluff.

9

Friday, September 30, 1881

Navajo Mountain

It was now full daylight. The night's rain had stopped, and the air was filled with that scent of freshness that Scotty enjoyed more than any other odor in all his wild home. For long moments he breathed deeply, savoring each breath. Finally, though, his eye on the countenance of his older brother, he broke the silence and spoke. "I see no sign of them here in this place."

His words, spoken quietly, almost reverently, nevertheless irritated his older brother. "Did I say that they would be here?" Posey questioned through clenched teeth as he continued to look around. "No! I merely thought it might be a possibility. Besides, it has been many long months since we have been in this place, and I thought it would be good to make certain that all is well."

Perplexed, Scotty did as Posey was doing. He looked around but saw nothing at all but the rocks, the earth, the trees, the bushes—all the things that had changed so little in the full circle of seasons since they, their two mothers, and Old Chee, had last ridden away from Navajo Mountain. Of course there was grass now, whereas before their horses and goats had cropped it to the earth. And of course the cold rains of the day before had stopped. These were the changes Scotty could see—the only ones. Certainly Poke and his sister Toorah had not been here, nor had anyone else in a very long time.

"Do you see it?" Posey asked quietly, his voice suddenly intense.

"See what, my brother?"

"Do you see that bit of wool where once the brush *wickiup* lived?" Without waiting for an answer Posey kicked his pony forward to where the brush shelter had stood. Lifting his leg over the pony's withers he slid to the earth, bent over, and in a moment was holding in his hand a bit of died wool that had been twisted into yarn.

"*Diné!*" he snarled fiercely, and then he spat with derision. "They have come to this place that is not theirs! They have scattered our *wickiup* until it is *topic-quay,* all gone, and they think by such efforts to keep us from returning to this place in the future. *Ick-in-ish,* I say, brother, that one day I will come back to this place, and then none of their fine horses will be safe!"

Still wondering that his brother's eyes could have spotted such a tiny bit of wool from such a distance, Scotty kneed his own pony forward. Overhead a buzzard wheeled in slow circles against the dark and tumultuous clouds, and a wind was blowing through the trees on the mountain above them, knocking a dead limb or hanging chunk of bark against a nearby tree. Though distant, the sound was obvious, for besides the wind it was the only sound Scotty could hear, and of a sudden this place where he had once lived, seemed terribly lonely, terribly ominous.

"My brother," he said, his voice very quiet, "*tooish apane,* let us hurry and ride from here."

"*Oo-ah,* yes," Posey replied, not noticing his brother's nervousness. "We will most certainly ride. We may have lost the tracks of the grizzly yesterday in the rain, but now I know where it is that he has gone. *Oo-ah,* and where he has also taken Too-rah." Posey turned and almost without effort leaped astride his pony. "Come, my brother, we will ride down the mountain to the *hogan* of the cursed child of the *Diné* who calls himself Bitseel."

Bluff Fort

"Are you getting along all right with Billy away from the fort all day?" Annie asked.

Eliza and Annie Maude Lyman, like almost all the other women and older girls in the fort, were helping in the production of the molasses. Eliza's assignment, the first since her baby's death and her bout with the whooping cough, was to sit and help chop the cane into lengths short enough to feed into the massive sugar press they had freighted in from New Orleans via Colorado. Annie Lyman had been assigned to assist her, and to watch over her in every other way possible.

Smiling, but without looking up from where she sat wielding the large butcher knife against the cane, Eliza nodded. "Actually, I think I'm doing quite well. I'm not coughing at all anymore, and little Willy never did come down with it. Besides, the cane beds aren't all that far away, you know. If I needed him, Billy could be here in less than an hour. Have you heard when Platte expects to return from Colorado?"

Annie's look was somber. "He told Adelia to expect him sometime yesterday or today. But then none of us knows for certain."

"No, we don't." Eliza's voice was filled with understanding. "Of a truth, Annie, it should be me questioning how you are getting along without your husband."

Annie laughed to hide her sudden tears. "I do miss Brother Lyman, Eliza, but I think I am doing much better than I have in the past. That little visit we had last spring was remarkably helpful."

"Visit?" Eliza's face was blank. "I . . . I don't recall—"

"Of course you don't. How could you be expected to recollect a single casual conversation out of hundreds we all have with each other. Besides which, you've had a few other things on your mind that would have traumatized the memory out of any of us. But I remember it, my dear—vividly! In fact—and I've been wanting to tell you this for weeks and weeks now—I'm learning to tell when the Holy Ghost is present, and I'm finally starting to have a little confidence in the impressions and feelings I receive when I pray."

Quickly Eliza looked up. "Now I recall our visit! You were struggling to understand why the Lord never answered your prayers!"

"That's right. And you and Billy showed me some verses of scripture that taught different ways of feeling the Holy Ghost when we pray. I've been concentrating on that all summer, Eliza, and I'm starting to feel some of those things you and Billy showed me—or at least one of them."

"Annie, that's wonderful! You really are feeling the Holy Spirit?"

"Well, I think I am. I do feel something when I ask the Lord for the power of the Holy Ghost to fill my heart, and every time I ask, if I have repented first, it is the same. But of a truth, Eliza, I do struggle to have real confidence in what seem to be the answers I receive."

Eliza nodded soberly. "Yes, that is difficult, isn't it—believing in ourselves. Billy says he thinks that is part of what the Lord is talking about when he promises that our confidence will wax strong in the presence of God."

"Brother Lyman showed me that passage of scripture way last spring, and I read it again just the other day." Annie smiled as she heaved another armload of cane into place between herself and Eliza. "But like everything else, it's a conditional promise. If our thoughts are virtuous and pure, and if we are filled with love for our fellow beings no matter who or what they are, then we can develop confidence in the Lord. Thanks to what you and Billy explained, I've been working on those particular things, and I feel like I am seeing a little progress."

Eliza looked away, her face immediately troubled. "Have . . . have you noticed areas where you cannot seem to get accurate information, no matter how hard you pray?"

"Have I ever!" Annie replied, not noticing Eliza's somber expression. "When I ask the Lord when something or other is going to happen, such as when Brother Lyman might be coming home, my impressions have never yet been accurate!"

"Yes, that is the same with me." Eliza turned back with a slight smile, though her face remained troubled. "I call it a problem with timing, and my experience has been identical to yours. The trouble is, I'm forever wanting to know when something or other is going to happen. I asked Billy about it once, and he told me he thinks part of the reason we can't get such information, is that an understanding of the Lord's timing of things is reserved for the prophets, and is revealed to them not when they seek it, but when God determines they need it. As an example, he read for me the account of Gabriel's visit to ancient Daniel, when the prophet was taught how to calculate the Lord's timing of future events."

Annie nodded her understanding. "Yes, and I recall Brother Lyman speaking of how the Prophet Joseph struggled to learn the timing of the Lord's Second Coming. In fact, he never did learn it. You said there was another reason?"

"Faith." The look of pain was back on Eliza's face, and again she turned away. "If . . . the Lord is going to reveal to us everything we ever think of asking," she continued quietly, "how would we ever learn to walk by faith?"

"Good question." Annie was still oblivious to Eliza's suffering. "Does Billy get answers concerning timing?"

Still looking away, Eliza shook her head. "Actually, he's told me he won't even ask the Lord for such information. His daily prayers—except for offering up praise and thanksgiving—are pretty much limited to questions concerning whether or not he has missed something for which he needs to repent, or if there are individuals in addition to Willy and me who are in need of his faith or his help."

"That's all?" Annie asked.

"Well, he told me once that sometimes he asks questions about religious, philosophical, or scientific issues over which he has been pondering. But I know he is careful to phrase such requests so that the Lord knows he isn't demanding an answer, and that whatever he receives will be for his own edification and growth. I believe he learned some of these things the hard way, but Billy is more than conscientious about the appropriate limits of his mortal stewardship."

Annie nodded soberly. "I think I know how he feels, for I made that mistake the other day when Brother Lyman announced to Adelia that he wanted to take little Albert with him to Colorado. I was frightened by the prospect, and so I asked the Lord if Brother Lyman was doing the right thing in taking the child with him." Annie Lyman giggled. "I swan, Eliza, I've never felt the Holy Ghost leave me so rapidly. Honestly, it was like a flatiron had been put onto my thoughts. Talk about a deadening of feeling! When I finally figured out what had happened and then asked the right questions, I was overwhelmed with the feeling that I had stepped beyond the bounds of my own stewardship, for I am not Albert's mother and don't preside over his father. In other words, I needed to repent."

Eliza's gaze remained far away as she fought with her emotions. "I know how you feel," she finally responded.

"It's interesting, isn't it," Annie continued, "how slowly and carefully the Lord teaches us his thoughts and his ways. Nothing ever seems rushed or hurried, and he doesn't reveal a single thing to any of us until we are absolutely ready to receive it—Eliza, dear, what is it? What have I said?"

"You've said nothing, dear." Furiously Eliza returned to her chopping. "The problem is mine, and I suppose it has to do with me not being ready to receive what I am asking for!"

"Eliza—"

"Well, I must not be! But all I want, is to understand what the Lord is doing with us! Only, nothing seems clear to me, not since . . . since Mary Eliza was taken from me!"

"Eliza, please, we don't need to talk about this—"

"But I want to talk, Annie! I feel as though I am going to burst with it! I pray and pray, and I feel nothing! And every time I say something to Billy, I start weeping, and I feel badly that he doesn't! Oh, Annie, why did our sweet baby have to go like that? Why did she have to twist about and suffer as she did? For that matter, why did she have to go at all? Couldn't the Lord see how much Billy and I wanted her—needed her? Other folks have oodles of children, so why would it have been so wrong for Billy and me to have two?"

"I . . . I don't know," Annie breathed as she reached to gently stroke her friend's back. "I still don't know why I can't have any!" Abruptly Annie's face brightened. "But at least you know the Lord is going to send you another little girl. How that thought must give you joy!"

In amazement Eliza looked at her friend. "How . . . how do you know that?"

"Why, Brother Lyman told me. He said the Spirit of the Lord rested upon him with great power the night of your baby's funeral service, and he could not restrain himself from prophesying to you and Billy that you would yet raise a daughter here on the San Juan."

"I'm sorry," Eliza stated almost woodenly as she turned back to the cane. "I didn't believe him then, Annie, and I believe him even less now that my thinking is more clear!"

"But, Eliza—"

"Annie, look at me! I'm nearly fifty years old, wasted away practically to nothing, and I don't mind telling you that I have lost all the strength and power the Lord ever gave me to be a new mother."

"But . . . but you'll regain your strength—"

"Perhaps." Eliza's eyes were filled with sudden tears. "But some things happened after little Mary Eliza was born, physical things that Maggie Haskel is only now explaining to me. Mark my words, Annie, your husband, Platte Lyman, is wrong! I will bear no more children, not in this life, and with this sort of an attitude, probably not in the next! And to tell you the truth, that is just fine with me. I don't want another child! I . . . I couldn't bear the thought that something else might go horribly wrong—"

Eliza finally dissolved into long, wracking sobs, and her own heart breaking with pity, Annie helped her to her feet and led her toward the privacy of Eliza's leaky little cabin.

Jackrabbit Canyon, Navajo Reservation

"Ho, brother, you were right. Those are indeed the ponies of Poke and the others."

Posey, crouched in the brush fifty yards from the *hogan* of the man Tsabekiss and his cursed son Bitseel, remained silent. He had not wanted to be right, not at all, for the hatred he felt for the son of the *Dinê* who dwelt in this place was so intense that he wished never to be near him. Ever since the young man Bitseel and his companion Hoskanini Begay had looked upon him with scorn while he and the others of Mike's band had been taking the life from the white prospectors two cycles of the seasons before—yes, and taking their wealth, too—Posey had nursed a hatred that would not go away for the arrogant Navajo youth.

Though he did not know the extent of the Navajo Bitseel's

hatred for him, he sensed it. And each time Bitseel made those strange noises with his mouth that were words to the *Dinê,* Posey felt more than offended and responded with the darting in and out of his tongue in an insulting manner. *Oo-ah,* yes, this felt good to Posey, too, for it was not hard to tell that the Navajo youth knew the meaning of the gesture and was infuriated by it.

"The Navajo has made Poke and the others welcome in his *wickiup,*" Scotty next offered his silent brother. "What do you suppose it is that they do there?"

"If I knew the answers to all your foolish questions," Posey finally snarled in response, "I would be back on the big river staying warm and eating my fill of fine food! Now be silent, and let me *shu-mi,* let me think!"

Grunting quietly Scotty withdrew a pace, wrapped himself in his warm robe, and settled in to wait. Posey saw this and said nothing. Near him *shpoomp,* some rabbitbrush, stirred in the chill wind, but it didn't matter. He would stay until he knew what Poke was doing with Too-rah and his enemy, Bitseel, in that round *wickiup,* and he knew that his younger brother would stay with him.

Far back and out of the way, one of their two ponies nickered, but the sound was so distant that Posey felt no fear. In the *hogan* such a sound would never be heard, and even if it were, he could easily beat the *wickiup's* occupants to the horses.

"Brother," Scotty whispered, "perhaps something moves among the ponies."

"Nothing moves among our ponies!" Posey practically spat his derision. "I hid them well enough, and they will be safe until we return!"

For a few moments Posey contemplated the scene, wondering about the whereabouts of the man Tsabekiss's herd of fine horses or flock of long-haired sheep. He also wondered that there were no other horses tied before the *hogan* but those of Poke and his small band. That was a strange thing, and he was just starting to ponder the meaning of it when Scotty crept forward once again.

"My brother," he said with some urgency as he gazed once more at the *hogan,* "have you determined what it is that Poke does with the *Dinê?*"

"I am certain he does in this place just what we do with the *Dinê* when they come to the big river," Posey answered haughtily. "Poke and his band are either playing cards and getting wealthy, or making a trade of venison and buckskins for the warm blankets woven by the Navajo."

Scotty grunted. "That is good to hear, my brother. I thought it might be something else, and I was growing worried."

"Something else?" Posey snarled with derision. "What did your foolish mind think they might be doing?"

"It was nothing." Scotty immediately scooted back to his former position.

"I wish to hear it."

"Very well." Scotty took a deep breath. "It was in my mind that the *nan-zitch* Too-rah is now a woman, old enough to be taken in marriage. I thought that perhaps the grizzly might be making a trade for her, selling her to one of the men of the *Dinê*."

And Posey, who had never entertained a more horrible thought in his life, was too stunned to even think of a suitable, sarcastic reply. All he could do was stare with increased hatred through the brush at the *hogan* of his enemy, while his heart grew darker and more filled with fear.

Bluff Fort

"Evening, Billy. Do you and Eliza have a moment?"

Surprised, Billy opened wide his door and stepped aside. "Certainly, President Lyman. Won't you come in?"

Stepping inside, Platte Lyman removed his hat. "Evening, Eliza. You're looking some better than the last time I saw you."

Eliza smiled graciously. "I'm feeling much better, too. I . . . we didn't know you had returned from Colorado."

"We just got in tonight—not more than an hour ago. How's little Willy getting along? He looks mighty peaceful there."

Billy and Eliza both looked at their sleeping son, though it was Eliza who spoke. "He's doing much better, thank you. He seems well past the danger of starvation, though he has missed your son Albert R. something fierce since you took him to Colorado."

"Albert's missed him as well. I'm pleased that they are friends." For a moment Platte rubbed his beard thoughtfully. "Billy," he finally pressed, "have you done anything about that riding problem we discussed?"

"Uh . . . no, I haven't."

"Well, no matter. Do you have access to that mule belonging to Dick and Parley Butt that you occasionally ride? Wonder, I believe you call it?"

Silently Billy nodded.

"Good. The last day or so I've been overwhelmed with the feeling that we need to find the trail to the top of Elk Mountain. We must have more graze for our livestock, and I believe that mountain is our answer."

"What about the Pahutes?"

Platte smiled. "Now that they're all camped down at Sand Island, I believe we'll be safe from them. At least that's what I'm hoping. I'll be taking one or two others with me in the morning to look for that trail, and I'd like you to accompany us. Eliza, will you be okay for two or three days without your husband?"

"I'm certain I will be fine."

"Good. Billy, will you ride with us?"

"I . . . uh . . . why, of course I'll go."

Platte smiled and extended his hand. "Wonderful!" he said, shaking Billy's hand. "I'd like to be on the way fairly early in the morning, if that suits you."

"It suits me fine."

"Good. I'll see you at the corral at three A.M. sharp."

And as Billy and Eliza watched in stunned silence, Platte replaced his hat, nodded courteously, and went out through the door and into the night.

10

Saturday, October 1, 1881

Jackrabbit Canyon, Navajo Reservation

"My brother, it is time to awaken."

Scotty was careful, for he did not wish to make much noise, and more importantly, he did not wish Posey to make much noise. They were too close to the *hogan* of the man Tsabekiss and his son Bitseel; and they were far too close to the grizzly Poke and those who rode with him.

The day was just graying in the east, and so they had been in this place of hiding part of one day and all of one night. For most of that time Posey had not slept at all, but had kept his mind at a fevered pitch with worry over whether or not the comely Too-rah was being sold to Bitseel as the Navajo youth's wife. Short of going into the *hogan* and asking, which he wouldn't do, there was no way he could know that. So he watched and worried about the *nan-zitch,* and Scotty watched and worried about his brother.

All night the fire had burned in the *hogan,* for Posey had chosen wisely and hidden with the night breeze coming toward them. Thus the wood smoke and occasional cooking smells had been on the air. This had not been easy for either of the youths, for neither of them had brought food on this journey, and Scotty was beginning to feel the effects of the prolonged fast. But at least there was water nearby—a small seep that Scotty had found during one of his numerous forays to see what else besides the lone *hogan* and sheep pens might be nearby. Posey had not been willing to move at all, but had sat almost without moving during the entire time of their being there, his eyes fastened on the east-facing door of the Navajo dwelling.

Scotty wondered at that, trying to understand the sort of power the foolish *nan-zitch* called Too-rah had somehow gained over his brother. He gave no such allegiance to anyone or anything else, and in fact fought viciously against every sort of restriction that Poke or anyone else might attempt to place upon him. Of course neither of the young men had ever been restricted in any way by their parents, and so even the concept of restraint was difficult for Scotty to understand. Yet he had seen Posey risk everything for a few brief moments with the girl, and laugh when he had thought of doing so again. And now this—

"My brother, it grows light."

Posey, deep in sleep, nodded once and then abruptly snapped his head up, his eyes wide with the memory of where he was.

"Has . . . anyone come from the *wickiup?*" he asked, adjusting his legs to ease the stiffness in them, but otherwise not moving even a little.

"I have heard a few things, my brother," Scotty responded, not wanting Posey to know that he had also slept, and had awakened only as the noises were about to come to an end. Still, what he had heard had been enough to tell him that there had been movement near the *hogan* and among the horses. But it had been too dark to see if anything of consequence was happening, and so he had not awakened his brother at that time.

"Why did you let me sleep?"

Scotty shrugged. "The sounds seemed to be nothing."

Hissing angrily to show his displeasure at his brother's decision, Posey hugged himself for warmth, for he had brought along no such sleeping robe as had his brother. Meanwhile his eyes strained to see through the gloom. But it was still too dark, and so the youth was forced to remain as he had been all night, anxiously waiting the growing light of day.

"When we return to the big river," he said suddenly, as if they had been speaking of this thing for many hours, "we will go to the dwelling of the tall, thin white woman and take from her the *tabby-nump,* the clock. It is a thing that will bring great pleasure to Too-rah."

Scotty considered this. "Will you still give the white woman the greenbacks?" he finally asked. "Or some other trade?"

Instantly Posey made the sign that he would not. "She fears me, my brother. I know, for I have seen it in her eyes each time we have entered that ugly dwelling that is their *wickiup*. That is enough to make the clock mine."

Scotty chuckled quietly. "And as I told you before, my brother, I fear the woman's husband. I looked into his eyes even as you were attempting to *co-que,* to shoot him with that poor rifle you had the morning he came after the horses. My brother, in his eyes there was no fear."

"There will be!" Posey snarled angrily. "One day I will find myself a fine, big gun, and then you will see fear in that man's eyes that will be greater than any fear you have ever seen! *Oo-ah,* yes! And you will see the woman cowering upon the earth before me as I smash out the brains of the ugly white-haired papoose she calls her son. Remember these words, my brother, for you will see that they will soon come to pass!"

And with that determined exclamation, the young warrior returned his attention to the vague form of the *hogan*.

Jackrabbit Canyhon, Navajo Reservation

"Topie-quay," Scotty breathed in amazement when the light had grown great enough to be certain, "they are all gone!"

"Yes," Posey growled angrily, "and you allowed me to sleep through their leaving. Hear this, you fool. From this day, you are no longer a brother to me!"

Shrugging as if to say that Posey's words had little effect upon him, which in fact they did not, Scotty crept forward after his brother. In the light of the morning they came at last to the *hogan* of Tsabekiss, which was indeed empty of any occupants. Inside, however, were many sheepskins and a few well-worn blankets, one of which Posey immediately appropriated for his own use.

While Scotty watched at the doorway, Posey kicked things

about, looking for anything else that might be of value. But there was nothing except for a few woman things, and these Posey would not even touch.

"Let us burn this place," he snarled as he straightened from his search, his eyes dancing with a fierce light.

"Very well," Scotty agreed easily. "Only, where will you get fire, my brother? With their departure the *Diné* have carried off all their hot coals, and with your *nan-zitch* getting farther away by the moment, taking the time to kindle a new flame seems a great waste of time."

Blinking at Scotty's thought, Posey stood irresolute. Finally, however, he made the sign of agreement. "We will hurry after the grizzly and his little sister," he said simply, and without a backward glance he strode from the old *hogan* and turned toward where he had chosen to hide their well-used ponies.

Jackrabbit Canyon, Navajo Reservation

"Ho, my brother," Posey said, too surprised yet for anger, "is not this the place where we hid our ponies?"

Scotty made the sign that it was so, though his eyes were busy looking up and down the meandering ravine. "They were here during the time of darkness," he responded quietly, wondering as he spoke what great witchcraft was at work in this place. "I came to them and led them to water."

"Perhaps you did not tie them securely." Posey's voice was like ice.

"I tied them well," Scotty protested, moving past his brother and trotting to where the two horses had been secured. "Come," he said quietly, "and you will see what has happened to our ponies."

Now getting angry, Posey strode forward and then stopped abruptly as he saw what his younger brother was pointing at. The tracks in the sand were plain, and Posey didn't even have to look closely to know that the one moccasin print, the large one, had been made by the grizzly Poke. The other, which had been made by the more pointed Navajo moccasin, he knew just as certainly belonged to Bitseel. Somehow in their leaving this canyon of the *hogan,* the two—whom Posey now thought of as his true enemies—had discovered this hiding place, and had taken the two ponies with them. The tracks going down the sandy wash were there to see. Which meant, and now Posey screamed his wrath and frustration as he realized it, that he and his foolish brother were afoot.

"It was you who led them to this place!" he snarled as he turned toward his brother. "It was—"

But Scotty was no longer standing behind him. Already he was fifty yards down the wash and trotting easily toward the place where the others had climbed over the edge and disappeared with their ponies.

And so Posey, whose anger knew no bounds, kicked viciously at the sand and started after. It would be a hard run, he knew, especially with the still-healing wound given him by the old cow. But no matter what else might befall him or his brother, he would catch up to those who had been foolhardy enough to take his pony!

Oo-ah! And when he did . . .

First Valley

"Is this about where you fellers got to the last time?"

"Aye, Kumen, within about a quarter mile." Hyrum Perkins was bending over a small fire as he responded, working on the simple meal the four explorers would be eating. An excellent cook, he delighted in such things, and was quite willing to leave other chores to his brethren. "Leastwise," he grunted as he leaned over to adjust the hot coals around the small dutch oven, "that's what Platte said."

In the not quite darkness, the stars were already showing overhead, and several coyotes were yipping their lonesome complaints to the heavens. It had been a long and tiring day, the men trailing north nearly fifty miles along the valley of Butler Wash. Now they were encamped on the edge of what they were calling First Valley, though in years to come it would take on the name, and be but a part of, a labyrinth of gulches, ravines, and small valleys known as Whiskers Draw.

"Well, so far, so good, at least in terms of the Pahutes," Kumen Jones opined from where he sat mending his saddle. "Mary was some concerned we'd run into them and have us an altercation."

"So was Eliza," Billy stated quietly as he finished staking the horses and mule nearby.

"I wouldn't much blame the Indians if they did raise a ruckus," Kumen then ventured. "This has been their country since who flung the chunk, and nobody takes kindly to trespassers."

Billy nodded his further agreement, thinking as he did so of Eliza's intense feelings concerning Pahute trespassers in their own little cabin. It was interesting, he thought, that here they were, doing the very same sort of thing.

"How's the cane harvest coming along?" Kumen asked, abruptly changing the subject.

"Eliza reckons they'll finish rendering the molasses within another day, or at the most, two."

"At least we got a good crop of cane." Hyrum Perkins smiled. "It's about the only crop that's done well."

"Thank goodness!" Billy responded. "When Platte was in Colorado he lined up a good price for all the molasses we can produce, so that cane will be an absolute blessing. Platte's planning on going back to Colorado next week with Jim Decker and George Westwood, to see what else we might be able to trade."

Hyrum nodded. "He'll work out something. Do you suppose he'll take little Albert with him again?"

"He plans on it," Billy responded. "Says he figures the boy's old enough to start learning the road. I hear Adelia's fit to be tied about it, and Eliza says she doesn't much blame her."

"How old is the child?"

"Coming on two, I reckon. And apparently old enough to start learning. I know Willy's learning a powerful lot, and he's even a few months younger than Albert!"

In the gathering darkness the compact fire gave off only a small amount of light, and could not be seen from more than a few yards away. Of course the weather was warm, so heat wasn't needed.

Nevertheless, a fire is a cheerful thing, especially in a big, empty country, and the three men were now huddled close, simply enjoying each other's company while they waited for the return of their leader so they could eat together.

"He's a mighty traveling man, is Brother Platte," Hyrum observed.

Kumen grinned. "Yeah, Hy, he is at that. From what I hear, he always has been. I don't know how many times I've heard him say that the best thing for the inside of a man is the outside of a horse. He believes it, too."

"That's because the doctrine is sound," Platte Lyman stated as he stepped quietly into the firelight, surprising all of them with his silent arrival. "I've never seen a problem with inner turmoil that a good trip on horseback couldn't help resolve. Speaking of which, no sign of Pahutes up yonder that I can see."

"Can you see any sign of the trail up through those rocks?"

Seating himself on his saddle, Platte nodded. "Maybe. Come daylight we'll find out for sure. That sop and 'taters smells mighty good, Hy. Hope you left the bark on 'em."

Knowing Platte was speaking of leaving the potatoes unpeeled, Hyrum nodded that he had.

"Good for you! Is she about ready?"

In response Hyrum lifted the lid and stirred the steaming contents, and soon the four men were busy refueling their trail-weary bodies. Later, after everything was cleaned and stowed away, bedrolls were spread out and the fire doused, and then the quiet talk began.

"This is a wondrous country, boys," Platte observed—"high, wide, and lonesome as a lost coyote. Still, she's God's country sure enough, and I can't think of a place I'd rather be than right here searching my way through it. Don't you agree, Billy?"

"I'd like it a lot better if I knew what I was about—and if Eliza and little Willy were here with me."

Platte and the others chuckled at Billy's dour humor. "Yes, there is that, all right. A man does get to missing his family. On the other hand, you seemed to handle that old mule just fine today. Where'd you ever get the notion that you couldn't ride?"

"Oh," Billy groused with his same quiet good humor, "by being bucked off one critter or another about a hundred and eighty-seven different times in the last two years. And by aching right now in every bone and muscle in my body, including a few I never even knew I had."

"Yeah, riding does take some getting used to. Still, Billy, I've a feeling you're going to need that skill, and would be wise to develop it."

"Which is why I was invited on this little jaunt?"

Platte smiled into the darkness. "In part, I suppose. Mainly, though, I thought you'd enjoy seeing some new country. Such sights certainly do stir my bones, I tell you what."

"We've all noticed that you're a traveling man," Kumen said.

"Yes, that seems to be true," Platte allowed. He leaned his head back, gazing for a moment upward into the star-shrouded heavens, his thoughts seemingly far away.

"Maybe it's all on account of I was born in a wagon box somewhere along the Platte River when our folks were coming west out of Nauvoo. Ma thinks that's when I got the wide outdoors into my bones."

"That where you got your name, then? From the river?"

Platte toed off his boots and wiggled his toes, allowing them a little freedom. "That's right."

"How'd you come by your knowledge of the gospel, President? You seem to know the scriptures mighty well," Hy observed.

"And you can explain and proclaim the doctrines of the Restoration better than most any man I ever heard," Billy added.

"Well," Platte drawled modestly, "if that's so, boys, then lay it to my ma. She nursed me from day one with milk filled with the testimony that Joseph was a prophet of God, and filled as well with the true principles of the gospel of Jesus Christ that Joseph restored. Her milk I was weaned of, but never the other."

"Who's your father, President?" Hy asked.

"Amasa Mason Lyman," Platte said.

"Isn't he the apostle who was excommunicated? Or is that the Lyman who is an apostle now?"

"Elder Francis Marion Lyman is our half-brother through Pa's first wife. He was only called to the apostleship last year."

Platte reached to stir the fire a bit before continuing.

"My father was called to the apostleship in 1842. As a point of interest, he also served a short time in the First Presidency with Joseph Smith. Then a little over ten years ago, in 1870, he was excommunicated for teaching some sort of questionable doctrine regarding the Atonement. He passed on about four years ago. I never heard the whole story about what happened, but I do know it's been mighty rough on our family. I know also that Francis Marion has redone Pa's temple work, and he is now back in the Church with all his blessings restored."

"Did you know your father well?" Billy asked.

Platte shook his head, seeming to warm to the subject.

"I knew him well enough, but he wasn't around much. As a young elder and then as an apostle he was called upon to fulfill several two- and three-year missions for the Church—fifteen all told—so he was gone on the Lord's errands for years at a time. Another thing. Pa was a big man, way too big for walking anywhere in comfort. Yet on one of his missions he walked over 2,000 miles, on others he was abused regularly and suffered all sorts of violence, and several times he was chained and imprisoned, occasionally for lengthy stays. For a fact he was imprisoned with the Prophet Joseph in Missouri through that long, cold winter of 1838–39, and he would have gladly accepted death with the Prophet had it come to that. I've heard the account from his own lips, several times, and the things those innocent men were forced to endure would make strong men shudder and cruel men weep.

"Pa loved Joseph Smtih. Ma used to read to us out of one of Pa's letters concerning the day he first met the Prophet, after taking thirty-five days to walk the 800 miles to Ohio, and I've memorized it. Pa wrote: 'When Joseph grasped my hand in that cordial way known to those who have known him in the simplicity of truth, I felt as one of old, in the presence of the Lord. My strength seemed to be gone, so that it required an effort on my part to stand on my feet.'

"A day or so later the Prophet told Pa that the Lord required his labors in the vineyard, and from that day in 1832 until his excommunication in 1870, Pa gave service beyond measure, never turning down a calling or an assignment. That, Billy, is why we saw so little of him."

Platte sighed deeply, his mind pondering his own words. "Of a truth, boys," he finally declared, "I carry the Lyman name proudly, and you can bet I always will."

11

Sunday, October 2, 1881

First Valley

"Looks like we have us a welcoming committee, President."

His eyes on the trail ahead, Platte Lyman nodded that he had already seen the half-circle of waiting Pahutes. "Looks as though I was right about the whereabouts of their hidden trail, too," he murmured quietly. "I just don't know how we missed it that first trip."

It was early, barely past daylight, and the four explorers had ridden little more than two hundred yards from their camp in First Valley when the dozen Pahute warriors materialized out of the rocks and juniper trees ahead of them. They were painted for war, each of them had his weapon at the ready, and as the explorers drew slowly nearer they could see the fierce scowls on the faces of the men.

"Do you know them, Kumen?" Platte spoke conversationally, showing no sign that the half-circle of Pahutes was causing him any concern whatsoever.

"Most," Kuman replied, also speaking in a normal tone of voice. "That fellow with the wide mouth and Berkshire boar neck is called Mike—Moencopi Mike. This is his band, or part of it, at least."

"I know Mike, all right," President Lyman said.

"Don't we all? The one next to him is a Sioux brave who calls himself Wash, and who has adopted himself into this band. Then you have Bridger Jack, Tuvagutts, Soldier Coat, Old Chee, Grasshopper, and then Hatch, who is Poke's grandfather—now, that's interesting, President. Poke and his four brothers aren't here, and neither is Jonah or Old Chee's two boys, Posey and Scotty. Makes a feller wonder where they are."

Instantly to Billy's mind came thoughts of Eliza and the fort, and as he rode behind Platte and Kumen and beside Hyrum Perkins, he began praying fervently for the safety of those at home.

"That's Old Baldy," Kumen continued, "him who was fixing to shoot Lem Redd with his broken pistol last spring. Looks like that's still his weapon of choice. That taller fellow there is called Brooks, and to tell the truth, I don't know the names of any of the others. They've all been in the fort, though—every last one of them!"

"What do you want us to do, President?" Hyrum Perkins asked softly.

Platte turned in his saddle and looked back at Hy and Billy. He smiled and said, "I used to ask my pa that question when I'd grow weary of a job he'd put me to, such as working our huge garden, and his answer was always the same: 'Just keep on planting potatoes.' That's it for us, too, boys. We'll just keep on planting potatoes and see how this thing plays out. But whatever you do, don't let them know you're nervous. I have the feeling they're waiting for some sign of weakness, and if we don't show any, and don't slow down, we'll be just fine."

"Just keep on planting potatoes," Hyrum breathed as they drew ever nearer the dark-visaged half-circle of men. "You with us, Billy?"

"As ever," Billy replied, trying to keep his mind on his pleadings for the safety of Eliza and Willy rather than his own nervousness in the face of this angry knot of Pahute warriors.

"I don't think we should try to break through their circle, President."

"You're right, Kumen. We shouldn't. I'll lead out and circle around Mike there, to the left. The rest of you stay close behind."

"As if we'd pick now to start wandering," Hyrum mumbled, bringing a slight smile to Billy's countenance.

"Mighty pretty Sabbath morning," Platte observed as he approached the Pahutes and turned his horse out and around them. "Given the choice, I do believe I'd rather be back to home, preparing a talk to deliver to the Saints. Howsomever, it's also a mighty pretty day to be riding through some of God's most handsome country. Don't you agree, Billy?"

"I do, President."

As the men rode forward around the outside of the half-circle, the scowling Pahutes turned their snorting ponies so they remained face-to-face with them. And so far as Billy could see, the dozen braves showed nothing in their countenances but seething hatred. None of them spoke, though, nor made any sound whatsoever, and after the four scouts had passed by them and were continuing up the trail into the junipers, the Pahutes remained where they were, apparently undecided as to what they should do next.

"What now?" Kumen breathed as they climbed through the trees and passed out of sight of the Indians behind them.

And almost in chorus, Platte, Hyrum, and Billy all replied, just as quietly, "Keep on planting potatoes."

Second Valley

"I don't know about you fellows," Billy said as they continued through the rocks and trees, seeking out what must surely be the trail to the top of the mountain, "but that seemed a little too easy."

"Easy?" Hyrum Perkins questioned. "Perhaps so, Billy, but as we rode past those fellows, every hair on the back of my neck was standing straight out."

"Same with me," Kumen agreed as he turned to check their apparently empty back trail. "And I'm still trying to get my shoulders to relax from expecting a Pahute bullet."

"How do you reckon they knew we'd be here, President?"

"From the tracks Joseph Barton, Orrin Kelsey, and I left when we came up here before, I imagine." For a moment Platte hummed a bit of a hymn. "That, and maybe they've been following us ever since we left the fort yesterday morning."

"But, we saw no sign of them!"

"Do you see any sign of them now, Hy? I don't, but the Spirit of the Lord keeps whispering to me that those braves are following us and that we are being watched."

Soberly Billy looked around. "I've been feeling it, too. But I also felt a protection back there, the same I felt in Butler Wash last spring when all those braves were swarming down around us."

"That's right, Billy," Platte agreed. "We are being protected! We're on the Lord's errand here, and so long as we don't thirst after their blood, the Pahutes won't have the power to spill ours. Ministering angels will see to it that they don't. But the moment we leave off doing the work of the Lord and start doing work such as will aggrandize and profit only ourselves, or the moment we begin thirsting after the blood of these poor, benighted souls . . ."

Platte did not need to finish, for all understood what the results of such selfishness would be, not only for themselves but also for their mission of peace. In silence, then, the four continued steadily upward, pondering deeply their own motives as well as the goodness and glory of God. Soon they emerged into what Platte called Second Valley, but which in years to come would be known as Milk Ranch Point. This they crossed without incident, to come at length to a ridge of rocks and trees on the north.

"Any of you see a trail here?" Platte questioned as he urged his horse first one way and then another, looking for sign.

"No trail," Billy called from where he was searching, "but I see plenty of pony tracks."

"Yeah, going in every which direction," Kumen groused. "Boys, they've hidden the trail but good! There's no way on this green earth we're going to find our way any higher on this mountain."

"President," Hyrum Perkins called quietly but urgently as he pulled his mount to a halt, "we have company."

Quickly the scouts gathered to confront a slender Pahute youth who had ridden his roan colt forward out of a copse of junipers.

"Kumen?"

"This is the one calls himself Henry, President—the same one Thales figures saved you boys' bacon that morning at Boiling Spring when he called out for the Utes to lower their weapons and not shoot their mormonee friends."

Slowly Platte nodded, and then he made the sign of greeting to the silent youth.

Soberly Henry responded in kind. "Me Henu," he said, speaking quietly but urgently as he endeavored to articulate his newly adopted language. "Me heap help! Pikey, pikey! Go fast!" And with that he pointed the direction the scouts should take if they wanted to continue upward.

As one, the four men turned in the direction the Pahute youth was pointing, but when they turned back to ask further questions he had vanished, somehow riding without noise back into the trees.

"Well," Platte said as he lifted his hat and scratched his head, "he's the disappearingest kid I ever saw."

"And the quietest," Kumen added. "Still, I reckon Henry wants us to go yonder. It doesn't look like the way of a trail to me, but I vote we trust him."

"Amen," Platte agreed for the others, and as one the four scouts kneed their mounts in the direction Henry had pointed.

Third Valley

"Is this the way you came before, President?"

Silently Platte surveyed the small valley, which would one day be known as an upper branch of Hammond Canyon. "Nope. I've never seen this country, boys. But then, we never got this high with our horses, either."

"There's Henry again, up yonder," Kumen said, motioning.

"Yes," Platte said as he touched spurs to his horse and turned it toward the Indian youth, "and he's acting more urgent than ever. We keep after him, boys, and Henry will lead us to the top of this mountain."

"You think the others are following?" Hyrum asked as they moved up through more trees.

"Well, Henry's being mighty careful about hiding from somebody, and it doesn't seem to be us. So, yes, they're back there somewhere, and we'd do well to expect them anytime."

Silently the men rode where the Pahute youth directed, wondering at his skill, and wondering, too, that he would show them the wonderfully hidden trail they were following. Certainly he was as Haskel had said, a true friend of the Mormons. And just as certainly the Indian youth had felt the power of the Lord's Spirit, confirming to his soul all the words that Haskel had spoken to him so many months before.

In almost total silence Henry continued to point the way, taking them up along the narrow backbone, hidden by trees, that led toward the top of Elk Ridge, and then along the high shelf to what would come to be known as Dwarf Spring. Many times he appeared and then just as quietly disappeared, but as the men rode ever forward across the luxuriant and nearly flat top of the mountain to Kigaly Spring and other good springs they were shown, they couldn't help but notice that Henry's face was agleam with the radiant light of true friendship.

More, the country they were being shown was almost as stunning as the friendship of the boy. Towering firs, thick stands of aspen they called quakies because of their ever-trembling leaves, and broad meadows filled with grass as high as their horses' bellies—it was a veritable paradise for livestock that the scouts had been led by Henry to "discover," and all knew they had found their summer range.

Nokaito Bench, Navajo Reservation

The Pahute woman called Peeb, which in the white man tongue meant *feather,* did not know what to do. She was not only growing larger with the child that was in her womb—her first, she kept thinking with justified excitement—but now her man, who had carried the *mericat* name of Jonah for all the days since he had slain with one fine shot a cowboy by that name, was behaving in a manner that was strange and most perplexing.

Normally a man of great strength and skill in the hunting of game and other manly pursuits, a man to make his woman proud, Jonah was suddenly behaving more in the manner of a woman. Yes, and this embarrassing change had come upon him in an instant, and only the day before. Many times since then, his eyes had grown wet with tears, and in the time of darkness he had whimpered frequently and cried out in terrible fear, and for some reason he had stopped feeling joy in her closeness. Now he wished only to be alone, to huddle beneath his sleeping robe and stare with wide and frightened eyes into the darkness.

Of itself the troubled mind of Peeb returned to the day before, when her man had crept fearfully into the silent *hogan* of Natanii nééz, who was known far and wide as the great *Diné* thief called Navajo Frank. Peeb had not gone into the *hogan,* but had remained astride her small burro. Yes, even when the woman of Natanii nééz had come forth to stand in the sun beckoning her to enter, Peeb had turned her eyes and remained mounted. It was where her man had told her to remain, and she had learned better than to disobey him.

But then Jonah himself had come forth, silently and with ashen face, and Peeb had known that something terrible had happened. Yes, in that dark *hogan* some great evil had come upon her man, and for the first time in her life, Peeb had known real fear.

Stumbling twice on his way to his fine pony, Jonah had pulled himself onto its back, turned it around toward the big river, and kicked it heavily in the ribs. Without a word Peeb had followed, and it was only later, when Jonah had fallen to the sand near a seep where they sought water for the animals, that his eyes had filled with tears and his lips had issued forth whimpering sounds like those of a hurt woman. Then, finally, Peeb had begun to learn a little of what had happened to her man.

Peeb had not heard the frightening words of the mormonee Thales Haskel on Sand Island two weeks before. She had not heard them because she had been exhausted from her duties and had fallen asleep. Neither had she known, then or since, how deeply Jonah had feared those same words. It was not the way of men of the People to speak of such fears to their women; in fact, it was not the way of men of the People to speak of anything to their women—unless it was to give orders or to shout angry reprimands when their orders were not promptly carried out. Peeb knew this, and was not troubled by it at all.

But with her man now lying on the sand near the seep in the land of the *Diné* for the second day, still trembling and ashen-faced, Peeb was beginning to realize that those words had something to do with the awful calamity that had befallen her man. Over and over he had repeated the mormonee's words, or small portions of them. And each time, as he mentioned all the mormonee horses and cattle he had stolen, he had trembled with fear, and his eyes had filled with those shameful, unbidden tears.

Yes, she thought wearily, this fine, strong man who was the father of the child in her womb, was *puck-kon-gah,* very sick. That much was obvious. Yet despite his rantings about the dying Navajo Frank and the powerful medicine words of the mormonee Haskel, Peeb did not have the least idea of exactly what was wrong with Jonah, or of what she might do to help him recover from it.

And so in the stillness of the late afternoon she sat helplessly by herself, trying not to listen to the terrified whimperings and foolish chatter of her man. On the morrow, if he still had not eaten or recovered in any way, she knew that she would drag him to his pony and tie him in place on its back. Then she would take him north across the big river and away from this land of such great evil.

No, she would not take him to the island from which they had left, for Peeb had no wish to have the others of the People see Jonah as he now was. Instead she would skirt the island and go on to the place where Poke and the others always made their winter camp. There, she reasoned, Jonah would be safely away from the evil of this land, and so could recover and become as he had always been! And that, she thought with a quiet sigh, was all she could possibly hope for.

Kigaly Spring

"President, this is the prettiest country I've seen since we left Cedar City two years ago," Kumen observed.

"And the greenest," Platte agreed. "Anybody seen Henry?"

The four scouts, finally camped for the night at what would be called Kigaly Spring, named for an old Navajo who kept his small herd of sheep nearby, realized that once again the slim youth had disappeared.

Platte, who had been kneeling at the fire while Hyrum sliced side meat and potatoes into a kettle nearby, looked up and then rose to his feet.

"Kumen and Billy," he called quietly, "bring the horses closer in. Of a sudden I'm having a troublesome feeling—"

"Somebody's up in those trees, President."

"I heard."

"Maybe Henry—"

"It isn't Henry. He's never made a sound all day that he didn't want to make. But whoever it is, boys, act normal."

Trying not to stare up through the quakies as he tied down his mule and Platte's horse, Billy realized that once again his heart was pounding so that it felt as though it would explode out of his chest. Would he never get used to this, he wondered? Would he never stop fearing danger—

Abruptly a horse and rider appeared in the copse of aspen above them, riding downward. He was followed immediately by a second rider and then a third, and soon it was apparent that the dozen warriors they had met in First Valley that morning had indeed been following them through the day. They were now stringing down through the aspen, single file, their faces even darker with hatred and anger than they had been before.

"They look to mean business this time," Kumen declared in sotto voce.

"And bad business at that," Platte agreed as the warriors rode boldly to the fire and circled about them.

Standing with the end of his mule's lead rope still in his hand, Billy searched the glowering face of Moencopi Mike, whose huge gash of a mouth was pressed tightly downward in a perpetual scowl of hatred. His dark eyes burned like smoldering fires, and Billy felt a shiver as he experienced close-up the hatred of the man.

What am I doing here? he found himself wondering as he glanced from Mike to Wash to Bridger Jack and to the others, *beyond the end of any known trail and at least fifty miles from the fort at*

Bluff. Yes, and Bluff itself is three or four times fifty miles from any help on whom we might call if these people mean to do us harm! Blinking at a bead of sweat that was dropping into his right eye, Billy continued doing his best to appear composed. *Besides,* his mind continued to run, *it is we who are trespassing on their lands now, and not the other way around. These are their precious hunting grounds, and we have been led here by a spy.*

Billy realized that Henry was not with these men, and again he wondered how the youth could manage to remain so unseen, even from his own people. Yes, and how he had ever had the courage—

"Boys," Platte said conversationally as he moved to stir the fire and add more wood, "the object right now is not summer graze, but how to somehow foil the great plan of murder and destruction these fellows have so obviously laid for us."

"Any ideas?" Kumen asked, busying himself with removing items from his packs, items of which he had no immediate need whatsoever.

"None at all, except to act natural and unconcerned. Hy, you need any help slicing them vittles into your pan?"

Hyrum grinned crookedly. "Not much, Platte. The way my hands are shaking, these spuds are pretty much getting sliced by themselves."

"Billy," Platte said as he seated himself on a rock while the Pahutes continued their fierce game of trying to stare the four scouts into submission, "you have any idea what sort of pines these are?"

"M . . . most are Douglas fir," Billy replied as he knelt and drove his mule's stake pin further into the loamy soil. "I think I also saw some white pines a little earlier, but I'm not certain."

It was not hard to tell what Platte was doing, and Billy admired the man for it. Here they were, four men literally surrounded by a dozen murderers—well, the leader of this gang was obviously Moencopi Mike, who had not only been one of the leading spirits in the murders of Jimmy Heaton, the Wilson brothers, John Thurman, Dick May, and who knew how many others during the big raid the previous spring, but who according to Thales Haskel and the Navajos had also slain the prospectors Mitchell and Merrick down in Monument Valley a couple of years before. Without doubt the man was a murderer, and seemed to delight most especially in shedding the blood of white men.

Now he was here on horseback playing the same deadly game with them, glaring downward with muddy eyes, first at him and then at each of the others, toying all the while with the stock of his pistol as if at any moment he was intending to pull it from his holster and begin firing!

Around Mike the other warriors sat their restive ponies, waiting for their leader to give the signal and begin the big things of which he had no doubt been boasting. In an instant they would respond in kind, Billy knew; and he knew just as surely that once Mike signaled, none of them would live more than a moment longer.

Yet something was holding Mike of the wide mouth back from his intended signal. With every fiber of his being he seemed to be exerting his will in silent conflict with these invaders of his hunting grounds, searching eagerly for any tremor of fear, for the least sign of any weakening under the weight of his wrath. Yet so far, he had not seen that for which he was looking. It was as if . . .

"Kumen, don't you think Billy is riding better than he has been claiming he could?"

Looking up from his saddle packs, which now seemed to need an awful lot of repairs, Kumen forced a grin. "Well, he hasn't been bucked off once since yesterday, at least that I've seen. I'd say he's doing some better, all right."

"So would I," Platte drawled. "Hy, what do you think?"

"I think we'd have to put him on an actual horse to see what he can do. Riding that sorry, worn-down mule isn't hardly a fair trial of any man's skill."

"That's a good point, too. Billy, you willing to swap mounts in the morning?"

"Not hardly," Billy declared easily as he propped himself on a log that had been dragged up earlier. "I heard you tell Bill Ball you was a mule man from way back, President, so your scheme to take Wonder away from me is mighty thin. I'll keep my own mount, and thank you to do the same."

Platte and the others chuckled, and meanwhile Moencopi Mike danced his pony about, all the while glaring downward at these stubborn Mormons who were somehow not afraid. The trouble was, he could not maintain such a fevered pitch of animosity forever, not when there was nothing to feed it on. And so finally, lest the others see him lose his dignity completely, the feared warrior grunted and kneed his pony forward, away from the fire. Without comment of any sort the others followed, and shortly they had gone into camp in a grove of oak perhaps fifty yards down the canyon.

Moments later the youth Henry emerged from the trees, and passing silently by the Mormons as if they did not exist, he rode down the canyon and slid from his pony. Then he joined the other Pahutes in their somber powwow.

"I'd give a ten-dollar gold piece to know what they are saying," Platte breathed as he watched the reunion near the blazing fire.

"They're probably cooking up something else to do to us," Billy responded in kind.

"Maybe, maybe not," Kumen declared. "One thing I do know, Mike's got to find some way of saving face. With those others painted and ready for war the way they are, you know he had to have promised them a big and glorious victory over us, with lots of booty. So far they've had nothing from all his promises but a long ride, and I think the old boy's in trouble."

"Could be," Platte agreed while he remained as relaxed as before. "Hy, how's dinner coming?"

"Give it another ten minutes, and we'll be ready."

"Good. I have a few loaves of Adelia's bread in my pack."

"You never mentioned any bread last night or this morning!"

Platte smiled widely. "Nope. I was saving them for the right moment, which I reckon is tonight. I also brought along a small jug of new molasses, which I figured we could have as a treat. So, once you're ready, Hy—"

"President, here he comes again."

"Here who comes? I thought—"

"Moencopi Mike. Difference is, now he's on foot, and alone!"

Instantly a wide smile appeared on Platte Lyman's face. "Well then, that's it, boys. Now I know what to do." And without further comment he rose to his feet and stepped to his bulging packs.

Kigaly Spring

"I'd say this fellow needs a new tactic," Hyrum Perkins observed as a still silent Mike hove to at the fire, his legs spread wide, his thick arms folded across his barrel chest, and his face as scowling and fierce-looking as ever.

"Either that or something new to think about," Platte agreed as he turned from his panniers holding a jug and a large loaf of his wife Adelia's homemade bread. "Billy, would you please hand me that knife Hy was using a little bit ago?"

Billy leaned to comply, and then watched in fascination as Platte cut a huge slice off the loaf of bread—not off the end as might have been expected, but from end to end, so that the huge slice removed a full quarter of the loaf of bread. With an elaborate flourish he uncorked the jug and poured molasses over the entire slice. Then, with a wide smile, he stepped to Mike and held out the slice to him.

For only an instant Mike hesitated, his face a study. But then without a word he took it from Platte's outstretched hands, lifted it, and closed his ponderous mouth over an entire corner.

To Billy's utter amazement the massive slice was gone in just a few bites, five or six at the most. And the Pahute had not even finished chewing and swallowing when Platte handed him a second slice, just as liberally cut and even more thickly smeared with molasses. This Mike ate with as much gusto as he had the first, and it had hardly vanished when a third slice was presented to his eager hands. That, too, disappeared into his huge maw, and he was smacking his wide lips with relish when the fourth and final slice of Adelia Lyman's loaf of bread was forwarded to him.

"You have any more bread, President?" Kumen asked.

"If I need it," Platte replied quietly as he watched Mike devouring the bread. "You fellows see the change in this man's face?"

"Well, he's too busy eating to frown, if that's what you mean," Kumen said.

"No, Kumen, it's more than that. Look at his eyes, and look at the softening around the corners of his mouth. Isn't it interesting what a little bread and molasses can accomplish?"

"*Nini tooitch tickaboo,*" Mike suddenly growled as he reached out and placed a sticky hand on Platte's shoulder. "*Nini tooitch tickaboo!* I like you!" And with a huge, satisfied belch, he turned and swaggered back toward his waiting fellows, ready to once again talk over his big plans regarding what to do with these strange people called mormonee, who had been so foolhardy as to invade his secret mountain retreat.

Kigaly Spring

"You certain you don't have any more bread, President?"

Platte lay with his head on his saddle, gazing upward. It was much later now. The stars to the north had swung fully halfway around the polar star, and he was feeling good.

"Nope," he replied softly, lest by chance any of the others might have drifted off to sleep. "Eight loaves was all Adelia sent with me. The molasses jug is empty, too. But it all seemed to be enough, wouldn't you say?"

Billy smiled in the darkness. "Maybe it was like the Savior's loaves and fishes—multiplied until it was enough to more than satisfy all twelve of those warriors."

"You could be right, Billy. All I know is that we had more than enough to pacify every last one of them; that, and to entice them into agreeing to rent us this mountain for the next hundred years for our summer graze."

Overhead a meteorite flashed briefly across the sky, followed almost instantly by another and then a third. Billy was surprised by the celestial activity, but waited in vain for a fourth. "Do you think they really understood what they agreed to?" he finally questioned. "I mean, some flour, some molasses, and a few head of cattle—it doesn't seem like much rent."

"Oh," Kumen said from his bedroll nearby, "we'll pay more than that, Billy, and you can count on it. You can also count on them knowing exactly what they were agreeing to. They may be savages to us, but they are anything but stupid!"

"You're right, Kumen. The rent they'll collect is far higher than what we agreed to pay."

Billy shook his head. "What higher rent? I don't understand."

"That's because you are so without guile," Platte declared kindly. "You see, Billy, our benighted landlords know we'll pay every fall as we have agreed, for that is our way. They also know we'll be bringing fine horses and fat cattle up here year after year to grow even more fine and fat—horses and cattle that will no doubt wander into the thickly wooded draws and canyons that drop away from this plateau in nearly every direction. The Pahutes know those draws and canyons like the backs of their hands, and they know we don't. Therefore, they'll simply help themselves to whatever they can find as well as whatever they can steal that hasn't wandered off—and do it with great impunity."

"That's right," Kumen agreed. "It's easy to track a thief on the half-naked desert hills down below us and nearer to Bluff. But up here in this thick grass and tall timber? Well, Billy, you get the picture."

"And we'll just let them get away with it?"

"Get away with what?" Platte responded with a wide yawn. "You see, Billy, it's all part of the rent. The Pahutes delight in it because they think they're getting away with something big, and we tolerate it because the true value of this mountain graze is most likely greater even than what they will take. In other words, we both get what we want, and we both go away happy."

"But . . . isn't that encouraging them to steal?"

In the darkness Platte shook his head. "Not at all, no more than filling our mission in Bluff is encouraging them to steal from us there. Remember, Billy, people pretty much do what they're of a mind to, and either enjoy or suffer the consequences thereafter. We need this summer graze, and so we bargained in good faith and gave them everything they asked for. Now we'll use the range and be blessed for it.

"Meanwhile, whether we like it or not, some of our stock will wander off this mountain and avoid our roundups, and that despite whether we have a dozen men herding every day, or none. The Pahutes, because of their natures and their traditions, are by and large going to take advantage of this weakness in our system. I could see it in their eyes tonight, and I know it's going to happen. Unfortunately, and Brother Haskel predicted this, they'll also suffer the consequences for those thefts. You mark my words, Billy, and see if it all doesn't come to pass just as I've said.[1]

"Well, look at that! There go three or four more shooting stars, all at once! Whoa! There's another! And another!" Platte was smiling widely, and both Billy and Kumen could tell it in his voice. "Glory be, boys! You sleep if you want, but this is rare, and I'm going to watch the Lord's fiery display!"

And with that, the darkened and star-shrouded encampments, both of Mormons and Pahutes, grew utterly still.

---

1. The discovery and exploration of Elk Ridge or Mountain, as well as the summer graze agreement entered into between the Mormons and the Pahutes, actually occurred in the year 1884, but was moved forward for the sake of our story. The results of that agreement—fine summer graze for the growing Mormon herds, as well as steady loss of livestock to Pahute and other thieves, continued for decades thereafter.

12

Monday, October 3, 1881

Cottonwood Wash

"Any more coffee in that pot?"

Looking up from the small stick he was whittling, the big man who was called Rob Paxman shrugged. "A little, maybe. Heft it, and see for yourself."

Lug Santoni, a small, nervous man with a swarthy complexion and an old knife scar given him by a laughing Union soldier—a long, jagged scar that caused one of his eyelids to hang half-closed, cursed softly. Without even half-moving Rob Paxman could reach out and heft the pot to make a quick check, besides which, he had been the last to fill his cup, and had ought to know how much was left. Instead, all he could do was sit around with that fool knife in his hands, whittling those idiotic willow whistles!

Ignoring the pain in his hip where the Tucson sheriff's bullet had flattened against the bone nearly three years before, Lug Santoni pushed himself off his soogins, limped halfway around the fire to avoid the tiny wisp of smoke it was making, and poured what was left of the coffee and some of the dregs, into his cup.

He could have been a little more careful of those dregs, he knew, for he and Rob Paxman could nurse two, maybe three more pots of coffee out of them before they were thrown away. They still had almost a quarter of a bag of ground beans left, of course, but the direction they would be traveling didn't bode well for picking up much more—not at least for a week and a half, maybe two. And that was assuming he stayed with Paxman, the miserable son of a range stud's road apple.

Drinking the virulent brew slowly so he could sift the dregs through his yellowing teeth, Lug Santoni contemplated the day that was passing by. Already the morning was half-over, and the heat in the wash was becoming oppressive, even beneath the shade of the cottonwoods where they were waiting.

"Don't be in no real hurry," they'd been told at least a dozen times by the foul-smelling Sugar Bob Hazelton, who from his camp down on the reservation had set them onto this rare opportunity. Of course he had set them on it only after they had agreed to split with him, which neither of the men had any intention of doing. "The Mormons in that fort are working fools, men and women alike. So let 'em get to their jobs afore you mosey in and start to asking questions." That's what the smelly fool had said, and Rob Paxman had apparently believed him entirely.

Squatting back on his saddle, Lug Santoni took another sip of the coffee, brushed a fly away from his face with his free hand, and contemplated once again the whittler across the fire. Rob Paxman might be fat in the middle and poor at each end, and lazier'n a spavined nag put out to new pasture, but he could draw that hogleg on his hip quicker'n a man could spit and holler howdy, and nobody'd ever yet seen him sitting on his gun hand. For a fact, while Lug hisself had been caught napping, Rob had outdrawn the badly cut Hazelton without half-trying, and Lug Santoni was still wondering that the evil-smelling fool wasn't spread-eagled out and rotting in the sun. But for some reason Rob had held his fire, they'd begun to palaver, and the upshot of it was that Hazelton had told them of the Mormons in the fort, and of the fine horses they herded from day to day and kept penned up in the fort most nights.

The thing was, Hazelton had no actual idea where the horses would be that particular day, and he wasn't at all anxious to be seen in the fort himself no matter what day it was. Claimed he was known there, in fact, and a visit would be unhealthy. Lug Santoni could believe that, all right, for it was obvious the sorry soul had run into some serious bad health somewhere afore—very serious. Lug Santoni understood that, for despite that he could pull his own iron quicker'n hell could scorch a feather, he had been forced to leave several burgs between two suns, and like in Tucson, once or twice he'd been shot, and then had come perilously close to dying of throat trouble. But he hadn't been hung—not yet, anyway, and he couldn't imagine what he'd do if he was ever put under somebody's knife the way Hazelton had been.

Folding his pocket knife, Rob Paxman put it in his jeans. Then, after a couple of taps with the willow whistle on a rock, he put it in his mouth and blew. The sound was clear, and even varied from note to note as Rob Paxman twisted the bark. Lug Santoni was always amazed by that, for he had never been able to get more than a single, thin screech out of one of those whistles. But Rob Paxman could actually play a few tunes.

"Reckon them Mormons are all working by now?" he asked as he rose abruptly to his feet, slipping his whistle into his vest pocket as he did so.

Glancing at the sun, Lug Santoni nodded. "More'n likely."

"Well then, Lug, my friend, let's the two of us ride into their fort on these sorry plugs of ours and see if maybe we can learn where that herd of theirs is being pastured today."

"We still going to be talking trade?"

"As ever," the big man said as he tossed his stiff saddle blanket and then his saddle onto the horse. "Anything to get 'em talking. And remember, don't mention Hazelton. We're just a couple of drifting cowpokes what need new hosses afore starting acrost the reservation."

"I hope that last part'll be a lie."

Rob Paxman grinned. "It will be. I ain't got no more intention than you, of sharing anything with our friend Sugar Bob. For a fact, Lug, onct we get them hosses we'll strike for the Mormon settlements out west of here."

"You know the way?"

"I do. I scouted the trail a few months ago coming out of Escalante, right after New Year's. Came near to throwing down on a party of folks what was headed this way; four wagons, a half-dozen fine-looking women, and some good teams and loose stock. Thing was, every time I got to where I could actual see 'em, there was all these menfolk scattered about and armed to the teeth, and I wasn't about to attack no army!"

"Mormons?"

Rob Paxman nodded. "Reckon so. I didn't know it then, though, not until Sugar Bob tolt us about the Mormon fort. Too bad, too," he laughed. "I'd like to have had two or three of them Mormon women."

Lug Santoni scowled darkly. "I'm surprised a few armed men restrained you," he declared with dripping sarcasm.

"It was more than a few, Lug. More like forty, maybe fifty. Onliest thing was, those fellers never left no tracks that I could see. They must have rode in the wagons, though why forty or fifty armed men would squeeze into four little wagons when they could travel horseback is beyond me. Another thing, them fellers never left no boot tracks walking around their camps of a night, neither. Oh, two or three men did, but that was all. Yet I swear it, Lug; ever' time I ever got a look at their camps—an' I followed 'em six or seven days—I was staring into the faces of the toughest looking bunch of hombres I ever did see. So I finally gave up on the project as a bad deal and struck off on my own."

"And met up with me."

Rob Paxman grinned. "That's right, pard, for the second time. Lucky day for both of us, wasn't it? So let's ride, and see if we can make this day even luckier!"

Lug nodded his reluctant agreement, and soon the two were heading south toward the mouth of Cottonwood Wash.

Sand Dunes, Navajo Reservation

"Do you see the *jeeshóó,* my father? The buzzards?"

Tsabekiss looked in the direction Bitseel had indicated with the traditional twitch of his lips, and for the first time noticed the low-circling birds of death. No doubt someone or something had died off in that direction, though like most of the *Dinê,* Tsabekiss feared death and had no desire to learn more. But his son was not so traditional, and it was not difficult at all for Tsabekiss to see that Bitseel wanted badly to go investigate.

"It is said," he cautioned, "that being near one who has died, invites trouble and destroys a man's *hózhó,* his balance."

"I have heard this thing, my father." Bitseel was unfailingly polite to his elders, and for this Tsabekiss was grateful. "Yet I wonder if perhaps it might not be good for us to ride a little out of our way—not to spend much time, but simply to *nishí,* to observe. Perhaps a thing has happened over there that we should be aware of."

Slowly Tsabekiss nodded. "Perhaps. But suppose it is a thing the cursed *nóódái* did on their way to my *hogan*. If it is so, now that we have honored them with food and lodging, we can do nothing about it."

Carefully Bitseel considered his father's soft-spoken words. Sometimes, his father was saying, it was better not to know a thing than to know it. On the other hand, as his fine uncle Natanii nééz had taught him before his terrible illness, there were many ways of extracting justice once a thing was known, and much time in which to accomplish it.

Smiling slightly, Bitseel turned in his saddle to look at the ragtag band of Pahutes who were following. For three endless days they had been in the *hogan* of his father, their *halchin* or odor making life most unbearable. It had also been amusing, for even as the one called Poke was endeavoring to sell his little sister to Bitseel, all the young Navajo's relatives had been making preparations for Bitseel to wed a comely Navajo maiden of the Standing Rock people.

In spite of those plans, which would culminate in just a few more weeks, old Tsabekiss had continued to act interested in arranging a marriage for the Pahute girl, Bitseel had continued to gamble with Poke and the others as though he had the same desires, and Poke had seemed absolutely certain that the purchase of his little sister would be completed at any moment.

Now, though, stripped of his wealth and still burdened with his baby sister, the surly Poke was growing less certain—

"If the *nóódái* are guilty of such a thing," Bitseel finally said to his father, bringing his mind back again, "then it is in my thoughts that they will not ride to that place with us. If we turn aside and they follow, then it would seem to me that they did not do whatever it is that we may discover."

Tsabekiss considered the wisdom of his son. Truly the young man had become a son to be proud of. Truly he had turned from the quest for revenge in order to have *hózhó* in his life. "What you say may be right," the father finally admitted. "Perhaps what has been done beneath those birds of death yonder, was done by the unseen *nóódâi,* who left their horses near our *hogan*. We have not seen those two, but from the looks on the faces of the others when the two horses were found, they must be very evil men."

Bitseel made the sign that he agreed. "Either very evil, my father, or very much despised." Abruptly he changed the subject. "How do you say about us riding to investigate what lies dead over yonder?"

After another moment's thought, Tsabekiss finally gave the sign, and soon the long cavalcade of Navajos and Pahutes was winding across the dunes toward where the buzzards circled so low in the sky.

Sand Dunes, Navajo Reservation

"*Belacani*." Tsabekiss was disgusted with what he was seeing, for there is nothing pleasant about the sight or smell of a body that has been dead for some time. He was even more disgusted because this unknown white man had invaded *Dinê tah,* the sacred land of the People. Tsabekiss had little patience with such invaders, and thought that in one way or another, all of them should be done away with.

As the long line of Indians following Tsabekiss and his son wound over the dune and spread out in a rough half-circle around the body of the white man, Bitseel left his father and rode closer. This one, who was sprawled head downward on the side of the dune, had been dead for two days, perhaps more, and already the buzzards had been at work on his swollen face and hands. Nevertheless the two bullet wounds in the center of the man's forehead were clearly visible, and offered ample evidence as to the manner of his death.

Looking at those wounds, Bitseel was instantly certain that the Pahutes had not been the killers of this man. They had guns, yes, but none were such good shooters as this, as they had proven time and again in shooting matches with men of the *Dinê*.

No, this *belacani* had been slain by another of his same evil race, and then left where he had fallen. Strangely, the killer had taken nothing from the man that might add to his wealth—at least none of his clothing, or his fine leather boots. Often since the *nóódái* had slain the two prospectors two years before, Bitseel and his father had come upon the bodies of other *belacani,* white men who appeared to have been looking for the white iron and gold that the first two had found. While one or two had been slain by men of the *Dinê,* most often they had been slain by others of the *belacani,* white men filled with such maddening greed that they had stripped the bodies of their victims of everything of value—even teeth filled with the gold they all seemed to crave. Neither Bitseel nor his father could understand this sort of greed, but more and more it seemed to them that the *belacani* were either devils or were driven by devils, and ought to be done away with or driven out of the land. Thus they had been quite willing to follow after Natanii nééz in his raids against the new *belacani* who had moved into the fort on the big river.

Sliding from his horse Bitseel climbed the dune, placed the man's hat over the toe of his moccasin, and then carefully used his foot to roll the dead man over onto his face. It was bad enough that the *belacani* had been left to rot in the sun and be consumed by the *jeeshóó,* but Bitseel was not willing that he be left to face what was being done to him. To the Navajo youth it seemed infinitely better that the man lie face downward, and so that is how he left him.

Kicking the now-polluted hat to the side, Bitseel was just coming off the dune when he spotted something glinting in the sand. Kicking it loose, he was startled to discover a fine, apparently new, rifle. As the watching Pahutes chattered in amazement, he lifted it, drew back the hammer, and blew sand from the barrel, levered a bullet into the chamber, and fired. The rifle worked perfectly, and Bitseel smiled as he held it up for his father to see.

Remounting but holding his new rifle most carefully in his free hand, Bitseel led out once again, feeling good that he was enjoying such amazing fortune. It was going to be good, he thought, when he would once again be sitting across the blanket from one or more of these filthy *nóódái*. Perhaps he might even be fortunate enough to find that cursed son of Chee, the one who seemed always to be sticking his tongue out at him in a most degrading fashion. Yes, he thought as his countenance grew fierce with determination, playing face cards with that one, would give Bitseel the greatest pleasure of all!

Bluff Fort

"Howdy, ma'am." Removing his sweat-stained hat, Rob Paxman smiled his warmest smile at the woman standing before him. "That's a fine-looking boy you've got there."

"Thank you. He favors his father."

"Begging your pardon, ma'am, but I'd have said he favored you." Reaching into his vest pocket, Rob Paxman took out the small willow whistle. "Here you go, son," he declared, leaning over and extending it toward the child. "It's a whistle. Put the notched end in your mouth, and blow."

"Thank you, sir—"

"Rob Paxman, ma'am."

"Thank you, Mr. Paxman. I'm afraid he's a little young for such doodads."

Rob Paxman grinned. "You work with him, ma'am, he'll figure it out soon enough. He has a bright look about him, mighty bright."

Sitting high in his saddle, Rob Paxman looked all around. "Don't see no menfolk hereabouts, ma'am. Our hosses are played out, and me and my pardner are headed out acrost the reservation . . . Well, ma'am, what we was hoping for, is a trade, but I don't see no animals hereabouts, either."

"No, our animals, the ones being rested today, are at pasture."

Rob Paxman smiled. "Good thinking, ma'am. Is that where the menfolk are—with the hosses?"

"Some, I suppose. The rest are here and there, working."

"Looks like you women are all working, too. What they doin' yonder, at the fire?"

"Rendering molasses, from that cane."

Rob Paxman smiled widely. "Ain't nothing better'n hot oven bread spread thick with molasses. Ma used to fix that for me, and I still favor it highly—I surely do. Ma'am, if you'll direct us to where your herd is, we'll stop pestering you and go see if maybe we can make a trade with your menfolks."

"Well, the horses are off in the Valley of the Butler today, but why don't you speak with Bishop Nielson? He's the one you'll be wanting to work a trade with."

"This Bishop Nielson feller's with the hosses?"

The woman shook her head. "That's him yonder, dragging up some wood for the fire."

Looking up, Rob Paxman saw an older man moving toward the fire, dragging some wood behind him. He was tall, maybe even taller than himself, and there was something wrong with his feet. But there was something else about the old man that was suddenly bothering Rob Paxman, something that put him in mind of the fearsome army he had seen on the trail a few months earlier.

"Thank you, ma'am," he smiled again, putting his doubts aside. "We'll talk to this Bishop Nielson feller." *The Valley of the Butler,* he was thinking as he clucked his mount forward, Lug Santoni following silently. Now all he had to do was find out where the Valley of the Butler was located.

———o—o—o———

Milk Ranch Point

"Well, Billy, it's been quite a trip."

Looking up from where he rode dozing in his saddle, Billy smiled as his friend Kumen dropped back to ride beside him. "I'll say it has," he responded. "Not alone did we see some wonderful country, but once again the protective hand of the Lord has been manifest in our behalf."

Soberly Kumen nodded. "As ever! I thought sure, when we met

those fellows in First Valley, that I was going to take a bullet in my back as we rode past them."

"You, too?" Billy chuckled quietly. "I could hardly breathe my heart was pounding so hard, and it took hours before the muscles in my shoulders relaxed. I don't know why such incidents make me feel so frightened, but I'm ashamed to admit that they do."

"No need to be ashamed, Billy. Not a one of us but didn't have pounding hearts and sweaty palms as we rode around that half-circle of angry warriors."

"But none of you looked frightened in the least!" Billy said.

"Neither did you." Kumen smiled a little sadly. "Sometimes I think it's amazing how we can hide our inner turmoil from each other. It'd be easier if we were like the women, more wide-open and willing to talk about anything at all."

Billy chuckled. "You sound like you have something you want to talk about, but don't know quite how to go about it."

Kumen ducked his head as though he were embarrassed. "I reckon that's about right."

For a few moments Kumen stared off into the distance, apparently trying to sort out his thoughts. Wisely, Billy let him think, and he was once again nodding off to Wonder's easy gait when Kumen finally spoke.

"Billy, do you reckon Bishop Nielson is inspired?"

"Of course I do!" Billy could not take the surprise from his voice.

"I do, too, but it's a bit harder for Mary to believe so, on account of the bishop is also her father. She's having a difficult time trying to decide when he's speaking as a man, and when he's speaking as a bishop."

Billy laughed. "President Young used to have people ask him that question all the time. When was he a prophet, as opposed to when was he a plain old simpleton, as he put it."

"Did he have an answer?"

"Actually, several. But the gist of his answers was that while he was always a prophet, his words were to be considered as the word of the Lord only when he was speaking in some sort of official capacity, either publicly or privately."

Kumen nodded. "That makes sense to me. Very well, now I have another question. Have you ever given thought to going into plural marriage?"

"What?"

"You heard me."

Sitting upright in the saddle and suddenly very much awake, Billy gazed at his friend. "I reckon that's true," he admitted with a sly grin. "You surprised me, is all."

"Well, have you?"

"Not ever. Tell the truth, Kumen, I've never felt that I should. I was lucky to marry Eliza, and she's all a man like me would ever want or need in a woman. Besides which, I've never received such a calling, and I don't know if I'd accept it if I did."

"Yeah, that's the rub, isn't it?" Kumen hunched his shoulders and twisted back and forth in the saddle, trying to ease his aching back muscles. "I've always felt the same."

Again Billy said nothing.

"You know how troubled Mary's been about not having any children?"

"Eliza's mentioned it a few times, and she's always remembering the two of you in her prayers."

"Does she really? Well, I do appreciate that. Thing is, more than four years have gone by now since we married, and we still have no children. So last Thursday after fast and testimony meeting I approached Mary's pa and asked him if he'd had any impressions on the subject, and if he thought it might be well to give Mary a blessing to have a family."

"And?"

Kumen sighed. "He'd had some impressions, all right. His feeling is that the Lord isn't going to bless Mary and me with children until I have done what I was told right after we got here to Bluff—to enter into plural marriage."

"Are you funning me, Kumen?"

"Not hardly." Kumen lifted his hat and scratched his head, then resettled it. "Pa Nielson and Platte Lyman called me in last May, when we were still living out of our wagon boxes. They told me the Lord had made it known to them that I was to enter into plural marriage, and further, that I was to do it with Lydia May Lyman, Platte's younger sister."

"Lydia May? But . . . she's so young!"

"Yes, she is certainly younger than Mary and me."

"Wh . . . why haven't you told me about it?"

"I haven't told anybody," Kumen exclaimed sourly. "Remember, Billy, Mary's father believes that we're men, not women, and are supposed to hold these sorts of things inside, working them out by ourselves! Naturally, I try my best to please him.

"Thing was, I had never considered such a thing, let alone with Lydia May. Fact is, I hadn't spoken with her more than a dozen times in my entire life, and that mostly to say howdy before meetings or adios afterward. More than that, however, I was troubled by how Mary would react, for I knew she had definite opinions about the Principle. It was fine for others, she was fond of saying, but not for her or me!

"Since I agreed with her, I didn't do much about it. Fact is, Billy, I didn't do anything. I didn't tell Mary about the call, and when Lydia May returned to the settlements with Platte last fall, I breathed a great sigh of relief. I had no idea she would be coming back with him, and when she did, well, it's been mighty hard for me to even look at her in all the months since. And I still haven't spoken with Mary about it."

"And you say the bishop thinks this is why Mary remains childless?"

Kumen shook his head. "Apparently so. Sort of strange, isn't it? Other folks have kids, plenty of them, with no strings attached. All they have to do is have them. But us? Oh, glory be. We can have posterity, all right, but only if I destroy Mary and most likely myself by entering into plural marriage."

"Have you said anything to Mary? Since last Thursday, I mean?"

"No, but I reckon I'm going to have to. She's full of questions about what me and her pa talked about for so long, and my 'Oh, not much,' just isn't going to cut it much longer. Fact is, if I don't tell her soon, she'll likely go to him herself, and to my way of thinking, that would make it even worse."

Billy nodded. "You're probably right. But I don't much envy

you, Kumen. I think that sort of announcement would be a terrible blow to a woman's sense of security and peace. Of course anyone ought to be able to get a testimony of it through prayer, but from what little I've seen, even a testimony doesn't make it any easier to live."

"Amen," Kumen breathed as he kicked his horse ahead of Billy's mule and started down through the rocks toward First Valley. "Amen, and amen!"

Sand Dunes, Navajo Reservation

"Do you see him, my brother?"

It had been many hours since Posey and Scotty had left Jackrabbit Canyon. The sun was already sinking lower in the western sky, and the two had been running without stopping since the loss of their horses. By now their thirst was great, but in a shady place near the trail of the horses they followed, they had found a small tank filled with rainwater, and that had helped. Scotty had also flushed out a rabbit, which he had somehow chased down and killed. The brothers had devoured its poor flesh raw, and that had eased their hunger somewhat. And so they had run on, and for the first time Posey was finding himself wishing he were a boy again, burdened with less clothing than these fine things he had been so proud to wear. But he had not been about to *tur-reb-by,* throw them away, not when at any moment they might come upon Poke and his favorite younger sister.

"My brother!" Scotty had now stopped running. "Do you see him?"

Glancing in the direction Scotty had indicated, Posey was startled to see a man—a white man—laying sprawled on his stomach on the side of a sandy hummock only a few dozen yards away. As a shadow passed over him he glanced upward, and only then did he realize that several buzzards were circling above—great birds of death that he had not even noticed during his running.

"The ones we follow, my brother? Either they *puck-ki,* killed this man, or they found him just as we have found him. Do you see how the tracks of their ponies go there?"

"I see."

Moving slowly Scotty moved slowly toward the corpse and moments later had rolled the man over with his foot. "This man has been dead longer than one sun," he said easily. "He was not killed by one of the People, and I do not think he was killed by the *Diné*."

"Why do you say that?"

"Because he still wears his fine clothing, which one of our people would most certainly have taken. And I do not think even the *Diné* can shoot so well as this." Scotty then pointed with his toe, and Posey noted the two bullet holes spaced less than half an inch apart in the man's forehead.

Filled with wonder at this thing he was seeing—at the accuracy of the unknown white man's shooting who had killed this man—Posey was still gazing downward when Scotty stiffened, turned his head a little, and grew still. Then he smiled with pleasure, climbed to the top of the hummock, and without hurry disappeared down the other side. Muttering softly Posey climbed after his brother, and stared with surprise at the saddled and bridled horse that was tossing its head nervously as Scotty approached it.

"The reins were tied in the brush," Scotty said simply as he led the horse back to where Posey stood. "I do not think either Poke or the men of the *Diné* heard it when they passed by, but the horse has been in that one place for many hours."

"Is there a rifle under the saddle?" Posey demanded, knowing full well where the white men carried their coveted weapons.

Scotty made the sign that there was no rifle there or anywhere else that he had seen.

"What is in those bags?"

"A few rocks, my brother. That is all."

Muttering that he would never understand the foolish ways of these white men, Posey strode forward and leaped into the saddle of their newfound transportation. "I will sit in the saddle," he said with righteous authority, not even bothering to look at his younger brother. "You may either ride behind me or run alongside. It is your choice, but I will be running this horse as hard and as far as it will go."

Humbly Scotty made the sign that he understood, pulled himself up behind Posey, and once again the two of them set off on the trail of Posey's *nan-zitch,* her fearsome brothers, and the cursed young man of the *Dinê* who rode with them—the one who may already have purchased the *nan-zitch* for himself.

13

Tuesday, October 4, 1881

Bluff Fort

"Morning, Eliza." Mary Jones was smiling mischievously. "Are you ready for another day of Indians, outlaws, rattlesnakes, and various and sundry other dangers and problems?"

"I don't find much humor in that today," Eliza responded as she pulled Willy's hand away from the pitcher of milk he was attempting to overturn. "Anymore, I don't believe I have the energy to keep fighting."

Chastened, Mary was instantly contrite. "I'm sorry, dear. It was a sad attempt at being funny, and unworthy of either of us. Will you forgive me?"

"Of course I will. But I swan, Mary, if this mission doesn't soon get a little less dangerous, I don't know what any of us will do. I am so tired of being alone without Billy, so tired of waiting for the next attack from that awful Posey, and so everlastingly heartsick because the Lord took from me my sweet little daughter—" Swiping with her kerchief at her sudden and unbidden tears, Eliza looked away. "Ha . . . have you heard from Kumen?"

Mary shook her head as she took a damp rag and wiped Willy's mush-covered face, while the child did his yowling best to twist away from her. "Nobody's heard anything, though Platte told Adelia he thought they'd be back by tonight." For a moment Mary gazed at the log wall, her mind far away. "The thing is, Eliza, I have a feeling something's wrong."

Instantly Eliza's tears sprang anew, her heart again in her throat. "Do . . . do you think something's happened to them?"

"Oh, no!" Mary responded as she realized how her words had been misinterpreted. "I didn't mean with all of them, Eliza, certainly not Billy. I just have the feeling that something is troubling Kumen, and every day the feeling grows stronger. I . . . well, I don't know what to do about it."

"Have you asked him what it is?"

Mary smiled. "Not hardly. He is so self-contained, and so proud of himself for what he considers his inner strength, that he'd be offended. So I suppose I'll just wait, trying to deal with my own inner turmoil while I wait for him to reveal his."

Taking a deep breath, Eliza forced herself to be cheerful. "Well, then," she declared as she cleared off the table and ushered Willy out the door to join Adelia Lyman and her son Albert, who both responded joyfully to Eliza's wave, "I have just the tonic for you, my dear. Hard work."

Now Mary laughed aloud. "Since when has candle dipping become hard work?"

"Since whoever figured out how to do it, first tried. But difficult or not, Mary, I can't tell you how pleased I am to have you helping me. I do miss you."

Quickly Mary reached to give Eliza a hug. "Thank you, dear. And I, you. Since Father outlined everything that needs to be done before winter, it seems like the entire fort is jumping with activity. The brethren are harvesting everything they can find to harvest, and there isn't a sister who hasn't been assigned one task or another that absolutely must be accomplished before the snow flies."

"I know," Eliza sighed. "Mine do seem such silly tasks, but I understand why they've been given me, and I appreciate Bishop Nielson's thoughtfulness."

Realizing once again that she had inadvertently said something hurtful to her more-than-fragile friend, Mary reached out and took her hand. "In spite of my teasing, dear, there's nothing silly about candles. I'm so tired of the smoke and horrid smell of those bitch lamps, that I nearly shouted for joy when I heard Platte had freighted in some cotton twine and tins of purified lard to make candles. Then when I found out you had been given that assignment—well, here I am, dear friend, officially assigned to be your assistant."

"Then let us be anxiously engaged," Eliza declared with what she hoped was a bright smile. "Do you know how to dip them?"

Now Mary was embarrassed for a different reason. "Actually, at home Mother always used store-bought paraffin, and so we rolled our candles between boards. I don't think I've dipped tallow candles in my life."

"Then this will be a good experience for you, Mary. As you can tell by smelling these lengths of wick, I soaked them in spirits of turpentine a couple of days ago and put them out in the sun to dry."

"What does that do?"

"It causes the wick to burn hot enough to consume itself above the tallow, thus eliminating the need for snuffing, as well as the smoke that snuffing causes.

"Also, yesterday I melted alum and saltpeter with the lard, one pound each of alum and saltpeter to each five pounds of tallow. Since the alum had first been dissolved in water, I had to boil the entire mixture until all the water had evaporated. That was also when I skimmed off the impurities."

"You'd think with purified lard there wouldn't be any impurities."

Eliza smiled sadly. "With lard as with people, Mary, no matter how much refining we go through, there are still going to be impurities. Look at me, and you will see a perfect example. Now, I brought several of these wire dipping-frames from Cedar, and you will see in a few moments how they are to be used. But first we must immerse each of these treated wicks into the melted tallow, and then twirl them in our hands until they are straight and stiff."

"And then they're attached to the dipping frames?"

"Exactly. Watch closely, now, for this is how it should be done."

Quickly Eliza dropped one end of a wick into the melted tallow, immersing it with a wooden spoon until only the fraction of an inch she held in her fingers did not get covered. Pulling the string forth she began twirling it rapidly, moving the wick up and down between her hands as the tallow cooled. In perhaps a minute the wick was firm and straight.

"Isn't that hot?" Mary asked anxiously.

"Not very. And even that isn't noticeable because of the rapid twirling. Are you ready to try it?"

Eagerly Mary nodded, and soon she had discovered that twirling a wick straight was not as easy as Eliza had made it look. Yet she persisted, and within a short time her wicks were about as straight as those twirled by Eliza.

"How many of these do we have to do?" she asked as the two of them formed wick after wick.

"I soaked more than a thousand wicks," Eliza replied. "I hope that will be enough to last all of us through the winter."

"A thousand wicks? Merciful heavens, Eliza, this could take us all day long!"

"Actually, we'll be lucky to get them all finished before next week. Now Mary, while you're twirling, I'm going to attach the straight wicks to this frame like this. Now I take the frame by its wooden handle, immerse all the wicks in the tallow, hold them there for a few seconds, withdraw them and lightly touch the bottom ends of the wicks to this board to remove the drippings, and then hang the entire apparatus in the window to cool."

"Here," Mary said as she jumped to her feet, "let me do the hanging, so you won't need to be bothered with all that standing and sitting."

"Thank you." Eliza smiled. "I'll get another frame ready, and by the time it is dipped, that one in the window should be ready for its next immersion."

"My word," Mary exclaimed in amazement, "how many times does each frame of wicks need to be dipped?"

"As many times as it takes to get the candles to the width we want. Bishop Nielson and I agreed that we should strive for one-inch candles, so you can see that will require a host of dippings."

"And a lot more tallow than you have in this kettle."

"That's right," Eliza nodded. "You can see why I said it would take at least a week to dip as many as I think we're going to need."

Mary shook her head. "And I thought I was volunteering to spend a day with you. Mercy sakes, Eliza, I do hope you won't get sick of my company before this project is through!"

"Or you, me." Both women laughed, and quickly they were once again involved in their work.

Valley of the Butler

"Well, it's a bit hard to tell, Bishop, but I reckon those are their tracks."

Bishop Jens Nielson sat in the buckboard, looking down. "Ya, I tink so, Yody. By yumping yehosephat, brudders, I yust should have known vat dose two owlhoots vas up to. But dat vone who spoke vith me, he seemed to be de finest sort of fellow. Can you tell, Yody, vich vay day vas going?"

Twenty-four-year-old Joseph Alvin Lyman, known to everyone on the San Juan as Jody, rose slowly to his feet, his eyes still on the churned-up earth. "They headed south, Bishop, so I reckon they're either headed onto the reservation like they told Hy's wife Rachel, or else they'll be doubling back up Comb Wash, climbing the Twist, and heading toward the settlements." Jody hesitated, stroking his bristly cheek. "Was it me, though, and I'd just stolen a dozen head of good horses, I'd head for the settlements."

The group of mounted men sat silently while their elderly leader removed his hat and contemplated the situation. There was not one of them who did not trust their bishop, not one who would not put forth their best effort to do as he recommended.

It was late in the afternoon, and most were anxious to either return to their homes in the fort or get on with the chase. Yet for several minutes Bishop Nielson remained silent, and the men simply sat their restive horses, waiting. Finally the crippled old leader replaced his hat and looked off down the Butler.

"Yody, I tink you vill be right. Ve vill find dat de owlhoots haff circled back up de Comb Vash, gone up de Tvist, und are headed for de settlements. Brudder Lem, vill you und Yody—"

"Well, hello, brethren," Platte Lyman called as he and his three fellow explorers came up over a rise and approached the group, their long exploring trip almost over. "Something the matter here?"

"Howdy, President." Lemuel Redd swung his horse about. "Hy, Kumen, Billy. Did you find the trail to the top of the Elk?"

"To the top," Billy grinned, "and then some. That mountain is covered with the best graze in the world!"

"Wonderful. Trouble is, now we may not need it."

In abrupt silence Platte and his party continued forward to join the others. "What is it, Bishop? What's happened here?"

"Vell, President," Jens Nielson replied, his expression forlorn, "I haff lost de herd."

"Lost it?"

"He means it's been stolen," Lemuel Redd declared quietly. "A couple of owlhoots snookered us good yesterday, and now every animal we had out here to pasture is gone!"

"What about the herders? Are they okay?"

"The thieves came when young Joe Lillywhite was here alone, and all they did was tie him up. He got free and ran all the way to the fort—took him all night and then some—and now Jody's just worked out the trail."

Platte nodded at his younger brother. "Good work." He then turned to Bishop Nielson. "You plan on sending some fellers after them?"

"Ya!" Jens Nielson responded emphatically. "I figure Yody und Lem vould be de vones to track dem down."

For a moment Platte was quiet, pondering the situation. "Bishop, two are good, but I'd like to increase the size of the party." Turning then, he glanced at his fellow explorers. "Billy, I know it's been a long ride, but would you and Hy mind joining Lem and Jody?"

Surprised, and quite naturally worried about being away longer from Eliza, Billy found himself finally nodding his agreement. Hyrum Perkins was not hesitant at all.

"Good. Bishop, you know the situation at home. Will Eliza and Rachel be okay without their husbands for another few days?"

"Ya, I tink so. Day vas both busy dis morning, und both seemed happy und vell. Besides, I vill vatch out for dem."

Platte nodded his appreciation. "Boys, Billy and Hy will need fresh mounts, and let's pool for them all the grub we have. No telling how long they'll be gone. Will a couple of you switch saddles for these two tired explorers, and give them a few moments to work the kinks out of their spines?"

As the men quickly fell to, Platte nudged his horse forward to the wagon. "Sorry to take over, Bishop, but I felt that the four of them would be needed."

"Tank you, President. I vas only vorrying about de harvest und de firevood gathering. Den, too, I vas tinking of putting Brudder Lem in charge."

"Good idea." Platte turned to Lemuel Redd. "Lem, will you take responsibility for this posse?"

Twenty-five-year-old Lem Redd nodded, thinking of the unfinished business of the harvest, scanty as it was turning out to be. Still, without their horses they were helpless, and so there was nothing but to track down the outlaws and bring back the precious herd.

"I reckon so," he stated quietly. "Hy, Billy, and Jody, you agree?"

"I do," twenty-nine-year-old Hyrum Perkins acknowledged in his rich Welsh accent. "It will be no trouble that we'll be having."

"We'll be all right, Bishop," Jody Lyman added as he climbed back into his saddle. "And we'll get the horses, too."

Billy eyed his new mount carefully, and then with even greater care he climbed aboard the long-legged horse and took up the reins. So far, so good, he thought as he tensed in preparation for the bucking he knew was coming. Yet when it didn't, he actually managed a slight smile.

"Billy?"

"Lem's fine, and I'll do what I can to help," he responded meekly.

"Ya," Bishop Nielson grinned, "dat iss de spirit! Vith a little sticky-to-ty, I tink you vill get de animals back yust fine. But brudders, go very slow, no hurry, und be very careful. Do not come up to dese fellows before you cross de river at Hall's und are in de settlements, for I tink dey are bad men. Ya, dey may smile purty und say nice tings, but I tink dey be killers. Dat is vy I say to leaf dem alone und stay back from dem ver dey cannot see you. Vonce dey are in de settlements, den you can get udder brudders to help you in making de arrests."

Lem Redd grinned. "We'll do 'er just as you say, Bishop. Let's go, boys, and see if we can chase those birds into a cage."

And without further ado the four reined their horses around and walked them south down the Valley of the Butler.

Comb Wash

"Did you fellers have a chance to say adios to your wives?"

"Aye, Billy, we did at that, though I had no idea it would be to the settlements I'd be going."

Billy and Lem Redd were rubbing down their mounts while Hy Perkins was bent over the small fire, working on the simple meal the four would be eating. Meanwhile Jody Lyman had walked a short distance along the trail, making certain the tracks continued the way the group anticipated them going.

In the deepening twilight bats were darting overhead, a nighthawk screeched as it winged by, and already a distant coyote was yipping its complaints skyward. To Billy it seemed such a peaceful evening, and he found it hard to imagine that he and the others were actually on the trail of desperate criminals. He was also thinking about Eliza, worrying about her fragile emotional state, and praying that the Lord would bless her while he was away.

"My wife was at the fire stirring preserves," Lem stated quietly as he responded to Billy's question, "so I was able to spend a couple of minutes with her. She reckons they'll finish preserving the berries they've gathered by tomorrow, or at the longest, the day after."

"At least we got a good crop of wild berries," Jody Lyman smiled as he walked in out of the gathering darkness into the firelight. "That and the cane are about the only crops that've done well."

"Not much to support a community on."

"Not much," Billy agreed. "Did either of you see my Eliza?"

"I saw her this morning when she sent your boy over to our cabins," Jody stated. "She looked to be doing well. Still mighty thin, mind you, but I didn't see that haunted sort of look that Nellie's been worrying about since your baby passed away. She's being kept busy, too, dipping candles with Mary Jones. At least that's what Nellie told me."

Billy nodded, his eyes on the younger man. "I was there when she received that assignment, so I'm pleased she's about it. Thanks, Jody. I appreciate the news."

For a time the men were silent, going about the chores that are part of every wilderness camp, finally eating the simple meal Hy Perkins had prepared, and then preparing for bed. Though they had not hurried their pursuit, they had come to the hidden and terribly precarious trail down the cliffs of Comb Reef with plenty of light to spare. Still, the thousand-foot drop had been hair-raising in the extreme, and Billy hoped he would never have to take that recently discovered trail again.

The terrible shortcut had saved them several hours, though, and true to Bishop Nielson's impressions, in Comb Wash the tracks of the fugitives and their stolen horses had been plain for all to see. Instead of going onto the Navajo reservation, the thieves had circled the end of the Comb Reef where it met the San Juan, and now they were moving back north and appeared headed toward Escalante and points beyond.

"Any of you boys concerned about chasing these owlhoots?" Lem asked after all had bedded down and grown still.

"I am," Billy admitted quietly.

"And me," Hy Perkins agreed.

"Why ever for?" Jody asked, and even in the darkness it was easy to tell that he was smiling.

"Because they're smart," Lem growled, "and because they're sidewinder dangerous. Seems to me we had all ought to be concerned."

"I don't see why, Lem." Jody was adamant. "We're four to their two, for pity sake; and besides, we have the good Lord on our side. We've always been protected, and the promise is that it will continue so long as we are righteous."

"True enough," Billy breathed. "On the other hand, Jody, so far as I know, the Lord has never clearly defined the parameters of that protection."

"The what?"

"The parameters, the boundaries. For instance, what does being righteous really mean? Can we break one commandment a day and still be righteous? Or two? Or might it even mean none? And does God's protection mean that we won't get hurt, or just that we won't be killed? Or might it mean that anything could happen to us, including death, but that we'll be protected enough to obtain our salvation and exaltation hereafter? You see, Jody, I'm grateful for the Lord's promise of protection. But I'm concerned enough about its true meaning, to go extra slow and careful."

"I hadn't thought of it like that," Jody admitted.

"Well, maybe that's why your brother sent Billy along as our elder statesman," Lem replied easily. "Fact is, I was some surprised when Platte didn't come himself, being the traveling sort of man that he is."

Jody chuckled. "He thought of it, he told me just before we rode out. But he also wanted to make another quick trip to Colorado and trail back more supplies, including the things for Billy's barrel filters. He told me he'd be gone by morning."

"He *is* a traveling sort of man," Hy Perkins agreed, remembering the intriguing description Kumen had used only a few days before.

In the darkness then Jody began to talk about his older brother, for whom he felt tremendous love and affection. He also spoke of his father, Amasa Lyman, and both Billy and Hyrum listened intently, not exactly meaning to, but nevertheless comparing young Jody's comments to those that had been made by Platte while camped in First Valley a few nights before.

"Anyway, boys," Jody concluded some time later, "that's the short of it. Platte's never had but three weeks of formal education in his life, but he sounds like an educated orator when he speaks."

"He does, at that."

"His real school, he says, is the great outdoors, where he somehow manages to learn and see things that other folks never even notice. He loves woods and fields and birds and animals, particularly dogs and horses, who seem to love him in return. He likes the rippling lake and the running stream far better than the pictures of them in books. He has never been able to abide being cooped for long in a house, but you'll never find him by a campfire, no matter where it is, that he isn't reading a book he's somehow managed to borrow." Jody turned his head to avoid a sudden streamer of smoke from the supposedly doused fire. "Platte says that sort of natural education doesn't saw a man off or stretch him out to fit some popular standard, but it develops naturally, without deforming the fine gifts he brought with him from the former world. He feels that with this natural education he can go forth to meet life and its battles without being mutilated and stilted by the artificial machines other folks call schools. So far, I reckon I'd have to agree."

14

Wednesday, October 5, 1881

Near Snow Flat

"Did you fellers notice anything strange about the tracks those boys left at the top of the Twist?"

The four Mormons had been walking their horses, and were now passing through the thirty-mile forest of pinion and juniper that had presented such terrible obstacles to their wagons a year and a half before. The stumps of the trees they had cut were now clearly evident, and each of them wondered without speaking of it, that they had actually managed to triumph and bring their families through.

"I noticed," Jody declared as his eyes scanned the trees ahead, "that their tracks were fresh—real fresh!"

"It's a thing I was considering also," Hyrum declared. "Is it waiting for us they be, or is it slow they are going because of our horses?"

"Good questions, Hy. Thing is, I reckon that may be why the bishop felt impressed to tell us to go slow. Those birds might very well be waiting for us, and I for one ain't interested in getting planted shallow without a reading, or being on the losing end of a powder-burning contest, either one."

Jody Lyman smiled. "Eloquent, Lem. Mighty eloquent."

With quiet chuckles they all continued forward, each of them more alert than before.

Trampled Water Canyon

It was the quiet time of the afternoon, less than an hour before sunset, and the two elderly men were sitting on their sheepskins outside the *atch í ́deezâhi,* the forked stick *hogan* that until recently had been the only type of dwelling the *Dinê* had known. Now other types, including those made of railroad ties, were making an appearance, especially over to the east where the railroad was being constructed.

But the two elderly men knew little of this, and cared even less. Nor was their concern the *atch í ́deezâhi* they now faced. Instead they were worried about the man who sat slumped near the east-facing doorway, and who hardly had the strength to even lift his head.

In appearance the man seemed as old as them, and perhaps older, for he was very frail and weak. Yet his gaunt frame, stooped back, and hollow chest were not due to the passing of many years. No, for not many days before, this man had been tall and straight, strong in his youthful vigor. Not many days before, this one had been known as Natanii nééz, the tall Navajo.

Then had come the terrible sickness, a strange disease that had wasted the tall one in an instant, or so he was claiming. Certainly it had terrified him, this sickness, and had left him seemingly helpless to fight it off. It was a frightening thing, too, for the family of Natanii nééz and for all of his relatives, of which there had once seemed to be a great many. But not now, not with this strange sickness eating the man away.

A great sing had been called, an Enemy Way sing that was supposed to drive the *chinde,* the devils, from this man so that he could regain his strength and continue his life. But few of the relatives of Natanii nééz had come to the sing. More unusual, few were even admitting that they were his relatives. And so there had been little power in the ceremony, little hope that it would do its work. The two old men seated on the sheepskins knew and agreed on this, though each had a different idea as to why it was so.

The night before had been the squaw dance, the traditional, joyous ending of the three-day sing. But there had been little joy, little even in the getting together of men and women, boys and girls, which coupling was also part of the great tradition of the enemy way.

Stunned at the way the sing had failed to rally the power of the People in behalf of the tall one, and fearful that they might also be affected by his evil malady, most of the few who had attended the sing had departed quickly, leaving only a handful behind. And of them all, only these two who had grown old seemed willing to sit through the day and discuss the extraordinary events they had been party to. The others who remained had traveled to the sing with these two, and so now they sat nearby in silence, waiting politely for the old ones to finish.

"It is said that a *belacani* witch blew a bone into him." Pahlilly, the younger of the two, did not take his eyes off the gaunt form seated by the *hogan*. "One of the *belacani* that the *nóôdâi* call mormonee."

"Do you believe this thing?" The oldest man's voice was high and thin, indicating the number of his years, but it was not weak or frail.

"I do not know, Father." Pahlilly was not actually the son of the old man, but the title used was one of respect, and he used it with great deference. "In all my years I have seen nothing like this that has happened to the one called Natanii nééz."

"Have you seen those who have had bones blown into them?"

"I think perhaps I have," Pahlilly replied thoughtfully. "At least, that is what has been said about them."

"In the seasons of this man's life he has seen much," the older of the two men declared. And he referred always to himself as if he were another, which humility befitted a man of his respected position. "This man has seen many who thought they were *biniszdin,* bewitched, who were then made well simply because they thought they would be made well. He has seen others die for the same reason. A man's thoughts are powerful things and can bring to pass many strange things."

Pahlilly considered this, but did not respond.

"From atop the mountain of his years this man has also seen true power—not the sort that comes because a man thinks or believes a thing, but power that comes when words are spoken and then obeyed by all of nature, despite the thoughts of him against whom the words have been spoken."

"You have seen this great thing?" Pahlilly looked keenly at his elderly companion.

"More than once."

Pahlilly was stunned. "Who but one of the Holy Ones has such power, that he can speak into the wind, offering only words, and see his words obeyed?"

The old man closed his watery eyes, and for a moment did not respond. When he did it was not to answer, but to inform Pahlilly—and those who were listening nearby—that he wished to make a telling. Silently, then, they gathered more closely so they could hear.

"Many snows and many grasses ago, more even than this old man can count, when he was but a child, he was taken captive by the *nóódái*—the Paiute people of the Mountain Laying Down Flat—the Kiabab."

Pahlilly gasped in surprise, for he had not known this amazing thing about the great headman who sat beside him. But the elderly one politely ignored him and continued his narrative.

"This man who was a child was made welcome in the *wickiup* of the chief of these people, and after a time was given the name Tanigoots, which in the tongue of the Paiute means one in whose mouth is always found the truth. So he grew after the manner of a man and, when it was time, took to himself a wife who was called Ungka Poetes and who was the daughter of a great chief of the Paiutes, a man who was called Kanosh.

"With Ungka Poetes this old fool found true *hózhó,* balance in the universe. No day began that found him fearful or afraid, no day ended leaving him sorrowful and lonely. Always his heart was joyful, always his mind sought ways to share such joys with Ungka Poetes. Yet all he did was not enough; no, never! Ungka Poetes was better skilled than he at sharing joy, and always she filled him with more of life's beauty than he could ever provide for her.

"And so the days of their lives slipped past, never hurrying, but never going more slowly like a man might wish. Then to Tanigoots and Ungka Poetes came a son, a fine youth who grew tall and skilled in the ways of the Paiute. To them also came a daughter, a sweet child as full of joy as her mother. The girl-child was called Maraboots.

"More seasons passed, Tanigoots became a chief, and then on a day that had seemed like all others, a runner brought word of a strange thing, a white man coming alone to the encampment of Tanigoots and his people. Many were afraid, for they had heard harsh tales of these strange people; others were merely curious. Yet none were prepared for the thin youth who rode boldly but alone into the encampment, spoke with ease in the tongue of the People, and called for a council of the chief men to be brought together.

"This council lasted many days, and the Paiute learned much. This youth, whose *belacani* name was Ira Hatch, explained that he and the others called mormonee knew *Shin-op,* the great Creator, for *Shin-op* had spoken to them and had given them a book of many words, telling of the old ones who had gone before the Paiute and others, including the *Diné*. Those old ones had been the People of *Shin-op,* the People of peace, and he had given them many words of power, which the mormonee now held."

"Who is this *Shin-op?*" Pahlilly questioned, not wanting to be rude but wanting desperately to understand the old man's telling.

"To the Paiute and all others of the *nóódái,*" the elderly man replied without hesitation, "*Shin-op* is the great Being who made and breathed life into this world and all who live in it. He is the son of the great *Towats,* and in his breath is all power over life and over death."

"I did not know of this great Being."

"He is not spoken of among the *Diné*."

Thoughtfully Pahlilly nodded his understanding of the old man's words.

"To Tanigoots and the others the things this white man spoke concerning *Shin-op* were also strange things, very strange. But as the days passed, the men and even the women could see that this man called Ira Hatch was truly a man of peace, just as he told us *Shin-op* wished all of mankind to be. Yes, and the heart of Tanigoots was touched by this young man, so that he knew the man's words were truly words of power. When the one called Ira Hatch left us he gave to the man Tanigoots the book he had spoken of, and to this day that book dwells in the *hogan* of the man Dah nishuánt.

"Not long after that, came a day of sorrow so great that even now the heart of the man who sits beside you, feels pain. Ungka Poetes grew ill and quickly took the long walk to the west into the land of the sky people, and the man Tanigoots was left alone with his children. For many days it was not possible for him to think, or even to see forward to the next dawning. But then to the encampment of the Paiutes came men of the *Dinê,* relatives of the boy that Tanigoots had once been. They were seeking their true headman, and with a certainty Tanigoots knew that this headman was himself. More, he knew that he must take up the journey not only to *Dinê tah,* but he must also take up the journey back through the years of his own life, journeying until he could truly become Dah nishuánt, a man of the *Dinê*.

"This was right, though there was much about it that brought sorrow. The son of Tanigoots grew a heart of flint when he learned that he might also become a headman. He thought of this as a great thing, one he could take without earning, and in only one day his heart grew cruel and hard, not alone to the People of the Kiabab but to his sister, who at twelve summers had become a woman, and whom he now considered a slave."

Pahlilly nodded his understanding. "In *Dinê tah* the woman Maraboots would surely have become a slave, for her mother was of the *nóódái* and not of the true People."

The old man made the sign that it was so. "Long did the man Tanigoots labor in his mind over this thing. He had no wish to see his daughter become a slave, but neither did he wish to abandon her to the People of the Kiabab, who would have treated her with even greater cruelty than would the *Diné*—this because she was a woman with no parents and no husband.

"Then into his mind came the thought: *give her to the* belacani *mormonee*. Give her to the youth who was called Ira Hatch. His people were men and women of peace, and so surely she would be beloved of them.

"A runner was sent immediately, and within seven suns the man

Ira Hatch was seated in the *wickiup* of this old man while the fine strengths of the woman Maraboots were explained to him. Afterward, through all the time of darkness, he went into the mountain alone, speaking his words of power with *Shin-op* and seeking the counsel of that great Being. Before daylight crossed the land again, Tanigoots heard a lone wolf calling from off in the trees, and he knew that *Shin-op* had answered the man Ira Hatch. Soon the mormonee returned, gave this one the rifle you see in his hands as payment for his daughter Maraboots, and the two of them rode away."

For many minutes there was silence, and Pahlilly wondered if the old man called Dah nishuánt had grown tired. But just as he was about to say something, the old man continued.

"This old man who was the father of the woman Maraboots has seen her only once in all the cycles of the seasons since that day. Long ago she accompanied the man Ira Hatch and other *belacani* mormonee into the land of the *Diné*. They were a people of peace, yet the son of Dah nishuánt, who had grown strong and had many followers, discovered the mormonee and set his heart to destroy them. In the battle he found Maraboots and sought to take her captive that he might enslave her and perhaps take her life. But the man Ira Hatch fought bravely for the daughter of he who had become Dah nishuánt, and his son was turned away.

"In his anger, then, for it was great, the tall, strong son of this old fool took another warrior of the People and together they found and took the life of a young *belacani* mormonee, a youth who trusted them and was betrayed by them.[1]

"As the other *belacani* mormonee fled the wrath of the son of Dah nishuánt and those who warred with him, they came by chance to the *hogan* of this old man who is seated beside you. It was then that he saw his daughter, and his heart was made glad. Yes, he saw that she was beloved of the *belacani* mormonee called Ira Hatch. More, she was beloved of all the people called mormonee, each of

---

1. For a fictionalized account of this experience and what followed in the life of the child Maraboots, see: Yorgason, Blaine M., *To Soar with the Eagle,* Salt Lake City, Deseret Book Company, 1993.

whom spoke to her with kindness and treated her with dignity. Besides Ira Hatch, this was especially so of a thin *belacani* who even then was called by the *Diné, bináádootízhi*—blue eyes. His *belacani* name is Haskel."

"The witch?" Pahlilly muttered in astonishment.

"Some say that, my brother, but it is not so. Like Ira Hatch and the others of the mormonee, Haskel speaks the words of *Shin-op,* words of power, and those words are always obeyed. He spoke those words into the face of the strong son of Dah nishuánt, who laughed and made a mock of Haskel. Yet within one season this strong son was dead—he, his woman, his sons and his daughter, his livestock, and even the great spring of water where he had placed his *hogan.* All have become as dust before the strong evening wind, carried away by the power of the words of the *belacani* mormonee."

Pahlilly was stunned. "Your son's name . . . he was called Peokon?"

"That is what he was called. He is one of the two warriors of the *Diné* who stole the innocent life of the mormonee youth so many seasons ago. Now Haskel has spoken the same words into the face of the other warrior who took the life of that mormonee youth, and no matter how many sings might be held, it will not matter. *Shin-op's* words of power have been spoken by the man Haskel, and they are being obeyed."

It was then, finally, that Pahlilly and those who sat nearby, understood that the old man who was called Dah nishuánt, was speaking of the gaunt man who sat still as death outside the door of the *hogan* across from them—the man who until so very recently had been known as Natanii nééz, the tall Navajo.

"Come," Pahlilly said to the others who had accompanied him as he rose abruptly to his feet, "we will cross the big river at the Crossing of the Fathers and ride to the fort that some say is there. It is in my mind to meet these people called mormonee—these people of peace. Yes, and it is also in my mind that perhaps we will hear a few of their words of power."

Bluff Fort

It was very late, after eleven, and Kumen, exhausted from the day's work, had just finished the nightly chores that Mary had left for him to do. The cow was milked, the calves and pigs fed and watered, the chickens watered, and even his dog had received several mouthsful of warm milk, squirted directly from its true source. Now Kumen was carrying his pail of warm milk toward his cabin, certain of what he needed to discuss with Mary.

For weeks he had been worrying about it like a dog worries about a bone, even sharing his concerns the day before with his friend Billy Foreman. But finally, only moments before, he had at last felt the inspiration of the Holy Spirit. He still didn't know what he was going to say to Mary, at least not exactly. But while milking he had begun remembering the day when he had been led by the spirit of inspiration to cross the river to retrieve his stolen horse. That inspiration had not only led him directly to the animal, but it had enabled him to communicate with the one called Frank, the thief, without any difficulty whatsoever. Not in all his life had Kumen spoken Navajo so well as he had that afternoon. No, and never would he have known exactly what to say, except that his words that memorable afternoon had quite literally been placed into his mind.

That being the case, he was now reasoning as he moved resolutely toward his cabin, the Lord would surely tell him what to say to Mary about their call to enter into plural marriage. All he had to do, therefore, was have the faith to just open his mouth.

Now, if only Mary would listen.

15

Thursday, October 6, 1881

Bluff Fort

"Eliza? Eliza, please wake up! I must speak with you! Now!"

Hurriedly crawling from the bed, Eliza drew on her robe and pulled open the door. "Mary," she said softly as the tearful woman stepped across her doorsill and into the darkened cabin, "what on earth has happened?"

Instead of answering, Mary simply burst into renewed sobs. Having no idea what might be wrong, Eliza closed the door and turned to stir up the coals beneath the white ash of the fireplace. Soon a couple of logs were burning brightly, and Eliza nodded with satisfaction. As she drew her rocker and another chair close to the heat and light, she noticed that Billy's Regulator clock indicated that it was approaching two in the morning. Thank goodness, she thought, that the commotion had not wakened little Willy, who was almost impossible to get back to sleep once he had been awakened.

"Very well," she soothed as she handed Mary a kerchief and then settled her in the rocker, "tell me what it is that has you so upset."

"Oh, Eliza, what am I to do? If I want children, then Kumen must take Lydia Lyman as a plural wife!" Abruptly the young woman grew angry, and her voice began to rise. "I can't bear it! I tell you, Eliza, it isn't fair, and I won't allow it to happen!"

"Shhhsh," Eliza urged as she held her finger to her lips. "Let's allow little Willy to sleep, Mary. Now, quietly tell me what this is all about."

Wiping her eyes and drawing a deep breath, Mary nodded. "Very well," she responded more calmly, "here's what happened. Tonight after he got home and did the chores, Kumen came in and told me he felt impressed that Pa should give me a blessing so I could have children. Well, it was late, but Pa's light was on, so I cleaned up and we went over. Kumen told Pa what he'd been thinking, and Pa agreed to bless me. While Aunt Kirsten went outdoors, Pa gave me a blessing, and in it he told me that if I wanted to raise Kumen's children, I must allow him to enter into plural marriage with Lydia May."

Eliza was dumbstruck. "Will . . . it be she who gives birth to these children? I . . . I mean, did the blessing—"

Mary shook her head. "No! Pa specifically said I would give birth to at least a son, but only on those conditions! Eliza, this isn't fair! It just isn't! And I won't submit myself to it!"

"But Mary," Eliza argued, feeling so torn it was terrible, "it was part of a priesthood blessing, revelation from the Lord through your bishop to you—"

"I don't care if it was the voice of God himself!" Mary stormed. "This is it! This is where I draw the line! I . . . I don't even know if the Church is true anymore. It surely doesn't feel true, not when it forces a man and a woman into something that feels so wrong, so—"

"You aren't being forced, Mary, and you know it. You've been given a choice. And you have every right to choose as you wish."

"Oh, certainly!" Mary's voice was so filled with anger and malice, and her countenance was so filled with bitterness, that Eliza hardly recognized her friend. "A fine choice that is! I give up everything except my marriage to come into this godforsaken land, and I stay here and suffer untold misery while others pack up and return to their easy lives! And how does the Lord reward me for all this . . . this sacrifice? By taking away my husband, the only thing I have left in this life, or by taking away my right to bear children, the only hope I have left. What sort of a god is that, Eliza? I ask you, what sort of a god would do such a thing? Not one I want anything more to do with, I can tell you that!"

Stunned by her vehemence and the amazing transformation of

her dear friend, Eliza didn't know what to say. It was almost as though she had become another person, one filled with darkness rather than light.

"Mary, I believe you need another blessing." Eliza's voice was trembling as she spoke.

"Another blessing?" Mary scoffed disdainfully. "That's a joke, Eliza, and not a funny one, either! The last blessing practically destroyed me, and I'll be damned if I'll have another! I won't—"

Stunned at her friend's burst of profanity, Eliza forced herself to continue. "Mary, dear, look in my mirror there. Do you see what I'm seeing? It seems to me you're battling forces outside of yourself, forces that are more than anxious to destroy you. And right now, Mary, I fear that they are winning."

"What? But I don't—"

"Answer me this, dear. Have you ever profaned in your life?"

"Of course not!"

"Yet you just did. That isn't you, Mary. I feel certain that you're dealing with an evil power that is trying to destroy you, and that is coming fair to succeeding. With all my heart, dear, I implore you to allow Kumen to give you another blessing, and let the Lord's power drive this evil from you!"

Suddenly submissive, Mary nodded her agreement. Silently she followed Eliza out the door and into the next cabin, where they found Kumen seated in the dim light with a sorrowful and dejected look on his countenance.

Quickly Eliza explained her feelings, then sat silently as Kumen laid hands on his beloved Mary's head, rebuked Satan, and then pronounced a few words of comfort upon her.

"Wha . . . what was that all about?" Mary asked when Kumen had finished speaking. And Eliza was astounded at the change in her friend's appearance—in the very tone of her voice. Where she had been angry, defiant, and bitter, she was now subdued, seeming at peace.

"Did you feel anything leave you?" Kumen asked softly.

Mary's eyes were wide. "I did," she breathed. "It seemed like a huge, dark cloud had engulfed me, was overpowering me, making me think I was about to smother or something. Then when you commanded Satan to depart, whatever it was, left me. But oh, Kumen, it was angry, and I felt like it was screaming at me! Was that the devil? Was I . . . possessed?"

"I don't know that you were actually possessed, Mary, but Eliza was right; you were certainly being tormented."

"But . . . why?"

Kumen smiled sadly. "I reckon because you gave the devil power, probably through your initial and quite negative reaction to your father's blessing. But I'm sure Satan's gone now, so don't worry about it anymore. Instead, why don't we pray for the strength to see this thing through?"

And a thoughtful Eliza, sensing that all would now be right for her friend, crept silently back to her home. Yet it was after dawn when sleep finally came, and before that she had pondered and prayed, not only for her dearest friend in all the world, who was struggling with such a momentous and terrible decision, but for herself. After all, if that slight relapse in Mary's attitude could give Satan so much power over her, then what might Eliza's own negative attitudes and fears have brought upon her own head?

Clay Hill Pass

"What do you reckon is taking that durn Mormon posse so long?"

Lug Santoni was crouched in some clay hummocks that overlooked the winding track cut and dug by the Hole-in-the-Rock pioneers a year and a half before. The dugway was a remarkable feat of engineering and labor, but such niceties were completely lost on the man, who had griped the entire way up the cut about its steepness and the dangerous ruts worn by the previous spring's runoff.

Big Rob Paxman, seated behind another large hump of clay nearby, was quite happily engaged in his perpetual and utterly useless whittling. Not a whistle this time because he had been unable to find any willows nearby, the man was slowly turning a limb of manzanita or mountain mahogany into a funny-looking chain, though what it might ever be good for, Lug had no idea. But already he'd carved out seven or eight links, one with a cage and a wooden ball inside it, and so it wasn't bothering him at all that the Mormons were so slow in coming.

Scrunching down Lug shifted his rifle and drew a bead on a distant stump, wishing for all the world that he could tighten the trigger and watch the bark fly. He knew he would hit the stump; he always hit whatever he aimed at. And his rifle, a Winchester Model 73, was the most dependable weapon he had ever owned. Too bad, he thought with a sudden grin, that the previous owner had been a little less experienced.

Shifting his gaze, he scanned the trail again, moving the muzzle of his rifle as easily as he moved his eyes. But still he could see nothing unusual—no sign of the pursuit they were certain would be coming.

"Rob, you got any good, smooth wallow-stones?" Lug asked, suddenly feeling thirsty.

"Just pick one up off the ground," Rob Paxman replied without looking up. "I only have one, and I bin thinking of sucking on it myownself."

"Just pick one up off the ground," Lug mimicked quietly as his eyes darted about the slope, looking for a small, smooth stone he could wallow around in his mouth to ease his thirst. "Maybe you ain't noticed, you big natural-born lummox, that this here hill is clay and soft rock, and good wallow-stones don't grow in such country!" Lug said this, all right, but he said it quiet, for there was no way on God's green earth that he wanted Rob Paxman to hear him. Especially not when Rob was above him and a little bit behind.

"No sign of 'em?" Rob Paxman suddenly asked as he folded his knife and slipped it into his pocket.

"Not ary a one that I can see."

"Interesting, mighty interesting." Rob Paxman rose to his feet and dusted himself off. "You know, Lug, I don't much mind if Sugar Bob Hazelton was wrong and those Mormon folks don't come. What I don't like, is that we ain't seen hide nor hair of that same Sugar Bob, who I was sure would be following us. To my way of thinking he's the chancy one, six ways from Tuesday more dangerous than a loaded polecat. There's a reason he was carved up by somebody or other, a good reason, and you can bet it wasn't on account of him setting no attendance records at Sunday School."

Lug Santoni did not reply, but in his mind appeared the vivid but terribly marred visage of Sugar Bob Hazelton.

"He said he wanted an equal cut of whatever hosses we stole," Rob Paxman continued, "and when we turned away from the reservation without giving his cut to him, I figured sure he'd be watching and come after us. Thing is, Lug, I've got me a squirrely feeling that when he comes, it won't be to palaver."

Slowly Lug Santoni looked around, more carefully this time. "You . . . uh . . . you think Sugar Bob might be figuring on bushwhacking us?"

"As ever. You see his eyes, Lug, when I got the drop on 'im? They was colder'n a banker's heart."

Lug Santoni considered that—considered it deeply. Rob Paxman wasn't endowed with much of the milk of human kindness, that was certain. And if he thought somebody else's heart was cold, well . . .

"Tell you what, Rob." Lug was already moving out from behind the clay hummocks. "I've plumb had it with waiting around on those Mormon fellers, throwing up ambush parties that nobody comes to. We got their horses, and the way I see it we're both mighty weak betwixt the ears to be dillydallying along trying to kill somebody what might not even be coming after us—especially when we can cross the river and hit those Mormon settlements, sell the nags, and start in to having us a riotous good time."

"I like your thinking, Lug," Rob Paxman agreed as he stepped down onto the rutted roadway and followed upward after his smaller friend. "'Cept for riotous. I ain't rightly sure I ever heard that word, and I am almighty sure I don't know what it means."

Bluff Fort

"I do hope the boys are okay."

"Do you think they might not be?"

Nellie Lyman looked up from her washboard. "I . . . I don't know, Rachel. Maybe it's that I didn't get to say good-bye to Jody, but I have this awful feeling gnawing in the pit of my stomach, and I can't seem to make it go away."

"Bishop Nielson says he instructed them to go slowly enough that they wouldn't catch the thieves until they have all reached the settlements and can get help. So they'll be safe enough, Nellie."

"I . . . I hope so. But . . . what happens if something goes wrong?"

Rachel Perkins, thinking of her own husband's danger, didn't answer, and Mary, standing next to her, thought of her experiences of the night before. "Then it'll be like everything else we've had to face since we were called on this peace mission," she sighed. "We'll just have to grit our teeth and bear it."

Though Mary knew that neither woman understood her veiled reference to Kumen's consideration of marriage to Lydia Lyman, she herself was close to tears. She thought she was beginning to feel peace with the idea, and yet every time her thoughts turned to it, she wept.

Of course, visits earlier that morning with women such as Adelia and Annie Lyman, Kirsten Nielson, and others who were already involved with plural marriage, had helped, and so had the things she had learned about Satan from Kumen's blessing given in the middle of the night. For a fact she was determined not to let the devil get his licks into her wonderful relationship with Kumen no matter whom the Lord called him to marry, and she was doing her best to exercise mighty faith in that regard. Yes, and she was also exercising great faith that Satan would be stopped from endeavoring to pollute her own mind, her own heart with doubts and fears.

"Speaking of trials," she finally declared, surprising even herself, "I'll say this, Nellie. I have received a witness from the Holy Spirit that has pacified me with the knowledge that Kumen and myself will . . . will be rewarded for our sacrifices, no matter how difficult they may prove to be." Lifting her apron hem she dabbed at her tear-filled eyes. "It will surely be the same with Jody and the others who have been assigned to take up the trail of those sorry horse thieves," she continued. "Whatever sacrifices the Lord may call one or all of them—or us—to make, will be amply rewarded by the Lord. We have that promise!"

Wiping at her own moist eyes with the back of a sudsy wrist, Nellie nodded. "I know that, Mary. I'm just frightened for Jody, and I can't bear the thought of him suffering or getting killed. I . . . I just hope that isn't what my feelings are all about!"

As the youthful Nellie Lyman returned to her laundry, she did not see the looks of apprehension and concern on the faces of the women around her. Not a one of them but knew exactly what the young woman was feeling, and not a one had the power to ease her burdens.

The South Bank of the San Juan

"You were right, my brother." A tired Scotty was standing beside the exhausted horse, which Posey had run until its legs were trembling and the foam of its sweat was flecked with blood. Now the heaving beast stood with its head hanging and legs spread, and Scotty knew it had little left to give. Of course this bothered Scotty no more than it did his brother, for it was the way of their people to make hard use of their ponies, and then to eat them when they had become good for nothing more. "We have made a big circle, and now we are all back here where we should have stayed."

Posey's look was grim, for big in his mind was the memory of the never-ending ride after Poke and his little sister, a ride of great danger and immense difficulty. From the place where they had found the horse and the dead white man, the tracks of those they followed had led them by a winding trail to the south and east between Nokai Mesa and No Man Mesa and on to Hoskanini Mesa where more of the *Diné* had joined Poke and the others. Traveling slowly this large band of Navajo men, women, and children had gone northeastward, finally camping at a spring less than a mile from what was called Hat Rock.

While Scotty had slept through the time of darkness, Posey had lain on his belly watching the distant encampment and fretting, wondering if he should try to sneak in closer and perhaps catch a glimpse of Too-rah, or if he should simply bide his time and determine where they were all going. Of course there was also the gnawing fear that some man or woman from either of the tribes might see him and spread the alarm. Such discovery would mean certain death, and Posey knew it. Especially now that Poke had discovered his and Scotty's horses near the *hogan* of the Navajo Tsabekiss, and so knew that he was being followed.

Finally wisdom had won out over valor, and Posey had spent the night lying still but inwardly seething and making vow after vow concerning the terrible things he would one day do to both Poke and the Navajo Bitseel.

Now it was the next afternoon, the two young Pahute warriors, nearly as exhausted as their hapless pony, were staring down off the bluff toward the river crossing where the tracks of the many horses obviously led, and Posey was once again ignoring his brother while wondering what it was that he should do.

"Do you see how it is?" Scotty, who the day before had guessed the ultimate destination of the others, was showing no mercy. Posey had scorned his idea then; Scotty had no doubt his brother would find a way to scorn it again now. Yet still he persisted. "The *Dinê* have gathered from every direction to come to this place where our people have been waiting to play *ducki* and to trade. Had we only waited, we would also have been there on the island to receive them. Yes, my brother, and we would still have our fine ponies that Poke and the *Dinê* have taken from us."

"Perhaps, but we would not know some of that country we now know, and we would not have this fine saddle and bridle, or even this fine pony, which I will now be able to use against the Navajo called Bitseel."

"Use?"

Posey smirked. "Of course! I know of no man who can beat me at *ducki,* the white man's game of cards. I will use these things as my wealth, and by my cunning I will take from that cursed one all that he has to wager. Then we will see to which of us the grizzly Poke would rather sell his favorite little sister."

A haughty smile creasing his face, the youth kicked the

exhausted horse into motion once again, certain he could urge the animal to get him to and then across the big river. And with a sigh that spoke volumes, Scotty picked up his leaden feet and followed after.

Bluff Fort

"Have you . . . thought much about what happened last night?"

Without looking at her younger friend, who had said nothing about their experience for most of the long and tiring day of washing and now the seemingly endless candle dipping, Eliza nodded. "I've thought about it almost constantly."

"So have I." Carefully Mary lifted a rack of freshly dipped candles and carried it to the open window to harden. "Truthfully, it is one of the most remarkable, and terrifying, experiences I have ever had."

Busily dipping more thickening wicks, Eliza nodded her understanding. "Are you feeling better about the things that were troubling you?"

Mary sighed as she returned to her chair. "If you're referring to plural marriage, I suppose I'm becoming resigned to it, though I don't know that I will ever feel okay. On the other hand, if you're referring to my encounter with the devil, then I am definitely not doing well! I am still frightened by the experience, Eliza, and my pleadings heavenward for understanding seem to be going unheard."

"I was troubled, too. I—"

"I suppose the thing that shocked me the most," Mary continued, not even noticing that Eliza had been speaking, "was how easy it was for the devil to get to me. All I did, for heaven's sake, was lose my temper, and I've done that plenty of times! What I said to my father and Kumen after that first blessing, though, was a caution, it truly was. It was even worse than what I said to you. Makes me ashamed to even think about it. But to be honest, I'm certain that's when old Scratch took over."

For a moment Mary looked at her friend. "What bothers me the most, though, is that I don't think I understand Satan. I mean, I suppose I have always believed in him—in the fact that he can tempt me to commit sin. But then again, maybe I haven't believed at all, for I have never in my life supposed that he could have such an effect on me as I experienced last night."

Eliza nodded her understanding. "I'm afraid you and I are in the same boat, Mary. Thinking back to all my rantings and railings against Billy while we were in Cedar and at the beginning of our trek here to Bluff, I'm certain as can be that I was also in Satan's grasp. Poor Billy must have been praying for months on end that the Lord would rebuke Satan from me."

"It's embarrassing, isn't it?" Mary said.

"Terribly." Eliza smiled sadly. "I simply detest this feeling of ignorance. If Satan can affect us all so easily, then I want to know how he does it!"

Carefully Eliza handed her friend another rack of dripping candles to be set to harden. "Willy is spending the night with the Lymans, though, so after we are finished with this vat of tallow, I intend to begin digging through the scriptures and maybe even Billy's daybooks."

"Then why don't I do the dipping," Mary declared thoughtfully, the exhaustion of her body suddenly gone from her mind, "while you start reading. That way, my dear, we can both learn together."

16

Friday, October 7, 1881

Bluff Fort

"Mary, there's little doubt that you have become a master candle maker."

Mary Jones smiled tiredly. Outside the night was graying into dawn. She and Eliza had worked and talked the whole night through, and it had now been more than twenty-four hours since they had slept. "That's because I've had a master teacher, Eliza; that, and hundreds and hundreds of candles worth of practice. Have you counted them yet?"

"No, but I know the number is well over six hundred. That's astounding, especially when I recollect how long it has taken me in the past to dip just a hundred or so. Of course we have frames hanging from every conceivable spot in this cabin."

"Which only you can reach," Mary smiled. "I swan, Eliza, for a woman in such a weakened condition, you are truly a working fool! I . . . I mean—"

"I understand what you are saying," Eliza laughed. "By the by, a little bit ago while you were dozing I thumbed through Billy's daybooks, and I can't find very much in them about the devil. I know he has some opinions on the subject, but without him here . . . well, I suppose we'll just have to wait for his return."

Mary nodded, her expression thoughtful.

"Another thing. I've been thinking of what you said to the

sisters yesterday, out by the washtubs." Eliza paused and stretched her back, easing her tired muscles.

"Yes?"

"That no matter the sacrifice we are called upon to offer, the Lord will reward us for making it?"

"I guess that includes this dreadful mission. Oh, how I wish we could all be released from it!" Eliza declared with as much fervor.

"Trouble is, a dear friend of mine likes to say that if wishes were fishes, we'd all be swimming in the San Juan," Eliza said.

Hearing her own words, Mary began to laugh, Eliza joined her, and their mirth continued until it was cut short by an unearthly shrieking—a shrieking that was all too familiar to Eliza. For some reason her sweet little Willy was starting to throw tantrums, terrible ones, and in a heartbeat she knew he was already up for the day and in the midst of a bad one.

"That's Willy," she breathed as she took her crutch and tiredly pulled herself to her feet. "Poor Annie. I wonder what stirred the child up this time." And with as much speed as possible she made her way out the door and across the commons toward the Lyman cabins.

Lake Pahgarit, Near the Cutoff to Hall's Crossing

"I'm sorry, Lem, but it's no good. I just plain can't do it."

Soberly Lemuel Redd regarded the smaller Billy Foreman, who was once again picking himself up from the ground and dusting the grime from his clothes. Jody Lyman had already roped Billy's runaway horse, and Jody and Hyrum Perkins were leading it back to where they had camped for the night near the lake.

"Maybe you're right, Billy," he finally admitted, shaking his head. "I've never known a man who couldn't ride a horse if he practiced it enough. But neither have I known a man who could be thrown so easily as that nag just threw you. That time it only did two little crow-hops, for crying out loud."

"I know," Billy Foreman admitted, sounding tired and humiliated. "But like I told you yesterday, this past spring I got thrown from Dick Butt's mule in just one jump. I don't know what it is, Lem, but a horse goes into the air and for some reason I lose all sense of balance. I wrap my legs around it, I hang on with both hands, and no matter! First thing I know I'm in the dirt, and somebody has to go and chase down the poor animal for me."

Lemuel Redd nodded thoughtfully. Perhaps Billy simply couldn't ride a horse. Why, he'd been thrown three times already that morning, and despite that Lem and Jody had watched particularly to give him pointers, neither could think of a thing to tell him. He seemed to be doing everything right—everything, that is, but staying in the saddle when the horse did anything but walk off with a quiet and steady gait.

The trouble with that, of course, was that for the life of him Lemuel couldn't think of how Billy might continue on this long and perhaps perilous journey. Only, the bishop and stake president had assigned them to chase down the horse thieves *together,* and Lem couldn't just leave Billy camped somewhere along the trail. They had to stick together in order to be obedient to counsel, and Lemuel knew it. But how?

"Any ideas?" he asked as he handed Billy his spectacles, which had been thrown aside in the latest brief melee.

"Yeah," Billy responded as he wiped his glasses and replaced them on his nose and ears. "You boys go ahead and I'll follow along on foot. Maybe after I've led that critter for a mile or so he'll gentle down enough for me to try it again."

"I don't feel good about leaving you behind us, Billy."

"And I don't want to slow you down. I just don't know what else to do—"

"The bishop told us to go slow anyway," Hyrum Perkins interrupted as he drew rein and dismounted to tighten the cinch on Billy's saddle. "After all, it's no race we are running."

"True enough," Jody Lyman agreed as he handed Billy the reins to his recalcitrant mount. "Besides, the tracks of those boys are still way too fresh to suit me. I think they keep laying for us, and if we aren't careful we'll wish we hadn't caught them."

Lemuel nodded, his eyes on the distant trail. "True enough. All right, Billy, you walk the kinks out of your animal, and we'll all stick together no matter." Lemuel smiled crookedly, almost apologetically. "But let us know when you think you're ready for more fireworks, and we'll all three have our ropes at the ready."

Billy smiled wanly at the man's dour humor, and shortly the four were once again on the trail of the horse thieves and the stolen animals.

Sand Island

Posey's mood was growing more foul by the hour! Not alone had he been unable to catch even a glimpse of Poke and his comely younger sister during their exhausting several-day foray into the land of the *Diné,* but now that he and Scotty were back on the island, both Poke and his brother Tehgre were once again heaping verbal abuse upon him at every opportunity. Again they were calling him *pu-neeh,* skunk! Not once or twice but several times they had mocked him with the name of the despised animal and mocked him, too, with their scornful laughter. To make matters worse, others of the People had taken up the chant, until Posey had grown so hurt and so angry, he could hardly keep himself from *yah-gi,* from crying.

Then had come the threats. As Posey had attempted to walk away with dignity, Poke had called him *shi-pun-ny moap,* which meant pesky or lightweight little mosquito. "*Poon-e-kee shi-pun-ny moap,*" the grizzly had snickered. "Look, pesky little mosquito, if I see you looking in the direction of my sister again, then *wite ung-i-nunk,* I will catch you with a rope and *pah-e-i,* drown you in the river! *Poo-suds-a-way-ah?* Do you understand?"

Of course Posey had understood, and so had everyone else. All had laughed, and he had fled to this place on the shore of the island, where the willows were thick enough to hide his shame, and where he had so long before, it seemed, killed the old mormonee cow. Now, his face black with anger, Posey was rhythmically hitting the cow's rotting carcass with his riding quirt. Surely, he was thinking, there was someway he could prove to Poke and his family that he was a man—that he was a feared and respected warrior. Surely he could find a way of showing what a great and wise man he had become . . .

Abruptly Posey realized that he had not yet seen a single person of the *Diné*. Where were they, he wondered? Where, most especially, was the despised one called Bitseel, the young man who was almost surely considering the purchase of the more than lovely Too-rah? Might they be together, he wondered? Might the trade have already been completed, so that the two of them were off alone somewhere in the willows, just as was he?

Blinking with the surprise and horror of such a thought, Posey lunged to his feet. He had to find them, his mind screamed as he lurched back toward the encampment. He had to find Too-rah, and if the dreaded trade had already been completed . . .

Unable or unwilling to even complete that horrid thought, Posey focused instead on Bitseel, vowing as he hurried through the willows that he would find the youth, somehow involve him in a game of *ducki,* and thereby strip him of every last ounce of wealth with which he might barter for the life of Too-rah. *Oo-ah,* yes! And then . . .

17

Saturday, October 8, 1881

Bluff Fort

"Kumen, you take care of Mary, you hear?"

From the wagon bench, Kumen smiled. "Don't worry, Eliza. We'll all be fine—all of us. You keep an eye on little Willy, and tell Billy we'll see him in a month."

In the early morning light, Eliza wiped away sudden tears. "You'll no doubt run into him on the trail, so you can tell him yourself. I . . . uh . . . I was wondering if you could do me a large favor?"

"Sure thing. Just name it."

"Not long ago I wrote the Co-op in Cedar City, ordering Billy and me a new cookstove, a Majestic. If you have time, Kumen, would you mind checking to see if they ever got my order?"

Kumen chuckled. "We'll do better than that, Eliza. If they have it in, we'll bring it back with us. It's paid for, I assume?"

"I'm paying for it with stock I have in the Co-op. There should be more than enough to cover it."

"Now, that's a good idea. Mary, you and Lydia May settled?"

"As . . . soon as I get . . . up here beside you—" Worming her way out from under the canvas cover, Mary settled herself on the wagon bench. Lydia May, right behind her, settled herself on a stack of blankets directly in back of the bench.

"Move 'em out!" Ben Perkins abruptly called from the lead wagon, and with the rattle of chains and creaking of wheels, all accompanied with shouting children and barking dogs, the three wagons began to move.

"You take care of yourself and Willy!" Mary called as she waved at Eliza. "Tell him we'll bring him some peppermints . . ."

Near Hall's Crossing

"You reckon those boys will try an ambush here, Lem?"

"Why not, Jody? They tried at Kane Gulch and Cow Tanks and Clay Hill Pass, and those're just the ones we know about. If I ever in my life saw inspiration, it was when Bishop Nielson told us to go slow and to go careful."

The four men, dusty from the long trail, were carefully making their way over the hills and along the gullies that would lead them at length to the rim above the Colorado River. Of course they didn't expect an ambush right there, for Charlie Hall and his son Reed were down below running their ferry, and folks from everywhere knew they were Mormon. But a mile or so this side of the river or the other side, either one, and as Lem Redd had already put it, all bets were off. These horse thieves were killers of the worst order.

"There they are, boys!"

Quickly reining in on the rimrock overlooking the river, onto which they had only just ridden, the four men stared downward in amazement. The two thieves had just driven their stolen horses off Charlie Hall's ferry on the far side of the river, and were even then turning them to follow the road that ran southwesterly along the riverbank toward the first big bend.

"Well, if that don't beat all!" Lem growled as he backed his horse out of sight. "'Cept for on the Hole-in-the-Rock trail, I never traveled so slow in all my born days, and despite it we've still caught up with those thieving hombres. Question is, did they see us?"

"They saw us for sure," Hyrum Perkins declared. "Didn't you see that big feller Paxman point his rifle up here at us?"

"I saw him," Billy admitted a little sourly. "Thing is, what do we do now?"

With a sigh Lem dismounted, lifted his stirrup, and loosened the cinch strap on his saddle. "We wait again, boys, and pray they were pointing at where we might have been, and not at where we are."

Above the Colorado River, near Hall's Crossing

"I hear your brother Ben's figuring on taking Mary Ann and the youngsters back to Cedar for the fall."

Hyrum Perkins nodded. "He may have already left, Billy. Fact is, we may run into him on our way back. Mary Ann's folks, the Williamses, live in Cedar, and she's been pining something awful to see them."

"That's Evan and Mary Williams?" Lem asked.

"That's right."

"Are they not members of the Church, then?"

"They be members, all right." Hyrum picked up a pebble and tossed it into a patch of low shad scale brush across the trail. "Evan became disaffected over something or other back in Wales, and to his meetings he hasn't been since. I reckon Mary does what Evan does because life's a bit more simple that way. Ben says they emigrated to Utah solely on account of his health, and because Mary Ann was here."

"You knew them afore? In the old country?"

Hyrum nodded.

Jody Lyman suddenly smiled. "Nellie says Ben's thinking of asking Sarah Williams, Mary Ann's younger sister, to be his plural wife. You know, until she was baptized in the San Juan last summer by Charlie Walton, I didn't have any idea Sarah wasn't a Mormon. Here we were six months together on that fool trek the winter afore, and you'd have thought we'd have time to learn everything about everybody involved."

"You'd have thought," Lem agreed. "Billy here is the one who told me about her not being a member."

"That's right," Billy admitted. "Seems Sarah and Eliza had a few nice talks, and it came out. Otherwise, I'd have never known it, either."

"The conversion and testimony of Eliza—everything that poor woman went through, in fact—had a powerful impact on Sarah's thinking. Sarah told me about it." Hyrum Perkins picked up another pebble and tossed it. "She also told me she thought Ben was going to speak to her about the Principle, and frighten her it did. Not of plural marriage, of course, but of her older sister, who it seems has a jealous streak where such things are concerned."

"Well, Sarah's a fine-looking little filly, that's sure."

"A lovely young woman, she is. But that is why she accompanied Platte, Bishop Nielson, and her brother, Thomas, back to the settlements last fall. She loves her elder sister, and would never hurt her."

"And still Ben's going to ask her to marry him?"

Hyrum nodded. "Write her he did, a month ago or perhaps two. Mary Ann agreed to give the union her blessing, but from what she's said to Rachel in the meantime, it be a blessing I would not be counting on."

"And I wouldn't be entering into plural marriage no matter how many blessings Eliza Ann gave me," Lem growled. "One woman's plenty to keep all the socks darned I can ever wear!"

Jody looked up, his face serious. "Why, Lem, Platte told me himself that he'd suggested you give thought to taking our sister Lucy Zina as your plural wife. Ain't that so?"

Lem Redd shifted nervously. "Givin' thought ain't the same as doin'." Then, abruptly changing the subject, he rose to his feet. "Billy, you've been sneaking a peek over that rim from time to time. Is it safe for us to follow?"

Billy, thinking of his friend Kumen's dilemma over the plural marriage issue, nodded. "Well, they're gone, Lem. Leastwise they're out of sight. Besides which, Charlie is rowing his ferry across toward us. To my way of thinking, that means it's time for us to follow."

After once again tightening the cinches to their saddles, the four mounted, and shortly thereafter were making their way down the slickrock cliffs toward the ferry at Hall's Crossing.

Hall's Crossing

"I'm sorry, brethren." Charlie Hall had rowed the four and their mounts back across the river, and now he was helping lead the horses off his ferry. "Reed and I had no idea those were your horses we were ferrying across a little bit ago, or that those two men were thieves. Why, that big feller is as sociable a man as I've ever met."

Hyrum Perkins nodded. "His name is Rob Paxman, and my wife, Rachel, said about him the same thing. She said he was charm itself with little George William, our son."

"Did they see us, do you know?"

Charlie Hall nodded. "I think they did, Lem. If they've been setting up ambushes all along, I'd go real careful if I was you."

"Well, that's what Bishop Nielson said to do. Give our regards to Sister Hall."

Charlie Hall smiled. "I would, but she's in Escalante—her and everybody else but Reed and me. Summers are too blamed hot here, I reckon. So they'll be back along about the middle of October."

"They're too hot on the San Juan, too," Jody Lyman agreed. "And altogether too dry. Trouble is, Elder Snow says we've been called to stay there, so I reckon for now, we will."

"Not if we don't get those horses back," Lem growled. "Mind if we stop yonder, Charlie, and fix us a bait of grub?"

"Not at all. But why don't you just come over to camp with us. Reed'll think he's died and gone to heaven if he can have another mathematical discussion with Billy here. Meanwhile the rest of us can eat a little something, have a game or two of jacks, and by then those boys should be long gone."

With a nod of agreement, the men turned toward the sheltered camp the Halls had established back under the rimrock overhanging the Colorado River.

The Colorado River, below Hall's Crossing

Lug Santoni was getting irritated. No, he thought with an inward snarl as he slapped at his arm, what he was getting, by jiggers, was mad as a stomped-on hornet! This was turning into far and away the worst experience of his already miserable life. Far and away! Angrily he tried to brush the ants off his britches, the huge, fiery red ants that seemed to inhabit by the thousands the pile of driftwood behind which he and big Rob Paxman had hidden themselves.

"Aarrgh!" he snarled beneath his breath as a sting that felt like a red-hot poker attacked his thigh. Of a truth, he thought balefully as he gave his leg a couple of good whacks and then glared at his seemingly peaceful partner, he was mad as a sow grizzly with two cubs and a sore teat! And ready by jiggers to do something about it, too! Happen that Paxman, the consarned nincompoop, hadn't suggested this blasted pile of driftwood in the first place.

"Kinda fiery, ain't they," Rob Paxman observed, still not moving a muscle to indicate he was even being bothered. "Sort of put me in mind of some ants I run into in Lousiana onct, 'cept they was a mite bigger and a whole lot meaner."

"Hummph!"

"Thing is, Lug, there ain't no better place for an ambush nor right here in this woodpile. It don't look like much cover at all, and when those Mormon fellers follow the road around that stand of willows yonder they'll have nowhere to go for cover, and we can pick 'em off clean."

Lug Santoni took another slap at his leg. "I thought we were through with ambushes."

Rob Paxman shrugged his massive shoulders. "We were, until they caught up with us. But I'm telling you, Lug, this here gooseneck is perfect. We can hear them Mormons coming long afore we can see 'em, and I hid our hosses on down the road a piece where they can't be seen or heard by those boys, either one."

Lug snarled as he smacked himself again, and then once more. "They best hurry, is all I've got to say. They don't, and these ants'll have me et alive."

"They'll be along, Lug." Rob Paxman gave his partner his

widest smile. "Just hold on a mite longer, and I'm telling you true, it'll be worth it for the both of us."

"It had better be!" Lug snarled evilly, and then he took another slap at his already burning leg.

The Colorado River, below Hall's Crossing

"You reckon we spent enough time at the Halls?"

"I hope so, Jody. I truly do." Without thinking, Lem Redd turned his mount up a narrow, brush-choked trail that cut across the narrow part of the gooseneck, his three companions following. Used by all who were familiar with it except the wagon companies, who had to follow the level but sandy roadway, the trail wound up through the point of rocks and then down the other side, saving two miles and a whole lot of the energy that plodding through sand consumed.

"If they be waiting again," Hyrum Perkins opined as the horses one at a time lunged upward over a three-foot sandstone ledge, "they'll be showing more patience than I've ever had."

"Or me," Jody Lyman admitted. "My Nellie says I'm always trying to hurry life along, and I reckon she's right. She says if I don't stop it then the Lord will stop it for me."

Hyrum grinned. "Rachel says the same thing to me. Says I don't take time to enjoy the good things, the simple pleasures the Lord has blessed us with. You know—sunsets, rainstorms, sandstorms, blooming flowers, long talks and walks with her and little George William—the sort of things women set store by. She may be right, too, but I can't recollect when I didn't feel in a hurry about whatever had to be done. Is that me, boys, or is that a gift the good Lord gave me?"

"It may be a gift," Billy drawled amiably as his horse topped the rocky backbone and started down the other side, "but it may have been given as a part of your weakness—your natural man."

"You trying to tell me the Lord gave us our natural man? Which same natural man is his enemy?"

"According to Moroni, God gave us our weakness so we would

be humble enough to keep praying until we overcome it," Billy responded. "And King Benjamin makes it fairly clear that that same weakness comprises our natural man, which also has to be overcome if we are going to return to God's presence. Maybe that's what Nellie is trying to tell you."

Jody nodded. "Makes sense, all right. I just don't know what to do about it—"

"Pssst!" Lem Redd hissed as he held up his hand, stopping the four of them in their tracks. "You fellers want to tell me what I'm seeing?"

Looking past him, both Jody Lyman and Hyrum Perkins drew in their breaths, while Billy just smiled as though he knew something the others did not.

"Is that our stolen horse herd down yonder in those willows?" Lem Redd's voice was very still.

"As ever," Jody acknowledged in little more than a whisper. "What do you think they're doing here?"

"I don't know, but I reckon we're about to find out. Go careful, boys. We don't want to get suckered into a trap."

And with that admonition the three drew their weapons, Billy pulled out the rifle he had been lent before starting, and then they urged their mounts on down the hill.

The Colorado River, below Hall's Crossing

"As far as I can tell, fellers, we've hit the jackpot."

Jody Lyman sat his horse, his eyes carefully scanning the sandy road, the willows, the rocks above them. "I think you're right, Lem. This ain't only our horses, but theirs."

"Saddles, packs, and all," Hyrum Perkins agreed as he, too, scanned the nearby terrain. "Where do you think they be, Lem?"

"I don't hardly know, Hy. Onliest thing I can see missing, besides the men, are their rifles. To my way of thinking, that means they're holding forth with another ambush. Don't you agree, Billy?"

"I do. Looks to me, boys, like the Lord has led us past the danger and delivered our herd into our hands."

Lemuel Redd grinned. "I'm with you, Billy. Pap always told me not to look a gift horse in the mouth, and I'm leaning that way now. My vote is to loose this bunch, our friends' animals included, and hightail it back to the ferry and across the river as fast as we can get there."

"Amen, Brother Redd. Amen and amen!"

The Colorado River, below Hall's Crossing

"You certain sure you tied them hosses up right?"

Lug Santoni, literally peppered with red welts from his bout with the ants, sat upright so he could better hear above the sounds of the river.

"Course I'm sure," Rob Paxman snorted. "Rope corral around the willows for the loose stock, and ours are tied good. Now get down, Lug, afore those boys come along and see you."

But Lug Santoni didn't move. Instead he continued listening, and gradually he rose to his feet. "Rob," he said slowly as he looked up toward the rocky hogback that rose behind them, "them hosses are moving, and they're moving fast!"

"You sure?"

"Sure as a spring robin watchin' a wormhole after a rainstorm. Not only that, but they're crossing over the top of this hyar hogback and heading back toward the river."

Cursing softly, Rob Paxman also stood up. "Well, come on," he growled as he started down the road. "I don't know how they got loose, but let's get our nags and go round 'em back up."

Lug shook his head angrily. "You ain't hearing me," he practically shouted. "Those horses ain't wandering! They're being driven! And that means our nags are being driven right along with the rest of 'em!"

"But who—"

"You know doggone well who!" Lug Santoni was fit to be tied, he was so exasperated with his big partner. "It's that confounded, dad-gummed Mormon posse, is who! Somehow they found a trail acrost this here gooseneck we're at the far end of, and while we've been setting here letting the ants eat us alive, they've got our hosses and are heading for the ferry and the far lonesome!"

Rob Paxman nodded. "I reckon you're right, Lug," he admitted humbly. And without another word he leaped across the pile of driftwood and headed on foot back through the willows toward the ferry.

The Colorado River, below Hall's Crossing

"Hy, can you and Billy get these animals to the ferry without us?"

"I reckon we can, Lem. Can you see them yet?"

Lem Redd shook his head. The animals were now off the sandstone hogback, through the willows, and with Hyrum Perkins pointing them, were trotting along the wide riverbank toward the ferry.

"Jody," Lem called as softly as possible while he dismounted, "let Hy and Billy take 'em to the ferry. Charlie and Reed can help load 'em, and you and I will swim it if we have to. You can swim, Jody, can't you?"

Jody Lyman nodded. "I can, and ol' Benny here is better than me."

Lem grinned as he pulled his rifle from the saddle scabbard and knelt in the sand in front of his horse.

"You thinking of shooting them?"

"Should be, Jody, but I probably won't. Scare 'em off, maybe, and that's about it. You?"

Jody Lyman, the reins to his horse in his hand, dropped to his knee nearby. "I'm not a killer either, Lem. Nor will I be, even if I am being killed. But firing to frighten them? That'd give me more'n a little pleasure."

"Good," Lem breathed as he raised his rifle, aiming a foot or so to the side of the approaching outlaws, "because there they come, sneaking through those willows yonder."

And with that, both Lem Redd and Jody Lyman opened fire.

—o—o—o—

The Colorado River, below Hall's Crossing

"You still see 'em, Jody?"

"I don't."

"Me, either. I reckon they've turned tail and run, so let's skedaddle on out of here and see if we can catch the ferry. Trouble is, those fellers ran too easy, and I— What in jumping blue blazes?"

"Those are some of our horses," Jody breathed as he turned around toward the ferry. "They must have gotten away from Hy and Billy—"

"Come on," Lem urged as he threw himself aboard his restive horse and spun it to head off the loose stock. "We don't have much time, Jody. Let's ride!"

—o—o—o—

The Colorado River, below Hall's Crossing

"Pull, boys!" Billy shouted as he stood anxiously with the horses, looking back. "Pull!"

Charlie and Reed Hall, kneeling with oars on either side of the ferry, dug at the water in unison. On board with the four Mormon posse members were twelve head of horses, including their own. In the water behind them swam the five animals that had escaped from Hyrum and Billy a little earlier. There hadn't been time to board them with the others, so lead ropes were put over each of the animals' heads, and now Hyrum knelt on the deck with the ropes in his hands, urging the animals to swim.

"You see 'em, Lem?"

"I don't, Billy," Lem Redd admitted. "But if they've climbed to that rim up there, we won't see 'em until we're halfway across. Then I'm afraid we'll be sitting ducks!"

"Well," Charlie Hall grunted, "we can't row any faster."

"I know it, Charlie. You and Reed are doing just fine. If those boys get on that rimrock, though . . . well, I hope we get out of this scrape alive, I truly do!"

Hall's Crossing

"They got our horses, Rob! I seen 'em. Mounts, pack animals, everything!"

"I know they did," Rob Paxman grunted as he scrambled up the steep face of the slickrock, trying to reach what he felt certain was the rim that overhung the river. "But we'll get 'em back, Lug. Don't you worry none about that! From this rimrock up here we can drill those Mormon skypilots clean, ever' last one of 'em. Then we'll be out of this country so fast our hosses'll be kicking the rabbits out of the way."

"We'll drill 'em clean if they don't shoot back, that is," Lug Santoni muttered sourly as he scrambled up the sandstone slickrock behind his big partner. "If only they don't shoot back."

Hall's Crossing

"Yipes!" Reed Hall, pulling on his oar, was staring wide-eyed at a bullet hole that had just appeared in the wooden deck of the ferry, not an inch from where he was sitting. "They nearly got me, boys! How about a little protection?"

As Reed continued his now practically frantic rowing, Lem Redd drew his pistol. The ferry was a little more than halfway across the Colorado, but the horses being dragged behind were slowing it down, and there wasn't much anyone could do about it.

"Like we figured, boys, they're up on that rim."

"I see 'em, Lem," Jody Lyman shouted. "But I don't think I can shoot and still keep these animals calm."

"You and Billy take care of the horses," Lem growled as he

studied the lip of the sandstone rim, "and I'll do the shooting. It seems to me those boys are mean enough to have reserved seats in hell, so from now on I'll do my best to see if I can punch their tickets for them. One, I won't stand still and watch them—"

The two outlaws bobbed up from behind the rimrock and both fired again, and Lem got off two snap shots of his own before they ducked back out of sight.

"Anybody hit?"

"Just the ferry again." Charlie Hall didn't even look up from his rowing. "Keep shooting, Lem. As long as you do, those boys ain't getting good shots a'tall!"

The heads bobbed up from behind the rimrock again, more shots were fired from both sides, and the ferry continued forward.

"I can help if it is what you want," Hyrum Perkins declared from the rear of the ferry. "I do not know if these horses are as valuable as a man's life."

"They ain't!" Lem was hurriedly reloading his weapon. "But they mean the world to our mission, Hy, so you stay with 'em. Besides, the way those boys are bobbing and ducking just from my pistol, I'd say they was all gurgle and no guts, with mighty cold feet for such a miserable hot country!"

Lem Redd fired again and again as more bullets rained on the ferry, reloading his pistol twice more and emptying it both times before the front of the ferry scraped bottom on the eastern bank.

"We're here, boys," Charlie Hall shouted as he tossed his oar onto the deck. "All hands ashore to pull this boat out!"

"These fool horses are going plumb crazy," Billy yelped. "Lem, Jody and I . . . are losing 'em—"

"No you ain't, Billy!" Lem shouted as he holstered his pistol and leaped for the gravel bank to help with the boat. "Just hang on until we can get the ferry grounded—"

"It be the left side of the ferry that me and the swimming horses are coming around," Hyrum Perkins shouted from where he had jumped into the neck-deep river. "We'll be heading for the willows—"

"Is she solid enough yet, Charlie?"

"Aye, Lem. Reed and I'll snub her down—"

The firing from the rim across the river, now that Lem was no longer shooting back, seemed continuous and bullets were thudding into the sand and kicking up dust nearby. "We're jake now," Jody suddenly shouted as the animals on the ferry deck, with bullets whistling all around them, somehow settled and began to follow him and Billy. "Man, but I wish I had my shooter out and a free hand to use it! Or better yet, my rifle—"

Plopping onto the sand and gravel of the bank, Lem was finally drawing a more careful bead. Of course he could also do better with his rifle, but there wasn't time to get through that knot of anxious horses.

"I'm hit!" Jody suddenly shrieked as he tumbled pell-mell off the end of the ferry and onto the gravel. "They got my leg, boys! I can't walk—"

"Take it easy, Jody," Reed Hall soothed as he dove beneath the horses' dancing hooves and onto the gravel beside the wounded man. "Let me take a look-see—"

"Is it bad, Reed?" Jody asked.

"Yeah, Jody, it looks bad—square into your leg, just above the knee. Lem, if you'll keep shooting, I'll drag him into the willows."

"But, we'll lose the herd—"

"I've got the horses, Jody!" Billy shouted as he tugged at the mass of lead ropes. "Just you worry about yourself!"

"Here, son," Charlie Hall called as he sprinted to the downed man, "let me help!"

And while Lem Redd fired again and again at the rimrock across the river, and while Hyrum and Billy scrambled to keep the horses together and get them into the tall stand of willows, Reed and Charlie Hall unceremoniously dragged young Jody Lyman into the willows behind them.

Hall's Crossing

"Well, they got our horses, ever' last one of 'em, so what do we do now?" Lug Santoni was mad enough to kick a wild hog barefooted, and right now his anger was directed at his big partner, who had proven himself so dumb he couldn't teach a setting hen to cluck. For a fact, Lug Santoni thought angrily, the chuckleheaded galoot wouldn't even make good buzzard bait, on account of no buzzard could possibly stomach him. Of all the miserable, low-down, stupid—

"I don't know about you," Rob Paxman replied abruptly, "but I'm going down to the river."

"You aim to try swimming it?"

"Not hardly. That's one thing I never learnt. You?"

"I never learnt how, neither," Lug Santoni declared. "I don't even bathe unless I have to! So, what do you plan on doing? Whittling willow whistles?"

Rob Paxman smiled his beautiful smile. "That weren't called for, Lug, and you know it. Now one of them Mormons has been hit, they'll be busy and maybe some of the hosses will get loose. If they do and then see me waiting, maybe they'll start back acrost the river so we can catch 'em."

"That's a whole lot of maybes," Lug growled in frustration. "Me, I'm going to check out that ferryboat captain's camp up under the rimrock. Could be there's women there that we can use for hostages—"

"And maybe something else besides," Rob Paxman added with a wink and a raucous laugh before turning to search for an easy slide down the slickrock.

Startled, Lug Santoni glanced at his cackling partner. In years past, the first time they had partnered up, he thought he had known the miserable soul. But this, this *lust,* was a whole new side of the man that Lug found himself considering truly evil, and the small outlaw didn't hardly know what to do about it.

"Pa used to say," Rob Paxman continued from the bottom of the slickrock where he was already walking away, "that there was only two things he was afeared of—being afoot and a decent woman. Me though, I'm only scairt of being afoot. That's cause I ain't never met me no decent woman!"

Again the man burst into his riotous, profane laughter. And again Lug Santoni, who after more than twenty years could still see the

Union soldiers who had cut his face and left him for dead before turning to rape and then kill his mother and little sister, vowed to wipe this monster from the face of the earth! He didn't know how he'd manage to do it, but when the moment was right . . .

———o—o—o———

Hall's Crossing

"His leg bone above the knee is all broken in slivers, Lem. As far as I can tell, there ain't nothing left of it—certainly not enough to set and splint."

Lem Redd and Billy Foreman, kneeling on either side of their suffering companion, glanced at each other and then down to Jody Lyman.

"Is the pain getting bad, Jody?"

Jody blinked his eyes and nodded. "She's fierce, Billy. Mighty fierce. I haven't ever had anything hurt like this, not ever! What . . . what do you reckon we should do?"

"Wait until dark, I think, and then start back. You agree, Lem?"

"I do. You up to it, Jody?"

For a long moment the wounded man was silent, clenching his teeth against the pain. "I . . . I reckon so, if that's the best."

"Is it a priesthood blessing you'd be liking?" Hyrum Perkins asked quietly.

His eyes squeezed tight shut, Jody nodded.

Without hesitation the three healthy members of the posse laid their hands upon Jody's head, and a loving blessing of comfort and power to endure was pronounced on their friend by Hyrum Perkins.

"I hope it wasn't out of line, that which I spoke," Hyrum stated a few moments later as he and Lem Redd checked on the horses.

"It was an interesting promise, all right. Physical comfort when it will be least expected but most needed, brought to him by a messenger sent by God. Sounds mighty straightforward, Hy."

Miserably Hyrum Perkins shook his head. "I . . . I don't know why I said that, Lem. It can't happen, and we both know it. In the hundred or more miles between here and Bluff there isn't one single thing but pure, harsh wilderness, with nothing of comfort anywhere. And the Lord knows the seeing and ministering of angels is a scarce thing. I . . . I wish I hadn't even said it!"

"Well," Lem drawled, "I think you were inspired, Hy. In a situation like this, and if I was the Lord, I'd for sure and for certain send an angel. Without one, I don't see how poor Jody is ever going to make it back home."

"I don't, either. But I'll tell you what it is that I be thinking. It is a wagon that Jody will be needing, and willing I am to leave now for Bluff, to get one and return. Besides, Billy's mighty good with Jody, and since you're captain you need to stay here, too."

"Good thinking, Hy, and I agree. Take your horse and one other, change mounts every twenty miles or so, and try not to stop until you get there. Jody and Billy and me will be coming along slow but steady, and we won't leave the trail by more than a few feet. That way we'll be easy to find when you return. And Hy, keep praying for that angel to come quick and give us a hand."

Hall's Crossing

"Oh, boys!" Rob Paxman called into the deepening twilight and across the muddy river, "you wouldn't leave two fellers like us stranded now, would you? Boys, you hear me?"

When his answer was nothing more than the constant, lonely murmur of the river, Rob Paxman kicked at a rock and swore viciously. "I thought Mormons was supposed to be God-fearing folks!" he shouted angrily. "Not horse thieves! Them saddled hosses and pack animals you took is ours, and you boys know it! Turn 'em loose into the river, and we'll call it good and never bother you again. Happen you don't, we'll press charges with the first sheriff we come to, and that's a promise!"

Again the churning, darkening river was his only answer. In hours the ferry hadn't moved from the far bank, and neither he nor Lug Santoni had seen hide nor hair of the horses or men that had crossed over. They had disappeared into the thick willows that lined the shore, and for all Rob Paxman knew, they had already found a secret trail out and were long gone.

Earlier the two outlaws had scoured the deserted camp of the ferrymen looking for anything that might be of value. But not only had there been no women, the camp itself had been unusually spare. There'd been a bait of grub, all right; some bedrolls, and a box or two that served as cupboards and table. But without horses they could pack little of it away, neither of them had a desire to remain there and wait for the ferry to return, and so at every turn the two had been frustrated.

And now Lug Santoni had gone wandering off.

"Oh, boys, you listen to me now!" Rob Paxman shouted again, trying to keep the desperation from his voice. "We wasn't ever shooting to kill, ol' Lug and me. We ain't killers! We was only tryin' to slow you down. You keep your hosses, only give us ours back, and we'll clear out and you'll never hear from us again! That's a promise from a man who never broke his word, not once in his whole and entire life! I swear it afore God Almighty! I surely do!"

Drawing a deep breath, the big man waited in vain for a reply. "As one Christian man to another," he then continued, "I plead with you to follow Jesus' admonition to turn the other cheek! We wronged you, and we admit it freely. So forgive us our sins the way you want one day to be forgiven of yours. You won't be sorry, boys, and you know it. Anybody who follows the Good Book the way you Mormons do is bound to be blessed for his good efforts and be rewarded.

"Boys? Oh, you Mormon boys! You know doggone well it ain't righteous to ignore a man thisaway . . ."

Hall's Crossing

"Jody, I reckon it's time to be moving. You up to it?"

"As . . . as much as . . . I can be," the wounded man breathed. "Isn't there anything that . . . that you can do for my leg, Lem?"

Lem gripped his friend's shoulder. "She's cleaned, splinted, and wrapped, but I don't know what else to do—'cept get you back to Bluff as soon as possible. Hy's gone to bring us a wagon, but that'll take him three, maybe four days. The farther we can go to meet him, though, the sooner we can get you off that horse."

"Lem, me and Reed will ride with you and Billy as far as the Lake country. Maybe that'll be of some help."

In the darkness Lem Redd nodded. "Thanks, Charlie. I reckon it'll take two of us to hold Jody on his horse, another to lead the herd, and the fourth just to find the trail."

"Well, Reed knows the trail fairly well, so why don't you and me do the holding and leave the herd to Billy? You ready, young feller?"

"I . . . think so . . ."

Carefully Charlie Hall and Lem Redd worked their hands under Jody Lyman's body, and then with great effort they lifted him off the ground.

"Ayyaaagh!" the man shrieked in terrible agony as his muscles spasmed, and then his body went limp.

"He's passed out, not died," Billy declared a second or two later. "That'll be good for all of us, but most especially for him. Reed, hold that nag still, so we can get the poor soul aboard."

"I'm trying, Billy. The horse must smell the blood."

"I reckon."

"Lem," Charlie called softly, "don't let him fall off the other side."

"Should we tie him down?" Lem Redd asked once the unconscious man was in the saddle and slumped forward over the horn.

"Naw, we might hurt him worse. We'll just ride close and hold him in place."

"Did you notice how hot he is?"

"He's feverish, all right." Billy pulled himself aboard one of the horses belonging to the two horse thieves across the river, which not only didn't buck but didn't even quiver. "You ready to ride point, Reed?"

"As ever. You have the loose stock?"

"I think so."

"Billy, you hang onto the lead ropes of those three animals I showed you," Charlie Hall called out, "and the rest will just naturally follow. Horses like company, and besides, they've already been over this trail, so it'll feel like going home to them."

"You think those boys'll wreck your camp, or maybe come after your ferry?" Lem Redd was peering through the darkness toward the west bank of the Colorado.

"They might, though there ain't much to destroy over there. Besides, the way that big one's been hollering and carrying on the past hour or so, tromping up and down that bank and kicking rocks ever which way, it's coming to me that neither one of them can swim. So I reckon the ferry's safe. Lem and me are ready, Reed, and so's Billy. Let's go!"

Slowly the horses moved out of the willows and into the slightly lighter darkness of the slickrock ledges to the east, Jody Lyman groaning even in his unconsciousness. It was going to be a long and terrible ride, they all knew, but at least they were on their way.

Hall's Crossing

"They ever answer you?"

Lug Santoni had come up behind Rob Paxman so quiet that the bigger man was unnerved. "How'd you do that?" he snarled. "You part Injun or something?"

"We're all part something," Lug replied quietly as he sat himself down on a small rock. Rob Paxman had a fire going, but there was nothing cooking, and Lug knew that such chores had once again been left up to him. Nor was there much in the ferryman's camp to choose from. A small sack of flour and a can of baking soda was in one of the cupboards, and in a barrel of brine was a bone with a bit of cured pork left on it.

Saying nothing, Lug mixed a little water and baking soda with some flour, set it to baking on the coals, and then sliced what little pork was to be had into a fry pan. "There ain't no coffee," he declared as he settled back onto his rock, "so I reckon river water will have to do us."

"Why, ain't that just fine!" Rob Paxman snarled. "No coffee, no horses, no women—no nothing! I'll bet it's a hundred miles to the nearest place where we can even steal something! I'll tell a man, Lug, we've got that no good Sugar Bob Hazelton to thank for this, and I intend to do it proper, first chance I get. No fooling, this is the dadblamdest streak of bad luck I ever did have! And I never have seed such a goshawful dry and forbidding country."

Rob Paxman swore again, viciously. "I figured to work on them Mormon skypilots' consciences a mite, get 'em to feeling guilty and come back acrost to help us sorry souls repent and see the light. But they ain't said nothing, so I reckon they're either holed up and waiting us out or they're already long gone on our hosses, the dirty, thieving buzzards!"

"Funny thing about the law," Lug responded amiably while he stirred the pork in the pan. "I find it passing strange how folks like us what live outside the law, always raise the most fuss and insist the loudest that good, honest folks like them Mormons acrost the river abide by every particle of it, no matter should it get 'em bushwacked by us, or not."

"Say, Lug, it ain't my fault most honest folks ain't got the brains of a medium-sized grasshopper!"

"No, Rob, I reckon it ain't, at that."

"You just wait until I get my hands on them sorry nincompoops, or on Sugar Bob Hazelton, either one! I'll learn 'em all a thing or two about crossing decent folks like you and me."

Reaching down, Lug slid the two pans from the coals, took a borrowed fork, and helped himself to maybe a third of the pork and hot bread.

"You want to wait around to get even with the whole lot of 'em?" he questioned as he began eating. "Or maybe do you want to get out of this here miserable country?"

Rob Paxman paused, a handful of steaming food halfway to his mouth. It was interesting, Lug thought, how he disdained using a fork, even when one was available. The man was so uncouth!

"You find some hosses, Lug?"

"Next best thing. I found a boat."

"I don't know nothing about boats!"

The smaller man grinned. "I do. This one's small, and it's old, but come daylight we can make some repairs and be out of here afore you know it. We'll take what food there is, and in two, three days heading downriver we're bound to find civilization of one sort or another. You game?"

Slowly Rob Paxman broke into his wide, all-encompassing smile. "As sure as a belch after a big meal, I'm game! Especially if it'll get us out of these confounded rocks!" And with that he reached down to the two pans and scooped out the remainder of Lug Santoni's pork and hot bread.

18

Sunday, October 9, 1881

The Mesa across from the Mouth of North Gulch

"Charlie, I don't think Jody can take much more."

It was not yet daylight, and the six Mormons and the recovered stock were crossing a wide, sandy bench bereft of all life but the nearly useless shad scale brush. Jody Lyman had been mostly unconscious for several hours, but when he wasn't incoherent, his constant pleas were for water and that he be allowed off his horse so he could die in peace.

Charlie Hall drew rein. "I think you're right, Lem. Trouble is, we've only come about eight miles, and that ain't much out of a hundred."

"If we force him to ride much farther, Pa, Jody'll die sure."

Charlie nodded at his son. "All right, Reed. We'll stop here, though what we'll do next is beyond me."

Sobbing in agony as he was lifted from the saddle, Jody Lyman passed out again when he was laid on the sand. Quickly Reed set out to gather some brush for a fire.

"Troubles?" Billy asked as he arrived with the horses and dismounted.

"Yeah," Lem muttered as he stood over their downed comrade. "Jody can't go much further, Billy. It isn't much of a camp, but I reckon we're going to have to stop here."

Grimacing at what he knew he was going to see, Billy squatted next to Jody and pulled aside the old shirt they had wrapped around his wound the afternoon before. "This is bad, Lem, mighty bad. She's swollen something awful."

Pulling his knife out, Lem slit Jody's trousers. Instantly the badly discolored leg ballooned outward. Jody groaned even in his unconsciousness, and tenderly Billy reached down and took his hand.

"Ain't we got any water left to wash that mess out with?" Charlie Hall was deeply affected by the gaping, putrefying wound and couldn't get past the feeling that somehow it had been his fault.

"Not if we plan on giving him anything else to drink." Lem looked to the east where the sky was growing with light. "He's emptied every canteen but one, Charlie, and that includes what was on those two yahoos' horses we managed to confiscate yesterday."

"That sun comes up, Lem, she'll turn hotter'n hades with the bellows pumping."

"Yeah, and drier'n the dust in a mummy's pocket." Lem Redd took the bedroll from behind his saddle and began gently working it under Jody's neck and head. "Thing is, the nearest water's at Lake Pagahrit, or at least the gulch this side of it. That's seven or eight miles."

"Same as back to the river."

Lem Redd nodded. "Yeah, but the trail to the lake's a whole lot easier. Charlie, either you or Reed ever been to the lake country?"

Charlie Hall shook his head.

"Lem, I'll go."

For a long moment Lem Redd regarded Billy. "No," he finally declared, "that wouldn't be too wise. Besides the fact that any one of these hosses could throw you at the next step, Billy, and maybe hurt you bad, I think you're needed with Jody. You have a way with wounded critters that the rest of us don't have, and Jody needs that as much as he needs water." What Lem didn't mention, but which was just as obvious, was that Billy Foreman, older than any of the others but Charlie Hall, was completely exhausted and practically ready to drop.

Rising, Lem loosed the saddle on his horse. "Give me fifteen, twenty minutes to sleep, boys. No, give me until the sun comes up. Meanwhile, gather every canteen you can find, and anything in those packs that might hold water. Then wake me and I'll go fetch it."

"You figure four hours?" Billy asked as he stroked the forehead of the suffering Jody Lyman.

"Between four and five, I reckon."

"H . . . hurry, Lem," Jody suddenly croaked, somehow reviving himself. "I . . . I'm in a bad way . . ."

Sand Island

It was only when Posey saw the fine new rifle in the hands of the despised Navajo Bitseel that he knew he had made the right decision. Yes, and it was as though he had made it long ago, and had spent almost every day of the past summer, preparing. Now all he needed was to somehow entice the Navajo into a game of *ducki,* at which Posey considered himself the master, so that he could break the arrogant youth and take that big gun unto himself. With a fine rifle such as that, he knew, he could not only obtain the things that would make the comely Too-rah his own, but he could also carry to the *katz-te-suah* mormonee the battle begun at the place called Boiling Springs so many months before.

All of them, Navajo and Pahute alike, were gathered together around a huge fire. There had been much feasting and much posturing, for though in general the two warlike tribes got along, there was not a lot of trust between them. That was especially true of Posey, Scotty, their father Chee, and the other followers of Moencopi Mike, he of the big mouth.

Years before, these renegade Utes had invaded the sacred homeland of Tsabekiss, his son Bitseel, and all their far-flung relatives, and had established a home of sorts on the slopes of Navajo Mountain. From there they had ranged far afield, stealing anything and everything they could from the industrious Navajo, and delighting in it. In turn the Navajo had despised all of Mike's band of Pahutes as lazy, indolent dogs—thieving abusers of fine animals, who were not at all worthy of being called human.

This antagonism had resulted a year or so before in a huge sing, an Enemy Way ceremony in which Bitseel had been the scalp shooter and which was designed to end Posey's life and to drive the remainder of Mike's band away from Navajo Mountain forever. Though Posey hadn't died, word of the hostile ceremony had reached him, and he had scorned it, as had his father and the others. Coincidentally, and surely it was only that, the Mormons had come into the country at that time, and Mike's band of warriors had almost instantly abandoned the mountain in favor of life near the unfinished fort on the San Juan. Tsabekiss, Bitseel, and the other members of their two clans saw this abandonment of Navajo Mountain a bit differently, of course, and were awed by the power of their big sing.

In spite of these differences, the two tribes, and their many bands and clans, continued to form occasional alliances with each other against their more wealthy neighbors, the whites. And once each year they gathered together at the ford over the big river near Sand Island, only a couple of miles downstream from where the Mormons had inadvertently settled, and there they sang, danced, boasted, traded—and most of all—gambled.

Posey, of course, knew all of this and considered none of it. Big in his mind had grown the thought of that fine rifle held carelessly in the hands of Bitseel, and except for occasional and fleeting thoughts of also keeping Too-rah from the Navajo youth, that rifle was the only thing in Posey's mind. He was going to obtain it for himself, and while he was about it, he thought grimly, he was going to show the upstart Bitseel a thing or two about both the general and specific superiorities of Pahute culture or the lack thereof.

Sand Island

Posey's appearance, across the big council fire on Sand Island, was almost enough to make Bitseel smile. In fact if it had not been for the diligent training of his uncle he would have smiled, and thus betrayed his consummate scorn and hatred for the short, ugly young Pahute. But Bitseel did not smile, did not betray his disdain for the young man with the strange, gaudy appearance.

"Do you remember that ugly little rooster?" he asked Hoskanini Begay as he twitched his lips in the direction of Posey.

"Ahh, the little one with the tongue of *tłíish bichohí,* the rattlesnake. This day, though, you are right. He does look like an ugly little rooster. I see you fingering your new rifle. Do you think perhaps you will shoot him?"

Bitseel smirked as he lifted his rifle and glanced at it. "Shooting him would be a fate he deserves, my brother. See how he holds his head high, as though he is the only *nóódái* rooster with red cloth woven into his long, ugly braids? The only one with a fine hat or other fine clothing? *Ho!* Truly the ugly little rooster needs something, though I do not think it is a bullet. Perhaps a little plucking would lower his head a little."

Hoskanini Begay chuckled. "Yes, and perhaps a lot of plucking would lower his head a lot. Do you remember that you owe me a fine hat, my brother? That one is very worn and very dirty, but because it belongs to that little *nóódái* rooster, it would be more than sufficient to pay the debt."

"Then it shall be yours," Bitseel vowed, watching Posey without seeming to see him, a fine trick shown him by his wise uncle before he had been stricken so terribly. And thus he was aware that Posey was also watching him. Or rather, Posey was watching his rifle. That startled Bitseel, and for the first time he noted that the young Pahute was unarmed.

For a few moments he played with Posey, handing his new rifle to first one man of the *Diné* and then another, each time acting as if he were giving the weapon away. And each time he could see very clearly the young Pahute's lust for the weapon he had so easily plucked from the sand two days before.

"He wants this rifle," he said to Hoskanini Begay as he kept his well-trained eyes on what was happening near the fire. "Since that is so, we will offer it to him."

"What? But I thought—"

Bitseel now smiled, but only slightly. "I will show it to him plainly, my brother, and at the same time I will show him a pack of cards. It is in my mind that the little rooster will agree very quickly to sit across a blanket from me."

"If you are right," the other Navajo youth stated, now understanding, "then the blanket to spread between you is here on my arm."

Sand Island

"Ho, my brother. The *poo-ye,* the eye of our enemy, is on us."

Posey, who had cleaned his fine, bright shirt and beaded leather leggings and moccasins as best he could in preparation for this moment, glanced across the assembled crowd toward the despised Navajo. He had not yet actually looked at him, but had instead been focusing his mind, trying to come up with a way of enticing the foolish one into a game of *ducki,* of cards. For the entire past summer he had been sharpening his wits and his skills at such games of chance on the lush heights of Elk Mountain, *ni-a-witch,* gambling with anyone who would play against him, and he was more than ready to take on this insufferable Navajo upstart who was both his enemy and his rival. *Oo-ah,* yes! As an up-and-coming chief over what would soon be his own band, Posey was indeed ready to trim this detestable Navajo in the way he had long dreamed of doing. The trouble was, he had been able to think of no way to entice the other into a game between the two of them alone—

Sand Island

Bitseel made his eyes wide and innocent, as though he were full of questions and doubts. Next he looked directly at Posey, as though seeing him for the first time, and when the other had finally raised his eyes from Bitseel's rifle to meet his gaze, Bitseel hesitantly showed the Pahute a pack of face cards with the king of hearts showing clearly as the bottom card.

For an instant the Pahute's eyes grew wide with surprise. Then they narrowed with scheming, and once again Bitseel almost laughed. This plucking was going to be *doo nantlá,* he could see now, much easier than he had expected!

———o—o—o———

Sand Island

"*Ho,*" Posey said to the Navajo youth as he made the signs of talking with his hands, "you look a little bored, my friend."

Bitseel eyed him narrowly. "And if I am?" he signed back.

"I saw that you have the white man face cards." Posey was being coy with his fluid hand-signs, for he did not want Bitseel to know how badly he wanted this thing to come to pass. "Unfortunately, I am not very skilled in the use of the cards. There is little time in our lives for such things as *ducki*."

Posey noted the sudden interest in the Navajo's eyes, and it was all he could do to keep the smile from his own dark countenance. This was working out better than he had hoped it would work out—much better! Soon that fine rifle would be his, and he and the comely Too-rah . . .

———o—o—o———

Sand Island

"Go and bring the others," Bitseel said to Hoskanini Begay as he took the folded blanket from him. "They will *baa bil honeeni,* they will find joy in watching this *nóódâi* rooster being plucked. Yes, and bring the little Pahute girl along with you."

"The *asdzâni* who has been riding with us these past few days? The *ch'ikééh,* the young woman who has been made available for marriage by her smelly brother?"

Bitseel smiled at his cousin's surprise. "She is not being brought for my sake, my brother. As I have told you in the past, I have no interest in that one. But I have heard that our ugly little *nóódâi* rooster finds her quite appealing. Bring her, but don't show her until we have plucked him thoroughly. *Ak'i'diishtiih?* Do you understand?"

Hoskanini Begay made the sign that he understood. And then, smiling widely with anticipation, he turned away to do his cousin's bidding.

Sand Island

"Do you have a blanket?" Posey asked his younger brother in sotto voce.

"I do not, my brother. But the Navajo appears to have one. See it there on his arm?"

Posey looked, and for an instant warning bells sounded distantly in his mind. But with a slight shrug the warnings were silenced, he made the sign that he was ready, and moments later the two young men were seated across the blanket from each other in a thick stand of willows. There they would be undisturbed, and there this drama could play out to its appropriate finish. Scotty sat slightly behind his older brother, and around Bitseel sat several other Navajo youths, obviously his friends. And though this was supposed to be a friendly game, not one of them, Navajo or Pahute, was smiling!

Bluff Fort

"I do wish the men would get back," Eliza declared as she and Annie returned to their cabins, little Willy dragging his feet along between them. Worship services were now over until after chores in the evening, and for a day of rest that was normally filled with light-hearted visiting, a somber mood had settled over the fort.

"Before he left, the bishop said that nobody expected word from them here at the fort for at least another week," Annie replied quietly.

"It . . . it just seems like there is so much danger, so much evil around us. Isn't it ever going to end?"

Annie smiled bravely. "One day it will, Eliza. We've been promised that by the Brethren, so we know it will happen.

Meanwhile, we're all so pleased to have those candles completed. It's nice to have something go right, wouldn't you say?"

"Yes," Eliza chuckled without much mirth, "I suppose it is. But I . . . Willy, child, you stop trying to pull away from me this instant! This is Sunday, and you will not be chasing after the Mackelprangs' chickens. Nor Josh Stevens's pig, either one. Besides, it's nap time, and you and I both need the rest!"

"Willy's getting to be a handful," Annie declared as she and Eliza fought the now screaming and ranting child.

"And how!" Eliza exclaimed in frustration. "Between his freedom-loving spirit and his terrible tantrums when he doesn't get just exactly what he wants, well, I swan! I just don't know what gets into him. I almost wonder if it isn't the devil."

Annie nodded as they led the shrilly screaming Willy through Eliza's door and toward his sleeping pallet. "All right, Willy," she warned, "you might as well stop this nonsense because you are not going out to play. Let's get these shoes off, and get you tucked in—"

"He goes to sleep amazingly quickly," Annie offered a few moments later when Willy's sobbing little frame had grown still.

"So would we all, happen we approached life with as much gusto as Willy does." Sinking back into her rocker, Eliza sighed deeply. "Fact is, Annie, anymore I go to sleep faster than him. He's wearing me out."

"Folks do say you have changed a lot, Eliza—"

Eliza smiled sadly. "Yes, I've gone from exhibiting or manifesting one weakness, to displaying another. I have to admit, I'm tired, and I'm discouraged. I haven't thought of it like this before, but I'm beginning to believe Satan is using Posey and most everything else in this country to cause me to want to abandon my mission. Fear has now become my greatest weakness, and I feel certain the devil knows it and is doing all he can to capitalize on it. Every time I submit to my fears, therefore, I give him more power over me."

"You really believe that's how Satan works against us?"

"Well, at least some of the time. I recollect Billy once saying that Satan's favorite method is whatever works. For instance, Mary's rebellion at her father's blessing worked against her, and my unreasonable fear has been working against me. I'm afraid, Annie, that the devil knows each of us well enough to work against us individually—or as Billy said—to do whatever works."

"Frightening, isn't it?"

"Yes, and I believe it gets worse. The more I study and pray, the more convinced I become that these satanic assaults against Mary and me and everyone else are not random acts by some wandering spirit that merely chanced upon us."

"What do you mean, Eliza?"

"I give it as my opinion that Satan assigns his forces to afflict and torment man just as we assign block teachers to help men and women become better—and demands one hundred percent participation out of them when he does it!"

"Do you think so?"

"Well, he never did believe in agency, so why should he give the freedom of choice to any of his followers today? I'm certain that's part of the hell of being under Satan's power or control—the buffetings of Satan, the scriptures call it.

"Anyway, I would imagine that the devil singles out a small child and instructs one or more of his evil spirits to watch and be ready to report whatever weaknesses that small individual manifests as he or she grows older. Then he waits."

"That's a horrible thought!"

Eliza nodded. "Yes. Horrible enough, hopefully, to motivate us as parents and Latter-day Saints to teach our children correctly and thoroughly, thus enabling them to have the power to overcome Satan as they grow older.

"Sadly," Eliza continued, "many of us don't teach our children like we should. And for that—for the unnecessary suffering our children will experience because we have not taught them thoroughly enough—I believe we will be held accountable. And that possibility, Annie, is truly frightening!"

"But, what should children be taught?"

Eliza smiled tiredly. "In a hundred different ways, they must be taught that righteousness is the only way to combat Satan, and that sincere repentance is the only way to achieve righteousness. And, we must show our children how we feel about our teachings by the righteous way we live. Satan begins working against them at such a tender age that it will take every ability we have, every ounce of priesthood power we can muster, to pull our families through this mortal experience without losing them."

"Wait a minute," Annie pleaded, looking more perplexed than ever. "I didn't think Satan had power over little children until they turned eight years of age."

Shaking her head while reaching for her copy of the Doctrine and Covenants, Eliza disagreed. "Actually, Annie, the scripture states that little children are not accountable for their sins until they reach the age of eight years. It never states that they can't commit sins, or that Satan can't entice them.

"Again, this is my opinion, but it seems to me that Satan begins his onslaught against each of us as quickly and as early in our lives as he possibly can—the moment we are capable of using agency to choose evil over good. Here in the twenty-ninth section of the Doctrine and Covenants the Lord says: 'But behold, I say unto you, that little children are redeemed from the foundation of the world through mine Only Begotten; Wherefore, they cannot sin, for power is not given unto Satan to tempt little children, until they begin to become accountable before me.' Did you catch that, Annie? '. . . until they *begin* to become accountable . . .' In other words, accountability appears to be a process, not an event, and so is being afflicted and tempted by Satan a process. Those who have reared children have told me they have noticed occasional, though very definite, satanic tendencies or behavior patterns in them, often long before they reach the age of eight years."

"My goodness, Eliza; that *is* a frightening thought!"

"It is. But it must also be remembered that little children are whole from the foundation of the world. They are redeemed through Jesus Christ, and cannot sin. I've been praying about this for days, and I believe it means that Christ grants unto all little children, up until the time when they have become fully accountable—about age eight—a thorough cleansing. And this is granted no matter what they have done prior to that time; for until they become fully accountable, their actions cannot be counted to them as sin. Made clean and pure and whole through the blood of Christ, little children are redeemed from the sins of the world, including whatever they might have done before the age of accountability that was not right. I believe that is what is meant by Satan having no power over them.

"After the age of eight, however, they are held accountable, and through the exercise of their own agency and their choosing of evil rather than good, they can become wholly subject to the power of the devil."

"I know Willy isn't yet two, but have you seen such tendencies in him?" Annie asked.

Eliza shook her head. "Not really, other than his terrible temper tantrums. If that's where they come from, then of course it is my responsibility to help him get past them."

Annie chuckled. "If that's the case, maybe I don't want children after all!"

"I'm not sure I blame you. This is terribly sobering! When I think of Willy's anger and contention, I recall the night of Mary's father's blessing, when the Lord promised her a child if she would support Kumen's call to enter into plural marriage. Why, she must have had an entire legion of those evil spirits with her that night! No wonder Kumen needed to rebuke Satan from her as he did.

"Worse, I think of my own behavior on our trek, and more importantly I think of the fear that fills my breast every time I see Posey and others of his ilk. Could that be spirits of fear that are troubling me, do you think?"

"I suppose, just as it could be spirits of anger and murder that are driving Posey, taking advantage of his natural weaknesses to destroy his soul and yours at the same time."

Eliza's eyes opened wide. "Glory be, Annie, that's something I have never thought of. Well, well, well! What an interesting idea! That satanic spirits might be the force behind Posey's anger. I'm going to have to do some praying about that idea, too."

Sand Island

"Are these *wahker* good enough for you?" Posey asked with a hissing sound as he tossed onto the blanket a handful of brass cartridges.

Instantly Bitseel made the sign of agreement, and soon his own handful of cartridges lay before him. Next he awkwardly shuffled the cards and clumsily began dealing them, indicating as he did so that he wanted to play a popular game the white cowboys called *cooncan*.

With a shrug Posey made the sign of agreement, though his heart was pounding with joy. This was one of the very games at which he had learned to excel, and now he knew without a doubt that everything this troublesome Navajo owned, including the fine rifle, would soon be his.

Back and forth the dealing went, each of the young men intent upon his play, and gradually the pile of cartridges shifted until at length Posey had them all. Bitseel's expression was pained as he gazed at his losses, but Posey was having the time of his life, and he lost no opportunity to jab his opponent.

"*Wahker topic-quay?*" he sneered. "Is your brass all gone? *Peshadny?* Have you nothing to say, *pu-neeh?*"

In answer Bitseel only looked more pained, more sorrowful. Haughtily Posey reached into the leather bag that hung from his neck and drew forth a handful of small silver change—white man money that he had gathered at the burning cabin in Colorado many months before.

Cursing under his breath, Bitseel turned to one of those with him, and soon a pile of small silver change that appeared about equal to Posey's pile lay on the blanket before him. Again the cards were awkwardly shuffled and dealt by the Navajo, and his luck did not get any better.

"*To-ege-shump!*" Posey sneered delightedly as he gathered in the last of Bitseel's pile of small change. "You are certain to lose! *Pe-nun-ko,* in the future, you would do well to remember that it is I who am *ne-ab,* I who am the great chief."

His face now dark with anger and grief, Bitseel made the sign to the Navajo to his left, and in an instant there were five silver dollars spread out on the blanket before him.

This much wealth startled Posey, but he recovered nicely and with great fanfare withdrew his own silver dollars and the two blood-stained greenbacks he had once offered the tall white woman for her clock—the two greenbacks that, with the dollars and the change, represented the sum total of his liquid assets. This money he defiantly tossed onto his own pile of silver and cartridges, and the Navajo made the sign that the amount was acceptable.

Deftly Posey shuffled the deck, allowed the Navajo youth to cut it, shuffled again, and then dealt—and in a moment his hand had won one of the five silver dollars. Bitseel glowered as Posey reached out and scooped it in, and for a moment Posey thought the other youth was about to quit the game. He had gathered up his other four silver dollars as well as his fine rifle, and the way his body was tensing, Posey was certain he was about to leave.

Instantly Posey pushed his pile of small change, and the silver dollar he had just won, back toward the center of the blanket. Then, to show his true good faith as well as his sincere understanding of Bitseel's bad luck with the game of *cooncan,* he indicated that he might be willing to try a hand of *monte* instead.

For a moment Bitseel hesitated, thinking deeply. But then with a sigh of resignation he dropped his four remaining silver dollars onto Posey's pot, and signed that he would be willing to try just one hand of *monte*—if Posey would go slow while he learned the nature of the game.

Posey, feeling as though he were about to burst he was so pleased—for after all, *monte* was the one game at which he truly excelled—waited patiently while the hapless Navajo fumbled with the cards and finally got them dealt properly. For a few moments then Posey toyed with the other, adding one of his two greenbacks to the pile and studying his cards as though he was unhappy with what he had been dealt.

For his part Bitseel was continuing to struggle, seeking directions from first one friend and then another, and setting all of them to arguing in their foolish tongue over what he should do. Finally, and very hesitantly, he took two more silver dollars from his friend and placed them in the center of the blanket.

Almost laughing, Posey matched the bet and then raised with the remainder of his cash, knowing that in a moment all of the money would be his, and that he could then go after the fine, big rifle gripped in the whitened knuckles of his adversary.

Calling, Posey watched the trembling Navajo spread out his cards, and with a triumphant smile he spread his own. In the same motion he reached for the pile of wealth, and was just starting to scoop it toward him when Bitseel reached out and spread more widely his cards, revealing a card Posey had not seen clearly a moment before—a card that now made it obvious to everyone that, somehow, the foolish Navajo had won.

With an expression of amazed joy on his face, Bitseel scooped the money out of Posey's hands and toward himself, still looking from one to another of his friends for continued instructions.

Dumbfounded, Posey took the cards and shuffled them vigorously, expertly. Back into the center of the blanket went the pile of cartridges, the youth of the *Dinế* cut the deck, and then Posey reshuffled and dealt the cards. In an instant, it seemed, the cartridges were also in front of the excited Bitseel, and Posey found himself snarling at Scotty to give him whatever money his younger brother might have.

Soon three more silver dollars, Scotty's entire fortune, were before Posey, and now he was demanding that he and Bitseel return to the game of *cooncan*. Reluctantly, the Navajo agreed, the cards were dealt, and before he had time to hardly even think of what was happening, Posey realized that all three of his brother's silver dollars were stacked on top of the pile of the amazingly lucky Navajo.

"Do you have any more silver? Any greenbacks at all?" Posey snarled at his squirming brother.

Quickly Scotty signaled that he did not, and now Posey was in a quandary. Here he was, in the middle of the biggest, most important game of his life, and suddenly he was both broke and humiliated! Somehow this inept and foolish Navajo had managed to have two good hands in a row, and this after hours of never managing to win a thing. Such luck shouldn't continue—it absolutely couldn't!

Again the warning bells sounded distantly in Posey's mind, and again he put them to silence. He wouldn't let this game end here! He just couldn't! Not with that fine big rifle sitting there so tantalizingly close, and with all his dreams of himself and the comely Too-rah so near to perfect fulfillment. To him this was more than a game—it was instead a great and terrible battle, and he must win! He must take back his money that the Navajo skunk had somehow managed to win, and he must cut some eyeteeth for this upstart enemy by taking his rifle and everything else he owned!

Only, he had no more money—

The Mesa across from the Mouth of North Gulch

"How far do you think Hyrum's got to?"

An exhausted but diligent Lem Redd, seated beside the suffering Jody Lyman, wondered that he and Billy could be thinking so exactly the same thoughts. Of course he had no idea, but he thought that, had it been him instead of Hyrum Perkins, he'd be at the fort by now and already on his way back. But every man was different, not alone in their endurance but in how they treated their mounts and for that matter how their mounts responded to them. Lem had grown up on horseback, and both Hy and Ben Perkins, colliers from the mines of Wales, had hardly ridden at all before emigrating to America. That would have given Lem an advantage, at least as far as riding went. On the other hand, the Perkins boys, both of them, were small but wiry and amazingly strong, and Lem suspected that their endurance might even be greater than his own. Certainly they had wielded both single and doublejacks almost without ceasing as they had cut out the Hole-in-the-Rock, and he had never been able to stay close to them in that department. It was—

"To my way of thinking, he should be on his way back by now."

Lem nodded. "I agree, Billy. There's also the possibility that he ran into somebody from the fort long before he got there; somebody with a wagon. That'd put him closer than ever."

"Now that's an interesting thought." Reed Hall, who was seated just a few feet away, studied the wounded man. "You boys think he'll last through another night?" he asked.

"Of course he'll last!" Lem replied with an easy lie, in case Jody was aware enough to understand him. "He knows Nellie is waiting back home for him, and he won't be abandoning her now. By the by, Reed, it was good thinking of you and your pa to stretch this blanket over Jody while I was gone. Sun's been hot enough today to singe the hide off a Gila monster. I reckon the heat might have done poor Jody in."

"It was Billy's idea. Pa and me just hauled them cedar logs back so we could drape the blanket over 'em and give Jody a little shade. Pa should be back anytime now with more logs to add to the pile I drug in a little bit ago. That way we should have wood enough to keep a fire blazing through the night."

"I hope your pa found water, too." Lem Redd thought of his own exhausting ride that morning, and of how rapidly the men and horses had gone through most of the water he had hauled back from Lake Pagahrit. Of course the sun was about to set, which would cool the air considerably and ease the need for water that all of them were feeling—at least until morning. And the cool of night might even help Jody's raging fever. But truthfully Lem was starting to lose hope for his good friend.

Jody's leg was now black and purple and swollen to perhaps three times its normal size, and the wound was festering and both looked and smelled awful. Much of the time Jody was delirious, too, rattling on about Nellie as though she was still Nellie Grayson Roper, and he was trying to talk her into marrying him and traveling to the San Juan all over again. He had also been doing a lot of jabbering about his older brother, Platte, whom it seemed from his ramblings he practically worshipped.

Platte was a good man, too, Lem thought as he watched over Jody. A bit standoffish around people, maybe, and awful quick to delegate work, so he could head out into the rocks and trees for a little exploring or traveling. On the other hand he had certainly improved the road east to the Mancos, and had now made enough trips back and forth that folks in Colorado knew him by name and trusted him enough to extend credit to the citizens of Bluff—no small accomplishment since most of the Colorado citizens seemed to pretty well despise Mormons.

"Beats me how these maggots can grow so quick in a man's wound," Lem grumbled as he took a small stick and once again began flicking larvae off Jody's wound. "Of course in this heat the flesh is putrefying fast, and that does draw the flies—"

"I think I picked out a hundred of them earlier this afternoon," Billy declared quietly. "Between that, shooing flies and bathing both his wound and his forehead, I didn't do one other thing while you were gone. I would have helped with the firewood, too, but—"

"You did just right, Billy. Jody needs somebody beside him all the time, and you have a way with sick folks—"

"Not this time, I don't," Billy breathed sadly. "Tell the truth, Lem, I don't have the least foggy notion what to do next. Not alone is the putrefaction growing worse, but I've never in my life heard of a bone being shattered any worse than Jody's femur. I . . . I can't imagine how it might ever knit back together."

Lemuel nodded his agreement with Billy's thoughts, but still he refused to give in. "The thing is, when he's of a mind to, the Lord can accomplish some mighty interesting things. About all we can do, therefore, is leave it all in his hands—"

"Lem?" Jody's voice was barely above a whisper, but for the first time in hours he sounded coherent. "Any sign . . . of Hy and the wagon?"

"Not yet, Jody. We'll build a big fire tonight, though, so if he comes along in the dark he won't miss us."

"Mi . . . mighty hard to travel this country in the . . . dark, Lem. Maybe he'll come in the morning. If he doesn't . . . I . . . don't think I'm going to make it."

"Jody, don't you be talking like that. Hy'll be back, and we'll have you in that wagon and home again afore you can say scat!"

"Maybe so. But I can smell my wound, and it . . . it doesn't smell good at all. I . . . I . . . Say, boys, where do you reckon that . . . that angel is? That the Lord was . . . going to send to comfort me? The . . . one you boys promised me in . . . in that blessing down by the river?"

"I reckon he'll be along shortly," Billy declared softly as he wiped Jody's brow again. And with all his heart he was praying that he was right!

Sand Island

Abruptly Posey reached down and loosed the fine, beaded moccasins that so elegantly graced his feet. Tossing them into the center of the blanket he demanded that they be matched by their full value in silver from the cursed Navajo's pile. Quickly the bet was agreed to, the cards were cut and dealt, the hand played, and when it was over Posey had lacked one ace of spades, and the young man of the *Diné,* who no longer looked so much astonished as he did smugly pleased, was placing the fine beaded moccasins upon his own feet.

Furious, though he let no muscle of his face betray the sting this gave him, for after all he was soon to be a proud chief, Posey removed from his head the fine hat he had taken from the dead white youth on the top of Harpole Mesa during the glorious battle in the LaSals. Scant moments later Bitseel had also won it, but instead of placing it on his pile to be wagered again he simply handed it to one of his friends as payment for an old debt of some sort.

Seeing the fine hat go beyond recall was almost more than Posey could bear. The muscles of his face twitched just a little with hatred and anger, but quickly he controlled himself. He must not give his enemy the satisfaction of seeing his discomfort! He must not allow the cursed Navajo to even begin to think that he, Posey, was close to being defeated. Instead he would remain in the game, and he would show the upstart from across the big river what real *ni-a-witch,* gambling, was all about.

After quick instructions Scotty was sent running, and short moments later was back with the dead white man's exhausted pony, still carrying its saddle, empty saddlebags, and bridle.

Without even rising to examine the horse or its accoutrements more closely, Bitseel disdainfully pushed a goodly portion of his wealth to the center of the blanket. When Posey signaled that the amount was satisfactory, the cards were shuffled and dealt. Posey nearly smiled at the fine hand he had dealt himself, and he nearly choked when it turned out that he had dealt his enemy a hand just one card better. And without a word Scotty handed the reins to one of the openly grinning friends of Bitseel.

Ducki becomes a mysterious anesthetic—deadening its victim to the blows he receives in the latter part of the game and at the same time inflaming him with a wild passion to continue on and win at all hazards. Dazed but still certain that he was going to triumph over this tall Navajo youth, Posey undid a couple of buttons and peeled off his beautifully brilliant red shirt—the one with the bullet hole so obvious in the front of it. Without a word or even a hint of a smile the son of the Navajo Tsabekiss took it, looked it over, put it back in the center of the blanket with a fairly large sum of silver, and easily won the pot.

Now more than half-naked, Posey stared in stony silence while Bitseel gathered shirt and silver unto himself. Glancing covertly around to make certain that none of his people save he and his younger brother, Scotty, were there to see his humiliation, Posey was relieved to see that nothing was stirring in the willows, not in any direction. Even better, the sun was far down the slope of the western sky, and if perchance he lost again—though he knew with certain surety that he wouldn't—he could at least escape into the darkness without Poke or his favorite little sister seeing his shame.

For long moments Posey considered the wagering of all he had left in the world—his fringed buckskin leggings with the fine and intricate beadwork down the sides. They were marvelous leggings, beautifully stitched and fit only for the proudest chief. More importantly, they were all Posey had left of his glorious newfound self—the dashing, dandy hero over which the more than alluring Too-rah had lost her lovely head. How would she respond if he should appear without them? Would she mock him, or laugh him to scorn? Surely her brother, the foul-tempered grizzly, would laugh and mock! But would Too-rah?

But what was he worrying about? This streak of winning being enjoyed by the cursed Navajo was just that—a lucky streak, a fluke! It was about to end, and no one knew that better than the young Pahute who would soon be chief. He had never suffered such a lengthy losing streak, and he knew that this coming hand would turn the tide. Then the cursed Bitseel would be humiliated properly, and afterward all things would work out for Posey, just as they had in his dreams.

Carefully he peeled off the fine leggings, and as he folded them neatly and laid them in the center of the blanket, his mind and heart were filled with hope and hate and the blackest of curses that he was mentally hurling at his impassive antagonist.

Naked now except for his breechcloth, Posey waited for the fumbling shuffle that had always been the best that Bitseel could manage. But no, something had now changed, something that Posey could not begin to comprehend. Picking up the deck of cards from the blanket, the Navajo youth, his movements almost fluid they were so smooth, expertly spread them in a beautiful fan. Instantly then he closed the deck, did a one-hand cut, riffled the deck, and handed it across to Posey.

"Cut them," he signaled.

Hardly breathing, Posey reached out and slowly cut the deck.

Almost without looking Bitseel restacked the cards, spread them in another perfect fan, closed it and did another one-handed cut, riffled the deck once, and then dealt the cards.

Still hardly breathing he was so astonished, so fearful, Posey reached, hesitated, and then withdrew his hand.

"*Ma'iichaan!*" Bitseel snarled with a look of utter disdain. "Coyote dung!"

Though Posey couldn't understand the words, he understood the meaning well enough, and so, steeling his nerves as best he could, he reached out and took the terrible cards in his trembling hands. Surely, his mind screamed, this would be a hand he could work with. Surely—

Yes! Already he could see that the cards he had been dealt were good. Almost perfect, in fact. Almost unbeatable! Hope rose in his breast as he called for, and miraculously received, the two additional cards he was certain he wanted. Yes! This was it! This was the hand that had eluded him, that he had been waiting for, the hand that would end the untimely run of luck enjoyed by his adversary. This was it!

Yet when the hand was called, he was somehow short a jack of hearts, and the fine, beaded leggings made their way across the blanket and onto the amazing pile of wealth that had been accumulated by the Navajo who no longer seemed quite so bumbling as Posey had first thought him to be.

For an instant there was absolute silence, and then the face of the youthful son of Tsabekiss slowly relaxed and broke into a wide grin. "*Hacoon!*" he urged tauntingly. "Come on!" Surely Posey had one more thing left that he could offer on the altar of his pride—a ring, a bracelet, perhaps some little trinket he had forgotten? With a flourish the youthful Navajo took up his big rifle and held it out for Posey's hungry eyes to see. One more hand of *cooncan,* he taunted, or even of *monte,* and he, Bitseel, would wager his fine new rifle against whatever Posey might place on the blanket. "*Hacoon!* Come on!"

Surely, the inflamed mind of Posey reasoned while he looked from the rifle to the pile of silver topped with two bloodstained greenbacks and the princely apparel stacked nearby, there was a devil in the *ducki!* There had to be, for never had he been so badly beaten, not since the grizzly Poke and his brother Hatch . . .

In a stupor of doubt and fear, the naked Posey stared about. It was not yet dark, but somehow he must keep out of sight until then, for who knew where the comely Too-rah might be wandering. Why, if she should happen to see him in the midst of his desperate humiliation . . .

Sand Island

"*Hacoon,*" Bitseel sneered again as Posey stared down at himself, naked now except for his breechcloth. "Come on! Surely there is something else of value that you wish to give us men of the *Dinê*."

Of course he knew that Posey did not understand his language, and so while those about him laughed and enjoyed this fine joke, he signed the same thing. The absurdity was, that the little Pahute fool actually wanted to continue. He still thought that he could defeat the great Bitseel. And so he sat there, his feeble mind trying to think of something else he could place in the center of the blanket.

"It is time for us to bring forward the *nóódâi ch'ikêêh,*" Bitseel said to the chuckling Hoskanini Begay. "It will be good for her to see this little rooster so thoroughly plucked. Is she close by?"

"She is near," his cousin responded with anticipation. "I will bring her."

"*Hacoon!*" Bitseel sneered again as Hoskanini Begay disappeared into the willows. "Come on! Surely you have some little thing you wish to wager. Some ring or other silver, perhaps a few coins, or even some cartridges. After all, without a rifle they can do you no other good."

The nearly naked Posey sat without moving, his eyes upon the blanket. Though he did not perfectly understand his words, Bitseel knew that the Pahute knew quite well what was being said. He also knew the youth's mind was still inflamed with the desire to win, to find some way . . .

"Here," Bitseel said maliciously as Hoskanini Begay returned, dragging the unsuspecting Too-rah by the arm, "I will throw in with my rifle this *ch'ikééh,* this young girl, against anything that you can think of to wager." And with that he pulled Too-rah down onto the blanket in front of the youth whose heart she had already won.

For an instant it was as though Posey did not recognize her. But then as their eyes met, his own eyes widened, his face darkened with humiliation and shame to be seen in such circumstances, and even as Too-rah was ducking her head to prevent him further embarrassment, Posey gave a strangled cry and leaped to his feet.

All the Navajos were laughing now, making a mocking of him as Posey stumbled away from the blanket and into the willows. And big in Posey's mind was the certain knowledge that the comely *nanzitch* Too-rah would never look at him in the same way again. Never would she see him as he truly was—a fierce and proud warrior of the People. Instead she would see only a naked man, reduced to nothing and humiliated in front of the cursed *Dinè*.

Unless, his frantic mind cried out, he could somehow redeem himself. *Oo-ah,* yes, if he could just come up with something of even grander proportions than his lost garb. Somewhere he must liberate some clothing from their current owner, the more dashing the better, and at the same time he must also acquire something to give the *nanzitch* that was so amazingly valuable that she would forever forget his temporary defeat and humiliation. For of a sudden, Posey was certain that this setback was just that—only temporary. If he could only think of a perfect gift . . .

And it was in that instant, while he was still stumbling almost blindly through the willows, that Posey thought once again of *tabby-nump,* the tall white woman's clock.

Sand Island

As the noise of Posey's heedless flight through the willows gradually diminished, Bitseel nodded with satisfaction. *Aoo,* yes, he thought smugly as he released the girl Too-rah and waved her off to continue with her own affairs, there were certain ways of destroying a man that were far more effective, and certainly more delightful, than merely putting a bullet into him!

Now, he thought, he must find that *belacani* gunman with the notch in his boot, the one who had done such unspeakable evil to his younger sister.

19

Monday, October 10, 1881

Harmony Flat

"You see okay, Josh?"

"Not hardly a lick," Joshua Stevens called into the predawn darkness ahead. "I can make out the team, Hy, but I can't see you at all. And the only way I know the spare team behind us is following, is because I can hear them. As Lem might say, it's so dark tonight all the bats stayed home."

Hyrum Perkins chuckled. "That sounds like him and Pap Redd both, for they seem to be cut of the same cloth. I think this is Harmony Flat, though in the dark it be difficult to tell. Hit any stumps, have you?"

"One or two, but not straight on. The horses seem to be steering clear of them."

"I've given mine her head, too. These animals can somehow see in the dark, where we can't. And since this old mare just went over this trail, it would seem she knows where she is going. I think we should change teams at Cow Tanks, though, and leave the used animals there to rest up."

"Sounds good to me, as long as we can keep going. From what you said, I would expect Jody's in a bad way."

"He was when I left, Josh. Mighty bad. I'm just thankful you and the Barton brothers were there in the Butler getting out that load of firewood. You being willing to come back with me without notifying Elizabeth, cut practically a day off the trip."

"Any of us would have come, Hy. I was just the most free."

"With you taking off like this, will Elizabeth be all right?"

"She'll be fine," Joshua responded. "She may be young, but she's tough as nails and doesn't need me to tell her what to do."

Hyrum smiled into the darkness. "It's interesting, all right, what this wild San Juan country is doing to our women."

"It is—about the same as another wilderness did to the women of the Book of Mormon. Now that I think on it, tough as nails pretty well describes all of them."

"It does at that, Josh. It surely does!"

In the silence between the two men that followed, the wagon continued creaking and bouncing forward through the slowly graying dawn toward Jody's agony.

The Mesa across from North Gulch

The elderly Navajo headman, who was called Pahlilly, glanced at the bright morning sky. *Jeeshóó,* buzzards, were still circling above the mesa that rose to his left. Nervously he fingered his *jish,* the medicine bundle that hung about his neck, almost unconsciously seeking the protection that he knew was there.

Pahlilly didn't like these birds of death; no man of the *Diné* liked them. And no man of the People liked being around those who had died. Death to the *Diné* was a great ending of things, a great ending of the *hózhó,* the balance, that a man worked all his lifetime to achieve. And always these huge birds signaled that death was stalking the earth somewhere beneath where they circled.

Yet there was something else on that mesa, something Pahlilly didn't fully understand, that had been drawing him closer ever since he had first seen the circling *jeeshóó* not long after first light. Nor could he explain it to the men who rode with him—his son and several others of his born-for clan who had attended the Sing. All he could do, therefore, was lead out until he understood what he was feeling; that, and nod his head with satisfaction that these others were willing to follow where he rode.

As with most of the mesas in this far-off desert country that existed between the two big rivers, the lower slopes of this one were littered with boulders, both huge and small, that in times past had broken from the caprock and tumbled downward. Working his way through them, Pahlilly found and then followed an animal trail upward, his horse carefully picking the way. It was not much of a trail, an occasional wearing thin of the soil where deer or perhaps a bighorn sheep or two had once passed. Yet to Pahlilly it was enough, and after a time he arrived, as he had known he would, at a narrow gap in the caprock through which his horse could scramble to the mesa top. There might be other such gaps, he thought as he dismounted to lead his horse, but they would be very difficult to find. And perhaps they did not exist at all. So, yes, it was a good thing to trust the wisdom of these *dini',* these animals who were as brothers to the People.

"Ho, my brother," his cousin who carried the war name of Hashké yíkaayá, He Went after the Warrior, questioned, "why is it that you chase after these birds of death?"

"I do not chase the *jeeshóó,*" Pahlilly replied mildly as he remounted and glanced up the gradual slope above the caprock to where the mesa apparently leveled off. "It is what they stalk that *bíníshkad,* I chase."

"Do you sense an enemy? The *belacani,* or perhaps the *nóódái?*"

For a moment Pahlilly sat his horse, considering. The heat of the morning was already strong, and in the distance two dust devils danced near each other—the Hard Flint Boys playing tricks on the Wind Children. Pahlilly watched the dancing columns of dust without seeing, his mind in another place.

"What lies upon this mesa may indeed be *nihe énaí,* our enemies," he replied to Hashké yíkaayá. "Yet I sense no danger; no, not to any of the *Diné.*"

"Still," the man questioned, "it might be a wise thing for us to have our weapons ready?"

Soberly Pahlilly made the sign of agreement. "That would indeed be wise, my brother."

Quietly the word was passed, each of the warriors made ready, and soon the group was following up a shallow wash toward the mostly flat top of the mesa.

Bluff Fort

"Excuse me, Charlie." Joseph Barton had removed his hat and was standing a little awkwardly inside Charlie Walton's open door, where a number of the Saints had gathered for their daily assignments. As clerk, and the only member of the bishopric left in the fort, Charlie had been given that responsibility.

Joseph and his brother Amasa had gone to the Butler late in the afternoon of the day before, to get out a last load of firewood that they had cut and left standing. Joshua Stevens, only hours home from his mail run to Colorado, had offered to go with them and assist their efforts. They had loaded the wood and had been on their way back to the fort when they had been overtaken on the road by the frantic Hy Perkins.

"Yes, Joseph? What is it?"

His hat in his hand, Joseph Barton glanced around the room. "I . . . I'm terribly sorry to report this, but there's been a shooting over at Hall's Crossing."

The gasps from Jane Walton and a few of the others were audible, and Joseph hurried on, not wishing to add to their worrying. "Nobody's been killed, but that lean-brained outlaw Rob Paxman and that other fellow who was with him have shot Jody Lyman in the leg, just above the knee, and Hy Perkins says he's in a terrible bad way."

With a strangled cry, nineteen-year-old Nellie Lyman buried her face in her hands. Jody's mother, her face looking stricken, reached over and drew her daughter-in-law close. "Nellie," she ordered the sobbing young woman, "you be strong, you hear? Jody will be fine!"

Quickly Mother Lyman then turned to Walter Lyman, Jody's and Platte's half brother. "Walter, you go fetch Platte. He'll be somewhere on the road between here and Durango."

"Yes'm." Eighteen-year-old Walter Lyman instantly started for the door.

"Walt," Joseph stated quietly, "Amasa'll have a good horse saddled and ready for you near the northeast gate by the time you get there. We both figured somebody would be going."

"Has someone gone after my Jody with a wagon?" Mother Lyman had shed no tears and seemed remarkably calm as she questioned Joseph Barton.

"Yes'm. Right off we emptied our wagon, and right now Josh Stevens is driving it behind Hy's lead, heading for the Crossing."

"Josh is driving the wagon?" Elizabeth Stevens was abruptly standing, her hand at her breast. Tenderly Eliza Foreman, standing next to her, reached out and took her other hand.

Joseph nodded. "Yes'm, Sister Elizabeth. He insisted, and since he fears nothing on this green earth—well, we were going to draw straws about who should go, but you know Josh. He would have none of it."

Slowly Elizabeth sank onto a chair, her eyes staring straight ahead. Her heart was pounding with sudden fear, and she was completely unaware that she was squeezing the life out of Eliza Foreman's hand.

"Hy figured it was about a hundred miles to where Lem, Billy, and Jody had stopped," Joseph continued, again addressing Charlie Walton. "Maybe a little less. Charlie and Reed Hall are with 'em, so there's plenty of help. If all goes well, and if Jody can stand the travel, they should be back here sometime Wednesday night or Thursday morning. We'd have been here sooner, too, but in the dark both our horses threw shoes, and we've had a dickens of a time ever since!"

Charlie Walton nodded. "Yes, Brother Joseph, you did fine. Brothers and sisters, it is in my heart to think that we should begin a fast, not just for Jody, but for Lem and Hy and Billy and Joshua, who will have the responsibility of bringing Jody home to us in safety. Sister Redd, will you lead us in a prayer to begin our fast?"

As Eliza Ann Redd stepped forward, Eliza Foreman was doing her best to understand her suddenly pounding heart. Something else was going to happen, she knew—something terrible that had nothing to do with Jody's being shot! To her, to Billy, to little Willy—Eliza simply couldn't tell. She just knew that something else was going to happen, for she could *feel* it!

Oh, mercy, she was thinking even as Eliza Ann was beginning her prayer, she had already lost her darling Mary Eliza! What would she do if something just as terrible happened to her darling Billy?"

The Mesa across from North Gulch

"I was mighty sorry to hear about your baby's death, Billy." Charlie Hall had just finished downing the slapjacks Billy had prepared for breakfast. "Losing younguns is almighty tough for any parent, but moreso on the women. Or at least that's how it seems."

Somehow Jody Lyman had lived through the night, but he was delirious again and growing rapidly more weak, and even with water and the blanket draped above him giving shade, Billy didn't think the wounded man could survive another day. And that was even if Hy Perkins somehow made it back with a wagon. Yet all of them had to do what they could, which for now was just continue to wait.

Now Billy stared off across the fire, his thoughts drawn away from the nearly dead Jody Lyman and back to the fort and to his suffering wife. "Eliza's had a rough summer," he admitted, "losing some dear friends in that Indian battle up at Pinhook Draw in the LaSals and then our baby. It surprises me, Charlie, but her grieving has been worse for her to get past than the whooping cough."

"Ma says women wear their grieving out in the open while men don't, so the women get over it better." Reed Hall looked up at Billy. "Folks do say Sister Foreman is coming along pretty well, though."

"You keep that close of tabs on us?" Billy was surprised.

"You're a friend," Charlie stated simply.

Billy nodded his appreciation. "Well, I don't think Eliza's over it, at least not yet. But she's a strong woman, and she'll come out of it just fine."

"The word we received at the Crossing was she had a premonition of trouble way last spring."

"She did," Billy replied quietly. "She most certainly sensed our baby's death. But more than that, I would say she also sensed the troubles we've had as a community. And of a truth, Charlie, I've never seen anything like it. Besieged on every hand by the elements as well as our thieving neighbors, I can't think of a day since early last spring when there hasn't been one crisis or another that has seemed to threaten our very existence."

"That's what we've heard," Charlie Hall agreed.

"Navajos, Pahutes, outlaws—this thing with Jody is very bad, for it is the first injury any of us has received. Now it seems our protection is not quite what any of us had thought it would be."

"Yeah, that's what surprised me, too," Lem Redd stated as he sat up from his bedroll, ready to face another grueling ride to the lake and back with what little water he could carry. "Up until now, I'd have said our worst enemy was that fool river. Or the ditch, which never seems to be finished."

"Or able to hold water even when we think it is," Billy said. Glancing at Jody, he sighed. "Jody isn't looking good, Lem."

Lemuel Redd stamped into his boots, rose to his feet, and with two steps and a snap of his wrist he roped his tired horse and quickly saddled it. "I know, Billy," he said. "But other than fetching water, I don't know what else to do."

The men grew still, and an awkward silence spread over the camp. Charlie Hall, in an effort to keep a conversation going in case Jody was listening, finally spoke. "You have any plans for the winter, Lem?"

"Probably I'll go to Colorado again and work on the railroad."

"You, Billy?"

"I don't know. Dick Butt and George Ipson are going to be sawing lumber up toward the Blue Mountain, and for a time they were pestering me to work with them."

"Pay wouldn't be as good."

Billy nodded. "I figured the same, and so I told them no—that it was a two-man job, and not three. But whatever I do, I'd like to be closer to home. The longer we're here in this country, the more frightened of the Pahutes Eliza is getting. She's especially terrified of that boy called Posey."

"He has a mean look about him," Lemuel Redd acknowledged.

Billy nodded his head. "He does. And he's only one of the reasons I'd like to stay closer to the fort. One thing I do know: I'll be almighty glad when we can control that ditch and raise some decent crops, so I can stay at home year round and be a gentleman farmer."

Lemuel Redd laughed quietly. "Well, don't hold your breath, Billy. I don't know if we'll ever beat that fool river!"

"At least it's something you can all pray for," Reed stated hopefully.

"Again," Billy breathed as he did his best to stifle a yawn. "I—"

A nearby rattling of stones alerted both Billy and Charlie Hall, and glancing up the two men saw a group of Navajo warriors riding toward them—all armed to the teeth and looking grim as death. "Lem," he breathed quietly, "we've got company."

The Mesa across from North Gulch

"They're armed, so I reckon they're a raiding party," Charlie Hall said, now standing near Billy and the suffering Jody Lyman.

"Maybe they're after our horses. Thales Haskel says the Navajo set store by good horses."

Standing beside his mount, Lem nodded. "Could be, Reed. For a raiding party, though, they're coming mighty slow and careful. More than likely they saw the buzzards, got curious, and have been following their sky-trail. Charlie, you recognize any of them?"

"The man in front looks sort of familiar, but I don't know who he is. Don't know that I've ever seen the rest of them."

Lem nodded. "All right. Reckon I'll go meet 'em, boys, and see what's up."

"Lem," Billy breathed into the stillness, "go easy. Our friend Hádapa came to raid and ended up saving Willy's life. Seems like many of the Navajo are good people, so maybe the Lord will allow the same thing to happen here."

"I was thinking that exact same thing," Lemuel acknowledged in similar quiet tones. Stepping away from his horse then, and intentionally not touching any of his weapons, the young Mormon leader walked slowly forward toward the dozen mounted men of the *Diné*.

———o—o—o———

The Mesa across from North Gulch

"There are not many of these *belacani*." The Navajo warrior who spoke was young, and in his voice was the sound of mocking. "And they do not camp wisely."

"That is so," the man whose war name was Hashké yíkaayá agreed as he glanced about the barren mesa top. Then, with a twitch of his lips, he indicated the more than a dozen horses that were grazing nearby. "But it is a wealthy camp, brothers. Very wealthy for so few *belacani*. Perhaps this wealth might be better put to use in *Diné tah,* the land of the People."

"My father, do we raid these few *belacani?*" the youthful member of the group asked.

Without looking at his son, Pahlilly regarded the three white men who were silently watching him and the fourth who was on the ground under the improvised shelter. Pahlilly, too, had noted the sparse camp, out in the open without shelter. He had also noted the tracks in the sandy earth, and from them felt confident that these four were the only *belacani* in the area. Finally he had noted the young man who had stepped forward without weapons in his hands, and who was now standing silently, waiting. He was young and either foolish or very brave, and the elderly Navajo sensed that he was not looking into the face of *nihe énaí,* an enemy.

"We do not know these *belacani,*" he replied at last.

"But they are weak, my father. They do not even hold weapons in their hands."

For the first time, Pahlilly turned from watching the white men and faced his son. "That a man does not hold a weapon in his hand, does not make him weak. Perhaps, my son, such a man displays an even greater strength, a strength that cannot be seen until it is used."

The young warrior sucked in his breath. "Is it in your mind, my father, that these *belacani* are they of whom old Dah nishuánt spoke when he gave us warning of their power—the people the *nóódâi* call mormonee?"

Turning back to look at the white men, Pahlilly made the sign that his son was correct. "It is in my mind that there is a reason why none of them have raised weapons against us," he replied softly. "I do not believe that reason is *nâszdid,* fear. Now come, my son, and let us see if we have arrived so soon at the end of our journey."

The Messa across from North Gulch

"*Ho!*" the old Navajo said as he held up his hand and looked down at Lem Redd. "Bad camp. Not good place."

Surprised that the man could speak English so well, Lem pushed back his hat and nodded. "It's a poor camp, all right. Our friend yonder, he couldn't go any further, so we just stopped. My name's Lem Redd, this man's Billy Foreman, this is Charlie Hall, and yonder is his son Reed Hall."

Slowly the Navajo nodded. "I am called Pahlilly. What wrong with man on ground?"

"He got shot—in the leg."

A ripple of interest passed through the group of Navajos, and Lem wondered how many of them were actually understanding him. Of course, if they'd been on the long walk to *Bosque Redondo* they'd spent a few years around whites, and Thales Haskel had said most of the Navajo had picked up more English than they were willing to let on.

"*Belacani* or mormonee?" the old Navajo suddenly questioned.

For a moment Lem Redd hesitated. He knew the Navajo feared the white soldiers that they called *belacani,* and most were doing their best to honor the treaty they had signed. He also knew, from sad experience as well as what Thales Haskel had explained, that the *Dinê* had little if any respect for the Mormons, calling them *'asdzáân*—old women.

But lying didn't come easily to Lem Redd, especially lying

about whether or not he was a Latter-day Saint. To him that seemed tantamount to denying his testimony, and he was not about to do that, not ever! Not even if it meant trouble or even death at the hands of these well-armed warriors.

"We're Mormon," he declared as he settled his hat back into place. "From the fort on the big river." And then he did his best to prepare himself for whatever might happen next.

The Messa across from North Gulch

Abruptly urging his horse forward past the young mormonee, Pahlilly rode to within a few feet of the blanket that sheltered the wounded man. Dismounting and leaving his weapons on his horse, he pulled the blanket aside and gazed downward.

"*Ajá ád bit a sit ání,*" he muttered, glancing at his son and the others who rode with him. "It is the bone above the knee, and it is broken in many pieces. This man is also *bitah honeezgia,* feverish, and the wound is *baa da'iilch'osh,* full of maggots."

Next he turned to Lem Redd. "What do for wound?" he asked, his deep voice filled with concern.

Lem Redd had also stepped to the side of Jody. He shook his head. "Other than washing it and keeping that wet rag around it, not much. We don't know what else to do," he admitted.

Wasting no time, Pahlilly took up an empty pot from beside the dying fire, motioned that Lemuel was to follow him, and then he started on foot across the mesa. Soon he had filled the pot with prickly pear leaves and was back at the desolate camp, where another of the Navajos had meanwhile rekindled the fire.

Working carefully, and making sure that Lemuel and Billy and the two Halls could both see and understand what he was doing, Pahlilly burned the spines from the cactus leaves and then mashed them in the pot, heating them as he did so. When all was ready he took the poultice he had made and spread it across the wound, both on top of the leg and underneath, where the bullet had emerged.

"Where water?" he asked when he had finished with the poultice.

"We're out," Lem replied grimly. "I was about to head for the lake country when you rode up."

Shaking his head with wonder, the elderly Navajo motioned for two of his men to come near. Handing them the canteens from Lem's saddle, as well as the now empty pot, Pahlilly gave almost silent instructions. Instantly the two abandoned their horses, turned, and trotted off the edge of the mesa.

"*Tó nahaltin,* it rained in this place two, three days past." Pahlilly was doing his best to educate these white people who knew so little of the ways of his country. "Water in rocks, not where sun strikes. Water stay many days."

In absolute amazement the Mormons watched as the two Navajos reappeared a short time later with the canteens and even the empty pot filled with clear water.

Taking one of the canteens, Pahlilly poured a little water into Jody Lyman's mouth, indicating to Lem Redd that it was to be done frequently but with not a lot of water.

"You speak him words of power?" he asked abruptly.

Surprised, Lem nodded. "We gave him a blessing, if that's what you mean. Several of them, in fact."

"Then he live," Pahlilly said simply as he turned back to his horse. With fluid grace he mounted and seemingly without instructions his horse pranced backward until it had assumed its position at the lead of the others.

"Thank you for your help." Lem Redd could think of nothing else to say, and he hoped the old man understood.

"Dah nishuánt tell Pahlilly, *belacani* mormonee friend," the old man declared from atop his horse, his face finally breaking into a smile. "Dah nishuánt wise. Pahlilly wise. Be friend with mormonee. Maybe mormonee speak words of power for friend."

Having little understanding of what he had just heard, but vowing to remember it and relate it to Thales Haskel when he could, Lem Redd smiled and raised his hand. And then without a backward glance he turned again to the aid of his wounded friend.

Bluff Fort

"Sister Lyman, I'm terribly sorry about what has happened to your son."

Eliza, finished with her day's work and also her chores, was finally picking up little Willy, who had spent most of the day with little Albert R. and the rest of the Lyman family. The baby-sitting was an informal arrangement, but it seemed to please the entire Lyman clan, and it gave Eliza the time she needed to accomplish all she was assigned.

For all concerned, it was a busy time of year. That day the men had finished building the icehouse, and in the morning they would fall to again, finishing the harvesting of everything they could find to harvest, including a half-dozen acres of wild hay that Platte and Dick Butt had found a few miles up Recapture. They were hopeful that would help make up for what the Navajo sheep had done to their winter range.

"The Lord has interesting ways of blessing and purifying all of us," Mother Lyman responded quietly. "Brother Joseph once received a revelation from our Redeemer stating that all things worked together for good to them that walked uprightly, and to the sanctification of the Church. Jody was always a good boy, and as a man he has never failed to walk uprightly. I am certain, therefore, that this will turn into a blessing, not only for him but for all of us."

Amazed at the strength of the elderly woman's faith, Eliza nodded. "I . . . I'm certain you are right, Mother Lyman."

For an instant then she paused, thinking of her own feelings and concerns. Again and again the terrible behavior of both Willy and Posey had come into her mind. At first upset that she was somehow linking them together, she was now beginning to realize that there was very little difference between Willy's temper tantrums, which could not be inspired by the Spirit of the Lord, and Posey's rages, which must surely come from the same evil source. And though there was also a vast age difference between her little son and Posey, was there that much difference in their understanding? Eliza didn't know, but the thought kept worrying her.

Then there was that new feeling of impending doom she hadn't been able to shake.

"Sister Foreman, you look troubled," Mother Lyman said.

Startled, Eliza sought for words to respond. "I suppose I am troubled," she finally acknowledged. "Lately I've been seeing some things—having the impression, I suppose, that Satan is working against both me and Willy, him with his temper tantrums and me with my fears. I . . . I think he might also be working with . . . others, and I don't know what to do about it—to stop evil from happening."

"Have you inquired of the Lord about it?" Sister Lyman asked abruptly.

"No." Eliza smiled wryly. "I'm afraid that I may learn something, either about me or someone else, that I don't really want to know."

"It can be a pickle, all right. Was it me, though, I believe I'd endeavor to rid myself of Satan's influence at every opportunity!"

Seeing the confusion in Eliza's eyes, Mother Lyman raised her hand. "Sister Foreman, I was present at a meeting of the Relief Society sisters in Nauvoo, in April of 1842, when Brother Joseph told us that he was about to deliver the endowment to the Church, which he did in the upper room of his store a few days later. But that day, Brother Joseph told us that the faithful members of the Relief Society should receive it with their husbands, that the Saints whose integrity had been tried and proved faithful, might know how to ask the Lord and receive an answer.

"Now don't you misunderstand me, Eliza Foreman. Priesthood is only conferred upon men, and this is according to the Lord's will and commandment. But all of us, men and women alike, have taken upon ourselves the name of the Lord Jesus Christ through baptism, and all of us have the right to use that name in calling upon God and doing other righteous deeds. This is a blessing to which we are all entitled."

Mother Lyman smiled kindly. "Now, I don't think anyone should be afraid to pray about things like this, my dear. Do you?"And shaking her head, a more-than-thoughtful Eliza took her son by the hand, and departed.

20

Tuesday, October 11, 1881

The Mesa across from North Gulch

"Howdy, Josh!" Reed Hall's voice filled with excitement as the wagon creaked to a stop near Jody Lyman's still form. "Long time since I saw you."

Joshua Stevens smiled warmly. "Hello, Reed. You and Billy been working on that ciphering he showed you back at the Hole?"

"A little. Mostly, though, we've been doing our best to keep care of poor Jody Lyman here."

Nodding his understanding, Josh Stevens looked down at the still form of young Jody Lyman. Hyrum Perkins was already off the wagon bench and kneeling over his friend, but had said nothing. "Are we in time, Hy?" he asked quietly.

"I . . . didn't think we would be," Hyrum Perkins responded as he caressed Jody's still hand, "but Jody's alive, Josh. He surely is."

Smiling his relief, Josh Stevens set the brake with his foot, wrapped the reins around the handle, and stepped to the ground. "Where's your pa, Reed?" he asked as he stretched his aching muscles. "Or Lem or Billy?"

"They're watering the horses," the youth replied. "Down off the mesa in some rock tanks the Navajos showed us. They'll be back shortly."

"Navajos were here?"

"They were. Yesterday. An old fellow name of Pahlilly, and a bunch of others. They were real friendly, too. Fact is, if it hadn't been for Pahlilly, I think Jody'd be dead by now. Pa and the others agree. That old man mixed up a poultice of prickly pear leaves for Jody's leg which we've been changing every two, three hours ever since. He's doing pretty well now."

"Is that what the Navajo used? Prickly pear leaves?"

"Yep, pounded up prickly pear leaves and a little water. That concoction of Pahlilly's has killed all the maggots in Jody's leg, stopped the putrefaction, and it even seems to have eased the pain some. Right now he's sleeping—"

"Am . . . not," Jody mumbled as his eyes fluttered open. "Howdy, Hy. You got back quick."

"I found Josh with Joe and Amasa Barton in the Butler, hauling out firewood for winter. Josh came with me while Joe and Amasa went back to the fort to spread the word."

"I . . . hope Nellie and Ma don't get too upset."

"They'll be fine once we return and they know you're okay. The one we're worried about is Platte. He does set store by you."

"Is . . . he home from Colorado already?" Jody asked.

Hyrum Perkins shook his head. "According to Josh, he is not. But no doubt it will be that Charlie Walton will send someone to find him and tell him about his favorite, and only, little brother—"

"Hello, Hy!" Lem and Billy had just come over the edge of the mesa, all the horses following behind. "You made good time! Howdy, Josh."

Joshua smiled. "Hello, Lem. Billy. You fellows all right?"

"Fine as frog's hair. Fact is, we've been living mighty high on the ill-gotten gains of our friendly neighborhood horse thieves, who kindly contributed to our comfort and well-being with their mounts, pack animals, and everything else they owned in this sorry world."

"Thoughtful of 'em," Josh responded with a grin.

"Mighty. But then, even owlhoots like them are sort of like a bob-wire fence—here and there you can find a good point if you look hard enough."

"Hy," Billy asked as Lem Redd paused to glance down at Jody, "you and Josh had any sleep?"

"All we need."

"Which means none a'tall." Billy grinned. "You've been traveling night and day, Hy, and you know it."

"Billy's right," Lem declared. "Off the rim yonder there's some shade, and several natural tanks with water in 'em. Charlie's there now, straining out the creepy-crawlies and filling our canteens. I recommend that you boys water your team and get a little shut-eye, after which we'll load Jody into the wagon and start back."

"We can start right now."

"Three, four hours from now will be fine," Lem reiterated.

Hy rubbed his face as he looked up from where he knelt. "Actually, I did sleep a little on my horse, Lem, and I dozed while Josh was driving. We spelled each other that way. All in all, though, you're right. We're both tired, and I think the horses are pretty well spent."

"They look it," Lem said as he began unhitching the team. "Here, Reed, give me a hand—"

"Hy?" Jody questioned from where he lay on the ground. "You . . . remember the blessing you and the others gave me, promising me a messenger from God, an angel?"

Silently Hyrum Perkins nodded.

"Well, I learned . . . one thing." Lifting his hand, Jody laid it on his badly wounded leg above where the poultice had been applied.

"What's that, Jody?"

Jody Lyman smiled weakly. "Angels," he breathed, "don't always come dressed in shiny white robes."

Sand Hills

"*Pikey! Tooish apane!* Come on! Hurry up!" Scotty had been rallying the young men of the various Pahute bands who had gathered to Sand Island—Sanop's boy, Bishop's boy, the two Grasshoppers, Paddy—he had been gathering them all, telling them about the great and wondrous thing his brother Posey was going to do once he was inside the mormonee fort. Of course Scotty was giving them few details, for he had not been given them himself. But nevertheless,

Posey had assured him that he was about to do *something* great and wondrous.

As a matter of fact, he had already pulled off what to any lesser Pahute warrior would have been a terrible impossibility. Left naked and penniless by the thieving ways of the Navajo Bitseel, Posey had somehow slipped through the willows and off the island without being seen—at least not by anyone who had been willing to spread the word of his shame. Approaching the fort during the time of darkness he had stolen the first horse he had come to—a stray whose mormonee owner had not yet been able to find it—and with it as barter he had gone to old Wash and obtained for himself a new outfit. Of course, it was not quite so bright and gaudy as his old one, not quite so fit for a chief. But these clothes were strictly white-man clothes. They were reasonably clean, fit Posey not at all, and they included a fine hat and a pair of tooled, high-top leather boots still wearing their previous owner's jingle-bobbed, silver-belled spurs. Of course the previous owner had no more need of such worldly things, and on Posey's feet they could be made to appear—and sound—very impressive.

Before daylight Posey had gone again—in bare feet, obviously—and stolen another horse, this one from one of the Navajo traders who had probably stolen it in the first place either from the Pahutes or from the mormonee. Now astride it with his spurs jingling merrily, Posey was already well across the sand hills and approaching the fort at a proud walk, traveling alone and in high style.

These things Posey had done, and the young warrior called Scotty, in spite of his doubts and concerns, was willing to admit them and sing Posey's praises because of them. He was also willing to admit—but only to himself and only silently—that Posey was a great fool who would wish before this day was out that he had never gone near the mormonee fort. Yes, for large in Scotty's memory were the words of power spoken by the old mormonee called Haskel, the words that had ruined Posey's big gun and that had prevented him from harming the mormonee brothers in the LaSals the previous spring. Of course others had then put them under the grass, but not Posey, who seemed powerless against the mormonee.

"*Pikey! Tooish apane!* Come on! Hurry up!" Scotty urged again as he whipped his pony after his older and hopefully superior brother. Scotty may not have known all the details, but without a doubt he did know where Posey was going. Somewhere the older brother had learned that the small man with glass before his eyes, the small man who was without fear, had ridden away and had not returned. That left the tall woman alone in her cabin with her ugly son. *Oo-ah,* yes, and with the big *tabby-nump,* the clock, ticking loudly on her wall . . .

Bluff Fort

"Dear Father in Heaven," a tired and worried Eliza was pleading as she rocked her crying son, "please bless little Willy with some peace. Help him to go to sleep, please, so I can concentrate on what I have been assigned to do."

Willy had been awake all night, crying almost continually, so that both he and Eliza were exhausted. Yet Eliza could find nothing wrong with her son physically, and her prayers over him had brought no relief whatsoever.

"Dear Lord," her softly breathed prayer continued, "if Willy is feeling the same thing as me, then wilt thou bring us both a little comfort? Bless Billy, please, and protect him and the others from harm and danger. I . . . I don't know what it is that is coming. All I know is, that no matter how many times I pray, I can't shake this terrible feeling of dread. Oh, mercy, Father in Heaven, what is it? What am I feeling from thy Holy Spirit?

"Please rebuke Satan from all of us, I pray, and keep him from our home. If Billy's supposed to do something, dear Father, then help him to know what to do. And if . . . if it's me that is supposed to do something, then take away my fear, I pray, so that I can think clearly enough to do it properly."

Bluff Fort

Without doubt heads were turning inside the mormonee fort as Posey rode slowly across the square, seated stiffly on the back of his horse. His head was high, and he was very conscious of the tinkling of the *tappa-arump,* the tiny silver bells that adorned his new spurs. His shirt might not have been such a bright red, and his Levis were not at all in the same class as his finely beaded buckskin leggings. But his new hat was a black one with a very high crown, his leather boots gleamed in the morning sun, and of course those tiny silver bells had a way of making everyone turn their heads just to see him pass by.

But Posey the warrior did not travel slowly just so the mormonee could watch him. No, his new horse was held to a walk only because he wanted his younger brother and the other young men of the People that he was gathering, to have time to come up with him. He wanted them all as witnesses of the great thing he was about to do—the great thing that would likely cause his name to be known forever, and most likely propel him to the level of a chief. Yes, and bring the comely Too-rah running to him from the grizzly Poke and his terrible brothers.

Such thoughts caused Posey's heart to beat faster, and so for him this was *ah-bat,* a great morning! The only thing that would have made it better would have been if he were holding a fine big gun in his hand, a rifle which he could have used against one or more of these *katz-te-suah,* these foolish whites. But that would come soon enough, he thought. Yes, and when it did, then he would truly be a chief!

As the hoofbeats of his followers pounded through the gate of the fort and came up behind him, Posey drew rein before the ugly log *wickiup* of the tall woman and sat still, waiting. He had seen no men in the fort as he had ridden in, which pleased him immensely. This day he wanted only the big clock; that, and perhaps to slay the ugly little child of the tall woman and thus throw another terrible scare into her as she was taught the true order of things along the big river. One day, he knew, all the mormonee would know that order.

But for now he was content to have the understanding settle on just one of them.

With dogs barking in every direction and his horse fidgeting nervously because of it, Posey sat in stony silence until the other Pahutes had brought their ponies to a dust-raising halt around him. Then without a look or a word directed at any of them, his brother included, the proud young warrior slipped to the earth and with jingling steps moved to the rough-hewn door of the small cabin.

"Ungh!" he growled as he threw open the door and stepped into the gloomy interior. "Heap hungry! Heap want-um food!" he announced.

Bluff Fort

Startled, for she had not understood the cause of all the commotion of horses and dogs outside, Eliza stared in fear at the glowering young Pahute. "Oh, Billy," she was breathing in desperation, her heart hammering, "why aren't you here when I need you? Oh Lord, my God! What am I to do now?"

"Heap hungry!" Posey snarled again as he took another menacing step into the room. "Squaw get-um Posey food. Heap hurry!"

Hastily pulling herself to her feet, Eliza put her suddenly silent child in the chair she had just vacated. Taking up the butcher knife she had used earlier to cut bread for Willy, which he had refused and thrown to the floor, she cut a thick slice of bread for Posey. This she hurriedly smeared with molasses and then held it out.

It was interesting, Eliza thought as she reached down to support herself with her table, how her mind was working. Her body was quite literally quaking with fear, and yet she had not reached for her crutch. She actually wondered at that. In her mind she was also praying fervently, pleading with the Lord to protect Willy and her and to send some sort of help. At the same time, she was noticing things about Posey that were intriguing to her—his new or at least different clothing that didn't fit him well at all, the fact that he was wearing boots and spurs with tiny bells on them instead of the moccasins she had never seen him without, and the final fact that he was alone in her cabin with her. Never before had that happened. Always his brother Scotty had been beside him. But this morning Scotty had remained outside on his pony, along with others Eliza could see through the open door, and for some reason this seemed extremely ominous to her.

"Dear Father in Heaven," she continued to plead silently as she watched the young man slowly devour the thick slice of bread, "please inspire someone to come and help me—either that or help me know what to do!"

There was something else about this young man that she was also noticing, Eliza realized rather abruptly. His eyes, which one would have expected would be on the bread, were not, and Eliza had the sudden, distinct impression that Posey had not come into her cabin for food at all. Rather, the food had been a ruse, giving him time to plan, to think through something else.

Besides, there was also that audience outside on horses. With a furtive glance Eliza verified that they were just that—an audience! Scotty and the other young men were peering in through the window and open door with great curiosity, yet they had not dismounted to follow Posey into the room.

Clearly those outside the cabin were waiting for something to happen, Eliza's mind was screaming at her, some great thing that would be at her expense that they could then boast of around their big fires for years to come. Thales Haskel had told Billy that such was their custom, and now Eliza realized that the youth Posey had come to accomplish such a deed. That was why he was being observed by the others! That was why he was eating his bread slowly instead of wolfing it down! That was why his eyes were not on the loaf of bread at all, but were darting back and forth from her son to the wall over near the fireplace.

The clock! That was it! That was what he had come for! In Eliza's mind now was the memory of that other afternoon when Posey had pulled out two one-dollar greenbacks and had attempted to purchase the Regulator clock from her. Of course it was not something he could have used, and Eliza had known that. That was why his attempt to purchase it had been such a surprise. In fact, if Billy had not happened home at that particular moment, she had no doubt that the precious clock would have disappeared out the door, and would most likely have never been seen again.

Now, though, the terrified woman realized that she had been given a warning!

Watching Posey's eyes, Eliza could actually see the decision forming in his mind—the decision that after his next bite he would step to the wall and remove the clock. This time, she knew, there would be no attempt to purchase it, no talking! The troubled young man, filled to overflowing with satanically inspired spirits of anger and hatred, would simply take it and depart.

The next thing Eliza knew, she had somehow crossed the room without her crutch and was standing in front of the clock, facing her adversary. She had said nothing, nor had he. But somehow she was there ahead of him, so that as he turned in the direction of the clock, he once again found himself facing her, and stopped in surprise.

"You may not have Billy's clock!" Eliza stated, her voice low. "It is not for sale, and you may not have it!"

His eyes widening with surprise, Posey took a step backward. He did not fully understand all Eliza had said, she was certain of that. Yet his eyes told her that he had most certainly received her message. For an instant he stared, and then as sudden anger flamed upward he stepped forward again, reaching out to throw her to the side so he could take Billy's clock from the wall.

Instinctively Eliza raised her hand to defend herself, and was as shocked as Posey to discover that she still held in her hand the butcher knife she had used to cut the slice of bread so long, it seemed, before.

Posey tried to stop his hand-thrust, but before he could do so his arm had come into hard contact with the blade of Eliza's knife. With an ear-piercing scream the Pahute jerked away, and then both he and Eliza stared at the deep, two-inch gash on his forearm that was already welling with blood.

Too shocked to even think of what she was doing, Eliza dropped the knife to the floor. Posey, beginning to feel the pain, shrieked again as his face twisted with anger and hatred. Stepping back, he took hold of his bleeding arm, shook it at Eliza as though it were terrible evidence against her, and then spun and grabbed little Willy by the hair, jerking him bodily out of the rocking chair.

Still shrieking, Posey slapped the boy, who was now crying in pain and fear. He was endeavoring to grab the child's ankles so he could dash his head against the log wall when Eliza, once again knowing full well what he was about and that the satanic spirit of murder had joined spirits of anger and hatred that had already taken possession of him, suddenly felt a great, inexplicable strength flood her body.

"Posey," she breathed fervently and almost silently, "in the name of the Lord Jesus Christ I rebuke you and the evil spirits who are motivating you, and command that all of you leave Willy and me alone!"

For another instant, perhaps two, nothing changed. Then abruptly Posey's hands went slack and little Willy scrambled away. Oblivious to the child's escape, Posey turned to face Eliza, perplexed by the power that emanated from the determined woman who stood in front of him. The fear had gone out of her, and seeing it unnerved him. She could see that even his countenance seemed to have gone slack. His mouth was hanging open, his eyes were wide and staring, and suddenly he began gasping as though he couldn't get enough air.

Without thinking, Eliza took up her crutch and moved a step toward the young Pahute, then watched in amazement as his face filled with fear. He began trembling, violently, then his legs abruptly gave way, and he collapsed in a heap on her canvas-covered floor.

Staring upward in shocked disbelief, Posey lifted his hands and cowered from Eliza, as though she were going to beat him into further submission. Willy, meanwhile, had reached the safety of the big bed, and there he sat, still rubbing his head where his hair had been pulled and wailing.

Eliza could see all of this, and could even see the watching Pahutes who were silently encircling her open door, their eyes glued upon her and her cowering foe. But not once did her gaze—her fierce gaze—waver or turn away from poor Posey.

"Get out!" she ordered firmly as she prodded the prostrate young warrior with the end of her crutch, almost tumbling him toward the door with the force of her shove. "Get out of here this instant! And don't you *ever* lay a hand on my son again!"

Bluff Fort

His eyes wide with fear and amazement, Scotty watched from the back of his pony as the tall woman pushed and prodded his trembling brother out through the door of the small log *wickiup*. There she put her foot against his backside and shoved, hard. Tumbling forward onto his face at the feet of the horses, Posey lay without moving in the dust, still cowering, still expecting the first blow from this woman whom he thought had been filled with fear. But instead the tall squaw stepped back into her cabin, picked up Posey's hat, which had fallen to the floor, stepped back through the door, and threw it into the dirt beside him.

Glowering menacingly in a way that Scotty could perfectly understand, the tall woman waved her crutch again, pointing at each of the mounted young warriors. Instinctively all of them backed their ponies away, and for the first time Scotty noticed that several white women and children, as well as one old white man, had gathered around them. Scotty also realized, for the first time, that the tall woman who had so thoroughly overpowered his brother, was no longer acting crippled. Yes, she was holding her crutch, but it was not on the earth supporting her, and she was not leaning against the log wall or anything else. She was standing alone, her crutch pointed at his hapless brother as she spoke to him with fierceness in her strange tongue, and on her face was the same expression Scotty had seen on the face of her husband.

There was no fear in the eyes of this woman, Scotty could see. Yes, there was *tobuck,* there was anger. But there was more than that—much more. In her eyes was the same courage, the same calm determination that her husband had shown that morning at the boiling spring when he had held Posey and himself under his rifle. This tall, thin squaw was not *katz-te-suah,* she was not foolish. She might be mormonee, she might be *mericat*, and she might even be a woman. But this squaw was also *te-a-now-er,* she was equal to any warrior of the People!

More, and this caused even Scotty to begin trembling, she could speak the same fearsome words of power that had once been spoken by the man called Haskel.

"*Ick-in-nish,*" Paddy snickered as he looked down at the still cowering Posey, "this one is *puck-kon-gah,* he is sick. Yes, he needs to be *nan-me-que,* confined to his bed!"

The other Pahutes laughed—all but Scotty. And then all but he yanked the heads of their ponies around and took off at a gallop, the hooves of their ponies throwing dirt clods in the air behind them.

As the other white women quickly gathered around Eliza, Scotty dismounted, intending to help his brother to his feet and onto the back of his horse. To his surprise, however, Posey jerked himself away from his brother's helping hands, crawled to the side of his pony, dragged himself up and onto its back, and seconds later that pony, too, was throwing dirt clods into the air.

Yet Posey was not riding after the others. He was not riding toward Sand Island and the comely Too-rah. Instead, he was urging his pony eastward, and suddenly Scotty knew that his brother was going away to deal with his shame, his humiliation, and that it might be a very long time before he would see Posey again.

What Scotty didn't know, was that he would *never* again see the Posey who had existed before that day.

PART THREE

THE GREENHORN

21

Monday, October 24, 1881

Bluff Fort

"Well," Billy said as he slammed the empty milk pail onto the floor of the cabin, "our cow's gone!"

"What?" Eliza, who had been waiting for the milk so she could feed Willy, was startled by the uncharacteristic disgusted tone in Billy's voice. Hardly ever had she heard him speak in anger. Surely, therefore, something was bothering him, something more than a lost cow.

"Has she wandered off?" she finally asked.

"Yeah, right into the hands of some miserable Pahute, more'n likely. At least that's what it looks like. Kumen's cow is gone, too, which won't make him happy once he gets back from the settlements. Thieves took them right out of the fort—while we were sleeping, no less! No dogs barked, nobody heard a thing. Yet the tracks of three good milk cows head straight toward Cow Canyon, pony tracks traveling right with them."

Eliza sat down to face her husband. "What're we going to do? With our poor diet, Willy needs that milk!"

"I know, hon-bun." Billy stared off, his expression thoughtful. "I reckon we can always borrow a little milk from somebody until we can get another cow. The thing is, how can I do that and still go to Colorado?"

"When are the men leaving?" Now Eliza's voice sounded tired, discouraged, and Billy suddenly realized that his attitude was infectious. Only, what in the world was he to do? How could he possibly leave his little family, especially when—

"Some are leaving as early as next week," he responded, forcing his mind back. "The thing is, Eliza, I don't want to go. I just don't feel good about leaving you and Willy alone for another winter! Especially not when we don't even have a cow anymore . . ."

Billy's voice drifted off, and for a moment or so, silence reigned in the cabin. The fall air, while not yet cold, was cool enough in the mornings that the fire in the fireplace felt good, and both Billy and Eliza stood facing it, their thoughts in a turmoil.

"Is anyone going after them?"

"After who?"

"The cows," Eliza exclaimed softly.

Billy looked up. "Yeah, Johnny Gower and Lem Redd, as soon as they can both be ready. I volunteered, but Charlie Walton gave the assignment to them. Thing is, milk cows the Pahutes usually butcher and eat right off, so nobody holds out much hope. I reckon that includes me."

Turning, Eliza took her crutch and moved to the small window, where she looked out at the distant yellow of the cottonwoods. Meanwhile Billy sank into Eliza's rocker. "Makes a body wonder when Thales Haskel's curse is going to take effect."

"What does Brother Haskel say?" Eliza asked without turning around.

"I quote: 'As soon as one of them gets mean enough, he'll die.' Thing is, I have no earthly idea what that means. The trick for us, hon-bun, is to not get mean ourselves. Love our enemies, I believe the Lord said." Billy shook his head and grinned wryly. "I suppose that includes milk-cow thieving Pahutes, don't you?"

"I suppose." Eliza sighed deeply, discouragement even more obvious in her voice. "Billy, I'm trying my best to have love for those people. The Lord knows that's true. But it isn't easy! This constant thievery is slowly killing every one of us, including little Willy!"

"I know, Eliza. Oh, how I know! But that's only part of why I don't feel good about leaving. The main problem has to do with prayer. No matter how many times I ask the Lord for peace, I can't get a good feeling about going!"

Eliza's look was bleak. "Well, I feel no peace, either. What's tragic, Billy, is that we have no choice. All you men have to work this winter if any of us are to survive, and the only work is in Colorado. That means you have to go, and we all have to put our trust in the Lord."

"I know that's the most sensible thing, hon-bun. Only—"

"Very well," Eliza exclaimed as she turned back toward Billy, "if neither of us feels good about you going, then I say it is time for a fast. Why don't we prepare ourselves for it, and fast this coming Thursday? That way I'm certain the Lord will tell us what you are to do—either that, or give us a good feeling about you heading off to Colorado."

"All right," Billy exclaimed, a smile finally lighting his face, "we'll do exactly that. But don't be surprised if the Lord tells me I am supposed to remain with you and Willy."

Shay Peak, Blue Mountains

"Well, Curly," Joshua "Spud" Hudson declared, waving his arm to indicate the vast panorama of country that was spread out below them, "just feast your eyes on that, would you? Wild country that stretches all the way from Indian Creek acrost to Beef Basin, then up past the Grabbens and the Needles and on acrost the Colorado to the Maze and Land of the Standing Rocks and—do you see it, Curly? There's Island in the Sky Mesa away off over yonder there, all hazy and blue up against them clouds, and this country of ours goes on beyond that to the Lord only knows where else and I can't tell because she's lost in the distance and I ain't been there yet." Dropping his arm, Spud took a deep breath. "Well, anyhow, she sure is a fine and purty country, don't you think?"

"Yes, sir, Spud," Curly Bill Jenkins agreed instantly as he looked northwestward from the high western slope of Shay Peak in the Blue

Mountains, "she surely is! I doubt many men have seen a sight more beauteous than this."

"Beauteous?" Spud growled instantly, looking askance at his riding companion and only remaining employee. "What in thundering blue blazes is *beauteous* supposed to mean?"

"Beauteous?" Curly questioned, acting surprised. In the past year or so he had come to know his boss quite well, and he wasn't about to let himself get railroaded into an argument or a lecture, either one. Few men had time for such lengthy extemporaneous discourses as Spud could deliver, and hardly anyone Curly knew had the disposition to endure them—himself most of all.

"Spud," he stated, reining the conversation onto more favorable ground, "I hate to say it, but your hearing's getting so bad you'll soon have to shout twice just to make yourself think you've heard an echo. What I said was, how lucky galoots such as you and me are, to look out over such a fine country as that is."

"Humph!" Spud growled as he continued to stare into the far distance. "Like fun you said that. Curly, I always took you for an honest man—"

"And I am one," Curly avowed sincerely, cutting his boss off. "Tell the truth, Spud, I was raised by my ma to make certain that my word was binding as a hangman's knot. Fact is, most folks swear I'm honest as a looking glass, and they ain't far wrong. Yes, sir, when I say what I say, you can take the fact that I said it and go straight to the bank! And when I don't say something and then don't say that I said it, even if'n I don't say it a hundred times or more in the same doggone day, you can take that to the bank right along with the other. I'm telling you, Spud, these are purdee facts that don't leave no room for coyotin' around the rim."

Apparently bewildered, Spud Hudson pulled his eyes off the distant country to glare at his sober-looking foreman. "Hell's tinkling hot brass bells, Curly," he finally grumbled as he kneed his horse toward a clump of quaking aspen where some cows were grazing, "you got more lip than an old muley cow. I never did encounter anybody with such a sad case of diarrhea of the jawbone!"

"Maybe," Curly Bill Jenkins muttered with a half-smile as he spurred his horse after his boss, for whom he had actually learned to feel great affection, "but all this verbal lather works like a charm against you, you bat-eared old buzzard-bait."

"What's that you're saying?" Spud snarled as he turned in his saddle.

"I said those slab-sided cows yonder in them aspen sure look like buzzard-bait," Curly shouted back, feeling delighted that Spud was actually starting to think his cinch was getting frayed—that he was getting old and hard of hearing when in fact the opposite was true. "Yes, sir," Curly continued, "despite a good summer them cows are so thin it looks like the good Lord's wrapped 'em in cowhide just to keep 'em from falling apart!"

"They look good enough to me," Spud growled without much enthusiasm as he turned back and shook loose his lariat. "Besides, I was going to tell you somethin', but now I'll be dogged if I will! Not after such inuations as you've bin insulting me with." Then with a kick and a halfhearted shout Spud was into the copse of aspen, which were starting to look skeletal now that their leaves were falling, and the cows, fat from the lush grasses of the mountain, were dodging and scattering out the far side with Spud right after them.

And Curly Bill Jenkins, doing his best not to laugh that he was getting so all-fired good at railroading his lovable but cantankerous boss, was trotting his favorite of all Spud's horses—a quick little mare he had taken to calling Betsy—not very far behind.

Blue Creek Point, Blue Mountains

"You got that bunch, Curly?"

Curly Bill, pleased as could be with how his little Betsy horse was moving the half-dozen cattle, raised his coiled lariat in positive response. Spud, who was keeping the seventy or so cows of the day's gather milling restlessly a little way back from Blue Creek Point, waited as Curly drove his bunch of cows toward him.

"I give us seventy-seven head in this bunch," he said a few moments later as the herds merged together. "What with the three hundred more down at the cabins, we're closing in on that five hundred head of cows what those old boys agreed to."

"What old boys was that?" Curly asked, feeling naturally curious.

"Why, didn't I tell you?" Spud asked, sounding surprised. "I'm certain-sure I did, Curly, 'cept with that wax buildup in your ears that folks've been warning me about on account of it being so doggone ugly to human folks but naturally attractive to those big old blowflies the way it is, I reckon you plumb missed it. Yes sir, big doings, all right, but I sure ain't got time to repeat myself. We'll hold these for the night there on all that grass along Blue Creek, and come morning they'll be fat and happy and content to stay put. Then if the blowflies ain't got in your ears, we'll ride back up Shay and see what else we can pop out of the brush up there. You got any questions?"

Twisting his finger in his ear, trying to get out the terrible wax buildup that he hadn't even noticed until Spud had started in to mentioning it, Curly shook his head. Durn stuff, he thought as he wiped his wax-coated finger on his leather chaps, who'd have ever thought earwax would attract those big blue blowflies? Or who'd have thought it'd cause him to miss hearing about some old boys what'd given Spud permission to round up five hundred head of his own cows? It was a sure-enough mystery, and it would do him well to get to the bottom of it as soon as he could.

Or rather, Curly thought gloomily, as soon as Spud felt like talking about it again, which just might be never, the way he had grown so cantankerous of late. The man had a bee in his bonnet, no two ways about it! And Curly Bill Jenkins, of a sudden afflicted with too much earwax to hear the straight of things, had no ghost of an idea what it might be about.

Bluff Fort

"I can't help but feel that I did a terrible thing, demeaning Posey that way." Eliza's voice was heavy and filled with sorrow and discouragement.

Billy, frustrated that after more than a year the fort was still unfinished, which as a direct result had led to the loss of his milk cow, was laboring by himself to set more heavy posts in the ground. Once the fort was finished, he was reasoning, he and the others might be able to keep their precious livestock safe for a change.

"Eliza," he growled as he struggled with a heavy juniper post, "we've gone over this a hundred times. You did exactly what you needed to do, and everybody who was there says so. Posey was in the wrong, and you did the right thing. Had I been home and seen what he was doing, I think I'd have done a lot worse!"

"I don't believe that for a minute."

"Well, you'd better believe it! No fool Indian is going to mess with my family, not while I still have breath!"

Eliza smiled wanly, certain that Billy's anger was more a result of the loss of their cow than anything else. "Two or three issues keep bothering me," she continued, putting Willy down so she could help balance the post while Billy filled in the dirt. "First, for days I had been praying that Satan and an array of his evil followers would leave Posey alone, just as I'd been doing for us and our home. Yet I know that Posey was possessed with at least the spirit of murder when he was after Willy, and I . . . I don't understand why."

Billy was digging again—another trench in which more posts could be placed side-by-side to form a fairly solid segment of wall. "Hon-bun," he explained as he continued his work, "a righteous person could try to pray Satan out of a wicked person every six or seven minutes, from now until the cows come home, but if that wicked person chooses to stay wicked, then Satan has the power to come right back. It couldn't be any other way, not if the Lord's law of agency is to be honored."

"I suppose you're right."

Billy nodded. "Of course I am. And you're right about Posey, too. A spirit of murder did have control of him, and I think it's had control of him for quite a spell. It surely did at Boiling Springs, and from what folks are piecing together, that same spirit would have been present when he was involved in those murders in Colorado."

"Others have told me that, Billy. More than once. Still, I can't help but think my own faith was lacking—"

"Eliza, we're talking about taking away agency again, which was Satan's plan from the beginning. Just because you or me or even President John Taylor is exercising faith over someone, doesn't mean the Lord will force that person into righteousness. Even when Alma's faith was sufficient to bring down an angel to call his son Alma the Younger to repentance, nothing was forced. Remember what the angel said to young Alma and his four equally wicked friends? The message was, 'Alma, go thy way, and seek to destroy the church no more, that their prayers may be answered, and this even if thou wilt of thyself be cast off.' Do you see, hon-bun? Alma was given specific commandments concerning others, but was left to do with himself as he wished.

"It has to be the same with your faith regarding Posey. He was prevented from hurting you and Willy because of your faith, as well as the promise of protection that we've all been given. But what Posey does with himself, is completely up to him. Thus far, it seems he's making some terrible decisions."

"But . . . what if he really was hungry? I know what that feels like, and maybe I just pushed him over the edge. Maybe when I cut him with the butcher knife—"

"When he cut *himself* against your knife, you mean? Eliza, you mustn't keep doing this to yourself!"

Eliza slowly shook her head. "I . . . I can't stop! Posey is a son of God, and God loves him. I know that, and I ought to love him the same! But I don't. I was angry at him, and I wanted to demean and hurt him, and that bothers me. Some of the people in the Book of Mormon willingly laid down their lives rather than oppose their slayers. Why should mine or Willy's lives be any more important than theirs?"

Billy was growing frustrated that his wife wouldn't leave off worrying about Posey and accept his point of view. "On the other hand, Eliza, Captain Moroni led other Book of Mormon peoples to fight for their lives and the lives of their wives and children, and Mormon says Captain Moroni was so righteous that his life shook the very foundations of hell forever." Billy paused in his work and looked up at his wife. "But hon-bun, this argument could go on and on, and nothing will be changed! You simply must stop thinking about it and get on with things!"

"I . . . I can't, Billy. I just k . . . keep thinking of different, better ways I might have handled Posey—"

"Howdy, folks! Kind of late for putting up walls, isn't it? Does this fine little lad belong to you?"

"Howdy," little Willy added instantly from his perch in the man's arms, using one of the few well-articulated words in his developing vocabulary. Then he said, *"Cliz bekigie."*

"Oh, my goodness!" Eliza exclaimed as she spun about. "Willy, where did you go? Thank you, Brother Haskel. Thank you!"

"Sister Eliza," the old Indian missionary replied with a wide smile, "you've no call to be thanking me."

"Cliz bekigie," Willy insisted. *"Cliz bekigie."*

"What on earth is he saying?"

Thales Haskel chuckled as he bent to set Willy on the ground. "He may not be too big yet, but this boy's a fast learner, and he talks pretty good. When we came past the icehouse he pointed the stuffed snake out to me, so I taught him how to say it in Navajo. *Cliz bekigie*. Snake skin. That's what he's saying. Here, Billy, let me give you a hand with those posts."

For a few minutes the two men labored together, setting several posts into the earth, closing up one of the several gaps in the fort wall.

"I understand you lost your cow this morning."

Billy nodded. "Pahutes, I reckon."

"Looks like. Well, I have a cow I don't hardly need, and she's just freshened. I got her milked a little bit ago, so come morning I'll show you which she is, and you can take over. Use her until you can get yourselves another."

"Thank you, Brother Haskel."

"No call to thank me." The man chuckled again. "That's on account of I'm tired of the milking and am thankfuller than somewhat to be shut of it. Owning a cow's more like wearing a ball and chain than anything else in this world! And I'd rather you called me Thales, since that's my given name. Either that, or Haskel, which is what the Indians call me.

"Speaking of which, I couldn't help but overhearing some of what you were saying about Posey in particular and our Pahute neighbors in general."

Billy nodded. "You heard right. Eliza's carrying a lot of guilt over what happened with Posey a couple of weeks ago."

"I heard about that, Sister Eliza, and I was right proud of you."

"That may be so, but I still feel like I somehow degraded him."

"You know," the old Indian missionary said after a moment's reflection, "I've been associating with Indians of one tribe or another for going on thirty years now, and I've known these renegade Utes or Pahutes for a good part of that time. While I consider some aspects of their lives, like squaw beating and abandonment, to be utterly wicked and depraved, I truly do admire other aspects of their lives. They may not believe exactly like we do, but many of them are true to what they believe, and a good many of them have spiritual experiences that would dumbfound us.

"There's something wondrous about their dancing and their singing that I cannot describe, but I know it is all sacred to them. I've listened to their singing, the perfect harmony of their voices, their chants, their movements. I've listened to their words, but their words don't begin to explain the sacredness and the importance of their songs. I'm convinced those things are greater and more magnificent than us white folks can imagine.

"I absolutely know that their mortal existence is sustained by the same divine power that sustains our own. They came from the same premortal world we came from, and they will go to the same eternal world hereafter. The justice of God, on which we depend, will in no case discriminate against them. The earth was organized as much for their use and benefit as it was ours, and they have as much right to be here and are as precious in the sight of the Lord, as we are. We know this, that the gifts of God which are most beneficial, are not just the gifts of good living from which we get temporary enjoyment. We are told positively that the first shall be last and the last shall be first, and it is up to us to learn what that means. But I ask you, which one did the Lord love most? The wealthy man who fared sumptuously on rich food, dressed in great splendor, and lived in a palace? Or the ragged beggar whose sores were licked by the dogs and who laid at his gate, begging enough food to keep him alive? Which one did the Lord love most, when he sent one to live with Father Abraham and the other to hell, where he lifted up his eyes in torment?"

Thales Haskel smiled. "All that being worthy of consideration, Sister Eliza, there remains one more thing to add. Now and then a fellow will come along who just naturally likes to be bad. He enjoys hurting others and creating damage and destruction. Such individuals are not a reflection of their society or culture, but are merely a reflection of their own selfish choices, their own pride, their own greedy nature. Lucifer was such a being, so was Cain who slew Abel, and so were Laman and Lemuel, Nephi's brothers.

"Now I might be wrong, but I've had my eye on young Sowagerie or Posey for some time, and it seems to me he's a far piece across the meadow of choices and is rushing headlong toward the river of darkness and destruction."

"Your curse," Billy breathed quietly.

"It weren't my curse, Billy, it were the Lord's! And some of those Lamanitish folks are starting to recognize that fact. Word is that Navajo Frank's terrible curse ain't going away, and their most powerful sings haven't helped him. I also heard of a Pahute called Jonah, one of Poke's band, who went to Frank's *hogan* to see for himself what *Shin-op* had done to the thief. Then Jonah came back across the river to his *wickiup* so filled with worry over what might happen to him on account of his own stealing, that now he's fixing on dying. If he does, then the next thing we'll hear—and you can mark my words on this—will be that Poke has kicked Jonah's squaw plumb out of his camp, which is the wicked part of Pahute life I was telling you about. Then there'll be no telling where she'll go or what will befall her when the cold weather gets here. Those fool Pahutes'll treat her like she's already dead, and then mighty soon she will be. So when a few bring the curse of God upon themselves, a whole lot more are called upon to suffer.

"Anyhow, Sister Eliza, those are my feelings on the Pahutes in general and Posey in particular. And it's why I said you did a good thing. Could be he's out in the rocks somewhere right now, licking his wounded pride and thinking maybe it's time he made a change for the better. Happen that occurs, sometime betwixt now and the eternities he'll come up and thank you for what you did for him—which includes not allowing him to shed the innocent blood of little Willy here.

"Now, Billy, it's too dark to do much more damage to this wall. But if you'd like, I'll come by in the morning—after you've milked my cow—and help you get a little more of this useless fort closed in."

Blue Creek Point, Blue Mountains

"You ever seen a meadow more lush than this one, Curly?"

Curly Bill Jenkins, through with both eating and cleaning up, looked out into the darkness beyond the firelight. "I reckon not," he said, trying to picture in his mind what the meadow had looked like before night had shut things down with its soft, chilly darkness.

And she's a dark one, too, he thought. No moon yet, the fire was down to hardly more than a few coals, they had no lantern. The only light was coming from the stars, of which there seemed to be about a million or two hanging above them. Yet the water in the creek was chuckling friendlylike, and now and then one of the cows would beller soft and easy, obviously paying no mind to the couple of hundred sociable coyotes that were yipping and ki-yiing from what seemed like just about every point on the compass.

Yes, sir, Curly Bill agreed, dark or not, she was a mighty purty meadow, set smack in the midst of a mighty purty country that Spud called his ranch—though Curly suspected that he'd never filed on a blamed inch of it. Still, it was Spud's by right of first and most recent claim, and all that purty country fed a herd of cows he had built up to between ten and fifteen thousand head.

"You know, Spud," Curly said, his brain suddenly swirling with a tiny bit of understanding, "I recollect the time ol' I. W. Lacy got to thinking on how wondrous and beautiful the country down around the LC looked to him. Way I remember, he waxed eloquent about it for hours and days at a time, or at least that's how it seemed to me.

Wasn't too long after that, though, that he was gunned down by that miserable Sugar Bob Hazelton over in Fort Lewis."

"You saying what, exactly?"

"I don't hardly know." Curly scratched his long, grizzly face. "Man starts making chin music the way you bin doing the past few days, and well, she sounds to me like you're maybe getting ready to move on and be gone."

"You think I'm going to die?" Spud growled menacingly.

"Not hardly, I don't! But then again . . ."

"Humph!" Reaching out, Spud dragged an old snag closer so that the biggest part of it was in the hot coals. In a minute or so flames started licking upward, and soon there was light enough that the two men could see each other across the fire.

"Sugar Bob Hazelton," Spud mused. "Now there's a mighty mean man!"

"Amen to that sentiment," Curly agreed fervently. "Amen, and amen!"

"You seen or heard of him lately?"

Curly Bill shook his head vigorously. "Ain't seen him since he shot my bedroll to doll rags a couple of months ago, and that wasn't a very pleasant encounter!"

"You saw him two months ago?" Spud questioned. "What happened?"

"Oh, the sorry nincompoop came out of the dark with his rifle practically blazing. I heard him coming, though, and got into the brush afore he started shooting. Otherwise I wouldn't be here today, I can tell you that!"

"He just started shooting?"

"As ever. Folks say he's gone plumb loco since Old Man Lacy took it to him with his knife, and I'd have to agree. After I got the drop on him, he said he was looking for himself a pardner. Then he started in to screeching and whining and jumping about like a bobcat walking on hot coals, and the next thing I knew, he took off running into the brush, still a caterwauling like he'd bin gut-shot. I ain't seen hide nor hair of him since. Reckon he's still around, though. I surely do. Bad pennies do keep turning up."

"That they do. Mighty unfortunate, too." Spud was still thoughtful, maybe more so than Curly had ever seen him. "Curly, you ever heard me threaten to sell this outfit of mine?"

"Yes, sir, about a hundred times."

"On account of?"

"On account of too many folks are coming in, taking up all the country that had ought to remain wild and free. And a man like you needs his elbowroom."

"That's exactly right!" Spud refilled his cup from the big, blue coffeepot he always carried. "Too many folks! Mormons, Injuns, Texicans, Coloradians, men on the dodge from the law, you name 'em. They just keep on a'comin', and they're all comin' right here!

"On account of that and that alone, when those two old boys from England made me an offer for the outfit last month, I saw my chance, took their money, and by the end of the week I'll sure be ready to run."

"You . . . sold the place?"

"Lock, stock, and barrel! All but five hundred head of cows, which I reckon'll give me a good start wherever I end up next. Yes, sir, Curly, the deal's done, and she might as well be signed in blood she's that firm! Ol' Spud Hudson'll soon be gone from this miserable country of the San Juan, and he'll be gone for sure and for good."

Curly was stunned almost to the point of being speechless. "I . . . well, I . . . Glory be, Spud! I just never thought you'd do it."

"That just goes to show you don't know me."

Curly was still shaking his head, trying to understand the verbal explosive his boss had just set off. "So . . . who are these old boys from England I'll be riding for? Or did you think maybe I would be riding on with you?"

Spud held up his hand. "Not with me, Curly. Where I go I go alone. Not that I wouldn't enjoy your company, mind you. Recalcitrant or not you're a hard worker, and of an evening you do carry on some enlightening conversations."

"So that's why you and me have been riding alone," Curly breathed, jumping to yet another understanding.

"Yep. It's why I'm now giving you that little mare you bin ridin', and it's why I let the other hands go over the last two or three weeks, never tellin' them the why of it or anything else. But you're a friend,

Curly, and it ain't right that I should ride off without so much as a warning about them bad pennies you brung up in your enlightening conversation a minute or so back."

Thoroughly confused once again, Curly kept still, and this gave Spud the opportunity of further explanation.

"Curly, I grew up punching cows for the Picket Wire outfit, over in southern Colorado. It was some of their strays that led me into this country in the first place, and I liked it so much I quit the Picket Wire and came here and built my cabins. Then I made my way up to Salt Lake City where I bought a couple of thousand cows, and within another year I was a rancher, and all of this fine empty country was mine. Leastwise that was the way of it until other folks started crowding in on me.

"What I'm trying to say is, all my life I've bin around good hands and bad ones, as well as one or two real sorry so-and-so's, like Sugar Bob Hazelton, who just ain't worth a decent man's time of day. Over time I've learned to spot all kinds of men a mile off, and to fight shy of the ones that looked to be trouble.

"Some time back I was contacted by the agent for a company called the Kansas and New Mexico Land and Cattle Company. They made me a purty fair offer, I got their price up a little, and that was when I met the two gents who mainly owned the outfit—brothers Harold and Edmund Carlisle, from England. They wanted a Utah base as the center of their Kansas and New Mexico operations, and they had more than enough ready money to cash both me and Peters out."

"Mr. Peters sold out, too?" Curly was astounded that he had heard none of this.

"He did. Last month me and him rode over to Colorado and signed the papers, and that was when I met my first Carlisle riders. Not the two brothers, Curly, who seem to be fine gents, but their riders. They're holding ten thousand head over there with more a'comin', and most of those boys are salty, Curly. Mighty salty. Fact is, I've about concluded they are a 'hurrah' outfit for sure, and I'm beginning to wish I hadn't done business with 'em."

"Bad pennies," Curly muttered, mostly to himself.

"As ever. Makes me wonder if the Kansas and New Mexico

Land and Cattle Company weren't after the high, wide, and lonesome, at least as much as they were after the grass and water of mine and Peters' spreads—you know, country where their riders could do as they please with no lawmen to make 'em toe the line."

For a moment Spud stared into the fire, and Curly stared with him. Curly was afraid of no man, and being the crack shot that he was, most fellers, including even the hard cases, stayed shy of him. But by nature Curly was a peaceable sort, and he found little joy in the association and rancorous lawbreaking of Sugar Bob and his ilk. So that's what Spud was doing, Curly realized with some surprise—warning him, telling him he would be better off long gone and out of there before the Carlisle riders showed up to claim the double cabins and everything else between there and Peters' Point.

Trouble was, where would he be long gone to, especially with winter coming on and him without any more of a stake than the little Betsy horse that Spud had just given him?

"You do what you're of a mind to do, Curly. But was it me, when those boys from the 'Three-bar' show up one of these days—"

"That their brand?"

"Yup. They've registered several, but that's the main one. Wide bars on the hip, side, and shoulder. Some fellers in Colorado were even calling them the Hip-side and Shoulder Cattle Company. Mighty convenient brand, too, seeing as how a running iron can turn most anything into a bar, especially if she's wide enough, which theirs sure enough is.

"Anyhow, Curly, like I said, you do what you're of a mind to do. I'll be gone as of next week, so if you decide to slope off in another direction, I'll give you papers on that little Betsy hoss."

"Thank you, Spud. I don't—"

"You bin a good hand, Curly, and I reckon I owe you more'n that. Pick yourself out a good pack animal, too, and take whatever else you need of supplies. I never promised those Carlisle boys any of that sort of truck, so take what you need to make yourself up a good winter outfit, and I'll give you a bill of sale for the whole shebang."

"That's mighty generous, Spud." Curly was having a difficult time thinking of what to say, let alone what to feel. This country—

this outfit—had become like home to him, maybe the best home he'd ever had. And Spud? Well, he'd become like a father to Curly, even though he couldn't have been more'n a year or two older and was about as sociable as an ulcerated back tooth. Still—

"One more thing, Curly. I can't abide a man getting all slobber-faced when he's fixing to say adios. Neither can I abide a man who ain't up and in the saddle by three-thirty in the morning, and who'll work until the job's done, no matter what. This job won't be done until we have five hundred head of cows down at the double cabins, and don't you forget it!"

Without another word Spud Hudson rolled over in his bedroll and was soon snoring softly, while Curly Bill Jenkins was left alone with the night and its millions of stars—to think and ponder over whatever in the world might become of him in his suddenly uncertain future.

22

Tuesday, October 25, 1881

Mouth of Cottonwood Canyon

It was still early, the sun not more than an hour high, and Billy clucked his team of mules forward, feeling good. Arising at a little after three, a little earlier than usual but not much, he had taken care of his shaving and other such oblations, done the chores, and hauled a dozen wheelbarrows full of the seemingly eternal supply of manure out of the corral and onto the Bluff community field, where he had spread it to dry and later be worked into the soil. A couple of the brethren had been out working on the fence around the five-acre field—a part of Lem Redd's tax assessment that the men of the fort worked off with donated labor—and so Billy had joined them for an hour, paying down a small bit of his own assessment. Joining Eliza then he had breakfasted, played a little with Willy, harnessed a spare team to a wagon, and was now on his way to a rock formation he had noticed a few weeks before, a weathered formation that was located up on the Bench.

Ostensibly Billy was going to select a slab of stone from which he could chip out a grindstone to replace the worn one in the chopping yard. But his real reason for going, though he had not explained this even to Eliza, was to seek a confirmation of some impressions he had been having of late, and an answer to his prayer concerning them—an answer that seemed to make no sense whatsoever.

Of course he could have done such praying at the fort, Billy knew as he guided the horses through the heavy sand, for much experience had proven it. But up on the Bench there was solitude, and without distraction Billy knew he could keep his mind more focused, enabling him to hear more clearly the still, small voice of the Lord's Spirit.

And keeping focused was hard enough during the best of times, Billy knew. Even during the midst of prayer his mind tended to wander off, to get itself involved in other worries and concerns—and even in silly things, such as he had been thinking of a few moments before. Such mental excursions, taken during prayer, he felt, must surely be a great disappointment to the Lord.

Curtailing such tendencies seemed a little more simple when he prayed vocally—something that was not always possible in populous areas. So the wilderness, just like the wild grove of trees to which Joseph the prophet had retired some fifty years before, looked to Billy to be an appropriate destination. For he had to be right about this, Billy knew. A wrong decision, one not inspired by the Lord or one that was inspired but slightly misinterpreted, could be catastrophic and even deadly for himself and his family. And that was why he was—

Mouth of Cottonwood Canyon

"Morning, Billy."

Spinning in surprise, Billy looked and then smiled at the stake president, who had ridden up on him so quietly that Billy had not even heard his horse's hoof falls. Of course the sand was soft and deep, and he had been very much engrossed.

"President Lyman, I didn't know you had returned. Did you find Jody a doctor?"

"I found one, all right. But it'll be at least two more weeks before he can get here, which isn't going to help Jody much at all."

"Yeah," Billy nodded, "he's in a mighty bad way—or at least he was last evening when I dropped in to see him. The flesh looks to be healing fine, but I don't know if there's enough bone left in his leg to ever knit together."

"The rest of us have the same fear," Platte admitted. "If he wasn't in so much pain, I'd haul him to Denver. But I don't think he could stand the trip."

"I can't even begin to imagine how he handled the pain from Hall's Crossing to here." Billy's eyes took on a distant look as he remembered the terrible journey with the wounded Jody Lyman bouncing along in the wagon. It was amazing to Billy that he hadn't been unconscious the entire way—either that or screaming with agony. Yet in his conscious moments Jody had remained almost stoical, his tremendous willpower enabling him to endure what few others could have managed.

"It was the many blessings you and the other brethren gave him," Platte stated simply. "Otherwise he *couldn't* have made it. No, for now he needs to lay still and heal. Then maybe after the doctor gets here and sees him, he can give us a better idea of what to do next."

Belatedly Billy swept a blanket and coat from the wagon seat into the bed behind him. "If you're going my way, President, climb aboard and sit down."

With a nod Platte Lyman rode close to the wagon, stepped from his saddle stirrup into the bed, and tied his horse's reins to the end gate. Stepping over the tools Billy had gathered, he slid into place beside the smaller man. "You looked mighty thoughtful when I rode up, Billy."

With a grin, Billy nodded. "You know me, President. I get to thinking on something, I can't let it go. Sometimes it's productive, usually it isn't. This time I'm afraid it was the latter."

"Now you have me curious," Platte chuckled. "What were you thinking about, if you don't mind me asking."

Billy's look was sheepish, but his heart was suddenly racing. He didn't want to discuss his negative impressions about going to Colorado—not yet, at least—not until he had received the certain confirmation he was seeking. Yet Platte's question had been so direct that he couldn't avoid it, not without lying. Unless, that is—

"Actually," Billy responded with a smile, "I was thinking about prayer. That, and pins."

"Pins?"

"Uh-huh." Billy quickly warmed to his subject. "Eliza was using straight pins to do a bit of mending for Willy this morning, she dropped one, and in the lengthy search for it I got to thinking about their minuscule size."

"And?" It was obvious that Platte was curious.

Snapping the reins of the two mules that were pulling the wagon, Billy turned them from the road and urged them up a sharp incline that would lead them out of the mouth of Cottonwood Canyon and onto the bench above Bluff. "You've heard of the ship *Leviathan?*" he questioned. "When it was launched a few years ago, it was touted as the greatest freighting ship ever built, carrying a little more than twenty-two thousand tons when fully loaded."

"*Leviathan,* huh? Like the beast of John's Revelation. Tell the truth, Billy, I've never heard of such a ship."

Billy smiled. "It doesn't matter. I only know about it because I read about it somewhere, and that sort of useless information seems to stick with me. Anyway, when I couldn't find that silly pin this morning, I got to thinking on how small pins really are. In fact, if my calculations are close, it would take two hundred of them to make one ounce."

"That's small, all right."

"Well, one thought led to another, and just a few minutes ago I was figuring that if a fellow dropped one pin into the hold of the *Leviathan* the first week of the year, two pins the second week, four pins the third week, eight pins the fourth, and continued doubling the number of pins dropped into the hold each week for the remainder of the year, he'd be in trouble."

"How so?"

"Well, figuring fifty-two weeks, and doubling the number of pins dropped each week, the total number of pins required would be four and a half quadrillion pins."

That anyone would concern himself with such a thing was astounding to Platte. Casting a curious look at Billy, and stifling a grin, he said, "You're sure about that, are you?"

Billy shook his head. "I think I'm right." He went on. "And at two hundred pins to the troy ounce, twelve ounces to the pound, and two thousand pounds to the ton, the poor soul who had been doing the loading would have 628,292,858 tons of pins, or tonnage enough to fully freight twenty-eight thousand ships the size of the *Leviathan*."

Platte stared at his traveling companion, not even trying to hide his amazement. "You figured all that in your head?"

"Actually, that's pretty straightforward mathematics, President. The trick is in carrying forward the right digits and keeping them all in order. I could easily have made a mistake or two in my calculations, though I don't think so."

Platte laughed softly. "Well, Billy, you do take the cake. No wonder you did such fine work at the Co-op back in Cedar."

Uncomfortable hearing such praise, Billy pulled at the reins, turning the mules toward a low sandstone cliff. "I just like to keep my mind busy, President," he explained. "I don't know what I'd do if I couldn't think."

"Yes, Bishop Nielson told me you had ordered in some books to study."

Now Billy's excitement became more real. "That's right—from the Montgomery Ward catalogue! In fact, I believe you freighted them in. This winter I hope to be studying the art of speaking, writing poetry, composition of writing, geography, derivation of words, general history, the histories of Greece and Israel, and of course the scriptures and study manuals for the Church. Actually I ordered them for the school, but since there's always more to learn, I intend studying them myself when there's opportunity."

"That's wonderful, Billy. I wish all the Saints were so inclined."

Again uncomfortable, Billy nodded at the cliff, which was looming closer all the time. "Uh . . . President, I don't mean to be taking you out of your way, but that cliff ahead is as far as I'm going."

"Then that's where I'm going, too."

"Excuse me?"

Platte Lyman chuckled. "When I stopped at your home to visit with you, Eliza told me where you'd likely be. Your project sounded intriguing, so I thought I'd see how you intend going about it."

"Cutting out a grindstone?"

"That's right. I'd noticed the grindstone at the woodpile was getting worn down, but I hadn't thought of anything so simple as cutting a new one off one of these cliffs."

"Well," Billy responded, "it's the same kind of rock, though this may be a little softer. A few weeks back when I was chasing our cow out this way, I noticed that this sandstone shelf is layered to about the right thickness for a grindstone. That got me to thinking about how it would be a simple matter to peel a slice of stone off and chisel it into a wheel. So, here I am. Of course we'll have to do a little blacksmithing on the treadle to make the stone fit, but Joseph Barton told me he thought he could handle that without too much trouble."

"Joe'll do a good job, and I'll feel a lot better leaving the womenfolks here in Bluff with a good grindstone. Is that the shelf where you intend to get your stone?"

"That's it," Billy said as he pulled his team to a stop and set the brake. More and more it was looking like this was not going to be a good morning to pray. Still, things tended to work out.

"See how loose that slab is? If you'll help me, President, I think we can rough cut it, get it loaded, and be on our way back within half an hour."

"Then let's get to it," Platte declared as he climbed to the ground. "And if there're enough good slabs, Billy, why don't we haul back two or three stones?"

With the hammer and a couple of chisels already in hand, Billy nodded his agreement.

Allen Canyon

"Up here, my sister! There are many fine roots in this place, and the digging is not so difficult as one might have thought."

The almost-fifteen-year-old Pahute woman who was called Peeb or Feather, now growing heavy with child, looked up the arid slope. There her younger friend, the maiden known as Too-rah, was already burrowing into the hillside with her digging stick. She was removing from the soil the bulbous roots of the kouse or biscuit-root plant, which they would later mash and dry into cakes that would be eaten during the coming time of cold.

Peeb smiled, thinking of how much she enjoyed the happy countenance and usually-singing voice of Too-rah. To Peeb the other maiden had always been as a sister, and in ways she was still closer to her than she was to her husband, the warrior who had taken upon himself the white-man name of Jonah, who now lay close to death in the *wickiup* down the canyon.

"My sister," Too-rah called from above, "do you come? Or is that child in your womb doing too much kicking again?"

Peeb laughed and used her digging stick as a climbing staff. "I come, my sister! But you are right about the other, too. This child that my husband planted within me is kicking in one place all the time, taking away my breath until I wonder that I can go anywhere at all."

With difficulty Peeb left the marshy bottom and made her way up the slope, leaving behind the piles of cattail roots she and Too-rah had already peeled and set to dry in the sun. Later, she would pound and grind these roots into a fine-tasting flour, and it would be one more thing she would use to feed herself and her husband during the coming season of cold. Why, already there was ice on the edges of the nearby stream in the mornings, and the old sleeping robes she used for herself and her husband were no longer sufficient to provide warmth. But for a year she had been stitching together tanned rabbit skins, pelts she had taken from rabbits caught in her own carefully placed snares, and as soon as she had gathered a little more cattail down—

Since coming to this secluded canyon, Peeb had also woven many baskets of the cattail fronds, and these she had filled with sunflower seeds that had already been ground to powder between stones she had found and prepared. That powdered meal, she knew, would make an excellent baby food once her unborn child was ready for it. There were also baskets of dried rose hips, chokecherries, currants, and elderberries, all of which would provide much-needed nourishment for her and her husband after the winter snows had come.

Peeb did not think of these things as great accomplishments, for they were as common to her as breathing—tasks and preparations she had been helping with since even before she could remember. After all, such preparations were the work of every woman of the People, each of whom existed that they might feed themselves and their gambling, warring, hunting men. Yes, and bear and then feed their children in the meanwhile. That was the way of things, the proper way. It always had been, and every woman who was wise, accomplished these tasks and found joy in the labor. Otherwise she would be beaten by a father or a brother or a husband until she learned. And that, too, was the proper way.

Of course, Peeb thought with a sly smile, beatings were not the way of the warrior who called himself Jonah, and that was much better than being proper. Yes, and in her heart there was such gratitude for her husband's kindness, such adoration, that there was nothing she would not do for him, no sacrifice she would not make.

Or rather, she admitted sadly as she dragged herself up the slope toward her friend Too-rah, that had been the joyous way of things before the mormonee Haskel's terrible illness had come upon her man.

Bluff Bench

"You said you wanted to visit with me?" With three good slabs of sandstone loaded in the wagon, Billy and his stake president were now headed back to the fort.

"That's right, Billy, I wanted to tell you that I could find only one barrel this trip. Still, I'd like you to make a filter out of that one if you will, just to see how it might work."

"I'll be happy to do it, President."

Platte nodded his satisfaction. "Additionally, Billy, most of the brethren are getting ready to head out for Colorado and the railroad, and Brother Redd and I were wondering whether you intend to join them."

Still uneasy about discussing his impressions and answers with anyone, Billy sat silently, trying to think of a way to respond.

"Billy, I don't mean to pry, but Lem and I must finalize our plans. I'm sure you understand that."

"I do, President." Billy sighed. "It's just that I'm not certain what I'm going to do."

"Meaning?"

"Meaning I don't know whether to go or to stay."

Platte nodded. "Was it me, Billy, and I'd come as close to losing my only son as you did last winter, and then to have lost my only daughter just a few weeks ago, well, I reckon I'd want to be staying, too."

"Maybe that's a part of it, President. Maybe it's even all of it; I don't know. What I do know, is that I keep having these feelings, these impressions, that I won't be going to Colorado."

"Have you prayed to discern the meaning of them?"

Nodding, Billy kept his eyes ahead. "I have, President, but I . . . I'm not certain of what I am being told. In fact, that was actually the reason why I came out here this morning—"

"And I came along and interrupted you," Platte offered.

"Well," Billy grinned, "things always happen for a reason."

"That's a fact. Would you mind telling me what you feel that the Lord has said to you?"

"Just that I'll be given something else to do that won't require me to go to Colorado. But that's crazy, President! There's nothing else in this whole blamed country that a feller like me can do—especially to earn cash money!"

"Not unless the Lord decrees it." Platte smiled and clapped his hand on Billy's knee. "But my advice, Billy? Trust the answers you have been given. Exercise faith, not only in the Lord, which I am sure you have in abundance, but in yourself. Have faith in the answers you feel you are receiving. Plan on staying at home, and then let the Lord fulfill his word. If you do, then he will."

As Platte climbed onto his horse and rode away, Billy sat in amazement. He had set out to pray for a confirmation, he was thinking, and the Lord had intervened and given him the very confirmation he had intended to ask for. It was just that it hadn't come in the way he had expected, and was therefore surprising. And that, he thought abruptly, was likely how his work for the winter would open up—in a surprising and completely unexpected way.

Bluff Fort

"Do you really know how to make a water filter out of that barrel and spigot President Lyman brought back from Durango?" Eliza asked.

Looking up from where he was writing in his current daybook, Billy smiled. "Sure do, hon-bun. Put in a perforated false bottom with the spigot set beneath it, and stack separate layers of sand, gravel, and charcoal above it. Cover the whole thing with cheesecloth or factory, weighted with a few stones, and there's your filter."

"But . . . how does it get water in it?"

Billy laughed. "Each pail any of us lifts from the well is poured into the top of one of the barrels. Then we lean down with our empty pail, turn the spigot, and empty what's already been filtered, from the bottom. As long as folks aren't in a real hurry for lots of water, such filters work fine." Billy tapped the tip of his pen on the bottle to remove the excess ink. "It's a real shame that Platte couldn't get more than one barrel and spigot for us. That'll give the Bluff citizenry little more than a taste of good water, and won't provide for our daily needs at all. Maybe if I think on it, though, I can come up with some other idea."

Eliza shook her head in wonder. "You continually amaze me, Billy Foreman. I can't believe all the things you seem to know."

"Well," Billy responded, his smile still in place, "my father used to tell folks that I'd stored in my head more useless tidbits of information than any two encyclopedias he'd ever read. I'm just amazed when some of it comes in handy now and then."

"Ahh, such modesty!"

Billy grinned at his wife's teasing sarcasm. "My, my. You do seem to be feeling better about things."

"Actually," Eliza replied, instantly serious, "I am. A lot better."

Putting down his pen and corking the ink bottle, Billy leaned back in his chair. "Do tell, fair lady."

After checking on their sleeping son, Eliza lowered herself into her rocker. "I don't know, darling. It helped to talk with you and Brother Haskel about Posey and myself, for that gave me a little different perspective. But there's more than that to it. Since last night I've been thinking a lot about my prayers—you know, the ones when I prayed about Satan and if he was affecting Posey and little Willy. Looking back, I realize that while the Holy Spirit did respond with information about what I was asking, it was mostly revelation about how the devil was affecting *me* that I was given."

Billy nodded his understanding, but remained silent.

"My impression is that I have been troubled considerably," Eliza continued, her voice more quiet than usual. "Certainly a spirit of confusion has been manifest in my life, for I have had so many conflicting thoughts not only about our mission here to this country, but about my personal beliefs as well. I . . . I've even found myself doubting that little Mary Eliza is really waiting for me in the eternal worlds, or that she is real at all. But confusion has played hand in hand with a terrible spirit of fear, and that has caused me the most problems."

"So, you're saying these spirits of confusion and fear have brought this upon you?"

Eliza sighed deeply. "I wish I could blame them. Unfortunately, just as Joseph Smith warned us, I'm the one who has been giving them power. I'm the one who must be accountable, for it is my own unrighteous thoughts and even actions that have combined to open up my soul to Satan's torments and afflictions."

"Eliza—"

"Billy, darling, when you told me what President Lyman said about having the faith not only to pray for answers, but to accept them when they come? Well, this is the information the Lord has revealed to me. Adelia Lyman told me yesterday when she brought little Willy home, that she sees an attitude among some of us that can best be described as, 'Love the Lamanites, hate the Indians.' It embarrasses me to admit it, Billy, but that is just exactly how I have felt. I read the Book of Mormon and feel a love for the Lamanites that I know is from the Lord. Yet at the same time I have a hatred and a loathing for these Indian peoples that was there before I ever started fearing them. They seem so uncivilized, so filthy, and some of their habits are so disgusting to me. Of course I know that I am likely just as appalling to them, but I have consoled myself with the conviction that I am a better, or superior, person. These are unrighteous thoughts!

"My own sinful deeds lean more toward gossip, that and little lies about how I'm feeling, told because I know it will engender greater sympathy. Sometimes I . . . I've even been glad to send little Willy off to the Lymans, for no other reason than because I wanted to do nothing but sit and feel sorry for myself.

"These are the things that have given those evil spirits power to afflict and torment me—to trouble my mind."

"Well," Billy responded quietly, "such things would do it, all right."

"And so," Eliza declared, suddenly brightening, "I've been repenting again! Is that troublesome to you, that your wife has to repent of so much or so often?"

"If you mean, do I feel badly that I married a mortal woman? The answer is no; not if you don't feel badly that you married a mortal man." Billy chuckled. "I do the same thing, Eliza. I am forever repenting of one thing or another. And I am forever being reminded by the Lord that my sinful actions, which I seem to repeat no matter how often I repent and think I have learned better, are giving the devil power over me. Worse, sometimes I know I have brought him into our home, for I have literally seen his evil influence spread from me to you and little Willy. To be honest, that's the hardest realization for me to deal with."

"But . . . you've dedicated our home, and have asked that angels guard the way of our passing. How can Satan or his followers get past that?"

Billy smiled a little sadly. "The same way they get past the personal protection your body should afford you, hon-bun. Strictly by invitation—mine in this case. I preside in this household, and when I come through that doorway in an unrepentant state, usually because of unrighteous or impure thoughts, I'm sad to say, the protection the

Lord has promised because of my priesthood is canceled, and those spirits climb into my coat pockets and ride happily in with me. Then they go to work on you and, to the degree they can, even on little Willy."

"Then when I'm in an unrepentant state," Eliza breathed, "they can accompany me where I go as well. That's true, isn't it?"

"I reckon."

"Oh, lawsy. That's probably why we've all been having such a difficult time. No wonder the Holy Ghost has been whispering that I needed to repent."

"And you have been."

Eliza smiled. "Well, at least for the past few days. Billy, darling, I can truly feel a difference! My heart is filling with hope once again, and more and more the world seems full of promise. More than that, Willy's temper tantrums have stopped almost completely, so that even Annie and Adelia have noticed." Eliza suddenly giggled. "I've even been asking the Lord to rebuke Satan from Posey. Of course I haven't seen him since the Lord sent him packing, but I hope he's been changing, too."

"With your strong faith," Billy smiled as he arose to prepare for bed, "there can be no doubt. But remember agency, Eliza. When you use your faith in behalf of someone else, attempting to bring about positive changes in their lives, it only works if *they* want it to. God exercises compulsion over no one, and neither may we—not, at least, when we are attempting to use the gifts and powers of God."

Eliza smiled at her husband. "I know all that, darling. But I have felt so good about doing it."

"Then I'm sure Posey is being as blessed by your great faith, as Willy and me." With a tender touch Billy lifted his wife to her feet and drew her to him, and as the candle flickered out, the two confessed with their kisses how blessed they had been to be led to each other.

23

Thursday, October 27, 1881

Sand Hills

The Pahute warrior who called himself Posey was a humbled young man. Not alone had the bone-thin white woman shamed him and driven him from her ugly log *wickiup* without so much as striking a blow, but now the comely Too-rah, she whose hand had fit so snugly and so perfectly into his own, and who had looked at him with such large and luminous eyes, had vanished without a trace.

For days Posey had been spying upon Poke's camp where she should have been, following it from a distance as the People moved slowly northward toward their late-season camping ground in Allen Canyon. Yet despite his best efforts to contact or even just to see the maiden, Posey remained frustrated. Not only had he not seen her, but he could not even find the prints of her moccasins once the band had moved along. So far as he could tell, Too-rah was no longer with Poke's motley band. What he couldn't tell, was where the young maiden had been taken.

Now Posey rode disconsolately across the sand hills of Bluff Bench, the stolen pony between his legs carrying him forward with no real destination in mind. To make matters worse it was raining, a steady cold drizzle that seemed to portend an early winter. The young warrior did not think much of that, but he didn't like the rain, and was thankful for the shapeless old hat he had found after his good one had been taken in that game of *ducki* by the evil and scheming Bitseel. At the very least, this hat was keeping the rain out of his eyes.

Since fleeing eastward from the mormonee fort on the big river Posey had spoken with no one, shown himself to no one. Instead he had flailed at his mount until it was nearly dead, and then he had dragged the staggering animal to a small spring in Yellow Jacket Canyon. There he would have starved if he had not eaten his horse, and there he had also thought many long thoughts regarding his recent experiences. Slowly, yet with marked progress, he had come to see that perhaps his brother Scotty, in spite of his slow and sometimes foolish ways, in this one thing might actually have been right. Instead of being weak and foolish as they appeared, perhaps the strange white people called mormonee might indeed have the terrible power of *Shin-op* in their words.

Certainly that is what the old fool known as Peeagament believed; as did Paddy's weak and foolish son, who was calling himself Henry. And just as certainly, if all the stories about them were true, it was what the tall Navajo who was called Natanii nééz, and the fine warrior of the People who had called himself Jonah, now believed. The mormonee called Haskel had spoken his words of power against them, and now they suffered! Was not that a great show of power? And just as Scotty had declared, had not Haskel's words, spoken against Posey's fine gun, also come to pass? Surely, Posey had concluded, one could not argue against such powerful words.

At the end of a week of such thinking, Posey had determined to share his thoughts with the maiden Too-rah, for he knew she would listen and tell him of her own thinking. Easily stealing another pony and riding to Poke's encampment, Posey had lurked in the brush and trees nearby, waiting for a moment when he might get alone with Too-rah. Yet now another week had passed, Too-rah had not been found, and Posey's face had changed. Now he was not thinking so much about words of power. No, instead he was thinking day and night about where Poke and his cantankerous brothers and old crone of a sister had hidden his beloved. For he had noticed, during his week of watching from cover, that while most of that fearsome family were always about the camp, Poke and his brother Sanop were gone. But this morning Poke and his brother had returned, and within an hour, Poke's two other brothers, Hatch and Tehgre, had ridden out, followed only a little later by the old crone sister, who had gone in another direction altogether.

Unfortunately the rain had made trailing any of them impossible, and so now, wet and discouraged, Posey was simply riding, wondering what he should do next. If there were only some way of knowing where Too-rah was hidden, or of maybe forcing Poke and his family to bring her back—

Suddenly Posey sat straight in the saddle, his eyes wide. Of course! The man Haskel spoke words of power! In fact, other than the scrawny mormonee woman, he was the only person that Posey had ever known who did. And if Haskel had such great power, why couldn't he be persuaded to use it in Posey's behalf?

Instantly Posey slammed his heels into the bony ribs of his newly stolen pony, and with a wild yell he turned the hapless animal toward the fort on the big river. At last a way was opening up.

Allen Canyon

"Are you not afraid of what the fearsome grizzly will do to you when he finds that you have come to this place?"

In spite of the rainy drizzle, Peeb and Too-rah were digging roots together on the rocky hillside, and were enjoying great success in their labors.

"I do not allow myself to think of Poke's beatings," Too-rah replied quietly.

"But . . . he may come at anytime. Surely he has been looking for you since you stole away from his encampment the night after the warrior Posey fled from the mormonee fort. Just as surely, Poke's wrath toward you will be great."

"Perhaps. Still, I speak words of truth when I say that I prefer Poke's beatings to the vicious anger of my older sister—she who has taken the place of our mother. Poke I can often hide from, but from that other, I cannot."

Peeb made the sign of understanding. "Her anger is always on her face, it is true; and there is no one of the People who has not seen it. And her shrieks fill even the bravest of warriors with fear. It is no wonder that she has never found a husband!"

"That is so."

For a moment both women were busy with their digging sticks, and in the stillness of the afternoon, the cry of a red-tailed hawk split the air.

"It is too bad that one such as yourself does not have the freedom of the wings of the air." Peeb was watching the slow circling of the hawk as she spoke.

"I have often wished I could fly away," Too-rah admitted. "But coming to this place in the dark of the night, riding fast on that young colt and not caring at all where I rode, felt much like a wing of the air must feel."

Peeb smiled sadly. "Truly it is a good thing to be free. Since my husband took me to wife I have known that freedom, and found much joy in it. But soon it will end for both of us, my sister—for me, when the warrior Jonah takes that long road to the west; and for you, when that fearsome warrior, who is your brother, returns to this place."

Too-rah glanced up mischievously. "Yes, and no doubt the sour one's anger will be even greater because she believes that I ran off with the warrior Posey." Abruptly the comely maiden's smile grew even more radiant. "And perhaps, my sister, that is the very thing I will do—"

Bluff Fort

"Brothers and sisters, since Bishop Nielson and his family haven't yet returned from the settlements, President Lyman has asked me to conduct the meeting tonight. Thank you all for coming."

Lem Redd paused, waiting until all had given him their undivided attention. "Thank you. Since most of our men will soon be gone for the winter, and since Parl, Josh, and myself will be leaving in the morning, President Lyman thought it might be wise for the rest of us to review our resources—what we have or hope to have that will carry us through the winter."

Eliza was nonplused at the buzz that followed, for she wanted to get on with the meeting and then get Willy home to bed. He'd been a little fussy of late, and she felt that perhaps some extra sleep would help. Only—

"As you are aware, our harvest was fair but nowhere near what we had hoped for. That's on account of our unfriendly old enemy the river, as well as its evil tributary, our ditch! But enough on that miserable story, at least until we have to start digging the ditch out again in the spring. If we go careful, there'll be grain enough for a pound or maybe a pound and a half of wheat a day per person, which isn't much. We also have a few hundred pounds of dried corn, which we'll share in like manner. We have three large burlap bags of pine nuts gathered, roasted, and shelled, and old Peeats, the wife of Chief Peeagament, has been showing some of the sisters how to fire cakes out of them. All of that'll help. There're a few melons left, and half a room full of squashes and gourds. We also have a certain amount of smoked meat, and of course there is always the hope for fresh meat during the winter."

"Yeah, if the Indians don't beat us to it!"

Lem Redd smiled. "That's right, Sam. We'll come back to those folks in a minute. If we're provident, brothers and sisters, and ration ourselves, and if the winter isn't too long or too deep, we should make it through at least as well as we did last year."

"Sounds mighty iffy," one of the men offered.

Lem Redd nodded. "It *is* iffy. Fact is, to stay on this peace mission is going to require every bit as much faith, from every one of us, as it took to get us here in the first place. That'll be especially so for you sisters, because most of you will remain here alone with your children for the balance of the winter.

"Of course the bishop will soon be here, Jody Lyman is here, President Platte Lyman is in and out as he needs to be, Thales Haskel will travel between here and Montezuma Creek, and as often as it is practicable, the rest of us who are over in Colorado will be coming home on a rotation basis. That will be of some help.

"The thing is, sisters, you'll be the ones who will be forced to keep up the chores and everything else that must be done. You'll also need to keep a sharp lookout for Indians or outlaws or both, and you'll have the responsibility of dealing with them if they come. Based on Sister Eliza's experience with Posey, the actions of the Pahutes last spring, and Jody Lyman's encounter with Rob Paxman and that other lean-brained fellow, we now know that at least some of our neighbors are more than willing to do violence upon us. We must guard against that—"

"How? How will we do that with all the men gone?"

"By our righteousness, Sister Mortensen. You know that as well as I do. Thus far we've all been protected wonderfully, but the Lord will grant a continuance of that protection only if we are all worthy of it. To that end, Bishop Nielson has encouraged us to be more diligent in our prayers, our attendance at our meetings, our love for our fellow beings, and so forth. Each of you knows what to do, so please do it, and all will be well with all of us.

"Now, a final note. Sometime around the first of the year President Lyman will once again be writing the brethren in Salt Lake City, informing them in plain language of our perilous circumstances—the river, the ditch, the poor crops, the Indians of both tribes, the outlaws—even a new threat of turning the whole San Juan country into a Ute reservation that we've been hearing rumors about. This much opposition has placed a terrible burden upon us, brothers and sisters, and in our poverty it is almost more than we can bear.

"It is President Lyman's feeling, and as a bishopric we agree, that the brethren will likely see the hopelessness of our situation and extend to all of us the releases that I am certain most of us have been praying for since our arrival a year and a half ago."

Again the buzz surrounded Eliza, this time louder than ever. Glory, she thought as she tried to hear everybody at once, wouldn't a release be wonderful! Wouldn't—

"But remember, such releases cannot come before next spring at the earliest, so it isn't time to begin packing just yet."

Lem Redd smiled, and most in the room chuckled.

"Questions or comments?"

"Do we still have bank credit over in Colorado?" Lem's wife asked.

"Miraculously, Eliza Ann, yes. President Lyman doesn't know exactly why, but the worse things seem to get here, the more willing to extend us credit those Gentile bankers and storekeepers become. Once again, however, I believe we are seeing the hand of the Lord in our affairs."

"We keep being told that Brother Haskel has pronounced a curse on the troublemaking Indians around here. I'd like to know if anything's happened," Parley Butt said.

"Thales? Would you mind answering Parley's question?"

Slowly the old missionary rose to his feet. "Well, you know what's happened to Navajo Frank, so I won't go into that. I've made a little medicine with Henry the past couple of days, and according to him, one or two of our biggest troublemakers are dying of various and sundry causes, including a young firebrand and thief who goes by the name of Jonah. Thing is, the rest are still laughing about it and planning more raids, which I reckon will continue until they keel over their ownselves. But Henry is our friend, and his father, old Paddy, is getting more friendly right along. Then, of course, there is old Peeagament and his wife, Peeats, and one or two of the other women. They'll do."

"Poke? Mancos Jim? Hatch and Old Hatch? Chee? Posey?" someone else called out. "What about them?"

"Well, Posey's disappeared. After his unproductive encounter with Eliza, and the Lord's power, he hightailed it for the high lonesome. We'll see if the experience humbled him or turned him bitter enough that he dies, too. Henry also says that Too-rah—"

"Who?"

"Too-rah. She's old Norgwinup's baby daughter, and Posey's true love. Seems she has disappeared—most believe spirited away by Poke and the rest of the clan because they don't like Posey any more than most of us. When Posey finds out Too-rah's gone, well, that could be another factor in what happens with him.

"As far as Poke is concerned, as well as his brothers and the others you mentioned, keep on being careful. Quite a number were involved in that big raid in Colorado last spring—Mancos Jim,

Wash, old Bishop, maybe Bridger Jack, Poke, and the rest of old Norgwinup's sons—"

"How many brothers are there in that family?"

"Five, I believe. Hatch, who is named for his granddaddy, is the oldest, and then there are the ones they call young Bishop, Sanop, and Tehgre. Poke is either the youngest or the next-to-youngest of the boys. Besides Too-rah, there's also an older sister, a rather mean and unpleasant women whose name I have never learned. Despite his not being the eldest, Poke seems to be the natural leader of the bunch, and the others all follow his lead. "Anyway, it seems to me any of these fellers'd just as soon kill us Mormons as those fellows they did kill. So in your kindnesses to them, you sisters, be careful, and if you see an Indian enter one of our homes, gather some friends and hustle over there quick. Pahutes, especially, don't much like to be outnumbered, even by women. That's about it, Lem."

"Thank you, Brother Haskel. Any other questions or comments?"

"What about winter graze?" Joshua Stevens called out.

"Well, you all know what the Navajo sheep did to that country out west, Josh. There isn't a twig or blade of grass left on it. So, we have that bit of wild hay we cut up on Recapture, the sand hills to the north, and whatever our critters can find out east of here. We hope it will be sufficient without our herders drifting too far away from the fort. If it isn't, well—"

"Might the Navajos create any more of that sort of trouble?"

"We hope not, Billy. As you no doubt know, the Indian agent who was so prejudiced against our people has been replaced by W. T. Shelton. Kumen has met him and reports that he is a broad-minded soul who is very much exercised over the plight of the Navajos, but who is just as sympathetic to our people and our troubles. He and the Navajo head chief, Manuelito, have promised Kumen that they will encourage their people to stay on the south side of the river, and will also do their best to stop the raiding of our people."

"That's all well and good, but can we trust these fellows?"

Lem smiled thinly. "I'll tell you what, Ed. About the only answer for that is to wait and see. But again, according to Kumen, and

Thales can verify this, Manuelito will measure up with the heads of any of our so-called civilized nations."

"Or stand taller!" Thales growled. "Folks, Agent Shelton is our friend, and that's all I intend to say. As for Manuelito, he has the love and respect of all who know him. If he'd had the proper training and background of some of what we call the 'more favored' races, he'd make most world leaders look like thirty cents change out of a dollar. He is quiet, unassuming, a born orator, and is wise and careful in his judgments. If we give him a year or three, we'll find that about all of our neighbors to the south will become as beneficial to our cause as has sweet little Hádapa."

"Kumen told me a young fellow name of Jim Joe is the same," Billy offered.

"That's true enough, Billy. Hosteen Joe has been raised by old Dahnish uánt, one of his uncles, and from what I hear is thrifty, careful with his means, and a hard worker. Kumen told me he looks upon lying or stealing as beneath his dignity, and is always frank, open, and straightforward in his dealings, either with red man or white. Several times he has helped Kumen regain property that other folks have stolen, including that big black horse that Bishop Nielson lost to Frank a while back. So, truthfully, folks, we are starting to get some friends."

"Any other comments or things the bishopric should know about?" Lem asked as Thales sat back down. "None? Good. Now folks, as your bishopric we feel that all of us are going to get through this coming winter in just one way—through the direct intervention and inspiration of the Almighty! Thing is, we all have to be worthy of it! If we are, then we will get through! Of that, in the name of the Lord Jesus Christ, I bear fervent and humble testimony.

"Sister Anna Decker, would you please close our meeting with prayer?"

24

Friday, October 28, 1881

Bluff Fort

"That's a fine-looking grindstone, Billy."

"Thanks, Joe." Both men were looking down at Billy's stone, which had taken him all the previous day to chip and chisel into a wheel. Now he had brought it by wagon to what they were calling the blacksmith shop—one of the empty cabins near the corral that had been converted for such use. Though primitive, it was complete with a forge, a large anvil, homemade bellows, two barrels of water, and a few tools. It wasn't fancy but seemed to do the job, and the Bluff settlers were more than happy to call it theirs. Most, in fact, were doing their own smithing.

Not Billy, though. He had watched farrier work or blacksmithing done a few times—the setting of hot iron tires on wagon wheels, the sharpening of tools, the shoeing of horses and mules, and the like, but he had never done any on his own. Of a truth he had been a little afraid of it, not so much of the work as of maybe doing it wrong. And so he had willingly let others take over when something had needed smithing, while he had covered for them by doing the more mundane tasks of daily life.

"The stone isn't perfectly round," Billy commented, "but the hole's well centered, and once it's on the treadle it should do the trick."

Joseph Barton nodded. "It'll do just fine. I dragged the treadle over here just after daybreak and cut it apart where it had rusted, after which I got rid of the worn stone. Platte brought in a little iron this last trip, and with that load of coal Monroe Redd hauled in the other day, our blacksmith shop's back in business."

"I'm glad to hear it," Billy said sincerely. "What can I do to help?"

"Pump the bellows, if you don't mind."

Nodding, Billy began pumping the homemade bellows, blowing the superheated flame onto a length of iron Joseph had thrust into the coals. "I'd hate to see the folks left for the winter without the means of doing a little light repair work," he commented. "Looks like the president brought back plenty of horseshoes, too."

"All sizes, and near ten pounds of nails. Oh yeah, he also brought back a new last and some other tools for repairing people shoes—that and a half-dozen tanned bull hides. They're thick enough that they should make fair-to-middling soles for most everyone's footwear."

Billy grinned as he lifted his foot and looked at the underside of his sole, where a gaping hole was obvious. "I'm glad to hear it. About the only thing I have left to stick between me and the elements, what with heavy paper being so precious, is rabbit skins. And they're so thin they wear through in about an hour of a feller doing nothing more than sitting on the porch and scratching in the shade."

"If you can find any in this durned country," Joe grinned in response. "Rabbit skins, porches, or shade, either one. Okay, Billy, keep pumping while we heat up this section of the treadle. Once both pieces are hot as we can get 'em, we'll make a joint here with a cold-weld, cool it, and then see if she'll hold. If she does, then I believe we can get the stone in place."

"Isn't that part of an iron tire?"

"It is," Joseph grunted as he hefted and turned the iron with his large tongs. "Platte found the wreck of a wagon somewhere along the trail a few weeks back, and brought home the iron tires, bolts and pins, and all four thimbles. Fact is, he was in yesterday pounding himself a new branding iron out of that length of iron tire over yonder—that and two bits for his bridles and a new blade for Adelia's kitchen knife. That's in addition to shoeing all four horses in his freight team."

Billy was astounded. "I heard all the racket while I was working on this stone, but I had no idea it was President Lyman in here making it."

"He was the one raising the ruckus, all right. He's a fine farrier, Billy, and not a bad hand as a carpenter, either. That new ox yoke there belongs to Hanson Bayles, but he told me it was Platte Lyman who took his adze and an old log, out in one of his camps one night, and roughed it into shape."

"Who curved those neck pieces?"

"George Sevy, before he left last fall. He had some hickory sticks under one of his wagons, so he soaked and bent a dozen of those neck pieces. Hanson bought two from him, and I hear Jim Decker bought a couple more. George was mighty handy, too."

"And you did the iron work?"

Joseph nodded as he bent over the heating metal, prodding the two pieces with his tongs. "Yeah, that's my contribution. Hanson wants to drive those two oxen he picked up out to Colorado. He figures to lease 'em to the railroad folks for the winter, and in that way pick up a little extra cash."

"Good idea," Billy nodded, wiping the sweat from his brow as he pumped. "When's he leaving?"

"Tomorrow morning. A bunch of us are leaving then. Somebody said you weren't figuring on going. Is that on account of Eliza and your little girl?"

Billy shook his head. "She's still not over the death of our daughter, true enough. But most families have to deal with that, Joe, and in time I think Eliza will be just fine. No, it's just that—"

"Excuse me, Billy, but these are ready. Put on a pair of gloves, take those extra tongs yonder, and when I have the treadle in place on the anvil, you lift this length of iron tire and hold it on the anvil where I tell you. Ready?"

Silently Billy nodded.

"Okay, here we go . . ." Carefully Joseph Barton lifted the treadle from the flames and, twisting it, laid the cutoff part along the top of the anvil. "All right, Billy," he said as he brushed on some flux, "lay that tire iron right here, square on top of the flux. That's it

. . . good!" With his free hand Joseph took up the large, rounded hammer he had made ready.

"Billy, if you can, move your head back a little . . . that's better. Now close your eyes, because when I start pounding, little pieces of this stuff'll fly off in all sorts of directions!"

Obediently Billy closed his eyes and turned his face away, and seconds later the tongs, his hands and arms—in fact his whole body—began vibrating with each terrific bang of the mallet. He could also feel the sharp, burning stings as tiny fragments of hot metal peppered his arms and neck.

"All right," Joseph breathed a couple of moments later, "that should do it, Billy. It isn't the best cold-weld I've seen, but it'll have to do."

Opening his eyes, Billy gazed at the joining of the two pieces of metal, welded simply by being pounded into each other. "How can that be called a cold-weld when the metal is so hot?" he asked as Joseph quenched the weld by pouring water on it, which sizzled into instant steam.

Joseph Barton chuckled. "Tell the truth, Billy, it may not be called that at all. But since Pa called it a cold-weld when he taught Amasa and me how to do it a few years ago, we've both just sort of stuck with it."

"Sounds good to me. But I still don't understand why it would be called a cold-weld when there is so much heat involved."

"Well," Joseph responded as he tested the joint to see that it had cooled properly, "this is how I understand it. A heat-weld is one where a hot gaseous flame melts flux and a special welding metal in between two other pieces of iron or steel, securing them without pounding or hammering. Trouble is, not many folks in our country have that sort of equipment. Fact is, I've never seen a heat welder, though I have read about them. But these cold-welds work fine for what we need, and they're the only kind of weld I've ever seen.

"Okay, let's pick up this stone of yours and slide it into place." The two of them labored to lift the heavy stone and position it. "There . . . Good job on that center hole, Billy. Looks like she fits." With a little more maneuvering Joseph pounded a couple of rivets into place, adjusted the iron leg with the new joint in it outward, and stepped back.

"There she is, Billy, better, almost, than new. Grab that ax yonder and give it an edge whilst I'm cutting off another length of this iron. That way we'll know what sort of stone this is going to be."

Without hesitation, Billy took up the ax and began pumping the foot treadle and thus turning the grindstone. And though a little out of round, the stone worked well enough to put a fine edge on the ax, leaving Billy pleased as could be.

For the next hour he watched Joseph Barton at his work, helping out as he was asked, and asking a bundle of questions regarding the forge and everything else associated with the shop. Knowing that Eliza and her girls were probably finished picking currants and waiting for him and his wagon, he finally bid his friend farewell and departed. But as he turned the team and wagon toward home, Billy was excited. For the first time in his life he felt confident enough to try a little smithing—another of the many tasks for which he had felt ill at ease when he had left Cedar City so long, it seemed, before. But now, he grinned as he snapped the lines to the mules, he was ready! Yes, sir! He would be back the next day when the majority of the men had gone. There were a dozen little things about his place that needed repair, some of them items that Eliza needed quite badly. And now, no matter whether he was going to Colorado or not, he was ready to see them fixed.

Bluff Fort

"My goodness, girls! That's a wonderful harvest of currants!"

Relief Society President Jane Walton stood inside her opened door, looking out into the bright afternoon sun. On the stoop were nearly a dozen pails of freshly picked wild currants, and around them were Eliza Foreman and the six young ladies the community affectionately referred to as "Eliza's girls," even though one of them was Jane's own daughter, Leona.

Beyond them, Billy Foreman was already back on the wagon

bench, a wide smile on his face. "Good luck, Sister Jane," he called as he snapped the lines to his team, "Eliza and the rest of 'em have nearly worked me plumb to death."

"Oh, sure we did," Lucy Nielson snickered, "asking him to load and unload eleven little pails of currants."

"Poor man," Lula Redd chimed in with a giggle. "He must have been done in by that strenuous snooze he took under the wagon while we were doing all the picking."

"Say, Lula," Billy grinned, "I had to hold the team, you know!"

"Of course you did." Adelia Mackelprang was enjoying the good-natured banter as much as any of the others. "That new pole fence would have broken right in half if those sorry mules had tugged on their lines."

"Well, it might have—"

"Okay, girls," Jane Walton interrupted, waving a chuckling Billy away as she spoke, "let's bring these currants in here. Good, now listen, so I won't have to say this twice. Sister Foreman was telling me the other day about you—how quickly you learn the things she teaches. Then the very next day my Charlie stumbled onto that patch of currant bushes you just stripped, and when I was telling Eliza about them, she asked if I could show her—and you—how to make preserves of the fruit. I agreed, but only on the condition that you girls do all the picking, and that each of you receive one jar of preserves when we are through." The Relief Society president smiled, and the girls laughed quietly, for they had been told how Jane Walton had really said it. "Anyway, from the number of pails, it looks like you have done a thorough job. I assume you have them washed and cleaned?"

"They're clean, all right," Mary Eleanor Lillywhite affirmed. "Even the green ones."

"Good! I'm glad you remembered to pick the green ones, too."

Lula Redd pulled a face. "Eliza told us to, though why remains a mystery. They're sour enough to pucker a witch's kisser!"

"Lula Redd, I declare! How you talk!"

"Well, they would, Eliza, and you know it."

"Perhaps, but your language, child—"

"I'm sorry, Eliza. I didn't mean to be vulgar—"

"The green fruit is what makes the juice turn to jelly," Jane interrupted as she lifted a pail onto her table and scooped out a handful of currants. "The tartness in green fruit—apples, currants, or anything else—is caused by something called pectin, and pectin is what gels the juice after it is cooked. As fruit ripens, however, the pectin turns to sugar. Of course the fruit tastes sweet when we eat it, but if cooked without pectin it can't gel, and will remain runny forever. By combining green and ripe fruit, however, we get both the sweetness and the pectin, and we end up with delicious, firm jelly, something we can spread on whatever we wish without fear of it soiling our clothes.

"Now, my daughter Frances, Mary Ann and Hannah Rowley, and Kate and Naomi Perkins are here to help us, and to learn the same things Eliza and I will be teaching you. Next year, each of you should be able to put up currant preserves on your own. Is everyone ready?"

Eagerly the dozen girls nodded, though Eliza noted that Lula Redd rolled her eyes as she complied. But then, Eliza thought with a wry smile, she herself would have done the same as recently as three years before.

"All right, girls, each of these stone crocks needs to be filled with currants, after which they will be placed in these tubs of boiling water. These wooden spoons are for stirring, and we have to boil the currants until they are all broken open."

"Do we stir constantly?" Sarah Jane Rowley asked.

"No, only occasionally."

"What's in that pot there at the back?"

Jane smiled. "Beeswax, Hannah, from Sammy Cox's bees."

"Oh, lawsy! Do you girls recollect when Cox's wagon tipped over backward coming up out of Cottonwood Canyon, and we had to gather all those dumb bees into bags!"

"I do! Thank goodness they were cold!"

"Amen!"

"Didn't Sammy take his bees when he left here?"

"Not all of them," Jane responded as she puttered about the stove. "Charlie bought a hive from him, and this year it has grown to three. We'll have some nice honey to share at our Thanksgiving feast."

"Are we going to do another drama?"

"No, Adelia. We're going to do a dance!"

"Perhaps we can do both," Eliza declared easily. "And maybe we can even hear from our choir. All right, girls, the next part of this project is outside."

"In the rain?"

"We'll stay under Jane's little porch."

"Yeah, if we can all fit under it."

"Can we just leave these crocks boiling?"

Jane Walton smiled. "I'll keep watch, Mary Eleanor. You go out and see what Eliza has to show you."

Obediently the dozen girls filed out into the commons, where Eliza was standing beneath the makeshift porch by two large burlap bags. "Girls," she said as she reached inside one of them, "this is an empty whiskey bottle, and in these bags are thirty-five of them."

"Thirty-five!" Lula Redd exclaimed gleefully. "Somebody sure went on a toot!"

"And how! Was that Billy, Eliza?"

"I hope not," Eliza laughed. "Actually, George Ipson stumbled onto these up near the LC Ranch, and asked Bill Ball if he might have them. As the cowboys had no further need of them, save for target practice, Bill Ball agreed and gave them to George."

"Boy, those cowboys sure must like their liquor!"

"What good are they to us, Eliza?"

"We're going to use them for our currants?"

"Don't tell me we're brewing currant wine," Mary Ann Rowley snickered, to the delight of the younger girls.

"Let's sell it to the cowboys when we're done. Bet we'd get rich off that many bottles."

"Yeah, we could sell the stuff at the Thanksgiving dance—at a dollar a bottle. We can invite every miserable cowpoke in the whole country."

"Girls," Eliza smiled, "that's enough. We aren't making wine, and you know it. We'll be using these bottles for our preserves."

"Well, I can see pouring it in those narrow necks, but I can't see how we'll ever get the jelly back out."

"That's why you're out here," Eliza stated with a wink at Lula's doubt. "Each of you take a length of this string, and one bottle. Good. Now tie the string so it makes a loop not quite as big around as the bottle. See? It must rest below the neck but just above the bottle's widest point."

"Like this?"

"Exactly, Leona. Now, once your string is tied, dip it in this coal oil and then put it around the neck of your bottle, like this."

"We're going to burn the strings?"

Eliza nodded. "Yes, Lucy. Now watch, because you're all going to have to do this in a minute or so." Striking a match Eliza lit her string and then waited until it had burned itself out. "Okay, as soon as the string is burned out, pick up the bottle by the bottom—like this so you won't get burned—and thrust the neck down into this bucket of water—like this."

"Wow!" two or three of the girls exclaimed as Eliza pulled the bottle back out of the water, the neck broken off cleanly where the string had burned. "Look at that!"

"Do you see?" Eliza questioned as she held the half-bottle up for the girls to see. "With the neck gone, we have a perfectly good jar for keeping our preserves. Now you do it, but stagger things, because there isn't room in that bucket for all the bottles at once. And they must be submerged when they are hot, or else they'll break jaggedly or even not at all."

Shortly the girls were creating jars of their own, and in a little while all were back inside—less two broken jars, which Eliza thought was remarkable—where Jane and Frances were squeezing the sufficiently boiled currants through a coarse cloth, holding back the pulp while letting the juice flow into a clean porcelain kettle.

"Do we only keep the juice, Sister Walton?"

"That's all."

"But . . . that seems like a terrible waste, throwing away all that berry stuff."

"We aren't throwing it away, Hannah. The pigs will make short work of it, believe me."

"All right, ladies," Jane declared as two or three of the girls took over squeezing the juice from the pulp, "the recipe calls for one and one fourth pounds of sugar per pint of juice. But since we aren't doing pints, and since we don't have any refined sugar, we'll be using molasses—about this much, I should think—which I am now stirring in and bringing to a boil."

"How do you know how much molasses to use?"

"By tasting it, Mary Eleanor, or by practice. I've done this enough times that I know about what to use, and it usually turns out."

"Will molasses taste the same as sugar, Sister Walton?"

"Pretty much, Naomi. Mainly what we lose is the color. Frances and I did some watermelon rind preserves on Tuesday—"

"Watermelon rind preserves? Yuck!"

"Actually, Lula, it is quite delicious. I was about to say, though, that with refined sugar, the jelly would be a clear green color. With molasses it is dark—about the same color, I would imagine, as your currant jelly will be."

"Folks actually eat watermelon rind preserves?"

Jane smiled. "It's Charlie's favorite, Kate. He'll be taking along a dozen jars when he leaves for Colorado in the morning. All right, girls, this froth or foam you see forming on top of the fruit must be skimmed off before it boils. Two of you take those porcelain skimmers and get it off. That's it. Hurry."

"Where do we put it?"

"In the slop pail with the pulp. It tastes awful, Lula, but the pigs seem to like it."

"They like anything!"

"Now what, Sister Walton?"

"Take that wooden spoon, Lucy, and see if it is congealing. As soon as it congeals, then we begin pouring it into your reformed whiskey jars."

"Don't we have to seal it?"

"Good for you, Mary Ann. That's right, preserves must be sealed, and sealed quickly. So, ladies, as soon as you have a jar filled, we'll pour a little of this melted beeswax onto the top, and then let it harden."

"Yuck! I hate beeswax! It sticks to my teeth!"

"You don't *eat* it, Adelia," Naomi Perkins snickered. "Beeswax floats!"

"That's right, Naomi. It does. And a thin layer of it, hardened on the top of these preserves, will seal them until you are ready to eat them—at our Thanksgiving feast or even much later this winter. Any questions?"

"Yes! Is this how all preserves are made?"

Jane Walton smiled. "Pretty much, Sarah. The recipes vary a little, and some folks like things sweeter than others. You can also buy Mason jars that come with rubberized lids that can be sealed by heating them. But when cash money's short, like it seems to be here in Bluff, then we use what we have available."

Bluff Fort

Posey's heart was filled with such fear, as he stood inside the door of the small cabin, that he could not stop trembling. Haskel was seated alone in front of the small fire, his bare feet stretched out toward it, and he had not looked up. Truly it was as Henry and the others had said. This old white mormonee had powerful medicine! Truly did his words have the power to make men do strange and marvelous things.

After a silence that seemed to last a lifetime, during which Haskel continued to stare without sound into the fire, Posey finally found the courage to open his mouth.

"Posey talk Haskel!" he blurted, his voice squeaking uncontrollably as if he were a small boy.

The old mormonee did not move, did not respond.

"Posey heap sad," the terrified young warrior forced himself to continue. "Allthesame steal mormonee horse, mormonee cow. Allthesame, heap sad!"

Haskel remained silent.

"Haskel have power, Posey need power. Haskel say where Toorah, Posey no more steal mormonee horse, mormonee cow!"

Nothing!

"Haskel make Pahute bring Too-rah back?" Posey's demands were now turning into less arrogant pleas.

Silence!

"Posey give Haskel tip-top pony, then allthesame no more steal, no more ever! Haskel say where Pahute hide Too-rah, Posey allthesame happy always."

Nada!

"Posey give Haskel tip-top pony, many many!" the young warrior pleaded, now getting desperate. "Haskel only make little medicine, just say where Too-rah. Then Posey allthesame no more steal, ever ever."

When even this unimaginably magnificent offer was ignored, the young warrior, not so much frightened anymore as he was discouraged, turned toward the door.

"Listen," Haskel suddenly said in perfect Ute, his voice so low and quiet that for an instant the startled Posey wasn't even certain the old man had spoken. Yet spinning about, he was shocked to see that Haskel had risen and was standing straight and tall, looking down at the much shorter warrior, his blue eyes seeming to bore right through him.

"You stop stealing," Haskel continued in perfect Ute, his voice no louder than before, but filled with all the power and authority Posey would ever want to hear, "stop lying, stop wanting to kill some man and get away with his outfit, stop wanting to kill the mormonee and steal their livestock, and *Shin-op* will love you. When *Shin-op* loves you, all your troubles will come out right."

Breathless, Posey waited for more. Surely this man of such powerful medicine would say more. Instead, however, Haskel folded himself back down into his chair and returned to his fire, so that almost instantly all things seemed as they had before—Haskel and his bare white feet ignoring him, the warm and stuffy cabin, everything.

"Ungh!" Posey grunted in disgust as he turned once again for the door and the drizzling rain. What a poor answer! There was no way to prove the old man's words, and he was still without any idea of where his beloved Too-rah might be hidden.

"Ungh!" he grunted again as he kicked his staggering pony viciously, urging it to hurry toward he knew not where. "Haskel has bad medicine!" Now he was snarling at the hapless animal. "Haskel's words have no power at all!" And in discouraged fury he flailed the sorry horse to even greater speed.

Bluff Fort

"What in the world are you doing?"

"Taking off this door hinge," Billy replied without turning around. "It's been broken since I put it on, and I figured it was time to mend it."

"But . . . that will take a blacksmith."

"I know," Billy replied with a wide grin. "Reckon it's time I learned how to be one."

It was nearly dark, the chores were finished, and Willy was already fast asleep. Eliza had taken up her darning needle and was working on Billy's socks, but Billy was not at his customary work, writing in his daybook. Instead he was bustling about like a man possessed, and Eliza could hardly understand why.

"Any particular thing inspire this?"

"Well, I did watch Joseph Barton for a time this morning. He's a fine blacksmith. Even helped him a little. And since the fort will mostly empty out come morning, at least of the men, I thought it might be a good time to get some things fixed up."

Eliza gazed at her husband. "Are . . . Have you changed your mind? Are you planning on following them in another day or so?"

"Why do you ask that?"

"Because of this flurry of activity. It's like you're in a hurry to get things done—before you leave, I mean."

Pausing, his expression serious, Billy looked up at his wife. "Hon-bun, I have no idea what I'm going to do. I feel silly as can be, not leaving in the morning with the others. I don't even have a good excuse for not going, though Joseph Barton instantly assumed I was staying back because you aren't over the death of little Mary Eliza."

"I . . . I'm not," Eliza whispered as tears of loneliness and grief sprang unbidden to her eyes.

"I know that." Billy stood and walked to Eliza, where he began gently massaging her shoulders. "I'm not over it, either. Every time I think about her I do just what you're doing."

"Maybe we . . . we'll never get over it."

"I don't think we will. For that matter, I don't think we're supposed to. That's part of being an eternal family. But President Lyman and others who have lost little ones, tell me that as time passes, it gets a little easier to deal with. I hope they're right!"

"Is . . . that why you're not going to Colorado?"

Billy sighed. "I don't know, hon-bun. Maybe. The whole time I was laying under the wagon today I was praying, trying to make some sense out of what the Lord seems to be telling me."

"The girls thought you were sleeping. So did I."

"Wish I had been. I think it would have been more productive."

"So . . . you didn't receive any further impressions?"

"I didn't, Eliza. It was the same thing all over again. I am not to go to Colorado this winter, for the Lord has another work for me to do. It may be taking care of you and Willy, for I didn't have a withdrawal of the Spirit when I asked that. But how I can do that and still earn cash money for the benefit of the community, I don't know."

"And we need cash money so very badly." Eliza thought again of her secret plan to give the community her savings, and almost had to pinch herself to keep from smiling.

Billy nodded. "Yes, hon-bun, we do. There's also the matter of food. In Colorado the railroad feeds me. Here at home I'm one more mouth to feed out of our extremely limited stores." Stopping his massage, Billy walked around and sat in front of his wife. "You see, Eliza, it doesn't make sense! Every ounce of reason and logic says I should be heading out with the brethren tomorrow."

"A few will be going next week, and Kumen and the others who have gone to the settlements will be going as soon as they return. Maybe you are supposed to wait, and go with them. Maybe all it is, is timing."

"Maybe," Billy sighed. "Thing is, I don't even get a confirmation when I pray about that. So . . ." Rising, Billy took up his screwdriver and returned to the hinge.

"So—what?"

"So, I'll keep busy doing whatever I can around here, for as long as I can. I reckon I can chop wood and haul manure and plant cedar posts around this fort until the cows come home."

"Or get stolen," Eliza said wryly.

"Yeah, that, too." Billy's grin faded, and he was silent for a moment, thinking. "My feeling, though, is that if nothing has presented itself by the middle of next week, then I'll know I was wrong."

"And you'll leave?" Eliza asked, trying to hide the catch in her voice.

"That's right, hon-bun. I simply must do my part."

"I . . . I know it," Eliza said as new tears sprang to her eyes. "But oh, Billy darling, I've already lost little Mary Eliza! I don't know if . . . if I can stand losing you again—even just for the winter."

25

Saturday, October 29, 1881

Duckett Ridge, Blue Mountains

Curly Bill Jenkins was just stepping into his saddle when he smelled the acrid odor of burning hair. For three days he had been camping near an old cliff dwelling under Duckett Ridge on the north edge of Brushy Basin, living off a yearling beef that Spud Hudson had given him, whittling doodads out of green tree limbs, and trying to decide whether or not to ride down to the LC headquarters to see if Bill Ball would give him a job. But now it had turned off cold—real cold—and he knew the weather was forcing his hand.

Curly was worried about asking for this job, though, for word had come up the trail that Bill Ball had got it into his noggin that Curly was in cahoots with Sugar Bob Hazelton, which in point of fact never had been, nor ever would be, true. Of course Mr. Lacy had believed the same nonsense, too, and had canned him once the herd of Texas cattle had been brought onto the LC in 1879. That was how he had ended up working for Spud Hudson.

But now Spud had sold out to the Carlisles and their "hoorah" outfit of ne'er-do-wells and outright owlhoots—wanted men who were bound to start drifting into the country sooner or later. And so Curly, who wanted no part of such an outfit or such men, had ridden south at the same time Spud had headed east. In the worst way he wanted a job for the winter—a good job working with good people such as Bill Ball was known to be. But even though the LC headquarters was only a few miles southeast from where he was now camped, located on a level bench in the high-walled canyon of Recapture Creek due north of White Mesa, Curly had still been trying to make up his mind about visiting when he smelled the smoke.

"Well, ol' Betsy hoss," he drawled softly as he pulled himself into the saddle and tested the breeze, "maybe we don't have to worry about no visit to the LC. Could be that Bill Ball and his outfit have come to us, and right this hyar minute are holding a branding party somewheres downwind. Wouldn't that be somethin', little hoss? Yes, sir, it would, and that's a purdee fact!"

Riding out of the secluded draw that was below the old Indian ruin, Curly headed generally south, going careful and quiet as was his nature, and pausing every little while to listen for the shouts of a branding crew and to test the air for more smoke. Thing was, the further he rode the more confused he became. Now and then the smell of woodsmoke and burning hair came clear, and he could hear cattle bawling all over the basin. But not once did he hear the shout of a human voice—the shouting and cursing so common to riders who were gathering, roping, throwing down, cutting, and branding cattle.

Within an hour Curly had grown so anxious that he left his horse and pack mule tied securely in a deep ravine. Taking his rifle he crept forward on foot, making his way through the thick brush and up the side of a small knoll where he hoped he would be able to see a little better. And as it turned out, he could. In a narrow draw not a hundred feet away from the foot of his little knoll, labored three silent men, all of whom were hard at work branding a small herd of cattle.

For a few moments Curly simply watched them, saying nothing and not moving at all. He knew none of them, of course, but that didn't mean much since he'd been out of circulation for going on three years. What he did know, after a little, was that they were using as branding irons a couple of the large, round rings from the ends of old cinch straps. With those makeshift irons, commonly called "running" irons on account of a man could use one on a cow and then run off in a hurry and not get caught with anything that even resembled a branding iron, the men were easily obliterating the LC brands on each of the cows, forming one of three wide bars that eventually graced the hip, side, and shoulder of each animal.

Rustlers! Bad pennies from the Carlisle outfit, doing their dirty work right there, practically under Bill Ball's nose!

Curly knew such cattle stealing was done, but most folks who rustled were content to take a cow now and then to eat, or else maybe they would brand with their own registered mark any and all unbranded calves they happened to run across. But this! This was bald-faced, wholesale rustling, for in a rope corral back up the ravine Curly could see at least fifty head that had already been branded. And in another rope corral milled at least a dozen additional head, all awaiting the same searing fate.

Slipping silently back out of sight, Curly descended the knoll and made his way forward until he was crouched just short of the lip of the ravine. All three men were now directly below him, not more than fifteen feet away, and all of them were at least a dozen additional feet from their horses and saddle guns. Of course they all wore handguns, but most men were not that accurate with such weapons, and Curly knew it. And even if it turned out that these men were, he thought with a wry grin, that didn't mean he had to give them a chance to prove it.

Waiting until the three had a cow down and were either holding it or using the heated cinch ring to burn the brand into the bawling animal's hide, Curly rose to his full, cadaverously lean height and stepped to within a foot of the lip of the ravine.

"Howdy, gents," he said amiably, and at the same time he levered a cartridge into the chamber of his saddle carbine. "Nice day for rustlin', ain't it?"

For an instant the men froze motionless in their awkward, bent-over positions, and Curly almost laughed, their frantic thinking was so plain. But then with a blur of speed one of the three spun upright, his right hand at the same time drawing his pistol from a tied-down holster slung low on his hip.

Without even lifting his rifle to aim, Curly fired, and even as he levered another shell into the chamber and shifted slightly to cover the other two, he had the satisfaction of seeing that his bullet had shattered the man's wrist and that his handgun had flown off somewhere into the rocks.

"You done crippled me!" the man shrieked in shocked disbelief as his two companions straightened and then stared at their friend's protruding bones. "You ignorant fool, you done crippled me for life!"

"I reckon so," Curly replied quietly as he watched the man grab at the wound with his other hand, belatedly trying to staunch the flow of blood. "I'm right sorry, too. If'n I was a better shot with this fool rifle I'd of hit where I aimed, which was right betwixt your eyes."

Curly saw the instant hope flicker in the eyes of the other two men, saw them measuring him and measuring also the degree of difficulty a draw against him would have, and he almost grinned again, it was so dad-burned funny.

"Seems to me," he drawled, almost hoping one or both of them would try, "that you two healthy hombres got you a choice. One, shuck your hoglegs into the rocks yonder and then help your friend, who is pumping out blood too fast to stay alive much longer, and who apparently ain't got the sense to twist a knot above his own wound. Or two, you can believe what I said about missing your friend's head, and have a try at me your ownselves. Oh, and you can do it one at a time or both all to once—whichever you want. It don't make no nevermind with me."

Curly grinned then, a wide, happy grin, for he hadn't felt so good since who flung the chunk. Or maybe even since Giggles LaFrench had sung all them hymns in an old-time, gospel-shouting, Sunday morning go-to-meeting. And seeing as how Giggles LaFrench had always broke out in giant hives even passing by a church, and also seeing as how she couldn't carry a tune in a bucket, no matter, that was some long time!

But Curly's confident grin, apparently, settled it. Slowly, so the happy cowpoke wouldn't misunderstand their movements, the two healthy rustlers gingerly pulled their pistols out of their holsters and tossed them into the rocks.

"Now your hideout guns," Curly ordered, still smiling widely. "The ones you didn't think I'd noticed. But do it careful again, and slow, because you hard cases make me real nervous, and I might jump to conclusions when you'd rather I wouldn't."

For an instant neither of the men moved, and so with hardly even a flicker of movement Curly fired again, blasting the hat from the head of one of the men and shooting low enough that his bullet plowed a short, shallow furrow in the man's scalp.

With a screech of pain and fear the man grabbed his head, discovered that he hadn't been killed but was indeed bleeding, and in another moment hideout guns had been produced by both of them and tossed into the rocks after the others.

"Now yer dying friend," Curly ordered, no longer smiling. "No doubt, he'll have a hideout, too."

"He can't use it nohow," the only man not wounded snarled angrily.

"Maybe," Curly snapped. "But you could! Now loose it from him! Pronto! Then we'll get this little party moving."

"But . . . but what about my arm?" the first man wailed. "I'm bleeding to death!"

"Talk to them," Curly intoned, nodding toward the others. "You boys have got my dander up, and I ain't feeling too much like one of them good Samaritan fellers this morning. Fact is, I wisht one of you would haul out another hideout gun or throw a toe-stabber at me or otherwise make a break for it. One less of you would sure make things a whole lot easier to manage."

Sullenly the men stared at Curly, who minded their anger not at all. Fact is, he was feeling better than he'd felt in years and years, and his disposition did nothing but improve as the men bound each other's wounds and then led out, under the cold, dark muzzle of his rifle, to where he had tied his animals.

"All right, boys," he grinned from the hurricane deck of his little Betsy horse, "all in step now, and be shure to sing along whilst yer marchin', beltin' 'er out good and loud:

One and a two and a shure enough three,
We're a heading on foot fer the ol' LC.
Come a ti yi yippie yippie yay, yippie yay,
Come a ti yi—

"What about our horses?" one of the men interrupted angrily, apparently seeing no humor in Curly's song.

"That's right, mister," the man pleaded who was most seriously wounded. "What with my arm all shot to doll rags like this, I can't never walk that far."

Curly smiled his infuriating smile once again. "I'm right sorry to hear that," he said as he pushed the three along. "Course if'n you don't, it'll sure save on the cost of rope onct we get to the ranch."

"Rope?"

"That's right. Way I figure it, you boys'll soon be climbing the Golden Stairs by way of a hemp neck-massage. Either that or by way of a bullet in the back on account of you ain't hurrying along in front of me quite fast enough."

"You him, then?" one asked as they anxiously quickened their stride. "You Bill Ball?"

"Me?" Curly Bill Jenkins laughed outright. "Not hardly. Compared to Bill Ball, I'm just a spring chicken. Bill Ball's got real fur on his brisket, boys. He was punching cows and dodging bullets afore he was even weaned, and now he stands out like a tall man at a funeral—all heart above the waist and all guts below. Way I heard it, his craw's stuffed fifty-fifty with creek-bed sand and fightin' tallow, and when he takes a swing, things either duck or go down flat."

Curly paused, looking ahead up a gentle, brush-covered slope. "Yes, sir, boys, Bill Ball's the real McCoy, and since yonder is him astride his favorite mule and coming straight at us, I'd say you're about to meet him face-to-face."

And for the first time since he'd been to church with Giggles LaFrench, or maybe even a long time before that, Curly Bill Jenkins started in to singing hisself.

South Bank, San Juan River

Grumbling unhappily, Sugar Bob Hazelton kicked a log onto the heap of coals that had, much earlier, been his fire. "Dad-gummed weather," he griped as he wrapped his arms about himself in a futile attempt at warmth. "One day she's hot enough by gum to raise blisters on a lizard's backside, and the next the wind shifts and she's so cold even the polar bears is hunting for cover!"

Kicking viciously the chilled outlaw sent another log onto the gray coals, and then another. At least there was a little smoke, he thought grimly, and a few spots of red-orange heat where the wind was reaching in with probing fingers, somehow tickling life into the dead-looking coals. Given a little time, maybe—

Nearby the insane outlaw's horse nickered once, and then again, giving its master what sounded like a horse-laugh. With a dour expression Sugar Bob glared at the lone animal. "It ain't no laughing matter!" he snarled angrily. "Hadn't bin fer that miserable Curly Bill Jenkins, I'd of had me a pardner to build up this dad-blasted fire for me; yes, and muck out all that fine silver ore down to the mine, too. Him and that gimped-up old silver-haired Mormon galoot from yonder at the fort! That's two of 'em what's done me out of a good working pardner, you miserable, ewe-necked crowbait!"

Staring off through the limbs of the cottonwoods, which were now losing their few remaining leaves in a hurry, Sugar Bob glared at the distant fort. "Miserable Mormons!" he snarled. "I ain't never done a bad thing to 'em, and what do I get in return? A little help? A decent pardner? A purty little woman to help me keep warm of a cold, cold night? No, by jings, I don't get none of that! All I get from that sorry old white-haired galoot and his sorry Mormon followers, is misery!

"Yeah," he grumbled, warming to his subject despite the weather and still talking to his horse, "and what about that four-flushing Rob Paxman and his snake-eyed pardner, Lug Santoni? Murdering double-crossers, the both of them, stealing all them Mormon hosses for me and then giving me the slip by heading west instead of south acrost the river here, to where I was waiting.

"Besides the hosses, I'd of had me *two* good working pardners then, you mangy old broom-tail, and they'd of done any doggone thing I'd have tolt 'em, too! And that includes building up my fires and fixing the grub and mucking out my silver! Either that, you snakebit old hay burner, or they'd of died on the spot and rotted to nothing where they lay. Serves the ornery so-and-sos right that the Mormons got their hosses back and sent 'em packing down the river. Good riddance is what I say! Good riddance, and I hope they've drowned somewheres in that turrible muddy water and are now a'burning in hell!"

His rancor spent for the moment, Sugar Bob grew still, his eyes again on the wisps of smoke from his useless fire, which promised heat but never seemed to deliver. Oh, he could have arisen and worked the fire to life had he been of a mind to, but the disfigured outlaw was of no such mind. Rather than warm himself by a real fire, he for some insane reason preferred watching the swirling smoke, shivering with cold, and cursing the entire dad-gummed world, which had in his demented mind, somehow turned, in whole and in part, against him. Especially the fool Mormons, yonder in their cozy cabins with dozens of good hot fires to keep 'em all warm, were against him, and Sugar Bob did not know what to do!

That was a fact, too! Everybody he knew was against him! Yes, and the whole evil scenario was driving him crazy! Not alone had Old Man Lacy cut and disfigured him and left him to bleed to death, but later on he'd had to kill poor old Dingle Beston just on account of general principles. Since then nothing had seemed to work out, no matter! After being driven out of Curly Bill's camp with a shot-up hand, he had somehow found his way to Twin Springs on the plateau top of Elk Ridge, where he had settled in to hide until his hand could mend and he could round himself up another pardner. For a couple of weeks he had camped there, too, more than half-starving and trying, meanwhile, to heal the wound in his hand and maybe as well the still-festering wound in his groin.

Trouble was, after those two weeks it had grown so cold of a night on the mountain that Sugar Bob couldn't stand it any longer, and so he had drifted south. Besides, the cold had got him to remembering the fine-looking little Navajo squaw he had done a little of his own carving on a few months before, and he was thinking maybe he could find her again, or another like her, to help warm up the rapidly approaching winter.

Back on the Navajo Reservation and practically starved half to death, he had found no squaws but had instead run into and finally talked that fool Johnny Molander into pardnering with him on his silver mine. He had also, he recalled with a grin, devoured most of the man's ample supply of grub. Then the next thing Sugar Bob knew, he had shot the ornery son-of-a-gun deader'n a petrified pasture flap-jack. For no good reason, either, or at least none that he could remember. There Molander had been, alive and laughing all easy-like whilst he was enjoying the sunset, all ready to go mine silver and make hisself rich, and then he was dead and Sugar Bob was leaving him behind in the sand and riding off laughing and cursing, and he still didn't know why he'd shot the man or didn't have him-self a new pardner, either one.

Next there were those two sorry hoss-thieves he had stumbled onto and tried to do a favor for, by sending them to the Mormon fort to steal all them hosses. Yeah, they deserved to be dead, them and that giant old white-haired Mormon what had taken his pistol from him and lifted him onto his hoss like a durned rag doll. And for what? He hadn't done nothing but eye them two Mormon women, though now he'd take his lusts a step or two further, by jings! Yes, sir, he thought with an insane grin, if that wagonload of berry-picking young Mormon females he'd been eyeballing in the rain the day before happened to come out again, or even better, if just one of them Mormon women was to come sashaying along that far bank, all alone—

26

Sunday, October 30, 1881

LC Ranch Headquarters

"That was good of you to bring them fellers in yesterday, Curly, real good. I know Mrs. Lacy and the Brumleys will be beholding, and it wouldn't much surprise me if they offered you some sort of reward."

Curly Bill Jenkins, sitting in one of the two leather armchairs facing the fireplace inside the LC headquarters cabin, nodded slightly but remained silent. Of a truth he was feeling about as expectant as a robin watching a wormhole, for the onliest reward he wanted was a job that would last through the coming winter, and he felt confident his capture of the rustlers would bring that to pass. Thing was, he had no idea how to bring the issue up with Bill Ball and still look like the hero he was presently being held out to be.

"You ever find out who they were?" Curly asked.

"Their names?" Bill Ball replied quietly. "They give 'em willingly whilst our cook, Old Rocky, was sawing off that man's hand and he was screaming his displeasure. His name's Boone Hogue, and according to the others he's supposed to be a real gunslick. Reckon now he'll have to learn to use his other hand—if'n he lives. The one whose hair you parted goes by the name Kid Slade, which I reckon ain't his real moniker at all. And the third of your lean-brained rustlers answers to Andrew Harvey Smith, which I reckon is his real name on account of I've heard of him somewheres afore, the Andrew being changed to Andy. The way they tell it, all three of them tough cases was minding their own business afore you came along and took unfair advantage of 'em." Bill Ball smiled easily. "Which only makes it fair, seeing as how that's what they were doing to the LC at the time. Onliest question I have, Curly, is did you shoot lucky or did you shoot a'purpose?"

Curly grinned. "Lucky, I reckon. I wasn't plannin' on creasin' that man's head—only shooting his hat off. And the other? The gunslick called Boone Hogue? I'd heard of him, but he was faster'n I thought he'd be. That's how come I hit his wrist and not his hand and pistol, which is what I intended to hit when I fired."

"You were lucky, all right," Bill Ball agreed. "Who taught you to shoot?"

"Not nobody. It just sort of come to me when I was a young'n. I ain't never even really learned to aim, at least not good and careful. I just sort of point, with pistol or rifle it makes no matter, and the bullets mostly go where I'm pointing. Back to home I won a few shooting contests and turkey shoots, but until yesterday that's about all the good it's ever done me. Think those boys will swing?"

Bill Ball shook his head. "Not likely, though we could have hung 'em here and been justified. Thing is, I don't hold to that. Give 'em their day in court, is what I say."

"That's a long ride to Fort Lewis."

"It is. But those leg irons will keep 'em quiet until the boys can get 'em there. They had more'n seventy head of LC cattle, Curly, most branded with big bars on the shoulder, hip, and side. You any idea who owns that brand?"

Curly stared at Bill Ball in shocked disbelief. "You ain't heard?" he finally asked.

"Heard what?"

"Bill, I hate to break the bad news, but Spud and Old Man Peters have sold their outfits to a couple of English brothers named Carlisle, who own the Kansas and New Mexico Land and Cattle Company. 'Cording to Spud, one of their brands is a bar on the hip, side, and shoulder, which they call the Three-bar."

Bill Ball looked stunned. "How soon does Spud leave?" he finally asked.

"A week ago. He headed east with five hundred head of cows

and no particular destination in mind. I don't know about Old Man Peters, but he may be gone, too."

"So." Bill Ball looked thoughtful. "That's why you were on LC range."

Curly nodded. "I bin camped at the head of Brushy Basin for a week, trying to screw up the gumption to come and ask you for a job. I'd finally made up my mind to do it when I smelt the smoke and run onto them rustlers."

"A job, huh? You any idea how many more of them Three-bar riders are in the country already?"

"I ain't got no idea a'tall. Spud did tell me, though, that they had ten thousand cows on pasture in Colorado with more a'comin'. He also told me he thought the Englishmen were square, but that the riders they had working for 'em was all a 'hoorah' bunch who looked over their shoulders at every section of straight road! He said he wisht, once he'd learned their natures, that he hadn't bothered to sell out to 'em. Thing is, he did, and the deal was already done."

For some time Bill Ball was silent, thinking. Finally he reached into his pocket, pulled out a pipe, stoked it, and fired it up. "Those boys who're taking your rustlers to Fort Lewis," he said after another few moments of silence, "have give me their notice. Being native Texicans they want no part of another high mountain winter, so once they drop the prisoners off they'll be heading south. I'm also missing another young feller, a happy-go-lucky son of a gun name of Johnny Molander, who won a cheap map in a card game over to Fort Lewis and couldn't rest until he'd followed it across the whole and entire Navajo Reservation."

"Huntin' for the lost Peshleki?"

Bill Ball eyed Curly narrowly. "You heard of it?"

"Who hasn't?" Curly shrugged. "Seen my share of maps to it, too. Thing is, Bill, lost mines don't hold much interest for me. I worked hard to become a cowman, and I'll be dogged if'n I'll throw it off to go chasing after some fool hole in the ground!"

Nodding, Bill Ball slumped into his chair. "I feel the same way. Always have. I did my best to talk Johnny Molander out of going, too. But he wouldn't talk for nothing, and he's been gone so long now that I'm afeared he won't be coming back."

"You think maybe he found it?"

Bill Ball laughed harshly. "You funnin' me, Curly? There ain't no mine—not now, and there never was! The onliest silver that'll ever come out of Peshleki is the silver that idjits like Johnny Molander keep paying for them fool maps. So no, he didn't find it. What he probably did find, is a bullet in the back from some other flea-brained nitwit who also wanted that useless map. It's too bad, too, because most likely we'll never really know what's happened to Johnny. His little dog what's bin pining around here something awful will likely die on account of Johnny's the only hombre he'll let get close, and somewheres or other Johnny's folks and maybe even his sweetheart will go to their graves a'wonderin' and a'worryin'."

Sighing, the LC foreman rose and stepped again to the window, his eyes on the cliffs rising beyond Recapture Creek. "Anyways, Johnny figured on being an extry hand this winter, so even without him I've got enough men to keep things going here on the home place." Softly Bill Ball tapped the windowsill with his fingers. "Thing is, Curly, now that you've told me what you have, I reckon I'm going to need a couple of men in a line camp betwixt here and Spud's range—probably somewheres up on Verdure Creek. You got you a partner stashed somewhere?"

Curly shook his head. "Ain't had one in years. Don't really believe in pardners, anyhow."

For a moment Bill Ball looked at him thoughtfully. "Interesting. Way I'd heard it . . . Well, I don't reckon that matters. If'n you'll take it, Curly, I'll hire you for the line camp, and see what I can do about scraping up somebody else to spend the winter with you."

"Is there a cabin?"

"I'll see that one's built and stocked with firewood and plenty of grub. Fact is, I'll get on it starting tomorrow. Either that or, if you ain't suspicious of haunts and we can find one close by, we'll close off one of them old Injun ruins and you can use it. You want the job?"

Curly grinned. "You know I do, Bill. And it don't make no nevermind to me whether I stay in a cabin or a ruin. Haunts ain't never bothered me yet, and I don't reckon they'll start now." Carefully, then, he drew a deep breath. "Howsomever, there's another little matter what needs to be cleared from the air—a little matter concerning you, me, and a polecat name of Sugar Bob Hazelton."

Curly watched Bill Ball's face stiffen, just as he'd known it would. But with dogged determination, for he did not like feeling accused of something for which he was not guilty, the tall, bald-headed cowpoke plunged ahead.

Allen Canyon

"Do you still think the warrior Posey will come to this place?"

Though the thirteen-year-old Pahute maiden Too-rah looked up at the question, the woman Peeb, a year older and a year wiser, did not, for she knew it was not polite to gaze into another's eyes when they were thinking of a response to a question. Nevertheless she was aware of Too-rah's glance, and she knew that her friend was troubled.

Behind the two women, a small fire burned in the early darkness, throwing light and heat both into the *wickiup* where the warrior Jonah lay in suffering silence, and against the women's backs as they sat together working. Before them, away from the *wickiup* and in the shadows cast by their own bodies, lay two robes made of rabbit skins, which Peeb had earlier stitched together into a double thickness. Now she and Too-rah were carefully stuffing cattail down between the robes, making a thermal blanket that even on the coldest of nights would hold her warmth and that of her husband and her unborn child.

Already such a down-filled robe was spread beneath where Jonah and she and Too-rah slept at night, and it had done wonders in holding back the cold that seemed to seep upward from the ground, oftentimes freezing people even though they were appropriately covered from above. Peeb had learned this great thing concerning warm robes from her grandmother, and she felt certain that her husband would already have died had it not been for that wonderfully insulated ground cover. In fact—

"It has been in my mind that the warrior Posey would come

here," Too-rah suddenly said, interrupting Peeb's thoughts. "The time of cold is rapidly approaching, the leaves have dropped, and it is in this place that Poke and his warriors always camp."

"That is so," Peeb agreed. "From the dropping of the leaves until the snow stays on the ground. It is then that they go back to the big river."

For a moment the silence held, the only sounds the popping of the fire and the distant splashing of the stream. For some reason even the coyotes were still, and for a moment Peeb wondered at that. "If the warrior Posey should come," she finally asked, "what will you do?"

"I will do as he asks," Too-rah replied simply. "It is in my heart that he is to be my husband, and so my place is to follow after him."

"Is that as you wish it to be?"

"My heart longs for nothing else." Too-rah smiled bashfully. "Unless it is that Posey be here now, his *moo-ninch,* his hand, folded strongly over my own."

"He is strong, like my Jonah, before—"

"Yes," Too-rah declared, attempting to take her friend's mind from the terrible sickness that was stealing away the life of her husband. "The warrior Posey is strong, and he is very, very brave. He has no fear, and sometimes that frightens me."

"I know your thinking." Peeb paused, her eyes staring out into the darkness. "My husband also had no fear, and thought it a great thing to make constant raids upon the mormonee along the big river. He, Poke and his brothers, the tall Navajo who is called Natanii nééz, Tuvagutts, Wash, Bridger Jack—"

"And the warrior Posey," Too-rah declared.

"Yes," Peeb agreed sadly, "and the warrior Posey. Now the strong words of the mormonee called Haskel have struck down the tall Navajo. Those same words have struck down my brave husband, and it is in my heart that perhaps Posey does not come to this place because he . . . because he has also been stricken. Have you also thought these things, my sister?"

Soberly Too-rah made the sign that she had indeed thought such things. "He who is called Scotty," she said, her voice hardly above a whisper, "told me that words of power were most certainly spoken against the warrior Posey."

"By the man Haskel?" Peeb asked fearfully.

"No, by a woman of the mormonee, against whom Posey had gone to make a raid. It was she from whom he fled."

"Perhaps this woman's words held little power."

"Perhaps." Too-rah sighed her discouragement. "Still, it is in my heart that all the mormonee, men and women alike, have great and terrible power in all their words. Scotty, after watching the warrior Posey flee in terror from the presence of the mormonee woman, told me that he believes this to be so."

"That a woman would have such power is a thing to be wondered at," Peeb admitted.

"It is. There is also another warrior, one called Henry, who believes the same as Scotty. Henry says the words of the mormonee were given them by *Shin-op,* the great creator, and that *Shin-op* taught the mormonee how to use the words so they would never have to fight. That is why no one has ever heard of a mormonee, man or woman, slaying an enemy."

Peeb looked at her friend in wonder. "Do you believe this great thing?"

"I . . . I do believe. The warrior Posey worried many days concerning how the mormonee, who carried big guns but did not once use them, took back their horses at the place of bubbling water during Moencopi Mike's big raid. Posey could not understand how it was done, and it filled him with anger. He worried more that his big gun would not fire at the mormonee when they came together at that place, and that the weapons of the other warriors of the People would not fire, either. These things troubled him greatly, for on the mountain he spoke of it often.

"Many times I have also heard Scotty tell the warrior Posey that it was the power of the mormonee words given them by *Shin-op* that did it, and Henry agrees with him."

"So does my husband agree," Peeb stated quietly, almost bitterly. "Before he stopped talking altogether, and before his mind started going off to so many strange places, he spoke of that great and terrible power, telling me that it was what was *e-i,* killing him. He had scorned and made a mock of the warning words of the mormonee Haskel by making more raids, and now he dies like an old man might die, slowly and painfully, and many years before his time. He believes, and I also believe! Now I fear that my husband will not live to . . . to see his first child."

And so saying, the woman Peeb covered her face and, coyote-like, began filling the night with her long and lonely wails.

27

Monday, October 31, 1881

Bluff Fort

It was interesting, Billy thought as he followed the obvious hoofprints of old Bess across the sand east of the fort, how short the days were getting. In a way that was good, for daylight came a lot later and darkness a lot earlier, and so there were less hours in which to do the backbreaking work that mere survival in Bluff seemed to necessitate. Of course it meant that more work had to be done by firelight and lamplight, but to Billy a good part of that was cozy work—reading, working on his study courses, playing with Willy, and helping Eliza as best he could. Those were the times he had dreamed of during the winter nights the year before when he had sat in the cave or elsewhere, hunkered against the cold and loneliness, and praying with all his heart that the winter would hurry and pass. And praying, too, that he and his precious family could soon be reunited. But now, he thought bleakly, it was getting ready to happen to all of them again—

It was growing pretty chilly, too, and the nights were downright cold. The water troughs in the fort, and the slower places on the river, all carried a morning fringe of ice. And this morning ice had even frozen in little crystals on the quilts where his, Willy's, and Eliza's breath had come in contact with the crisp, cold air. There was no doubt about it; once again it was time to start wearing his nightcap and dressing for winter.

The livestock was feeling it, too. It was harder now to get the cows into the milking stalls in the corral, and it seemed harder for them to let down their milk so Billy and the others could take it from them. As for the horses, they had a hump in their backs every morning, and now practically every one of them crow-hopped when they were first mounted. Some also put up a pretty good job at bucking, though to Billy it seemed one and the same.

And that, simply put, was why he was trailing Thales' cow, old Bess, afoot. Despite his hundreds of miles horseback the past few months, as he and others had chased the Pahute horse thieves to Boiling Spring, climbed and explored the Elk Mountain, or gone chasing after the two horse thieves who had shot Jody Lyman and then escaped down the Colorado River, Billy remained uncomfortable in the saddle. It wasn't that he disliked riding. To the contrary, he found the experience exhilarating. It was the bucking and crow-hopping he hated—that, and the picking himself up out of the rocks and cactus that inevitably followed. So he rode when he had to, walked or took a wagon when he could, and enjoyed as much of the country as his senses could take in, no matter.

"Well, Bess," he breathed as he finally spotted the wandering cow, who had snagged the end of her rope between two large rocks, "at least you picked a pretty morning to wander off. You ever seen a clearer sky? Or brighter yellow on what's left of yonder cottonwood leaves? Or felt a sharper nip of old Jack Frost in the air? Mercy sakes, Bess, but the Lord's put you and me into a wondrous world, filled with more beauty and mystery than a fellow can hardly imagine! Why, there're so many things I'd like to know, to understand—

"Say, what's that yonder, across the river? Smoke, you think? Well, Bess, old girl, I'd say you were right. Somebody's camped over there, sure enough, right near where Navajo Frank's hidden trail comes down off the bluff. Reckon it must be some of our Navajo neighbors—maybe even Frank and sweet little Hádapa. Too bad Kumen's not back from the settlements. He'd know right off who they were, and maybe even cross over and have a good sit-down with them."

Turning back toward the fort, the cow in tow, Billy forgot the smoke and began thinking instead of his neighbors. By now Lydia May would have become Kumen's plural wife in the St. George temple, and no doubt the whole party was well on their way back to Bluff, hurrying to beat the snow that made travel over the mountains so difficult.

For a moment Billy wondered how the newly reorganized family would be dealing with things. He didn't think he'd be dealing with it very well, and neither would Eliza. For a fact, Billy couldn't even imagine how his dear Eliza might react—

Abruptly Billy's mind stopped, and then he knew! He wouldn't be there with Eliza and little Willy—not for visiting with the Joneses, not for arguing the principle of plural marriage, and not for anything else! There would be no job for him except in Colorado, no way to earn even a dollar of cash money unless he followed the rest of the brethren east to work for the railroad. The impressions he had received, the answers to prayer he thought he had been given, had obviously been mistakes. That, or maybe he had been outright deceived—fooled by the devil with some of his crafty lies. That seemed more likely, in fact, because the answers had seemed so firm, so direct. How could he make a mistake about that?

So no, it had to be that he had somehow been deceived. Only, what had he done that had given Satan such power over him—

"Morning, Billy. Did old Bess get away again?"

"Howdy, Thales." Billy had been so deep in thought that he hadn't even noticed the Indian missionary's approach. "Yep, she did. But I was lucky. Her rope caught between some rocks, so I didn't have much trouble finding her."

Thales Haskel nodded. "She's a wanderer, all right. Mighty pretty morning to go searching for her, though. Clear, fresh, not even a breath of wind to stir what's left of the leaves."

"I noticed that. Fact is, earlier I saw a smoke over across the river, near that hidden trail—rising straight upward. Even a little breeze and I likely wouldn't have seen it."

"Smoke, huh?"

"Yes, probably some of our Navajo neighbors. I was thinking if Kumen was back, he would probably know just who they are. Maybe you do."

Soberly the thin old man pushed back his hat. "Nope, as a matter of fact, I don't. When you figuring on heading out east, Billy?"

"Well," and Billy unaccountably dropped his eyes as he said it, almost as if he were ashamed, "Joe Lillywhite, Sam Mackelprang, and Amasa Barton said yesterday at meeting that they're leaving Wednesday morning. I . . . uh . . . I reckon they'll make good company."

"They will . . . if'n that's where you're supposed to go." Carefully Haskel readjusted his hat down over his eyes. "Well, adios, Billy. Don't let old Bess pull no more shenanigans. I learned her better. More important, remember to always trust the Lord, no matter! And when it comes to riding instead of walking or taking a wagon, don't forget the power of the Lord's priesthood. That's what Noah used."

With that the Indian missionary and interpreter touched his horse's flanks and rode off, and Billy was left with a puzzled look, trying to make sense of what the old man had said—of what in the world Haskel thought Billy was supposed to do.

"Dear Father in Heaven," Billy breathed fervently as he moved toward the northeast gate of the fort, "keep Satan away from me, and please help me to understand—"

Bluff Fort

"See window, Pa? See window?"

Billy, finishing the gruel Eliza had fixed for breakfast while he had been chasing down the cow, smiled at his son. "Why sure, Willy, I suppose I can show you what's brewing outside. Come here, and . . . whoa, you're getting so big I can hardly lift you!"

"All he wants to see is that smelly snake skin," Eliza grumbled as Billy picked up his suddenly excited son. "*Cliz bekigie!* I expect I hear that fifty times a day."

Carrying his son to the window, Billy grinned as the child pointed in the direction of the icehouse and began repeating the Navajo words again, over and over.

"He's sure-enough got it down, all right. Reckon it's time for Brother Haskel to teach him something else."

"I thought that's what he was doing yesterday, when he and Willy went for a little walk after meeting. But I haven't heard any new words, so I don't know."

"Outside, Pa? Outside?"

"A little later, Willy, when the sun warms things up a bit. See? Right now there's still ice on that barrel yonder by the well."

"Ice."

"That's right. Ice. Ice means it's cold outside." Billy smiled at his son and tickled his tummy, bringing forth a paroxysm of giggles. "You know, hon-bun," he said as Willy strained to see more of what was outdoors, "it's too bad Platte couldn't get any more than that one beer barrel and spigot. The water coming out of that filtering system tastes a lot better than before it went in."

"I'm certain I can taste the beer."

Laughing, Billy turned and came back into the room. "Not much, you can't. Platte carried brine water all the way from the Mancos just to kill the taste."

"Billy?" Eliza was keeping her hands busy, and not looking toward her husband. "What are you going to do?"

"Today? Well, I figured I'd clean some manure out of the corral and then see if I could do a little more blacksmithing. Saturday I even mended a packsaddle somebody had left there. Now I know how those blamed things are put together. In fact—"

"Smithing isn't what I mean, Billy, and you know it."

Sighing, Billy put his son down on the bed, where he began tickling him again. "I don't hardly know what to tell you, Eliza. No matter how hard I pray, I can't get a good feeling about going to Colorado. Neither can I get approval to go spend the winter with Dick and George at the sawpit." Billy shook his head as Willy crawled away and slid his feet onto the floor, then toddled to the fireplace. "Thing is, nothing else has opened up, and time's run out. Putting things off, I've done every single thing I can think of, to help you and the other sisters be ready for winter. Now it looks like I have no choice but to leave."

"When?" Eliza's voice was small, and afraid.

"I told Thales a little bit ago that I was going to leave Wednesday morning, with Sam and the others."

"But . . . what about your feelings, your direction from the Lord?"

Again Billy dropped his gaze. "I must have been wrong, hon-bun. I reckon there's nothing else but to admit it."

"Do you really believe that?"

"What choice do I have?" Billy's voice was suddenly hard, which surprised Eliza. "If a man's being deceived, the best thing he can do is face it and move on."

"Oh, Billy, darling—"

"Ahh, hon-bun," Billy soothed as he stepped to his wife and took her in his arms, "I'm sorry. I truly am. I . . . I think I'd give about anything in this world if I could just stay home with you and little Willy. But I can't. We have an obligation to these folks. We're part of this peace mission, and I have to do my part to keep it going, just as much as they do."

"I know that, Billy. It's just that—" Eliza took a deep breath. "I wasn't going to tell you this, not yet, at least. But awhile back I wrote the Co-op in Cedar, asking them to exchange my . . . *our* shares for a new cookstove—a Majestic. Kumen's going to try and bring it back with him."

Billy was thrilled. "That's wonderful, hon-bun! It'll make it so much easier for you to keep the cabin warm. Besides, you won't have to bend over so much to do the cooking, they're a ton cleaner, and—well, stoves are a blessing to about everybody in the fort! No fooling, Eliza. I think you did just the right thing!"

"I . . . I'm glad you think so. I also wrote my bank in Salt Lake, asking them to transfer all my funds to the bank in Durango. Billy, I'm going to donate everything to the mission."

"Why," Billy declared, now truly astounded, "that's wonderful of you! Only I didn't know you had any such funds."

"It's the money I got from the sale of my millinery shop. I . . . I was saving it . . . in case our mission didn't work out. But folks here are in such terribly awful shape, and needing cash money so badly—well, it just seemed like the right thing to do."

"You're wonderful!" Billy exclaimed. "To be so generous, hon-bun."

Eliza shook her head. "It isn't a bit more wonderful than what everybody else is doing. Thing is, Billy, if we donate all that—the use of our stove and all the money—wouldn't it be enough to allow you to stay home with us this winter?"

Surprised, Billy looked at his wife. "Why, I don't hardly know. I suppose . . . well, are you, ah, are you certain you'd feel good about that?"

"Why wouldn't I?"

"Because it wouldn't be a donation anymore, Eliza. It'd be a buyout. You'd be purchasing my company for the winter. Which is fine, as far as it goes—and there would be nothing I'd like better. But what about all the other lonely sisters here in Bluff—the ones who haven't been blessed with money like you have? How will they feel when they see what your money has purchased for you?"

"But . . . they'd benefit just as much as I will! The money is going to be for them, to purchase the things they need."

"All except the company of their husbands and fathers and brothers and sons."

"Well, I think this is a foolish discussion!" Eliza declared, upset by Billy's reasoning. "If people are going to be as little as you think they'll be, then . . . then . . . well, then they're all a bunch of narrow-minded fools! I'll give them my money and you can just go to Colorado! Willy and I won't ask for a single thing!"

"Eliza—"

"I mean it, Billy. And I don't want to talk about it anymore, either! Don't you have manure to spread somewhere?"

Billy sighed and picked up his hat. "I'm sorry, hon-bun. I didn't mean to upset you. We'll do whatever you think is best, and I'm sure it will all work out. How soon is the money supposed to get here—to Durango, I mean?"

"I don't know." Eliza's voice was now quiet. "It was the president of Main Street Bank that I wrote to, but I haven't heard from him." Pulling her large kettle of heated water from the fire, Eliza began the task of scrubbing the dishes. "Of course," she added thoughtfully, "with mail being the way it is—"

"*Báàh bee nehelgéshí*," Willy suddenly shouted as Eliza picked up the butcher knife she had used to cut the bread a little earlier. "*Báàh bee nehelgéshí!*"

"What is he saying?" Eliza asked, confused.

Billy chuckled. "He's pointing at that knife, so I reckon it's Navajo for bread knife or butcher knife—something like that."

"*Bááh bee nehelgéshí,*" Willy said twice more, and then again.

"Well, hon-bun," Billy smiled as he clapped his hat on his head, "at least he isn't saying snake skin anymore. Haskel's given him something new to drive us crazy with."

"See the *Bááh bee nehelgéshí,* Ma?" the child asked earnestly, tugging at his mother's apron. "*Bááh bee nehelgéshí?*"

Abruptly Eliza started to laugh, with relief Billy joined her, and for both of them the world was starting to look a little better.

Bluff Field

"Say, girls, where you headed?"

Billy, working with Amasa Barton and Joseph Lillywhite on the brush, juniper, and willow fence that they hoped would surround the Bluff field before they departed eastward, paused to wipe his brow. The nights and mornings might have cooled off considerably, he had been thinking before the two girls rode up, but the afternoons were still plenty warm.

"Lula, you aren't going after more currants, are you?"

Both Lula Redd and Sarah Jane Rowley, who were riding double on the horse, laughed and waved their pails in the air. "You guessed it, Brother Barton. All we need is a little bush, and we can fill these in a hurry."

"You're not going very far, are you?"

"Not even as far as the Jump, most likely. Eliza said she is sure she saw another currant bush when we were there the other day, so Lula and I are going to see."

"Your folks know?"

Lula rolled her eyes. "Yes, Brother Lillywhite, we told our mothers. Our fathers are already gone."

"I'm glad you told your mothers," Joseph Lillywhite declared soberly. "Still, you'd best keep an eye out for Indians."

"Or any other strangers," Billy added.

"We will." The girls' reply was in singsong, and Billy knew they'd had their fill of instructions. "If you can squeeze any extra fruit into those pails of yours," he grinned, "bring some home for us."

"What's the matter, Billy?" Lula teased. "You and Willy already gone through that jar of preserves we gave you?"

"No," Billy's smile grew wider, "but we might by tonight."

Laughing, the two girls rode eastward, and after remarking about the amazingly sassy manners of modern youth, the three men returned to their work.

Bulldog Canyon

"Howdy, boys." Bill Ball sat on his big mule, gazing down at the two men who were about finished digging a pit into the side of the hill. "Dick Butt, ain't it?"

Removing his hat and wiping the sweat from his forehead on a grimy sleeve, Dick Butt nodded. "Yes, sir, that is my name. This is George Ipson, and you'll be Bill Ball."

"Have we met?" Bill Ball asked in surprise.

"No sir, not officially. But I saw you once from a distance, the boys at the fort tell of your help with the cribs, and talk of the mule you ride gets around, too."

Bill Ball grimaced. "No doubt spread by that tax-collecting Lem Redd."

"He's one of 'em, all right." Dick scrambled out of the pit and stood upright, stretching his back. "What can we do for you, Mr. Ball?"

"I didn't know you Mormons were going into mining."

Chuckling, Dick Butt gave a helping hand to George Ipson, who also scrambled out of the deepening pit. "We aren't, though I suspect if one of us found a good vein of ore, we would be. No, Bill, this hole is a logging pit, not a mine. George and me are figuring on cutting some of these Ponderosa pines this winter and whipsawing them into good, smooth lumber."

"You roll the log acrost the hole?"

"That's right. Endwise. Then one of us stands atop the log and the other beneath it, in the pit, and we work the saw back and forth down the length of the log together."

"Sounds mighty tiresome, especially for the fellow down in the pit who has to eat and breathe all the sawdust."

"We'll trade off," George Ipson stated confidently. "And no matter how tiresome it is, or how dirty, it can't be any worse than cutting ties for the railroad. Even better, there's a chance for a good profit in this business, because there isn't another like it anywhere in the country. That's something else the railroad never offered us."

"Well," Bill Ball drawled, "it should work, happen Injuns and other unruly sorts don't drive you out of the country first. I hope she does work, despite that it leaves me somewhat disappointed."

"Oh?"

Bill Ball nodded. "When I was down to Bluff working on them cribs last spring I had a talk with your Danishman bishop about maybe hiring myself a hand or two for the winter. Turns out I do need one. He recommended you, Dick, and somebody a day or so back tolt me I could find you here."

"Bishop Nielson recommended me?"

"That's right. He said you was a top hand with hosses or cows, either one, was tough as nails, and was an honest man, to boot. You figure you might be interested?"

For a moment Dick Butt and George Ipson looked at each other. "Much obliged, but I don't hardly think so," Dick finally answered as he turned and looked back up at the man. "George and I have pretty well made our plans."

"I was afraid you might say that." For a moment the foreman of the LC looked thoughtful. "Well, then, I have another proposition for you. Word's out that a new outfit is moving onto Spud Hudson's range, a hoorah outfit, they say. To keep our cows shy of buzzards such as them, I've got to put me a line camp somewheres up on Verdure Creek. I was thinking of maybe using an old Injun ruin, but I've bin scouting for two days now and ain't found one that'd even begin to do the trick. That means I've got to have me a cabin, and I've got to have 'er quick. How'd you boys like the job of building it for me?"

"Cash money?" George Ipson asked.

"As ever. A hundred dollars if you can get 'er done within the week, and I'll even send up a long, tall galoot name of Curly Bill Jenkins, to help."

"How big?"

"Curly or the cabin?"

Dick Butt grinned. "The cabin."

"Not very, and not fancy, either. Dirt floor, sod roof, and a couple of cowhides stretched over some poles for a door and window. But she'll need a fireplace, most likely mud and willows like you've used on some of those cabins down to the river. That's on account of I ain't got any extry stoves to drag up there to Verdure, and these boys will need a little warmth. She'll also need a lean-to shelter for the horses and a couple of corrals, one close in like a pen and the other somewhat bigger. Will you do 'er?"

"We'll do 'er," George Ipson replied, unintentionally adopting the cowboy's slang. "The fireplace may take into next week, though."

"And I'll make the pay a hundred and twenty-five."

"Thank you," Dick Butt stated. "Are you still short a man?"

Bill Ball nodded his affirmation. "You have a suggestion?"

"I do, happen you're of a mind to hire a man who knows livestock, is tough as they come, and is a whole lot more honest than I'll ever be."

"You know such a feller?"

"I do. He ran the Co-op back in Cedar City for a time, and I never saw such a hand with stock. He doesn't beat 'em or overpower 'em, mind you, for he's a little feller and that just ain't his style. What he does do, is sort of get under their skins or into their heads, so that he somehow thinks like they do. I don't know how he does it, and I don't think he knows, either. But I've seen him figure right away what was wrong with sick cows that had the experts stymied, and do the same with horses. More than that, he can somehow tell a good animal from a worthless one, and to me that's his best trait. Tell the truth, Bill, I never once saw him make a mistake. Course he's quick to say he don't know a whole lot and can't ride worth sour apples, and in that he's sure enough right. But he's a quick learner, so that's something I wouldn't worry very much about."

"Is he a hand with a gun?"

Dick and George smiled at each other. "Not according to him," George responded. "Fact is, he never carries one. But when we rode amongst those Utes and Pahutes after our horses last spring, he got the drop on a couple of them renegade murderers and never budged until their weapons were lowered and cooler heads had prevailed."

"I still can't hardly imagine how you boys pulled that one off, without even one shot being fired."

"Well, one Pahute tried twice, aiming to kill this feller I've been speaking of. Both shots misfired, and that was when our man took over and got the drop on the shooter and his brother. After that they never let out a peep."

"Sounds like a real hombre!" Bill Ball grinned. "What might his handle be, and where might I find him?"

"His name's Billy Foreman," Dick Butt declared as he replaced his hat, "and I reckon of an evening he'll be found at home, there in the Bluff fort with the rest of the Saints. Unless, of course, he's already headed off to Colorado to work on that fool railroad."

"Reckon I'd best hurry, then," Bill Ball declared, and with a wave of his hat he was off, his big riding mule pointed southward toward the Rio San Juan.

South Bank, San Juan River

Uncomfortable in the afternoon heat, which had already replaced the week of early cold weather, Sugar Bob Hazelton woke with a start. He'd slept a good two hours, he thought as he rose to his feet, and in that time the shade from the cottonwoods had shifted, leaving him to burn.

"Dad-gummed sun!" he snarled as he fished around for his

canteen. "It don't do its work proper of a morning, then it fries a feller to death in the afternoon!"

Lifting the canteen he took a swig of the tepid liquid, and then with an oath he spat it out. "Water!" he snarled as he wiped at his mouth with his dirty sleeve. "I'm getting sick to death of drinking water! What I need, by jings, is a good jug of whiskey!"

Jamming the cork back into his canteen he tossed it in the direction of his saddle, not caring in the least if he ever saw it again. For now his mind was running, thinking of the whiskey he'd drunk in his life, both good and bad, and of how it didn't seem to matter one way or the other.

"What I'd ought to do," he muttered as he picked up Dingle Beston's army binoculars to take another gander at the distant Mormon fort, "is mix me up a batch of my own rotgut, like old Dingle and me did, down to Texas. Yeah, then I could drink me all the booze I wanted, and sell the rest to the fool Injuns. That'd sure-enough prime the pump of my prosperity, all right. Then maybe I could even buy me a woman to warm my blankets of a cold winter night!"

Grinning at the thought, Sugar Bob actually began mixing the concoction in his mind—a mixture that was by no means original with him—three plugs of chewing tobacco, two ounces of strychnine, six bars of good lye soap he could steal from any settler woman in the country, two or three hats full of sagebrush leaves, and maybe a pound of red pepper. Dump all that into half a barrel of unstrained river water, pour in two gallons of straight alcohol, stir in a rattlesnake head or two, and there she was! Injun whiskey! Mixed together and allowed to sit for a week or so under a sun as hot as this one, Sugar Bob thought as he wiped his brow and felt his mouth actually starting to salivate, and the resulting brew would raise welts on a creek-bed rock or cause the dead to rise up and shout hallelujah! Yes, sir, he grinned as he stared absently through the stolen binoculars, it would—

What was that? There, across the river and beyond those willows. It was a horse, a bay, and it was carrying a white woman! No, by jings, it was carrying *two* white female critters, all gussied up in pretty pinafores and bonnets. Even better, they were alone, and headed directly toward him.

Dropping the binoculars to the earth and forgetting the whiskey altogether, Sugar Bob Hazelton slipped through the willows and splashed as quietly as possible across the three or four meandering channels of the river, shallow now in the late fall. He did not worry about quicksand, he did not even worry that he had left behind his horse and his fine rifle. His side arm was weapon enough against a couple of women, he was certain, and with one or both of 'em in tow, he could always ride their bay back across the river to where his own nag was staked out.

Two dad-gummed women, by jings! And white women, to boot! Why, they'd be enough to warm any man's cold winter nights—

South Bank, Jan Juan River

Now that they were coming onto him, drawing closer, Sugar Bob could see that the two riders on the bay weren't exactly women. No, sir, they were little girls, all scrawny and pinched-looking and not round and comfortable-looking in the least. Why, even together they weren't a match for that little Navajo squaw on whom he'd had so much fun with his knife a couple of months back.

Still, he thought, clearing his mind of useless memories, a man in his position couldn't afford to be choosy. Especially not after what that sorry old I. W. Lacy had done to him. Besides, there were two of 'em coming at him through the willows, all giggly and stupid, and together they had ought to equal one good blanket companion in any man's language!

Hunkering down in the willows, Sugar Bob waited. They weren't in any hurry, that was sure. And from their laughter the two girls were having an almighty good time of it, too. Fact is, they were paying so little attention to things that he could probably stand right up and holler "Boo" at 'em, and they wouldn't even see him. Of course he wouldn't do that, but he could have, and he knew it.

Somewhere back in the bluffs across the river a crow gave a

raucous screech, and behind him a chunk of sandy bank gave way and sluffed quietly into the water. These were normal sounds, and Sugar Bob paid them no mind. Otherwise it was silent on the river bottoms, not even a breeze to stir the willows. But the girls were drawing closer, thirty feet away now, maybe even twenty-five. He couldn't see them, but their happy voices gave them away, and once again the outlaw's mouth was beginning to salivate. In another minute, perhaps two, he'd sure-enough be set for the winter!

Now! he thought as his hand reached for his holstered pistol, it was time—

"Looking for this, brother?"

Spinning to his feet, Sugar Bob Hazelton found himself facing a thin old man of medium height, who was holding Sugar Bob's most recently stolen pistol in his hand. But that couldn't be! his mind screamed as he groped again and again for the missing weapon. *It just couldn't be!* He'd heard nothing! No footsteps, no movement of willows, no whisper of metal against leather as his gun was pulled. Nothing! Yet his holster was empty, and that hogleg dangling in the old man's hand, was sure-enough his!

The two girls entirely forgotten, the dumbfounded outlaw whined in frustration and reached for his toe-stabber, a long-bladed weapon he kept slung between his shoulder blades. He was good with that knife, and fast—

"Now you'll be looking for this," the old man said quietly as he touched with his moccasined toe the handle of Sugar Bob's knife, which was buried to the hilt in the sand. "Since you'll be leaving these parts, I didn't reckon you'd have much need for either of 'em anymore."

Then, while Sugar Bob stared in stupefied amazement, the old man tossed the pistol out toward the river, where it splashed into the quicksand-laced water. Before he could draw another breath, the stunned and thoroughly shaken outlaw watched his knife arc out in the same general direction, to splash into the murky water with hardly more noise than had his pistol.

"Why, you miserable, low-down—" Sugar Bob started to snarl. But then he noticed the man's eyes, icy blue and piercing in a way he had never before seen, and his cursing quickly died away. This man, whoever he was, was dangerous, he could see, more dangerous than any man he had ever encountered. Why, he was even more formidable than that tall old Mormon galoot with the gimped up leg what had picked him up like a rag doll—

"Who . . . who are you?"

"You'll not be bothering the children," the old man stated by way of reply. And his voice was so low, so quiet, that Sugar Bob had to strain even to hear it. "Your name's known, Robert Hazelton, and there's a sheriff in yonder fort who has papers on you. You even look in the direction of those two girls again, and me and that sheriff won't rest until you're swinging from this here cottonwood."

More stupefied than ever, Sugar Bob could only stare. He was known! Somehow this frightening old man knew his name, and was warning him of the intention of the law.

"Was I you," the old man continued as his gaze transfixed the erstwhile outlaw, "I'd fork that sorry pinto you have staked across the river and make tracks. Even then I fear it'll be too late."

"Wha . . . what do you mean?" Sugar Bob stammered, not even noticing that the two girls had ridden up and pulled rein and were silently watching the proceedings.

"You have a bloody past, Robert Hazelton, a cruel and bloody past that cannot be overlooked. Neither will you be able to escape it—not in this life, not in the next. You have offended some of God's sweetest innocent ones, you've planned on offending more, and it would have been better for you if a millstone had been hanged about your sorry neck and you'd been drowned in the depths of the sea."

"But—"

"I'm sick nearly to death with the evil of you, Robert Hazelton. Far rather would I be dealing with the most bloodthirsty Pahute or thieving Navajo, for they are only acting according to the false traditions of their fathers, and not the satanic evil that drives you.

"Now skedaddle! Shoo! In the name of the Lord God of Israel I tell you to take your pestiferous soul and be gone! And don't you even *think* of coming back to bother these folks again!"

Unable to speak, to respond, or to resist in any way, the famed outlaw turned and stumbled toward the river. His crazed mind, abruptly clear, demanded his obedience and thus his departure, and he couldn't begin to fight it. Neither could he hear, as he splashed woodenly across the shallow water toward his camp, the heartfelt gratitude expressed by the two little girls as they followed their beloved Brother Haskel toward a distant bush—one that was absolutely loaded with currants.

28

Tuesday, November 1, 1881

Kane Springs

It had been a good week for the men who called themselves Bridger Jack and Wash, a very good week. Good friends and fine warriors, they had spent the week gathering mormonee cattle from the breaks to the east of the sand hills. They had then driven them to this fine place of watering—the very place where the *mericats* had first come up to them following the big raid the previous spring—and on the morrow they would begin pushing the cattle over their secret trails through the LaSals and into the shining mountains of Colorado. But first, they had both agreed a little earlier, a few hands of *ducki* would be in order.

Bridger Jack, who was Pahute, was a peaceable sort of man who did not delight in bloodshed and who avoided every situation where it might be required of him. In fact he had not even taken part in the Big Raid of the previous spring, and was not happy that so many whites and Utes had been killed. Rather he was an explorer, a man who enjoyed seeing firsthand the far and lonely country, and already two separate mesas where he had lived for a time were being called by his name.

Wash, a Sioux brave who had been captured by the Kiowa as a child and then traded to the Utes who had raised him as one of their own, was of a more volatile nature, and most recently had been involved in what was already being called the Pinhook Massacre.

Yet these two friends were raiders of the first order, and from the moment when the man Haskel had disappeared into the darkness of Sand Island after uttering his big words the month before, they had thought no more about them. Instead, they had raided on through the fall, taking mormonee horses and cattle and whatever else they could get, and now they had come to this fine camp where they were resting before their big drive into Colorado.

Hand after hand of the white man cards had been played, and neither of the men had been a clear-cut winner. Rather, it had become a time of laughter, of fine jokes, and a time to bask in the warmth of true friendship. But then the mood changed, for all the luck seemed to be going the way of Bridger Jack. He smiled with satisfaction as his cards began consistently beating those of the surly Wash, and in time he even cackled delightedly at his good fortune. For Wash, the fun had gone out of the game, and he grew increasingly more sullen, more dark with anger. Finally, the veins throbbing in his neck and forehead, the surly Sioux could take it no longer.

"*Attow-knots,*" he seethed in insulting tones. "Crow! Do you think that I do not see that you are cheating?"

Surprised, Bridger Jack laid down his cards. "I would not cheat you, my brother," he declared. "It is one of those runs of the cards; that is all."

"*Tu-wish-erer!*" Wash snarled. "Liar! What is that card hidden beneath your leg? Are you a witch, that your evil magic has hidden that card beneath you?"

Ignoring the name-calling and looking down, Bridger Jack was startled to see a card protruding from beneath his leg. He must have dropped it, he thought, as he picked it up and turned it over. The ace of spades—the white man's card of death. "Ungh," he grunted pleasantly as he looked up at his friend, holding the card before him. "I did not know this ace was there."

Not only was Bridger Jack sincere, but more, he was ready to cancel all debts owed by his friend and start the game over, or at least he was ready until he saw the big pistol held firmly in the grip of Wash.

"*Wagh,*" he breathed as he groped without looking for a weapon of his own, his eyes still fixed on Wash's pistol. And he was still groping when that same pistol exploded in his face, blowing Bridger Jack back onto the earth and snuffing out his life.

As the echoes of the shot faded away, Wash stared in horror at the bloody remains of the man who had been his only true friend during all the long seasons of his life. Yes, and as he began to wail in an anguish of soul that would not stop, the warning words of the mormonee Haskel came suddenly to his mind. "Perhaps," the man had said on that evil night on Sand Island the moon before, "those who continue to steal from the mormonee friends of *Shin-op,* will kill each other—"

And with that stark realization, the heartbroken wails of the suddenly lonely mankiller, grew noticeably louder.

Bluff Fort

"Howdy, Willy." Closing the door to keep in the warmth, Billy scooped his grinning son into his arms. "You and your ma have a nice night?"

"Nice night," Willy replied with a wide smile, at the same time tugging at Billy's beard. "*Dághaa? Dághaa?*"

"What's he saying?" Billy asked as he turned to Eliza. "Has Thales been here again?"

Eliza nodded. This morning. Willy was tugging on his beard, so he taught him how to say it in Navajo. He claims Willy's a born linguist."

"Well, I reckon that's so. Say it again, Willy." He guided Willy's hand to his beard. "What's this?"

"*Dághaa. Dághaa.*"

"Good job, Willy! Mmmmm. Something smells good!"

Eliza smiled. "Then you must surely be hungry."

"I am." Billy smiled back, set down his son, and shrugged off his coat. "Nothing like a night with the horse herd to work up a hunger. What'd Thales want?"

"Oh, a couple of things."

"Such as?"

"Well," Eliza stated matter-of-factly, "he told me that the Navajos have changed Navajo Frank's name from *Natanii nééz* or the Tall One, to *Ch'ééh disdziih,* which means one who can't get his breath."

"That fits, all right. And it sounds like you've been learning a little Navajo yourself. You say that real well, Eliza. By the way, did Thales find out if it was Frank and Hádapa who were camped across the river?"

"Why, no! Haven't you heard?"

Billy looked puzzled. "Heard what? Who was camping there, you mean? I've been out on the bench, remember? I haven't heard a word. Besides, you said Thales came by for a couple of reasons. What else did he need?"

"He came to thank you. For warning him."

"Warning him?" Now Billy was completely perplexed. "Hon-bun, I don't have the least foggy notion of what you are talking about."

"I'm talking about the camp you spotted yesterday and told Brother Haskel about. Billy, that was the outlaw Sugar Bob Hazelton over there, spying on us!"

"Sugar Bob Hazelton? The fellow you and Mary ran into?"

"One and the same. When Lula and Sarah Jane rode out yesterday afternoon to look for more currants, they probably looked to that horrid man like easy pickings. Leastwise he surely went after them."

Billy was aghast. "He tried to kill them?"

"No, he tried to steal them—to take them with him."

"But . . . but they're just little girls!"

"According to Brother Haskel, that beast doesn't much care how old a girl is, so long as she's a girl. And, yes, that's what he was intending to do. Take one or both of them away. Of course he hadn't counted on Brother Haskel, who disarmed him and sent him packing."

"Had he hurt the girls?"

"Not even a little. He was still lying in ambush when Brother Haskel stopped it. The girls watched the whole episode, and Lula said it was the most amazing thing she had ever seen."

"Watching Thales at work, is. I wonder if he pronounced one of his famous curses?"

Eliza shook her head. "Not that the girls heard. Brother Haskel just told the man he had a cruel and bloody past which he couldn't escape, and then he ordered him off. I guess Hazelton left without a word, all white-faced and shaky-legged, wading across the river for his horse."

Billy shook his head in disbelief. "I can't imagine this happening—or that I hadn't heard about it, either one. Boy I hate how things happen when I'm gone, even for just a few hours! But the girls—they're okay?"

"Oh, they're some upset, and I imagine they'll be a little more cautious after this. But yes, they should be fine."

Dumbfounded and his mind whirling, Billy could do little more than shake his head. "Thales and Sugar Bob Hazelton," he mumbled. "Who'd have thought it? And I'd imagine that before he sent him packing, he first of all put the fear of God into the man. With his piercing eyes and intense gaze, and that almost silent way he has of speaking, he could do it."

Eliza nodded her agreement. "Well," she then concluded, her words piercing Billy's very heart, "I can't tell you how thankful I am that Brother Haskel is around."

"So am I," the small man stated quietly as he stared out the window, his heart heavy for a multitude of reasons. "So am I, my dear Eliza, especially since in the morning I'll be gone to Colorado—"

Bluff Fort

"Oh, Billy, are you certain you need to leave so soon?" Eliza was almost in tears, and she couldn't seem to stop herself.

"That is the arrangement I have with the Lord," Billy replied with a sigh. "I don't think it's ever appropriate to make deals with him, but I had a feeling the other day that if no job had presented itself by today, I would leave in company with the brethren who are departing for Colorado tomorrow morning. That's what I promised the Lord that I would do.

"Besides, the fence around our field is now completed, meaning the livestock can be pastured closer to home without constant herding. The fort is as finished as we can get it without a lot more cedar posts, and you know it's too dangerous to go all that way alone. Other than that, and digging on that fool ditch, there isn't much left for me to do except be with you and Willy."

"Isn't that enough?" Eliza whispered.

"Oh, hon-bun, it sure enough would be if I had my druthers. But we're part of a mission, you know that. I couldn't live with myself or you and Willy, either one, if I wasn't making an honest contribution."

Eliza sighed deeply. "I know it, Billy, and I don't mean to complain. I've just been so hopeful about you finding work that was closer to us." Abruptly Eliza brightened. "Well, enough of feeling sorry for myself! I've been thinking, Billy, and I'm afraid you are right about my money—you know, donating it and then having you spend the winter here at home. I was wrong to even think of it in the first place, and I was more wrong to get upset when you tried to show me the straight of things."

Billy's expression was serious. "You've had a change of heart? What made you change your mind?"

"Prayer. You know how we've talked about contention and lying as being two of the names or assignments of Satan's evil followers?"

"I do." Billy smiled wryly.

"Well, have you ever heard of a spirit of resistance? As in encouraging a mortal to resist truth, resist good counsel, or resist the direction of priesthood leaders?"

Billy shook his head. "I haven't, but it sounds like a job I'd assign out if I was the devil."

Soberly Eliza nodded. "So would I. When I prayed this morning I asked the Lord to forgive my sins, and then I asked him to rebuke Satan and any of his followers and cast them from me. In an instant I had the feeling not only that a spirit of resistance had been troubling me, but that it was also the source of many of my difficulties during the trek. So I asked God why it kept coming back, and my feeling was that it was on account of certain weaknesses I have—part of what the Apostle Paul and King Benjamin call my 'natural man.'"

"Which they also say is an enemy to God."

"That's right, and now it makes sense to me. When I manifest those weaknesses it gives Satan power to come after me. My behavior, for which I am most certainly accountable, is displeasing to God, and in that sense my natural self is stepping forward and, to a certain extent, at least, I have become God's enemy.

"Anyway, after those impressions, and after that spirit had gone, I had the strongest feeling that the money had been the Lord's all along, not mine, and that the devil had been lying to me about it. I was still trying to get used to that idea when the feeling came that if I was going to give it back to the Lord, I couldn't set up any sort of conditions on how it might be used or I'd lose every blessing associated with it.

"So," she said as Billy's smile grew, "as hard as it is to say it, I think you're right to leave in the morning for Colorado."

"And the money?" Billy pressed.

"It goes to Bishop Nielson, one hundred percent. And if I can do it—if we can get that much cash money out of the bank in Durango—then I'll donate it without him or anyone else even knowing where it's come from. That's what I promised the Lord this morning."

"Good for you," Billy said as he sat down at the table and started tugging at his pocket. "And you feel good about your decision?"

Eliza laughed. "Good? Except for you leaving, I feel wonderful! I've been feeling wonderful all morning long, like I don't have a care in the world."

"Well," Billy drawled with a chuckle, "that gives me a little peace of mind, too." Carefully he then unfolded a Salt Lake City newspaper that had arrived the week before. "Hon-bun," he said gently as he turned the paper so Eliza could more easily see it, "I reckon you'll want to read this little article I found last night when I was lazing around the fire up on the bench."

Stepping to his side, Eliza read where Billy was pointing.

MAIN STREET BANK FAILS!!!
NO FUNDS LEFT! EVERYTHING LOST!
BANK PRESIDENT ARRESTED FOR FRAUD AND THEFT!

"What?" she questioned, looking up and not reading the rest of the article, "I . . . I don't understand."

Tenderly Billy took his wife's hand. "Eliza, that's the bank you told me was yours, Main Street Bank, and according to this, it has gone broke. Your money, along with the money of everybody else who banked there, was stolen by the president, and now it's gone."

"But . . . but I'm going to give it to the bishop," Eliza said, unable to get her mind around the fact that such a thing could happen.

"I know that was your intent, hon-bun, and so does the Lord, who is bound to bless you for what you wanted to do. But I reckon us poverty-stricken but eternally rich Bluffites must not have needed it after all. Don't you think?"

"I . . . suppose we . . . didn't," replied a stunned Eliza as she sank into the rocking chair, her hand still locked in that of her husband. "I suppose we didn't."

And then, to Billy's relief, Eliza began to laugh.

Bluff Fort

"Might you be Billy Foreman?"

It was dusk, and Billy had only just completed the chores, milked old Bess, and strained the milk for supper. Now he held little Willy in his arms while Eliza was busying herself with a ladle, stirring the iron kettle that hung over the fire.

"I am," Billy replied as he gazed up at the tall man who stood before him, holding his Stetson in his hand.

"I'm Bill Ball, foreman of the LC cattle spread, headquartered north of here off White Mesa on Recapture Creek. Mind if'n I step inside?"

Billy smiled. "Of course not, Mr. Ball. Do come in."

Bill Ball stepped into the factory-ceilinged cabin and was

immediately struck with the tidiness of the place. The cabin at the LC was larger, but there had only rarely been a woman in residence, and so the place had the cluttered, dusty look of menfolk about it. But here, even with only a canvas floor, everything was neat and tidy, and the dried sunflowers on the table, which had been carefully set with china, silver, and crystal, added a touch of beauty that Bill Ball found amazing.

"Mr. Ball, this is my wife, Eliza, and our son Willy."

"Pleased to meet you, ma'am," the LC foreman said as he bowed slightly toward Eliza, who curtsied in response. "You, too, Master Willy. Here. Reckon I have me a willow whistle you might like to toot a little."

Silently Willy took the proffered whistle, and Bill Ball took the chair at the table that Billy had indicated.

"Would you share supper with us?" Eliza asked as the man settled himself.

"If there's enough, ma'am," Bill Ball smiled, "I reckon there ain't nothing I'd like better. Our cookie's a fine sawbones and dentist, but not much good in a kitchen. I only hired him on account of he's all stove-up and can't do much else, so what he fixes does get tiresome."

"Your wife doesn't do the cooking?" Eliza asked in surprise.

"Ain't married, ma'am. Planned on it onct, but my intended passed away real suddenlike, and since then I just ain't felt much interest in it."

"I'm sorry to hear that."

"Yes, ma'am, at the time it was a mighty hard thing. But then most folks face hard doings now and then, so it doesn't do much good to complain. No offense intended, but I noticed you use a crutch, ma'am. A recent injury?"

Eliza chuckled. "Not very, though of a cold morning it gets to feeling recent."

"Frostbite," Billy explained as Eliza dished up the simple fare she had prepared. "She lost all but one of her toes, and some of each foot, in the snows of Wyoming back in '56. She was with a handcart company, crossing the plains."

"In 1856, was it? You must have been mighty young, ma'am. Three, maybe. Or four?"

Now Eliza laughed outright. "Mr. Ball, it's a wonder to me you don't have women chasing you from daylight to dark, the way you carry on. Of a truth I wasn't yet twenty, but I was close, and that's enough said."

Bill Ball nodded politely, Billy offered a simple blessing over the food, and soon the four in the cabin were busy eating.

"Mighty tasty," Bill Ball stated a little later when all had finished and Billy had placed the dishes and silver in a pan of water for soaking. "I ain't had fresh, warm milk in half of forever, and maybe then some. Did you know I was coming?"

Surprised, Billy looked up. "Not at all, though we have heard of you—of the work you did on the cribs last spring. Once we even saw you, and you, us. Amongst the Saints you're well thought of, Mr. Ball."

"I'm pleased to hear that. I thought you might have been expecting me on account of all the finery you had your table set up with. I don't reckon I've seen serviettes since Mrs. Lacy and her daughter fed me onct back in Texas. And I don't reckon I've ever seen a finer, more delicate set of crystal."

"Thank you," Eliza replied, blushing a little.

"The table wasn't set for you, though," Billy added quietly. "Despite that conditions here are primitive, and we are so very limited by poverty, Eliza is a woman of grace and refinement, and this is one of the ways it shows. There have not been more than two or three nights since our wedding that she hasn't set our table in exactly this way, and you will perhaps have noted that little Willy is already being shown proper table manners." Billy smiled. "Eliza's intentions, I believe, are to see that both Willy and me become gentlemen, no matter that it takes the rest of our lives for either one of us to accomplish it."

"Oh, I don't know," Eliza replied slyly as she looked at Bill Ball. "I should think Willy will learn his proper manners within four or five years, though ten or twelve might be needed for my husband."

Bill Ball chuckled at the good-natured exchange. "Well, ma'am, if you were learning me, it would take a lifetime and then some. And if I have my way with your husband, that ten years could get stretched out a little, too."

Billy and Eliza looked at each other, though neither spoke. Both had wondered at the cause of Bill's calling on them, but they had been too polite to inquire, waiting for him to explain.

The time had come, and Bill went on: "Billy, last spring I spoke to your Bishop Nielson about maybe hiring a hand to work cattle for me this coming winter. He recommended Dick Butt, who turned me down a couple of days ago on account of he and another feller are planning on spending the winter sawing lumber."

"George Ipson. I knew they had such plans."

"Dick Butt recommended you—said you were the best man with cow and hoss critters he'd ever seen."

Stunned, Billy looked at the tall Texan. "Me? Mr. Ball, I don't have the least notion about cowboying. Besides, it's all I can do to stay in the saddle of a dead horse, and a live one's plumb impossible!"

Bill Ball chuckled at the joke. "Dick said you'd react this way. Thing is, Billy, cowboying a man can learn. What he can't learn is his natural gifts. It's your gifts I'm wanting for this winter.

"Now, I can't pay a whole lot—a dollar six bits a day cash money. But the LC has as fine a pantry as I've ever seen, and once a month I'd be more'n happy to pack a mule or two with supplies and deliver them here to the fort—to you, ma'am, as part of your husband's pay."

"But . . . but I couldn't take something that the other folks—"

"Eliza," Billy said softly, "we'd have Mr. Ball deliver the supplies to the bishop, just as you intended doing with your money. That way the Lord can still use you to bless everyone here."

Bill Ball's eyes narrowed slightly. "You'd truly do that? And not keep the supplies for yourselves?" It was obvious that the Texan was surprised, and maybe even doubtful.

Eliza smiled. "It'd be the only way we could accept your offer, Mr. Ball. But, still, it would be greatly appreciated."

"Well, you Mormon folks surely are a wonder. Howsomever, I'll agree to that. Now to the last item on the agenda—yer pardner. Billy, you'll be spending the winter in a line camp at a place called

Verdure, near fifty miles north of here. I've already hired a tall, lanky son of a gun name of Curly Bill Jenkins to pardner with you. He's an opinionated cuss who don't hold much with anything he doesn't personally agree with, and is quick to tell folks about it, too. But he's a fine cowhand, honest, and almighty handy with a gun. Fact is, afore I hired him he winged and then captured three rustlers single-handed, and they were supposed to be bad men."

"Sounds like a tough customer, all right."

"As ever. Thing is, Billy, he don't like Mormons, and is quick to say that, too."

"Then why are you hiring me?"

Bill Ball smiled. "Because I do like Mormons, and I happen to be the boss. But don't you fret too much about Curly. Onct he gets to know you and Eliza, his prejudices'll disappear like the morning mist, and—Oh, I plumb forgot. Maybe you shouldn't introduce him to Eliza."

"Why in the world not?" Billy asked, not seeing the twinkle in Bill Ball's eyes.

"Folks," the Texan replied with great seriousness, "like me, Curly's a bachelor. But unlike me he's always on the prowl. I swear that man would ride a hundred miles to a dance, and then just stand around scratching his britches and looking. Afore he's through I reckon he'll have checked underneath ever rock and behint ever tree for that future and everlastingly beautiful Mrs. Curly Bill Jenkins that he believes is out there waiting. And until he finds her, there ain't a good-lookin' woman in this country what's totally safe.

"Which is why I'm thinking, Billy, that maybe you hadn't ought to introduce him to Eliza here . . ."

It was a moment before either Billy or Eliza realized that the man was teasing them, and as Eliza found herself unaccountably blushing again, Bill Ball's slow grin spread from ear to ear.

"Well, ma'am," he said as he abruptly rose to his feet, "you and Billy think on it. If'n you're willing, Billy, I'll be riding back to the LC in the morning, and you'd be welcome to ride with me. Oh, and one other thing. If there's ever a need for you to come home for a bit, then have at 'er. No notice necessary. Curly'll do fine for a few days without you. And, Eliza, ma'am, if you and little Willy ever get up toward the LC, you plan on staying for as long as you've a mind. That place sure could use a woman's touch, particularly a woman like you."

And with another smile that might or might not have meant he was teasing again, Bill Ball shook hands all around, clapped his Stetson back on his head, and ducked out through the door.

29

Thursday, November 3, 1881

Mustang Spring

"Well, Billy, that old mule sure-enough gave you a toss."

Dusting himself off, Billy looked at Bill Ball and nodded. "Told you I wasn't much of a rider."

"Oh, you can ride, all right. I saw plenty of evidence of that yesterday. What you can't do, it seems to me, is stay on an animal what is pitching and bucking."

"Isn't that the same thing?" Billy questioned without much rancor. "You certain you still want me?"

"Depends. What you figurin' on doin' next?"

Billy gave a sour look at old Sign, which was the mule he had determined to ride to the LC. "Do? Why, he'll be fine now that he's had his say. So, I suppose I'll remount and wait for you to tell me what you want me to do—go or stay."

Bill Ball chuckled. "Get aboard, then, Billy Foreman, for you're my man. I'll not abide a quitter, not ever! But as long as a man is working on betterin' himself, I can tolerate his shortcomings 'til doomsday."

With a nod Billy walked to the mule, which was standing quietly a dozen yards away, and swung aboard. It was early of a frosty morning, hardly past daybreak, and after having camped at Mustang Springs for the night, the two were once more on their way. The road—which was more a trail than a road, for Billy was certain there had been precious few wagons over at least this part of it—had led east up the San Juan to the mouth of Recapture and then turned north to follow up that winding canyon. Just beyond Mustang Springs it twisted eastward out of the canyon by way of a rude dugway, which they were now headed for. It then turned northward, skirting White Mesa as it wound toward the head of Devil Canyon and Verdure Creek, after which it bore northeastward in the general direction of what had been Spud Hudson's double cabin place, but which was now being called the Carlisle outfit. Long before that, however, a separate trail snaked westward to the LC headquarters on Recapture Creek, and that was where he and Bill Ball were headed.

"It seems to me," Billy said, more thinking out loud than holding actual conversation, "that the colder the morning, the more these animals buck before they can be ridden."

"Why," Bill Ball exclaimed after a moment's thought, "I reckon that's so, though I hadn't thought much on it."

"Well, I have to think on it," Billy grinned wryly as he adjusted his spectacles. "I've been wondering, though—do you suppose they buck and pitch and crow-hop about just to warm themselves up—to get their blood flowing, so the work we're about to demand of them won't hurt them?"

Now Bill Ball gazed down at the smaller man who was riding beside him. "Dick Butt tolt me you were a thinking man, Billy, and I'm starting to agree with him. That makes a lot of sense, though it's something I ain't never even considered."

"I don't know if it's true," Billy said self-consciously. "It might be simply that when a horse is cold, it hurts to have a man and a saddle on its back."

"Hurts?" Bill Ball guffawed. "There you go again, Billy Foreman! I ain't never thought of that possibility, neither. But now that I think on it, that notion's just as sensible as your first one. Which is right?"

Billy shook his head. "I don't know, Bill. Maybe both, maybe neither. The twist in the rope is that some animals buck when its warm or cold, no matter. Maybe they just like to buck. As for old Sign here, though, I think he bucks because the saddle and me hurt him when it's cold, and he needs to stretch himself out to ease the pain. To test my theory, though, I'm going to see if I can work him from the ground each morning before I saddle him. Maybe it'll help, and I won't get thrown so much."

"Good idea." For a moment or so the two rode in silence, and Billy looked around, enjoying the view of new country. It was a marvelous land, he was thinking, filled with rocks and trees and a thousand steep-walled gorges and arroyos where water had sliced and cut and worn through the ages, obeying always the demands of gravity and dropping ever lower in elevation. On the mesa tops, though, and also on the flats at the bottoms of the narrow, twisting canyons, the abundant grass grew belly deep to a tall horse. Though rough, the country was a stockman's paradise, and Billy could understand why it was drawing ranchers from all over the world.

"What is it about being thrown that you don't like?" Bill Ball asked abruptly.

"What's to like?" Billy responded instantly. "It hurts; it's embarrassing; I don't want to deal with broken bones; and if I break these specs I'm in deep trouble—"

"Right there's your problem, Billy. Ever' time you mount, you look jumpy as a bit-up old bull in fly time. An animal senses that. I been trying to figure it, and I think what you're really worried about, is them spectacles. You're so nervous about maybe breaking 'em that you act like a chippy in church—too stirred up to enjoy the show."

"You could be right," Billy admitted slowly.

"Could be, is right. So before you mount, Billy, try this for an experiment. Take your specs off, wrap 'em in something soft like a wad of buckskin, and stash 'em in your saddlebags. Then mount up and see if'n you can maybe enjoy the show—in other words, stay on board until your hoss knows you mean business."

"All right, Boss, I'll give it a try." Billy chuckled softly. "And even if it doesn't work, if I can't see where I'm headed, maybe it won't hurt so doggone bad when I land."

White Mesa

"So, Billy, are there actual Mormon fellers there in the fort who have more than one wife?"

Pulling his appreciative eyes back from the wide, nearly level mesa, which looked to Billy as though it would make a wonderful townsite, Billy nodded to his new boss. "A few. And I reckon there'll be more."

"Do tell."

Billy smiled as he urged his smaller mount to keep abreast of the huge mule Bill Ball was riding. "Well, Bill, when folks get called to enter into the Principle, which recently a few of our people have been, then pretty much they go ahead and do it. Some don't, but most are obedient."

Bill Ball shook his head. "I don't reckon I understand. Get *called?* What in thunderation is that? Way folks talk, purty much any Mormon what has a hankerin', can be married to any number of others."

"Not hardly. At least that's not the way the Lord has commanded us to live it. The way it works is, that a man is called in by his priesthood or Church leader, who issues him the call to enter into plural marriage. There may or may not be a suggestion at that time concerning who his plural wife might be. The man then presents the idea to his first wife, and if she is agreeable, then either of them might contact the woman who is the candidate for being his next wife. Or, if no suggestions have been given, the husband or his first wife may suggest a candidate. The woman is then approached, and if the Lord bears witness to her that such a course of action is his will for her, then she—and they—proceed."

"So it isn't something that's forced?"

"Not if hearts are pure and the Principle is entered into properly."

Bill Ball's face showed his amazement. "Who'd of thunk it? That sure ain't the sort of orgy-fied life a feller gets to imagining. How about a woman? Can she have more than one husband?"

Billy chuckled. "Not in the Mormon church. You see, Bill, ours is a patriarchal society, with worthy men holding the administrative rights to the priesthood, and able with their wives to assist their posterity to attain the fulness of the blessings of the gospel. To that end, each child must be able to clearly identify his—or her—parents. But if a woman were to have several husbands, none of her children could be certain of their parentage."

"By thunder, that's so, but I'd never have thought of it." After a pause, Ball said, "Uh . . . Billy, do you have any other wives than Eliza?"

"Not hardly! Nor do I expect to!"

"You don't want any others?"

Billy shook his head and smiled. "Bill, when I found Eliza I was more lucky and blessed than I can say. And talking her into marrying me—well, that took an amazing miracle. We've been married now going on four years, and I couldn't be happier with my—or the Lord's—choice. I don't need another wife, Bill, I truly don't. More than that, though, I've asked the Lord, for I know that the thought has worried Eliza, and I can tell you with confidence that I don't believe I will ever be called upon to go through that particular hardship."

Bill Ball looked stunned. "You . . . you asked the Lord? Like you're some kind of a prophet or something?"

Billy laughed. "Not me, Bill. I'm just little Billy Foreman, and nobody knows that better than me. Thing is, like you and everybody else on this earth, I'm also a son of God. I was created by him in the premortal worlds, and he knows me now as well as he knew me then. If I have a question and ask it in faith, he is more than happy to respond to me."

"Ask and ye shall receive," Bill quoted quietly.

"That's correct. But I also believe worthiness enters into the picture. In other words, if we want his divine responses to our questions or requests, we must also be willing to do his will."

"If any man will do my will," Bill breathed. "So, you're telling me I could do the same thing?"

Billy smiled. "No reason why not—at least none that I know of."

"Well, I'll be a suck-aigged mule! Who'd of ever thought such a thing?"

"Who indeed?" Billy grew sober. "Now, before we get to the LC, I have a question or two for you. Like I told you at the fort, I have never worked cattle—well, except in and around the Co-op in Cedar City. I really don't know the first thing about it. What good can I possibly be to you and your hands?"

Bill Ball shrugged. "Who knows? Dick Butt said you was a fast learner, and he said you had a way with hosses and cows. I expect things will work out, and you'll fit in just fine."

"Until then?"

"Well," the LC *segundo* drawled easily, "the boys, particularly your pardner Curly, could make things a little warm for you, all right. They do like to prod a greenhorn, and nothing pleases 'em more'n some rank trick or other that they manage to pull off. But if'n you'll go easy, Billy, and don't let 'em hoorah you into something your better sense tells you to avoid, then you'll come out of it just dandy."

"Any pointers on what to look out for?"

Bill Ball grinned. "Well, she's too cold fer rattlers in your bed, and since Mormons don't drink, they can't work on getting you drunk and making you do something stupid thataway. So I don't know. One thing, though. You sure ain't got much of an outfit—no boots, spurs, hat, gun, Levis, bandanna—Well, I reckon you can expect a little ribbing over that."

"I have a pistol at home, but I didn't think to bring it."

Bill Ball smiled. "No matter. For now, you can wear an old one of mine."

"Bill, I don't hold with gunplay, and would just as soon not wear one."

The eyes of the *segundo* narrowed slightly. "I don't hold with gunplay, neither, and don't you forget it. But to a cowpuncher, Billy, a gun's a tool of the trade, nothing more, nothing less. It can help you get out of all sorts of tight spots that don't have a thing to do with another human critter. It helps in moving ornery cow-critters along. And a gun in hand helps more'n somewhat to keep old loafer wolves like that crazy Sugar Bob Hazelton at bay."

"He showed up at the fort a couple of days ago, apparently spying on our women."

"Sugar Bob? Why, that miserable, low-down skunk—" Turning, Bill Ball glared at the smaller man. "Wisht I'd of knowed that, Billy;

I surely do. There ain't a man alive what deserves killing more'n him!"

Billy nodded but remained silent.

"He's the smooth-talking gent what took the life of my sweet Laurie Yvonne, her that was Mr. and Mrs. Lacy's only daughter." Bill Ball's face was set, and his voice was low and deadly-sounding. "Had his way with her first, and then she kilt herself from shame. But it was Sugar Bob what done it, just as sure as he shot Mr. Lacy last year in that saloon over to Fort Lewis. Billy, I hope to heaven your Mormon women will take care against that dirty sidewinder. He's mean as they come, and I can tell you this—my Laurie Yvonne ain't the only woman whose blood is on his hands!"

"Thales told him he had a cruel and bloody past."

"Who's that?"

"Thales Haskel, an old missionary to the Indians and an interpreter who is living at the fort. Apparently he disarmed Hazelton and then sent him packing."

"Disarmed him? How? That miserable gunslick's fast as they come."

Billy smiled. "Thales doesn't use guns, Bill, not in that way, at least. According to the girls Sugar Bob was trying to bushwhack, he just took Hazelton's gun and knife from him and tossed them into the river. Then he rebuked him and told him to skedaddle. He did."

Bill Ball shook his head in near disbelief. "You Mormons are a wonder, you surely are!"

"Well, Brother Haskel's special, Bill, and that's a fact. He knows no fear, and his eyes can bore right through you. I can't imagine anyone standing up to him, face-to-face, without wavering. His real power, though, is in the Spirit of the Lord, and that he uses with wonderful efficiency."

"Well, that sure must be so, all right—Haskel and all the rest of you, to boot."

For a few moments they rode in silence, and Billy could see that Bill Ball was thinking this thing through—that, and dealing once again with his own personal grief, an agony of soul that must never have gone away.

"Anyhow," the tall *segundo* stated suddenly, as though Sugar

Bob Hazelton had never been a topic of discussion, "before the winter's over, Billy, I'm sure you'll have picked up some sort of outfit. You are going to need a better coat, though, for this is cold country where you'll be going. I have a coat left behind by Mr. Lacy, there's a rusty old pistol hanging inside the door to the bunkhouse, and somewheres there may be some old boots. At least that'll be a start."

"I'd be grateful," Billy stated thoughtfully. "I truly would." And while Bill Ball grew silent again, Billy pulled a pencil stub from his shirt and began scratching a few scribbley lines in his daybook.

LC Headquarters, Recapture Creek

"You done what?!" Curly Bill Jenkins was not pleased with the news delivered by his new boss, and of a sudden he didn't give two hoots and a holler if the man knew it or not. "You hired that funny-looking little feller out there on the veranda as my pardner?"

"That's the straight of it." Bill Ball was not wavering, not even blinking, and that made Curly even madder.

"Jumping blue blazes, Bill! What'n double deuce did you go and do that fer? That little feller ain't no cowpoke, and you knowed it when you brung 'im up here! He ain't got no proper saddle boots; whatever he claps on his head's the poorest, most miserable excuse fer a hat that I ever did see; he cain't see a lick without them specs hanging off his nose; and he flat out tolt us he ain't rode hosses much and ain't never run cows 'cept around a corral in his whole and entire life! What'n bonnie-by-howdie am I supposed to do with a sissy like that?"

"Work with him. Help him learn."

"Help him learn!" Curly was so angry the veins in his neck were standing out like cords. "By jumpin' Jehoshaphat, Bill, I won't do 'er! Fire me now if'n you want, but I won't! Why, that there little feller's a . . . a . . . well, dawgawn it all, he's a dad-blasted, Bible-thumpin', Mormon!"

"I know that, Curly." Bill Ball remained supremely calm. "It's partly on account of him being a Mormon that I hired him."

"It . . . what?"

"You heard me. I don't know what you have against those Mormon folks, but I'll bet a month's wages it ain't nothing more than pure ignorance. I've been down to Bluff Fort and worked with 'em a mite, and I found 'em to be fine folks. They're thorny as cactus, too; brave enough to stand up to the Navajo and runnygade Pahutes we have around these parts without killing 'em or getting killed, either one. Besides which, man or woman either one, they're the hardest working so-and-sos I ever did see."

"Well, that don't cut it with me, Bill. It just don't cut it at all! I rode down to a Mormon dance onct, there at that fool fort—you was there with me as I recollect—and they wouldn't even allow me on the floor! All them purty women standing about, some of 'em single, too, and needin' a good man like me, and they wouldn't allow me in but what I first had to give up my pistol and make a solemn promise not to raise no ruckus no matter what else happened!

"Well, sir, I wouldn't do 'er! A man ain't even half a man without he has his hogleg on his hip! He's practically nekked! And what in hell's tinkling hot brass bells do they expect a feller to do fer a little fun if'n he cain't raise no ruckus at a dance? That's when it come to me about them people, Bill, and that's when I rode away and never looked back. Ever one of them Mormon sons was greedy cowards, hogging up all them women and not letting no poor honest cowpoke like me have a chance at 'em."

Chuckling, Bill Ball rose to his feet and walked to the window. "Be that as it may, Curly—and I won't argue their religion with nobody—I have it on good authority that this Billy Foreman, despite that he's a Mormon and wears spectacles and ain't got enough of an outfit to spit on, has a way with cow and hoss critters that'll make a man wonder. That's the kind of man I want in this hyar outfit, and that's the kind I got!"

"Not to pardner up with me, you didn't!"

Slowly Bill Ball turned around to face his newest hand, his eyes suddenly hard as steel. "You best walk a little slower, Curly Bill Jenkins, and tread a little more lightly." In three steps Bill Ball was directly in front of Curly, staring him eyeball to eyeball. "Now, you'll go to that line camp as pardners with Billy Foreman, and you'll act like you like it! You hear me? And a month from now, if'n you ain't bin proved dead wrong about him on all counts, I'll double yer wages fer the winter, haul you back here to the ranch, and let you sleep and eat yer life away until spring. Deal?"

Too astounded to say anything, Curly Bill Jenkins simply nodded. A winter with nothing to do at double the pay sounded good, mighty good! In fact, already his mind was starting to consider insurance plans that would more certainly guarantee the outcome. And that, by howdy, was when he began to grin.

Bluff Fort

"Afternoon, Eliza. Any word from Billy?"

"Not yet." Eliza smiled as Willy ran to Nellie Lyman and began shouting Navajo words at her.

"My goodness. Are these real words Willy's using?"

Eliza shrugged. "I don't hardly know, Nellie. But Brother Haskel says the boy's a natural linguist, and it's him doing the teaching. So I suppose they must be close."

"That's marvelous. Maybe soon we'll have a whole fort full of people who can communicate with either tribe the way Adelia can with the Pahutes. By the by, Jody appreciated so much having Billy drop by before he left. Billy has such a gift for lifting people's spirits, and he can be so everlastingly funny. Several times Jody has told me how glad he was that Billy was along to help bring him back to the fort."

"Billy says Jody's a pretty special young man. By the way, how is he? I've not been to see him in nearly two weeks, and I'm truly embarrassed. Are things looking any better yet?"

Nellie's gaze dropped. "Not really. The bones just aren't healing where that bullet shattered them, and so the flesh won't heal, either. We keep hoping and praying, and of course when his mind is clear, Jody seems determined not to lose his leg. But often the pain is so terrible he can't bear it, and that's when his mind goes.

"Poor Mother Lyman is nearly worn out with worry and loss of sleep, but she won't consider anything but that she stay right there beside him. Mercy sakes, Eliza, I could feed him and so forth, and I am his wife. But Mother Lyman won't hardly even hear of it. She's right there every minute, and when she isn't, Platte or Annie or Adelia have been. Of course now Platte's gone to Colorado to talk to whatever doctors he can find over that way. He's even thinking of going all the way to Denver if he can't find satisfaction any closer. The thing is, how would we ever get Jody that far? Even moving him to clean causes so much pain he can't take it. Oh, bother! I just don't understand why the Lord allows things like this to happen."

"To sanctify us," Eliza said wryly. "Billy says that's what Brigham Young always said. Suffering is sanctifying. Sounds like a terrible doctrine, doesn't it." Eliza smiled. "I've thought about it a little, though, and I suppose it works that way because trials and ordeals tend to expose both the best and the worst in all our natures. That way, if we have the presence of mind to consider it, we can strengthen our best traits and eliminate our worst ones. Trouble is, I don't usually have that much presence of mind."

Nellie laughed. "Neither do I! I'm usually either complaining or feeling sorry for all of us, probably myself most of all, and I don't even realize it until it's too late to stop. But Platte said something the other day that made me feel a little better. He said these kinds of trials are a way the Lord has of helping us to offer up sacrifices when we would otherwise be disinclined. All we need is to endure them as well as we can from moment to moment, and the Lord will find a way of rewarding us when it is time."

Eliza nodded. "That is comforting, isn't it?"

"Tell the truth, Eliza, no matter how this turns out with Jody's leg, I've got a feeling this particular sacrifice is going to last the rest of our mortal lives. Glory, but that thought scares me to death! I . . . I don't know if I can hold on."

Reaching out, Eliza drew the young woman to her. "Of course you can, Nellie. Remember what you just said. You only have to do it one day at a time."

As she comforted Nellie, Eliza thought for a moment of her own sacrifices—the giving up of her family to accept the Lord's gospel; the partial loss of her feet in the snows of Wyoming; the giving up of comfort and civilization so she could accept her present calling to the San Juan; the loss of her baby daughter—

As tears of loneliness started instantly from her eyes, Eliza took a deep breath and steeled herself against the greater loneliness she was now battling—the loss of her sweet husband's joyful company for the next several months. Glory be, as Nellie had so eloquently put it. How on earth could she possibly endure the long, cold months of winter? How could Willy? It was almost as if—

"Oh, by the by," Nellie suddenly exclaimed as she pulled away from Eliza's hug, "the brother that came through from the settlements this morning? Charlie Hall sent a message with him for Jody. A few weeks back a fellow staggered off an old boat and into Lee's Ferry, which is down river from the Halls. According to reports he was a smaller man, sort of dark complexioned, and about all he had by way of possessions were the weapons and other personal effects of his deceased partner—a man by the name Rob Paxman. It seems Paxman drowned, or so the story went. The folks at Lee's Ferry didn't know about our horse thieves and Jody's shooting, so they traded him a horse for one of the guns, and now he's gone."

For a moment the young woman worked to control her emotions. "Eliza," she asked softly when her lips had nearly stopped trembling, "when do you think the righteous in this country will ever see justice?"

With her question left hanging, for Eliza could not begin to answer it, the emotionally exhausted young woman turned and walked away.

30

Friday, November 4, 1881

LC Ranch Headquarters

"Well, boys," Curly Bill Jenkins exulted as he strode into the ranch kitchen, swept off his hat, and bowed low his cadaverous frame, "say howdy to the newest lazy hand on the LC, all set for a winter's worth of fodder without a lick of work."

The room, filled to overflowing with LC cowhands and Old Rocky, the cook, grew instantly still. To a man they knew what was up, and to a man they agreed wholeheartedly with Curly's plan, whatever it might turn out to be.

"What'd you do with that poor Mormon greenhorn?" Young Bob Hott, not even trying to hide his grin, was still doing his best to sound sincerely concerned.

"Curly probably set him aboard ol' Hurricane," Ervin "Slim" McGrew drawled solemnly, "and then turned him loose."

"Naw," Henry "Hank" Goodman argued good-naturedly, after aiming at—and missing—the nearest spittoon. "Curly'd never do that! He ain't no *murderer*."

"That may be so and it might not," one of the Ptelomy brothers offered. "But was it me huntin' a warm bunk and plenty of winter feed, I might just consider it."

The other Ptelomy brother guffawed. "You'd do no sech thing and you know it! Ma'd have your hide if she knowed you were even thinking on it. Still, there are plenty of other ways—"

"So, what'd you do, Curly?" Old Rocky was a cantankerous,

dirty, old man with little patience for anyone, and now it showed. "Fess up, man, or we'll figure all you got is more smoke than a wet wood fire."

"That's so, Curly!" James Frink was grinning ear to ear. "Instead of standing there quiet as a breast-fed baby, you had ought to be talking so fast we kin smell the sulfur. Speak up, man, so's we kin all be impressed with your amoozing wisdom."

"You mean amazing, Jimmy."

"No he don't! He means amusing."

"I don't mean neither one, you flannel-mouthed numbskulls! I mean—"

"Whoa up, there!" Curly growled as he slapped his sombrero back atop his bald dome, bringing about a silence that was brittle as glass. "The whole lot of you fellers have more lip nor a muley cow, and I ain't exaggeratin'."

"That may be so," Bob Hott allowed, "but heretofore, Curly, you ain't been 'zactly hog-tied when it comes to making chin music yourownself."

Curly grinned. "That's true enough, Bob, and it were no less true this morning. All friendlylike I worked the kinks out of that little Mormon sissy's mule for him, on account of he's scared to fork a bronc, and then I sicced him after that ol' splayfooted runnygade cow what's been ruling the breaks north of here the last year or so."

"No, Curly! Not old Splayfoot! You didn't!"

Curly grinned at Louis "Red" Pauquin's sarcasm. "I did so, Red, and I admit it. I drawed him a picture in the dirt of what her track would look like, and then I sent him out to fetch her. Moreso, I tolt him Mr. Ball wanted that ol' runnygade and her brood brought in pronto, on account of she might die she's getting so old and feeble. I also tolt him that I didn't have time to help him, and that he was on his own until the job was done."

"But . . . chasing that slick runnygade'd break the heart of any decent puncher what's fool enough to try."

"Yeah, and kill his hoss, to boot!"

"Maybeso," and Curly's grin grew wider, "but that sissy ain't a puncher, boys, and that's the rub. Bill Ball hadn't no right to drag him in here and pardner him up with me in the first place, and we all know it! That's why I done what I done."

"Well, leastwise the part about that Mormon skypilot being on his own's the gospel truth."

"So's the part about that old runnygade having a brood, so at least you ain't no liar."

"No, sir, I ain't," Curly's grin continued. "But I am lazy, boys, as any honest cowpuncher has a right to be. That's why I figured it was high time to pull the sissy's picket-pin—afore he got hisself any false notions about being up to the work the rest of us take such pride in. Besides, Bill Ball made the rules, so now I'm fixing to spend all winter here in the cabin in front of a big old fire, takin' my ease, pickin' my teeth and doing her up proper!"

And with that, a smug Curly Bill Jenkins sat down to his well-earned morning feed.

The Breaks between Johnson and Recapture Creeks

It was almost noon, after nearly five solid hours of searching, before Billy finally ran onto the tracks of the old splayfooted cow. "Well," he breathed into the stillness of the November day, wishing as he looked around that he had brought along a canteen, "this track isn't fresh, but at least I know this splayfooted critter's real. Come on, Sign, let's see if we can scout up something a little more fresh."

Moving in widening circles he rode and walked, leading his mule, for another hour before, to his amazement, Billy did find fresh sign. He was atop the little mesa between Johnson and Recapture Creeks when he found it, and the tracks of the old cow and her brood, which he guessed comprised another five head of various ages and sizes of cattle, were pointed toward the drop-off into Johnson Creek. And so, holding his saddle pockets to keep them from making a racket, Billy followed after. He didn't know how far ahead the cattle were, but he felt certain that they were close, and that he would come up to them within another few minutes.

Meanwhile his mind was replaying his conversation with Curly

Bill Jenkins, whom he had found to be surprisingly affable. The man might be a Mormon-hater of the worst stripe, but that morning he had been genial as could be, and Billy could feel nothing but gratitude that he had offered to take the cold-morning kinks out of old Sign. Moreover it had taken him less than two crow-hops to calm the animal, after which the mule had traveled peacefully enough to satisfy even the worst sort of greenhorn. Of course one couldn't predict what the mule would do for the rest of the day, but there was no doubt it was growing tired—so much so that Billy was regularly walking now, leading the exhausted animal so it could gain a little rest. Because of that, Billy expected no further trouble.

But Curly Bill Jenkins? Well, he had explained quite clearly what Billy was to do, even drawing a fine likeness of a hoofprint in the sand so Billy would recognize the ancient cow's track when he came on it. He'd even warned Billy that the feeble old animal had once been what the punchers called a "runnygade," a long-legged, long-horned Texas cow that was more deer than anything else. Now, though, Curly had assured him, she had grown old and weak, and Bill Ball was concerned that she lay down and die with none of the LC hands the wiser.

Of course Curly hadn't been able to help with this urgent search, having been given a previous job to do. But he'd told Billy where to look, and even encouraged him to take along a slab of bread in case it took longer to find the cow than was expected.

Of a truth Billy had been on the lookout for a little "rawhiding" at Curly's hands, but he felt quite satisfied that it hadn't happened—which relieved him greatly. Of course Curly and the others might be waiting for another day or a better opportunity. Such deviousness was certainly possible. But to Billy this looked like a straightforward assignment—a chance to bring in an old cow and her brood—and he felt more than thankful that Bill Ball, and Curly, had started him out with a job he could probably do.

Where the mesa broke away into Johnson Creek Billy lost the tracks again, and after another hour's futile search, cutting another big circle, he gave it up and paused to eat some of the dry bread. That cow had gone down off the mesa somewhere, Billy knew as he sat on the rim looking over the brush-choked canyon. But where it might have been—

Suddenly he saw movement below, in the willows, and in another moment Billy was certain that he was gazing upon his charges—the old splayfooted cow and her five different calves. Noting where they were he took up Sign's reins and walked away from the rim, heading south for a notch he had discovered earlier where he and the mule might make their way to the bottom.

The trouble was, no matter how quiet he moved, no matter how carefully, when he reached the place in the willows there was only a jumble of tracks—no feeble, dying, old, splayfooted cow, and no calves.

With a long sigh Billy glanced at the afternoon sun, wiped his brow, and began circling again. Finding at last a trail going out of the canyon on the east side, he followed it up, as expectant as ever of coming on the old cow within the next few moments. Up, up, through the hills, rocks, and brush he followed, until the tracks came at last to the base of a cliff, where they again seemed to disappear.

Now worried that the afternoon was slipping away, and wishing that he had drunk from the creek when he had been near it, Billy did his best to ignore his raging thirst while he moved back and forth along the base of the cliff, looking for some sign that the cattle had been there.

Finally, just as his mind was telling him that it was time to give up and head back, he saw another fresh track—-a splayfooted one, at that. Back down to the creek he then rode, following the tracks expectantly and finding, again in the willows, only the place where the animals had been sleeping during his search up near the cliff.

With a sigh of weariness, he led Sign to the water and allowed the mule to drink, after which he himself laid down and took up several hands full of the refreshing liquid, both drinking and then wetting thoroughly his grimy face and hair. "I don't know, mule," he breathed as he stood and looked around at the still canyon, "this splayfooted cow doesn't seem all that feeble. And she sure doesn't act like she's about ready to drop over and die. Still, I reckon we had ought to give it one more try—"

For the next hour and a half Billy kept after the splayfooted cow, following the fresh tracks with almost breathless interest. Back onto the mesa she led and then eastward toward Recapture, up and down and crossways, through every gully and around every tree and sandstone boulder, until finally she turned down a trail into Recapture, where again her tracks vanished.

Going afoot to the edge of the canyon Billy peered down, and soon was rewarded with a view of the animals, who had made the mistake of holing up in a boxlike alcove in the cliff, and from which there seemed to be no escape.

Again walking his lathered and exhausted mule, Billy made his way to the bottom. Mounting then he rode to where he had seen the cattle, absolutely certain that they would be gone again. But no, to his everlasting surprise they were all there, old Splayfoot and her five recalcitrant progeny, heads drooped and tongues hanging as though they were as tired as he and Dick Butt's poor mule surely were.

"Wore you out, did we?" Billy grunted as he forced his dried and cracked lips into what he hoped was at least the semblance of a grin. "Well, no matter, you poor, suffering critters. All we've got to do now, is follow this canyon down."

Rounding them up Billy started the cattle drifting, his smile still intact. Though it was obvious by now that Curly had indeed been hoorawing him, Billy felt forced to smile at the humor of it. The splayfooted cow, which was every bit as much of a "runnygade" as Curly had declared, was anything but old and feeble. Moreover she was savvy as they came, and knew the country they had covered, better than any man could know it.

By now it was past sunset and turning darker, and the supposedly exhausted cow was suddenly showing the whites of her eyes and swinging her head and dangerous-looking horns from side to side as she pushed at her various grown calves—a sure sign of her mean and contrary nature.

This worried Billy and so he tried to keep the mule close. But the old cow was now moving faster, her descendants with her, and in the growing darkness it was all Billy and Sign could do to keep up.

Then, as they passed a stand of cedars, old Splayfoot made a break and headed through the trees. Urging the dragging mule into a stumbling run, Billy finally headed the cow a quarter of a mile farther on, but now the darkness was getting thick as pea soup, and it was all Billy could do to see anything.

Taking advantage of the darkness the cow made another run, and within moments she and her entire brood had disappeared, making good their seemingly well-planned escape.

For a long time Billy simply sat in the saddle, doing his best to control his anger as he listened to the sounds of the night. He was angry, and he was the first to admit it. Not alone had old Splayfoot and her progeny bested him and his mule without any effort whatsoever, but that smiling, affable Curly Bill Jenkins had rawhided him something proper! Such rawhiding was cruel, it was deceptive, it was unkind. But most of all, Billy thought grimly as he reined the mule around and sent it shuffling toward the LC, it was embarrassing! Curly had spotted his weakness and had nailed him with it, and in spite of his supposed intelligence, Billy hadn't even seen it coming!

"Well, mule," he muttered as his countenance grew more dark, more determined, "that old cow hasn't seen the last of me yet; nor Curly, either! Tomorrow I'll be armed, and if we can't drive that critter in, Sign, then by all that's sacred we'll be dragging her! And that, my tired old friend, is a promise!"

Allen Canyon

"Ho, brother, there is no sign of the little skunk in this place!" The Pahute warrior Sanop, Poke's younger brother, having twice encircled the area on foot while his sharp eyes scanned for sign, now pulled himself onto the back of his pony. Like Poke and the others, he had fully expected to find the shamed Posey hiding near the maiden Too-rah, who had also shamed Poke by making a successful flight from his encampment. Now she must be dealt with in order that an example might be made, and this bothered the older Pahute warrior not at all. "I do not think that the *katz-te-suah* little one who calls himself a warrior, has been here," he concluded.

"*Ungh!*" Poke grunted as he looked from his youngest sister to

Sanop and then back again. "That is good—for him." He glared menacingly at Too-rah but completely ignored Peeb, who stood at her friend's elbow. "Is there any sign in this place of the warrior who is called Jonah?"

"That one is in the *wickiup,*" Sanop responded somewhat fearfully, backing his horse slowly away from the brush-covered dwelling as he spoke. "He is there on his sleeping robes, but his mind wanders in strange places, and he speaks words that I do not know. He looks very *puck-kon-gah,* very sick."

"He dies from the power of the mormonee Haskel's words," Peeb declared boldly, speaking out even though she had not been bidden to do so. "Like the tall Navajo, my husband made many raids against the people called mormonee, and now this suffering is what the great *Shin-op* has put into his life."

Poke held himself still, not for an instant deigning to look at the pregnant young woman.

"The mormonee are *Shin-op*'s friends," Peeb continued, her voice rising. "He has given them words of great and terrible power, and has sent them to the big river to be our friends and to show us *Shin-op*'s way."

"Peeb is right!" Too-rah was now speaking for the first time, and her voice was trembling with her passion. "The man Haskel said that those who would not be friends with the mormonee would die. The Navajo called Peokon would not be a friend, and now he is dead. You all know this to be true. The tall Navajo would not be a friend, and if he dies or not, his life has already ended. You know this as well. Now this fine young warrior who is called Jonah, who followed you and others in his hatred of the mormonee, has felt the weight of the mormonee words and is also close to the dark road of death—"

Poke's fury at his defiant younger sister, and at the truthfulness of her words, finally erupted. "Then I say that the fool called Jonah is already *e-i,* already dead!" he thundered. "Those are Poke's words of power!"

With a vicious kick the Pahute leader sent his horse at the two young women, lashing at them with his rope as he lunged past. Peeb was sent sprawling by the horse's shoulder, but Too-rah took the full weight of the heavy rope and was knocked immediately unconscious, falling perilously close to the fire.

His anger still at a fever pitch, Poke reined about and sent his squealing mount crashing into the lone *wickiup,* his intent the utter destruction of all who opposed him. But the terrified horse turned slightly aside, and though a portion of the *wickiup* and all of Peeb's baskets of stored food were destroyed by the crazed animal's pounding hooves, somehow the dying warrior who was called Jonah, remained untouched.

"Bring that one with us!" he ordered Sanop as he reined aside and pointed at his sister's sprawled form. "Whether that little skunk who calls himself Posey has been in this place or not, he shall not have my father's youngest daughter. She belongs to the warrior Poke, and he will sell her to whom he wishes!"

Then, with a fierce war whoop, the fearsome grizzly leaned down and caught up a burning stick from Peeb's fire. This he tossed onto the demolished brush *wickiup*.

"No!" Peeb shrieked as she saw the flames start up. "No—"

"*Wickiups* of the dead are always burned," Poke laughed harshly as he watched Sanop throw the still unconscious Too-rah over his horse's withers and then mount behind her. "Come, brother, and let us return to the encampment down the canyon. In another sun, or perhaps two, this place will be cleansed and ready for the coming of the People! Then we will plan even bigger raids against the *katz-te-suah* mormonee."

31

Saturday, November 5, 1881

LC Ranch Headquarters

"Say, who'n blue blazes is the hombre what is tromping around in hyer?"

Billy, up and dressed and now lacing up his newly soled shoes, quietly identified himself to the growling Curly Bill Jenkins. It was around three in the morning, he knew, his typical time of arising. But obviously these LC hands, as they called themselves, were used to a little later hour.

"It's me, Curly," Billy replied without much concern for the man's interrupted sleep or anything else that might be troubling him. "Daylight's a'burning, and I have things to do."

"But . . . it's the middle of the gol-durned night, you Mormon idjit!"

"I reckon." Billy's voice was calm, even quiet. But in him was a seething determination and a fixed purpose, and he wanted nothing more than to get out of that bunkhouse and get back after that splayfooted cow.

Not much had been said the night before when he had returned late and exhausted. Curly had asked where he had old Splayfoot and her brood corralled and what he'd been doing with himself to look such a grimy mess, but none of the others had said a word. In fact they hadn't even looked at him, though Billy was astute enough to know they were all grinning and winking at each other when his back was turned, and having a riotous good time. And Curly Bill, who still sounded as polite and concerned as a man could sound, was no doubt the worst of the lot.

Not that Billy actually cared, he told himself. What he did care about, were Eliza and Willy and the rest of the Saints. To them he owed a diligent effort to learn this fool job and to do it right, and it all had to begin with the rounding up and bringing in of that splay-footed brindle cow.

Outside he lighted a lantern, moved to the tack shed, and packed outside his saddle, bags, and other gear, which he carried to the corral. The night before he had taken the old pistol down from above the bunkhouse door, checked the action to make certain it worked, and pocketed a handful of cartridges. This was now stowed in one of the bags. He had also taken from the kitchen another loaf of bread, which was stowed in the other bag, though he had been unable to find a spare canteen anywhere. Back in the tack shed again, he added to his accoutrements a coiled, hard-twist rope, one that looked to be an extra, and a crudely made pair of thick leather chaps that were dust covered and laying on the ground in a corner. The leather was stiff and hard, and they were awkward to wear, but he knew they would make a world of difference to his legs as he beat the brush chasing after those miserable cattle.

Again at the corral Billy had little difficulty bridling and saddling his still-tired mule. Leading her to the trough he let her drink, took a long draught himself from where the water trickled in, and then he faced up the canyon. "Well, Sign," he breathed quietly as he blew out the lantern and hung it from a handy peg, "I'm sorry to have tuckered you so bad yesterday. Thing is, there's nothing for it but to go and get the job done, no matter. I'm not going to ride you, though, at least not at first. We'll both walk, and—

"Well, what's this? Gopher, is that you, boy?"

Reaching down, Billy felt the wiry fur of a little mixed-breed dog that he had first seen just the day before, who was now standing with wagging tail, sniffing at Billy's legs. Apparently the dog had belonged to the missing Johnny Molander, but had come wandering back to the ranch a few weeks before, giving rise to the idea that the missing Johnny must be dead. Unfortunately, the little part terrier had allowed no one else to adopt it, snapping and growling whenever anyone tried, and so earning the rancor of the ranch hands. Now it subsisted on occasional table scraps and bones, taking the more-than-occasional kick from an irritated cowpuncher's boot, and accepting it all as the price it had to pay to stay alive.

"Well, Gopher," Billy declared to the still-silent dog as he scratched it behind its ears, "if you need a friend, then I'm your man, for I don't suppose anybody's happy being lonesome. Howsomever, I'd better be making tracks. You stay here, boy, and I'll see you later on."

Obediently the still-silent dog stepped back. A little surprised that the dog had seemed to understand him, Billy straightened upright, took Sign's reins in hand, and led him northwestward into the early-morning darkness.

LC Ranch Headquarters

"Any of you fellers seen Billy Foreman this morning?"

Again the LC hands were in the chuck hall, stuffing their gullets, as Curly liked to put it. But with Bill Ball standing tall in the doorway and glowering at them, their mood went instantly from festive to sober.

"Didn't see him," one of the Ptelomy brothers declared without looking up.

"But we sure-enough heard him," the other brother added. "He was up and out of here almighty early."

"Which was some strange," Bob Hott added, "seeing as how he looked limp as a neck-wrung rooster when he got in last night. You'd of thunk he'd of wanted a little rest."

"His sorry old mule needed it, too," Slim McGrew agreed. "That mangy critter looked weary as a tomcat tromping in mud."

"Well," Curly declared laconically, speaking for the first time, "I hate to break the bad news, Bill, but that same sorry mule is as missing as your man is. Reckon they've both headed south fer the winter."

Though the room remained silent, there was not a man who was not grinning inwardly and who didn't want with all his heart to guffaw with the others at their rare success in running off the greenhorn. *One day,* they were all thinking with glee—*that was all that little Mormon pantywaist had lasted.*

"So," Bill Ball said as he leaned against the door frame and pushed back his hat, not minding at all the cold air he was allowing into the room, "you reckon you've won the bet, Curly?"

Curly fought to keep his face sober, to hide his mirth. "Well," he drawled in response, "he *is* gone, Bill. And you did say inside of a month, as I recollect."

"I did," Bill Ball admitted, his voice sounding sad and thereby delighting his riders. "One thing, though. For a man riding south, that mule's tracks head off in a mighty peculiar direction."

"Huh?"

"Billy was heading northwestward, Curly, back in the direction he rode in from, last night. Was it me, I'd say our little Mormon feller's on his way to bring in that old splayfooted brindle cow, which I reckon you tolt him I wanted him to do.

"So whenever you're ready, Curly," and Bill Ball smiled and pulled his hat back down as he said it, "I've got a couple of bogs that need mucking out today. Reckon it'll take you, and all the rest of you boys working with him, to get 'em mucked out proper."

And with those cannonballs having been fired and exploded, for no cowpuncher hated anything worse than digging post holes and mucking out muddy, cow-trampled bogs, the tall *segundo* turned and walked quietly away.

Recapture Creek

It was just coming daylight when Billy reached the place where he had lost the cattle in the darkness of the night before. But now old Splayfoot's tracks showed clearly, and Billy nodded with satisfaction. The brindle-colored cow seemed to have made a beeline for her favorite stomping grounds from which he had driven her, and so Billy did not even attempt to follow her trail. Instead he mounted the docile Sign and rode rapidly, arriving within half an hour at the area of Recapture where he had cornered the cattle the first time.

Climbing a cliff on foot, he looked about, and in short order spotted not only the leggy brindle cow and her brood, hidden off in some cedars, but he spotted as well the little dog Gopher, which had apparently been following him all the way from the ranch.

"Here, Gopher," he called softly as he descended from the cliff. "Hey, boy, come on over here, and let me give you a scratch."

Obediently but very gradually the little dog approached, groveling and wagging its tail in the most pathetic but hopeful sign Billy had ever seen. "Hey, little fellow," he said, squatting on his haunches and holding out a chunk of bread, "you don't need to fear me. I'm not going to kick you, I promise. I just wish I had something better than this bread to offer you."

Carefully, and with tiny whining noises the little dog inched close, sniffed the bread, and then gulped it down. Meanwhile Billy was scratching and petting the mangy little animal behind its ears, and within another couple of minutes man and dog had become fast friends.

"Well, Gopher," Billy said as he rose to his feet, "time to get back to work. Old Splayfoot's a'waiting, and I've got it to do. So just follow along like you've been doing, and by tonight I'll have you back to the ranch."

In reply Gopher wagged his tail, and with a grin Billy mounted, once again taking hold of his saddlebags so they wouldn't cause noise, and urged his mule forward.

Recapture Creek

"All right, you splayfooted old critter," Billy muttered as he eyed the cattle from a hundred feet away, "if you're going to run, have at 'er, because I'm going to catch you just the same."

The old cow, her head held low, was watching Billy intently. Her five offspring, which ranged from a yearling calf to two nearly grown bulls, both with their mother's distinctive color, were either pawing the earth with anxiety or chewing their cud nonchalantly. But none of them, Billy felt, had the savvy of the old brindle cow.

Slowly Billy untied his borrowed rope and shook out a good-sized loop. He was not a roper and he knew it. In fact, in a hundred or more throws in the corral back at the Cedar City Co-op, he had caught only three animals. And they had been horses being held in a corral. But now he was going against a huge old cow with horns fully five feet across, who considered herself a daughter of the wind and who acted accordingly. Yet somehow, he thought as he clucked his mule into motion, he had to get close enough to make a good toss.

Billy didn't even see the little terrier make his move. The first glimpse of movement he caught took place a moment or two after he had begun his careful approach, when the dog seemed to materialize out of the ground directly in front of the old brindle cow. It did not bark even then, but growled fiercely as it proceeded to back the cow and her followers through the cedars and toward some cliffs.

Once, the old cow swung her ponderous head and started to make a break. But to Billy's complete amazement the little dog leaped into the air and clamped his jaws tightly on the muzzle of a startled old Splayfoot. In pain the old cow began shaking her head and bellowing, pawing the dirt and spinning about in a desperate attempt to rid herself of the horrid creature on her nose. But Gopher seemed to have a death-grip where it hurt the cow the most, and Billy was certain the little animal was going to die for his efforts.

Suddenly, though, and without warning, Gopher let go and sprang free, and a moment later he had backed the wounded old cow up against the cliff, from which position she was now giving the dog her full and complete attention.

"Well, I'll be doggone," Billy breathed in wonder. "If that doesn't beat anything I've ever seen! Somebody's trained you mighty good, little feller, and that's a fact! Probably Johnny Molander, I should reckon. All right then, I get the message, Gopher, and I'm a'comin'—"

Recapture Creek

Even with the old cow being held relatively still by the growling Gopher, it took Billy three tosses to get his loop over the animal's horns and snug around her neck. Snubbing her as tightly as possible to one of the cedars, he then looked around for the five offspring.

"Why, Gopher," he asked in amazement, "where'd they all go?"

For they were indeed gone, all five of them, having disappeared from the scene as quietly as ghosts. But a moment later Gopher was on their trail, and soon Billy and Sign were also winding up through the rocks and the trees, topping out shortly on the flat crown of the mesa.

It took Billy half a mile to head the five cattle, and even then he would not have come close to doing so if it hadn't been for the amazing instincts of the little terrier. He could not only chase cows and subdue them, Billy was noticing, but he even seemed to think like them, anticipating and then heading off their every move. The dog was amazing, and as the five escaped cattle were driven back down into Recapture to where their surly mother was tied, Billy felt drawn to the animal more and more.

"All right," he breathed as he dismounted and headed for where the cow's rope was wound around the tree, "now comes the hard part, Billy Foreman. Somehow you've got to get her down and tie her head to her foot, just like you've seen Dick Butt and some of the other cowboys do back in Cedar. That way she can travel but not freely, she won't be able to escape again, and you and Gopher can drive the whole bunch back to the ranch."

Saying it turned out to be one thing, however, and doing it quite another. Again and again Billy's hands were burned with the rope as he attempted to pull the cow closer to the tree and she tried to pull herself away from it. Several times she made a run and threw herself when the rope came taut, and several other times Billy actually got close enough to pull her down by twisting her tail. That was always close, but each time Billy managed to come out on top, exhausted but summoning strength to continue his efforts. Finally, though, old Splayfoot had wound herself close enough to the tree that she had no more room in which to fight. When Billy twisted her down that time she stayed, and so yanking the rope away from the tree he pulled her hind foot forward and tied the rope around it, tying her head to her foot and effectively hobbling her.

"There, you miserable cow!" he grunted as he rose to his feet to wipe at his grimy face. "I had ought to tie you up short as possible, but I reckon after such a battle you deserve at least a little mercy, so I'll give you about a foot of latitude and hope you'll be appreciative."

For answer the brindle cow, still on her side, rolled her eyes and panted as though she were nearly dead.

Sweating and panting from exhaustion himself, Billy staggered toward his mule, Gopher at his heels. Mounting, he turned to watch as old Splayfoot rolled and heaved herself to her feet. With her progeny in tow she then moved out at Billy's urging, and all went perfectly well—for a few steps. Then, to Billy's horror and probably little Gopher's chagrin, Billy's poorly tied knots began to slip loose.

With her head and foot now enjoying full freedom, the long-legged brindle cow swung her head once and was off, Billy's long rope in tow, and her always willing offspring pounding along behind her.

Sick with anger and frustration, Billy kicked the valiant Sign in the flanks and took off after.

Recapture Creek

For the next several hours Billy felt certain he was living a nightmare. Down Recapture they went, two miles and then three, and then with a suddenness Billy could not believe they turned up through the cliffs and onto the mesa, which he and the animals charged across like a runaway freight train. Old Splayfoot was the engine, her brood were the cars, and Billy and Sign were the caboose, just about that far behind. And in and out and all over the landscape scampered little Gopher, doing his best to bring the mad bovine charge to a halt.

But once again, Billy saw, old Splayfoot was proving her savvy. Her nose still sore from her earlier encounter with Gopher, she now refused to lower it or place it anywhere near the menacing dog. More, she kept herself and progeny always in the open and on the move, never allowing the terrier to back her into a corner or against a cliff. It was an amazing performance, and Billy's emotions ranged all the way from anger and absolute frustration, to out-and-out admiration. He would never have supposed that cattle could be so observant, so apparently astute. But this one old cow called Splayfoot, whether from pure instinct or outright brilliance, was out-maneuvering him at every turn.

In and out of both Johnson and Recapture Creeks she charged, up and down through the cliffs, and back and forth across the mesa in between. She was like a child's toy that was run by a spring, wound tight and destined to go so far and run so long with nothing to relieve the monotony but the wind at her back. And Billy, his poor mule growing more and more exhausted by the hour, could do nothing but keep on following.

Once he lost the tracks when he, Sign, and Gopher all paused at the same moment for a drink in Johnson Creek, and another time he wasn't paying attention and ran amok of a cedar tree, being knocked from the saddle and jarred so hard that it was ten anxious moments before he was certain he wasn't dying from lack of air. It was nearly an hour later before he saw the cattle again, and then the chase resumed as before, the freight train charging ahead in the same horrid order.

When the benumbed Billy was certain they had inscribed all the capital letters and drawn several huge profiles across the top of the mesa, which works of art unfortunately occupied most of the day, that part of the program came to a sudden and complete halt. With a wild snort old Splayfoot suddenly made a beeline straight across the mesa and then down a narrow, winding track into Johnson Creek, following a route that had heretofore seen only bird traffic, and that not very often.

Thankful that Parley Butt had shod Sign only a week before, Billy inched the mule down the hairline of a trail, feeling certain on more than one occasion that both he and his mount were capsized and gone over the edge of the terrible precipice. Even Gopher seemed cowed by the trail, and slunk along behind as Billy urged the mule forward. Finally doing away with ceremony and giving Sign its head, Billy simply clung to the saddle for dear life, until at long last he was delivered safely to the rocky bed of the canyon.

But now Sign was used to the lead and refused to give it back. More, the old brindle cow had finally got the mule's dander up. So away it went on its own, Billy simply hanging on, down the hill as from a catapult, over this rock and through that tree, traveling all the time like an arrow from a bow. Then without warning the cows sashayed to the right, up against and along the cliff, and Billy came within a gnat's eyelash of losing his precarious seat as the mule followed suit.

For half a mile Billy's leg was brushing the rough sandstone cliffs, then the animals turned back down, crossed the creek in the worst possible place, at least for a man and a mule, and ran up and along the cliff on the other side, thus subscribing a great and meandering circle. A mile and a half later they crossed the creek again, and, to Billy's horror, headed back up the same practically nonexistent hairline of a trail he and his dog and mule had barely survived, coming down.

Up the winding track and across the mesa they thundered again, then down, around, back up, and across the mesa going the other way, the old cow intentionally picking her way through the roughest country this side of the River Styx. And so it continued until an hour before sunset, a chase so monotonous that Billy lost track of the number of times, with only minor variations, that it was repeated.

Finally, after staggering up a long, winding canyon out of Johnson Creek, poor old Sign stopped and stood trembling. Unable to take another step, let alone carry Billy, the mule hung its head in exhaustion, and Billy knew he was now afoot.

Beside him little Gopher stood all a tremble, his tongue hanging out and his breath coming in short, ragged pants. Yet his eyes were bright, and as he lifted his head to look at Billy he seemed actually to be talking, urging the man to get moving before old Splayfoot went again into hiding.

Nodding his agreement Billy took the bread, divided what was left between himself and the dog, and then pulled the rusty old pistol from the saddlebags. "All right, Gopher," he muttered as he thumbed cartridges into the magazine, "if that fool critter won't go one way, then she'll surely go another. Let's move!"

And with a farewell pat on the neck of his faithful mule, Billy and the little terrier headed off toward Recapture together.

Bullpup Canyon

"Well, fellers, this hyer bog-muckin' is sure how I wanted to spend the day."

"You could be riding pardners with that sissy little Mormon."

"Not me, boys. That there's Curly's job, and he's got the wool on his brisket to get 'er done."

"I'm telling you fellers," Curly responded grimly, "I won't need to. That little sissy ain't got sense enough to spit downwind, and as fer being a cowman, he don't know dung from wild honey. He's gone and left us entire, and I don't reckon we'll ever see him again."

"If'n we don't, then I reckon he stole that rusty old lead-pusher from over the door."

"Yeah, and them old chaps what used to belong to Johnny Molander."

"That Mormon stole Johnny's chaps? Why, that no-good—"

"Hank, them chaps was wore out and you know it. We bin using them to clean our boots on for near a year. Johnny tolt us to."

"It don't make no matter! If that little skunk took 'em without so much as a by-yer-leave—"

"If he took 'em to wear so's he could go after old Splayfoot, then I say more power to 'im!"

"He ain't going after old Splayfoot!"

"Not, leastwise, in this life!"

"Well, his tracks sure headed off in that direction. I know, cuz I checked."

"So did I. But so what? He won't round up that old runnygade, fellers. No one ever has."

"Well, if'n he does, he'll be saltier nor Lot's wife."

"Jest like we're all acting techy as teased snakes," Slim McGrew growled as he slung another shovel of mud.

"Or muddier nor a Comanche's blanket," Bob Hott averred with a snort, declaring truth and for the moment ending the conversation.

Ducking his head, Bill Ball did his best to hide his grin. Like the others, Bob Hott was filled with sarcastic bad humor, and he wasn't worried about who knew it. He had left home at fourteen to become a cowpuncher, was already a top hand in anyone's book, and he hadn't yet seen his eighteenth birthday. Most of the other LC hands were not much older, and any of them would tackle any job—provided it could be done from the hurricane deck of a horse. But mucking out bogs couldn't be done that way, and there wasn't one of the men who was enjoying what he was presently doing.

Not that punching "cows," which meant either sex of bovine to a cowboy, was expected to be glamorous or exciting. Most days began by four in the morning and consisted of eighteen hours or so of picking maggots from stinking sores around a cow's horns, pulling steers from bog holes, being pounded half to death by the unfriendly gaits of various mounts, getting lashed and beaten by tree limbs or gored by angry cattle, losing whole thumbs or fingers when rope dallies around saddle horns went wrong, and sweating through fiery summer days or freezing through interminable winter blizzards, no matter. Cowhands fought prairie and forest fires, stopped dangerous stampedes, rode all day without food or water, "laid out" all night without a bed, and "rode herd" in rain or sleet—all without a murmur. Of a truth it could be said of any of them, as Curly had so eloquently put it regarding Henry McCabe: "Fer a feller who's gone through so many close shaves, I don't see how he ever saved his whiskers." Under such stern working conditions, courage was prized above life, and weaklings were quickly weeded out, for each man knew that one coward could endanger the lives of an entire outfit.

No, Bill Ball thought as he worked silently beside his grumbling men, despite that they were "rawhiding" Billy Foreman pretty badly, these hands of his were neither cruel nor unkind. No one was more generous, with time or money, than a puncher. They would share anything with a fellow rider. Loyalty to the "iron" or brand was unstinting. Concern for the cattle, the property of their outfit, came first, and each of these men would in an instant shrug off any consideration of risk to his own life or limb to do his job.

High in each of their codes was square dealing, and not one of them but believed that his word was his bond. Yet they were clannish, for their work made them so. Soft-spoken and reserved with strangers, they had the reputation of being taciturn and reticent by nature, which they most surely were not. There was no more boisterous, skylarking, hard-swearing bunch than a party of cowboys gathered around a campfire or in a bunkhouse.

These things Bill Ball understood, for despite that he was *segundo* for this outfit, he was nevertheless one of them, doing as they did and feeling as they felt. His one advantage, besides his being older than all but a couple of them, was that he could evaluate his men from a slightly different perspective—the more lofty view of an employer. And that was why he had hired Billy Foreman in the first place. Bill Ball had seen something in the little man that was fine and good, and he felt certain it would show itself to both Billy's, and to the LC's, advantage.

But first, he thought grimly as he lifted and then threw another shovel made heavy with mud, the little Mormon had to somehow prove himself—

Recapture Creek

For the first time since his rope hobbles had slipped off the recalcitrant old cow, Billy felt a little excitement. She was on the edge of the canyon not fifty feet away, moving slowly through the last of the vanishing sunlight and hardly keeping ahead of her five offspring. She was also limping badly, her tongue was hanging out, and she looked every bit as exhausted as Billy felt.

As he lifted the old pistol and brought it to bear—for until that moment he'd had every intention of shooting the animal on sight—Billy felt a familiar stab of pity. She looked so wretched and wasted, as did her pathetic progeny, that he simply couldn't do it.

"Well, let's go, Gopher," he breathed tiredly as he thrust the pistol beneath his belt, working to the left of the cattle so they wouldn't get even a little spooked. "I reckon now, maybe, they'll drive."

To Billy's surprise, when he reached the brindle cow her splayed hoof had come down on the rope, and she was standing, hardly even paying him attention. Offering up a quick prayer of gratitude for even small favors, Billy waved his arms and shooed her off the rope, after which he and Gopher easily turned her and started her and her brood toward the ranch.

"Thank you, Lord," Billy breathed as he stumbled after the cows, willing his tired body to keep moving, "until a little bit ago, I wasn't certain I would ever win the day—"

But alas, the prayer of gratitude was uttered too soon. Passing a small canyon leading down to Recapture Creek, the old brindle cow abruptly turned and went down, faster and faster until like a runaway freight she plunged into the jungle of growth at the bottom.

Feeling for the first time in his life like cursing, Billy took the trail again, this time afoot, up and down and across Recapture and out in the parks east of there, which was a new course altogether. And there in the waning daylight, he finally got a glimpse of the cow and her charges again, not too far ahead. Fifteen minutes later, however, he lost the trail altogether. In spite of the gathering twilight he made a big hunt and finally found it again, saw that she was headed off toward a place the cowboys called Mudd Spring, and so with a sigh of utter discouragement he turned and went back after his mule.

Recapture Creek

It was nearly dark when Billy, once again astride his courageous mule, came up to old Splayfoot again. Using every ounce of strength it had left, old Sign tried to head and stop the cow—to no avail. Next Gopher got into the act, growling near her nose as if he were a whole pack of ravenous wolves. But old Splayfoot merely snorted, lifted her head above the dog, and plunged on, not even in the least intimidated.

And that, Billy knew, was the last straw! With a fervent plea heavenward that the Lord would direct his aim, Billy pulled out his pistol and cocked the hammer.

"Giddup, Sign!" he shouted as he kicked the poor mule in the ribs, "bring me up alongside of her, and that's all I'll ask!"

Amazingly, Sign did just that, lifting its head and thundering forward until Billy was riding only feet away from the lumbering old brindle cow, who with one swing of her ponderous horns could have impaled the mule on the spot.

"Okay, Sign, hold it steady . . ."

Then, to the amazement of Billy and probably Sign and Gopher, too, old Splayfoot once again got her foot on Billy's still-dragging rope. Down she went in a tangle, her offspring came crowding over the top of her in a mass of confused hooves and horns, and by the time Billy got his faithful mule turned and headed back, the old mother cow was just pushing shakily to her feet. And coming to the awful realization, as she did so, that a vicious little animal with sharp teeth and a fierce growl had once again fastened himself to her nose.

"Good job, Gopher," Billy breathed as he swung down from the saddle. "You too, Sign. I'd say you've earned a rest." Then, with no further thought or even sense of pity, he stepped up to the exhausted, trembling bovine, lifted the rusty pistol, and fired.

LC Ranch Headquarters

"You fellers see what I see?"

The question hung in the still night air, for the moment unanswered. Bill Ball and his hands, finally finished with their terrible job, had just ridden up to the corrals. It was hours past dark, and not a one of them but was cursing Bill Ball and every other foreman who had ever ordered them to do such unmanly and inhuman labor. But at least the spring was now clean, and—

"I see 'er, Slim, but I don't hardly believe it."

Again utter silence reigned.

"That, fellers, is old Splayfoot," Bob Hott finally muttered. "I seen her onct, and that's sure enough her."

"And them's what used to be her calves, too," Jimmy Frink observed. "I wasted a whole and entire day a few weeks ago trying to catch that three-year-old bull yonder, figuring to cut him and maybe gentle him down some. Now here he is looking peaceful as a church-goer on a Sunday morning!"

"Yeah," one of the Ptelomy brothers muttered, "and his ma's lookin' sorrowful as a bloodhound's eye. I don't reckon she's ever bin corralled."

"What do you think now, Curly?"

"I don't think nothing!" the cadaverous cowpuncher snarled, still unable to accept what his eyes were revealing to him. This just couldn't be so! It just couldn't.

"Well, I'm a'thinkin'!" Bob Hott averred. "First of all, I'm a'thinkin' that this hyer is the most amoozing thing I ever seen. And what I want to think next is how that little greenhorn done it."

"He shot 'er!" The speaker was the cook, Old Rocky, and he was seated on the step of the chuck hall, where he had remained, until then, unnoticed.

"Billy Foreman shot her?" Bill Ball questioned narrowly as he looked back at the huge old cow. He had been just as astounded by the sight as any of the others, and of them all was feeling the most pleased. But this news of the cow being shot, roused his *segundo* instincts and raised them bad. "He hadn't better have shot her!" he growled. "Besides, Rocky, she's a'standing right here."

"He shot her through the withers, Boss, right up betwixt her shoulder blades. Purtiest shot I ever did see—in one side and out the other, slick as a whistle. Done it with that old rusty hogleg, too. And it didn't hurt her a bit, at least not permanentlike, though it did take all the spunk out of her. Yes, sir, Boss, a Civil War surgeon couldn't have did it better, and I had oughta know. I useter be one."

"And she's not hurt?" Bill Ball pressed in disbelief.

"Not that I can see, 'cept maybe her pride. Fact is, the little feller's already daubed both holes full of axle grease, so's the blowflies won't get in. Course her nose is some tore up where that mutt Gopher grabbed aholt—"

"Johnny Molander's mutt?"

"Same as. Reckon he left with Billy this morning. Maybe it was on account of the little feller wore Johnny's chaps, I don't know. I do know the mutt wasn't around all day, and a little bit ago when Billy and his mule limped in behint these hyer cows, why, there he was, wagging his tail and walking tall beside 'em."

"So," Ervin McGrew breathed, shaking his head in disbelief, "Billy and the dog actually brought these runnygades in?"

"As ever, Slim. Now he's sawing logs to beat the band over in the bunkhouse, and old Gopher's sawing 'em right alongside him. Neither of 'em even stopped to eat they was so tuckered. Setting here trying to figure what they must've went through, I don't reckon I blame 'em!"

"Well, I'll be double dogged."

"Yeah, Red. Me, too." Bob Hott shook his head and dismounted. "Like I said, boys, any man what can bring in old Splayfoot, here, has to be salty as Lot's wife! And that's a purdee fact!"

32

Sunday, November 6, 1881

Bluff Fort

"Ohmagosh, Ma!" Nine-year-old Hyrum Fielding, who had been staring out the meetinghouse door and wishing worship service would end, was so excited he couldn't contain himself. "Bishop Nielson's back! And here come the Joneses, and . . . and . . . Ohmagosh, Ma! There's folks with 'em that we don't even know!"

"Hyrum Amos Fielding! You are not allowed to speak in that manner, and you know it!"

Cowed only a little, young Hyrum Amos glanced away from the stern looks of his mother, Ellen Hobbs Fielding, and his father, who was also called Hyrum Amos. Following the devastating spring floods, the Fieldings, members of the original Hole-in-the-Rock expedition, had moved to Montezuma Creek with the Hydes and others, and there they had actually managed to raise a small crop. Now they were back not only to collect some personal belongings that had been left behind, but to visit dear friends and perhaps encourage one or two of them to join the smaller settlement at Montezuma Creek.

"Hy's sure-enough right!" Zachariah Decker, also nine, was instantly at the open door. "It's the bishop!"

"And there sure-enough are some strangers with him," ten-year-old Billy Mackelprang agreed loudly. "Two, three—no, five wagons and a whole passel of livestock!" And that, whether it was meant to or not, quite effectively ended the meeting.

Bluff Fort

"Oh, Mary, I can't tell you how I've missed you!"

"And I've missed you, Eliza." Mary Jones, who was now standing in Eliza's cabin, gave her tall friend a huge bear hug. "And my goodness, Willy," she exclaimed as she lifted Willy up into her arms, "look how you've grown! Do you remember your Aunt Mary? Maybe you don't, what with all this dust on my face. But at least it'll come off—"

"*Cliz bekigie,*" Willy interrupted as he pointed toward the distant icehouse door. *"Cliz bekigie!"*

"My goodness, child, who taught you to speak Navajo? Eliza, he just said rattlesnake!"

"I know," Eliza chuckled. "Brother Haskel has been teaching him. He says Willy has a real gift for it. Now, Mary, dear, how are you getting along? I mean, with the . . . the—"

"With Kumen being married to Lydia May?" Mary finished in a quiet voice. "Eliza, dear, I want to talk with you about it, but now isn't the time. Remember how easily we can hear each other through these common walls?" Abruptly the young woman brightened. "But come with me at once, my dear. I am simply dying to show you your new stove!"

And with a tiny squeal of delight, Eliza hugged Mary and then followed her and Willy out the door.

LC Ranch Headquarters

For some time Billy simply sat on the veranda of the bunkhouse, wondering what to do with himself. There was not a soul in sight, and so far as he could tell, Old Rocky the cook was the only man besides himself who was present. Of course he had slept in, not even wakening until shortly after six. But that was not surprising, considering the ordeal he had endured the past two days. What had surprised him, was that all the cowhands were up and gone, and he had not even heard a whisper of their departure.

For a time he had wondered if they might not have come home

the night before, though Old Rocky had set him straight on that score. The cook had also informed him, calling him "Mister Foreman" as he had done so, that all the chores had been done, the wood chopped and the water drawn, and that he was to consider the day a Sunday and use it as a day of rest. All of which Billy thought strange, especially since it *was* Sunday, and he hadn't been called Mister in practically his whole life.

"I don't know, Goph," he muttered as he scratched behind the little terrier's ears. "I reckon I shouldn't have shot old Splayfoot, after all. The only thing that makes sense about them ostracizing me like this, is that Bill Ball is fixing to fire me."

In response the little dog looked up and thumped his tail on the porch floor, then inched closer so Billy could scratch more easily. At this Billy chuckled, wondering again at the seeming intelligence of the dog. And then his mind was wandering again, trying to understand what was going on.

Bluff Fort

"Oh, Mary! That's the most beautiful stove I've ever seen!"

Mary Jones smiled as she stood beside her friend, who was gazing under the tarp of the wagon. "Well, you picked it, Eliza. All we did was freight it here to Bluff."

"Did it cause you any trouble?"

"Not a bit. Of course, we didn't have to haul it down through that horrid Hole-in-the-Rock, for that portion of the road is now utterly abandoned. Then, too, we had plenty of help for the few times when we bogged down."

"You mean the new families? Are they really here to stay?"

Mary chuckled. "Well, at least that's their intention. Of course no one has told them much about our grim monsters, the river and its tributary—our ditch. And neither is very much being said about Lamanites and outlaws. But whether they stay or not, Eliza, they are simply wonderful people. I know you will love them!"

"I'm sure I will. Who are they?"

"Well, Samuel and Josephine or Jody Wood, who have come from Cedar City—"

"I remember Jody!"

"Yes, and she remembers you."

Suddenly Eliza's eyes widened. "Oh, my goodness, Mary. That was back when I was not at my very best—"

Mary laughed easily. "All she remembers about you, Eliza dear, is good. And I've pumped her full of so much more of your goodness that she's fairly bursting to see you again!"

"Mary—"

"We also have with us Kumen's cousin, Frederick I. Jones, and his wife, Mary, and their young son."

"Kumen's cousin?"

"Yes, and Fred's every bit as feisty as Kumen. Oh, and Mary's maiden name is Mackelprang."

"Sam Mackelprang's sister?"

"Right. That's why she's over yonder hugging poor Adelia to death." Suddenly Mary clapped her hand over her mouth. "Oh, dear! I suppose Adelia being alone, means that Sammy has already gone to Colorado?"

"He," Eliza responded quietly as she turned and picked up her son, "and most everyone else."

Eliza had quite effectively hidden her suddenly tearful eyes, but she was not able to deceive her best friend. "Oh," Mary declared, easily changing the subject, at least for the moment, "and those folks with the one wagon trailing the other are William Adams and one of his wives, Mary Barbara. They also have four sons, who are apt to be anywhere. William's first wife, Mary Ann, has chosen to stay in Parowan, so his family is now terribly spread out. I shouldn't wonder if they hardly ever see each other again."

"How very sad!" Without warning, Eliza began to giggle. "I'm sorry, Mary, dear, but what on earth are we to do? You said both new women are named Mary, and if we add you and the several other Marys in this fort—"

"Then hollering out one name should get a whole lot of attention," Mary chuckled, concluding that now was the time to ask—

before Kumen had the chance to come over and do it. "By the by, should I assume that Billy has already gone to Colorado?"

"Actually, no," Eliza responded, doing her best to sound positive. "Bill Ball came during the week and hired him to be a cowboy, up on the LC—"

"A cowboy?" a young man asked as he turned and stepped toward the two women. "Your husband's an honest-to-goodness cowboy?"

"Eliza," Mary grinned, "I'd like you to meet George Albert Adams. He is seventeen and has expertly handled our stock the entire journey. George Albert, this is Eliza Foreman and her son, Willy."

"Pleased to meet you, ma'am. Willy."

"Likewise, I'm sure."

"Uh . . . I'm a cowpuncher myself, ma'am." The young man had his hat in his hand, and he seemed very nervous. "I ain't bad, I reckon, for Pa and us have ranched all our lives. But still, ma'am, I've sure got a hankering to meet me a real, live, Texican cowpuncher."

"Then the next time Bill Ball comes to the fort, George Albert, I'll introduce you. He's the foreman on the LC, the ranch where my husband is now working—"

"Did I hear you say Billy's working for the LC?"

"Hello, Kumen!" Eliza beamed as the young man embraced her. "Isn't it something? He's being paid cash money, and each month Bill Ball will be sending a packload of foodstuffs down here to the fort."

"Why, that's a wonderful blessing!" Kumen was obviously pleased. "Has . . . uh . . . has Billy learned yet to stay in the saddle?"

"He hadn't when he left," Eliza responded with a perplexed smile. "But with his great faith, I'm hoping that's now changed. If it hasn't," and now she shrugged helplessly, "then I'm afraid he's going to have a very long winter—"

LC Ranch Headquarters

It was late afternoon, Old Rocky had fed him two huge if not altogether appetizing meals, and Billy was wondering if everyone at the LC ate that much all the time. Not that any of them looked it, exactly. But there just seemed to be so much food—

On a desk in the main cabin he had found some paper and a quill pen with ink, and being absolutely bored to tears, he sat down and commenced a letter to his wife and son.

"My dearest Eliza and darling Willy," he wrote, already wondering what he might have to say. After all, he'd been gone less than a week, and—

"I take pen in hand to express to you both my love, and to tell you that I would far rather be there with you, than where I am. Not that I am being treated badly, mind you. Far from it. I have been fed twice today and feel stuffed as a Thanksgiving turkey. I am worried that if this continues I will soon grow out of my britches."

For a moment he paused, looking out the window and collecting his thoughts. "The LC ranch is in a lovely place," he continued, "built on a bench above Recapture Creek with cliffs behind it and a wondrous view from the front. There is one place not far from the cabin where I think I could see you, if only my eyes were better. Certainly I can see all the way to the tall rocks on the Navajo Reservation, though they are quite faint with distance.

"There are many trees about, principally of juniper or cedar and pinion. But there are also the large trees called Ponderosa that Dick and George are sawing somewhere near here. It is those trees, I believe, out of which the buildings of this ranch have been put together. The work has been done well and carefully, at least for the most part, and I suspect it will stand the test of time rather well.

"We have, besides the main or headquarters cabin, which is quite spacious and pleasant and where I now sit, a long bunkhouse that sleeps twenty men, a chuck or mess hall and adjoining kitchen and cellar, a barn or horse stables with adjoining tack shed and corrals, two outhouses, and a smokehouse. In addition to the nearby creek there is also a well and pump, so that water can be obtained from either source. There may be more to the LC off in other places, but these are all the buildings I have seen.

"The men here, whom everyone calls hands—"

"Are you making out all right, Mr. Foreman? Kin I get you anything else fer chuck?"

Looking up, Billy smiled pleasantly. "No, thank you, Rocky. I've eaten quite enough."

"Well, the boss said to feed you up proper, which is what I'm aiming to do."

Billy continued smiling as the cook closed the door behind him, after which he continued his letter.

"The men here, whom everyone calls hands, seem like very good men, honest and hard working. Their language is certainly colorful, and is more like Pap and Lem Redd's than anything else I have heard. Almost all of them seem too fond of tobacco, though, and I suspect if there were whiskey around, they would imbibe quite freely of that, too. They are mostly quite young, in their teens or early twenties, I should guess. One young feller, Bob Hott, hasn't even started shaving yet, though Bill Ball says he is looked upon as a top hand.

"My partner, Curly Bill Jenkins, has anything but curly hair. Rather, he is bald as a billiards ball, is tall and gaunt-looking with deep-set hollow eyes, and his shoulders are rounded and stooped, I suppose from trying to stay a little shorter when he was a growing youngster. He is also bowlegged from so many years in the saddle, and I believe he emphasizes that when he wants to impress others such as yours truly. According to Bill Ball, Curly is also a top hand, and is quite a shooter with either handgun or rifle.

"Speaking of which, I had to shoot a cow last night, which may turn out to cost me this job. There is a custom among these hands which they call rawhiding, in which they test a new man by playing jokes on him to see what he is made of. I have been through a little of this already, being sent after a vicious old cow that is known in these parts as a 'runnygade,' their word for renegade. She is a Texas longhorn, brindle colored (yellow-tan, speckled with white), ornery as can be, and every bit as tall as my mule. For two days I chased her back and forth through a terrible country not too far from here, never getting very close, and finally last night, with the help of a little mixed-breed terrier they call Gopher on account of the hands tell him to 'go for' his own food, I caught the cow and her five offspring.

"Though tired she would not drive, so finally I placed a bullet through her withers to humble her, and in that condition drove her back to the ranch.

"Truthfully, though, I do not know if I have done the right thing. I am certain the men were rawhiding me, but perhaps I did not respond properly enough to suit their strange fancies. Besides which, I lost my temper several times and almost said things a Latter-day Saint ought not to say, for which I feel very badly. Now today I am being ignored by all except the cook, Old Rocky, and he keeps calling me Mister and trying to feed me. Gopher, however, is staying at my side, so at least I have one true friend. The rest of the hands are nowhere to be found. So perhaps you see the straits I am in and the feeling I have that the Lord may be forced to withdraw his blessing of this job. Certainly I do not know what to do or where to go, or even if I am still employed.

"But allow me to change the subject and tell you a little about Old Rocky, since he is the only other hand I have actually had much contact with. I do not wish to be guilty of libel on the old man's character, but some things about him are too remarkable to pass by without notice.

"Apparently he was a surgeon in the War between the States, but those glory days are long past, and I think Bill Ball has hired him as cook out of sympathy, though it is hard for me to generate the same. He wears an undershirt for all the time that is stiff with dirt, and as to his person, he looks as if he might never have been diluted with water since the last time. He smokes and chews tobacco, and when expectorating he often bedaubs the front of his already polluted clothing. His language is quite vile, and except for when speaking to me, he seldom says anything of a redeeming nature.

"He is not in the least handsome, and with his grizzled gray hair and beard clipped and notched close to his head, he looks perfectly hideous. He wears a slouch hat and a pair of big shoes, and as a fitting climax to all the rest, a pair of overalls several times too large, of which he uses but one button, halfway around his waist, to where the front is lapped around to the button to make them tight enough to stay on.

"At close range the olfactory nerve is shocked, and strongly confirms what sight has already indicated. He is slouchy and careless beyond description, and it appalls me to think that he is the man who has been assigned to fix my meals. But allow me to give you an interesting example of his mannerisms.

"I saw him, the first night I was here, attempt to use a hammer. He picked it up and then made to moisten his hands with saliva. But it all went on his wrist, a disgusting sight, though he noticed it not at all and began hammering. In the kitchen I later noticed his bed, the pillow of which appeared to have lost flexibility and was almost black with dirt. For obvious reasons I did not dare look that closely at his blankets.

"I am sorry that such sights fill me with disgust, Eliza, but I fear you have spoiled me with your cleanliness, your fine manners, and your dainty, feminine ways. Isn't it strange that of all the hands who labor here on the LC, it is this man who has spoken with me the most, and who has shown me the most courtesy? Perhaps there is a lesson in this, that I have yet to learn.

"Well, the sun is setting after what has seemed a long day, almost as long as the two that preceded it. The soreness in my muscles is nearly gone, and good old Sign seems to have completely recovered from carrying me so far through such treacherous country. Oh, and one other good thing. So far, no one but Bill Ball has seen me thrown from the saddle. I hope and pray that will continue.

"Will you please give each other big hugs and kisses for me, and know that I would give them to you if only I could.

"Your affectionate father and husband, Billy Foreman."

LC Ranch Headquarters

For an hour Curly Bill Jenkins sat in the darkness, thinking. Somehow the puny little Mormon had managed to make a fool of him, at least in the eyes of some of the hands, and Curly did not like that even a little. He liked even less the fact that the little sissy had somehow managed to round up old Splayfoot and her brood, and drive the whole and entire bunch back to the ranch. It wasn't possible, but he'd done it. And that in spite of the fact that he was so green he'd have needed one leg tied up before he could even be given a haircut.

In continuing disbelief, Curly again shook his head. That morning early, every last one of the men, Bill Ball included, had made a beeline upcountry to where old Splayfoot had been known to hang out. There they had joined together their considerable breadth of cow-sense and tracking abilities, determined to find out by what impossible fluke of luck the little Mormon had come to accomplish what all of them had heretofore thought of as, if not impossible, then at least far too difficult and time-consuming to ever even try.

Hours and hours later they had sat in stunned silence on the little mesa between the two creeks, scratching their heads and trying to believe what they had all discovered to be true. There had been no fluke of luck, no easy or fortuitous accident. Old Splayfoot's tracks were everywhere, all of them less than two days old, going up and down and back and forth and around and around, over the mesa and across and between the two creeks until the men had grown dizzy just following. And all of the cow's distinctive tracks were either covered with the narrow hoofprints of a mule and the paw prints of a dog, or else they were overlaid with the equally distinctive prints of Billy Foreman's home-soled shoes. In other words, they all had to finally admit, Billy, both aboard his mule and then on foot, had simply worn the fool cow down, following her without letup for two grueling days, finally winning the battle of wits and will to which old Splayfoot had subjected him.

Again Curly shook his head, trying to figure it out. No man would do that. No, no man *could* do it! He'd know better, by jings, than to even try. It was too dangerous, too hard on a good horse, too impossible to avoid bloody contact with the runnygade cow-critter once she'd got her dander up and turned back against him from ambush the way they always did. Besides which, no man had that sort of walking strength, that sort of endurance. Even if he wanted to, which Curly doubted any man would. No, sir, no human critter could possibly walk down a long-legged, far-traveling, fast-walking, wild runnygade Texas longhorn. *It just couldn't be done!*

Yet somehow that sniveling little sissified Mormon had gone and done it. More, he had gone and made Curly look like a fool for having told him to do it in the first place—which in Curly's considered opinion was by far the worst offense.

So, he thought as he stared out into the darkness beyond the bunkhouse, his jaw set and hard, it wasn't over yet, not by a darn sight! Still, he had to come up with something foolproof—some surefire way of rawhiding the little greenhorn into quitting. And he would, too, just as soon as the right idea came trailing along—

33

Wednesday, November 9, 1881

LC Ranch Headquarters

"There's gonna be a dad-gummed show this morning, boys," the lanky Curly Bill Jenkins declared to the other hands in the chuck hall, his grin spreading across his face. "It's taken me two days to set this up proper, but now that I have, she's gonna be a dinger!"

Ervin McGrew shook his head. "Curly, you still after that little Mormon feller? Even after he done brought in thet runnygade Splayfoot like you asked?"

"It ain't the Mormon, Slim." Jimmy Frink was only partly teasing. "Curly's got so old and stove-up with the arthritic rheumatiz that he cain't face another winter in the saddle. That means his onliest hope fer a warm fire'n an overstuffed chair, is driving poor Billy Foreman out of the country."

"I ain't so old and stove-up that I can't stomp you into the ground, Red, and don't you forget it!"

"Yeah!" one of the Ptelomy brothers snickered, "and that's with both arms tied behint his back."

"And both laigs broke in a dozen places," the other brother added gleefully.

Curly's face was now red with anger. "Go ahead, you miserable galoots, and make fun whilst you can. I've got that sissified little Mormon all set up to fly without no wings, and if'n I have to enjoy his squawking and flopping all by my lonesome, then by double jings, that's exactly what I'm gonna do!"

"Fly, huh? Whatcha going to do, Curly? Throw him off a cliff?"

"Don't forget, fellers. He is a gol-durned skypilot. Maybeso he kin fly further'n we think!"

"Yeah," Bob Hott laughed. "After all, he sure-enough rounded up them cows all by his lonesome, so he probably can fly. Where's the cliff, Curly? This I'd like to see."

"Out to the corral," Curly replied smugly. "I told the little greenhorn that Bill Ball wants him to take a certain hoss and ride it today."

"I sure hope it ain't Hurricane," Bob Hott immediately protested, his voice revealing his concern. "You know that outlaw critter ain't never been rode."

"Or even hand-held by just one man," Slim McGrew agreed. "Not at least without practically killing whoever was dumb enough to get too close."

Curly's grin widened. "You know how Bill Ball's been bragging on this Mormon feller being a real cowpoke ever since he drug in those few lame cows? Well, I take that personal. Maybeso Bill Ball can outride me six ways from Sunday, and maybeso he's even the boss. But I'm telling you boys, that durned little greenhorn got lucky, and he ain't no more a cowpoke than a green willer is a full-growed Ponderosa. Besides, I take being a cowpoke as an honorable profession—somethin' to be earned and feel proud of. I'll be double-dipped in a sheep vat if I want to be crowded into the same loop with a no-nothing, do-nothing little Mormon sissy like Billy Sanctimonious Foreman. That's why I aim to prove onct and forever that he won't never be a cowpoke, and that I want a real man with me at the line camp this winter. Seems to me Hurricane's about the best pardner I could find to get 'er done."

Curly's companions were aghast. "But . . . but Hurricane'll kill him!"

"If'n Billy Foreman's stupid enough to get that close to an animal what's showing the whites of his eyes the way Hurricane's already doing this morning, since me'n Hank and the two Ketchum boys saddled him, then for sure he ain't no cowpoke, and I reckon he deserves pretty much what he's going to get."

Ervin McGrew was furious. "Well, I don't reckon that at all!"

The protesting youth shoved his chair back and rose, determined to get out to the corral and get Billy's attention. "And I'm gonna—"

"You ain't gonna do nothin,' Slim!" Curly's grin disappeared instantly, to be replaced by a menacing scowl—"Nothin' but watch and enjoy the show with the rest of us. You get my drift?"

Slowly the young man clapped his hat on his head. "I get your drift," he responded sullenly. "But despite that Bill Ball ain't here today, when he finds out what you done, well, I ain't siding you for nothing. As far as I'm concerned, Curly, for this stunt you're on your own, and that's a fact."

"Fine with me," Curly growled. "Now, shaddup and get outside, the whole dad-gummed, miserable bunch of you, 'cause this is gonna be funny!"

LC Ranch Headquarters

Billy Foreman was seated at the grindstone, putting a fresh edge on an ax. Already he'd chopped about half a cord of firewood, and now he sat methodically pumping the treadle and honing the blade, his work careful and deliberate. It wasn't that he was intentionally working slowly, or at least he didn't think so. Rather it was that he was suddenly in big trouble, and he needed time to think things through.

Earlier Curly had approached him, all sweetness and light, and informed him that Bill Ball, who had ridden out earlier, wanted him to give his mule a rest and try out a new horse that day, a fairly gentle old nag. More, the horse he was to try had already been saddled by the more-than-thoughtful Curly, and was now awaiting him in a chute back of the corral.

What Curly didn't know, was that Billy had seen him and two other hands saddling that same gentle old nag a little earlier, and having the devil's own time of getting it done. Moreover, Old Rocky had already introduced Billy to that same horse the previous Sunday during his bored wanderings, revealing its well-earned name and uttering a dire warning to Billy or anyone else who was fool enough to even approach the animal alone.

So now Billy sat whetting the ax and thinking, wondering what would be the best thing for him to do. It was another attempt at rawhiding him, that was certain, and a vicious attempt, at that. But now that he was wise to it, what should he do? How should he respond? His very ignorance had won him a few friends the week before, especially because he had been blessed to bring in the renegade cow and her brood. So, should he exercise his faith and just have at it with the outlaw horse, trusting in the Lord to turn things out all right the way he had before? Or would the Lord want him to exercise good judgment and simply refuse?

All morning he had been praying about the situation, seeking fervently for some whisper of the Holy Spirit that would tell him what to do. But so far, he thought grimly, no response had come. Not unless—Well, maybe that was it; maybe that *was* his answer. Now that he thought of it, every time he had asked the Lord what he was to do, Billy had ended up thinking of how he had gone out after old Splayfoot and had actually brought her in. Was that his answer? Was the Lord in fact telling him to simply walk into that corral and climb aboard a horse that not only had never been ridden, but that seemed bent on destroying any man who tried?

Oh, glory, Billy thought as his heart started hammering within his chest and his foot stopped its steady pumping on the grindstone's treadle, *what if the Lord is actually going to require of me the ultimate sacrifice?*

The Beehives, Allen Canyon

The Pahute woman called Peeb did not know what to do. In fear she crouched hidden in a crevice in the huge rock formation in Allen Canyon that was called by some the Beehives, wondering. The terrible Poke and his brother had slain Jonah, taken sweet Too-rah, and then gone away. But then, after a few days, the whole band had returned to this place, and now Poke was looking past her as if she were not there. *Oo-ah,* yes, and more, once he had knocked her rolling with his passing, and had continued on without so much as looking back to see what harm might have been done to the very pregnant girl.

He should have looked back, Peeb knew, for tradition had it that any woman who was as big with child as she, merited a certain amount of respect. But the great Poke had shown none; no, not since she had sheltered his sister Too-rah and spoken defiantly of the mormonee words of power that had been spoken by the man Haskel.

Of itself the troubled mind of Peeb returned to that day when her man, who had carried the *mericat* name of Jonah for all the days since he had slain with one fine shot a cowboy by that name, had crept into their *wickiup* and taken to his sleeping robes. Though he was *puck-kon-gah,* sick, Peeb had not understood what was wrong with him. Now, however, she knew! Now that the great warrior Jonah had finally lost his breath to the evil Poke and taken the long journey into the land of the sky people, Peeb knew.

The sharp hooves of Poke's horse might have brought Jonah's death, yet they had not been what had ended his life. That had been done simply through the words of power that had been spoken by the mormonee called Haskel. The warrior Jonah had stolen from the mormonee people without ceasing, and so the great *Shin-op* had turned away his face and allowed Jonah 's breath to escape, and now the man was dead.

Dutifully Peeb had finished burning the *wickiup* after Poke's vicious attack and her husband's death. She had also burned the contents of the *wickiup,* including the stored food and the two fine sleeping robes that had also escaped Poke's fire. Then for several days she had sat in silence, shivering with the cold but hardly moving, until Poke's band had finally arrived to set up their own encampment. Shyly, then, and with head hanging as befitted one of her new widowed status, Peeb had presented herself for their mercy.

At first Peeb had hardly even noticed that she was being ignored. But then had come the beginning of true cold, the child had not yet been ready to come forth from her womb, and no man among Poke's people had expressed any interest in her.

Even her beloved friend Too-rah could not help, for she was no longer with Poke's band. She was simply gone, and no one spoke of it. At first Peeb had wondered if Posey might have come for the maiden, but when she discovered that Tehgre, one of Poke's brothers, was also missing, as well as the harsh crone who was his oldest sister, Peeb knew. Too-rah had been taken away to a place of hiding, either that or to be sold as another's wife, and so would never be seen in the encampment of her family again.

Peeb had officially begun her starving then, not because she wanted to starve, but because no one would give her anything to eat. And that was when she had finally realized that no one of the band, man or woman, was speaking with her. Worse, she was given space in no *wickiup,* and so of a day she scrounged about the canyons and hillsides looking for berries or seeds or roots or insects or anything else that might sustain life, and of a night she sat huddled in a ball as near one of the dying fires as she could get without being ordered away.

Quickly she had grown dirty but hadn't noticed, thin because she had no longer been able to move about as easily to find food to eat, and tormented because she had no idea why she was being treated by the others as she was.

And now had come this day, big and awful in her mind as was the grizzly, Poke. To her utter and complete amazement, Peeb had watched from her cleft in the rocks as the women had packed the camp onto their scrawny ponies and dogs, the children had run about everywhere screaming with the excitement of another move, and the men had gambled stoically until all was made ready. Then without a backward glance, Poke and his entire band had ridden off down Allen Canyon toward Cottonwood—into lower, warmer, country—and Peeb had been left utterly and completely alone!

Now, as *tabby,* the sun, climbed toward midday, diffusing upon the confused woman what little warmth he was able to muster, Peeb knew. She was *e-i,* she was dead! The fearsome grizzly had declared her to be dead just as he had her husband, and so now it was no longer possible for any of the People to even see her. She, too, had taken that long road into the land of the sky people, and all that was lacking was her realization that she had indeed left her body behind.

The thing was, she found herself thinking as she tried to make herself smaller and therefore warmer, why did she still feel the cold? Or why did she feel the hunger that gnawed within her belly? Or why, more importantly, did she still feel the child within her womb, the child who even at that moment was kicking and straining against her ribs?

The woman called Peeb did not know the answers to these things. What she did know, now that she was alone in the canyon, was that she must somehow find something to eat, some robe or matt of grass or strip of bark to cover herself and keep her warm. In other words, she must find some way to keep her dead body going until her child was born, or until she found herself in the land of the sky people where she knew she should now be.

These things, she reasoned, could be better accomplished if she stayed close to the people who had left her behind. Truly she would need to gather what strength she could find and follow after them.

But first, her stomach, which was dead, was telling her over and over again, the woman Peeb needed to find some little thing to eat—

LC Ranch Headquarters

Billy removed his spectacles, carefully wrapped them in the soft buckskin Bill Ball had given him, and set the bundle on the ground at the base of one of the corral posts. There were men about: Bob Hott, Jimmy Frink, Slim McGrew, and others, and of course Curly was across the corral, busy doing something with one of the fence poles. In fact all the men were busy, and none of them seemed in the least interested in what Billy might be doing.

Yet, Billy thought grimly as he climbed the pole fence and paused for a moment at the top, every man jack one of them was no doubt watching him intently, ready to enjoy the rodeo. Or *circus* might be a better description, Billy thought as he glanced for a moment at Hurricane.

Of a truth the animal was magnificent. In fact, he should have made someone a wonderful mount. But no, something tragic had happened, some terrible event or series of events that had turned the horse into an outlaw—a man-killer. And now he, Billy Foreman, a sorry little clerk turned pioneer, who couldn't even stay in the saddle of poor, old, gentle Sign when the mule gave a morning crow-hop, was expected to walk out there and climb on that horse and ride him?

"Oh, dear Lord," Billy breathed as he turned and climbed down the inside of the corral fence and planted his feet hesitantly inside, "please help me know what to do—"

"Look at that," he heard Curly sneer as he turned and began to walk slowly forward. "The sorry fool don't even know what that hoss is going to do to 'im. Why, if he wasn't snubbed to them posts tighter'n the snarl to a bulldog's mouth, he'd be dead already. And," he snorted, "Bill Ball says he's got him a way with animals."

Slowly Billy moved forward, his hand outstretched, his heart racing. Even without his spectacles he could see the animal rolling its eyes, and his ears had no difficulty picking up the horse's snorts of anger.

"Dear Father in Heaven," he breathed again, "I'm trying to exercise faith that you've told me to go ahead with this, but please tell me how—"

Abruptly Billy's mind was filled with a memory, a time when, in company with Brigham Young, he had paused for refreshment in the small community of Nephi. There'd been an older man there that day, Edward Ockey, who with his grown son Heber, had been gentling a wild horse in a nearby corral. Billy remembered it because folks in President Young's party had expected to see some wild bucking and riding. Instead, though, they had watched the young Heber literally talk the horse into submission without so much as his even climbing aboard.

To most of the people the event that afternoon in Nephi had been a disappointment, but Billy had found it intriguing. In fact that evening he and Heber had talked for several hours, learning that they had both been born on the plains en route to Utah and that both were attracted to books and learning. Heber had revealed to Billy that his method of training horses had been brought by his father Edward from England, and consisted in actuality of a quiet contest of wills between man and animal. Usually the process, which did not break a horse's spirit, took from several hours to several weeks, though

Heber said he had actually seen wild horses become completely subdued and submit to being ridden in an hour or less. The difference, it seemed to Heber, had been what sort of treatment they had suffered at the hands of other men.

Now, as this memory raced through Billy's mind, he found himself actually picturing the things Heber Ockey had been doing with the wild horse on that long-ago day, visualizing each step.

"Whoa, big fella," Billy breathed as he slowly closed the gap between himself and the terrified, angry horse, "I'm not your enemy, and I mean that sincerely. I have no intention of hurting you, and I'm certainly not very anxious to ride you. But you see, that's my job, and so it's something that must be done."

Moving ever so slowly Billy drew nearer, his hand outstretched toward the straining animal. He was aware that Curly and the others had now gathered behind him, lining the outside of the corral fence and watching what each expected would be the little Mormon's immediate demise. But at least they were watching silently, Billy found himself thinking, so for the moment both he and Hurricane could ignore them and concentrate on each other.

"You hear what he's saying to that hoss?" one of the men suddenly questioned in sotto voce.

"Not a word," another whispered, the whisper carrying easily to Billy's ears.

Part of the humor in their action, Billy understood, was the simple joy of rawhiding a greenhorn. Bill Ball had said it was done all the time. But this—getting an actual Mormon greenhorn to try and ride this particular animal—was more sinister, and had even deeper motives. It seemed likely that Curly was the instigator, though why made no sense to Billy, no sense at all.

"Get ready, boys," Curly suddenly muttered. "I reckon the fur's about to fly!"

"Yeah," someone else agreed. "In another minute or so, what that little greenhorn's been a'jawing about with that hoss, just ain't a'going to matter—"

He's probably right, Billy thought as he slowly inched his open hand toward the big horse—for now that Billy was close, he was surprised by how tall the animal was. Its head towered over him.

Sixteen hands, maybe seventeen, and very well formed. This was a beautiful horse! And he was as terrified as he was beautiful, Billy thought grimly. Either terrified or angry—so much so that his eyes were showing mostly their whites—he was lunging violently about and trying to use his hooves to trample. If his head hadn't been tied securely in both directions, his powerful teeth would have already taken off Billy's hand and no doubt a great deal more.

Yet what choice did he have, Billy found himself wondering? The Spirit seemed to have told him to do this, and now that he was so close, the only thing he could think of, was to lay his hand on the trembling, straining animal's neck. It was a fool idea, though, for if Hurricane somehow broke free—

"When it comes to riding, don't forget to use the priesthood," Billy heard as his hand gently touched the horse. It was Thales Haskel's voice, and for a split second Billy thought the old man was there beside him, telling him what to do. But then he remembered that Thales had spoken those words the last time they had met in the fort, and that they had made no sense at the time. But Thales had also said something else, something about Noah—"That's how Noah did it," he had said. That was it! "That's how Noah did it." Of course! Noah had no doubt used the priesthood to gather together and subdue all the animals—

Softly then Billy began speaking again, his hand resting lightly on the neck of the still-trembling, fighting horse. He chose his words carefully, purposefully, speaking peace and blessings in the name of the Lord Jesus, explaining again and again what he intended to do, and doing it in the most tender tones he could possibly utter. And slowly, as Billy continued speaking his own words of power, the horse began to relax.

Moments later, when he felt that it was time, Billy loosed the horse's bridle with its cruel Spanish bit, which he gently removed and dropped to the ground. He did the same with the main lead rope that had been tied around the horse's neck. Then, very carefully, he reached down and began untying the ropes that had held Hurricane so securely.

LC Ranch Headquarters

What followed, as Curly allowed some time later, was the biggest quiet since Giggles Aplenty had showed up in church of an Easter Sunday morning. And seeing that Giggles hadn't been in church or even been seen abroad in daylight in a dozen years, that was some quiet. Still and all, the quiet wasn't sufficient for the men of the LC. All they could see was Billy and Hurricane standing side by side in the narrow chute, Billy slowly untying ropes, and they couldn't hear a dad-blamed thing. For three or perhaps four minutes—a terribly long time to the waiting cowboys—there was no other movement from within the chute, and no sound. More, they were concentrating so intently on Billy and the outlaw horse that none of them heard the soft hoof falls of another animal walking up and stopping behind them.

But then, abruptly, the tie-downs were loose and Billy was backing out of the chute, one of the ropes coiled in his hand, and Hurricane snorting and tossing his head and following.

"What the double-deuce?" one of the watchers muttered, and then all stared in silent wonder as Billy waved his arms and started the horse trotting and running and bucking and kicking around the perimeter of the circular corral, while he stood still in the center, simply turning and watching the big horse move.

Then, to the ranch hands' even greater amazement, Billy took the coiled rope and tossed it at the outlaw horse, not to catch it, apparently, for the rope didn't even have a loop. No, all the little Mormon wanted, it seemed, was for the rope to snake across the horse's withers in front of the saddle, and then for the startled animal to snort and kick and escape out from under it.

"Well, if that ain't the craziest, durn-fool trick I ever did see—"

Hearing but paying no mind, Billy repeated the procedure again and again, tossing the rope, waiting for it to fall from Hurricane's back, and then coiling and tossing it again. And every time the rope flew toward the horse and then hit him, he snorted and bolted in fear.

"Say, you durned nincompoop! Ya cain't ketch 'im if you ain't got a loop in your rope!"

"Yeah, that's so!" Curly agreed instantly. "What's the matter, you sissified little Mormon? You sceered of that gentle old nag?"

"I may be wrong, Curly, but it seems to me that's Billy Foreman in the corral with that outlaw, and not you. Makes a feller wonder who it is that's sceered."

The low voice, from behind the men, caused all the boys to wheel guiltily and gape up at the man who sat horseback behind them. "Howdy, boys." Bill Ball grinned and pulled his pistol out of its holster, which he then cocked. "Curly, what'n tarnation's Billy doing in there all alone with Hurricane?"

"He . . . uh . . . I . . . uh—" Curly stammered, absolutely unable to respond.

"Billy," Bill Ball then called, his voice quiet but carrying, "why don't you drop that rope and skedaddle on out of there?"

"Why, Curly said you wanted me to ride this horse today," Billy replied innocently as he continued his efforts with the rope. Neither did he take his eyes from the circling animal.

"Well, Curly was mistaken about my orders. Howsomever, since you've already brought ol' Hurricane out of the chute and got him saddled, why don't we have Curly here take the kinks out of him?" Bill Ball shifted his gaze to the lanky cowboy, if not his pistol. "Go ahead, Curly, climb inter that corral and show us what you can do."

While Curly Bill Jenkins forced his mind to grasp the reality that he had just been ordered to ride the famous and unridable outlaw, Bill Ball smiled at his new hand. "Meanwhile, Billy, why don't you and me mosey over and pick three or four head out of that bunch of hosses yonder."

"But Bill," one of the cowboys yelped, "them's *our* mounts!"

"They *were,*" Bill Ball agreed as he reached to open the gate, and then noticed that Curly Bill was still standing by the pole corral, staring at the outlaw horse. "Curly, you ain't got very far. Something wrong?"

"I . . . uh . . . I—"

"Looks like Curly's bin stricken with a stroke," Slim McGrew opined seriously.

"Or taken a sudden case of arthritic rheumatiz," Bob Hott chortled.

"If it's all the same," Billy declared softly, finally taking the pressure off the man who was to be his partner, "I truly do like the looks of this horse, Bill. Give me a little more time with him, will you? I'd like to try out his gait."

In the profound silence that followed, Billy continued his patient work with the outlaw horse. Strangely, though one hour passed and then two, none of the hands turned away, and none spoke. Instead they watched and waited in silence, as captivated and maybe even agitated by Billy's rope tossing, as was the snorting outlaw bronc.

But then, when everyone was certain this nonsense had no point, but was going to go on forever, the big horse suddenly slowed to a trot and then a walk, while Billy continued to toss the rope across his withers. Thirty interminable minutes later, Hurricane snorted and bobbed his head a few times and then stopped altogether, his muscles quivering. And even when Billy tossed the rope one last time, he did not move.

At that Billy coiled his rope, turned his back on the animal, and waited. For what seemed to be several long minutes, Hurricane merely stood, his head high and his eyes watchful. But when Billy didn't turn, and didn't even throw the rope at him, the big horse finally grew restless. Two or three times he bobbed his head, snorting each time as if he wanted Billy to look. When that still didn't happen, the animal, still bobbing its head and snorting, began walking slowly toward him.

"Now it's comin'," Curly Bill Jenkins breathed, unaccountably feeling every bit as concerned for Billy's safety as Slim McGrew and Bob Hott had appeared earlier. "Unless somebody stops it, that crazy hoss is gonna kill 'im—"

Once again speaking quietly but keeping his back to the horse all the while, Billy stepped first one way and then another, purposely moving away from the outlaw. And to the amazement of the dumbstruck cowboys, who now included the *segundo* Bill Ball, the famous mankiller simply followed. It was as though he wanted Billy to turn and pay more attention to him, and he wasn't going to let up from following until the frail Mormon did so.

"By Tophet, would you look at that?" Pat Ptelomy muttered in absolute amazement. "In all my born days I ain't never seed the like!"

"Nor likely will again," his brother Mike Ptelomy agreed with an oath. "Look at the way we're a'gawkin' at 'im, boys. Why, that there little feller's drawin' more stares nor an albino runnygade with two heads and a sweet disposition, and he deserves 'em jest as much!"

"He still ain't rid 'im, though!" Curly growled, unaccountably getting irritated again. "This is just a cheap trick. Keep an eye on Hurricane, for that'll be the real show. That's when that there hoss'll show his true colors! You mark my words—"

Fifteen more minutes passed and then twenty, going as slow, one of the watchers declared, "as wet gunpowder being lit by a cold fuse." But Billy persisted, walking in front of Hurricane first one way, then another, and finally walking beside the animal and leading him here and there with a slight touch of his hand.

"Well, Curly," Bob Hott finally muttered, "I bin keeping my eye on ol' Hurricane right along, jest like you said, waiting fer the real show to start. Way it appears, though, ol' Hurricane ain't going to look away from that little Mormon feller fer nothing less nor the Second Coming."

"Even then," Slim McGrew added sarcastically, "I reckon the Lord would have to show up on the handlebars of one of them new-fangled bicycles being rid by a tame Russian bear, to draw so much as a walleyed blink out of that nag. Curly, you about ready to give up?"

"You boys just hang on and wait—"

Abruptly Billy leaned on the saddle, talked quietly to the outlaw horse for another moment or so, and then swung aboard.

"He-yaah!" one of the observers yelled in anticipation, and then he grew silent as a thrown-away feather duster, which was about the same quiet as everybody else was experiencing, at least according to what Jimmy Frink would tell folks later. Hurricane was standing still, Billy Foreman was leaning over the saddle horn patting the outlaw's neck and still talking, and nothing much else was happening.

"Well, I'll be double-damnable dipped in sheep dip," Curly Bill Jenkins mumbled in amazement. "I'd of never believed this if'n I hadn't seed it with my own two eyes, and I ain't altogether shure I believe it anyhow."

But Curly was to see even more, for at that moment Hurricane started to walk around the corral, first one direction and then, at the touch of Billy's knee, the other. Soon he was trotting, and a couple of minutes later he was moving at an easy gallop, with Billy Foreman seated firmly in the saddle.

"He's a fine horse," Billy called out, for a moment raising his voice so Bill Ball and the others could hear him. "Bill, I'd consider it a privilege to ride this animal while I'm working for you."

"Ride?" one of the Ptelomy brothers ejaculated as he yanked off his Stetson and slammed it onto the ground. "By jings, Billy Foreman! I ain't seed a show like this since Buck McSwoon torched the stage curtains when Miss Rosy Applebottom was a singing and dancing fer Judge Roy Bean. And Buck only torched the curtains on account of the judge had hanged his brother fer no cause other'n a few little murders, besides which Buck could see the gleam in the judge's eye and wanted Miss Rosy fer hisself. Mormon greenhorn or no, Billy Foreman, I'll work free the whole and entire winter and let my wages buy that nag so's you kin have him fer keeps! I'll be dawged if'n I'd have believed it, but you shure-enough earned 'im!"

"Deal me in on that hand and stop being so durn selfish," the other Ptelomy brother growled. "Otherwise I'll tell Ma on ya—"

"You kin have all my chips, too," Jimmy Frink added enthusiastically.

"No need for that, boys." Bill Ball was pleased, and showed it by the way he uncocked and then holstered his pistol, which he admitted later would have been used for either Curly Bill Jenkins or the outlaw Hurricane—whichever had caused the most trouble first.

"From now on," he growled as he gathered up the reins to his big mule, "Hurricane's Billy's hoss, and he can do with 'im as he wants. By tonight he'll have the papers to prove it. Now daylight's a burning, boys, so I reckon we had all ought to get back to work."

And in surprisingly good humor, the men, Billy Foreman and Curly Bill Jenkins included, obeyed.

Bluff Fort

The four men sat upon the earth, their mouths silent as they politely gazed past each other over the small fire. It was dusk, and the three Navajos had arrived almost two hours before, seeking *'aleeh,* a conference, with Thales Haskel. The old missionary and interpreter had responded to them without hurry, kindled a fire in a secluded spot near the fort's corrals, and there he had fed them from a pot his wife Maggie had brought to them.

"Bináá doot ízhi," the oldest one of the three finally declared, using his venerable age to break the long silence, "it is a good thing that these old eyes can see you once again."

With his hands, Thales Haskel made the sign of humility and respect. "I am also pleased to see you, Dahnish uánt. The cycles of the seasons have been good to you."

"And to you," the elderly man responded politely.

"It was you who gave us back our lives," Thales declared slowly, "when that one who was a warrior of the *Dinê,* thought he would take them from us. For that gift I thank you once again."

Dahnish uánt grew sad. "That one thought he was a warrior, but he had no *hózhó,* no balance. Do you have word of the woman Maraboots, the one who was daughter to this old man?"

"I do not." Actually, Thales had heard a rumor that the Pahute woman had passed away—during, or shortly after, the birth of her fifth or sixth child. But the rumor had never been confirmed, for he hadn't seen Ira Hatch, Maraboots' husband, in several years, and so of a truth he didn't know. But there were other things—

"I do know the woman Maraboots is the mother of many fine sons, all of whom are growing rapidly into manhood. They are sons to make a man proud."

The old man nodded, and Thales could see that he was pleased. "Over the seasons of this man's life," Dahnish uánt said, abruptly getting down to the business at hand, "this one has seen many things. He has seen words of power spoken by many among the *Dinê,* and sometimes those words are fulfilled and sometimes they are not. He has also seen words of power spoken by the *belacani* soldiers such as Rope Thrower, words that are enforced by the rifle and the torch, and sometimes those words are also fulfilled. But there is much unhappiness with those words, and much sorrow, for the *belacani* soldiers have no more *hózhó* than many of the *Diné*."

The old man continued, "He has also seen words of power spoken by the ones the *nóódâi* call mormonee, words that bring much happiness with them, for the mormonee are indeed men of *hózhó*. It is true that sometimes these words bring sorrow and even death to certain others, but that is because *ńdiistsóós,* those others have chosen. Such a choice was made by the son of this old man, and now such a choice has been made by Natanii nééz."

"I have seen the tall one," Thales Haskel admitted. "He came to ask that I write a letter to the Holy One the Utes call *Shin-op,* asking that the words of *Shin-op* be taken back."

"Have you done this great thing?"

"I have mentioned it," Thales Haskel replied. "But who am I to make such a request of the Holy One? Who am I to see into the heart of Natanii nééz? Am I the one who can say that his heart has changed? No, I am only Haskel. It is *Shin-op* who must decide."

Briefly the old man smiled. "Your words are true, my brother, just as the words of Jacob Hamblin and Ira Hatch were true so many circles of the seasons back. Truly have the mormonee come to be friends with the *Diné*. Truly have they come to show us the way of the Holy One the *nóódâi* call *Shin-op*."

"You also speak words of truth, Dahnish uánt," Haskel said.

"This old fool does not think the one called Natanii nééz will steal from the mormonee again," the old man finally declared. "But Bitseel, the nephew of him who was once the tall one, has grown angry with the mormonee, and his heart has grown hard toward their words of peace. There are others among the People who feel the same. But most of them are young, Haskel, and so it is to be hoped that the great *Shin-op* will give them time to learn a few things before his words of power strike them down."

"Yes," Thales Haskel agreed, "such a thing is to be hoped for."

"Haskel, is it in your heart to know that this old fool is a true friend of the mormonee?"

This time Thales Haskel signed his answer. "Yes, I know this."

"The man called Pahlilly is another friend, and in time there will be many others. It is in the heart of this old one to ask that the mormonee be patient with the *Dinê*. Do not fight them even when they do foolish things. Wait upon them instead, my brother, and soon it is to be hoped that all the *Dinê* will see that it is good to be friends with the mormonee."

"We will do what we can do," Thales Haskel replied quietly, looking into the watery eyes of the old man. His glance was penetrating, and Dahnish uánt shifted uneasily. "Now," the interpreter and missionary said abruptly, "there is more you wish to know. Ask what you will, my father, and if I can, I will give you answer."

Silently the old man made the sign that he was pleased with Haskel's insight. "My brother," he said, pointing finally to his right, "this man is now called Jim Joe. He is the husband of my granddaughter, and he is a friend to the mormonee our people call Red Beard."

"Yes, I have also heard this thing from Kumen Jones."

The old man nodded his satisfaction. "This one is the son of Jim Joe, and is called Hashk é y ázhi, Little Warrior. These two have also seen the power of the words spoken by Haskel, Red Beard, and the others, and they, too, think of themselves as friends of the mormonee."

"It is good."

"In times past this old fool has related to these two all that he remembers of the words of the man Ira Hatch—words concerning the true name of the one you now call *Shin-op*. Yet his memory has gone away with his years, and he cannot recall all those words. He cannot recall the true name of the Holy One." Dahnish uánt took a deep breath. "It is this old fool's desire that you repeat for us the words of Ira Hatch."

For a time Thales Haskel studied the three Navajo warriors, and then slowly he made the sign of agreement. "The true name of the Holy One the Utes call *Shin-op*," he said quietly, "is spoken in our tongue, as *Jehovah*."

Abruptly the old Navajo blinked, and then a great smile crept over his face. "That is so," he breathed, his old voice so low it could hardly be heard. "It is good to have a memory return, my brother. But on its heels has come another memory—one that is much, much older. Many cycles of the seasons past, more cycles even than many old men together can remember, a man of brightness, a man of power so great it could not be known, came among the ancestors of the *Diné*. They stood in awe of this man, and feared to use, or even to think, the name for him that he gave them. Instead they asked his childhood name, thinking it would be less fearful. That name which he gave them, Haskel, is now back in the memory of this old fool, where his father so carefully placed it even before he was captured by the People of the Kiabab." Again the old man was beaming. "It is called in our tongue, *Yeh ho vah*."

34

Thursday, November 10, 1881

Trail of the Ancients

The young Navajo warrior who was called Bitseel did not know where he was going, at least not exactly. He knew he was riding northward, and that was after a full day of riding eastward past the big rocks of *Dinê tah,* the land of his people. Then he had turned north and crossed the big river at the place where it would one day be called Mexican Hat, after which he had climbed the terraced reaches of Cedar Mesa and continued northward along the Trail of the Ancient Ones, which skirted the yawning depths of Grand Gulch. Now it was well into the afternoon of his second day on the trail, and he was standing without movement on a rocky promontory, looking northward across a vast forest of juniper and pinion. In the distance but growing much closer were the two jutting knolls atop Elk Mountain that were known as the Bear's Ears, and as he gazed thoughtfully in their direction Bitseel began rubbing his *jish,* his sacred medicine bundle, that hung by a thong about his neck.

Two days before, in the time of darkness that was long before sunrise, he had seen those very formations in a *neishheel,* a dream. Bitseel did not think of himself as *bil âhât 'i,* a visionary. Yet this, he felt, had been more of a vision than a dream, for not only had he been shown those two hills up very close, which in actuality he had only seen from a great distance, but he had known exactly where to ride in order to reach them. Moreover, and thoughts of this caused him to finger his sacred bundle even more vigorously, in his dream he had also seen—or been shown by the sky people—a set of footprints in the earth near those two hills, one of which was notched exactly as had been the boot print of the evil *belacani* who had stolen both balance and life from his beloved younger sister.

Though coming at an awkward time—in only five days he was to be part of a great Sing after which he was to take a young maiden of the *Dinê* to wife—Bitseel knew that he had to follow the way of his dream, the way shown him by the powerful sky people. Taking nothing in the way of food or water, he had simply arisen and stolen quietly from the *hogan* of Tsabekiss, his father.

Soon astride his favorite horse, Bitseel had ridden eastward into the chill fall morning, following almost exactly the trail he and Hoskanini Begay had followed two years before when the *nóódâi* had slain the two *belacani* prospectors named Mitchell and Merrick. This time, though, he had traveled much faster, pausing only to water his mount at various springs, and occasionally to eat a root or other edible plant he had happened to chance upon in the course of his journey.

Thus, in less than two days, the young man Bitseel had traveled far and come to the rocky promontory on Cedar Mesa upon which he now stood.

Though it was afternoon rather than morning, he took a little pollen from his *jish* and sprinkled it into the cold breeze, sending with it a prayer to the sky people for continued guidance. Then, certain that he was on the course to those two hills that he had been shown, the young Navajo warrior slid back onto his horse, turned, and made his way down into the trees. Somewhere ahead, he knew, was the evil white man who had violated and slain his small sister. The sky people had shown him this great thing, and now it was up to him to find the man and do with him as the *Ye'i* might direct.

Kane Gulch

Gaunt and hollow-eyed, the outlaw Sugar Bob Hazelton was a frightened man. No, he was more than frightened; he was terrified!

Not alone was he slowly starving to death, having been unable to find anything to eat in several days, but in that same time he had not slept for even a moment. Oh, he was tired, all right, and feeling limp as a neck-wrung rooster. But try as he would, Sugar Bob couldn't bring himself to close his eyes. There were too many people out there, way too many! And every last one of 'em wanted him dead!

Staring out into the chilly silence of Kane Gulch, he once again did his best to figure out what was going on. Of a truth, though, he couldn't, for it made no sense. He didn't know the people who were trying to kill him, or at least he didn't think he did. And most of the time he couldn't even figure where they were. When he'd see one of them it would be only a glimpse, and no matter how fast he was with his rifle, by the time he fired, they would be gone! Worse, not once had any of them—and already he'd counted almost a dozen, men and women both—not once had any of them left behind a single track, or even the least indication of where they might have gone. It was infuriating to the crazed outlaw, and maybe even maddening.

The one thing he did know, he thought sullenly as he listened for some sound from behind him—the direction from which they always seemed to come—was when their sneak attacks had started. Eleven days before! That's when they had started showing up—right after that worthless Mormon fellow with the cold blue eyes had sneaked up behind him, stolen his knife and handgun, and tossed both of them into the consarned river!

Sugar Bob should have killed him on the spot—he knew that now. He should have killed him with his bare hands! But for some reason he hadn't quite been up to it. For some reason, even while he was thinking about doing it and flexing his hands to squeeze the life out of the scrawny fool's neck, his feet had been stumbling into the river and back across it. Then instead of pulling out his rifle and letting go with five or six well-placed rounds, his hands had been saddling his riding horse, and he had gone pounding up that narrow, hidden trail, leaving behind his pack animal, food, and all the other truck he'd managed to steal and otherwise accumulate during the previous couple of years.

That'd been bad enough. But that night, as he'd sat hunkered over a hatful of fire somewhere on the reservation pretty near freezing to death and only keeping warm on account of he was dreaming of the next woman he was going to find and use up, the first attack had come. Sugar Bob had heard a noise from behind, spun with his rifle ready, and caught a glimpse of a laughing woman in the same instant he had fired.

Instantly feeling bad that he'd killed the onliest female in five years what had come to him of her own free will, Sugar Bob levered another cartridge into his rifle's chamber and stepped out to see who she might have been. Only, there had been no one there—no body, nor even any tracks left in the soft sand.

Bewildered and upset, he had kicked around some in the semi-darkness, hollering and screaming and raising a pretty good ruckus, seeing if maybe he could spook her into breaking once more into the open. Failing, he had slowly returned to his fire and hunkered down again, but before too long he had heard something else. Again he had turned, rifle in hand because that fool Mormon had thrown away his only pistol, which would have been faster, glimpsed a man standing there laughing at him, and fired dead center into the idiot's heart. Only, somehow he had missed again, for once more there was no body in the sand, no trail of blood, or anything else that he might follow.

From that moment until this, as he had ridden hard from one likely looking hideout to another, Sugar Bob had been on guard, not sleeping but holding his rifle at the ready and going through round after round of ammunition as his laughing attackers had kept on coming. Again and again he would glimpse the same one or two people, sometimes three or four times in an hour all through a day or night, and again and again he would hole them dead center, the same as he had done plenty of times before. Only, no one of these newest folks had ever been killed or even wounded, which troubled him greatly. The only good thing, he thought with minimal satisfaction, was that he was so dad-gummed fast even with his rifle, that none of them had ever had time to shoot him.

Then the next day his attackers would change, somehow, and he would be shooting at a couple of different folks. Only he couldn't kill them any better than he had the others, and he couldn't make them stop their crazy laughing.

Lately—maybe in the last day or so—Sugar Bob had been getting the feeling that his attackers were not strangers. Though he couldn't see any of them for long enough to make certain, in his brief glimpses he was starting to think that maybe he had seen them somewhere before. He was also getting the feeling that their laughter was not just mockery, but actual happiness. But that made no sense either, for how could a person, especially one of the white women he had seen, be happy being all alone in the miserable darkness of a cold, Navajo Reservation night?

It was—

With a start Sugar Bob rolled to his feet, his rifle in his hands and already firing. Again nobody was there when the smoke had cleared, but this time his horse's head was up, ears forward and nostrils distended, and the outlaw knew something had changed.

Leaving the animal and darting up the wash in which he had camped, Sugar Bob scrambled up one rocky hill and then another, doing his best to find a clearing in the trees from where he could see who had moved into his exclusive but odoriferous neighborhood.

Below him and to the east rose the sharp little hill called Salvation Knoll, where on Christmas Day two winters before, George Sevy and three other Mormon explorers had finally got their bearings and found their way to Montezuma Creek, thus saving their own and nearly two hundred other lives. To the west and still below him, the country widened out into a brush-covered area called Grand Flat, where the Mormons had camped during their terrible trek eastward from the Hole-in-the-Rock a few months later.

Sugar Bob knew none of this, and wouldn't have cared if he had. As he scrambled up through the rocks and trees of the steep foothills, roughly following what he didn't even realize was an ancient pathway that would see use for another hundred and more years to trail cattle to the top of Elk Mountain, he was thinking only of a mighty cold camp that was now being invaded by some enemy who was looking to get himself killed. Or at least that was what Sugar Bob was muttering half aloud as he scrambled even higher toward the rimrock of Elk Mountain and the twin formations known as the Bear's Ears. What he was actually thinking, in his insane way, was anybody's guess!

Kane Gulch

Bitseel, off his horse, was kneeling in the sand while his hand feverishly fingered his *jish*. This was powerful medicine he was in the midst of, almost more powerful than a man dared consider. For there in the earth before him, just as he had seen in his dream, were two *belacani* boot prints, the one showing the same notched sole that had become so familiar in his mind when he had been seeking his lost little sister.

Standing, the Navajo youth looked carefully around. He noted the horse that was tethered where it could not get to the nearby water, the battered saddle and dirty blankets over against some rocks, even the smoldering fire where logs too large to catch flame were sending up thin tendrils of smoke. It was a white man's camp, all right, thoughtlessly laid out and offering hardly any protection from the chill wind that was whipping up out of the south.

There was also an odor that lingered about the camp, a terrible odor that occasionally assailed the nostrils of the young man. He didn't know what it might be, for he had never smelled anything like it, but he was relieved when the wind occasionally took it another direction, and he didn't have to suffer with it.

Moving carefully he left his horse standing freely, and with his fine rifle in hand he began sorting out the tracks left by the evil man with the notched boot. It was obvious that he had been alerted by something, probably Bitseel himself, and it was just as obvious that there were no weapons left in the camp. Therefore the man was hidden somewhere nearby, armed and ready to fire. Thoughtfully Bitseel examined the country, thinking what he himself might do. No doubt, he concluded almost instantly, the man had climbed up through the rocks and trees, and by now had positioned himself for a shot at Bitseel. The Navajo youth understood this clearly, and he also understood that he must not simply follow the tracks, for that would be what the man was expecting. Instead he must follow the evil one's thoughts, and they could only be known by the *Ye'i,* the sky people, who had brought him on this dangerous quest in the first place.

Again Bitseel drew a pinch of pollen from his *jish,* and with a murmured chant he sent it into the gusting wind. "Let beauty walk before me," he breathed quietly. "Let beauty walk behind me. Let beauty walk all around me." Then the young man grew silent, clearing his mind and allowing the sky people to once again establish his *hózhó,* his balance with all things.

The thought that came to Bitseel then, and this should have been no surprise, was of the Enemy Way ceremony almost two years before, that he had been a part of. In his mind he could see Hosteen Yazzi drawing the Corn Beetle and Big Fly with his colored sand, and he could see himself stretching out in the place of Corn Beetle while the Singer chanted the songs of Changing Woman and her twin warrior sons.

Bitseel had been the scalp shooter for that ceremony, a great honor for one so young, and he could still remember the words of the four First Songs and the Coyote Song, which he and the others had chanted to conclude the great sing. He was remembering, even as his eyes and mind probed up the steep, juniper-covered foothills while trying to think like the evil man with the notched boot, the words of the powerful Coyote Song. Murmuring them quietly he stepped out, climbed for a moment or two, and then moved quickly to the side, away from where the tracks showed plainly in the sand.

In almost that same instant there was a vicious *whap* in the air near his head, followed by the sharp *crack* of a rifle, and Bitseel knew that the sky people were indeed guiding him. The thoughts of the white killer had warned him to move, he had done so, and thus he had not been shot. Now he had only to follow those same thoughts a little longer, he knew, and he would be led to the man who had done such terrible things to his younger sister.

Kane Gulch

Cursing viciously Sugar Bob Hazelton levered another round into the chamber of his rifle. Then he rose to his feet and glowered down the slope. Once again the disfigured outlaw had missed a shot that even a child should have made, and once again the man he'd been shooting at, had vanished. This time, though, he'd had more than a glimpse. And also this time, if he hadn't known better, he'd have sworn that the fool he had fired on, had actually ducked!

And that was another thing, he thought as he turned and scrambled upward, looking for an even better vantage point. This for sure and for certain wasn't Navajo country, and in fact was far from it. But that feller down there in his abandoned camp, in the few seconds Sugar Bob had had time to examine him before he had fired, had looked to be Navajo!

"Durn fool Injuns," he muttered as he moved up toward a rocky outcrop that was maybe three hundred feet above his last position, "now I got them sneaking up on me, along with everbody else! Worse, ever' last Injun alive is slicker'n a bunkhouse rat when it comes to sneaking up on folks!"

Pausing in the lee of a juniper to catch his breath, the outlaw then moved more carefully, stepping from rock to rock as he sidled upward to come at length to the outcropping. It was a dandy ambush, too, with good cover and a fine, late afternoon view of everything below. Squatting quickly he thrust his rifle into position, and then he settled in to wait, a silent laugh creasing his disfigured face.

"Come on ahead, you miserable heathen!" he grunted a few moments later as his patience started wearing thin. "Just on account of I don't normally leave enough tracks to trip an ant, don't give you no leave to lose my trail. All you have to do is climb this hill, you fool redskin, and afore you know it you'll be saddling a cloud and heading for the happy hunting grounds."

Carefully the insane Sugar Bob Hazelton scanned the pinion- and juniper-studded slopes below, looking for any type of movement, any motion at all. That he had missed with his first shot was disconcerting enough, but now, for some reason not being able to see the confounded red fool—

Kane Gulch

Still fingering his *jish,* the sacred medicine bundle that helped give him access to the sky people, Bitseel climbed steadily upward. Though his rifle was in his hand he did not carry it at the ready, neither did he make any attempt to hide the way of his going. Instead, he simply climbed, choosing of course the easiest route as he made his way upward.

In his mind continued the words of the Coyote Song, the chant that was part of the Enemy Way ceremony, and Bitseel found himself wondering, as he climbed, if in some way he and the wily old Trickster hadn't somehow come together. But mostly he didn't think at all, except in the way of remembering the words that wouldn't seem to go away.

He was also conscious that at any moment he might hear the wicked *whap* of another bullet passing by. He didn't know that he was dealing with the wrath of an insane man who was neither seeing nor hearing reality. He did know, however, that he had been shot at once, and that a second effort would most certainly be made. Yet for some reason he felt no worry, and when no further shots rang out, his heart knew peace. Truly were the sky people showing forth their power!

Continuing steadily upward, Bitseel climbed around and past a rocky escarpment, turned, and was not at all surprised to see the evil *belacani* with the notched boot crouching there only a few feet away, looking away, surveying the country below.

In wonder Bitseel stopped and stared, his mind questioning how he had managed to climb past the white man, passing almost directly under him, without being seen. Truly there was power in those who were assisting him! Truly had there been power in the words of his father, old Tsabekiss, who had counseled him to cease thirsting after the blood of this man, but instead to seek his own true balance with the universe. Then, he had been told, the all-powerful sky people would do with the evil one as they wished—

Kane Gulch

Sugar Bob did not know what made him turn. Maybe it was a noise, though no sound had registered in his ears. And maybe it was simply a feeling, a sense of danger. But turn he did, and was dumbfounded to see the Indian not twenty feet away, a little above and behind him, simply standing and watching him, his rifle resting in his arms.

For the length of a heartbeat the outlaw was too shocked to react. Somehow his mind could not grasp the fact that this Indian—this *young* Indian—had climbed the hill directly under his deformed nose and gotten behind him. Or even that he was now standing there in full view, not ducking and vanishing, but watching. It wasn't possible! It simply wasn't, and Sugar Bob knew it. Still, his brain was screaming at him, it had happened, and now he had to react! He had to do something—

With a speed that had become legendary, the outlaw swung his arm, leveled his rifle, and fired, the swing and the firing one smooth movement that took hardly more than a second from start to finish. "There!" he sneered as a second bullet followed instantly after the first, "that'll learn you, you sorry excuse—"

But then the suffering outlaw grew still, his eyes wide and staring. For where he had fired—where the youthful Navajo warrior had been standing only seconds before—once again there was nothing! No body, no blood, NOTHING! Somehow, in less time than even the famous Sugar Bob Hazelton could shoot, the Indian had vanished! He was there and then he was not, and nobody could do that unless . . . unless—

With a whine of fear the outlaw lunged to his feet, his rifle ready as he stared wildly about. But there was no one near that rocky outcropping but himself, no one at all! In terror then he tore off his coat and vest to lighten his load, kicked off his boots to better hide his tracks, and then he started running. Frantically he scrambled upward and across the steep slope, fleeing the outcropping in his stockinged feet and striving with every ounce of strength and knowledge to reach the beetling rimrock of Elk Ridge, a thousand feet above, without leaving any tracks the Navajo could follow.

If he could just get to that distant, overhanging rim, he reasoned as he ignored the battering his feet were taking, and get hunkered down in those rocks where he could see everything below—

Kane Gulch

His sense of awe increasing, the youth Bitseel dropped the hastily discarded boot with the telltale notch in the sole, turned, and once again began climbing steadily after the frantic outlaw. He did not hurry, nor did he hide. He merely climbed, almost literally stepping in the dim but obvious tracks of the one he had so longed to kill. Yet now such thoughts had no place in him—not in his heart, not in his mind. Instead he had become more of a watcher, a spectator, wondering even as he was following the man, what the great and powerful sky people intended doing with the *belacani,* or assisting the man to do with himself.

To Bitseel, taught thoroughly by his father and his numerous uncles in the ways of the *Dinê,* one thing was a certainty. Because of this man's great evil he had lost his own *hózhó,* his balance with all other things. Thus he would most certainly destroy himself, for that was the only direction he could go. The single question that remained in the mind of the youth, therefore, was how it would happen.

Elk Ridge

Sweat pouring from his body despite the chill wind, the insanely frantic Sugar Bob Hazelton at last reached the out-thrusting rimrock of Elk Ridge, from which he intended killing that fool Navajo. Clawing his way upward on the forty-foot cliff, on what was most certainly an ancient trail he had stumbled upon—a stroke of luck if ever he had seen one—Sugar Bob emerged at last onto the top, where he stood for a second to catch his breath.

His torn and shredded feet hurt, but he ignored them, and

because he was wet with sweat and wore no coat, the cold wind quickly chilled him through. But this he also ignored, choosing instead to look for the best place to set up his ambush.

Below him the country stretched off to the south and west, covered either with the rolling juniper and pinion forest through which the Hole-in-the-Rock pioneers had chopped their way nearly two years before, or dropping dramatically into the yawning depths of Grand Gulch. And way beyond, obscured almost totally in the haze of distance, lay the San Juan River gorge and, even farther away to the south, the giant buttes of Monument Valley.

Behind him at no great distance rose the twin knolls called the Bear's Ears, and northwest of them, his old camp at Twin Springs. But these things Sugar Bob did not see, did not even consider. Neither, in fact, did he see the rest of the vast and awe-inspiring panorama. Instead, his wildly shifting eyes were probing the steep hillsides that dropped away from forty or so feet below him, for there, he knew, his enemy would soon be climbing.

Casting about, the outlaw selected one vantage point and then, almost immediately, another that looked even better. Dropping to his stomach he wormed forward through a labyrinth of small boulders and brush, his fine Winchester held out ahead of him, until he was at the very edge of the rim but not skylined above it.

Though the wind there was fierce and cold, blowing up through the rocks and making enough noise to obscure most any sound below, Sugar Bob put it all from his mind. He could endure the cold, and his hearing, while good, was nothing compared to his sharp vision. That had never in his mortal life—at least not until eleven days before, he recalled with a shudder—let him down. Feeling satisfied that such a thing could not possibly continue, the supremely confident outlaw began once again his murderous vigil, his wary eyes watching and probing, his finger pressed expectantly against the trigger of his stolen rifle—

Elk Ridge

As before, Bitseel climbed steadily, following the white man's tracks until he was led to the ancient trail. Recognizing it for what it was, the youth thanked for their wisdom those old ones who had gone before. Then he climbed carefully but without hesitation upward through the rimrock, reaching without difficulty the spot where the trail emerged on top. There, as before, he paused to look around, and he was not at all surprised to see the white man only a few yards away, lying prone and carefully scanning the country below.

For a moment Bitseel fingered the trigger of his own rifle, wondering if that was the way the sky people wished things to be. It would be such an easy shot, he knew, for the man had his back to him, and had no idea that Bitseel had once again climbed to a place that was behind him.

But no, he thought with sudden clarity, a bullet in the back of the evil *belacani* wasn't the way. Neither, he was just as certain, was a bullet in the man's front. Instead, he now knew, those great beings who lived above and had such incredible power, had another idea, a much better one, though the youth had no idea what it might be.

Perhaps—

Then Bitseel noticed a dark round boulder, about the size of a man's head or a little larger, that lay a few feet to the rear of the tensed and waiting *belacani* and to his side a little, closer to his feet. It was a strange little boulder, and seemed somehow blurred or indistinct, as if it were shifting or moving—

Elk Ridge

Again Sugar Bob Hazelton did not know what made him turn. But when he did, and saw the Navajo youth standing behind him as before, simply watching him, his insane mind snapped. Instead of turning to fire his rifle, the stunned outlaw simply scrambled to his tattered, bloody feet, and stared.

This was unbelievable! It couldn't be happening! There was no way on this green earth that this crazy Indian could have followed him—that or gotten behind him again, either one! Why, so far as he knew, only he, the great Sugar Bob Hazelton, was skilled enough to pull such a stunt. For a fact, his insane mind reminded him, he alone could follow a wood tick acrost solid rock! Or even, by jings, could hunt down a whisper in a big wind. He had never in his life met anyone who was as good as himself, and it just wasn't reasonable that this fool Navajo kid who still looked green enough, now that he could be seen up close, to need to free up both hands before he could even pucker and spit—

Suddenly Sugar Bob's mind seemed to freeze. This dad-burned Navajo, just like all those laughing idiots who had been sneaking up on him the past eleven days, looked familiar—mighty familiar! Somehow he put Sugar Bob in mind of that handsome little Navajo squaw what he had used for a few days and then taken his knife to afore she had escaped—

Sugar Bob blinked to make certain, and abruptly it wasn't a rifle-carrying warrior he was facing at all, or even that sorry little squaw with blood all over her face and arms and naked chest. Instead it was sweet little Laurie Yvonne Lacy, her belly swollen with his child, standing with hands outstretched as she pleaded with him to do the manly thing and marry her.

About to reply, Sugar Bob rubbed at his forehead—and was dumbfounded to see two prostitutes he had used down in Fort Worth—used and then killed because they had wanted him to pay. Then they were gone, and he was staring instead at the unarmed fool on the street of Fort Stockton he had killed, and then that fat Mexican barkeep the other side of the Rio Grande who wanted two silver dollars for his awful booze but got instead a couple of lead pills from Sugar Bob's pistol.

Now rubbing viciously at his eyes, Sugar Bob found himself staring at Old Man Lacy, who was standing where Laurie Yvonne had been only a moment or so before, his eyes still flashing anger over what Sugar Bob had done to his only daughter. Opening his mouth to try and explain why he had abandoned her, Sugar Bob found himself talking not to I. W. Lacy but to his old pardner, Dingle Beston. And then Dingle changed, somehow, and the man standing before him was Johnny Molander, who had thought with his map that he was going to be rich, and had instead ended up dead.

Sugar Bob was still cringing from the unspoken accusations in the eyes of all he had seen, when again it was the little Navajo squaw who was standing before him, the one he had taken from her sheep and done such vile things to. Now she was here with him again, her eyes filled with a great and terrible sorrow—

These were the people! These were the ones who had been sneaking up on him the past eleven days, laughing at him and making a mockery of his efforts to kill them. But none of them were laughing anymore, he saw as his eyes widened with fear. They had stopped laughing, and he couldn't kill them because every last one of them was . . . was already dead!

With a moan of fear Sugar Bob stepped back, and in the stepping his bootless foot landed on, and then sank into, the dark, slowly moving boulder that Bitseel had noticed only a moment or so before.

For an instant nothing happened. But then, as the outlaw looked down and saw his bare foot and lower leg covered with a writhing mass of rattlesnakes—suddenly angry reptiles that had balled up against the cold, and were even then trying to extricate themselves and seek out permanent dens in the beetling rocks, absolute horror replaced the fear that had stricken the face of Sugar Bob Hazelton. The mass of rattlers, with bared, venom-dripping fangs, were already attacking the bloody object that had intruded into the midst of their twisting bodies, and in another instant the pain of their bites reached his insane mind.

Now Sugar Bob screamed, emptying his lungs even as he began kicking violently and firing downward, trying desperately to dislodge the dozens of biting snakes. Forgotten was the bloody little Navajo girl and his host of other victims. Forgotten, too, was the Navajo youth who looked so much like the girl and who had somehow tracked him down. All the disfigured outlaw could think of, as he tried to jerk and hop back from the attacking reptiles, was that despite his skills and his careful planning—despite his superior intelligence and cunning, he was being killed!

Somehow, his mind screamed in frustration, things had continued going against him, so that no matter how hard he had worked, no matter how smart he was or how fast he could yank out a handgun or flip up a rifle, he was being planted shallow without a reading!

He was being killed!

Somehow Old Man Lacy and his sweet little daughter, or maybe it was Dingle Beston or those two Texas whores or that fat barkeep or maybe Johnny Molander or maybe even that comfortable little Navajo squaw from down on the reservation, had come together with these horrid snakes to do him in—

Elk Ridge

The youth Bitseel stood still. The screams of horror that had come from the evil *belacani* even after he had backed off the rimrock to vanish in a forty-foot drop, his foot still swathed in rattlesnakes, had ceased. Now there was only silence on the mountain—the silence of the wind moaning over the rocks and moving on toward the Bear's Ears behind him. Even the few rattlesnakes left behind, Bitseel observed, had discovered holes and were disappearing, and the young Navajo found himself, of a sudden, feeling very much alone.

Still—

With humility he pulled another pinch of pollen from his *jish* and tossed it into the air. "Let beauty walk before me," he breathed quietly as he looked upward. "Let beauty walk behind me. Let beauty walk all around me." Finally, his voice filled with reverence, he concluded: "In beauty, it is finished."

Then without a backward look, or even a glance over the rim at the battered body of the outlaw *belacani* who had so devastated his family, Bitseel turned and started back down the ancient trail. His goal was the distant *Dinê tah* and the *hogan* of his wise and kindly father. There the born-to and born-for clans of his parents would soon be gathering for the Sing and also his wedding, there the lovely maiden of his dreams would be waiting, and Bitseel could hardly wait to get there.

35

Friday, November 11, 1881

Bulldog Canyon

"Why'n double-deuce are you always reading something?"

It was nearly ten o'clock of a Friday morning, and Bill Ball had told Curly and Billy to take a wagon load of supplies to the new line camp in Verdure. Seeing no way out of it, Curly had agreed, though he had by no means given up his opinion of the little Mormon who was seated beside him on the jostling wagon, poring over an old newspaper. He'd been reading it for at least an hour, Curly knew, and before that he'd had his nose buried in a dumb book. Which was fine, Curly supposed, if a man was alone and off in the wilderness somewhere, with nothing better to do. But if he was supposed to be partnering with somebody else and working together, or if there was a job needing doing, no matter, then a man hadn't ought to go sticking his nose into no books or newspapers.

"It's a fine way to pick up a little learning," Billy finally answered, interrupting Curly's sour thoughts.

"In that old newspaper?" Curly snorted. "Why, it's yellow and tore and it ain't even all there. How could a man get any learning out of that? Besides, I ain't never seen much use in newspapers, least ways beyond using 'em to line an outhouse or start up a good, warm fire."

"Can you read?"

"I can read my name, and that's good enough!"

Billy smiled. "Whatever we have, usually is good enough—until we find out there's something better. Then most folks won't rest until they have it. That's called human nature."

Curly looked crossways at the little man, trying to figure out what he'd just said. "Mister," he finally growled, "I hope you ain't implicating that I don't know what I'm missing."

"I wouldn't think of it, Curly." Billy had to fight to keep a straight face. "But I am telling you that there's information in this old newspaper you would most likely find interesting."

"Such as?" Curly questioned doubtfully.

"Well, for instance, I was just reading about the gunfighter, Billy the Kid."

"No fooling? There's something about old William Bonney in there?"

"A little. This reporter says he escaped from jail this past May, while under heavy guard, and then was shot dead in Fort Sumner, New Mexico Territory, in July."

Curly was thunderstruck. "Billy's dead? Well, if that ain't enough to turn the berry bushes blue. I never thought *anybody* was fast enough to take out Billy the Kid. Bet whoever done it, had to shoot him in the back."

Billy looked at his lanky partner. "You speak as if you knew him."

"Well, going on three years back, I met up with 'im onct or twice. He put it out that his real name was William H. Bonney, that he hailed from New York, and that he'd killed a man for every year of his life. I reckon some of that was true."

"Yes, the paper reports that he was twenty-one, and had killed twenty-one men."

Curly nodded. "Yeah, he was a bloodthirsty little pup, all right. Too bad somebody didn't put out his lights a lot sooner. I don't like killers and I don't like liars, and the Kid was both. One of them nights I was telling you about? He'd been drinking, and I reckon it sort of loosened his flap-box. Purty soon he was spouting off about one thing or another, mostly making fun of the poor souls he'd shot, when he upped and said his real name wasn't William Bonney after all, but Henry McCarty. The next morning he threatened to shoot anybody who ever told it, but I figured, who wanted to know anyhow? And I never said nothing. But no sir, I didn't like him much at all. What else does it read in that fool paper?"

"Well," Billy continued, hoping this was the breakthrough he had been hoping for, "according to this same reporter, there's another shoot-out brewing in Tombstone, down in Arizona. You've heard of the Earp brothers—Wyatt, Virgil, and Morgan. Well, them and a gambler named Doc Holliday are pitted against a bunch of owlhoots including the Clantons and McLowrys and a Billy Clairborne and others. There's already been bloodshed, and this reporter thinks more is coming, maybe a lot more."[1]

"I saw Wyatt Earp onct, when I was trailing cows up from Texas. He was sittin' at a bar with an ugly cuss of a woman folks called Calamity Jane, and she was outdrinking him two shots of red-eye to one. She was a calamity, all right."

Billy chuckled. "Well, you do seem to have been around. Bill Ball says you're a real hand with guns, too. Maybe you're one of these famous gunfighters."

Curly shook his head. "Not hardly. I don't hold with gunfightin'; don't hold with killin' folks, neither. But we do live in a bloodthirsty country hereabouts, and a man can't be too careful."

"It's bloody back East, too," Billy stated soberly. "There are articles in here regarding President Garfield's assassination this past July, and the murder of Russia's czar back in March. Add to that a bunch of anything but square dealers named Texas Charley Bigelow, Nevada Ned Oliver, and promoter John Healy, all from back East, who have formed the Kickapoo Indian Medicine Company and hired three hundred Indians—none of them Kickapoo, it says here—to sell their oil, salves, cough cure, pain pills, wart killer, and the like. According to the paper, most of that stuff is made from alcohol, sugar, milk, and cocaine, and won't do a body a lick of good."

"Some folks'll do anything for a buck," Curly acknowledged.

"Then our whole country's been in a drought so bad the cattle ranges in Texas, New Mexico, and Arizona have dried out, New

1. Actually, the famous shootout at the O.K. Corral, on the outskirts of Tombstone, had already occurred, on October 26, 1881.

York City ran plumb out of water, and folks in Pittsburgh, Chicago, and a dozen other eastern cities have been dropping like flies all this past summer from heat exhaustion. To my way of thinking, it all adds up to the troubles and sorrows of the Last Days."

Instantly Curly was angry. "Listen, you! I don't hold with no Bible-thumpers! Especially Mormon ones!"

Billy sighed with discouragement over his foolish mistake. "You don't have to agree with me, Curly. However, all a man needs to do is look around, and he'll soon see what is happening."

"All I need to see," Curly snarled, feeling certain that Billy was now trying to convert him, "is that with cows getting killed off in Texas and Arizona the way droughts do, the price for good beef had ought to come up pretty good right here on the LC. I reckon that's news that Bill Ball ought to have."

And with a vicious snap of his lines, Curly uttered a wild, Comanche yell and urged the four-horse team to greater effort.

West of Salvation Knoll

"Well, friend Hobbs," Walter Joshua Stevens breathed into the cold morning as he scanned the steep slope ahead of him, "that's where they've gone, sure enough."

In response his high-stepping bay gelding bobbed his head once, and then again, letting his rider know that he agreed.

"Thing is, boy, that's the steepest dad-gummed slope in miles, the rise must be two thousand feet, and that rimrock way up there at the top is sheer cliff! Why would a bunch of no-good cows decide to hightail it straight up a mountain like that, especially when they could have stayed here on the level and run for a hundred miles?"

Shaking his head when the gelding did not respond, Joshua nudged the animal into motion, threaded his way through the cabin-sized detritus that littered the bottom of the slope, and to his surprise found himself at the base of an old trail that angled upward. From more than twenty-five or thirty feet away it could not be seen. Yet somehow his forty head of cattle had found it and disappeared upward, leaving the tired young man with no choice but to follow.

He had a right to feel tired, too, as did his gelding. Scheduled to leave for Colorado and a winter's work on the railroad, word had come that the camp at the railhead would pay top dollar for up to fifty head of good beef. Joshua had immediately offered his own small herd, and had set out immediately for the Grand Gulch Plateau, where he had left them to get along on their own through the winter.

And they'd got along, all right, he thought grimly as he dismounted and began leading the gelding up the hidden trail. Two weeks of freedom and already they figured themselves to be wild cows. One sight of him and Hobbs, and they'd thrown their tails in the air and skedaddled, and all he'd seen since had been tracks and scattered splotches of steaming dung.

Pausing for a breather, Joshua Stevens looked upward. The trail he'd stumbled onto was amazing, following the contour of the steep hillside as it climbed, working its way around rocky outcroppings, but not for a moment appearing eroded or rain-washed the way a poorly made trail might appear. Yet it was an old trail, very old, and one not created by animals. How Joshua knew that he wasn't certain, except that it had the feel of a man-trail, not nearly so steep or abrupt as deer or mountain sheep might make it.

What excited the young man, though, was the possibility that the trail would lead to the top of Elk Mountain. Though Platte Lyman and some of the other brethren had explored the mountain a few weeks before and pronounced it covered with what looked to be the most wonderful summer graze in the world, they had been able to find only one way up, and that was through those tortuous canyons to the east where the Pahutes seemed to be in control. But this route, which according to the tracks of his own cattle would make a fine stock-trail, was more direct and easy to access. Best of all, he had seen absolutely no sign of Pahutes, not anywhere!

Upward the man and horse continued, the cattle-tracks leading the way, climbing until he came to a bend in the trail where he looked down in surprise. Almost at his feet, not more than half a dozen feet from the trail, lay a pair of finely tooled boots. They were worn but by no means worn out, and they were laying sprawled as if hastily discarded.

Now being more careful, Joshua Stevens looked around. But he was alone, of that he was quickly certain. The owner of those boots was gone, as if—

At that moment the young Mormon saw the track—a man wearing a holey sock with two toes hanging out, had pushed the front of his foot into a spot of soft earth as he had climbed. From that Joshua knew the man had been in a hurry, had been down on his luck, and, yes, he was not being careful about where he stepped. A dozen feet up the slope lay a broken prickly pear cactus leaf, and after that Joshua began to find little spots of dried blood—dark brown stains, which soon increased in size until it was obvious the man's feet were being torn to doll rags even as he fled upward.

Fled? But who might he have been fleeing from? And above all, who was "he"?

Fifty or sixty feet higher Joshua found a moccasin track—Navajo, he thought—and then it all sort of began to make sense. A white man, likely a cowboy, was being stalked by a Navajo warrior—

Thing was, the warrior wasn't stalking. The tracks, where they had not been obliterated by his own cattle, showed that the Navajo had been simply climbing, not ducking or crouching or doing anything but climbing the old trail. Meanwhile the deepness of the white man's tracks, as well as their erratic spacing and the stains of dried blood, showed clearly his heedless flight.

As Joshua and his gelding finally approached the steep rimrock or cliff that marked the top of what was called Elk Mountain, the youthful Mormon slowed and began going more cautiously. After all, he didn't know who might be above him on top of those cliffs, or what, and he had absolutely no desire to turn his lovely Elizabeth into a grieving widow. Far better to take his time—

There! Something was over there in the rocks, something lying still as death—

Still leading the gelding, Joshua moved off the trail and toward the low pile of detritus. What he could see clearly, he thought, looked like a hand and an arm, or at least it had that look. Yes, he thought as he inched closer, there was no doubt about it. This was the body of a man, a white man, sprawled in death at the foot of the forty-foot rimrock.

And then, abruptly, Walter Joshua Stevens stopped cold, his eyes wide with the horror of what he was seeing in the cold morning air.

Long Canyon

"Of all the dad-gummed miserable, rotten luck!" Curly and Billy were crowded under the wagon, examining where Curly had just burst out the front end of the reach by running one of the front wheels into a rock he had not bothered to avoid. They were halfway up the dugout going out of Long Canyon, and Billy could not imagine a worse place to have a breakdown.

More, storm clouds were building off to the south and west, the temperature was dropping rapidly, and Billy felt certain the warm weather they'd been enjoying the past few days was about to change.

"Well," the lanky cowpoke continued, "there ain't nothing for it but to pack what we can on two of the horses and cache the rest until we can get back for it. Then we can ride on to Verdure Creek."

"Why don't we just fix the wagon?"

"Fix the wagon!" Curly guffawed scornfully. "Fix it with what, you flannel-brained Mormon idjit? You think you're gonna carve a new reach out of one of these hyer cedars?"

Patiently Billy shook his head. "I was thinking more along the lines of boring a new hole for the kingbolt in the old reach," he said as he pulled out his pocket knife. "I'll do the boring if you'll get a fire started somewhere close by."

"A fire? If'n you're that cold already, then I reckon you've got a long winter ahead of you."

With effort Billy curbed his tongue, holding in what he felt like saying. "It isn't for me," he said as he reached up and began twisting his blade back and forth. "You'll need to heat that kingbolt there until it's red hot. Then we can use it to burn the hole through the reach and do it to the correct dimensions."

"That there's one of the stupidest, flea-brainedest ideas I ever heard! That reach is four inches thick and made of hardwood, and it'll take you until a week from tomorry to even dent it."

"Just heat the bolt," Billy responded patiently as he lay on his back in the rocks, boring upward into the burst-out reach. Trouble was, he was thinking as Curly grumbled something and began unhooking the teams from the now-dragging tongue, the man might just be right. The wood was very hard, and the longest blade on his knife was just past three inches. Neither could he get at the reach from the top, not without taking apart most of the wagon. That meant he'd have to burn through the last inch of the reach, and Billy wasn't at all certain it could be done.

Still . . .

It took almost three hours for Billy to bore out what he could of a new hole. Meanwhile the storm had continued to develop, and Curly, who had grumbled and moaned the whole and entire time, had unloaded the wagon so it could more easily be maneuvered. He had also heated the kingbolt until it was glowing red, and with the aid of tongs found in the toolbox he now handed the bolt to Billy.

"Temperature's droppin' faster nor a gut-shot elk!" he mumbled as he looked at the threatening sky while rubbing his arms against the cold. "I still think we should of packed what we could and skedaddled on out of here."

"You may be right," Billy mumbled as he twisted the hot bolt back and forth in his new hole. There was no difficulty in burning out the part he had bored with the knife, he discovered, but before it could burn on through the rest of the reach, the bolt had cooled too much, and Billy finally pulled it from the hole.

"We're going to need to heat it again," he said quietly.

"What in thunderation for?"

"Because it cooled before it burned all the way through. However, Curly, we're nearly there. Another hour, maybe two, and we should be loaded and on our way."

"Yeah, and wet enough to bog a snipe! This storm's building fast!"

Billy chuckled grimly. "We'd have been wet anyway, Curly. That was determined when you smacked the wheel into that boulder."

"Are you telling me this was my fault, you sniveling little—"

"Curly," Billy interrupted, his exasperation finally showing, "my name's Billy, or sometimes William. You want to call me something, call me one of them. Now, are we going to get that bolt heated again or continue wasting time?"

An hour later, as they were being pelted with hail and rain combined, the two miserable men worked the reach back into place, slid the kingbolt through, and checked to see that the tongue hounds would not break when the animals again began to pull. Everything appearing satisfactory, they hurriedly reloaded the wagon, fastened the teams' double trees back in place, and once again Curly gave his fierce rendition of a wild Comanche yell.

At least, Billy thought as he clung to the side of the jolting wagon and shivered beneath the slicker he was finally wearing, his new partner would have to admit that the sissified little Mormon had accomplished something beneficial.

Dodge Springs

In amazement Billy examined the vast panorama of country into which he and Curly were rolling. It was now late in the day, but at least the storm had let up, and the sun was brightening the western sky. Of course that did nothing to raise the temperature any, but it did serve to give a little hope, and that was something Billy desperately needed.

A few miles ahead of them Verdure Creek flowed east toward the deep Montezuma Canyon, which gathered the waters of the Blue Mountain watershed and carried them down to the San Juan. The joining of the small and greater watercourses formed a pie-shaped triangle of higher ground to the southwest, composed of hundreds and hundreds of acres of rich, arable land. Pines, pinions, and cedars grew heavy along the rims of the canyons, but thinned out on the top to sage and grassland. To Billy it looked like one of the best farming and ranching areas he had ever seen, and he felt pleased that Bill Ball and the owners of the LC controlled the operation of it.

"Curly, what's this country called?"

"Spud Hudson called it Dodge Point, or Dodge Springs."

"Spud Hudson's another rancher in this country?"

"He was."

Amazed that his partner was still acting surly in spite of all that had happened, Billy shook his head. What in the world would it take, he was wondering, to win the man's friendship? Of course maybe he never would, but would end up spending the winter in company with a man who not only disdained him, but openly disliked him. That was not something to look forward to, and Billy found himself almost wishing he had gone with the rest of the Bluff brethren to Colorado. The fly in that ointment, though, was that the Lord had most certainly revealed that this was the job he wanted Billy to take. Of course there could be a hundred different reasons why that might be, but somehow Billy couldn't make himself believe that one of them would be so that he would suffer through an interminable winter with this surly character.

"Reckon this is as good a place as any to rest the horses," Curly suddenly declared as they came around some oak and onto some springs. "After that, we'll push on to the line cabin."

"This is Dodge Springs?"

"I reckon so," Curly growled as he jumped down, and that was all he intended to say.

As Billy also jumped from the wagon to help, Curly hurriedly unhitched the two teams of steaming horses from the wagon tongue. Then he took from him the lines Billy had just picked up and led both teams to the springs, where they were allowed to slake their thirst. Afterward Curly put them to graze on the thick grass, after which he hunkered down against one of the wagon wheels, pulled his sombrero down over his eyes, and relaxed.

"What sort of grass is this?" Billy asked as he examined the forage, not really interested in the grass but simply trying to figure out how to communicate with this cantankerous man.

"Spud called it bluestem. I reckon that's good enough."

"For the likes of a sissified Mormon like me, you mean?" Billy chuckled without much mirth, for he was getting tired of the man's surly attitude and had finally determined to say something about it. "I declare, Curly. I don't know who filled your head so full of nonsense about us Mormons, but that's exactly what it is. Utter and complete nonsense! There's not a one of us that isn't a plain, ordinary human being, just like everyone else on this green earth, with gifts and talents and weaknesses a'plenty. And so you'll stop worrying yourself to death over it, I'll tell you something else. I not only believe what I believe, but I'm convinced you have just as much right as me, to do the same. In other words, I'll not be trying to convert you to Mormonism, Curly Bill Jenkins, and that's a promise!"

"Humph!" Curly responded and then offered nothing more.

"Something else you'd better hear," Billy declared after he had dragged up a dead cedar and started a fire under it, intending at least to get himself a little warmer. "I told Bill Ball when he hired me that I didn't know a blessed thing about cowboying or ranching, either one, and I told him the truth. I do know some few things about livestock, though, because in my former line of work I had to learn it. Bill Ball seemed to think that was sufficient, and he hired me."

"Well, it ain't nowhere near gonna be enough," Curly growled from beneath his hat, "and that's a promise I'll make to you! This work takes a man with real fur on his brisket—"

"Rather than a small, sissified Mormon like myself," Billy once again finished for the man, sarcasm now dripping from his voice. "Well, Curly, we'll just have to see. But I'll tell you this; don't you ever look behind you expecting to be alone, for it won't happen. No matter where you go or what you do, I'll be somewhere behind you watching and learning, meanwhile doing my best to hold up my end of the load."

"And if you can't?" Curly snarled bitterly.

Billy smiled as he held his hands out to the growing flames, but not with joy or out of humor. "If it turns out I can't, then I'll leave of my own accord. But I won't be driven off by you or anybody else, Curly Bill Jenkins, rawhiding or no. And that's a fact you can take all the way to the bank!"

And with that, Billy turned away to more fully enjoy the fire.

36

Saturday, November 12, 1881

Bluff Fort

Early morning, Eliza was thinking as she stripped the cream from old Bess's udder, was her favorite time of day. Not only was it usually quiet, allowing her to think and even pray without interruption, but her mind seemed clearer, and she was better able to focus. Of course, she thought with a wry grin, the Lord had promised those very things in a revelation to the Prophet Joseph, so it made sense that she would discover them to be true.

Just like all the other revelations the prophets had received through the ages, one after another, folks from one age to the next had discovered them to also be true. Well, not all folks, Eliza thought then. But certainly those who wanted to know. It was just as the Lord had promised in the Book of Mormon—people received according to their desires. Good or evil, mental darkness or further light and knowledge from the Lord—even how much further light and knowledge—all was determined, and granted, according to an individual's true desires.

All was inexorably linked to the doctrine of agency—and of the final judgment. Based upon his or her desires, each individual freely chose and subsequently reaped the rewards for or suffered the consequences of their choices. And those choices, compiled one day and made readily accessible to a person's memory, would determine the reward that individual would receive in the final judgment.

These were sobering thoughts, which Eliza had been pondering a great deal of late. Especially this was so since the death of her sweet little Mary Eliza. Oh, how that precious little infant was missed! How Eliza's heart ached each time she was thought of, each time she was mentioned by herself or another. It was as if the pain and loneliness of her baby's death would never go away, would never diminish. After all, it had now been more than two months, and Eliza's tears still flowed freely—especially at night when the wind was blowing and Billy was not there to take her in his arms and comfort her.

Glory! Eliza thought as she stopped milking, wiped at her eyes and then took a deep breath, endeavoring to regain at least a semblance of control, would life never get any easier? Would her arms and heart never stop longing for that sweet little daughter? Would her long winter nights never stop being so lonely, so empty?

Already it seemed as if Billy had been gone forever! Yet not even two weeks had passed since he had ridden off, and there were still at least four months to go! Four interminable months when she would spend her nights comforting a lonely little boy while weeping her own tears of loneliness, longing, and grief.

And yet, Eliza thought as she took another deep breath, the Lord had promised comfort to those who mourned. Yes, and he had also promised that death would lose its sting. Were those promises to be fulfilled only in eternity? For Eliza was certain they would be fulfilled then. But what about now? her heart seemed always to be crying out. Couldn't she receive at least a little comfort now? A little peace?

Before his departure for the LC, Billy had promised her those very things in a wonderful blessing. So she knew they would come. But when? Would she be forced to live the rest of mortality in agony? In loneliness? In sorrow? Or would the Lord somehow stretch forth his hand?

"Please, dear Father," she breathed as she pressed her cold forehead into Bess's warm flank and closed her eyes, "please take away from my heart this terrible loneliness."

Cottonwood Canyon

Exhausted and discouraged, Posey urged his latest mount up the sandy canyon bottom. He knew that Old Chee and his two wives were camped somewhere ahead, and he had reached such a point of failure that, unmanlylike, he had begun fighting tears and longing for a little solace from his mother.

For many days and many nights Posey had searched, wearing out one stolen pony after another as he pursued his desperate search for Too-rah. In his travels he had spied on every camp of the People from the mormonee fort all the way eastward along the big river and on into New Mexico. Someone had told him Hatch and Sanop had been seen in that direction, but finding nothing he had turned northward onto the Ute Reservation in Colorado, where he had next nosed through every camp from Merriano Springs to Pine River. He had met Utes who had known of Poke and the rest of old Norgwinup's family, but either they wouldn't or they couldn't tell him a thing about the old man's baby daughter—the comely but utterly vanished Too-rah.

He had then turned back west and ridden to Navajo Mountain and the country of old Tsabekiss, the despised Navajo Bitseel's father. Finding nothing but a rumor that Bitseel had recently taken himself a wife, Posey had frantically reversed his direction again, returning to the neighborhood of the fort where he had spied for a time on Bitseel's new *hogan,* a foolish dwelling that the despised one had built across the river and a little south of Bluff.

When at length he had determined that Bitseel's new woman wasn't his own Too-rah, for he now thought of her as his own, the exhausted but much relieved Posey had crossed the river and passed by the fort, intent only on continuing his hopeless search. But finding a game of *ducki* going on outside the log walls, he had stopped to watch, laid a dollar against somebody's bet, and won.

"Skunk bait!" somebody had hissed from the other side of the blanket, after which the person had laid five dollars on an ace of diamonds.

Startled, Posey had stared into the taunting eyes of Bitseel, who was daring him to cover his bet. Having just won, Posey fished out his last money and rose to the challenge. After all, it had a fifty-fifty chance of becoming sufficient answer to its own insult. But his medicine was still bad, for the next flip of the cards gave the ten dollars to Bitseel, and once again Posey had nothing.

"*Ay law! Pu-neeh shi-nizen!*" Bitseel gloated in the Ute tongue as he took up the money. "Well, I declare! I do like skunk meat!"

In bitter wonder Posey had stared at the young Navajo. "Where did you learn to say that?" he half-demanded, half-pleaded.

"*Nine kotch pe soogh away,*" Bitseel had responded innocently and again in perfect Ute. "I don't know." But that, of course, had been a lie, for the Navajo had known. He had learned it from a Ute or a Pahute, a particular individual who took evil pleasure in calling Posey a skunk. That, of course, would have to have been the grizzly, Poke. The question that remained, however, was one Posey couldn't answer. Was Too-rah being held where Poke and Bitseel had been together? Or had the despised Navajo learned those words during Poke's earlier expedition into *Dinê tah,* the expedition when he had hoped to sell Bitseel his baby sister?

With an exhausted sigh Posey kicked his stumbling mount over a low hummock of sand in the bottom of Cottonwood Canyon, and abruptly found himself face-to-face with three fine horses—shod and therefore owned by the mormonee of the fort he had left behind only an hour or so before.

Without thought Posey grabbed his hard-twist rope to take for himself a new horse or two—and in the next instant he was rehearing the words of the man Haskel. "You stop stealing and *Shin-op* will love you," he could hear in his mind. "When *Shin-op* loves you, all your troubles will come out right."

For a moment Posey continued to shake out his loop, making ready to throw. Of a truth, however, old Haskel's words had begun to sound more and more appealing, especially since nothing else Posey had tried was working. Maybe if he actually did quit stealing mormonee horses . . .

With a grunt the tired young warrior recoiled his rope and kicked his spavined mount on up the canyon, leaving the tempting animals behind. After all, his own exhausted mind was now telling him, if it would help him find the comely Too-rah, anything was worth trying once—

37

Sunday, November 13, 1881

The San Juan River

Tuvagutts was a happy man. As the elderly Pahute thief rode eastward along the big river with his packs bulging, he could think of nothing more that life could offer, nothing better. Not alone was his new camp perfectly hidden in a little canyon some five or six miles ahead where the mormonee never came, but from it he could spy and strip the sand hills north of the mormonee fort, of any of the fine animals pastured there. *Oo-ah,* yes, and from the sand hills it was a simple matter to take such animals onto McCraken Mesa and from there into Colorado, where his Ute brothers were always ready for more cattle, more horses.

This day, however, he had been after other things—better things, at least for the moment—than horses and cattle would ever be. Some weeks before, while he had been poking around looking into this or that, he had stumbled onto a fine patch of *shan-te-cut,* watermelons, being grown by the mormonee of the fort. This patch of melons was in another small canyon cut back into the sandstone bluffs, out of the way of watching mormonee eyes, and it was watered by a small seep that kept the melons growing even when the mormonee did not have time to tend them.

Old Tuvagutts had kept his sly old eye on these melons, waiting for them to turn ripe and sweet. Finally that was accomplished, but when he had gone to raid them, they had already been harvested by the mormonee and taken into their fort.

Frustrated by the people who would do such evil things to him, Tuvagutts had sat on a rock to think things over—and had realized he was not alone in the small box canyon. From behind some large boulders near the seep or spring had come the plaintive cry of a young calf. Investigating, the old warrior saw not alone a lost stray that no doubt belonged to one of the mormonee, but he saw as well the purchase price for the melons he had been craving.

A little later his hopes had been confirmed, for the young mormonee who was watching over the melons at the fort, had been happy to trade several of them for the struggling calf. More, the mormonee fool had even helped Tuvagutts load them into the packs on his flea-bag of a pony. And so now he was headed back to his secret camp, riding near the log and stone cribs in the big river where the mormonee were foolishly trying to take out water to make little floods over their ground. Tuvagutts almost laughed aloud at the foolishness of such people, for anyone with any sense at all should know that rivers flowed where they would, and made their own floods when it was time.

Yes, he thought as he laid the quirt to his tired old pony to remind it that they were not yet near his camp; people with eyes to see, even if they were only the foolish *mericat* mormonee of the fort, should easily know such things. Yes, if they were more like him, they would be aware of everything that was happening around them at all times.

Unfortunately, old Tuvagutts was too busy congratulating himself—far too busy. Instead of watching what was going on about him as he should have been, or instead of giving heed to the strong words of warning spoken by the man Haskel down on Sand Island a few weeks earlier, which he absolutely should have been doing, the old Pahute's mouth was busy speaking unkind things against the white fools in the unfinished fort, and his mind was visiting the same tragic place. And that was why he did not see even a part of what was coming up behind him.

The Jump, San Juan River

"Ho, my brothers," one of the four Navajo warriors declared in quiet tones, "the old fool is alone."

"Yes," another one agreed as he edged his fine horse around a clump of greasewood, "and he does not look behind him. Truly this *nóôdâi* who is called Tuvagutts, is an old fool."

The four warriors, wise in the ways of stealth and even wiser in the lay of the country, did not know what was in the bulging packs the old Pahute's horse was carrying. What they did know, was that Tuvagutts had emerged from the *belacani* fort with those loaded packs, looking very pleased with himself, and so they also wanted whatever was in them. Hence they rode carefully and quietly, waiting for the time when the old man would turn from the river and ride up into the juniper-studded hills. That way he could be approached unseen from several directions at once—that way their surprise raiding of the old man would be complete.

Though none of the four had been at Sand Island to hear the warning words of the mormonee called Bin á á doot ízhi, Blue Eyes, his words had nevertheless been noised abroad in *Dinê tah*. So had the confirmation of those words been spread by the great Natanii nééz, who claimed that his days of raiding, and perhaps the days of his life, were ended because of them. Still, these four were strong warriors, sufficient unto themselves, and so none of them had given those words so much as a second thought.

Besides, they were not raiding the mormonee, not any of them, and so Haskel's words were as the wind, here and gone again with nothing changed at all.

Unless . . .

"*Nch'i,*" one said as he glanced at the others, "a strong breeze has come up."

Feeling it themselves, the others looked about, and were amazed to see a small, dark cloud rumbling and flashing away behind them, only a little to the southwest. It was not a big cloud, or very dangerous looking, but it did surprise them, for it had not been there only a short time before.

"*Kós haleeh,*" another one breathed a moment later as he looked back and upward, "it is going to get cloudy in this place, too."

"Yes," another agreed with a slight smile. "And *bee niki-da'diltsi,'* we may get caught in the rain."

Though it was a little cloud, it was dark and fast-moving, and the four raiders were amazed at how quickly it caught and then overtook them. In fact they were not yet near the cedar-studded hills where the trail turned upward when the lightning began flashing about them and the thunder was suddenly rumbling and throwing fear into their mounts.

"This storm is *bá háchi!*" one shouted against the thunder. "It is angry."

"Yes, my brother, and *bá ntseeshdá,* I am worried about it."

By now it was obvious to the raiders that the old Pahute had also noticed the storm, and in the process he must have noticed them. Anxiously he had begun flogging his scrawny old pony, and without warning he now turned from the trail and urged the animal upward onto the hillside where no trail existed.

Without comment the four quirted their fine horses after him, no longer even considering the storm or the need for stealth. After all, rains came and went, and this man they chased was only an old Pahute. Despite the fury of this small storm that was now upon them, the Navajo warriors still wanted whatever it was that old Tuvagutts carried in his packs.

For a moment, perhaps two, the old man was out of their sight in the trees. Then they emerged from the junipers into a small clearing, and were just in time to see the worried Pahute flogging his pony toward the trees on the far side. And there, in the trees toward which he was riding, sat two other Pahutes on their equally scrawny ponies, waiting for the old fool to arrive.

"*Hiyeee!*" one of the Navajo warriors screeched to show his valor, and in that same instant there was a blinding flash of lightning in front of them and a peal of thunder so loud and deafening that the four terrified Navajo horses leaped straight into the electrically charged air and then bolted squealing in four different directions. And all the while the four brave Navajo riders were doing their best to simply hang on.

Back together moments later, all were soaked thoroughly, and yet each was determined to press on after the missing old man and his packs. Yet they went hesitantly across the clearing, almost fearfully, for not only could they not see any of the three Pahutes, but the air was still charged with electricity, and there was as well a fearful odor in the air, an odor none of them had ever smelled.

Abruptly their horses began squealing and trying to bolt again, and as the Navajo raiders fought to bring them under control the rain ended, the cloud swept on by, and the afternoon sun broke through.

"Ho, brothers," one breathed as his pony gradually grew still, "what is this thing yonder in the rocks that has frightened our horses."

The others looked in the direction indicated by the man's twitching lips, and then in wonder they slipped from their trembling mounts and crept forward.

The sight that met them, a great red blotch upon the earth, sent a shiver of fear along each of their spines. Yes, for the great blotch was made of blood and hair and hooves and hands and no doubt the remnants of two overly filled packs of watermelons! Staring at the ground before them, their eyes wide with fear and a growing understanding, none of the four went any closer. Nor did they need to, for all could plainly see that this scrambled horror on the earth was the mortal remnant of old Pahute Tuvagutts and his loaded ponies that they had been following—at least before the fierce lightning had done its work.

No one said anything as they turned and threw themselves aboard their fine horses; not one of them even opened his mouth. Yet big in all of their minds, as they turned to flee the terrible scene, were the warning words of the man Haskel, his strange and powerful medicine. The old interpreter had said that maybe lightning would strike those who raided the mormonee, just as he had said they might be withered up like dry grass. The powerful Natanii nééz had been withered up like dry grass, or so it was said by those brave enough to visit his *hogan*. He was still alive, it was said, but not by much, and no one knew for how long. Yet everyone knew that the once powerful man—who had gloried in his raids upon the mormonee—had most definitely been withered up!

And now the old Pahute thief called Tuvagutts had been struck by lightning? He, and perhaps both of the other Pahutes, for they were just as gone as old Tuvagutts. It was surely a thing to be considered. Yes, and it was a thing to be spoken of quietly in the *hogans* of the People, but only in the winter, they knew, and only when nighttime fires had burned very low.

"*Hiyeee!*" one of the erstwhile raiders screeched again, his voice filled with wonder and fear, and in a heartbeat the four were racing heedlessly for the safety of the big river and their sacred *Dinê tah*.

Verdure Creek Line Camp

The trouble with Billy Foreman, the sour-minded Curly was thinking as they rode single file, was that he couldn't figure the man out! He'd tried—oh, how he'd tried, and had gone from disgust to grudging respect and then all the way back to hate and on to disgust again. Now, as he cantered his mount down into the Verdure Creek bottoms and toward the new and well-stocked line cabin them other Mormon fellers had thrown up, he felt confuseder'n a slave trader giving the keynote speech to a convention of abolutionists. Tell the truth, Curly had no more idea than a creek-bed boulder how he felt about the man.

With Curly's own grumbling help, Dick Butt and George Ipson had done a fine job of building the cabin that now loomed ahead of them. They'd used good Ponderosa logs notched at the corners for the walls and heavy sod they'd dug out a little lower down Verdure Creek to overlay the log and willow roof. They'd taken the time to saw planks for both the door and a shutter for the window, and these had both been covered with stretched cowhide to help keep out the wind. They had also chinked the walls, though with the straight logs the need had been minimal, and they had built a mud and willow fireplace that was big enough to heat the small cabin just fine.

Inside they had planked two bunks, one on each wall going away from the fireplace, put a rough plank table in between the bunks, and provided two well-cut sections of log for chairs. They had also laid a few flat stones in front of the fireplace to make a hearth. These things had been extra, and a pleased Bill Ball had paid the two men extra when he had seen them. So the cabin, which was roughly eight by twelve feet, was a good one, snug as could be, and Bill Ball was certain his two outriders would now spend a fairly tolerable winter.

While Curly and the two Mormons had been building and finishing the cabin, Bill Ball had sent three more cowhands up from the LC to build a corral and lean-to behind it, and to lay in a minimal supply of firewood. The rest, Curly thought sourly, would be up to him and the useless little Mormon. Still, with fresh water from the creek only a few steps away, he and the strange little man riding ahead of him were supposedly set for the winter.

Though the late afternoon skies were now clear there was a skiff of snow on the ground, maybe an inch or so—snow that had fallen since he and Billy had snaked the wagon load of supplies up from the ranch two days before. Curly was still shaking his head over how the little fellow had known how to fix that burst-out reach, but it had held just dandy for the rest of the journey to the cabin and then back to the ranch, and that in spite of the fact that they were blazing a new wagon-road a good part of the way.

And that, to Curly's way of thinking, was precisely the problem. Besides that he was so short he had to borrow a stepladder just to kick a grasshopper on the shinbones, an hombre with any smarts at all would know that the little fellow wouldn't—no, *couldn't*—have sense enough to spit downwind. Or find a cow if she was in his own bunk. Or cut her from the shade of a tree after she'd gone lame in all four legs. Yes sir, by all rights Billy Foreman should have been plenty ignorant without him or anybody else having to make a job out of proving it.

But that was exactly what was happening. Not alone had he rounded up them blasted runnygade cows and figured out how to tame and ride old Hurricane without the least sign of trouble, but he'd also become bosom buddies with Johnny Molander's little dog—the same as would snap the fingers off any other hombre who reached out to touch him! Those things, plus no matter what sort of trouble came up or how hard or dangerous was any task that Curly had told him to do, somehow the little Mormon greenhorn had managed it just dandy and come away smelling sweet as lavender water and twice as useful. It was absolutely perplexing!

Of course he was always apologizing and admitting to things he didn't know how to do—things such as tossing a rope or bulldogging and throwing a wild cow. Without his fool spectacles he was blind as a snubbing post and couldn't work for sour apples. And with his own good eyes Curly had seen the little man try to ride one of the more gentle nags on the place—and end up sailing off into the air with his hind legs a'kickin' like a migratin' bullfrog. Fact is, he'd been throwed so high, Curly recalled with a grin, that he'd expected to see St. Peter's initials whittled on the little Mormon's boot-soles after he'd come back down.

But even after that amazing exhibition, or maybe because of it, Curly was beginning to wonder if the little feller wasn't an honest-to-gosh cowpoke in disguise, maybe even a legendary wild bronc buster that none of them had happened to hear about. Yes, sir, he was actually starting to think that this whole and entire affair might be a huge rawhide job on the unsuspecting LC hands—set up by the little Mormon and Bill Ball to get the last laugh.

Whether that was so or not, Curly thought as he followed Billy, Hurricane, and the little dog through the snow toward the cabin, he had still come to appreciate the smaller man—a little. He was a fair hand around a fire, he didn't ride Hurricane hard or otherwise hurt him, he was gritty enough to stick to a job until it was finished, and he was clean.

He was also pleasant and friendly, even of a chill morning when a man had a right to grouch and complain afore he got hisself outside a cup of hot java. Nothing had seemed to rile him except Curly's attack on his religion down at Dodge Springs, and he was always on the lookout to do something nice for somebody else, Curly included!

But he was still a dad-burned, Bible-thumpin', Mormon skypilot, and Curly hadn't hardly ever heard one good thing about the Mormons—not from anybody! Besides that, Billy was married and he had a child, a little boy, at least according to Bill Ball, and both of those things were foreign concepts to the perpetually single, lanky cowboy.

So Billy wasn't a partner to Curly Bill Jenkins, not even hardly.

Oh, he'd likely do to spend the winter with, so long as he couldn't be driven off and Bill Ball wouldn't have it no other way. But as for being a partner the way one or two others had been . . .

One thing, though, Curly thought as he approached the corral, pens, and lean-to shed at the side and rear of the cabin, since he'd been rebuffed about his fool religion a few days before, the little feller had kept his distance and hadn't talked too much—just like he'd promised. Curly had feared Billy would all the time be arguing religion or thumping his Bible trying to convert him. Not only had that not happened, but since Dodge Springs the little feller had grown silent as a tree full of owls at noontime, being friendly but not speaking any more than Curly had been speaking to him—and maybe even less.

Naturally loquacious and outgoing, Curly couldn't understand that. Neither could he understand the unreasonable reaction of the other LC hands to Billy's own private roundup of old Splayfoot or his apparent taming of the outlaw Hurricane. Not alone had they all offered to buy the dad-gummed hoss for Billy, but now every time he and the little Mormon got back to the ranch, why, there on Billy's bunk was more foofaraw from those same awestruck cowpokes. It was all used, of course, but it was plenty serviceable, and now Billy had spurs and two pair of boots, one pair that fit him good; a shirt and leather cuffs; a pair of Levis and some good chaps to protect them; a pliable rope, and a doggone good Stetson that was just the right fit. Of course he was also wearing Old Man Lacy's sheepskin winter coat what Bill Ball had given him, and to look at him a feller'd of thunk he was a regular cowhand.

Of course the two of them hadn't yet done any actual cowboying, but that was scheduled to commence afore dawn the next morning.

"Doggone little Mormon runnygade!" Curly grumbled to himself as he approached the pole gate Billy had left open for him before he'd vanished beneath the lean-to, "I don't know what it is, at least not exactly. But sure as sulphur stinks bad, that confounded little greenhorn is up to something that ain't no good."

38

Monday, November 14, 1881

Verdure Creek Line Camp

"Of all the rotten, low-down, dirty—I'm a'telling you, Curly Bill Jenkins, if it weren't for bad luck, you'd have no luck at all! I knowed we shouldn't of dragged that fool wagon up here!"

Billy was standing beside the just-saddled Hurricane, his bedroll or, as Curly called it, his soogins, tied behind his saddle. Now, in the slowly spreading daylight, Billy glanced at the taller man who was so vociferously chastising himself. It was unusually cold, the ground was coated with ice, and just moving about in the corral had soaked Billy's boots and feet something fierce. In fact it had put him in mind of the trek they had made from the settlements two winters before, when he had thought his feet would never warm up again. Now he was beginning to wonder if that would be his annual fate. "Something wrong?" he asked anxiously.

"Wrong?" Curly snarled, the anger in his voice fairly dripping. "Oh, not hardly, not unless a feller considers that betwixt now and whenever, we've got more packing to do than old lady Levine, and I forgot to throw in a pack outfit when we was loading that wagon."

"A packsaddle?"

"As ever!"

"Not even a tree?"

"Nothin'!"

Billy gazed up into the loft at the rear of the lean-to where they had stored their gear, his mind racing. He knew they had only two riding saddles, so that was out. But he also knew, from his experience at the blacksmith shop back in Bluff, that even a rudimentary packsaddle might be constructed out of materials at hand.

"I might be able to make one," he finally ventured, "but to do a half-decent job, it'd likely cost us a good part of a day."

"Make one?" Curly guffawed, thinking of the burst reach Billy had repaired but then immediately forcing the humbling and therefore unwanted memory from his mind. "Nobody alive just ups and makes a packsaddle! Besides, we ain't got a good part of a day! We're behint the eight ball already, and ever' doggone hour gives that hoorah Carlisle outfit more time to rustle LC cows—especially yonder in the Brushy Basin country where I caught them other varmints! That's why I let Bill Ball talk me into using that goldurn wagon in the first place—to hurry things along."

"What do you suggest, then?" Billy asked.

"Why, I reckon we just do as we can," Curly growled as he tugged his hat down tight. "We ain't even got an extry riding saddle, but somehow we've got to load this hyer mare with war bags, a tarp, pots and kettles, and what chuck we're taking, including that hind quarter of beef hanging yonder. I don't suppose you know anything about packing?"

"Well, I—"

"Ahh, never mind!" Curly was completely disgusted, and he wanted the little Mormon to know it. "You're useless as a wart on a purty gal's nose! Now unless you're willing to hold this sorry mare so's she can't do no prancing around, why, just keep out of my dadgummed way."

Billy took up the rope to the mare Curly had indicated, patted her neck, and ran his hand down onto her front legs. "Is this our pack animal?"

"Yeah! Her name's old Fudge," the lanky cowboy snarled, his mood growing more foul by the moment. "She's also my second string, behint my little Betsy hoss. What of it?"

"She looks badly spavined, Curly. Look at her hocks, here. See the swelling? I don't know if she's up to the task."

"Slim said that colt of hers run her ragged when they brung the two of 'em up here," Curly growled. "That's the onliest thing what's wrong with her! She's rested now for two days, though, and'll get our gear to the basin and be my second string, just fine! So, hold 'er against that fence if you're gonna do it."

Lifting an old saddle blanket and placing it on the mare's back, Curly next placed the two war bags across it, as well as a gunnysack of grub and the quarter of beef, all of which he covered with the tarp. This was lashed in place with a lap-cinch made of another gunnysack. Next he "borrowed" Billy's extra pair of Levis, and with that and a short length of soft-twist rope, he secured a huge coffeepot, mugs, and a deep iron skillet and finished tying down the pack—at least as well as it would tie without the wooden trees of a packsaddle to fasten it to.

"All right," he snarled as he yanked the lead rope from Billy's hand, "get the gate, Mormon, and don't get too far behint me!"

Nodding politely Billy took Hurricane's reins and trudged to the gate. There he dropped the poles and stepped aside as Curly cantered through, his little Betsy mare lifting her feet high and handsome. The spavined mare came next, already looking spent, and her colt frolicking after. Putting the poles back in place, Billy stepped out in Curly's tracks, leading Hurricane to work the stiffness from his muscles. The silent but ever observant little Gopher trotted at his side, checking every few moments to make certain Billy was still nearby.

Within a couple of hundred yards, however, Billy came upon a grounded Curly, using usswords, as he might have put it, that would have sizzled bacon. Already the pack had slipped, and several minutes were now spent in redoing and retying everything handy. Worse, by the time they had remounted and ridden to North Fork, which was less than an hour further on, the old mare seemed about ready to lay down and give up the ghost.

"Curly," Billy ventured as he gazed at the trembling animal, "old Fudge doesn't look like she has much more in her."

"She'll be fine as soon as she warms up."

"Maybe," Billy replied, wondering how an hour of travel could have failed to warm anything up. "But I don't think so."

"What do you want I should do?" Curly snapped as he turned in his saddle and glared at his companion, "put the pack on that dad-gummed outlaw you're forking?"

"I think Hurricane would take it. So would old Betsy. Either way, one of us is going to end up afoot before much longer."

"We ain't got time for walkin'. Happen you're right—and I don't hardly think you will be—we'll just throw the pack on that fool colt."

In alarm Billy looked at the yearling animal, wondering how an unbroken horse would treat their pack. But Curly was already forging ahead, yanking on the mare's rope as he dragged the staggering animal after him. Eight or ten rods later, however, the old mare's legs slowly buckled beneath her, she lay down and rolled onto her side, and thereafter she refused to move.

"Well, I'll be double- and triple-dunked in bad-used sheep-dip," Curly groaned as he turned about and yanked again and again on the old mare's lead rope. "Get up, there, Fudge! Get up, you miserable old sorry excuse for a half-empty bag of buzzard bait!"

"She looks about as robust as a sick kitten, all right," Billy opined quietly.

"Nobody asked you!" Curly barked as he slid down and attempted with his hands and long arms to work the quivering mare back onto her feet. "Get up, Fudge! Get up, you miserable—"

"We can sure give Hurricane a try," Billy said when the old mare still couldn't move. "And maybe I ought to throw together some sort of a packsaddle. It wouldn't take too much—"

Angrily Curly shook his head. "I tolt you, Mormon! We ain't got time for none of that packsaddle foolishness, and I ain't waiting around for you to hoof it afoot all the way to Brushy Basin!" With great dexterity Curly threw himself back aboard his Betsy horse. "We're going to tie our pack on the colt, and that's final!"

Shaking out a loop Curly set out after the frisky animal, who seemed to have other ideas and would not allow itself to be roped. After about ten minutes of Curly and the young horse going back and forth in every imaginable direction over about two acres, however, the colt dashing and prancing and Curly burning grass and trees and everything else within range of his red-hot language, Billy gave little Gopher some quiet directions. Shortly thereafter Curly's rope settled over the head of the suddenly subdued yearling colt, and he became a satisfied man. Or nearly so.

After tying his bandanna over the colt's eyes to settle it down, and then snubbing it tight to a tree, Curly stepped back and wiped his forehead. "There! That'll settle yer milk, you short-coupled, young broomtail!" Then he turned and yanked the pack, gunnysack lap-cinch, cups, pots, pans, and everything else, from the still-prone mare.

"Want some help?" Billy questioned from aboard the patient Hurricane.

"Not hardly!" Curly's mood was not getting better, and more and more he was cussing Bill Ball and everyone else who had maybe convinced this fool Mormon that he might become a cowhand. "Your kind of help's useless as knotholes in a bob-wire fence! So you and that dad-burned hoss and dog just stay shy of this colt! I don't want none of you to go spooking it!"

Grunting and swearing, Curly then packed the motionless animal, meanwhile looking to Billy like he might be about to drown in his own sweat it was dripping off him in such profusion.

"There," he breathed when he at last gave the pack a final tug and then untied his bandanna. "Reckon that ought to hold!"

Mounting his little Betsy horse Curly took the lead to the colt and once again led out, climbing the rise that led to Hell's Hole and the area between Recapture and Johnson Creeks, where Billy had had such an amazingly lucky time chasing that old runnygade Splayfoot and her brood. But the colt seemed to lead well enough with the pack on its back, and both Curly and Billy began to breathe more easily as they crossed the summit, skirted to the south of Hell's Hole, and began the sharp drop down through the cliffs into Recapture.

"Curly," Billy suddenly called urgently from behind, "the pack's slipping—"

Spinning, Curly saw that it was so. Turning little Betsy he tried to get back, but his sudden action, as well as the slipping pack, spooked the yearling horse. Frantically the animal pulled loose its lead rope, and then it seemed to go crazy, thinking perhaps that it was a pinwheel in a Fourth of July celebration. War bags, beef, ropes, Levis, gunnysacks, flour, salt, beans, cups, pots, skillet—everything on that horse—went off in every possible direction, and the yearling colt went highest and farthest of all.

In stupefied amazement both men watched until the colt was all the way down to the creek. There it abruptly stopped and began cropping grass as if nothing had happened, so finally the men moved. Still silent, Curly started down after the young animal, and Billy, spying a beaver dam down on the creek a few yards beyond the horse, began casting his eyes along it for a few good sticks.

"Whatcha doin'?" Curly growled a little later as he tied the captured colt's lead rope to a nearby tree. Billy was seated on the ground near the beaver dam, his knife out and one of several dried sticks in his hand.

"Waiting to see how long it'll take for our pack to be gathered up," Billy drawled as he worked to smooth one side of the stick.

"Now, you lookee hyer!" Curly snarled. "I ain't takin' orders from no dad-gummed Mormon skypilot—"

"I never gave an order," Billy interrupted amiably. "I merely voiced a wonderment. My theory, though, is that a packsaddle won't do much good if the packs are scattered from here to breakfast."

"You're actual' thinking of making a packsaddle?" Curly found himself wondering why he was surprised.

"This is the second side of the front crosstree," Billy replied nonchalantly as he held up the limb he was working on. "Those two limbs there'll make a fine rear crosstree, and smoothed a little, those two logs right here'll make fine fenders."

"How you gonna fasten 'em together?" In spite of himself, Curly was hoping this fool Mormon could pull the project off. Already the day was half-gone, that doggone colt was crazy enough to pull the same stunt again, and he sure didn't feel up to no walk the rest of the way to the basin. No sir, if this little Mormon could actually fix a burst-out reach, then maybe by jings he could also put together a workable packsaddle!

Of course he'd then need the two war bags and everything else that fool colt had scattered abroad.

"Green pegs should do it," Billy finally responded to Curly's question. "Then when we get a little rawhide we can tie it tight."

In less than two hours, the rough-looking packsaddle was finished and settled securely on top of the old saddle blanket on the back of the again-blindfolded colt. It was single-rigged with a belly-band made of Billy's Levis, and was more fully secured with a gunnysack breast collar and a simple breech or hip strap made of rope wrapped in Curly's oldest shirt sleeves, which he had seemed quite happy to donate to the cause. Shortly thereafter the two war bags, the quarter of beef, and the gunnysack containing all the grub Curly had been able to salvage were beneath the tarp, and all of it, including their cooking and eating utensils, were tied to the cross-trees with expertly executed diamond-hitches. With a satisfied nod Billy indicated that the outfit was ready to move.

Without a word—for Curly could clearly see that the little Mormon was no novice packer and it sort of unnerved him—he took the bandanna from the colt's eyes, untied the lead rope, and kicked his Betsy horse into motion. He did not look back, he did not say "thank you" or "well done," and above all he did not smile or cast even a sideways, wall-eyed glance at the little fellow who was now dragging himself aboard the outlaw Hurricane.

But he was thinking. In fact he could no more stop his mental perambulations than he could have stopped that fool colt from strewing their gear over half of creation a couple of hours before. And what he was thinking, by jings, was the same as he had thought after the little Mormon behint him had rounded up that wild runnygade cow or tamed without a buck or a crow-hop the meanest outlaw nag in all of San Juan County. The fellow was either weasel-smart and as full of information as a mail-order catalogue, which didn't look too likely happen a feller just glanced at him; or his craw was so full of sand and fighting tallow that it wouldn't chamber a winter-dried pea, no matter.

Either way, Curly thought with a nervous grunt, he himself was now being rawhided but good by the slickest cowpuncher and bronc buster this side of wherever. Worse, the little feller was probably even a gunslick, maybe even the fastest in the country! Yes, sir, the man might be small and he might be a spectacles-wearing Mormon, but to Curly's new way of thinking he was gritty as creek-bed sand and so tough he'd eat off the same plate as a rattler!

In other words, he thought grimly as he kicked his little Betsy horse up through the cliffs toward the mesa and Johnson Creek beyond, Billy Foreman was a man over whom Curly Bill Jenkins had ought to rethink his opinion!

Cottonwood Canyon

"This bad thing is so, brothers! We saw it with our own eyes!"

Posey, struggling up as if from a drugged sleep, stared out of his mother's *wickiup* to see Hatch and Bishop, Poke's two oldest brothers, mounted on two of the mormonee ponies he had passed by earlier, and surrounded by his father and the others of Mike's and old Chee-poots' encampment. The men were endeavoring to explain what great thing had happened to them, and it was obvious to Posey that they were excited.

It was late in the day, and for an instant Posey wondered where he was and how he had managed to sleep so long after *tabby* the sun had topped the cliffs to the east. But then the memory of his exhausting search returned, as well as the bad feeling in his heart toward Hatch and Bishop and their evil family, and quickly he scrambled to his feet and hurried toward them.

"How was this warrior called?" Old Chee asked as Posey strode nearer.

"He was the warrior Tuvagutts!" Bishop replied. "The two of us saw him riding fast toward us, his panniers heavily loaded. When he did not see us even though he looked straight at us, we thought perhaps his mind was gone and that we should take his packs from him to protect them."

Some in the crowd nodded their agreement; others chuckled.

"There was a small *pahger-nump,* a cloud," Hatch went on, "that was filled with fire. It came fast toward us from the south, *o-no-nint,* the thunder, making a hungry growl, and I thought the storm was *pah-wi yoahts,* walking as the wolf walks."

"Just as old Tuvagutts came near," Bishop took over, "there was a terrible roar and then *coo-nah,* fire, filled the air. Our ponies went down in a heap and us with them, and when we got to our feet our ponies ran off in a hurry and there was a great *paquy-nary,* a great stinking, in the air.

"We looked for the old fool Tuvagutts to see what had happened to him, and where he had been there was nothing but hooves and hands and feet—those, and a great red splotch upon the earth."

"Where was this place?" Posey questioned, not thinking of the late Tuvagutts so much as he was the possibility that Hatch and Bishop were riding from where they and Poke had hidden his beloved Too-rah.

"Off toward the big river," Hatch replied evasively as he swung his arm in a long line, sweeping from east to west. "It was in a clearing in the trees."

"What is the matter, *pu-neeh?*" Bishop sneered, his old rancor suddenly back. "Is our little sister lost to you?"

Furious, Posey started forward. But as his younger but larger brother Scotty wrapped his arms about him to stop him, Posey was more than arrested by strong words that came from behind him—words repeated by old Paddy's son who was calling himself Henry.

"Tuvagutts died according to the words of Haskel, Brothers," Henry declared with conviction. "Did he not say that perhaps *Shin-op* would send the fierce and vivid lightning to kill us if we continued to steal from the mormonee? *Wagh,* Brothers, you know that he did, for you heard those words of power with your own ears!

"Now the two of you ride horses that belong to the mormonee, horses that you stole from *Shin-op's* friends. The man Haskel promised that those who stole from the mormonee would die! It is in my heart to wonder in what terrible way the great *Shin-op* will now take your lives!"

And Posey, the memory of Haskel's words suddenly ringing like wild bells in his own memory, felt a strange chill run through him, causing him to forget all about old Norgwinup's two evil sons who were there on the stolen mormonee horses, their faces filled with new fear.

Haskel's words did have power, he knew! Yes, they were words of truth! More importantly, only the day before, he, Posey, had stopped stealing mormonee horses and cattle, which meant that now *Shin-op* loved him. Therefore, he was certain, he would soon find his beloved Too-rah, and then all his troubles would turn out right—

39

Tuesday, November 15, 1881

Cottonwood Canyon

The *poo-chits,* the stars, were hanging like dainty lanterns in the velvet blackness above him when Posey opened his eyes. *My-toge,* the moon, had already set so it was late, perhaps an hour or so before dawn. Yet something had awakened the anxious youth, some sound that was not normal. But as he strained his ears into the darkness he could hear nothing—nothing but the wind, the coyotes, and the plaintive cry of a distant night bird.

He was still camped with his father's people at the foot of a high cliff in Cottonwood, a cliff where no trail led to the top. Over that cliff's brow, towering high above them on the east, the desert winds moaned and sighed, sounding at times almost like a human voice. Now, as Posey stared upward beyond the cliff toward the myriad of twinkling lanterns, wondering in the meanwhile what the grizzly had done with his comely baby sister, Posey imagined that he heard a voice calling from the rim high above—a soft voice that was calling his name!

With a start the instantly revitalized warrior was on his feet, his whole being straining with the effort to better hear what had brought him to instant consciousness. Yet a second or so later, when a mourning dove for some reason started from a shelf of the cliff a little above him, Posey sighed and relaxed his vigil. It had been the bird, not little sister, who had been crying into the darkness.

Yet some moments after he had retired again, the *katz-tinzeer,* the soft sound, came again! Instantly he was back on his feet, his whole body quivering with the tension of what he must surely be hearing. And then he heard it again—twice! It was indeed the voice of the lovely Too-rah, and twice more she called his name!

"*O aakerom!*" he called back as he started with a spring for the black wall of the cliff. "Yes, I hear! Where are you?"

"Come and get me!" Too-rah called in great excitement from high, high above. For some reason her voice seemed muffled, yet her words were as plain and unmistakable to Posey as any words had ever been.

"I am coming! I am coming!" he shouted into the night as he stumbled over brush and rocks and beat his way to the looming base of the cliff.

For a moment he cudgeled his brain in an effort to think of the cliff as he had seen it in the light of *tabby,* the sun, searching in his memory for a way up its imposing face. Yet when nothing came he started up anyway, groping with his hands and feeling with his feet as he moved blindly upward, his pounding heart in his throat. Too-rah was there! Somehow she had come back, and had managed to find him in the camp of his father and his mother.

"Too-rah, where are you?" he yelled as he pulled himself ever higher, trying to get the maiden to repeat her cherished words.

No answer came!

"Where are you?" he called again, this time more frantically, then pausing and listening with his whole being. But again there was no answering voice, nothing but the throbbing of his heart, his labored breathing, and the soft sighing of the wind as it drifted over the distant top of the cliff. In the hush of darkness it was only silence that answered him, mocking the harsh and pleading sound of his voice.

Too-rah is dead, his mind began screaming at him! It had only been her spirit that had called out to him, somehow reaching toward him from along that lonely and fearful road to the west.

Still he climbed, groping his way into a narrow canyon that stretched upward. The gray dawn revealed a way he might continue his climb, at least if he was very careful, and so as the sky above him slowly brightened he inched his way upward, his raw and bleeding fingers probing the way.

Most of the region at the top, once Posey had finally reached it, was sandrock or slickrock, bare and smooth. Yet in a little hollow where sand had been drifted in by the wind, Posey found the clear imprint of moccasined feet—Too-rah's feet! He was certain of it! Yet why should she have been there? And why should she have been running in the inky blackness of the night? For in another spot he found a second footprint, and then a third—planted so he could easily discern that she had been moving in great and desperate haste.

Then over top of Too-rah's fourth print Posey found the larger, deeper track of a man! Stunned, he bent down and studied every detail, reading in the signs what had happened, where Too-rah had gone. He worked slowly, carefully, and so it was some time before he found the mark of horses' hooves in another place, and even one more partial track of Too-rah. But the horses' hooves seemed to lead nowhere, and finally he lost them on the hard surface of the rock.

Still, he thought as he straightened his aching back and stared about him, maybe Too-rah was not dead! Maybe she had escaped from the watchful eyes of her family and had been hunting him through the night. Or maybe Poke had sold her, and she had fled from the man who had bought her, only to be caught and dragged away just as she had come upon Posey's listening ears. Could that be, he wondered? Could she have come so close only to be snatched away forever?

In his long and desperate hunt for this comely will-o'-the-wisp, Posey had found himself wondering, from time to time, if he might have lost his reason. Now, unbidden, that thought came again. The tracks he had seemed to see, and the voice he had seemed to hear—might they have had their existence nowhere else but in his tired and overwrought mind?

Ump-i-o. Desperate as he felt, Posey was not certain. But large in his heart were his feelings for the lovely maiden, feelings that would not go away. And so with a sigh he made his way around the cliff and back down to the encampment of his family. There his pony was now rested and ready to take up the trail once again. And on its bony back, he vowed, he would continue his lonely search forever!

Bluff Fort

"Eliza!"

Filled with her usual hustle and bustle, Eliza Ann Redd sat down next to Eliza Foreman. The afternoon sun was warm, and so Eliza was seated outdoors where she was restitching a worn nightshirt for little Willy. Besides, with the new stove in place in her cabin, there was far less light than before. Of course she loved the warmth and the ease with which she could cook on the marvelous new stove. But of a truth, it seemed a waste to light as many candles as it took to give her as much light as the fireplace had once provided.

"How's Billy getting along with his cowboying? Have you had any word from him yet?"

"One letter, written about a week and a half ago. The others are doing something to him called rawhiding, which he expects to get through."

"Yes," Eliza Ann laughed. "The old hands used to do that to the greenhorns on Pap Redd's place back in the settlements. It usually turned out to be quite humorous."

"For all but the greenhorn, I imagine. Have you heard from Lem? Did he and the others get to Colorado okay?"

"I received a note, not a letter, but they seem to be all in one piece, and were to set out after more railroad ties the next morning. Oh, Eliza, I do hate spending another winter alone!"

Soberly Eliza nodded. "So do I, my dear. When Billy left, it felt like I was losing my little Mary Eliza all over again."

Instantly sympathetic, Eliza Ann Redd reached down and pulled Eliza against her. "I . . . I'm so sorry, Eliza, dear. I didn't mean—"

"I know you didn't," Eliza declared as she straightened, took Willy's nightshirt, and dabbed her eyes. "I just can't seem to get over my grieving!"

"Well," Eliza Ann bubbled, obviously trying to brighten the mood, "why don't we talk of something fun? I haven't had the time to tell you, but you were an absolutely wonderful villain in our little production this past week. And of course Willy traipsing around with you, made it even better. I had no idea you were so theatrical!"

Eliza smiled ruefully. "I'm not, Eliza Ann. That was my true nature showing through."

The woman giggled delightedly. "That may be your opinion, but it isn't Lula's or any of the other young women in this fort. I truly believe they think you can walk on water! Why, this latest idea you've conjured up, as part of your Young Lady's Retrenchment Society lesson for the older girls, has Lula more excited than anything you've ever done. Just think of it! Having these children braid their own horsehair hackamores, bridles, lead ropes! Why, the child thinks she's destined to be a cowboy. Grandpa Redd would be fit to be tied!"

"And how do Mother and Father Redd feel about their daughter's ambitions?" Eliza was fairly certain she already knew, but didn't see any harm in asking.

Eliza Ann smiled. "You do get right to the point, don't you? Yes, Eliza, we're a little concerned, but only because Lula won't help out with the domestic chores—not unless we reward her with something she can do out of doors."

Sighing, Eliza Ann Redd shook her head. "Well bother, Eliza, I don't know why I worry about her so much. And it certainly isn't your fault. To be truthful, I was as big a tomboy as she is, though I was more into climbing trees and throwing fisticuffs with the boys. It wasn't until I started into womanhood that I began to see the value of some of the more ladylike graces. I . . . well, I suppose I was hoping to steer Lula clear of such foolishness as I indulged in, but I'm sure she will be fine."

"She will be, Eliza Ann. But if you want, I can tell her she is too young to attend my classes—"

"Oh, no, you won't! Lula looks forward to those classes all week long, and you've taught her some wonderful skills that I certainly don't have. Besides, Lem ate every speck of those currant preserves you helped her to make, and has taken a solemn oath from her that she will put up twice as many jars next year. So please, Eliza, allow her to continue with her attendance.

"By the way, will Billy be home for the Thanksgiving dance next Thursday?"

"I don't know, but I don't think so." For a fact, it had seemed so impossible that Eliza had not even given it a thought. Besides, what with the play and all little Willy's demands, there had simply been no time. "He's hardly been at the LC long enough to ask for such a favor," she continued, actually starting to wonder.

"Well," Eliza Ann declared, looking sad, "I do hope he comes. He's become so good at calling the dances, and we would love to use him for this one. Lula and Sarah Jane Rowley have given out those handprinted invitations to every man, woman, or beast who has even come near the fort." Eliza Ann giggled again. "Truthfully, though, some of those folks hadn't better show up. Why, there was one man Lula told me about, and she was even pinching her nose while she was telling me, he smelled so awful—"

"Oh, no! I hope it wasn't that terrible Sugar Bob Hazelton again! Lula's already had one brush too many with him!"

For a moment Eliza Ann's eyes widened in fear. Then, quickly, she relaxed. "I'm certain it wasn't," she breathed. "Lula didn't say a thing about it being him, and as disgusted by him as she was, I'm certain she would have. That girl shows no restraint whatsoever in her speech!"

"Then we'll see if we can work on that during our classes," Eliza promised, and with a hug of sincere friendship the two women returned to their separate duties.

Bluff Fort

"Well, that looked like an interesting conversation."

Eliza looked up, mock shock on her face. "Mary, it is not polite to be eavesdropping."

Mary Jones chuckled. "I didn't say I'd heard anything. I admit only to have watched it."

"But you're dying to know what was said, aren't you!"

Again Mary laughed. "Actually, I'll bet I can guess. She thinks poor Lula's tomboy ways can be laid at the feet of a certain Eliza Foreman."

"Why, you *were* listening in!"

"No, but she said the same thing to me, just yesterday. I tried to set her straight, and I hope you did the same."

Wondering about how many others of the sisters the young woman had spoken with, Eliza nodded. "So far as I could tell, we came to a meeting of the minds. It was interesting, though—"

"Mary! Eliza! Did you hear?"

Looking up, the two women saw an anxious Elizabeth Stevens hurrying toward them. In fact she was so anxious that she wasn't even holding her skirts up and out of the dust, and both grew instantly concerned.

"What is it, Lizzy?" Mary questioned as she rose to her feet. "Is everything all right?"

"All right?" the young woman repeated as her face broke into a smile. "It's more than that! It's wonderful! Joshua came by a little bit ago, trailing our herd of cows to Colorado—"

"I thought he'd already gone!"

"So did I, but he came back after the cattle when he heard there was a market for them. Anyway, you'll never in this world suppose who he found up near the top of Elk Mountain. Ladies, he stumbled onto that evil man you encountered a couple of months ago right here in the fort—the same horrid man who tried to lure Lula and Sarah Jane to their deaths!"

"He encountered Sugar Bob Hazelton?" Eliza was stunned. "Oh, Lizzy, I do hope he took care—"

Elizabeth Stevens laughed. "No, no, you didn't let me finish. Joshua encountered Sugar Bob Hazelton's *body!* He is dead!"

"But . . . how? Who could have killed him?"

"That's the horrible part. Nobody killed him, not unless a body figures one of God's destroying angels had a hand in it. Joshua said he fell off a high cliff."

"What's so horrible about that?" Mary was starting to sound disgusted with the younger woman.

"He wasn't alone, is what. That evil man fell, all right, but it wasn't the fall that killed him. He either landed in a mess of rattlesnakes, or he got into them before he fell, because Joshua counted more than fifty bites on his bare legs and feet—"

"Bare legs and feet? What happened to his boots?"

Elizabeth shook her head. "I don't know, and I didn't think to ask Josh. Anyway, besides all those bites, there were two dead snakes, one right under him. Joshua says his legs were swollen something terrible, which is why he figured the man hadn't died right off. He also says he has never in his life seen such a look of horror on a man's face!"

Eliza shuddered. "I don't blame him! I absolutely loathe snakes—"

"I'll bet it wasn't the snakes," Mary breathed from beside her. "I'll bet he was horrified by his first good glimpse of hell!"

"I don't know," Elizabeth replied as she adjusted her bonnet. "All I know is, Brother Haskel's curse sure must have worked, for that evil man is dead! I just thought the two of you would like to know—Oh, there's Eliza Ann. I'd better put her and Lula's minds to rest as well."

Turning, Elizabeth hurried off, and in thoughtful silence Eliza and Mary returned to their work.

Brushy Basin

"Good beans," Billy commented as he sat on a rock by the small fire, savoring a little supper.

"Mmmmm."

"And this sourdough does hit the spot. There's a little gravel in it from when that colt dumped it over near Recapture, but not so much that it's dangerous to a man's teeth. No offense, Curly, but you're a fine cook, and I do appreciate it."

"Mmmmm hmmmm."

Perplexed by this man who was supposed to be his partner, Billy grew silent. It had been a long and harrowing day, beginning long before daylight and ending only a short time before, leaving him tired, worn, and no more haggard-looking than he actually was.

Throughout the morning Curly had seemed to be doing the work of several men, with Billy following along as best he could, up and down hills, over cliffs and rocks, around and through trees, every bit of it at breakneck speed, doing all the lanky cowpuncher could to either kill them both off or round up every cow-critter they happened onto.

Bunched together these cattle were set to drifting eastward toward the distant Verdure Creek drainage. On their own they wouldn't go far, but as the basin was emptied, they would be gathered into a fair herd, and this Curly—and hopefully Billy—would push all the way to their winter graze down along the Montezuma Creek drainage.

Surprisingly, Billy's Hurricane horse had turned out to be a natural at the job, as had little Gopher, and so Billy had quickly learned to give the animals their head and just hang on. Of course he was no hand at all with a rope, and that did limit him. So did not wearing his spectacles, for in the thick brush and trees of the area he'd have lost them in a minute, especially the way Hurricane carried on once he'd spotted a fleeing cow. So the spectacles had remained with his bedroll, and all day Billy had been riding mostly blind and hanging on for dear life.

Sometime around noon, in a second skiff of snow that had fallen during the night before, Curly had spotted the tracks of three animals he had recognized as old-time runnygades. Long-legged Texas longhorns, these wild animals were heading at a fast clip for the top of a black knoll on the west side of the basin.

Bill Ball had told both of them that he wanted those troublesome, practically worthless animals out of the country, and so with a wild whoop Curly had gone after them, with Billy, Gopher, and Hurricane not more than a jump or two behind.

Near the top of the knoll the renegade cattle had separated, and so had the two men, Curly going one way and Hurricane taking Billy the other, pell-mell down the side of the knoll where it seemed that the trees and the brush were the thickest. In an instant Billy had lost his hat, and in another had known he could never dodge all the trees and that Hurricane didn't expect him to. What the animal expected, it seemed obvious, was for Billy to hang on and absorb the blows of the trees and limbs as they came. And somehow the horse had seemed to have the uncanny ability of knowing which trees and limbs Billy's body could break and which were too stout—and then somehow avoiding the latter.

Of course the ride had been anything but pleasant, for not alone was Billy getting pounded practically to death by horse and trees and limbs, but within seconds he had also felt as though he was like to being drowned in snow. It had coated every square inch of his clothing, matted the hair on his bare head, and was plastered on his frozen face. It had also melted down his neck and inside his clothes and in his shoes. It was even packed beneath him on the saddle, so that by the time he was down off the knoll he was riding two or three inches higher in the saddle than when he had started. Thoroughly miserable, he was soaked and cold and going numb.

Nevertheless, the ride had been deadly earnest business, and despite that Billy had been bruised and battered and uncertain, even, of what was going on, at the foot of the knoll where the trees thinned, somehow his rope ended up in his hand, a loop made, and the bitter end tied to the horn. Breaking clear of the trees, he saw for the first time the cow Hurricane was after.

It was a roan-and-white steer with a bald face and a roan splotch over one eye, with horns maybe four or four and a half feet across. As Hurricane brought Billy alongside, he could see that like old Splayfoot, the rangy animal was every bit as tall as his horse's withers. Worse than Splayfoot, though, every two or three strides this steer would hook with its left horn, trying to catch Hurricane in the side or shoulder, though each time the horse managed, somehow, to avoid being gored.

Twice Billy had thrown a loop and missed, and then Hurricane and Gopher had taken over. First the little terrier had slowed the animal down. Then, crowding the steer with his shoulder, the horse had bumped it just right and knocked it over. But Billy had been so surprised that he hadn't reacted, and in a heartbeat the steer was back on its feet and thundering ahead. Moments later and another quarter-mile up the draw, however, Gopher and Hurricane had done it again, and this time Billy had been out of his saddle and doing his best to hold the steer down and tie its hooves with his peggin' string.

An hour later when Curly had finally arrived, Billy had been sitting astride the downed but poorly-tied steer, freezing to death and waiting, apparently not knowing what else to do. Without saying a word or showing any expression whatsoever, Curly had retied three of the hooves together, pulled a small saw from his saddlebags, dehorned the animal, placed a rope around the bleeding stubs, and snubbed the animal close to a tree. Then he had loosed its hooves.

"We'll come back after it tomorry," was all he'd said as the steer had lunged to its feet to begin fighting the rope, and Billy hadn't heard another word from the cowboy for the remainder of the day. Even now, as the two huddled close to the fire. Doing their best to thaw out, Curly's strange silence continued.

"That was quite a ride after those runnygades today," Billy finally ventured.

"Yup."

"I think ol' Hurricane's been ridden before; either that or he's one terribly smart horse."

"Mmmmm."

"Same with little Gopher. Johnny Molander's trained that dog to a fare-thee-well!"

"Uh-huh."

"Is there a reason for leaving those three cows snubbed to trees like we did?" Curly called everything, steer or otherwise, a cow, and Billy was trying to pick up the man's sometimes colorful lingo.

"Yup."

"Would you mind explaining it to me?"

"Yup." And with that, the enlightening conversation ended. Curly crawled into his blankets, pulled his tarp over himself in case it snowed again, and was soon snoring.

And Billy, who was feeling more sorrowful than frustrated, massaged his aching muscles as he sent a plea heavenward, stretched out under his own blankets and tarp, thought for a few moments of Eliza and little Willy, worried for a few moments about the morrow being as bad as the day he had just survived, and finally did his best to get a little rest.

40

Thursday, November 17, 1881

Brushy Basin

Of all the doggone befuddlements, Curly Bill Jenkins was thinking as he sat on a ridge watching Billy Foreman making a run after some cow-critters across the flat below, that scrawny little Mormon feller was harder to figure than a crosseyed skunk spraying sweet perfume. There wasn't a solitary thing about him that added up! He was a sure-enough greenhorn, but still didn't leave tracks enough to trip an ant! He was a Bible-thumping skypilot, but wouldn't preach! He was a sissified little man who couldn't see beyond the end of his nose, but who when it came down to it was gritty as eggs rolled in sand and got the job done fine whether he could see or not! And no matter what Curly had tried, the scrawny little man wouldn't rawhide for nothin'!

So for two days now, Curly had been trying a new tack. First of all he'd stopped speaking to the man, which was good for two reasons. One, he didn't want little Billy Foreman rawhiding him in some secret or sneaky way that one day would blow up in his face. And two, in case the little hombre really was a greenhorn, he didn't want to be giving him no free education in the fine profession of cowpunching.

And the second thing he had been doing, in case Billy Foreman was either one of the two main suspects—greenhorn or otherwise—was going out of his way at every opportunity to show the little man what a highfalutin' specimen of true manhood that he, Curly Bill

Jenkins, actually was! And he'd done a fine job of it, too—even if he did say so himself.

In the frosty mornings he'd used a "hooleyann" or fast loop to catch up their mounts before the horses could even think of ducking or twisting away. Few men could actually throw such a loop, and he wanted Billy to see how good at it he actually was.

Both days Curly had also insisted on working the kinks out of each of their animals, though he knew full well he'd never be able to stick on Hurricane for more than a minute. That was because the outlaw horse was not only a pile-driver—humping his back and coming down with all four legs stiff as ramrods—but he was also a sun-fisher, twisting his body sometimes all the way around while in midair; and a spinner, which meant he went up in the air and then whirled backward on the way down. Obviously a feller never knew which of those tactics the outlaw would use next, or even if he might invent a new one. All of which was why he couldn't be ridden.

Except, of course, by that scrawny little Billy Foreman.

In the brush, their responsibility was to rope and throw the largest of the animals, and to gather them and the rest into a single bunch for branding, cutting, castrating, and dehorning. Afterwards the cattle were loosed and driven toward where the herd would be gathered.

Two men usually did the roping and throwing of the larger cows, one throwing his loop around the horns and the other the heels, and then riding in opposite directions and "stretching" the animals to the ground.

Curly, however, had been doing this by himself, using a roping technique called "going over the hump." The trick was to cast a Blocker loop in such a way that it curled over a running critter's back and circled down just above the ground, where on the next bound both front feet would be thrust through it. Roped in this manner, any cow-critter, no matter its size, would somersault and lie breathless and prostrate until the roper could secure three of its legs with a peggin' string.

Occasionally Curly had missed with this most spectacular of throws, but mostly he hadn't, and that fact pleased him immensely.

Next had come the roping, branding, and cutting of the calves or mavericks, which was normally accomplished by up to five men. Two "ketch" hands usually did the roping, two "flankers" stood by the fire to catch and hold down the calves, and then the "brander" or "iron-man"—yelling "Hot iron!"—slapped the branding iron, which was kept glowing cherry-red in the fire, onto the bawling animal's side.

For the past two days, though, Curly had been doing the whole shebang by his lonesome, allowing Billy no more responsibility than to help bring in the cattle, tend the fire, and watch. The lanky cowboy would ride his Betsy horse quiet through each gather, heel-rope the calves and drag them to the fire where he'd leap down, throw them onto their sides, and then brand them. Still kneeling on the bawling calves he would then take up his knife and cut the earmark of the LC into their ears, after which he'd castrate the males, smearing the wound with axle grease, and also dehorn the larger, maverick animals of both genders. All this, except the dehorning, was usually accomplished in five minutes or less, a very good time indeed, and Curly felt sure that the little man was being duly impressed.

Now, as he urged his little Betsy horse down off the ridge and toward Billy Foreman, Curly was feeling tired but good. Yes, sir, he thought with a sly grin, maybe his tongue *was* hanging out a foot and forty inches. After two days of doing what he'd done, it had ought to be! But dad-gum it, he'd put on one wingding of a show for that scrawny impostor—a show that wasn't yet over. When it was, by jings, then little Billy Foreman, greenhorn or not, was going to know that he—Curly Bill Jenkins—was thorny as cactus served cold and meaner'n a stepped-on, hydrophobied polecat!

And that way, he felt certain as his smile grew even wider, he'd be certain of spending the winter, if not exactly lying around eating free food, then at least being shown a decent amount of respect.

———o—o—o———

Spring Canyon

"What do you know, old woman? Speak to me, or you will be starting early along that dark and lonely road to the west!"

Not intimidated, the kindly old Pahute woman who was called

Peeats merely laughed at Posey's ferocious threats. After all, she knew him and his brother both, and she had no fear of either of them. Of course she did have information for Posey, information she wanted him to have. But she would tell it only on her own terms, and not upon the surly young man's demands. After all, he had treated as his enemies the mormonee people of the unfinished fort along the big river. But Peeats, a warmhearted soul under even the worst of conditions, had developed a great love for the mormonee people, and had taken it upon herself to help them in every way she could.

For many days, however, a bitter feud had been raging between her grandsons, Paddy and his cousin Neepooch Grasshopper, the only sons of her two daughters. Old Peeats knew that the cause of the feud was Neepooch Grasshopper, who despite the warning of the man Haskel, had been raiding from the mormonee people until he could no longer find anything to steal. Therefore he had turned to preying upon his own people, beginning, tragically, with his cousin. As Paddy had been recently left fatherless, Neepooch had taken him for easy prey, and was now paying the price.

Paddy was by nature a lot like his grandmother, a great soul who honored the words of *Shin-op* as he understood them. Fearless without boasting, he wanted to treat everyone right and live in peace. Generously he had forgiven his cousin the first time he had stolen from him, and the second also. But when Neepooch had stolen Paddy's horses the third time, and had spurned all efforts at peace by striking him and leaving him for dead, Paddy had taken his father's old triggerless gun and declared war to the death!

Up and down the country the two cousins had hunted each other with rising wrath, old Peeats and her daughters fretting in high anxiety over which would be first to find the other. Peeats, of course, favored Paddy, for Neepooch Grasshopper was surly and cruel, and would cast her aside as quickly as he would his cousin if ever the need should arise.

In his rising fury, Paddy had sworn that he would never stop until he had killed Neepooch, and likewise Neepooch had sworn that he would go until he had slain Paddy. So in every direction across the land the two cousins had hunted each other, Neepooch after Paddy and then Paddy after Neepooch, all the way from Peter's Point on the north to beyond the big river to Moencopi on the south, and from Lake Pahgarit on the west to McElmo's Wash and Mitchell's infamous trading post on the east.

Now in the midst of his own desperate search, Posey had chanced upon the camp of old Peeats and her daughter, Paddy's mother. It was hidden in the greasewood in a fork of Spring Canyon where Paddy could stop for supplies or a fresh horse without exposing himself, and was along the way to Tank Bench, where Posey had been heading.

"I will help you, son of Chee-poots," the old woman croaked in her squeaky voice, "if you will take a fresh pony to the one they call Paddy."

"Why should I waste my time with that?" Posey was still sounding arrogant. "I have more important things to do, and you know it."

The old woman cackled at the response, exposing her almost toothless gums. "You will wish to take him a fresh horse because my grandson Paddy has seen the maiden who is called Too-rah!" she declared gleefully. "He told us this, the last time he came to our camp. He did not tell us the place where he had seen her, but perhaps he will tell you—if he thinks you are his friend."

His heart hammering with the wondrous possibility of getting a proper clue, Posey eagerly took in his hand the rope of a fine young pony. With fierce set of jaw and new determination he then left the old woman in the greasewood and rode away, fearful not alone now for Too-rah, but that Neepooch Grasshopper might find Paddy before he did, and take from Posey his once-in-a-lifetime chance of finding out what he wanted most of all things to know!

Where in this broad, wide land, he found himself wondering for the thousandth time, had the evil grizzly secreted his doe-eyed baby sister? And how in the world could Posey hope to track her down?

Brushy Basin

Come a runnin' all yo' cowboys
An' listen to my tale,

And I'll tell you of some trouble
On the old Chis'um Trail.
Hippi ya, hippi yi, hippi ya!

With the sun low behind him and his Betsy horse's nose headed toward camp, and with a gather that already numbered more than a hundred and fifty cows drifting slowly toward the Verdure, Curly was feeling good. Though by choice he and his mare had been working practically alone, still they had performed miracles in that Brushy Basin country. Yes, sir, another day, or maybe a day and a half, and it would be cleaned out entire! Even better, Curly knew that he and his exhausted little mare had impressed Billy Foreman. Even if the little man turned out to be the most seasoned cowhand in the country, he had to be impressed. And that, by jings, left Curly grinning like a jackass eating cactus! Or singing like a confounded coal-mine canary!

Oh, we rounded up the cattle,
Then we cut out all the bulls,
An' branded all the dogies,
An' throwed 'em with the culls.
Hippi ya, hippi yi, hippi ya!

I dumped my roll of beddin'
Near the old chuck-wagon's tail,
For the outfit was a headin'
Up the old Chis'um Trail.
Hippi ya, hippi yi, hippi ya!

Now all Curly had to do to finish the job, he thought as he finally stopped singing, was to sling a little of what he had always slung best—

"Say, Mister! Where do you keep your hogleg?"

"Excuse me?" Billy Foreman asked dumbly.

"Yer hogleg," Curly drawled. "You know, yer hardware, yer lead-pusher, yer bean-slinger, yer cutter, yer artillery!"

"Ahh," Billy smiled. "You mean my pistol. It's here, in the saddlebag."

"Fat lot of good it'll do you in an emergency, hid away in a dadgummed saddlebag. Can I take a look at it?"

"Of course." Reaching behind him, Billy pulled the rusty old weapon out and handed it to Curly. He was surprised by the request, of course, for Curly had shown no interest in anything about him since Monday when he'd noticed the spavines on old Fudge and then put together their makeshift packsaddle for the colt. Of course since then the lanky cowboy had been busier, as he might have put it, than a little dog in tall oats, so that might have been part of it. And he'd been doing a yeoman's job, too. In fact Billy had never seen a man work harder, and he'd found himself wondering if being a cowpuncher always required such intensity of effort. But that hadn't explained Curly's silences at night, nor his aloof expressions whenever Billy and his "doggone pets"—as Curly was now calling Hurricane and Gopher—had managed to do something right. His only other reaction besides looking aloof, on such occasions, had been to redouble his own efforts, constantly leaving Billy behind in his dust—

"She's in mighty sorry shape."

"It's about how I found it," Billy admitted.

"Well, at least ya got five beans in the wheel, so ya done something right."

"By beans you mean cartridges?"

"Yeah," Curly sneered. "Lead plums. Blue whistlers. Them as is supposed to bed the other feller down permanent, and send him to hell on a shutter."

"I don't hold much with what you fellows call gunplay."

"Izzat so?" Curly said. "Why, that may be, I reckon. But I ain't never seen a purtier shot than the one you put through the withers of that old splayfooted cow. A quarter of an inch either way, back or forth, up or down, and that old runnygade would still be laying where you shot her."

"It was pure luck," Billy admitted humbly.

Curly was smirking. "I reckon it was. How come you ain't never oiled this piece?"

Startled, Billy looked at the pistol in Curly's hand. "Oiled?"

"Yeah, like this'n hyer." And in a fraction of a second Curly had drawn his own pistol, left-handed, from its holster. For a few seconds he twirled the weapon on his forefinger, after which he brought it level as if pointing at some imaginary target. "The sheen on the metal's oil, which I slather on everything but the grips at least onct a week. I do the same with its twin and my Winchester, and then I use 'em as often as I can to keep 'em in practice."

With a slight flip of his wrist Curly handed Billy's sorry-looking revolver back to him, butt first, after which he began twirling his own weapon on his forefinger then passing it back and forth in the air between his hands, pausing occasionally—and always perfectly—to bring it to the level as if he were about to fire.

"This hyer's a gun I've had a long time. It's set on a hair trigger, but that's because I don't pay much attention to it when I'm shootin'. I look at what's going to get hit, and in less time than a feller can blink, it does. This old hogleg's kept me out of the graveyard more'n onct."

"You've been in gunfights, then?"

"Here and there, though to tell the truth I don't much hold with 'em, either. I reckon Ma learned me better. Course, there are times . . . Well, yonder in that gully is where I came on them three yahoos from the Carlisle outfit what was burning their mark on the hips, sides, and shoulders of a bunch of LC cows. That time, though, I used my Winchester, and it done all right."

"Bill Ball told me you didn't kill any of them."

"Didn't need to. Leave that up to the law, is what I always say."

Again the revolver was spinning in Curly's hands, back and forth, and for the first time Billy heard the rapid chirping of a squirrel that their riding had disturbed. It seemed to be thirty or forty feet away, in a clump of scrub oak they were passing, though Billy had seen no sign of movement in the oak whatsoever.

For a second longer the weapon spun on Curly's trigger finger, perhaps two. Then in a heartbeat the weapon was leveled, and a streak of fire and smoke streamed from the muzzle, while the sharp report caused Hurricane to dig four dents in the ground, he jumped that quick. Somehow Billy managed to remain in the saddle, and scant seconds later Gopher was panting before him, the headless body of a squirrel dangling in his jaws.

"Dad-gummed dog!" Curly moaned even while he was mentally exulting in the fine display of shooting he had just shown the little man who was supposed to be his partner. "Never could stand eatin' nothin' what had dog slobber all over it!"

With that he spun his pistol back into its holster, smiled with the satisfaction of a job well done, and spurred his little Betsy horse ahead of Billy and toward camp.

Bluff Fort

"Brothers and sisters," Kumen Jones declared as he stood before the small group of Bluff Saints, "thank you all for taking part in our fast and testimony meeting tonight. It has been an honor for me to meet with you again, and I have been uplifted by your spirits. I only wish I were not leaving on the morrow for Colorado, but for a time we must all live this way, as most of you well know."

"Will any of you men be back next week for Thanksgiving, Kumen?"

Kumen shook his head. "I'm certain some of the brethren will be back, Mary, but I doubt it will be Brother Wood or Brother Adams and his son, or myself. However, we'll all do our best to be home for Christmas!

"Now, there has been a development with the Utes or Pahutes, which Bishop Nielson wishes me to discuss with you. I know we've been hearing rumors about this for more than a year, but this seems to be factual, and so the bishop wanted me to pass it along. When we passed through Escalante a couple of weeks back, we learned that this past September, according to a September 12th copy of the *Ouray Times,* which was handed to us, a good part of the Utes left Colorado and moved into Utah."

"What? But—"

"The article," Kumen declared, at the same time holding up his hand for silence, "reads: Sunday morning the Utes bid adieu to their old hunting grounds and folded their tents, rounded up their dogs, sheep, goats, ponies, and traps, and took up the line of march for their new reservation (in Utah), followed by General McKenzie and his troops. This is an event that has been long and devoutly prayed for by our people. . . . Eastern people can now come to this section in the most perfect security. It throws open to the dominion of white men one of the most fertile and beautiful valleys in all Colorado, a valley that will be to those of us who are so fortunate as to become owners of its broad acres, a happy land of Canaan."

"Do you know the valley they abandoned?"

Kumen nodded. "I do, Jane, and there are actually three of them, though I believe they join together. They are the valleys of the Uncompahgre, Gunnison, and Grand rivers. New communities already forming there are Montrose, Delta, Dallas, and Grand Junction. More importantly, at least for us, is that this group of Utes who moved into Utah is the northern bunch, under Chief Ouray."

"Well, they must not have come here, or we'd have seen them."

Kumen nodded. "That's correct, Jody. They went north of here, up toward where the Green River comes out of what they're calling the Uinta Mountains."

"So we don't have to worry about it?"

"Actually, Eliza Ann, we do. You see, the same political and military forces that drove out the northern Utes, are working feverishly to do the same with the southern band. If they succeed—and President Lyman tells us they have powerful friends in Washington who are in complete agreement with their plan—the southern Utes' destination, which has already been announced to them and most of Colorado, is right here in our own San Juan County!"

"Here!?" several exclaimed at once. "But . . . we can hardly deal with the Indians we have now—"

"We know that."

"So, what do we do?"

"Why, Adelia," Kumen smiled tiredly, "we do as we've always done. We work hard, we pray hard, and we leave these sorts of crises in the hands of the Lord. Bishop Nielson only wanted me to tell you so that you would know what to pray for, each time you gather together."

"What if it turns out the Lord wants them here?"

"Well, some days I think they deserve it."

"Or we do, which is even more discomforting!"

There was general, but subdued, laughter, for most who were in attendance had longed for the day when they might be released from their persistently difficult missions. So far, though, such a release had not been forthcoming.

"Any other questions?" Kumen asked when the laughter and the buzz had abated.

"Will you be taking mail with you in the morning?"

"Of course we will, Lula. Even for your father." Kumen winked at the young girl to let her know he was teasing. "Any of you who have messages or letters or even parcels," he then continued, being more serious, "see that they are here at the meetinghouse by daylight. That's when we hope to get under way.

"Now, any other questions?" Kumen looked around the silent room, nodded, and smiled. "Very well. Before we conclude, I have a little something to say, after which Bishop Nielson wishes to take a few moments.

"There is once in a while a man who appreciates his wife and his mother, but the majority of us just don't know how. I expect we will have to get well on into the next estate before it dawns on us just where the woman's place is in the general scheme of things.

"In addition to the hardships and privations of ordinary pioneer life in a rough, sandy, rocky country with the bare necessities and none of the luxuries of life, long distances from railroads or neighbors of any kind (with the exception of the Indians, many of whom are saucy and mean), you sisters have not only stuck with it but prospered. Frequently us menfolks can get away from these primitive and dreary surroundings, but you sisters are tied down with bonds stronger than the thickest chain. Since coming to this country I have said many times that only once have I been thankful that I was not born a girl, and that has been all the time!"

Kumen waited while the members of the congregation either chuckled or nodded knowingly.

"Now you are up against this determined effort by the influential people of Colorado and elsewhere to give the whole of San Juan County to the Indians. This will act as a hindrance to the development of our country, and you sisters will be the hardest hit, for it will greatly delay the time when more and better conveniences can be furnished you. No one of you can feel like making permanent improvements while the specter of having to pick up and move on again, stares you in the face.

"And now, after naming and describing the foregoing trying conditions, we have the most soul and body testing experience of all to name, which is the bearing and caring for the souls of men. The majority of you are young married women, and all of you believe in being obedient and fulfilling the first great commandment given to our first parents—to multiply and replenish the race. Well, your record fully shows your faith and works along that line. Here again we brethren have to remove our hats, make as graceful a bow as we can, and say, 'All honor to womanhood, all honor to motherhood!' I also say it, in the name of the Lord Jesus Christ. Amen.

"Bishop Nielson, we now turn the time over to you."

"Brudders und sisters," the elderly Jens Nielson said as he pulled himself to his feet with the aid of his cane, "I yust haff to say dat I am pleased vith your spirits, und your villingness to sacrifice. Ya, der iss not a vone off you dat does not haff sticky-tu-ity, und so our mission vill be successful no matter vhat de old devil trows at us.

"Next veek vill be a vonderful celebration, vith dramatic readings und presentations, music from de vard choir, more good food dan ve can shake a stick at, und a dance dat vill last the whole night through. As most off you know, Billy Foreman hass gone to vork for de LC Ranch, in de mountains avay north off here. Dat's important because Bill Ball promised, as part of Billy's pay, to send a mule-load off supplies down here vonce a month. Both Billy and Eliza haff been gracious enough to direct me to disburse dose tings amongst our people as dey are needed. Vell, de first mule-load vas delivered yesterday, und der vill be some tings for dinner next veek dat might yust surprise you."

Tenderly the elderly bishop smiled. "Eliza, ve're beholding to you, und ve tank you sincerely, for ve know dat offer vas made to you und Billy. Bill Ball also hired Dick Butt and George Ipson to build him a line cabin up on de Verdure. He paid dem a hundred and tventy—five dollars—cash money—vich George delivered to me de udder day. Not bad, for a veek's vork. Dose boys vere inspired to go up into that country to cut logs, and it is obvious dat Billy vas inspired in de same vay. In dis manner de Lord iss blessing us all, und vill continue to do so.

"Now, brudders und sisters, I haff a final tought. Vith udders off my family I haff been to de settlements to take part in de ordinances off de holy temple. It vas a long und difficult journey for all off us, particularly de vomenfolk, und took almost two months off our time.

"But brudders und sisters, I feel to prophesy dis night dat it vill not alvays be so! Ya, vone day ven I vas on my vagon seat und praying about de harshness off our journey, de Spirit off de Lord rested upon me und told me dat der vas a day coming in vich der vould be a holy temple raised unto de Lord in dis very country. I do not say vhen, or even precisely vhere, but I say it, brudders und sisters, und you may go to your homes und write it down. Vone day soon, de Lord vill see dat ve haff a temple here in dis San Juan country, so dat ve may all go as often as ve vish, und partake off de sacred ordinances derein.

"Ya, und even de Indians—all dose who vish to do so of all de tribes—vill partake off dose ordinances along vith us. Dat I vas also shown. Den vill ve be one people, und der vill be no more vars and disputations among us!

"Dis I say by de spirit of prophecy und in Jesus' name. Amen."

41

Sunday, November 20, 1881

The Horn

From the quiet look in the eyes of the Pahute known as Paddy, Posey knew that the big chase was finally over. The thieving Neepooch Grasshopper was somewhere lying faceup on the ground with a bullet in his head, another victim of Haskel's powerful curse just as surely as he had been the victim of Paddy's broken gun. Posey knew that, and in the knowing felt again that chill of certain knowledge he was starting to grow accustomed to. More significantly for the young warrior, and he knew this just as well, with Neepooch Grasshopper dead, Paddy had no more need for the fresh mount Posey had been dragging around the country.

It was late afternoon, and the two had chanced upon each other on a rocky and cedar-crested promontory of Bluff Bench that was being called, at least by the powerful mormonee from the fort on the big river, The Horn.

Uncomfortably Posey looked at the other warrior, not much older than himself but seemingly much stronger and more powerful. That Paddy had never shown much affection for him, Posey knew. That he disdained all who stole, from the mormonee or from anyone else, was even more obvious. Therefore, Posey thought timorously, Paddy might just turn out to be friendly.

"*Impo ashanty?*" Paddy demanded when he saw that Posey meant to stop and palaver. "What do you want?"

"I ran into your mother and your grandmother in the greasewood,"

Posey declared with not a little pride in his own goodness, for not once in his travels had he ridden the horse he had been sent to deliver. "They sent this fine pony for you to ride."

"Ungh," Paddy grunted as he took the rope from Posey's hand.

"Posey is no longer a thief," he then declared of himself. "Posey believes the words of the man Haskel. Posey loves *Shin-op; Shin-op* loves Posey. Posey now a heap-good Injun!"

Paddy remained silent, making no comment or offer of payment or reward. Seeing that he was going to have to ask for what he wanted, despite his newfound goodness, Posey went at it in the Pahute way—the long and roundabout way. Speaking slowly, he told of following the crooked trail of Paddy and Neepooch Grasshopper to Marriano Springs and all throughout the reservation and elsewhere. No, he was not spying; he expected never again to speak a word of it to anyone. But there was something very important that Paddy had learned in those same travels, which Posey most desperately wanted to know.

"What is that?" Paddy asked quietly.

"Old Peeats told me you had seen Poke's baby sister, the maiden Too-rah," Posey finally admitted. "I am interested in knowing where she might be found."

"That is a thing I do not know."

Posey was stunned. "But . . . old Peeats told me that you had seen her."

"Well, that was many weeks ago, and that camp was due to move right away."

Posey made the sign of understanding. "Though they may have moved, I would like to know where they were at that time."

Again Paddy grunted. "It will do no good for you to know this thing. The fierce warrior called Hatch, or the one called Bishop or even the one called Tehgre, stands to guard her at all times. As well, she is never out of sight of her older sister, that crone whom many declare to be a witch!"

Involuntarily Posey shuddered, believing every bit of the gossip. "That may be so," he pressed despite his fear, "but I would still like to know where it was that you saw the maiden Too-rah."

"Very well," Paddy agreed, digging his heels into the ribs of his pony as he spoke, and starting away, "but it will do you no good to know. It is perhaps eighty miles from here, maybe a little more, hidden in a clump of cedars near Paiute Springs—near where you and those other fools put that white man under the grass after your wonderful big raid on that other white man's horses this past spring."

Paddy did not even try to hide the disgust in his voice, and Posey noted it and felt an uncomfortable and certainly unusual sense of shame. Nevertheless he had what he had sought for so long—a real clue as to the whereabouts of his beloved Too-rah, and so he put the other from his mind and watched the successful cousin ride away.

Now, he thought grimly, all he had to do was ride the eighty miles to Paiute Springs!

Verdure Creek Line Camp

"To my dearest Eliza and darling Willy, Greetings to you from your husband and father at Verdure Creek. I am seated on a log bench in the snug little cabin built by Dick and George here on Verdure Creek, and I think it will do for the winter much better than the cave where I wintered last year. It is well-chinked with mud and grass, which I know you can appreciate, and the fireplace is small but draws as good as can be expected. The door and window are only stretched hide, but they will do. We are located in a long, narrow valley beneath high stone walls that run west to east, and I believe it will be a little warmer than the surrounding country. Already it has snowed on us two days, but the storms are passed for the moment and the weather is quite warm.

"It is Sunday evening, and we have only just arrived at this place an hour or so ago. Despite that it is the Lord's day we have worked hard since just after three A.M., bringing our gather of cows the remainder of the way out of the Brushy Basin country, so that they are now scattered along the Verdure, eating to their hearts' content. In the past week we have gathered almost a hundred and fifty head—a goodly number according to my partner Curly Bill—and besides we drifted almost twenty head of hip, side, and shoulder cows up over Duckett Ridge and onto what is being called Carlisle Range.

"I am now fast friends with my horse, Hurricane, and little dog, Gopher, and the three of us make a fine team. They are very patient with me, and I think in time they may make a fair cowhand out of me. Interestingly, since the day I first climbed onto his back, Hurricane has never bucked or tried in any way to unseat me. (I have once been thrown, but I will come to that in a moment.) I can only conclude that it is because of the blessing I gave him, for of a cold morning he humps his back something fierce, and four days in a row he has thrown my partner hard. I find this passing strange, not because of the horse but because of Curly, for a week ago he did nothing but scorn me. Now he no longer speaks to me, except in occasional slang monosyllables, but nevertheless he does all in his power to ease my burdens and make my life comfortable, including taking the morning kinks out of Hurricane. It got so bad by Thursday night last, what with him endeavoring to do all the work and leaving me none, that I determined to go my own way thereafter and do what I could to help. So, I have done just that.

"And I must say that chasing cows is the hardest, most dangerous sort of work I have ever attempted. So that you will understand, I will give you a for instance of one day's efforts. Last Friday, while Curly wrangled the horses, I fixed what he calls a 'bait of grub' for breakfast, after which he went one way and I another. I rode down a gulch or arroyo or ravine, I hardly know how to tell the difference, and at length came upon two small bunches of cows. Between the quick feet of Hurricane and the amazing savvy of Gopher I got them together and brought them back up through the thick sand of the gulch—a very hard drive, I assure you—and got them all into a side arroyo near camp where we had put up a makeshift brush fence and corral. I then rode up the gulch and stumbled on three more bunches, totaling about twenty cows. One of them was an old bull renegade that was determined to stop the others, and so for a time he and Hurricane and Gopher had it out. When he was finally toppled and tied down, I sawed off his horns and cut his ears, after which I snubbed his head hard against a thick cedar and rode off, leaving him to be humbled by the pain. Through the week Curly has done the same with half a dozen of the older, more recalcitrant animals, and the tactic seems to work.

"Coming back toward camp one of the calves went crazy, so I somehow got a rope on it following a pretty good run and jerked it down a hill all the way to the bottom, where I sat on it and then marked and cut it. Driving the others was mighty vexing, for they seemed wild as deer and several times two old cows tried to do in both me and Hurricane. But the horse was wise to their ways, and we also got these to the corral.

"By that time Curly was there with a big bunch, and he was already cutting and branding, so I worked at what I think is called flanking calves and working the irons until all the animals had been cut, earmarked, and branded. We then drifted them eastward across Johnson Creek and up onto the mesa toward Recapture, after which we returned to the Basin and went again to our work.

"Trying to recall it all now is like harking back to a bad dream. Some cows I found were bogged near Johnson Creek and I had to get them out, which meant we all had to go into the bog together. You can bet I was a sight to see. Others were alone and wild and mean as can be, and kept us all hopping as they did their best to gore us.

"In another place at the head of a small ravine I had gathered three steers and four cows and then ran into a bunch of hornets. The cattle stamped about and worked their tails back and forth and bellowed like fury, Hurricane kicked and jumped to get shut of them, and I ended up unhurt but seated on the ground. It is the only time I have left Hurricane's back unintentionally. I soon discovered why the animals dislike the hornets, though, for they crawl up into their hair and make much trouble, stinging again and again. I thought their stingers would come out like a bee's after one mighty effort, but they don't, and so the hornets remain armed and ready to attack the next quivering muscle. For some time my gloved hand acted as a swatter for all concerned, and though I was also stung a few times, I am pleased to report that we ridded the countryside of a good many of the pests.

"Then there were the sly and sneaky wild cows, gathered in bunches but using the brush and trees to hide and avoid capture.

None of them desired to go toward our corral, and so it was a terrible chore for Hurricane and Gopher to get them there.

"One bunch of wild ones after another we found. While Hurricane would get me behind them, Gopher would seem to be everywhere, nipping and snarling and grabbing their noses until they were bunched and all moving together. Then he would hold them while Hurricane and I would fly after and bring back another bunch, which we would then endeavor to join with the first. I do not know who taught these two animals of mine what to do, but they expect me to know as much as they do, and the results are sometimes humorous and always exhausting. If my eyes weren't being filled with sand while struggling to tie a cow downed by Hurricane, then I was having my face and clothing ripped from my body by sharp tree limbs while at the same time feeling my spine and neck snapped in a hundred places by the leaps and twists and turns of my noble horse. And always I was hanging onto the saddle horn for dear life as Hurricane matched stride for stride the evasive and dangerous wild ones that comprise a good part of our LC gather. I shudder to think what sort of a cowboy I look to be.

"By dark of that day, I could hardly move I was so tired and sore, but still Curly insisted on cutting, marking, and branding thirty more dogies, his word for calves of whatever size. And again, all he would allow me to do, while he roped, tied, cut, marked, and branded, was to flank and work the irons.

"Meanwhile the weather had warmed that day and become oppressive, and when we finally thought of supper we found our haunch of beef to be full of maggots and flies. Thereafter on the trail our meals consisted of water, flour, and beans, with a great deal of coffee for Curly.

"For some reason the heat that night continued oppressive, very warm and close, and somehow 10,000 bugs, ants, mosquitoes, gnats, and various and assorted other creatures had escaped the frost and snow so that they could gather together and attack me. In spite of the need, you can suppose I did not get much rest.

"All that is one day in the life of your father and husband, a sorry, novice cowpuncher who would a hundred times rather be with you. But please allow me to speak a little more of my partner, Curly Bill Jenkins.

"The man has me very much confused, for while on the one hand he behaves quite rudely, on the other he almost seems to be showing off, trying to impress me. I have pleaded with the Lord to help me understand, and my only impression is that I am somehow a threat to him. Of course that makes no sense, for we are in his element, not mine, and he is wonderful at it. A day or so ago I saw him shoot the head from a squirrel so distant I could not even see it—this with a pistol and without even pausing to take aim. His riding is equally wonderful as he seems to become one with his little mare, and I have never seen a man who is so accurate with throwing a rope, even from the back of a wildly charging horse. Add to that his sheer physical stamina as he goes endless hours without stopping, and the man is absolutely amazing! So why I should be a threat to him, I cannot begin to say.

"I have even wondered if he has somehow got the idea that I am some sort of ringer—something like a fake Billy Foreman—though from my numerous mistakes I can't imagine why he might think such a thing. Still I am trying to be polite, though I have taken a cue from him and now hold my own council most of the time. But when I am not praying for the two of you, I am beseeching the Lord to help me know what to do about Curly.

"In closing, my dears, as I sat aboard Hurricane on a hillside the other day, all three of us catching our breaths after a terrible run after some wild ones that had miraculously left me alive, I gradually became aware of a vast silence that seemed to engulf my whole world. For a time I sat pondering, and then I had the strangest feeling that our dear little Mary Eliza was near. While we never saw her in life, the gentlest breeze made me think of her voice, and I realized how fortunate I was to have her on the other side of the veil so she could come near whenever she wished.

"Since then, it seems as though I see her in everything; in the quietness of the morning, the song of a bird or the flash of its wings, the beauty of a flower that has already gone to seed—well, she seems to be everywhere, and so in a way I have not lost her at all, but she is mine more than ever. When Bill Ball and I left Bluff we rode past the hill where we laid her tiny body. If I were to say this aloud, folks would think I am crazy or at least out of line. But I don't care much to be near her grave. She isn't there, and I know it. Instead she is somehow where we are—you, me, and Willy—and I know she is finding joy in our presence as much as we should be finding it in hers.

"I hope and pray, my dear Eliza, that you are also feeling her presence, and are finally able to find joy in her heavenly exaltation.

"I won't deceive you, though, and say that I don't miss you and Willy, for I do—terribly! When I am alone that pining seems to grow more acute, as it did yesterday when I paused to simply drink in the country. As often happens, some lines began to form in my mind, and I scribbled them down. Eliza and Willy, my dears, I hope they will express to you the things I am feeling while we are absent from one another.

Alone in a solitude vast and still,
My thoughts to a home life fondly turn;
And wish for the time of joy to come,
When ne'er again from my dear ones I'll
roam.
Alone in the mountain's silence, deep,
To my eyes that crave love's answering
glance;
Behold the rocks and lonely hills,
And distant buttes whose gloom enchants.

"To the two of you, my dear ones, and to the heavenly spirit of little Mary Eliza, whom I know is with us and watching over us during this lonely time of our separation, I send my deepest love and bid you fond adieu. You are always in my heart!

"Your affectionate husband and father. Billy Foreman.

"P.S. I will be thinking of you during your Thanksgiving feast and dance, and hope that you will eat some extra bread pudding for me."

Bluff Fort

"Eliza, my dear, what on earth can be the matter?"

Pushing herself up from her bed, Eliza hid her tear-stained face from Eliza Partridge Smith Lyman, who had knocked and then opened the door on her own.

"I . . . I am sorry, Mother Lyman," she sobbed. "I . . . just—"

"My dear girl," the older woman soothed as she sat down on the bed beside Eliza and put her arm tenderly around her quivering body, "whatever is wrong?"

"I . . . I'm just being foolish—"

"You let me decide that, dear. Now talk to me, please."

Blowing her nose, Eliza took a deep breath and then another. "It is so silly! I merely st . . . stopped by to give a little something to Sister Decker and her new baby daughter. But . . . out of nowhere it was . . . like holding my own little Mary Eliza! Only their child wasn't dead, she was alive, and . . . and . . . Oh, Mother Lyman, why did the Lord have to take my baby away from me?"

"Because she didn't need this mortal experience, my dear, and you know it. But that isn't the point, at least not right now. The point is your pain, and it is neither foolish nor silly! You have lost a dear, sweet infant daughter, part of your very being for nine long months, and it is the most natural thing in the world for you to grieve after her."

"But . . . will it never end? I am so happy for the Deckers, but I know they are now feeling terrible after my display of—"

"Yes," Mother Lyman chuckled, "they were worried and told me, so I came to check on you."

"Will . . . will it always be like this when I see a new baby?"

"Perhaps, at least until the Lord gives you another—just as my son Platte promised."

"But . . . that can't be!" Eliza was amazed that Mother Lyman knew of the foolish prophecy. "Look at me! I am well past my childbearing years!"

Again Mother Lyman chuckled. "Yes, and so was Abraham's wife, Sarah. Perhaps like her, you need to exercise a bit more faith."

"I . . . don't believe I have any faith—at least not anymore. This is just too hard, especially with Billy gone, and the terrible pain of her death cuts me through like a knife! It never lets up! I simply can't stop thinking about her, wondering about her, missing her—"

"Yes, I felt much the same when the Prophet Joseph was slain by that mob in Carthage. I didn't think I could live after that, and I didn't think the Church would survive, either one. But God has a way of healing even the worst of wounds, and I know he will soon heal yours."

"I don't know how you can say that. I'm not—"

"Oh, but you are, my dear Eliza! You are always doing for others, giving friendship and whatever else you have to give. Why, the way you love the little girls of this fort, or the way you took in our sweet Hádapa when the rest of us were too fearful—"

"So was I!"

"Of course you were, and yet you reached out anyway, giving of your love and accepting hers, and showing us all that Christ and his Spirit can be in any of us, no matter the color of our skin. For a fact, you remind me of my dear friend, Jane Elizabeth Manning James. Have I ever told you about her?"

Silently Eliza shook her head.

"Well, then, listen carefully. Jane is a woman of African descent who joined the Lord's church in Buffalo, New York. Despite the prejudice and persecution of the times, she made her way to Nauvoo where she and I became acquainted. Even though slavery was still rampant, she was a free woman, and yet she endured terrible things at the hands of white people, many Latter-day Saints included. How ashamed I feel when I hear of such incidents, which no doubt she continues to endure.

"When the Saints came west across the plains, Jane came with us—she, Hark Lay, Oscar Crosby, Green Flake, and others of their race—fine Latter-day Saints and courageous pioneers! Yet all of them continued to struggle with the prejudices that exist in this wicked world, battling daily to overcome hatred and replace it with pure love.

"Then came a winter day when I and my children were literally starving for want of food, and there was none to be found anywhere. Somehow Jane heard of my plight, and though she had but four cups of flour left to feed her own needy family, and though others were constantly turning their backs against her great needs, yet she took half of all she had—two whole cups—and freely gave them to me.

"Somehow we lived on, Jane and I and our families, and there is not a day goes by but what I thank the Lord for sending Christlike individuals like Jane Elizabeth Manning James, to show me the Lord's loving way. Oh, how I pray that she will one day be blessed and honored for the wonderful woman she is!

"My dear Eliza, you are the same. Despite prejudices, despite fears, despite sorrows of the heart that only Christ can comprehend, you have the faith to reach out and love others, and I honor you for that. More importantly, the Lord honors you, for you are truly a woman who spends her life in God's service."

Smiling brightly, Mother Lyman gave Eliza another hard squeeze. "And that, my dear, is how I know that the Lord will yet take away your grief and your sorrow. Then will joy unspeakable be yours, and all of us will be able to rejoice with you just as your heart has longed to rejoice with the Deckers. Am I making myself clear?"

Dabbing at her eyes and once again cleaning her nose, Eliza slowly nodded.

42

Tuesday, November 22, 1881

Verdure Creek Line Camp

"They look good, Curly, mighty good!"

"Yeah, them cows're fat enough, all right. Three years ago down to Texas there weren't enough grass to chink between the ribs of a sand flea. But here? Well, the graze is so thick the rabbits have to climb trees just to see out. I'm telling you, Bill, I ain't never seen range conditions any better."

Curly and Bill Ball were seated their horses on the south rim of the Verdure Creek canyon, gazing down to where Billy Foreman was hazing a small herd eastward toward their winter graze. Bill Ball, who had come to check on both the men and the stock they had been gathering, was already on his way back to the ranch, Billy's letter to Eliza in his saddlebag.

"Prices are good, too," Bill Ball acknowledged. "If things hold up the way I expect, by spring, range cows will be selling at from thirty to thirty-five dollars a head. Curly, that's 300 percent more than old I. W. Lacy paid for the cows we drove in here back in '79!"

"Three hundred percent!?" Curly breathed. "Some folks are gonna get mighty rich."

For a moment the men sat in silence, watching the scene below but thinking other things. Finally Curly tugged down his hat brim and took a deep breath. "Bill, I just got to ask you a question."

"Fire away."

"I'm a'gonna. But doggone it, Bill, I want a straight answer, and no coyoting around the rim!"

"Why, Curly, that does startle me. You know I ain't never misled you in your whole life. Why should I start now?"

"Because this may be different. You just might want to color this thing up redder'n a Navajo blanket. But if I have your word of honor—"

"You have it!"

"All right!" Curly took another deep breath. "Have you and that little feller down there, what gives out his name as Billy Foreman, been a'rawhiding me?"

Surprised, Bill Ball sat for a moment, considering his lanky cowpuncher's strange question and somehow feeling rankled by it. "Why in thunderation would you think that?" he finally asked.

"Why in thunder—Now lookee hyer, Bill! I ain't no greenhorn and you know it. Fact is, I'm older'n you by ten years, and I been setting that much longer on the hurricane deck of a hoss. In my time I been rawhided good, and I've give it out the same! But I ain't never been bamboozled like this time!"

Soberly Bill Ball shook his head. "Curly, have you fallen somewhere and hit your head?"

"What?"

"I know you've been working the kinks out of old Hurricane ever' morning, just for exercise, I reckon. Billy tolt me. So maybe you smacked your head against a rock, or maybe one of them Texas runnygades got your brain cavity with its horn. Whatever, something turrible has sure addled your think-box!"

"I ain't crazy, Bill! Ain't nothing or nobody what's stolen my rudder!"

"Then why in tarnation you knocking around like a blind dog in a meat market?"

"Because I've got it figured that you and that little feller down there have been rawhidin' me, is why!"

Curly was so upset the veins were standing out in his neck, which Bill Ball found amazing. Even more amazing, was that the long, thin cowpuncher was so convinced of his accusations.

"How have we done that?" Bill Ball finally asked, fighting hard just to keep from laughing at the poor man's explosive expression.

"You know doggone good and well how! Billy Foreman ain't no greenhorn the way you tolt me he was, not in any way a'tall! Oh, he gives a good shake at it, acting like he can't ride or shoot, wearing out three hats just to get his campfire a'burnin', and losing enough hide ever' time we head out after a few old cows, to half-sole an elephant.

"Thing is, Bill, the real side of him just keeps on poppin' up, and a feller can't auger against it. Like him shooting that old runnygade cow in the withers and bringing her in. That there's an old-timer's trick and you know it. I seen old Charlie Goodnight do it onct, and he tolt me a man had to have real fur on his brisket to even give it a try! I sure wouldn't! Then there's that outlaw hoss and dawg what no one could even touch until he comes along. But slick as the bark on a willow whistle he got 'em both eating out of his hand. Since then he's fixed an unfixable wagon reach, made us a fair-to-middlin' packsaddle—"

"I saw that, and wondered where it came from."

"I'll just bet you did!" Curly wanted to keep the sarcasm from his voice, but he couldn't hold it back. "He chopped and stacked more wood yesterday than I've chopped in a whole winter, and made it look easy! Then you had ought to seen the way he brung in them cows over to the Basin, pretending he cain't rope and then knocking 'em rolling with his hoss and dawg and then setting on their necks until he could get their feet tied and so on.

"I'm telling you, Bill, I near worked myself into a reserved tread on them golden stairs to heaven whilst we were in the Basin. I put on the goldurndest rodeo show any cowboy has ever put on, liked to killed myself in the process, and that with only one riding hoss to do it. But not onct—and I'm telling this serious—not onct did that little feller ever get out of my shadow! He was always there, acting cool as a skunk in the moonlight but showing more by jings cow-smarts than a yearling calf's mother! I still ain't sure if I ever actual' kept ahead of him!

"So I want to know, Bill, and I want it straight and plain. He ain't no greenhorn, his name more'n likely ain't Billy Foreman, and he probably ain't even no married-off, kid-raising, Bible-thumping Mormon skypilot, neither! So, just exactly who in by howdy, is he?"

"Well, Curly," Bill Ball drawled by way of response, "since you've figured it ever' which way from Tuesday, and since you've painted the particulars in such bold and beautiful strokes, I reckon it's time to come clean."

"I knowed it!" Curly crowed with a satisfied grin.

"You sure-enough did! Contrary to what I may have led you to believe, the true name of that little feller down yonder, is Billy Foreman, though I reckon his ma called him William, back when he was born. Worse, he's an honest-to-gosh, practicin' Mormon, what lives in the Mormon fort down on the San Juan with the rest of them people, and he has one wife named Eliza and a tow-headed little son name of Willy, who is learning to speak Navajo better'n the Injuns. This letter in my saddlebag here, which you could have read on account of Billy didn't have no way of sealing it if you could only read, is addressed to the two of them."

"Bill, if you're a funnin' me—"

"I've told you God's own truth, Curly, and now I'll add a little more to it. Until he and Eliza joined the wagon company that came into this country two years ago, Billy Foreman was a clerk. That's right! A pen-and-ink wielding clerk! First he clerked for Brigham Young up to Salt Lake City, and then he clerked for a co-operative store in a community called, I believe, Cedar City. He can't throw a rope for sour apples, he's still learning to stay aboard a hoss, and I know for a fact that the onliest time he's ever fired a gun in his life, was when he shot that old runnygade cow through the withers.

"On the other hand, that little man is weasel-smart, and what he ain't learned from books, don't hardly need to be knowed. He knows cows and hosses front, back, and sideways on account of he reads about 'em. That's why he's got so many wrinkles on his horns. Besides that, he chopped railroad ties for a living last winter, got the drop on a couple of runnygade Pahutes this past spring and stopped 'em cold without ever firing a shot, surveyed a five-mile-long ditch the Mormons are still digging on, chipped a fine grindstone for his folks out of a handy cliff a few days afore he come up here, and is learning himself to speak Spanish and maybe half a dozen other things besides. Them're the things his wife tolt me whilst she was padding out my belly with some of the best grub this side of forever!

"In short, Curly, despite his size and his spectacles, that little fellow's a real hombre! He just don't look it!"

Stunned, Curly could only stare ahead. "He . . . he really is married?"

"To a woman who's purty as a little red wagon in a flower bed."

"And he has a kid?"

"A fine little boy. Come to think on it, Eliza mentioned they'd had a little girl, too. I think a couple of months ago. But she's passed away."

This news shook the lanky cowboy. "No foolin'? They had a poor little girl what died?"

"That's what she tolt me."

"And you and he ain't bin rawhidin' me?"

"Not even in the least little bit!"

"So little Billy Foreman ain't no gunslick nor bronc buster nor cowpuncher in disguise, either one?"

"No. But he ain't no greenhorn, neither!"

"Then what in thunderation is he? I'm a'tellin' you, Bill, if'n all you say is true, then I've dragged that feller near enough to hell to smell the smoke, and all the time he was so quiet about it you could hear daylight a'comin'. What kind of a feller could have the grit to do that?"

"The kind with real fur on his brisket," Bill Ball replied quietly. "What you and me and the boys have been seeing, Curly, is a man with the gumption to step out and try something new, no matter."

"Yeah, and the brains to make it work."

"If we'd ask Billy about it, though, I've a notion he wouldn't call it gumption or grit or brains, either one. He'd probably call it faith, the same as the rest of them Mormons call it. And more'n likely, Curly, he'd be right."

"Well," Curly drawled as he took off his sombrero and looked at it hard, "I'll be a dad-gummed, slab-sided son of a mountain jackass! Who'd of ever thunk it?"

And with that question left hanging in the clear mountain air, a slap of his hat against his horse's rump, and a wild Comanche yell to move things along a little faster, Curly Bill Jenkins turned away from his boss and spurred his little Betsy horse back down into the narrow valley of the Verdure.

Double Cabins, Northeast of Blue Mountain

When Posey saw the white man through the trees, he did not know how to proceed. He had been doing his best to remain unseen as he had ridden northward toward Paiute Springs, not wanting to advertise his presence lest Poke and the others hear of him and remove Too-rah to another location. Yet he knew this cowpuncher, whose name was King, had seen him, for he had turned aside and was now riding directly toward the lonely Pahute.

For an instant Posey smiled, thinking of how easy it would be to put the white man under the grass. But then just as quickly he cast the thought from his mind. Perhaps King was mormonee! Yes, and perhaps he also spoke words of power! Now that *Shin op* loved him, it would do Posey no good whatsoever to even make an attempt on the white man's life! After all, he needed all the help he could get!

Posey had been on horseback for an entire night and almost the whole of the next day, struggling desperately to get to Paiute Springs before the Norgwinup clan might get it into their heads to move and take their baby sister to another location. He might have ridden the eighty miles from The Horn in less time, but his horse had already been exhausted, and besides, he had needed an additional mount for when he found Too-rah.

Returning to Cottonwood he had picked up two fresh mounts from his younger brother Scotty, saddling one for himself and concealing on the other an additional saddle under a light pack, lest prying eyes discern his purpose. Then he had ridden north, riding furiously through the night and then going more slowly and carefully through the day, avoiding meanwhile the main trails as he continued northward.

Already at a disadvantage because so many days had passed since Paddy had seen Too-rah, Posey was at an additional disadvantage because the Norgwinup clan had dragged no *wickiup* poles that would have left a lasting mark, meaning that it was going to be impossible for him to find any sort of trail. All he could do, therefore, was find more eyewitnesses, and it was that alone that kept him from fleeing the oncoming white cowpuncher.

"Where Pahute camp?" Posey asked as the man drew rein and shook out the makings. "Maybeso find camp heap fast."

"No sabey," King replied indifferently.

"You seeum this camp over here?" Posey asked next, pointing off toward Paiute Springs.

"I saw no smoke."

"How many days ago?" Posey pursued.

King indicated with his fingers that the Pahutes had left perhaps ten days before.

"You seeum go?"

"Over here, me seeum trail." The cowboy pointed toward the Blue Mountain. Then, becoming more interested and ready to speak, he admitted that he had met the camp's occupants.

Posey listened with open mouth. "How many?"

"No sabey, maybeso ten."

"How many squaws?"

"I don't know. One squaw all same here." King then held together his wrists, indicating that one of the squaws had her wrists tied with a rope.

Posey leaned forward with wide eyes. "What's a matter rope?" he questioned, almost lost in the vision inspired by King's words.

"Injun talk, squaw all time run away," the cowpuncher explained. "Talk, five days huntum, rope fixum, no more run away."

His mind whirling, Posey stared past the man King and off into the distance. Too-rah had tried to get away! For five days she had been free! And where had she gone? To the cliff overlooking Cottonwood and the encampment of his father! Too-rah had tried to go to Posey, had tried in the darkness of that last night of freedom to find him. But when she had called out to Posey, her brothers had heard and then found her, and had taken her back. Now the comely baby sister was hobbled like a horse!

With fury and resolution boiling in his veins, Posey forgot all about King and about how easy it might have been for him to put the white man under the grass. Instead he wheeled his tired horse and rode off, his second mount in tow, and even the harsh and callow laughter of the cowpuncher did not trouble him.

Posey was most certainly getting closer—

Bluff Fort

"A Leatherstocking dinner?" Eliza actually chuckled at the thought.

"Why, yes." Annie Lyman was nonplused. "Jody Wood brought all five volumes of James Fenimore Cooper's Leatherstocking novels with her, and I've been reading them ever since. Again and again they speak of the wonderful dinners the hero helps provide for folks on the frontier, and I thought it might be fun to duplicate his menu, at least as well as we can."

"And I agreed with Annie's suggestion," Jane Walton declared as she stepped to the side of Platte Lyman's second wife. "With most of the men gone, we must do something to spice up this Thanksgiving feast!"

A dozen of Bluff's remaining citizens, all female, were gathered at the meetinghouse/schoolhouse for the evening, where they had been practicing the dramatic presentation the rest of Bluff's and Montezuma Creek's citizenry—as well as whomever else might happen by—would see on the afternoon of Thanksgiving. There would also be dramatic readings by several of the young people, a short concert by the Bluff choir, and a dance that would last through the night. And, of course, there would now be a Leatherstocking dinner.

"Very well," Eliza laughed again as she reached down and picked up her sleepy son, "it sounds perfectly wonderful—I think. But I haven't read those novels in years, and I can't remember—"

"Fenimore Cooper's feasts involve all wild meat," Annie declared brightly, "so obviously we'll need to do a bit of substituting. In the fictional feasts they ate venison prepared several different ways; they ate antelope, porcupine, hedgehog, as Pathfinder called it, and beavertail, which he termed 'toothsome.' They also ate grouse and sage hen, fresh trout and salted trout that tasted like mackerel, and of course all the wild garden truck they were able to find."

"In *our* dinner," young Lydia May Lyman Jones picked up, "we'll substitute beef and pork for venison and antelope. But we do have porcupine, we have both fresh and salted fish out of the San Juan, and Adelia suggested that we substitute dog for hedgehog and horse for beaver tail."

"Dog?" two or three echoed in disgust.

"Yes, like the Pahutes eat it. And even horse, if one of ours gets to looking terribly sickly by Thursday."

Now several of the women were shaking their heads and pulling faces.

"I don't think we should bother with those." Newcomer Ann Bayless, who was the sister of Hanson Bayless and who had come in with the bishop's wagon company, could not even imagine eating dog. "But I'll tell you something we can eat. This morning I shot a brace of ducks down by the river, and—"

"*You* shot them?" Mary Jones questioned.

"Why, yes," Ann responded brightly. "I've been shooting game birds for years. Father taught me to do it. Anyway, I'll donate the ducks and see if I can get some more before Thursday. I'd prefer eating them to tackling dog and horse."

"So would I!"

"And me! But Annie, what about the grouse and sage hen you mentioned?"

"I'll go with Ann after the ducks," Harriet Ann Barton declared softly. "Along the way, maybe the two of us can also scare up a few sage hens. They're plentiful in the hills above the river. Besides, Joseph saw a grouse up in Cottonwood a few months ago, so maybe we'll be lucky and see another."

"Harriet Ann," someone asked incredulously, "do you also shoot?"

"Of course I do—when I need to! I can't imagine that any of us doesn't. After all, sisters, it's a hundred miles to the nearest store, and there probably isn't a butcher shop even there. So, what is more reasonable than to assist in the procuring of food for ourselves and our families—at least when the opportunity arises?"

"If you see a fat tom turkey, Harriet Ann, shoot it, too!"

"That's right. We don't have a turkey for our feast!"

"No, but we have plenty of chickens, so I suppose they'll do."

"I suppose. But they aren't nearly as tasty—"

"Is Joseph coming back for the feast?" Harriet Ann was asked in the silence that followed.

"I wish he were, but I don't know. How many of the men are returning?"

"Lem Redd said he thought he'd be back."

"My Charlie will be coming, too," Jane Walton declared.

"He'd better! Without his fiddle, we won't be having much of a dance."

"Who's going to call it?"

"Yes, Eliza, is Billy coming back?"

"I . . . I don't know," Eliza replied as the empty ache of loneliness rose instantly within her. "But I hope he does—"

"So do we!" Lydia May laughed. "Those two men can get me to sashaying something awful!"

"It's awful for us poor older vimen to vatch you, too!"

Kirsten Nielson was funning her, and Lydia May knew it. "Older, smolder," she teased. "I'll never see the day when I can cut the rug like you and Eliza!"

"Cut it, maybe," Eliza smiled as she turned for the door, Willy already asleep in her arms. "But don't ask tired old ladies like us to help rebraid it before morning."

"Or me, either," Jane Walton declared as she opened the door for Eliza. "I'll do a little dancing, I suppose. But please spare me the tireless shenanigans of those Blue Mountain cowboys the little girls have invited!"

"Yes, like Billy Foreman!" someone teased from behind Eliza as she stepped outside. And Eliza, smiling at the thought of Billy acting like a Blue Mountain cowboy, wondered if this night she could keep her loneliness at bay.

43

Wednesday, November 23, 1881

Paiute Springs

The *wickiup* near Paiute Springs, once Posey had crept near enough to see it clearly, was not hidden at all. Rather it was in plain view of the white man's trail across the canyon, and the audacity of such openness stunned Posey more than he could say. Three saddled horses were tied to a tree nearby, and by the sounds coming from inside the *wickiup,* Posey knew that a game of *ducki* was in progress.

He crept nearer. The big lure of those cards, and the values staked on their colors, encircled that *wickiup* full of people with hypnotic fingers, drawing ever more tightly around them. Worse, it was having the same effect upon Posey, and it took every scrap of his will to keep hidden and away from where he could actually see the game.

"You lie!" roared a familiar voice, and after a moment Posey placed it as belonging to one of old Rooster's sons, a man whom he had met on Pine River during the course of his seemingly eternal search for Too-rah. The members of the Rooster clan were famous thieves, and in Posey's presence they had bragged of their many successful forays against the mormonee people on the big river. In fact, they had declared boldly, they were even then making preparations to return for another winter's fine raiding against the womanlike white people of the unfinished fort.

Now Posey was remembering these things, realizing that old Rooster and his sons had been serious. At least one of them had most certainly returned to the San Juan country, and would soon be engaged in robbing the mormonee of whatever he could find to steal. Perhaps, Posey then thought, old Rooster and his other son might also be around—

Seconds later another voice had been identified as belonging to Rooster's second son, and only seconds after that, a third voice grunted in such a way that it might as easily have said, *"Pu-neeh!"* The grizzly Poke was in that lodge with the Rooster boys, and he was also in the game!

In another moment Posey had also identified the rasping voices of Hatch and Bishop, two of Poke's brothers, but though he listened with bated breath and crept even nearer, he could not identify the guttural exclamations of Tehgre. Neither, he finally decided, could he hear the voice of Sanop.

What could that mean? Where were the last two of old Norgwinup's vile sons? And where, most of all, was the lovely maiden for whom he had pined so long? Posey was certain she was not there, for all the squaws were crowded into the doorway of the *wickiup,* their necks craned, their eyes intent upon what was happening inside. But even by looking at only their backs, Posey could see that Too-rah was not among them!

Suddenly Posey understood. Old Rooster was not there. Sanop and Tehgre were not there. However, Too-rah's other three brothers had ridden their ponies in from their hidden camp to join the two Rooster brothers in this game. Therefore, his captive beloved and the others must be somewhere else—possibly close by!

As the game increased in its furious intensity Posey backed away and crept to his jaded ponies. Then, still hampered by the necessity of remaining unseen, he began making a giant circle around the camp, looking for tracks. Bending low toward the ground as he rode, no marks on the ground escaped his keen eyes. Yet nowhere—

Abruptly he stopped. Three sets of pony tracks had come in from the thick cedar country on Peter's Point, off to the north. Hardly daring to imagine that this might at last be the hiding place of his beloved Too-rah, Posey nevertheless made eager haste toward the larger and more dense growth of timber that rose menacingly in the distance.

Peter's Point

Only a little later, a dog barked from somewhere ahead in a thick stand of trees, and Posey pulled his ponies to a scrambling halt. He had come perhaps three miles, and he was still on the trail of those ponies. But now he was faced with a quandary! It was late afternoon, and he was certain this was the camp for which he had been hunting for what had seemed to him, forever! But as the cowpuncher King had told him, Too-rah would be a prisoner, probably bound both hand and foot, and Tehgre and perhaps even Sanop, as well as their evil crone sister, would be on guard. These were fierce fighters, great warriors, and except for his *weitch,* his knife, and an old pistol he had traded for that might not even work, Posey was unarmed. How could he possibly face such enemies?

Of course, since the maiden of his dreams was bound, he reminded himself as he sat his pony irresolute, perhaps Poke's wife and his ugly old crone sister had been considered guard enough. Perhaps Tehgre and Sanop were off on some business of their own, far away, and he would have to face no one but the two squaws!

At all events, the grizzly Poke was not there with his terrible hog string—at least not at the moment. But he would come! With darkness he and his two brothers, and perhaps even the others, would be back at this camp! And the darkness would make escape even more perilous than the daylight!

Hiding his two ponies in the forest, Posey stilled his hammering heart and crept toward the barking dog. In recent weeks he had become an expert at spying on lonely camps, and now he put to use all his considerable skills.

Soon the one dog was joined by a second and then a third, and Posey thought the cacophony of sound would surely advertise his presence. Still he crept forward, his mind resolute! No matter whom he had to face, no matter how many dogs he had to fight, he was going to free his beloved!

This was a tremendous moment—the supreme moment of Posey's young life! For his beloved Too-rah he was facing death itself, and doing it with eager anticipation. Assuring himself of his pistol and his knife on his hip, and finally standing upright, he marched into the small clearing and straight for old grizzly's den.

Three yellow curs met Posey halfway, fighting ferociously to rend him asunder. With kicks and swings of his knife the youthful warrior fought them off, continuing meanwhile toward the doorway of the brush and hide *wickiup*. And there in the rude entrance he came face to face with Poke's squaw, who had been waiting to see what might have been disturbing the dogs.

"*Pu-neeh!*" she screeched in fury and amazement, at the same time urging the yellow curs to greater anger. "*Skunk! Polecat!*"

An instant later Too-rah appeared behind her, trying to come out into the clearing. Without hesitation she ordered the dogs back, at the same time reaching past Poke's squaw with a stick to join Posey in his terrible battle against them. But her hands were tied, and she made poor headway against the snarling and snapping animals.

"*E-iqueay!*" the old squaw shrieked as she grabbed at Too-rah, endeavoring to force her to the ground or back inside. "Die!"

"*Te-we-ne!*" the maiden responded pleadingly as she fixed her eyes on her youthful savior. "Make haste, Posey! *Tooish apane!* Hurry!"

Spurred by the comely one's pleas as well as by the look in her eyes, Posey kicked the dogs right and left. With his knife he stabbed one of the furies in the side and leaped toward the struggling women. Two of the dogs attacked him again and he tripped and fell to the earth, and it was then that he heard the voice of someone calling and coming from a nearby camp that he hadn't even seen.

Somehow on his feet again he stabbed a second dog, twisted past Poke's wife, and in a moment had snatched the maiden Too-rah from her ferocious and determined sister-in-law. Slashing the rope on her wrists he pushed her behind him and turned with bleak countenance to face Poke's wife and whomever else might be coming from that second camp.

"*Tooish apane!*" Too-rah pleaded as she grabbed at Posey's arm and began pulling. "Tehgre! He is coming! So is my sister!"

For an instant Posey paused, letting Too-rah's words sink in. Then he took her soft and willing hand in his own and practically dragged her past the downed dogs, across the clearing, and through the maze of trees and brush, to where he had hidden the two ponies.

Somehow this seemed to the young warrior, perfectly right! Somehow it seemed to be a logical continuation of that wonderful dash he and Too-rah had made together up through that thicket of birch willows on the LaSals when the two of them had escaped the Colorado posse's hail of bullets during the big raid. All his waiting and hoping and hunting had deferred their hope, but now it was intensified a thousandfold and more!

Panting and eager and thrilled to the very fingertips, they reached the two ponies. Quickly boosting Too-rah into the hidden saddle of the one, Posey then sprang onto the back of the other, and in that instant someone came crashing through the brush behind them, a wild war whoop rending the early evening air.

In one jump Posey's newly energized pony struck a lope, and Too-rah's mount, still tethered to Posey's saddle, was drawn behind. Through brush and trees, over rocks and up and down precipitous banks they fled, trying desperately to put distance between themselves and the howling camp behind. Their destination was the mountain of the Elk and the tall timber of its backside, but to get there they still had to pass directly by the camp of the Rooster boys and their big game of *ducki*. Otherwise they would have to create their own trail, and in such a situation as they now faced, that was not a good idea.

"Does Tehgre have a horse?" Posey shouted.

"No," Too-rah replied breathlessly, "but he will get one soon enough! Then he will warn Poke, and they will all be after us!"

Down a juniper-filled swale Posey went, looking for a way off the rim and down into Peter's Canyon. But the cliff was too high, too steep, and on toward the Rooster boys' camp they were forced to go.

Suddenly they were greeted by the sound of gunfire, exploding very close! Instinctively ducking and pulling their ponies in another direction, the fleeing young couple next heard, through the jumble of trees, the pounding of many hooves—approaching them!

Whipping out his old pistol and holding it at the ready, Posey and Too-rah drew rein and sat toe-to-toe on their quivering and steam-blowing ponies, hoping their stillness would hide their presence. On came the pounding hooves, through dry limbs, over brush and rocks, the murderous *whack* of whip and quirt mingled with panting and grunting of horses straining to the utmost point of exertion.

There was no way for Posey and Too-rah to remain unseen, no way for them to avoid the next barrage of bullets. On the one side of them was the fifty-foot drop into Peter's Canyon, on the other the enemy camp of the two Rooster boys. And Posey and his beloved Too-rah were caught in the middle!

"Be ready!" the comely maiden hissed as she grabbed Posey's knife from his belt and held it before her, ready for use. And then together the two of them held their ponies still and waiting—

Bluff Fort

"Hádapa?" Eliza, who was just preparing to go find little Willy, could hardly imagine that the beaming Navajo woman had come all the way through the fort without being noticed or sung out about. But apparently she had, for she was standing at her door, a small burro waiting patiently behind her.

"My goodness, girl, come in out of the cold!"

Willingly the young woman stepped inside, and Eliza closed the door.

"What that?" she asked in her amazingly improved English as she pointed with her finger.

"That, Hádapa, is a stove."

"Stove?"

"That's right. It has fire inside it, for cooking, and now our home stays warm much longer."

"*Hogan* warm. Hádapa build new *hogan*. Ver' warm."

Gently Eliza pushed the Navajo woman into her rocker. Then she turned and took a seat on the bed. "You have a new *hogan?*" she then questioned. "Why, that is wonderful! Is it closer to the fort? Is it nearby?"

"No, not nearby. Ver' far, two day."

Stunned, Eliza felt almost as if she were about to burst into tears. She loved this woman, dearly, and now it seemed like she was also losing her—

"I'm sorry, Hádapa. We will miss you—all of us!"

"Hádapa miss 'Asdzáán nééz—" Abruptly the woman stopped, then smiled. "Hádapa mean 'Liza; many days Hádapa miss 'Liza, miss Billy! Hádapa love 'Liza, love Billy! Hádapa love all mormonee. All mormonee love Hádapa. Most, though, Hádapa love Haskéts 'oósi, small Slender Warrior." The woman's smile vanished as she glanced toward Willy's sleeping pallet. "Is small Willy child . . . is he—"

"Willy is just fine! In fact he is right now with Brother Haskel, no doubt learning more Navajo and making a big pest of himself in the bargain. But, my goodness, dear. Where have you learned to speak English so well?"

"Husband speak mormonee tongue ver' well, teach Hádapa fast."

Eliza nodded. "That's right. Frank does speak English—"

"Husband not Frank," Hádapa said forcefully as she interrupted Eliza.

"I . . . I mean Natanii nééz—"

"Not Natanii nééz! He mean, ver' mean. No get better, no get kind. Hit Hádapa, hit ver' hard, Hádapa leave. Hádapa go ver' far, build new *hogan,* find new husband. Now Hádapa happy!"

"You . . . you've remarried?" Once again Eliza felt stunned.

Without thinking Hádapa made the sign for yes. And there was such happiness in her face, such peace, that Eliza could hardly contain herself. "Who is he, my dear? And how did you find him? I want to know everything about it!"

"He called Hashké yitaayá," Hádapa replied almost shyly. "It mean, He Walked among the Warriors."

"Hashké yitaayá," Eliza repeated carefully. "That sounds nice. Oh, Hádapa, I do hope he is a good man for you! You so deserve a good man!"

"Hashké yitaayá is good man, 'Liza; ver' good! Ver' strong!" Rising to her feet the young Navajo woman then turned her side to the wondering Eliza, after which she pressed her clothing tightly against her bulging abdomen, which until that moment had been perfectly hidden. “See, ’Liza? Already he bring small one to Hádapa. Fill empty womb. Hashké yitaayá ver’ strong, ver’ strong indeed! Now Hádapa ver’ happy!”

With a squeal of joy Eliza rose and threw her arms around her beaming friend, and then her pent-up tears finally came.

Camp of the Rooster Boys

Through the trees came Poke and Bishop, riding as if from the very devil himself. But they were strangely silent, and they rode with their eyes cast behind them even more than they rode looking ahead. More strange, they were not riding straight for the two runaways, but at an angle that would take them past, with at least thirty feet to spare. And most strange of all, not once did either man—the grizzly or his gravel-voiced brother—look in Posey’s and Too-rah’s direction.

Quietly the two hunched down over their horses’ necks, muscles tensed and waiting, determined to sell their lives dearly for the freedom and togetherness they both craved. But without so much as a pause, the two fearsome warriors crashed on into the cedar and pinion forest, and in moments all that remained of their passing was a rapidly dissipating cloud of dust.

In wonder Posey urged his pony forward along the back trail of the two men, Too-rah silently following, and shortly they came to the *wickiup,* which only moments before had housed the wild and ferocious game of *ducki*.

Slowly the young couple drew rein, their eyes wide with surprise and fear. Before them on the ground, his body sprawled in gory death, lay one of the two sons of Old Man Rooster. A few yards away lay the body of his brother, and sprawled in the doorway of the *wickiup* was the fearsome Pahute called Hatch, Poke’s eldest brother. All had been shot to death, and all had died as climax to the supposedly innocent game of *ducki*.

The squaws had already begun their death wails, and it took the two young runaways only a moment or so to discover the tragic tale. In a burst of anger over Poke and the other sons of old Norgwinup cheating at their infamous game, the participants had boiled out of the *wickiup* and into the clearing. There the two Rooster boys had summarily emptied their pistols, shooting and killing Hatch. Without fanfare Poke and Bishop had then slain the Rooster brothers in another hail of bullets—only to remember, apparently, that old Rooster and others of his clan were encamped nearby.

Filled with sudden and terrible fear for their own lives, the remaining sons of old Norgwinup had then fled, and it was that same headlong escape that had boiled itself through the rocks and trees near where Posey and Too-rah had crouched waiting on their ponies. Likewise had the fierce shooting they had heard only a moment or so before, been directed at others and not at them.

With somber faces Posey and Too-rah turned from the camp of death, each of them knowing that once again the powerful words spoken by the man Haskel had been fulfilled. Thankfully they themselves were not guilty of stealing mormonee horses, mormonee cattle. Thankfully they themselves were friends of the great *Shin-op,* and he was friend to them! Thankfully the words of old Haskel were for them and not against them!

A little later, when the runaways somehow found a place to get off the rim and down into Peter's Canyon, they were further convinced of *Shin-op's* love and took the new trail eagerly. Straight for the tall timber they then fled, knowing that the pine needles and tall grass of the mountaintop, even though it was cold and covered with snow, would soon hide the way of their passing. And knowing, too, that the great *Shin-op* was truly guiding their way.

Though it would be winter on the Elk Mountain, Posey felt, there were deep, warm canyons beyond the Bear's Ears, Woodenshoe Butte, and Deer Flat. There the two who were already thinking as one, could hide in great and wonderful comfort as well as security. And immediately before them and the friendly mountain for which they now rode, lay blessed freedom—that, and the sheltering, beckoning arm of night.

Wagh!

44

Thursday, November 24, 1881

The Foothills East of South Peak, Blue Mountains

"You see that spot of color yonder?" Curly asked as he pointed off down a wide swale. "That's a tom gobbler down there, chawing on them acorns under the snow. Betcha he come here looking for hens and got sidetracked."

Doing his best to see where Curly was pointing, Billy could see nothing that resembled a wild turkey. Despite that it had snowed again the day before, depositing several inches and turning the higher country icy white, Billy could see no spot of color splashed against it. Even with his spectacles on, he was beginning to understand that his vision was nowhere near that of the lanky cowboy.

Suddenly Curly reached up and pulled his hat down tightly on his forehead. "He's out of range of my hogleg, I reckon, so set tight, because I'm a'going after him!"

"But . . . we just butchered a whole beef."

"Yeah, but this is Thanksgiving!" Curly growled, and with a slash of his spurs sent his little Betsy horse down through the oak. In wonder Billy followed, his mind trying to understand his strange partner.

Early that morning they had butchered a small steer, which Curly had downed with one shot to the head. It took quite a knack to butcher a beef on the ground, but with a minimum of words Curly had directed the labor as the animal was roped and rolled onto its side, gutted and skinned, and then quartered with an ax. Keeping only the hind quarters and the ribs from the front quarters they had carried the beef to the cabin where they had wrapped it in a tarp and hung it to cool. The hide they had then salted, rolling it as tightly as they could and then tying it to one of the shed rafters. Later it would be scraped and tanned, but not until after the gathering of LC cattle from near the Carlisle spread had been completed.

Now they were middling high in the foothills to the east of South Peak, in country where grew both pine and oak, and in half a day they had made a good gather of forty-seven head including nearly two dozen calves, which they had also cut, marked, and branded. They had been hard after two more bunches, sly old runnygades and their offspring who were being given up by the snow, when Curly had spotted the wild turkey.

With a gentle nudge Billy let Hurricane know he wished him to follow his tall, thin partner, and so willingly the big horse started down the hill. Without a sound Gopher also followed, ranging far out to the side as well as back and forth as he made his way down through the thick clumps of leafless oak and brush.

Still both confused and bemused by the cowpuncher ahead of him, Billy was discovering that he thoroughly liked the man. While in certain respects he was absolutely impossible to understand, in others he reminded Billy a great deal of both Dick Butt and George Ipson. Both bachelors, in many respects they were like overgrown boys, full of noise and fun. Curly Bill Jenkins was the same, whooping it up over one thing or another whenever he was happy, and acting surly and getting his feelings hurt over nothing at all when he wasn't.

Of course he was a real man and a top hand, no matter. And no one had ever better accuse him of being a kid! But there were definitely times, such as right then, when Curly acted more adolescent than adult, and when Billy could do nothing but follow after and see about picking up the pieces.

Curly had reached the bottom of the swale and had just started up the far slope when Billy finally saw the turkey. It was a huge bird, and it was now fleeing in alarm, its long legs churning and its wings slightly open and dragging as it fled ahead of Curly's little mare.

"Wahooo!" Curly yelled joyfully as he bent low over his saddle horn, his heels urging his little Betsy horse forward. "You see this hyer turkey now, Mister? The way he's working them legs of his, ain't slow!"

Abruptly caught up in the chase, Hurricane leaped the bottom of the swale and pounded up the far side, inching his rider ever nearer to the low-riding Curly. And meanwhile the big old tom was almost keeping the same pace, his own rapid strides as long as the mare's jumps.

Amazed that the wild gobbler didn't fly, Billy was just wondering why Curly hadn't drawn and fired his pistol, when the bird abruptly took to the air. Lifting her head, little Betsy looked as if she wanted to fly, too, and Billy almost laughed it seemed so comical. Instead, however, she responded to more of Curly's wild yells and hat swings and somehow managed to stay mostly beneath the wildly flapping bird.

For half a mile the bird stayed in the air until, exhausted, it dropped back to earth where it landed running. "Yipiii ti yea!" Curly exulted as his mare again began to crowd the big bird. "Kii yii yii!" Undaunted by Curly's wild yells, the turkey wasn't through, not by a long shot. With the lanky cowboy on its tail feathers, Gopher not far behind, and Billy not far behind that, the huge bird seemed to be pumping its legs faster than ever. Billy was amazed at how much ground it could cover, how fast it could run when pressed.

Abruptly it launched itself into the air again, and once more Curly kept his little mare practically under it. Still, it didn't take much, for Betsy had that turkey in view and was treating it just as she would a fleeing calf. She knew her job, and she wasn't about to let a little thing like fifteen or twenty feet of air keep her from it.

Again the old tom lit running, this time after only a quarter of a mile, and Billy thought that the bird must surely be tiring. Hurricane's breathing was heavy, so was the mare's, and flecks of foam were already flying from both animals' mouths. But the tom was still running in fine form, and so across the hills and swales, in a great circle toward lower country, the two cowpunchers were led.

Now no longer shouting but riding silently, Curly had settled into the serious business of riding the huge bird into the ground. The patient Gopher was doing the same, and Billy had also forgotten his other tasks, the fleeing gobbler being his and Hurricane's sole objective. And time after time, it took to the air, beating its ponderous wings for a quarter of a mile before landing on the run and covering another quarter of a mile in that way. It was an amazing sight, an amazing experience. Both horses were flecked with foam and Gopher's tongue was hanging far out, and Billy found himself wondering how many miles they had covered and how long it would take them to get back to their drifting gather. He was also amazed by the number of cows they stirred up as they pounded past—cows he knew that he and Curly were going to have to come back for, before the winter had set in for good—

"There!" Curly shouted from a hundred feet ahead, bringing Billy's mind back to the chase, "yer mouth's open, ya dad-gummed bird! You might be faster'n chain lightning with a link snapped, but I got ya now!"

Shortly the gobbler was on the ground and running again, but now its wings were spread wide and its strides were much shorter. Worse, it was being harried by little Gopher, who had finally caught up to the actual chase. Now dodging rather than merely fleeing, the huge bird actually ducked between the moving legs of Curly's mare, endeavoring to escape this newest sort of danger.

"Call off yer dawg!" Curly yelped as he whipped out his pistol and held it pointed upward.

"Gopher!" Billy yelled instantly, after which he whistled shrilly, bringing the little terrier to an abrupt stop.

For the next few seconds Curly and his little Betsy mare whirled about, trying to extricate themselves from the still-dodging bird. Then in a flash, the .44 belched fire and smoke, and by the time Billy had pulled rein in the bottom of the ravine where the chase had ended, the headless bird was making its last fluttering kicks in the snow.

"You know how to clean a bird?" Curly asked as he whirled his pistol back into its holster.

"I've cleaned 'em," Billy drawled, intentionally making himself sound like the lanky cowpuncher.

"Then git down and clean another, why don'tcha, whilst I see if I can get our bearings."

Shortly Billy was handing the eviscerated bird, legs first, to the grinning cowboy. Deftly he tied the huge turkey to his saddle, after which he watched as Billy cleaned his hands in the snow and crawled back onto Hurricane.

"Doggone fool bird," Curly then grumbled as he nudged his horse into motion. "Led us back practically to where we started, which was right thoughtful of 'im, if stupid. Still, I reckon his meat'll be so tough we'll have to sharpen out knives just to cut the gravy!"

And with another wild yelp of triumph, he pushed his little Betsy horse into a good hard lope.

Verdure Creek Line Camp

It was the quiet time of late afternoon, just before sunset, the gather they had made that day was on its bed ground, and Curly Bill Jenkins was seated across the fire from Billy Foreman, slowly pulling the feathers from the big tom turkey so it could be set to roasting through the night. The line cabin was behind them a few yards, but the fireplace was too small for the huge turkey, and so they had opted to eat outside. And each of the two men, not by accident, were enjoying the solitude in silence.

"Howdy, boys!" a voice shouted from the willows maybe a quarter of a mile off, bringing Curly to his feet in a hurry. "Smells like supper!"

The man wasn't much closer but was coming right along, and without hardly even moving, Curly snaked his rifle into his hand. "You recognize the voice?" he asked Billy quietly.

Having dropped the spoon he'd been using to stir their supper of beans, Billy shook his head. "I don't," he replied as the man hove into sight.

"Me, neither. Maybe he's with that Carlisle bunch and maybe he ain't. But I'll tell you this much. That gent's hoss must've died about a year ago and is being dragged along under him just fer general principles. Just take a look! That there's the most scrawny, ewe-necked crowbait a body ever did see. Same with that sorry-looking mule he's dragging behint. Not alone is it packing about three times its own weight, but that mule has the meanest look in its eyes I ever did see. Mister, you stay shy of the hooves of that critter, you hear?"

"I hear," was all Billy said. But suddenly he was sniffing the air. "You notice anything else peculiar?"

The breeze was blowing from the man's direction, and an instant later Curly Bill grimaced. "As ever! That old boy, whoever he is, ain't had a bath in a month of Sundays—or maybe a year of 'em. He smells stronger'n a wolf den in the morning, which is somewhat whiffy. I don't know about you, but I'm standing clearer of that feller than I am his sharp-hooved mule!"

"Howdy, boys," the man said as his cayuse plodded up and he heaved himself down from what must have once been a saddle. "What's up?"

Curly Bill cast his eyes heavenward, but not much had changed since the last time he'd looked. Same skyline, same smoke and sparks from the fire, same blue that he knew would soon be darkening and breaking out in stars. It wasn't much, he thought, with which to open up a sociable and enlightening conversation. "Not a whole lot that's new," he drawled, still with no inkling of the trouble he and Billy Foreman were soon to be facing from this man who gave every appearance of being a prospector.

"That's a fine-looking turkey," the man observed.

"Yep."

"Figurin' on cooking it tonight?"

"Yep."

"Over a fire it'll take most of the night."

"Yep."

"That's why yer also cooking them beans."

"Reckon so."

"Well, you fellers got any extry? Beans, I mean?"

"I reckon we do, if'n you don't mind the aftereffects." Curly said this without hope, for even on his upwind side the man was odoriferous, and Curly suspected he wouldn't be minding any such problem at all. What was also becoming worrisome to the lanky cowpuncher, was whether or not the man would light and set and decide to take up permanent residence, which would force him and Billy Foreman to go live somewhere in a cave.

"Good beans," the prospector said by way of being sociable once Billy had dished him a plate and then stepped quickly back. "Yep. Good beans. A man can go a long way on a meal like this."

"He's right," Curly Bill said to no one in particular. "Far, and a whole lot faster, too. Beans do seem to push a feller along."

The stranger, ignoring Curly's remark, continued lining his flue like he was stoking up for a long, hard winter.

"Cows around here?" he asked as he finally emptied the plate, dropped it, and picked up the pot.

"Some," Billy answered, knowing that cattle were everywhere around them, most in plain view; and knowing too that his partner was suddenly wondering what the two of them would now be eating. Curly did like to eat, beans were his favorite, and Bill Ball had not sent a whole lot else with their provisions.

"Good grass, I reckon," the prospector said around another mouthful of grub.

"Somewhat." Billy was also growing worried about their supper.

"Surprised you boys is still here," the man said as he wiped the pot with the last shreds of Curly Bill's sourdough bread, which he had also been chowing down on. "Surprised, for a fact."

Curly eyed the man like he'd lost something. "Mister," he then growled, "you're a chuckle-headed, rattle-brained, flannel-mouthed idjit! Just where in thunderation else would we be?"

"Good beans," the man replied as he dropped the now-empty pot, wiped his mouth on his filthy sleeve, stretched, scratched himself a little, and then hoisted himself back aboard the hair-covered bone yard that he called a horse. "Yep. Good beans and bread. Reckon I owe ya."

"Somewheres else we had ought to be?" Curly asked again, trying not to sound riled. "Somewheres other than here, I mean?"

But the prospector had said his piece, had left his stench and a couple of empty pots, and was moving off. Billy was feeling grateful for small favors, but not Curly. Usually smart as a bunkhouse rat and, at least of late, talkative as a dead tree, he chose that moment to turn foolish and wax even more loquacious.

"Mister," Curly called out, "I asked you a question. You et our beans, you et our bread, you fouled our camp with your powerful scent, and for payment I want an answer. I don't want no oratory. I don't need no verboose and extravagant reply. But by jings I do want an answer, and I want it now! Savvy?"

Slowly the prospector turned around in his saddle, belched, and looked hard at Curly Bill. "Somewhat touchy, ain't ya?" he asked.

"Somewhat."

"Dangerous maybe, too?"

"Maybe," Curly replied. "Now, about that other place you think maybe we had ought to be?"

The prospector grumbled, twisted a little more, reached deep into his hip pocket, and pulled out a folded paper. "Don't know what's happened to common hospitality," he growled. "Here. You read it. I'm headin' for the high lonesome where a body feels welcome. And don't feel too bad about missing them beans and bread. They wasn't as good as I said."

He belched again, tossed the paper on the ground, Curly Bill launched himself in the prospector's general direction, and the mean-eyed mule, the one that Curly had forgotten about entirely, of a sudden lashed out with both hind hooves and gave it to him solid, right in the breadbasket.

Curly groaned and went down, the prospector cackled as he leveled his carbine at the stunned Billy, and then with another belch he was off into the willows up the creek, still laughing.

"Happy Thanksgiving!" he called out a moment later, and then he laughed even harder, his cackle finally fading into the distance.

"Shucks," Curly gasped after Billy had dragged him back to the fire and had worked on him for long enough that the sky had grown dark in the meantime, "what happened?"

"Not much," Billy replied as he picked up the paper and held onto it instead of throwing it into the fire, which turned out to be a major mistake. "You got kicked by a jackass is all."

"Oh," Curly replied in a wheezy sort of way. "Thank goodness that's it. For a minute there I was sure I was kicked by a jackass. When did it get dark?"

"While you was looking for your lost breath."

"Oh. What's the paper say?"

"Thanksgiving dance tonight," Billy replied after quickly reading the fine printing on the handwritten invitation. "At the meetinghouse in Bluff. Funny, but I'd forgotten all about it."

"Big doings, huh?"

Billy smiled. "I'll say! Drama, readings, music, more food than a man can imagine, and then a dance. Too bad it's so late. It would've been fun to maybe kick up our heels a little, and I sure am pining to see Eliza and little Willy."

"I got kicked out of one of them dances you Mormons throw," Curly groused. "They wanted me to give up my hogleg."

"Yep," Billy admitted quietly. "Mormons do have a strange idea about wanting their women and children to stay alive and healthy. Just good, clean fun is our dance motto down to Bluff."

"Humph!"

"You'd have sure enjoyed the dance, though, happen you'd have stayed. There're some fine women there in Bluff. Good dancers, too."

For a moment Curly looked away, his mind racing. "Feller onct told me them dances you folks throw, last most of a night." Now he looked at Billy again. "Is that so?"

"Well, at least until morning chore time."

"You think they'll have a turkey for their feast?"

"Not likely, but there're plenty of chickens."

Groaning and holding his ribs, Curly sat up. "Then we're goin'," he said.

"We're what?"

"We're goin'."

"Curly, that's fifty miles if it's a foot!"

"Don't matter. Don't matter if the hosses is tired. Don't matter if the crickets is tired, too, with their tongues hanging out a foot and forty inches. We're going."

"But Curly—"

"You need to see your wife and son, don't you?" the cowpuncher and turkey-chaser asked as he struggled to his feet. "And I ain't bin to a dance with real white women in two years. I ain't getting any younger, either, and a man's got to think of his future."

"What about these cows—the ones we're supposed to be moving onto their winter graze in the morning?"

"Happen there's some purty young gals at that dance, or even some old maids or widows, I had ought to be looking."

"But . . . there aren't—"

"And even if there ain't, a man's got to keep in practice."

"Big day tomorrow right here, Curly."

"First, howsomever, I need me a bath and a shave."

"Bill Ball said we need to move those cattle. We'll need our rest to do it, and so will the horses."

"And I don't have a clean white shirt," Curly continued as if Billy hadn't even been there. "Sure got to have a clean white shirt for them fine Mormon women. What time is it?"

Billy pulled out his pocket watch. "After dark," he replied after a moment's thought. "Too late to be heading for Bluff, that's for certain."

"We'll make it," Curly declared. "We kin cut acrost White Mesa, and I know a few other shortcuts besides." And with that he strode into the cabin, pulled out of his saddlebag his dirty white shirt, grabbed his razor and stropped it on his latigo strap, and headed back outside for the creek.

Billy, having already learned that there were times when his new partner wouldn't move even for a forest fire, sat back to watch.

"What'cha gawkin' at?" Curly snarled as he lathered his face and began scraping.

"You."

"Oh, good. I thought for a minute you was gawkin' at me. Should've knowed better, I reckon."

"I reckon."

Finally shaved, Curly stripped and waded into the icy creek. Shivering, he whooshed and scrubbed and scrubbed and whooshed in the dark of the chilling water, rubbing with an old curry brush until Billy thought he would wear his skin away.

"Cold?" Billy asked sympathetically.

"Yep," Curly responded through chattering teeth.

"You look it."

"You don't have t' watch!"

"Nope."

"Then why don't'cha quit?"

"Because you look cold."

"I had ought to," Curly groaned. "Fact is, I'm colder'n a Montana cowboy caught without boots nor britches in a blue norther."

"You look it."

"Still gawkin', are you?"

Billy grinned. "Yep. Seems like gawking at you is considerable better than joining up."

"You already have you a woman," Curly groused. "You don't need to worry about such things as scent." And with that little below-the-belt punch he splashed from the creek and pulled on his long johns and britches. Then he set to work with that same curry brush on his dirty white shirt.

"Need a light?" Billy asked amiably.

"Nope."

"Powerful dark."

"Yep."

"Awful dirty shirt."

"Yep."

"Might miss something in the dark."

"Might."

"Want me to light the lantern?"

"Nope!" And by the tone of his voice Curly made it known that his decision was final.

Once his shirt was washed, he took an old pair of flannel long johns out of his warbag and with them lifted a hot rock from the side of the fire. Smoothing his wet shirt on a log he then commenced ironing it with his hot rock.

"Man can't meet no women in a wrinkled, dirty shirt," he muttered, sounding somewhat embarrassed by what he was doing. "It ain't fittin'."

"Nope. Reckon it isn't."

"Man shouldn't wear a wet shirt on a night ride, either," Curly continued. "Might lead to consumption."

"Might," Billy agreed, still fighting to keep his expression sober.

"Ma showed me onct how to do this."

"Thoughtful of her."

"Yep."

"In the dark, too?"

"Course not!" Curly snarled this last reply.

"Want me to light that lantern now?"

"Nope."

"Why not?"

"Waste of oil. Don't need it. I done this enough I reckon I can do it just fine in the dark."

"I reckon."

Shortly Curly had his shirt ironed and on, his string tie in place, his vest buttoned and his hair slicked down. Then, smelling of bear-grease and lavender water and feeling more miserable, as he put it, than a razorback hog trying to strop itself on a broken fence post, Curly saddled up, shrugged into his winter coat, and climbed aboard his horse.

"Let's git."

"My hair isn't combed, Curly, and my own clean shirt is still in my saddlebags."

"Slick your mop down quick, then, and get your duds on. I ain't waiting around for no grinnin', retarded, Mormon supposed-to-be cowpoke."

With that he slapped spurs and was gone, and Billy, after hastily looking to his own appearance, saddled his already tired Hurricane horse, whistled for Gopher, and headed out after his strange new partner.

Later he would try and remember that ride to explain it to Eliza, but only bits and pieces would come to his memory, and they were of country so rough it didn't seem passable, and of darkness so thick he hardly ever saw Curly in front of him.

"No moon tonight," he said at one point when he knew Curly was close by.

"Nope."

"Powerful dark for riding."

"Hosses got a sixth sense for this sort of thing."

"You certain?"

"Bet them women'll look purty tonight. 'Sides, I ain't met your Eliza yet. Only fittin' I should meet the wife of the man I'll be winterin' with."

"Man could get killed on a ride like this."

"I should meet yer little boy, too. Me and Willy should be pals. Maybe he'll even want me for his godfather."

"Not if you're killed riding hard and fast in the dark. And how did you come to know their names?"

"Them Mormon women ever marry irreligious cowpokes?" Curly was a master at avoidance, Billy had long before decided.

"Not if they're dead."

"Maybe I should get myself a little spread first—a cabin and two, maybe three hundred cows. I hear women like men what have a little outfit of their own. I reckon it'd be the same with Mormon women."

"Can't work a spread if you're pushing up grass from the underside," Billy argued.

"Hummph!" Curly responded. And except for once when his horse slipped and he let out with a string of pronouns and adjectives and dangling particulars that would have peeled the hide off a dead man's boot, Curly never said another word. His Betsy horse got the message, though, for it turned as cautious as if a scorpion had fallen down its throat and was lodged in its gullet, and stepped along from then on lighter than a flea on a mean dog's nose. Curly was pleased at this, and by the time he was leading Billy across the Bluff Bench toward the fort a few hours later, he was warmed up enough to have removed his winter coat, and felt practically ready to burst forth in song.

"I tell you, Billy," he suddenly declared, surprising his partner by using his true and actual name, "there's nothing like the thought of a purty woman to make a man start to whistle, provided of course he's still young enough to pucker."

With that he did whistle, and he was still whistling moments later when they had dismounted and were passing through the light from the open meetinghouse window, the legs of the tom turkey gripped tightly in his hand. Then Curly stopped dead in his tracks, looking downward. His whistle died on his lips, and he didn't even look through the glass to observe the revelry of the Saints.

"What's up?" Billy asked, feeling puzzled.

"Not much that's new."

"Besides that."

"I knowed it!" Curly Bill sounded upset, and Billy could tell it.

"Good. Knowed . . . I mean, knew what?"

"I knowed it! That's all, I just knowed it. Fine night for a ride," Curly then said, looking around.

"Turns out, it has been."

"Will be again, too. Reckon that little Betsy hoss of mine needs another good blow. Adios, Billy. Give this hyer bird to the folks with my regards. Say howdy to Eliza and little Willy, and try'n get back up yonder tomorrow, or the next day at latest. I'll push them cows down into Montezuma whilst I'm waiting."

Stunned, Billy took the bird and watched as Curly turned and strode back toward where they had tied their horses. "Where're you headed?" he asked as he caught up with his partner's long strides, the turkey dragging behind him.

"Back."

"But, the dance is yonder, Curly, and she's still in full swing."

"Can't go, Billy. Not now."

"Why not?" Billy was surprised at how riled he was getting. "Listen to me, Curly Bill Jenkins! I've come a ways tonight, following you. I've risked my neck a hundred times, I've put on my one and only white shirt, and I'm raring to cut a few shines with my Eliza and get a hug or two from little Willy."

"Yep, you should. But I can't do 'er with you."

Stumped, Billy grabbed the tall man by the arm and spun him around. "Why can't you, you long, tall galoot? Tell me straight out, so I'll understand."

"Yep," Curly said, once again looking downward. "I sure did know it."

"Oh, for the—! Curly, what in thunderation did you know?"

"I knowed all along I should have listened to you," Curly said quietly, his voice sounding stricken. "About the lantern. Bill Ball said you was weasel-smart, and I've knowed it too, just from watching and listening. You're the onliest man I know what uses language so polished a feller could skate on it, with words running no more'n eight to the pound, no matter. Yes, sir, with you being that dad-gummed smart and me a'knowing it, I sure should have let you light off the lantern and give me a little illumination."

Billy said nothing, only waited.

"Look at this here," Curly said as he held out both arms. "A woman likes a man with a clean shirt, and mine ain't. In the dark I washed one sleeve twice, the other not at all. It's still blacker'n a burnt boot, so I reckon I'm going back to finish my laundry. Adios, Billy. I'm gone."

"No you ain . . . aren't," Billy muttered as he grabbed his partner's arm, spinning him around once again.

"I aren't?"

"Nope. We're partners."

"That why you about amputated my right wing the way you jest grabbed me and spun me about?"

Billy grinned. "It is. Now, you look to me about the same size as Bishop Nielson. Wouldn't surprise me if he has two or three extra shirts. I'll go speak to him, and in a few moments I'll introduce you proper to Eliza and little Willy. After that you can cut the rug with those lovely Mormon women all you're of a mind to."

Slowly Curly broke into a wide grin. "You'd do that for me?" he asked, hardly daring to believe.

"This once, I would!" Billy looked serious as he handed the huge old gobbler back to the much taller man. "After all, it isn't my shirt you'll be sweating on and wearing out at that dance yonder, but the bishop's."

Curly guffawed and Billy smiled with him. "All right, pardner," he drawled, for the first time in Billy's memory using that particular word, "let's head on back!" And together the two men, each eager for a different reason, started once again toward the Thanksgiving dance.

PART FOUR

CURLY BILL'S CHRISTMAS

45

Wednesday, December 21, 1881

Verdure Creek Line Cabin

"I'm telling you, Bill, there goes the doggondest pardner this old son has ever had! It's going to be a lonesome few days without him."

"Pardner?" Bill Ball questioned as he stood outside the cabin door with his employee, watching Billy Foreman ride away. "You trying to tell me, Curly, that you ain't any longer interested in my offer of double wages and a free bunk for the winter?"

"Not on your life, I ain't! Besides ever'thin' else Billy's been a'learnin' me by doing his studying out loud, he's been coaching me personal in ciphering and letters. Yes, siree, Bill, that little hombre's got more smarts than a tree-full of owls! He thinks by spring he'll have me reading and doing a few figures besides. Then, by jings, I can keep a tally-book using more than just little marks to count up!"

"How about religion, Curly? He learning you any of that?"

For a moment Curly looked troubled. "Well, we auger it from time to time, if that's what you mean."

"Billy argues his religion?"

Now Curly looked pained, and his reply was more a sigh. "For an actual fact, no. I auger it and stomp around with my dander up, raising a ruckus, whilst Billy just sort of smiles at me and talks it, plain and quiet. And even that ain't hit it square, Bill. It's more like he breathes it, thinks on it ever' doggone minute, even when he's asleep, and sort of acts religious by instinct, not even having to try."

"In other words, he's what the Good Book might call a righteous man, or a man without guile."

Curly looked crosswise at his boss. "Why, I reckon them's fittin' words for it, though I was thinking more along the lines of goodness. Bill, that little feller's got more dad-gummed good in him, just natural-like, mind you, than I'll ever conjure up a'purpose in my whole doggone miserable life! I mean, I never by nature do anything for folks and by nature Billy don't know how not to! What I can't figure out, is if all that goodness has anything to do with the religion them folks practice down at that fort!"

Chuckling at Curly's dilemma, Bill Ball turned and led the way into the snug cabin. Outside the wind was whipping the leafless scrub oak and aspen and drifting the foot of snow that was already on the ground, and as Bill Ball and Curly each poured themselves a steaming cup of coffee, both men knew that a new storm was soon to follow. For a fact they had even talked of accompanying Billy Foreman to the fort, but had decided against it on account of the amazing savvy the horse called Hurricane had demonstrated. If anything or anybody could get Billy Foreman through a storm, it would be that horse. Of course there was also little Gopher and the pack mule loaded with supplies that Billy was leading, both of which had some savvy all their own. Billy was in good hands, so to speak, they felt, and wouldn't need anyone to accompany him.

"He tolt me that you'd give him a week off. Is that so?"

"Sure is." Bill Ball sighed with contentment. "I reckon I can stand a little peace and privacy for that long. Billy know anything about your plans?"

"Nope." Curly tossed a couple of logs onto the fire burning in the fireplace, sat on one of the bunks, and pulled off his wet boots. These he placed on the stone hearth. "Durn feet are cold," he grumbled as he laid back and stuck them toward the fire.

"I was going to say we had a few miles yet to ride," Bill Ball observed as he sat on one of the square-cut logs, being careful not to get mud or water on the Navajo rug the boys had spread over the dirt floor. "Hard to do fer a feller with his boots off, though. What's yer count, Curly, and where about is most of the stock located?"

For a moment Curly lay with his hands under his head, staring at the willow ceiling. "Near as I can figure, Bill, in the month we've bin here, Billy'n me've gathered just under four thousand head. There's probably a hundred head in the basin we couldn't get; runnygades, mostly, and maybe a few more'n that. There are also a few north of here, in the foothills. Maybe between one and two hundred. Most of what we got, though, is down off Dodge Point, either in Dodge Canyon or the Montezuma Creek drainage. Day afore yesterday Billy found the tracks of fifty or sixty head going up Long Canyon, so there may be more in that country, too. We just ain't had time for a good look-see. Does that tally with what the boys have in Recapture and Devil Canyons?"

Stretching his own feet out toward the fire, Bill Ball nodded. "Pretty much. We've got a few hundred head scattered through Bulldog and Bullpup canyons, too, but the numbers work out to near eight thousand head—about what we're supposed to have. Either you or Billy seen any strange hoss tracks?"

"All sorts of 'em, north of here, in Halfway Hollow and acrost Montezuma on West Boulder Point and in Boulder Canyon. One bunch of fellers sat up there on the Verdure Creek rim a'lookin' us over right here, but they never did come down fer coffee. But yeah, Bill, I'd say the Carlisle bunch was here."

"Any sign of rustling?"

"None that I've seed."

"Well, keep your eyes peeled, Curly, just in case. By the by, when Slim was in Fort Lewis doing our chasing for us, he learnt that your three rustlers had been left dancing on the long end of some mighty short ropes."

"They hung 'em?" Curly asked in surprise.

"As ever. Seems they'd been tried and convicted fer murder but had escaped and then joined up with the Carlisles. Least that was the story their *segundo,* a salty young feller name of Latigo Gordon, give out."

"So they actual' died of throat trouble," Curly mused, shaking his head in wonder. "Ain't that somethin'! Do you doubt that Latigo feller's story?"

Bill Ball shook his head. "No reason to. I met Gordon onct, and he seemed purty straight up to me. Leastwise *he's* a cowman, whether his British bosses are or not. Anyhow, the army was happy to see your rustlers brought back in, you kin bet."

"Interesting," Curly breathed. "Makes sense now, why they'd come into this country so early."

"It does. No better place for a man to hide. Have you cut any Indian sign?"

Curly nodded. "Billy and me follered some pony tracks—Pahute, I reckon—that was headed for Dodge Springs. They kilt one cow whilst they was there, but it was old, and they weren't a big bunch and didn't stick around long. Too cold, I reckon. Looked to me like they was headed generally south, toward the river."

Bill Ball nodded his understanding, knowing that the lower elevations toward the San Juan were always warmer and were quite often without snow. "Bob Hott followed a big trail a couple of days back, following the drainages but moving from northwest to southeast acrost Mustang and down into Alkali Canyon. He guessed there might have been thirty Indians in the bunch, maybe a few more, plus a pretty fair herd of horses and goats. No way of telling for sure, but my guess is it's Poke's band, heading for that big old winter campground where Nancy Patterson Canyon empties into Montezuma. That's where Poke's spent the last two winters, I know that. Could be your bunch were headed for the same camp."

"Could be." Curly looked thoughtful. "I just hope Billy doesn't run into 'em. A few of those braves on the scout can be a fearsome thing."

"As ever. 'Course Billy's faced a few of them warriors afore, and it didn't seem to slow him much. I reckon we can ease our minds on that score, too." Now, though, Bill Ball looked a little pained. "As head line rider for the LC, Curly, there's something else you had ought to know. Slim McGrew and the Ptelomy brothers cut the trail of a shod horse yesterday."

"Another of the Carlisle boys?"

"Could be, though the tracks was way south of where Spud's range is. Thing is, that hoss was either wandering or whoever was on him was being almighty careful about mixing up his trail. The boys followed him fer a spell, but it was coming on dark so they had to give it up. As far as they could tell, the tracks finally dropped off

Mustang and kind of wandered down into the head of Horse Canyon."

"Nothin' down there that I know of."

"Me, neither." Bill Ball turned and poured himself another cup of coffee. "They was going back today for another look-see, but I told 'em not to bother. Trouble is, I wasn't thinking about Billy heading home. But his road goes right past the mouth of Horse Canyon."

Curly's expression was bleak. "It also crosses the trail of that big band of Pahutes what Bob Hott found. Bill, I know we cain't neither one of us go chasin' down there to side the little feller, and I know he wouldn't like it if we did! Still, for my peace of mind I got to ask you a question, and I'd appreciate a straight answer the same as you give me last time. The way things always sort of work out for Billy—breaking Hurricane without even one little buck, gentlin' down runnygade cows whilst he's setting on top of 'em and fumbling to tie their legs with his peggin' string—"

"What? He sits on cows after he's roped 'em?"

"He ain't roped none of 'em a'tall, Bill, or so he says. Claims he ain't no good with a rope. Claims ol' Hurricane knocks them cow-critters over for 'im, and then he piles out of his saddle and sets on 'em until he can get 'em tied, their ears nocked, and their horns sawed off."

"He actual' sits on 'em?" Bill Ball seemed thunderstruck.

"I'm tellin' ya, that's it. Then he sort of twists their necks a mite with one of the horns so's he won't get gored, but other than that he just sets on 'em and talks whilst he's tying up their legs. Or sings. I've heard 'im do both."

"And all without a rope, you say?"

"None that I've ever seed."

"So you've actual' seen Billy do this?"

"More'n onct I've hid where he couldn't see me, and watched. I'm telling you, Bill, it's the dad-gumdest thing a feller ever did see! That little dawg of Johnny Molander's grabs aholt of the cow-critter's nose and slows it down, and then that Hurricane hoss sashays up and throws a shoulder into it, and over the critter goes, ever' time! Then quick as scat Billy grabs his saw and piles onto its neck, hooks a leg around one of the horns to twist it good, and then he leans way back and wraps his peggin' string around three of the legs, just like he knows what he's doing. After that he nocks the ears and saws off the horns, and then he puts a rope around the bleeding horn nubs and snubs the critter up to a tree, purty as a picture."

"Such a thing don't hardly sound possible."

Curly chuckled without much mirth. "It don't look no more possible than it sounds. And to hear Billy tell it, he never did it afore in his life until that dawg and hoss showed him how, right there under my nose in Brushy Basin."

Curly took a deep breath. "But that there's the rub, Bill, and it sort of trails around the rim and meanders all the way back to his religion again. What I mean is, I can see how Johnny Molander might have trained the mutt. But how can an outlaw bronc what's never been ridden or trained, either one, have the smarts to go knockin' over wild cow-critters, one after another, and then stand around bein' patient whilst Billy sits on 'em until they're tied up, nocked, and dehorned?"

"I dunno." Bill Ball was staring into the fire, trying to picture in his mind what Curly was describing. "Does he use his rope when he gets his mount of a morning, or don't he?"

"Naw, he just goes out and gives a whistle or a holler, and here his hosses come a'hoppin'."

Again Bill Ball was surprised. "I sort of figured Hurricane for a trick like that, but the other hosses he rides?"

"There's only two—Muffin and Sky Lark—and they do the same. Besides that, I ain't never seed a buck or a crow-hop out of any of 'em, not onct! And I bin a'watchin'. 'Course Billy does walk 'em around a bit afore he mounts, but I can't see what good that does. Anyhow, it's the doggondest, dad-blasted thing I ever saw. But it ain't no stranger'n him setting on wild cows or riding breakneck over steep ledges and through trees and brush so thick you cain't see daylight without his specs but never onct getting spilled out of his saddle. Well, Bill, I bin sort of . . . ah . . . wondering—I mean, I'd sure like to know what you think."

"About what? Go on, man. Spill it!"

"Well, this is sort of embarrassin'. But to tell the truth, I bin sort of wondering if all this amazing activity ain't on account of his Mormon religion."

"Meaning what, exactly?"

Before answering, Curly studied Bill Ball's face carefully, and could see nothing but genuine concern. "What I mean is, with all his natural goodness and such, do you suppose Billy actual' does have a pipeline direct to the Lord God Almighty, and that there are maybe a few hundred honest-to-gosh angels flapping their wings hereabouts, working with him and helping him to stay alive?"

"Why would you think that?" Bill Ball was doing his level best not to grin at his head line rider's cogitations. "I mean, besides that he seems to be performing regular miracles."

"On account of he's always praying, talking to the Lord and sitting there real quiet afterwards, just like he's being talked back to. Oh, he don't know I'm watching, on account of he don't kneel down until he thinks I'm sawing logs fer real. He also prays when he's off alone in the hills, for I've seed him do that, too—actual kneelin' down prayers. Besides which and like I already said, the little feller's so doggone good, always happy and friendly and willing to lend a hand, and he just happens to be hitched to the handsomest and kindest woman this side of creation, with a little boy to match, that it all makes a man set up and wonder. If it's so, Bill, that all of this is on account of his religion, then things'll make a little more sense to me, and I won't worry no more about his safety on that there trail to Bluff."

Bill Ball chuckled and rose to his feet, put down his cup, and shrugged into his coat. "So, you've met Eliza and their little boy?"

"Yep."

"When was that?"

"Thanksgiving night. Billy and me made a fast ride to Bluff with a fresh turkey, I danced up a storm with ever' Mormon woman I could get aholt of, and then we fogged it on back up here the next day. Like I said, it were a fast trip. That Eliza Foreman's a mighty fine-looking woman, if a little poor in flesh, and it ain't too hard to see how she and Billy feel about each other. I just hope the future Mrs. Curly Bill Jenkins will be that adorin' of me. And Willy? By Tophet, Bill, I ain't never seed a brighter-faced boy nor that little kid!

He and his ma are the genuine articles, all right, which is why I'm a'doin' for 'em all what I am. Speaking of which, you brung the stuff I ordered?"

Bill Ball grinned. "Sure as shooting. Slim got it when he was at Fort Lewis, and it's in my right saddlebag. You get that other done?"

"As ever, and except fer trying to get 'er done when Billy weren't around, it wasn't as bad a job as I thought it'd be."

For a moment Curly lay silently, gazing into the fire. "Anyhow," he said as he looked at the LC foreman with strangely haunted eyes, "that's it. On account of maybe a thousand different things, I just couldn't help wondering about Billy."

"Yeah," Bill Ball nodded quietly, "I reckon I understand. Taken all in all, he's purty near too good to be true."

"That's it—exactly!" Curly rolled off the bed and drew on his wet boots. "Thing is, I can't find nothing to make me think he ain't. True, I mean. Oh, he denies that he's anything remarkable, flat out. And I ain't ever caught him doin' anythin' other than what he says he does." Curly grinned sheepishly. "I even made a mark on his throwing rope onct, to see if it'd be coiled up different by nightfall. It weren't."

Curly shook his head at the memory. "Billy claims he ain't worth a pinch of snuff in a high wind when it comes to cowboying or loving his neighbors, either one. But he's a mighty fine hand, you can take my word on that and ride it all the way to the bank. And he's always doin' things for me, Bill, things I'd never even think of doin' for no other man." Curly sighed deeply. "Maybe one of these days . . ."

Abruptly Curly clapped his hat on his head and swung wide the door, showing his readiness for more work. "Now if only that little banty rooster of a pardner of mine kin just get hisself home alive—"

Bluff Fort

"We'll miss you, Jody—you and Nellie both. But you know you'll be in our prayers."

For a moment there was silence. Most of the women and girls in the fort had already said their good-byes to the cheerful young man whose leg had been shattered by the outlaw's bullet almost two months before. Now it was Eliza's turn, and like several of the others, she was finding it difficult to control her emotions. Yes, she would miss both Nellie and Jody, for they were such sweet people. But more, she understood perfectly well the hopelessness of Jody's condition. The femur of his leg, fractured into so many small pieces, was not mending or coming together. Worse, slivers of bone were continually working their way out through the barely healed flesh of Jody's leg, creating fresh sores and leaving the poor man in constant pain. Yet he never complained, and according to Nellie, only groaned and moaned when he was asleep. Otherwise, folks had little way of telling that he was suffering.

"Well, Sister Eliza," Jody replied from his cot as he gave a crooked grin, "I do appreciate that. Tell the truth, I reckon prayer is about all I have going for me right now."

"President Lyman says the doctor over in Denver is a good one."

"So he tells us," Nellie responded quietly.

"He's had some good success with badly broken bones," Jody added to cover for his wife's discouragement. "You just watch, Eliza. I'll be back by spring good as new, ready to start digging on that fool ditch."

Again the silence stretched out. In the rear of the two wagons that Platte had readied for the trip to the railhead in Colorado, had been loaded supplies, a tent, and such other items as would make the journey as comfortable as possible. The front wagon had been stuffed with blankets and pillows, and it would be on these that the wounded Jody Lyman and his wife Nellie would ride. Walter C. Lyman would do the driving and bring the wagons back to the fort once Jody was on the train, and Platte would ride alongside the outfit, doing the scout work.

"Is Mother Lyman accompanying you?"

"Not hardly," Jody grinned. "I'd rather have her worrying here, than worrying and fussing over me there."

"Besides," Nellie added, "she's not really up to the journey, what with that chest cold she's been battling. But you can imagine that she doesn't like the idea of being left behind!"

Eliza chuckled. "I'll just bet she doesn't. If it were Willy who had been shot, I know that I—"

"*Ajáád bita sitání, niheesto!*" Willy suddenly declared from his mother's arms, at the same time pointing down at Jody's bound leg. "*Ajáád bita sitání, niheesto!*"

"Willy, what on earth—"

Jody chuckled. "It's all right, Eliza. He's just reminding me that I have a broken leg. Brother Haskel taught him to say it the other night."

"What he's actually saying," Thales Haskel said as he strode up, "is that your thigh bone has been shattered. And I couldn't say it any better. Come here, Willy, boy, and let's give your mother's arms a rest."

In an instant a beaming Willy had gone to Thales Haskel's arms, and then the old interpreter's look turned sober. "The Lord bless and keep you, Jody. I don't know how much good that doctor will do you, but I do know that you'll be fine."

"I know it, Brother Haskel. Both Platte and the bishop have promised me that in blessings."

"So did Billy, Lem, and Hy Perkins after you had been shot," Nellie reminded him.

"So I understand, though I don't have much memory of those days." Jody looked up at Eliza. "Next time you write to Billy, Eliza, would you please thank him for me? Except for him and the others, not to mention Chief Pahlilly and his men, I'd never have made it! Isn't it something, how much the Lord requires us to lean upon others!"

"Or how difficult it is to do so!" Eliza said.

"That's so," Thales agreed. "But I've come to believe it's all a practice, teaching us to be humble enough to lean on the Lord. After all, his Atonement's a gift, but it'll do no good unless we're each one willing to receive it. Well, young man, adios. I'll be seeing you soon."

"So long, Thales. Keep learning that kid Navajo."

"Do I have a choice?" Thales chuckled, and with that he turned and carried little Willy away.

"I'll give Billy your message," Eliza then replied as she reached down and took Jody's hand. "It's too bad you aren't waiting another day or two, though. Then you could tell him yourself."

"Yeah, Annie told me he was coming home for the big Christmas shindig." Jody grinned again. "Tell him to eat my share of the feast too, will you?"

"I'll do it, Jody. And God be with you—"

Fiddler's Green

The two young warriors sat their ponies without moving, only their eyes probing about. The snow was falling heavily, as it had been for some time, and that should have made their task more simple. Yet so far the two had found nothing, and they were growing weary of the hunt.

The canyon they were in, a large and open meadow on Recapture Creek at the mouth of Ute Canyon that was surrounded by high sandstone walls, had held their encampment only one day before. Now their band had moved down the stream and onto McCraken Mesa to the east—all but the two of them. They had been given other instructions because certain evidences had been seen, and so now they waited.

"*Wagh,*" one breathed as his pony snorted and stomped a hoof, "the snow continues to hide the earth, my brother. That rock ahead in the trail will be nothing but a mound of snow, as will everything else in this country, and all will be hidden."

The other warrior made the sign of agreement but remained silent. Big in his mind was the wrath of he who was called the grizzly. Poke it was who had sent them forth, and it would be Poke to whom they would report when they returned to the encampment. It would not be wise, he was thinking, for the two of them to return having found nothing. Yet the snow was most assuredly growing more deep—

"My brother," the talkative one spoke again, "I do not think the one who is *e-i,* dead, still follows. I have seen no sign of her passing in many days. It is in my mind to say that we have ridden far enough. It is in my mind to tell the grizzly that the woman truly is *e-i* this time, and that he need be concerned no longer."

"All this may be so," the quiet one replied slowly. "Yet if Poke says that the woman who is dead, still breathes and still moves about, then who am I to argue? Then again, perhaps one of the foolish mormonee will come along this trail they have made. I tell you, my brother, that such a kill would be a good thing for all of us."

The talkative brave's eyes brightened. "What you say is true. Yet we do not know that such a one is coming, or even if such a one is out in this storm at all."

"No, we do not know this thing," his companion admitted. "Nevertheless, my brother, it is in my mind to say that we must remain in this place at least a little longer. *Oo-ah,* yes, and we must be very observant. Whether a white man comes this way or not, I am more worried about the woman. I do not know how easy it is to see one who has already taken the long walk to the west, to the land of the sky people."

The talkative warrior sucked in his breath as a worried look appeared on his painted face. "Yes," he breathed, "I had not thought of things quite like that. Is it possible that this one we have been sent to *puck-ki,* to kill a second time, moves about us even now? Is it possible that the woman leaves no trail because it is her spirit that follows us?"

Now it was the quiet one's turn to look worried. "Brother, these are strong thoughts, worthy of consideration. Perhaps we should turn and ride slowly back down this stream, not ceasing our vigil but remaining ever watchful for that troublesome one who perhaps must be slain again."

Anxiously the warrior brought his old rifle up and cocked it. "*Pie-ka,* come. Let us go from this place, but let us go carefully—"

And it was at that moment when the rock in the trail ahead of them—the rock that was now almost wholly covered with snow—decided to move.

Fiddler's Green

The Pahute woman Peeb—she who had been the wife of the warrior called Jonah—could not keep her mind about herself. Though she was no longer cold, it seemed as if she was somehow buried in snow. And though she could not remember her last meal, she no longer felt even the slightest pangs of hunger. And her terrible journey, the one that was taking her from Cottonwood to the big camp at the mouth of Nancy Patterson Canyon, seemed to be stretching on eternally!

Yet her child was still within her womb, kicking feebly, and so the woman Peeb doubted that she had taken that long journey into the land of the sky people. Instead she must still be living, which would mean that she had to hurry to the big camp where the two canyons came together—the camp where someone would show her how to birth and take care of her baby.

Summoning all her strength, then, she pushed herself up from the frozen ground, staggering to her feet. She was not yet at the big camp, she was certain of that. And yet out in front of her, their forms blurry and indistinct, sat two, maybe three, horsemen.

Perhaps these were indeed the sky people, she wondered as she raised a feeble hand in greeting. Perhaps she *had* taken that long journey to the west.

But then Peeb's world was filled with noise, a great and terrible roaring, and for some reason she was back on her face in the snow.

46

Thursday, December 22, 1881

Bluff Fort

"Ma, when's Pa coming home?"

Ignoring the drizzling rain that was falling outside, Eliza looked down at her son. He was sitting on a woven Navajo rug that Bill Ball had sent down for them to put over their canvas floor, pushing one stick across it with another. And Eliza was watching for when the roof would begin to leak so she could roll the rug up and crawl with Willy onto the bed—still the only dry corner in the home.

"Ma, when is he?"

Smiling, Eliza shook her head. "We haven't had a recent letter, Willy, but he promised at Thanksgiving he'd be home before Christmas. That's in three more days, so it should be soon."

It was amazing to Eliza how Willy was starting to speak in whole sentences, and that he was able to understand pretty much all she was saying. Of course sometimes both she and others had a little difficulty understanding him, particularly when he broke into Navajo.

"Ma, is Pa going to dance?"

Eliza laughed. "He might, Willy. If the storms aren't too bad and he gets here in time. Then we'll all go to the Christmas dance together."

"Curly dance?"

Briefly Eliza thought of the tall, lanky cowboy, who had seemed so enamored with little Willy. "If he comes, I suppose he will. But your father told me he was going to ask for a whole week this time, so somebody will have to stay with the cattle. That'll be our friend Curly."

"Curly have Christmas?"

Eliza smiled. "Of course he will."

"Christmas fun. Willy love Christmas. Ain't that right, Ma?"

"*Isn't* that right," Eliza corrected absently as she thought of her son's other words: *Christmas fun. Willy love Christmas*. Oh, mercy! Would things ever get any better for them? For any of the Saints who had been trying to eke out a living on the miserable San Juan?

It wasn't so much not having anything that bothered Eliza. She'd dealt with that in the past and had always come through such trials just fine. But this was different, very different. Not alone did she and the others in the fort have little with which to face Christmas and the long winter months afterward, but few of them felt any real hope that things were ever going to get better. The old river was sure to stay the same grim monster it had always been; the awful ditch would fail several times over the course of the next spring and summer; crops would undoubtedly be sparse and meager, if they grew at all; Indians and outlaws would continue their thievery and cruel threats; perhaps the Utes would be sent in by the government to take over all of San Juan County; and come next fall, Billy and the other menfolk would be forced to leave their families once again, to go begging the Gentiles for work and maybe even a little cash money. It was all so degrading, so terribly oppressive and pointless.

For a moment she glanced at Willy's empty sock, hanging on the wall above and behind the new stove, and large tears started from her eyes. Not alone would it remain mostly empty come Christmas, but by all rights there should have been another on the wall beside it—a sock belonging to little Mary Eliza.

Now Eliza's tears were falling freely. She no longer thought of her deceased child every minute like she had through the fall. But when she did think of her—which was still at least hourly, she supposed—the empty loneliness returned, and Eliza was left desolate.

Part of it was because she had never been able to hold the child close to her, to feel her suckling at her breast, to smell and feel the sweetness of her tiny breathing. Never had Mary Eliza been able to grasp her mother's finger, to smile, or even to open her eyes. These things had been denied Eliza, and were part of the reason why she continued to feel so devastated.

But the other part, which when she thought of it made things seem almost unbearable, was that now Eliza understood that her childbearing days were past. She had finally and most certainly grown too old, and in many ways too feeble, to bear more children. Maggie Haskel was convinced of the same thing. Willy, at least on this earth, would remain her only child—the only posterity she would ever give her darling Billy!

With a quick sob Eliza lowered herself into the rocker that Billy had unpacked so many times during their never-ending trek from Cedar two eternal years before. What an awful trip that had been! Eliza actually smiled through her tears when she thought of it, it had been so bad. Who would have imagined that things were only going to get worse here on the San Juan? Especially for her! Especially because she had been forced to bury her only daughter on that ugly, rocky knoll—

Missing Mary Eliza had been and was even yet a physical pain, too—an aching that actually hurt her mortal body. Eliza would never have supposed such a thing until experiencing it herself, and now that she had, she found herself completely unable to describe it to Billy or others. But women such as Adelia Lyman knew and understood, for they had also been through it, and just watching them carry on gave Eliza a certain measure of strength.

Billy did the same thing when he was around, for despite his own sorrow over Mary Eliza's death, his soul was by nature happy, filled with joy. He was such a good man, so tenderhearted and thoughtful—

"Oh, dear Lord," she sobbed as she reached down and drew a surprised little Willy to her breast, "please protect our Billy. If it is raining here, I know it will be snowing in the mountains where he is, so watch over him and bring him home to Willy and me in safety. It . . . it doesn't matter that we don't have anything for Christmas—not if the three of us have each other! So please, dear Father in Heaven, bless him to come home in safety."

47

Saturday, December 24, 1881

Verdure Creek Canyon

"Heeyah!" Curly shouted as he rode the trail away from the Verdure Creek line camp. "Heeyah, little Betsy hoss, let's ride!" Having said adios and Merry Christmas to his *segundo,* Bill Ball, he was now on his way south, where he was certain his welcome would be even warmer than the climate.

Though the snow had stopped falling and the sun was out, it was already sloping down the western sky, and before long, Curly knew, it was going to be colder'n one of his spinster Aunt Matilda's pecky-type kisses. And it was already near enough to that, he thought without rancor. That was why he had two red bandannas tied around his neck, his fleece-lined coat buttoned tight, thick gloves on his chapped and calloused hands, his chaps oiled and strapped tight around his jeans, rolled-up burlap in front of his legs, and his battered Stetson pulled down over his ears. Looking more like a bear than a man, he cared not at all, for he was on his way to cut the rug at the Christmas dance at Bluff, and nothing on earth could have made him happier.

Nothing, that is, except for seeing the faces of Eliza and Willy Foreman—yes, and Billy, too, when Curly handed over the Christmas presents he'd been secretly gathering for the past month.

Around Curly the world was snow and ice and barren trees, mostly scrub oak and scattered Ponderosa pines here on the mesa top, and he kept his eyes squinted against the glare from the sun lest he go blind before night settled down around him. But he'd planned on leaving late this way, he thought with a grin, knowing that he could get right to dancing when he got to Bluff, and not have to waste no time palaverin' with folks whilst things were gearing up to start.

His Betsy hoss was raring to go, too, for her ears were forward and her dainty hooves were fairly skipping over the icy trail, eating up the miles like they didn't even matter. "Hiyaa, Betsy hoss!" he shouted joyfully, "this hyar sure can't be the best you can do! Why, if'n you was to rise up like an eagle and fly us to the fort, I wouldn't be a bit surprised!

"Bless, you, Spud Hudson," he hollered into the wind, "fer being a good and generous man! Maybeso my stirrups are practically draggin' on the ground my legs is so long and she is such a small critter. I still ain't never rode a finer hoss, which I don't think there is in all this wide and wondrous creation!"

Grinning with the joy of what lay ahead, Curly whooped and hollered a few more times, his little Betsy hoss replied with a couple of spontaneous bucks and hops, and then the two of them were on their way for certain and for sure. He was Curly Bill Jenkins, a tough son of a gun who was ready to prance and to howl. Maybeso he was getting a little long in the tooth, and maybeso there was more gray in his beard than a man might want to admit. Maybeso, too, his nose had been broke more than once, and his left ear was crooked where he'd sewed it back hisself after a runnygade's horn had ripped it loose. And maybeso finally he'd slept too many nights in the rain and the snow, and that of a morning his lumbago and his rheumatiz were getting sort of fierce. All that was as nothing, for he was still who he was, tall in the saddle and fast on the draw—head line rider for Bill Ball and the LC.

It didn't matter that he'd been in the saddle and hard at a man's work since he was fourteen. It didn't matter that he'd trailed huge herds of cows up the Chisholm Trail and the Goodnight-Loving Trail, either one, and come out broke and the worse for wear every time. It didn't matter that he'd even trailed thirsty cows over the *Jornado del Muerto* and nearly dried hisself to death for lack of water. It didn't matter a'tall! Tonight, he thought with another whoop and a grin, he'd join the festivities with the Mormons and jig it up good. Tonight, by Tophet, he might just take one of them purty little Mormon gals and sweep her clean off'n her feet! He would, that is, if the floormaster'd let him do 'er. And if the man didn't, he thought with another wry grin, then he'd do the best he could, and that would be just dandy.

And over and above every other blessed festivity, he thought happily, he'd enjoy each breathless moment of suspense as Billy and Eliza and that fine little Willy child opened the gifts he'd either made or sent all the way to Fort Lewis to have Slim McGrew get for him more'n three long weeks before—

Horse Canyon

Quickly the hours and the miles slid by, and it was full dark and coming on six in the evening and Curly and his little mare were foggin' it down the valley of Recapture when the cowboy thought he heard the sound of an ax striking wood. He'd have doubted it even so, but his Betsy hoss's ears twitched when his did, and so he was forced to pull rein so's he could listen. Not that it would have mattered much to somebody else, he thought grimly, but he was head line rider for the LC, by jings, and it was up to him to know what was happening on the range.

Shortly the sound of a striking ax came again—not the sharp, even sound of a good bite into the wood that an ax swung by somebody like Billy Foreman might make, but the tinny, uneven sound of someone chopping wood that didn't have the least tiny notion of what they were about. By the time it came a third time, Curly knew the sound of chopping was coming from a ways up what must have been Horse Canyon, and he knew that whoever it was, would be in trouble. He could have gone on even so, but since there was still plenty of time to reach the dance, and since going on sure wouldn't have been what a man had ought to do, Curly nudged his little Betsy hoss, and she left the trail in a jump.

A mile up-canyon, and he was riding toward a rough-looking

little cabin he hadn't even known was there, and even in the dark he could see a woman's skirts swishing back and forth as she stood out in the yard beating at the firewood with her ax.

"Evening, ma'am," he growled as he dismounted and strode through the snow toward her. "Reckon you could use a little help."

Without another word Curly took the ax from the woman's exhausted hands and, toeing the whacked-up log to a better position, he began chopping. One swing. Then without a murmur he strode to the grindstone, started the squeaking equipment to turning, and in a short time had put a good edge on the battered ax.

Now the chips began to fly, and as Curly got into the rhythm of it, the stack of firewood began to grow—one cord after another—just like Billy Foreman had chopped. Of course real cowpunchers didn't much like such work, preferring to do only what could be done from the back of a hoss. Still, there were those rare occasions—

After a time, Curly sank the blade into the chopping block to stop the rust, and then he began hauling much of the huge pile of wood into the cabin, where he also stoked the smoking fireplace with a fresh supply of logs. That done he gathered the chips into the wood box for kindling, his eyes probing everything he could see within the cabin while he worked.

In the rumpled bed lay a sallow-faced man, his eyes sunken and closed. "My husband," the thin, tired-looking woman explained to Curly's unasked question. "He took sick near a week ago, and he ain't been up since. Good thing the old plow horse somehow brung him home. Otherwise he'd of died, and we wouldn't of known where he was at. He ain't died yet, but we still don't know what's wrong."

"You Mormon folks?"

The woman shook her head. "Not hardly. Is they any of them about?"

"Some. Down at the fort on the San Juan—maybe twenty, thirty miles from here."

The woman's hair was graying and partly loose from its bun, her thin dress was more patches and rags than whole cloth, and now that she was out of her husband's boots she was barefooted and mud-splattered. Studying her face, Curly could see that the worn woman was probably not as old as he had originally thought.

So far as Curly could tell the cabin was of recent but very poor construction, a "raw-hide outfit" he would have called it under other conditions, and everything within it spoke of age and hard use. These hard-pressed people were homesteaders, he could see, and this place was likely the latest in what had been a long string of bad choices, bad luck.

"You got kids, ma'am?" he asked quietly.

The woman, her eyes empty and hopeless, nodded toward the loft. "Two. Girl and then a boy."

Glancing upward Curly saw four eyes, all large and round, peering down at him from out of the darkness.

"They was hungry and augerin' on account of it's Christmas and there weren't much to eat, so I put 'em to bed early."

"Christmas," Curly breathed in surprise, looking around the small room as though he was seeing it for the first time. "Where's yer tree, ma'am. Kids got to have a tree."

"Ain't got one," she replied, sounding more discouraged than ever.

"Be back shortly. Man's job anyhow." Curly gave the woman what he hoped would be a reassuring grin, and put the dance at Bluff far from his mind, for he was certain they would not even yet be started. Then he was outside and on his little Betsy hoss, with ax in hand and a gleam in his eye, and they were winding up-canyon, looking for a suitable tree.

"There she is," he said a little later as he propped the stubby pinion in the center of the room, "as fine a Christmas tree as I ever did see. Also happened to flush out a little buck deer whilst I was out. He's gutted and skinned, and I'll fetch him off my hoss whilst you start to decorating the tree."

"Ain't got no way of decorating it," the woman declared with even greater sadness.

"Sure you do," Curly said as he remembered the seemingly unending years of his own childhood poverty. "Reckon I still got a little time, so I'll help."

Shrugging out of his heavy coat and plopping himself down on a broken chair he started asking for things—little bits of this and hands full of that, and soon the tired-looking woman was getting him just about everything he asked for. Nor did it take a terrible long time, for despite his lumbago and his rheumatiz, and despite that the dance in Bluff was by then in full swing and all them purty gals and old maids and widows was laughing and having a grand time without him, he was still head line rider for Bill Ball and the LC, and there weren't nothing his gnarled hands couldn't do. Besides which, his anxious mind reminded him, there weren't any way he'd expect less of hisself than to do it, and that despite the fact that this particular Christmas Eve was a Saturday, and Billy had told him the bishop closed the dance down at midnight sharp lest his flock be found dancing on the Sabbath.

"All right," he said a little later as he picked up his fleece-lined coat and shrugged back into it, "there's yer deer all butchered up and set under yer eaves to cool and freeze proper, ma'am, and there's yer Christmas tree, decorated and with a bit of candle on most every limb. Put your things fer the kids under it and light 'er off in the morning, 'cause I've got folks a'waitin' and it's time to ride."

"Ain't got no things fer the kids." The woman's almost groan stopped Curly in the doorway, and slowly he turned back around. "Say it agin," he demanded quietly, hoping he'd heard wrong but knowing all along that he hadn't.

"Ain't got no things fer the kids."

Curly sighed quietly. "Well, ma'am," he drawled as he cast a pitying glance up toward the dark loft where the extra-wide eyes still stared back down at him, at the same time pushing thoughts of his friends in Bluff out of dead center in his mind, "kids cain't wake up of a Christmas morning without there's a little something fer 'em under the tree."

Looking up, he waved his hand. "You kids get to sleep now. Ya hear? Scoot!"

In an instant they had disappeared, and Curly turned and winked at the tired-looking woman. "Reckon I got me that little something we was speaking of," he whispered, "out in my saddlebags."

Shortly he was back inside again, and the woman gazed in wonder as he reached into his bags. "Here's some cloth and thread and needles," he stated quietly as he brought forth two bundles tied up in brown store paper—the two bundles that had been for Eliza and the purty little gal he was sure to have met at the dance. "I ain't much on stitchin', ma'am, but fer a needle-and-threader like you look to be, there's enough here to make you and your little daughter a purty fair dress."

Back went Curly's hand, and this time when he drew it forth he held two pieces of wood, carefully and painstakingly carved. "This critter," he explained as his mind tried not to think of little Willy, "is a runnygade Texas longhorn steer, smartest and meanest animal ever born." Carefully the lanky cowboy pushed the head and neck of the carving, which he had drilled out, onto a dowel that was protruding from the steer's body.

"That'll do it," he grinned as he handed the finished gift to the woman. "It's fer yer son. I carved it myownself, and tell 'im if he's almighty careful he can turn the head back and forth, just like it's a real, live runnygade."

Curly pushed his hand back into the saddlebags again, searching one side and then the other. But this time he found nothing, which he had known all along was what would be there. "I don't have nothing fer your husband, ma'am," he explained sadly. "But when he wakes up, you tell him I sure did wisht him a merry—Wait a minute. Wait just a doggone minute!"

Down went Curly's hand into the pocket of his own Levis, and when it came forth again it was holding his good carving knife—the one he had been thinking all along would go to his partner, Billy Foreman. "Merry Christmas, ma'am! Give this to yer husband. Adios, now, 'cause I reckon I got to go."

Without another word Curly was out the cabin and climbing aboard his little Betsy hoss, and then he was urging her back down-canyon, toward the road to Bluff. "Don't know what time it is," he muttered with a sudden grin of renewed anticipation, "but I reckon we'll still get in a swing or two, Betsy gal. So raise yer skirts and come a'skippin', all you fine-lookin' Mormon gals, old maids and widows included, fer Curly Bill Jenkins is on his way!"

Fiddler's Green

And he would have been, too. Yes, indeed. Only Curly had pushed his little Betsy hoss hardly more than another couple of miles when he, and his quick little mare, both heard another sound. But this one was different from the distant chopping of an ax. Way different! It was loud, and it was close—too close, as a matter of fact—for such a terrible, awful scream.

In an instant his little Betsy hoss was pitching and bucking, and in that same instant Curly's well-oiled pistol had somehow found itself into his hand, which had also somehow become glove-free. Later, he couldn't recall having removed his glove or drawing his hogleg, either one. But then later on the lanky cowpoke couldn't recall a whole lot of what would soon be happening. About all he could recollect, when he tried to talk about it at all, was that terrible awful scream, added to the certain knowledge that there was a catamount or lion close by, and that he and his little Betsy hoss were about to get pounced on for sure.

Thing was, nothing moved, nothing jumped, nothing pounced. His horse finally still but with muscles quivering, Curly held back, looking and listening. And that was when he heard, coming faint from the far side of an old cottonwood blowdown just off the trail ahead of him, the brokenhearted sound of someone's tears.

"Well, I'll be double-dipped in dew-claws," Curly muttered as he fingered his pistol and urged his mount toward the old blowdown ahead. "What in thunderation else can possibly go wrong of a cold Christmas Eve?"

Very carefully, then, he drew rein and leaned out of his saddle to peer onto the far side of the log—

48

Sunday, December 25, 1881

Bluff Fort

"Billy? Hello in there! Billy Foreman, sing out if you're to home."

Throwing back the quilts and stumbling groggily to his feet, Billy fumbled first for his spectacles and then for a match. "Eliza," he called softly as the candle flared and then steadied, "wake up, hon-bun. Someone's here."

Frantically Eliza crawled from the bed and wrapped herself in one of their warm quilts. Meanwhile Billy was struggling to pull his trousers up under his long nightshirt.

"Who . . . who is it?"

"I don't know, hon-bun. But Gopher's at the door, and since he's not even growling, I figure it must be a friend. Thing is—"

"Billy, you awake?" the voice called out.

"I am now," Billy said softly as he moved to stand beside the little dog. "Who is it?"

"Yer pardner, you dad-gummed cowpoke! It's me—Curly Bill Jenkins. Open up, will you? Afore I freeze to death out hyer!"

Hurriedly Billy opened the door, and seeming to stagger a little, the heavily bundled cowboy pushed past him and into the chilly room.

"Curly, what on earth are you doing here?"

In answer Curly merely held one gloved finger to his lips, indicating that they needed to talk quietly. "Build up the fire in that stove,

Billy," he said with solemn urgency. "And Eliza, ma'am, if you wouldn't mind heating a little water?" Then, without even waiting for an invitation, he lowered himself carefully into a chair.

"But—"

"Do 'er, Billy." Curly looked pained, maybe even hurt. "I . . . I'll explain things by and by."

Without further questions Billy soon had a fire blazing in the stove, with the oven door open to let out the heat, and a silent Eliza had filled a kettle full of already warm water from the stove's reservoir and moved it to directly over the flames.

"All right, Curly," Billy pressed as Eliza lowered herself onto the edge of the bed, her eyes wide with concern, "what are you doing here?"

Reaching out one still-gloved hand, Curly scratched for just a moment behind Gopher's ears. The dog then relaxed, and so, it seemed, did Curly. "I . . . figured to come to the dance," he breathed tiredly.

"The dance? But . . . but it's the middle of the night, Curly, practically three in the morning! Look at that clock up there, and see for yourself. I told you the dance ended at midnight on account of it's now Sunday."

Curly grinned an exhausted grin. "It's also Christmas, ain't it?"

"Yes, but—"

"Well then, I set out to bring you and Eliza and little Willy some Christmas gifts. Bill Ball and me and the rest of the boys, we bin planning it for a whole month, and I was given it to do."

Stunned, Billy looked at his wife. "Curly, you and the other fellows had no need to do such a thing. We're getting along just fine—"

"Don't you worry none." Curly was holding up his one hand again. The other seemed locked across his chest, and he was sort of leaning into it like a man might lean into an injury—perhaps a gunshot wound—that was causing him pain. "You ain't going to be overburdened with gifts, no how. Met some homesteaders a little bit ago, up-country a mite in a place name of Horse Canyon. They was down on their luck, way down, and everything I had for you folks I ended up forkin' over to them."

Billy smiled broadly. "Why, Curly, that's just what you should have done!"

"Maybe it were and maybe it weren't." The longer Curly sat, the more tired and worn-out he looked, and he had still not removed his coat or hat or gloves. "Thing is, pardner, instead of gifts for you folks like I'd planned, all I brung you and Eliza, is trouble."

Again Billy and Eliza looked at each other, neither of them having the least notion of what the unpredictable cowboy was talking about.

"After I'd left the homesteaders' place," Curly declared, his voice still subdued, "I met me a woman."

"What? Up in that country, on a night like this? But—"

Again Curly held up his gloved hand. "Not no white woman, mind you. This one was a squaw, a Pahute I reckon. She was just a little bit of a thing, still a kid, and she was about as stove up and solid-froze as any human critter I ever seed. Looked like she hadn't had no chuck in a month of Sundays, she was so ganted up and ribby. Worse, her feet and legs, under them leather wrappings she had on, were stone-cold blue but going on black, with big splotches of white where the flesh was froze solid."

"Oh, Curly—"

"She was alone out there in the snow and the bushes and the dark, screeching and moaning with the pain of being froze, I reckoned, and it took me a while to figure out she had even bigger problems than that."

While Billy looked stunned, Eliza's hand came quickly to her mouth.

"I . . . I done what I could," Curly breathed, unaccustomed tears starting suddenly from his eyes, "only it weren't much and it weren't nowheres near enough. After a bit of jabberin' and makin' no sense a'tall, the poor little critter of a sudden give out with a long sigh, and I reckon that's when her soul headed out fer the happy hunting grounds, which I hope by now she has found."

Now Curly's expression turned bleak. "Well, that skeered me, her dying thataway, and in a panic I reached down to turn her over—to see if maybe I could do somethin' else. That's when I found the bullet hole, high up in her chest and going clean through that she'd somehow stuffed with a bit of grass trying to stop the bleeding, and that's when I finally figured out what had kilt her."

Tears were now coursing down Curly's cheeks and into his beard, and now both Billy and Eliza were sorrowing with him.

"Thing is, folks, that little gal was tougher'n boot leather, for when I worked out a little of her backtrail I seed that she'd been crawling a long ways after she had been shot, maybe miles and miles, afore she ended up behint that old cottonwood blowdown. It hadn't snowed all day long, of course, so her trail was plain as could be, off the road a little and punctuated here and there with the blood from that big ol' hole in her chest. It was a wonder to me the wolves or coyotes hadn't got 'er, cause if they're given a blood-trail like that to follow, especially in the hungry season—well, they just never miss! But she were lucky, I guess, for there weren't no sign of them critters nowhere, despite how far she'd crawled.

"Still, it were easy to tell she'd wanted to get somewheres, I could see that, and she'd wanted to get there mighty bad. Thing is, I had no good idea where or why, and it finally come to me that it was something I wouldn't never know."

Curly took a deep breath. "Back at her body I was just fixin' to pull some bark down over her and bury her as best I could, when she moved again. Well, that skeered me a little more and I jumped back, for even if'n I don't believe in haunts I can tell when a person's dead and their spirit is flown. She was and hers had, and I knew she hadn't ought to be moving again.

"Gettin' up my courage and tellin' ol' Betsy hoss to mind her manners and stand still and not come no closer no matter I was fool enough to try it, I snuck back around and took me another peek behind that log."

"And?" Eliza pressed, as caught up in Curly's tale as was her husband.

Dropping his gaze, Curly stared at the floor. "And she moved again, ma'am. Her legs moved." The LC cowhand paused and took a deep breath. "I . . . I'm right embarrassed to admit this next, fer it ain't fittin' fer a man to . . . to do what I done. But I . . . well, I lifted up the edge of what was left of her skirts to make certain of what I was seeing—the tops of her poor, scrawny legs where she was moving 'em, I mean—fer moonlight and cold can play some strange and terrible tricks on a feller's mind! And . . . and—"

"It's okay, Curly," Eliza soothed as she stepped close and placed her hand on the trembling man's coat-covered arm. "You did just right. The woman was dead and you had to make certain."

Curly raised his eyes and looked at Eliza, his countenance still stricken. "I . . . I reckon I know that. It's just that . . . that—"

Unable to continue, for his tears were falling again, Curly furiously used his teeth to remove his one glove. Then, reaching carefully inside his coat and once clean white shirt, he gently brought forth a tiny, withered-looking object.

"It's a baby, ma'am," he said tenderly, holding the limp little form out to Eliza. "When she died, that poor, shot-up little mother had just finished having her this scrawny little baby girl. I bit through the cord on account of I didn't have my knife no more, and I worked on her not much but some—'bout the same as I would a little dogie calf. The child's still alive, I reckon, but just barely. And since she ain't got no folks, at least not anymore, I . . . I didn't know where to take her or what to do with her. And then it come to me, Eliza, ma'am, that I should maybe bring her here to see if you might want to be her ma. I mean, I thought that maybe on account of you lost that other poor little gal—"

Curly stopped then, for it was obvious that Eliza and Billy were no longer paying him the least little bit of attention. Instead they were both on their feet and at the table, Eliza rubbing and washing the tiny child in warm water and Billy holding his fingers under her withered little body, saying a brief but heartfelt prayer. And wonder of all wonders to the hardened and crusty old cowpoke, who was no longer quite so dead set certain about the nonsense called the Mormon religion, but who was absolutely convinced that his scrawny but upstanding little partner had a direct pipeline to the Lord God Almighty and half his herd of holy angels, no matter, Billy had blessed the child to keep on living! And was now thanking the good Lord that he, Curly Bill Jenkins, bone-hard brush-buster of wild runnygades and head line rider for Bill Ball and the LC, had that night been in tune with the same Lord God Almighty and so had delivered to them the finest and sweetest Christmas gift either of them could ever have imagined—the little daughter they had been promised so many long and lonely months before by some feller name of President Platte De Alton Lyman.

And Curly was still wondering at that—wondering and rubbing Gopher's ears again and hanging for dear life onto a sleepy-eyed little Willy child who had crawled of a sudden onto his lap and snuggled down hard, when the tiny infant who was now in Eliza's arms, began to cry.

Yes, siree, the lanky cowpoke grinned as the wonderful, joyous warmth in the cabin forced closed his tired eyes, it was sure-enough turning out to be one wingdinger of a Christmas!

EPILOGUE

Tuesday, May 16, 1882

St. George, Territory of Utah

"Well, my dear," Elder Erastus Snow was commenting to his wife, "the world is certainly a busy place. So much is going on that a fellow can hardly keep track of it all."

Propped up by the pillows in her bed, Artemesia Snow smiled. No matter how old and crotchety she got, or how ill, sweet Erastus was always there doing for her, reading the newspapers, discussing the things that troubled him about his assignment over the Church in southern Utah and Arizona, and just being sweet. He was also terribly busy, but that didn't seem to matter. He wanted to be near her during this that she felt was her last illness, and Artemesia was pleased to have him.

"According to the papers we received by dispatch this morning—"

"Elder Snow?" his personal secretary said, "I'm sorry to interrupt, but the First Presidency has forwarded you a packet of information about the new Edmunds anti-polygamy law that President Chester A. Arthur signed into law this past March."

"Thank you, James. I do want to see that."

"There's also a letter from President Platte Lyman, of Bluff. I know you have been especially concerned about those folks, and so I thought—"

"Don't apologize, James. Open the letter, please, so that I may read it right now."

The clerk smiled. "It's already been opened, sir, by the Brethren in Salt Lake. They've included a note. Here you are."

Taking the letter, Elder Snow read the entire missive without comment. Finished, he read it again, more slowly, and then stared off into space, his mind busy. "Well, my dear," he finally declared, "that dream the Lord gave me last spring, concerning the grave danger being faced by the Saints on the San Juan? It has been fulfilled to the letter. Since that time they have constantly been under attack or threat of attack, and it is a wonder to me that they have not all perished."

"But . . . who has attacked them?"

"Everybody, it seems. Pahutes, Navajos, outlaws, the muddy and treacherous San Juan—President Lyman reports that any or all of those forces have been arrayed against them day and night ever since they got there. Yet they have managed to persist in their mission, and they wisely attribute their safety to the Lord. But they are weary and impoverished, my dear, and their numbers have grown so small that they are finding it practically impossible to go on. President Lyman is once again pleading for a release so that the Saints can move on to a less hostile environment."

"I don't blame them a bit!"

Erastus's voice was filled with sorrow. "Neither do I. The thing is, this other note says that the First Presidency have made this a matter of prayer, and their impressions are that the Saints in San Juan are to continue their mission."

"Oh, no!"

"That's what it says, my dear. President Lyman has been written to that effect. But the Brethren wish me to join with Elder Moses Thatcher and take up a journey to the San Juan this fall, after the weather has cooled again. They wish me to speak in the name of the Lord, and promise the Saints that if they will be faithful to their calls and assignments, the Lord will surely bless and prosper them."

"Oh, Erastus, not another journey into that terrible country! You know how difficult it was for you to recover from your last journey there."

"It'll be all right, my dear. The Lord will strengthen me just as He has always done. By the way, Brother Lyman does mention a little good news. Apparently Billy and Eliza Foreman, who as you may recall lost a baby daughter last spring, have adopted an orphaned Indian child—a baby girl. Brother Lyman says that though she has some sort of health problem she is a beautiful child, and he has never seen Eliza and Billy so happy."

"That's wonderful," Artemesia beamed.

"Yes, it is." Erastus Snow nodded at his wife. "And you can count on it, my dear. No matter the difficulties they may encounter, the Foremans will be eternally blessed for this endeavor!

"But now, let me think for a moment. What must I do to prepare for this next journey—"[1]

---

1. Artemesia Snow, wife of Apostle Erastus Snow, died in St. George on Thursday, December 21, 1882. At the time of her passing, Elder Snow was traveling with Elder Moses Thatcher on a lengthy tour that ranged from San Juan County, Utah, to Maricopa County, Arizona. It is unknown when Elder Snow received word of his wife's passing.

HISTORICAL NOTE

Because various aspects of the preceding story beg an historical explanation, may I offer the following. As 1881 ended for the exhausted citizens of Bluff, there were a great many who were losing hope that anything would ever change. Yet in the world around them, change was occurring constantly, and most of the San Juan settlers were hard-pressed to even imagine what was going on.

Drought was still plaguing the cattle ranges of Texas and the Southwest, and part of New York City was expected to be illuminated by electricity in the coming fall. In fact the offices of financier J. P. Morgan were already so illuminated. A man by the name of H. W. Seely had obtained a patent on an electrical flatiron, and a young fellow named Schuyler Skaats Wheeler, twenty-two years old, had invented an electric desk fan.

A scientist named Robert Koch had discovered that tuberculosis was caused by a bacteria, and that it was a communicable disease. Walt Whitman had published a new work titled *Specimen Days*; Mark Twain had just released a new novel called *The Prince and the Pauper*; and the most popular story of the day was called *Pinocchio, Little Wooden Boy*, about a puppet who came to life only to have his nose grow longer every time he told a lie.

A new company called Van Camp Packing was selling cans of commercially packaged pork and beans; and the Hatfield-McCoy feud in Kentucky and West Virginia was heating up again, with more murders all around. And finally, the major U. S. railroads had adopted a standard time with four separate time zones—Eastern,

Central, Rocky Mountain, and Pacific—each an hour behind the other as one moved west.

For the LDS settlers of Bluff, 1881 was the first of several pivotal years. Not alone did their attempts to tame the San Juan River as well as their own irrigation canal utterly fail them, but such efforts failed every year but one thereafter. Finally, after six or seven years of enduring the starvation and abject poverty this caused them, they turned from a farm-based economy to livestock, establishing large, community-owned herds of both cattle and sheep.

They also began spreading outward from Bluff, though not without a price. In 1885, Amasa Barton and his wife, Parthenia Hyde Barton, took over a trading post located ten miles west of Bluff at what was called the Rincon, where Comb Ridge plunged into the San Juan River. Shortly thereafter Amasa was shot and killed by a disgruntled Navajo, becoming the only member of the missionary community to ever be slain by Indians of either tribe.

In 1887, to counter the effects of escalating troubles with the rampaging cowboys/outlaws of the Carlisle outfit, the Bluff settlers boldly established a new community on what had heretofore been considered Carlisle range at the foot of the Blue Mountains. There "Latigo" Gordon, foreman for the Carlisles, had earlier built a saloon for his eighty or so riders, which he called "The Blue Goose" and which became the most infamous watering hole in the southeast corner of Utah.

Called by the former Bluff settlers first, Hammond, and then Monticello, this tiny new community of peace-loving Mormons struggled against constant harassment from the cowboys. Yet they plowed fields, planted crops, and built homes, using the legal system, as well as their faith in the Lord's promised protection, to oppose guns, rustling, stampedes, drunkenness, and most every other form of intimidation and debauchery the Carlisle outfit could throw at them.

While there was a great deal of bloodletting among the cowboys during those years, the Mormons were protected from the gunplay until the 1891 July 4th dance. At that dance a man named Tom Roach became intoxicated and killed his friend Joe McCord. He then held the dance party at gunpoint while he robbed them. Seeing the robbery, Frank Adams ran to Charlie Walton's home and obtained a rifle. Coming back, he and Roach fired at each other. As it turned out, Roach's gun was empty, and Adams's round went awry and hit Relief Society President Jane Walton near her heart, killing her almost instantly. As with Amasa Barton and the Indians, Jane Walton thus became the only one of the San Juan missionaries to lose her life to gunplay.

Deep drought during the 1890s caused the big ranchers of the area, including the Carlisles, to lose interest in the country of the San Juan. In 1896 they sold the lion's share of their interests to their foreman, "Latigo" Gordon, who had married a Mormon girl and wished to settle down. Despite all that Gordon had purchased, it is estimated that the Carlisles drove from the country 30,000 additional head of cattle.

In that same year Jody Lyman bought out all the interests of the LC Cattle Company, except 22,000 head of cattle, which were driven to Dolores, Colorado, and points beyond. Within a half dozen years a third San Juan County settlement was established on LC land atop White Mesa, a few miles below the old LC headquarters. First called Grayson after Nellie Grayson Roper, Jody Lyman's wife, the town's name was later changed to Blanding. Its first actual settlers were young Albert R. Lyman, son of Platte Lyman, and Albert's bride, Mary Ellen "Lell" Perkins Lyman. In 1902 these newlyweds set up a tent on White Mesa and, all alone in what was still a howling wilderness, began construction of their first home.

The Pittsburgh Land and Cattle Company had purchased the ranges surrounding Coyote or LaSal from the McCartys and others in 1884. Using the Cross H brand that had belonged to Green Robinson, the PCC was soon running 20,000 head of cattle on the LaSal Mountains. During the drought, this company was sold to the partnership of Cunningham, Carpenter, and Prewer, who changed the name to the LaSal Cattle Company. Shortly thereafter Prewer was bought out, and the name was again changed—to the Cunningham and Carpenter Cattle Company. They then sold out to a consortium of Mormon businessmen—Lemuel H. Redd, J. A. Scorup, and others. Meanwhile, J. A. Scorup had joined with Andrew Somerville to buy up the country around Indian Creek, which they also began ranching.

Thus, by shortly after the turn of the century, the Bluff Saints and others who had joined them, were finally realizing the promises of prosperity made by their Church leaders so many years before.

Posey's quest to locate the kidnapped Too-rah, which lasted over a year as opposed to the relatively short time portrayed in this book, ended as described. For as long thereafter as Too-rah remained alive, Posey worked diligently to be friends with the Mormons. Too-rah was a kind and benevolent young woman who endeared herself in many ways to those of both races. Together she and Posey brought forth two sons, Jess and Anson, and it seemed to the Mormons as if their troubles with Posey were finally over.

However, one morning after several years of wedded bliss, Posey lifted what he thought was an empty pistol and playfully fired it at Too-rah. Mortally wounded, Too-rah lay in terrible pain while Posey frantically sought out Aunt Jody Wood, who had been called by Bishop Nielson to serve as the community doctor. Unfortunately, Aunt Jody could do little beyond offering brief comfort, and Too-rah passed away from her wound.

Posey's sorrow knew no bounds, and to make matters worse, the still-terrifying Poke ordered Posey to repay him for the death of his baby sister by taking as wife the older crone, the ugly sister who had done so much to keep Too-rah from Posey a decade and more before.

Soon Posey's old bitterness toward the Mormons had returned, other Pahutes with similar attitudes joined his band, and from then on, no one was ever certain of their safety when the Pahute leader was around.

It was at the schoolhouse/courthouse in Blanding, in 1923, that Posey interrupted the trial of a young Pahute that was then in session, by firing a pistol at Sheriff Bill Oliver. Missing at almost point-blank range, and no doubt cursing all the while at old Thales Haskel's forty-year-old promise that he could never kill a Mormon, Posey and his followers fled from town and vanished into the gulches and canyons south and west of White Mesa. Quickly gaining national attention and drawing all sorts of dignitaries and soldiers to Blanding, Posey's little war proved to be the last Indian uprising in

America. The action ultimately culminated in Posey's death, as well as the end of the intermittent forty-three-year battle he had waged against the Mormons.

Until the mid-1880s, Bill Ball remained a true friend to the Mormons, employing several as cowboys and doing all in his power to help them. In that year, however, some outlaws he had fed and sheltered through the winter, repaid him by stealing a herd of horses and vanishing into the wilderness west of the LC headquarters. Recruiting Kumen Jones and six or eight other Mormon men to ride with him as a posse, Bill Ball tracked the outlaws to a spot called Navajo Springs, where the outlaws were leisurely eating lunch. All the posse but Bill Ball wanted to draw down on the three thieves and order them to surrender; however, Bill feared such an approach might cause harm to some of his Mormon friends. So, the posse remained at a distance and followed the horse thieves up Comb Wash until after dark.

Early the next morning Bill detailed Kumen and some of the others to block any escape up the Twist, but the outlaws escaped another way by going up the south side of Red Canyon. Bill and the remnants of his posse followed, Bill leading, and so he was the first to ride into an ambush the three had set. Instantly Bill Ball fell, mortally wounded by the men he had befriended, and James B. Decker sprang from his saddle only a fraction of a second before a bullet tore into the wood and leather beneath him. In the confusion that followed, the three outlaws then withdrew and escaped.

Bill Ball was buried not far from where he had fallen, and despite the continued efforts of the Mormons and later a much larger posse of cowboys, the three murderers were never apprehended.

Though the Billy Foreman character has been fictional in all three volumes of *Hearts Afire,* the experiences ascribed to him in this volume, both in the fort and later on the range as a cowboy, were based upon the experiences of Albert R. Lyman, as recorded in Lyman's meticulous journals. Though young Albert rode the range some twenty years later than my account, conditions in the San Juan country had hardly changed, and he felt the job was a sore test of any man's mettle.

In the course of time, young Albert rode or associated with

Erwin "Slim" McGrew, Bob Hott, and the other cowhands that I have ascribed to the LC Ranch, and upon whom I have based the fictitious character Curly Bill Jenkins. Kumen Jones wrote that these young men from back East, who were involved in the cattle industry in southeast Utah, were fairly well educated, had been brought up in good Christian homes, and were men who stood for law and order. Though they didn't understand the Mormons' endeavoring to help the Indians, from a purely business point of view it made good sense to maintain friendly relations with both tribes, which they did. That fact alone naturally added strength to the forces for peace in San Juan. Thus the Mormons of Bluff looked upon these men as companions and friends, riding with them frequently, and in many cases learning the cattle business from them.

In fact, Bob Hott purchased the K Lazy T brand from the owners of the LC, ran cattle with that brand out of Verdure for several years, and then sold out to his friend and neighbor, Joseph Barton. Today the land, and the K Lazy T brand, are still in the Barton family.

Non-Mormon homesteaders also came and went in San Juan County, and the remains of one such homestead vanished long ago from Horse Canyon, where Curly Bill Jenkins is described to have stumbled upon that destitute family on a cold Christmas Eve.

Peeb and Jonah, fictional names for an historical Pahute couple, the man of which perished because of Thales Haskel's curse, provided me a backdrop in which to describe prevailing Pahute family relationships and attitudes. Widows if not immediately remarried were simply abandoned to die, and orphans or otherwise unwanted children suffered the same fate. Despite the wrath of some of the Pahutes, several San Juan settlers took in these suffering waifs, and so Curly's decision to give Peeb's infant to Eliza merely reflected what the Mormons tried, always, to do.

As far as the fictitious Sugar Bob Hazelton goes, there seemed to be no end to the nefarious crimes committed against both Indians and whites by the various outlaws and bad men who occasionally called San Juan County their home. The depravity shown Bitseel's younger sister in my story was a composite of several accounts I came across during my years of research for the story, though so far as I know, nothing of this sort befell the family of old Tsabekiss and his son Bitseel.

Large numbers of rattlesnakes rolled into balls for warmth was not an uncommon sight in the San Juan country during the colder weather, particularly in the higher elevations. A settler in a neighboring state once reported finding the remains of an unknown person who had apparently met his end through their numerous bites, and after a little reflection, that seemed as good a way as any for me to end Sugar Bob's sorry career in San Juan County.

The doctrine of plural marriage, though actually practiced by a very small percentage of Latter-day Saints, and though outlawed entirely by the Church in 1891, played a significant role in the lives of the San Juan Mormons a decade earlier. Some who lived it found great joy and happiness, others struggled just to hold their lives together. The conversations I have created in book three between Eliza Foreman and Annie Lyman, Mary Jones, and the Williams sisters, who both married Ben Perkins, are based upon the journals and records of Adelia Lyman, Kumen Jones, and Sarah Williams Perkins, and almost word-for-word reflect their personal attitudes and experiences.

It should be pointed out that, in fulfillment of her father's promise, Mary Jones did give birth to a son, whom she named Leonard, and who grew to be a fine man. Meanwhile Lydia May Lyman, Kumen's plural wife, gave birth to nine children. Then tragedy struck when Lydia May perished in a fire started by a dropped lantern. Without hesitation Mary took over the rearing of Lydia May's large family of small children, loving them with such unstinting devotion that in later years every one of them bore record of their eternal devotion for their beloved "Aunt" Mary.

After less than a year of caring for the crippled and cantankerous Natanii nééz, the Navajo woman I called Hádapa left him and took as her husband another man, one who gave her children and made her a happy woman indeed. It is interesting that in the various accounts of her life that I came across in my studies, no one seems to have recorded her true name.

Jody Lyman never recovered from the terrible bullet wound inflicted above his knee by Rob Paxman. Though he lived for many years, he did so as a cripple, enduring constant pain as well as numerous surgeries, none of which seemed to do him much good. Yet through it all, he and his wife, Nellie, raised a fine family, and never lost faith in the power of the Lord to heal, whether in this life or the next, it did not matter.

That said, I had the feeling as I did my research and put this book together, that the story my characters were in fact playing out, was one of survival amidst grueling, unending hardship, with an ever-increasing faith serving as the lubricant that enabled all the groups to reach toward a frictionless future together. As we enter the year 2000, that has, for the most part, been achieved.

Blaine M. Yorgason

ANNOTATED BIBLIOGRAPHY

Abbott, E. C. (Teddy Blue), and Helena Huntington Smith. *We Pointed Them North: Recollections of a Cowpuncher.* Norman: University of Oklahoma Press, 1982. A very readable first-person account of driving herds of Texas cattle north into Montana, and of subsequent adventures there.

Acton, Zelma. *Oral History.* Interviews conducted by Deborah Fellbaum and Shirley E. Stephenson. Utah State Historical Society and California State University, Fullerton, Oral History Program, Southeastern Utah Project, 1972, 1974. Zelma Acton gives much information regarding the Utes and their customs.

Adams, Allie, and Lloyd Adams. *Oral History.* Interviews concerning Jens and Kirsten Nielson, conducted by Deborah Fellbaum, Utah State Historical Society and California State University, Fullerton, Oral History Program, Southeastern Utah Project, 1972.

Adams, Ramon F. *Western Words: A Dictionary of the American West.* Norman: University of Oklahoma Press, 1981.

Askins, Charles. *Texans, Guns and History.* New York: Bonanza Books, 1970. Contains considerable information about the Texans who may or may not have made their way into the San Juan country during their flights from the law.

Baker, Pearl. *Posey the Pahute.* Unpublished manuscript, 1986. This manuscript contains a brief history of Anglo/Indian relationships in the nineteenth century, as well as much information about Posey.

Beckstead, James H. *Cowboying: A Tough Job in a Hard Land.* Salt Lake City: University of Utah Press, 1991. With a foreword by actor Wilford Brimley, this text details cattle and cowboying activities in Utah from its earliest days. It is liberally illustrated with period photography and is an enjoyable read.

Blankenagel, Norma Palmer. *Portrait of Our Past: A History of Monticello Utah Stake (Formerly San Juan Stake), 1882–1988*. Private Publication, 1988. This volume contains numerous photographs, historical anecdotes, and summarizations. The interesting format is topical rather than chronological, making the historical flow difficult to follow.

Burton, Alma P., comp. *Discourses of the Prophet Joseph Smith*. Salt Lake City: Deseret Book Co., 1965.

Carter, Kate B., comp. *Heart Throbs of the West*. 12 vols. Salt Lake City: Daughters of Utah Pioneers, 1951. These volumes, as well as all other DUP publications, contain numerous journals, diaries, and reminiscences of the Pioneer West and its people.

——— . *Our Pioneer Heritage*. 20 vols. Salt Lake City: Daughters of Utah Pioneers, 1958.

Crabtree, Lamont J. *The Incredible Mission: The Hole-in-the-Rock Expedition/San Juan Mission Story and Trail Guide*. Private Publication, 1980. Lamont Crabtree uses numerous photographs and maps to describe each portion of the trail as it was in 1880 and then as it appears today. He lists the members of the expedition, omitting some of the names given by David E. Miller but including names Miller does not give. Crabtree also lists the ages of the expedition participants.

Daniels, Doug, and Ruth Meo. *Uriah and Annie Butt: Interviews concerning the early Bluff experiences of Willard George William (Dick) Butt*. Utah State Historical Society and California State University, Fullerton, Oral History Program, Southeastern Utah Project, 1978.

Dary, David. *Cowboy Culture: A Saga of Five Centuries*. New York, Avon Books, 1981. Contains some good information on trail herds and the art of driving cattle.

Ehat, Andrew F., and Lyndon W. Cook, eds. *The Words of Joseph Smith*. Provo: Brigham Young University Religious Studies Center, 1980.

Foster-Harris. *The Look of the Old West*. New York: Bonanza Books,

1975. This is an excellent examination of how all sorts of things looked in the nineteenth century—forms of transportation, horse and rider accoutrements, weapons, clothing, and the small items, such as quill pens and inkwells, which were part of day-to-day living. The book is lavishly illustrated by Evelyn Curro.

Gottfredson, Peter. *Indian Depredations in Utah*. Salt Lake City: Private Printing, 1969. Contains an interesting vocabulary of the Ute dialect as it was understood by early Mormon scouts and Indian missionaries.

Grant, Bruce. *The Cowboy Encyclopedia*. New York, Chicago, San Francisco: Rand McNally & Company, 1951. Entries concern almost anything one would want to know about both the Old and the New West, from the open range to the dude ranch.

Hafen, LeRoy R., ed., *Colorado and Its People: A Narrative and Topical History of the Centennial State*. New York: Lewis Historical Publishing Company, Inc., 1948. Dr. Hafen provides excellent accounts of the Thornburgh Battle with the Utes, the killing of Indian Agent Nathan Meeker, and the Ute capture of his wife, daughter, and others.

Horwitz, Elinor Lander. *Mountain People, Mountain Crafts*. New York: J. P. Lippincott Company, 1974. This book gives excellent information concerning cabin and furniture building, toy making, and musical instruments as they are handmade by people of the southern Appalachian Mountains.

Hurst, Michael Terry. "Posey." Unpublished screenplay, 1977. Written from Posey's perspective, this fictionalized account is based entirely on known historical events.

Jamison, Richard L., comp. *The Best of Woodsmoke: A Manual of Primitive Outdoor Skills*. Bountiful, Utah: Horizon Publishers, 1982. This is a collection of articles originally published in the magazine *Woodsmoke,* which deal with the methods of survival used by ancient Native Americans and other primitive peoples.

Jenson, Andrew. *Church Chronology*. Salt Lake City: Deseret News Press, 1899.

Jones, Francis W. *Oral History*. Interview conducted by Pat Whitaker. Utah State Historical Society and California State University, Fullerton, Oral History Program, Southeastern Utah

Project, 1972. Francis chronicles experiences of his parents, Kumen and Mary Jones, at the Hole, some interesting aspects of polygamy, and gives considerable information about his parents' Navajo acquaintances.

Jones, Kumen. *Writings of Kumen Jones*. Edited by Albert R. Lyman. Compiled and published by Edward (Ted) Jones, 1363 Harrison Avenue, Salt Lake City, Utah 84105 (1-801-581-1384), Mr. Jones has copies of this work available upon request. Kumen Jones was one of the original Hole-in-the-Rock pioneers, and his writings are a wonderful evidence of the determination of those people to remain true to their callings despite the incredible difficulties they encountered.

Kelly, Charles. "Chief Hoskanini." *Utah Historical Quarterly,* July 1953. An excellent account of the ways and mannerisms of this powerful Navajo headman.

Lavender, David. *One Man's West*. 3rd ed. Lincoln: University of Nebraska Press, 1977. A wonderful, first-person account of life as a working cowboy in and near the San Juan country of Utah and Colorado.

Lyman, Albert R. *Aunt Jody*. Serialized in the *Improvement Era,* 1958, 1959, 1960. An account of the life and accomplishments of Josephine Chatterly Wood, pioneer nurse and doctor for San Juan County.

——— . "Dick Butt: Sheriff of San Juan, Stories of Willard George William Butt." Unpublished manuscript, 1957. Details many of Dick Butt's experiences both as a Hole-in-the-Rock pioneer and frontier lawman.

——— . *History of Blanding, 1905–1955*. Private publication, 1955. Written to commemorate the fiftieth anniversary of the city of Blanding, Utah, this is mainly a reminiscence.

——— . *Indians and Outlaws: Settling of the San Juan Frontier.* Salt Lake City: Bookcraft, 1962. It is impossible to say enough good about the prolific work of Albert Robinson Lyman. The son of Hole-in-the-Rock expedition leader Platte De Alton Lyman and his wife, Adelia, he was carried as a baby over the treacherous road by his mother during the summer of 1880. During his ninety-six years of life he not only helped pioneer San Juan County, including being the first white settler of the community that is now called Blanding, but he also knew or was acquainted with practically every resident of the county, Mormon, Indian, or Texan. Mr. Lyman authored numerous books and articles about these people, almost all of which have been published.

——. *The Last Fort*. Serialized as "Fort on the Firing Line" in the *Improvement Era,* 1948, 1949, 1950. Written from the Mormon perspective, this is an account of the up-and-down relationship between the Mormons, the Navajos, and the Pahutes of San Juan County.

——. *Man to Man (Voice of the Intangible)*. Salt Lake City: Deseret Book Company, 1962. A fictionalized account of the author's own youth in wild San Juan County.

——. *The Outlaw of Navajo Mountain*. Salt Lake City: Deseret Book Company, 1963. This is a somewhat fictionalized account of the life of the Pahute known as Posey.

——. *The Piutes of the San Juan: Shadow of Peogament, Peeats, and Peeogament*. Private publication of three unpublished papers compiled into one by Ky Lyman Bishop.

——. "Platte De Alton Lyman." Unpublished manuscript, copy in possession of Edward and Valerie Platt.

——. "Journals." Volumes 1–4. Unpublished manuscripts, the originals of which can be found in the Department of Special Collections, Harold B. Lee Library, Brigham Young University, Provo, Utah. These journals, of which there are forty-two volumes of which I am aware, as well as seventy-two volumes of "thoughts" that were written during the same time period, reflect this prolific writer's personal day-by-day experiences in San Juan County through most of his ninety-six years of life. The copies I used were graciously made available to me by Albert's son, the late Karl R. Lyman, and his lovely wife, Edith.

Lyman, Albert R., and Gladys Perkins Lyman. *Oral History*. Interviews conducted by Charles Peterson, Gary L. Shumway, and Stanley Bronson. Utah State Historical Society and California State University, Fullerton, Oral History Program, Southeastern Utah Project, 1970, 1973.

McLoughlin, Denis. *Wild and Woolly: An Encyclopedia of the Old*

West. New York: Doubleday and Co., 1975. An amazing compilation of facts regarding the varied characters, places, and events that made up the Old West.

Monaghan, Jay, editor in chief. *The Book of the American West*. New York: Bonanza Books, 1963. This large book contains excellent articles by such renowned writers as Dale Morgan and Ramon F. Adams concerning the exploration and settlement of the American West. Articles are included on Indians, mountain men, outlaws and cowboys, the cattle trade, and the settlers as well as an entire section on modern Western art.

Nielson, Edd, and Ida Nielson. *Memories*. Interview conducted by Deborah Fellbaum. Utah State Historical Society and California State University, Fullerton, Oral History Program, Southeastern Utah Project, 1972. Edd was the son of Joseph Nielson, who came through the Hole.

O'Brien, Alberta Lyman. *The Story of Sarah Williams Perkins*. Private Publication, 1993, copy in possession of Edward and Valerie Platt.

Olsen, Larry Dean. *Outdoor Survival Skills*. Provo: Brigham Young University Press, 1967. This volume contains excellent material concerning edible plants of the Mountain West, as well as primitive toolmaking, shelter building, small animal trapping, desert water collecting, and so forth.

Palmer, Emma Stevens. *Recollections*. Interviews concerning Walter Joshua Stevens, conducted by Gary L. Shumway and Jessie L. Embry, Utah State Historical Society and California State University, Fullerton, Oral History Program, Southeastern Utah Project, 1973. Joshua Stevens was born 21 December 1856, in Pleasant Grove, Utah, to Walter Stevens and Abigail Elizabeth Holman. With his younger brother David Alma he was called on the San Juan Mission. He married Elizabeth Kinney before leaving, and the trip was their honeymoon.

Perkins, Cornelia Adams, Marian Gardner Nielson, and Lenora Butt Jones. *Saga of the San Juan*. San Juan County Daughters of Utah Pioneers, 1968. In this heavily illustrated volume, the authors trace the history of San Juan County from every perspective, including geologic. The book focuses on Mormon settlement, however, and pays little attention to Navajos, Pahutes, and non-Mormon cattle ranchers.

Peterson, Charles S. *Look to the Mountains: Southeastern Utah and the La Sal National Forest*. Provo: Brigham Young University Press, 1975. An excellent history of the San Juan country, with a strong emphasis on Mormon/Indian/cowboy relationships and their effects upon the land.

Pinckert, Leta. *True Stories of Early Days in the San Juan Basin*. Farmington, New Mexico: Hustler Press, 1964. Gives some details on the Colorado portion of the San Juan country.

Platt, Lyman De. *The Ancestral Heritage of Benjamin Perkins and His Two Wives, Mary Ann Williams and Sarah Williams*. Private publication, copy in possession of Edward and Valerie Platt.

Potter, Edgar R. *Cowboy Slang*. Seattle: Superior Publishing Company, 1971. A delightful source of western lingo, with terrific illustrations by Ron Scofield.

Rickey, Don Jr. *$10 Horse, $40 Saddle: Cowboy Clothing, Arms, Tools, and Horse Gear of the 1880s*. Ft. Collins, Colorado: The Old Army Press, 1976.

Redd, Charles. *Short Cut to the San Juan*. Denver: Westerner's Brand Book, 1949. An excellent abbreviated history of the San Juan expedition written by the son of Lemuel H. Redd Jr. and Eliza Ann Westover Redd, two of the expedition's members.

Redd, Leland. *Oral History*. Interview partially concerning Jens Nielson, conducted by Louise Lyne. Utah State Historical Society and California State University, Fullerton, Oral History Program, Southeastern Utah Project, 1972.

Shelton, Ferne. *Pioneer Superstitions, Old-Timey Signs and Sayings*. High Point, N. C.: Hutcraft, 1969.

Shelton, Ferne, ed. *Pioneer Proverbs: Wit and Wisdom from Early America*. Collected by Mary Turner. High Point, N. C.: Hutcraft, 1971.

Smith, Cornelius C. *A Southwestern Vocabulary: The Words They Used*. Glendale, Calif.: Arthur H. Clark Co., 1984. Separated into "Spanish Words and Terms," "Anglo Words and Terms," "Military Words and Terms," and "Indian Words and Terms," this is a very helpful glossary.

Smith, Joseph Fielding, comp. *Teachings of the Prophet Joseph Smith*. Salt Lake City: Deseret Book Co., 1977.

Tanner, Faun McConkie. *The Far Country: A Regional History of Moab and La Sal, Utah*. Salt Lake City: Olympus Publishing Co., 1976. A topical, intently readable history of the early difficulties in San Juan County.

Trager, James, ed. *The People's Chronology: A Year-by-Year Record of Human Events from Prehistory to the Present*. New York: Holt, Rinehart, and Winston, 1979.

Tyler, Ron, and Bank Langmore. *The Cowboy*. New York: William Morrow and Co., Inc. This is a compilation of previously published articles and book portions dealing with the early American cowboy, illustrated with modern photographs.

Vernam, Glenn R. *The Rawhide Years: A History of the Cattlemen and the Cattle Country*. New York: Doubleday and Co., 1976.

Walker, Don D. "The Carlisles: Cattle Barons of the Upper Basin." Salt Lake City: *Utah Historical Quarterly,* vol. 32, no. 3, Summer 1964, 268–84.

Wallechinsky, David, and Irving Wallace. *The People's Almanac*. New York: Doubleday and Co., 1975. Besides a great deal of information, this volume contains a perpetual calendar that is helpful for establishing day-dates.

Watts, Peter. *A Dictionary of the Old West, 1850–1900*. New York: Alfred A. Knopf, 1977. An illustrated dictionary pertaining to the common language of cattlemen, frontiersmen, scouts, cowboys, gamblers, miners, and others during the last half of the nineteenth century.

Wellman, Paul I. *Death on Horseback: Seventy Years of War for the American West*. Philadelphia and New York: J. P. Lippincott Co., 1934. Contains interesting information concerning the Utes and what is known as the Meeker Massacre.

Winslowe, John R. "Gold Canyon, The Most Lied about Mine in the West," *True West,* August 1966. Contains considerable information about the mine near Navajo Mountain known as the "Lost Peshleki."

Wood, Frances, and Dorothy Wood. *I Hauled These Mountains in Here*. Caldwell, Idaho: Caxton Printers, Ltd., 1977. An excellent account of the Colorado freighting business of David Wood. Because his business was so widespread, the book also covers the major mining towns, road and railroad building, and facts concerning a host of other prominent characters too numerous to mention.

Yorgason, Blaine M. *Hearts Afire, Book One: At All Hazards*. Salt Lake City: Deseret Book Co., 1997.

——— . *Hearts Afire, Book Two: Fort on the Firing Line*. Salt Lake City: Deseret Book Co., 1999.

——— . *Hearts Afire, Book Three: Curly Bill's Gift*. Salt Lake City: Deseret Book Co., 2000.

——— . *To Soar with the Eagle*. Salt Lake City: Deseret Book Co., 1993. Though not intended at the time of its writing, this historical novel, dealing with Indian missionaries Thales Haskel and Jacob Hamblin and their encounters with the Navajos Peokon and his father, Dahnish uánt, during the mid to late 1850s when George A. Smith Jr. was murdered, is actually a prequel to the *Hearts Afire* series.

Young, Karl. "Wild Cows of the San Juan." Salt Lake City: *Utah Historical Quarterly,* vol. 32, no. 3, Summer 1964, 252–67.

Young, Norma Perkins. *Anchored Lariats on the San Juan Frontier.* Provo, Utah: Community Press, 1985. This very readable account of the settlement of San Juan County, laced with journal entries from the various early participants, also contains numerous excellent photographs.

Young, Otis W. *Western Mining*. Norman: University of Oklahoma Press, 1970. This is an informal account of prospecting, placering, lode mining, and milling on the American frontier from Spanish times to 1893.

Young, Robert W., and Morgan William Sr. *The Navajo Language: A Grammar and Colloquial Dictionary.* Albuquerque: University of New Mexico Press. The second portion of this huge, scholarly volume converts English words and expressions into Navajo.

——— . *A Family History: Joseph Franklin Barton and Harriet Ann Richards Barton*. Private Family Publication, 1994. Containing copies of original letters and journals written by two of the Hole-in-the-Rock participants, this volume provides interesting details I have not found elsewhere.